# 1633

★

# 1633

## DAVID WEBER
## ERIC FLINT

1633

Copyright © 2002 by David Weber & Eric Flint

A Baen Books Original

Baen Publishing Enterprises
P.O. Box 1403
Riverdale, NY 10471

ISBN: 0-7434-3542-7

Cover art by Dru Blair

Distributed by Simon & Schuster
1230 Avenue of the Americas
New York, NY 10020

Production by Windhaven Press, Auburn, NH
Printed in the United States of America

To Sharon and Lucille,
for putting up with us while
we disappeared into this book

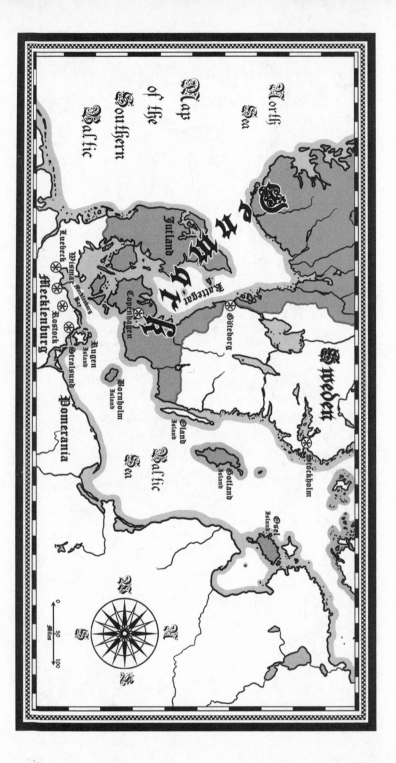

# Part I

*That is no country for old men*

# Chapter 1

"How utterly delightful!" exclaimed Richelieu. "I've never seen a cat with such delicate features. The coloration is marvelous, as well."

For a moment, the aristocratic and intellectual face of France's effective ruler dissolved into something much more youthful. Richelieu ignored Rebecca Stearns entirely, for a few seconds, as his forefinger played with the little paws of the kitten in his lap. Rebecca had just presented it to Richelieu as a diplomatic gift.

He raised his head, smiling. "A 'Siamese,' you call it? Surely you have not managed to establish trade relations with southeast Asia in such a short time? Even given your mechanical genius, that would seem almost another miracle."

Rebecca pondered that smile, for a moment, while she marshaled her answer. One thing, if nothing else, had become quite clear to her in the few short minutes since she had been ushered in to a private audience with the cardinal. Whatever else he was, Richelieu was possibly the most intelligent man she had ever met in her life. Or, at least, the shrewdest.

And quite charming, in person—that she had not expected. The combination of that keen intellect and the personal warmth and grace was disarming to someone like Rebecca, with her own basically intellectual temperament.

She reminded herself, very firmly, that being disarmed in the presence of Richelieu was the one thing she could least afford. For all his brains and his charm, the cardinal was almost certainly the most dangerous enemy her nation faced at the moment. And while she did not think Richelieu was cruel by nature, he had demonstrated before that he was quite prepared to be utterly ruthless when advancing what he considered the interests of his own nation. *La gloire de France* was a phrase which rang splendidly—but, like a sword, had a sharp edge to those who stood in the way.

She decided to pursue the double meaning implicit in the cardinal's last sentence.

"'Another' miracle?" she asked, raising an eyebrow. "An interesting term, Your Eminence. As I recall, the most recent characterization you gave the Ring of Fire was 'witchcraft.'"

Richelieu's gentle smile remained as steady as it had been since she entered his private audience chamber. "A misunderstanding," he insisted, wiggling his fingers dismissively. Then, paused for a moment to admire the kitten batting at the long digits. "My error, and I take full responsibility for it. Always a mistake, you know, to jump to conclusions based on scant evidence. And I fear I was perhaps too influenced at the time by the views of Father Joseph. You met him yesterday, I believe, during your audience with the king?"

Another double meaning was buried in that sentence as well. Subtly, Richelieu was reminding Rebecca that her alternative to dealing with *him* was the rather childish King Louis XIII—or, even worse, the religious fanatic Father Joseph. The Capucin monk was close to Richelieu, and was also the leader of the harshly intolerant Catholic lay organization of France known as the Company of the Holy Sacrament.

Rebecca controlled the natural impulse of an intellectual to *talk*. In this, as in so many things, her far less intellectual husband had trained her. Mike Stearns was a trade union leader in his origins. So, unlike Rebecca, he had learned long ago that the best tactic in negotiations is often simply to say nothing.

"Let the other side do most of the talking," he'd told her. "On average, I'd say anyone's twice as likely to screw up with their mouth open than closed."

The cardinal, of course, was quite familiar with the ploy himself. Silence lengthened in the room.

For an intellectual, silence is the ultimate sin. So, again, Rebecca found herself forced to *keep it zipped!*

She took refuge in memories of her husband. Mike, standing in the doorway to their house in Grantville, his face somewhat drawn and unhappy, as he bid her farewell on her diplomatic journey to France and Holland. The same face—she found this memory far more comforting—the night before, in their bed.

Something in the smile which came to her face at *that* memory defeated the cardinal. Richelieu's smile never wavered, true. But he did take a deep breath and, gently but firmly, set the kitten down on the floor and left off his idle playing.

"The 'Ring of Fire,' as you call it—which brought your 'Americans' and their bizarre technology into our world—was enough to confuse anyone, madame. But further reflection, especially with further evidence to base it upon, has led me to the conclusion that I was quite in error to label your . . . ah, if you will forgive the term, bizarre new country the product of 'witchcraft.'"

Richelieu paused for a moment, running his fingers down his rich robes. "Quite inexcusable on my part, really. Once I had time to ponder the matter, I realized that I had veered perilously close to Manicheanism." With a little chuckle: "And how long has it been since *that* heresy was condemned? A millennium and a half, ha! And here I claim to be a cardinal!"

Rebecca decided it was safe enough to respond to the witticism with a little chuckle of her own. Nothing more than that, though. She could practically *feel* the cardinal's magnetic personality drawing her in, and didn't doubt for a moment that Richelieu understood the power of his own charm quite well. By all accounts, the cardinal was a chaste man. But 'seduction' was a term which had more than one application. Time after time, Richelieu's rise to power and influence had been eased by that personal grace and charm—and, with other intellectuals, the suppleness of his mind. Were she not, for all practical purposes, the envoy of a nation at war with Richelieu, she would have enjoyed immensely spending a few hours with one of Christendom's most prodigious intellects discussing the theological implications of the strange event which had brought an entire town of people into 17th-century Europe from a place centuries in the future called "the United States of America."

*Silence, woman! Obey your husband!*

And that thought, too, reinforced her own serene smile. In truth, Mike Stearns was very far removed from a "patriarch." He would be amused, Rebecca knew, when she told him of her self-admonition. ("I will be good God-damned. You mean that *for once* you listened to me?")

It was another little defeat for Richelieu. Something in the set of his smile—a trace of stiffness—told her so. Again, the cardinal ran fingers down his robe, and resumed speaking.

"No, only God could have caused such an incredible transposition of Time and Space. And your term 'the Ring of Fire' seems appropriate." Very serene, now, his smile. "As I'm sure you are aware, I have long had my agents investigating your 'United States' in Thuringia. Several of them have interviewed local inhabitants who witnessed the event. And, indeed, they too—simple peasants—saw the heavens open up and a halo of heatless flame create a new little world in a small part of central Germany.

"Still—" he said, abruptly, holding up a hand as if to forestall Rebecca's next words. (Which, in fact, she'd had no intention of speaking.) "Still, the fact that the *event* was of divine origin does not lead to any certain conclusion as to its *purpose*."

*And here it comes,* thought Rebecca. *The new and official party line.*

She was privileged, she realized. Her conversations with the courtiers at the royal audience the night before had made clear to her that France's elite was still groping for a coherent ideological explanation for the appearance of Grantville in the German province of Thuringia. Having now survived for two years—not to mention defeating several attacking armies in the process, at least one of them funded and instigated by France— the Americans and the new society they were forging could no longer be dismissed as hearsay. And the term "witchcraft" was . . . petty, ultimately.

Richelieu, she was certain, had constructed such an ideological explanation—and she would be the first one to hear it.

"Have you considered the history of the world which created your Americans?" asked Richelieu. "As I'm sure you also know, I've obtained"—here came another dismissive wiggle of the finger— "through various means, several of the historical accounts which your Americans brought with them. And I've studied them all, very thoroughly."

*That's a given,* thought Rebecca. Somewhat glumly, because it was only a "given" in retrospect. At the time, it had never occurred to her, or Mike, or any of the leaders of their new United States, that history books would rapidly become one of the most prized objects for espionage. Technical books, yes; blueprints, yes; *anything* which would enable the United States' opponents to steal some of their incredible new technology. But . . . *high school history textbooks?*

In retrospect, of course, the thing was obvious. Any ruler or political figure in the world, in the summer of the year 1633, would eagerly want to see what lay in store for them in the immediate years to come. And the consequences of that knowledge would be truly incalculable. If a king knows what will happen a year or two from now, after all, he will take measures to make sure that it either happens more quickly—if he likes the development—or doesn't happen at all, if otherwise.

And in so doing, of course, will rapidly scramble the sequence of historical events which led to that original history in the first place. It was the old quandary of time travel, which Rebecca herself had studied in the science fiction novels which the town of Grantville had brought with it also. And, like her husband, she had come to the conclusion that the Ring of Fire had created a new and parallel universe to the one from which Grantville—and the history which produced it—had originally come.

As she ruminated, Richelieu had been studying her. The intelligent dark brown eyes brought their own glum feeling. *And do not think for a moment that the cardinal is too foolish not to understand that. He, too, understands that the history which was will now never be—but also understands that he can still discern broad patterns in those events. And guide France accordingly.*

His next words confirmed it. "Of course, the *exact* events will be different. But the basic framework of that future world is clear enough. I believe we can summarize it with that term you favor so much: *democracy.* Or, as I would put it, rule by the masses. Because, to be frank, *all* the various political structures which that future world exhibits show the same basic characteristic. The authority of an established aristocracy and royalty discarded; all power vested in the 'people'; whether that people be called 'citizens' or 'the proletariat' or 'the Volk.' No rein, no check, no limits of any kind placed upon their desires and ambitions."

The wiggling fingers, this time, were not so much dismissive as demonstrative. "All the rest follows. The massacre of six million of your own fellow Jews, to name just one instance. The atrocities committed by such obvious monsters as Stalin and those Asian fellows. Mao and Pol Pot, if I recall the names correctly. And—let us not forget—the destruction of entire cities and regions by regimes which, though perhaps not as despotic, were no less prepared to wreak havoc upon the world. I will remind you, madame, that the United States of America which you seem determined to emulate in this universe did not shrink for an instant from incinerating the cities of Japan—or cities in Germany, for that matter, who are now your neighbors. Half a million people— more likely a million, all told—exterminated like so many insects."

Rebecca practically clamped her jaws shut. Her instincts were to shriek argument in response. *Yes? And the current devastation which you have unleashed on Germany? The Thirty Years War will kill more Germans than either world war of the 20th century! Not to mention the millions of children who die in your precious aristocratic world every year from hunger, disease and deprivation—even during peacetime—all of which can be quickly remedied!*

But she remained true to her husband's advice. There was no point in arguing with Richelieu. He was not advancing a hypothesis to be tested, here. He was simply letting the envoy from the United States know that the conflict was not over, and would not be over, until one or the other side triumphed. For all the charm, and civility, and the serenity of the smile, Richelieu was issuing a declaration of war.

And, indeed, his next words: "So it all now seems clear to me. Yes, God created the Ring of Fire. Absurd to label such a miraculous event a thing of petty 'witchcraft.' But he did so in order to warn us of the perils of the future, that we might be armed to avoid them. That we might be steeled in our resolve to create a world based on the sure principles of monarchy, aristocracy, and an established church. Perils of which, my dear Madame Stearns, you and your people—meaning no personal disrespect, and implying no *personal* sinfulness—are both the agents and the embodiment."

The cardinal rose gracefully to his feet and gave Rebecca a polite bow. "And now, I'm afraid, I must attend to the king's business. I hope you enjoy your stay in Paris, and if I may be of any assistance please call upon me. How soon do you plan to depart for Holland? And by what means?"

*As quickly as I can, by any route available.* But she restricted herself to a hesitant, almost girlish: "I'm not really sure. Travel from here to Holland is difficult, given the nature of the times."

Richelieu's charm was back in full force, as he escorted her to the door. "I strongly urge you to take the land route. The Channel—even the North Sea—is plagued with piracy. I can

provide you with an escort to the border of the Spanish Nether-
lands, and I'm quite sure I can arrange a safe passage through to
Holland. Yes, yes, France and Spain are antagonists at the moment.
But despite what you may have heard, my personal relations with
Archduchess Isabella are quite good. I am certain the Spaniards
will not place any obstacles in the way."

The statement was ridiculous, of course. The very *last* thing the
Spaniards would want to see was a diplomatic mission headed by
the wife of the President of the United States perched in Holland,
which the Spaniards had been trying to reconquer for half a century. Little, that United States might be. In physical size, simply
the old regions of Thuringia and western Franconia—a small
enough piece of Germany. Granted, by German standards the
United States was an important principality. Only Saxony had a
larger population. But its population was not even remotely as large
as either France or Spain's. Still, that same new little country had
shattered a Spanish army at Eisenach and the Wartburg a year
earlier. The idea of an alliance between the United States and the
United Provinces . . . would be enough to give nightmares to any
Spanish official.

"Perhaps," was all she said. Smiling serenely, as she passed
through the door.

# Chapter 2

After the door closed, Richelieu turned away and resumed his seat. A moment later, Etienne Servien came through a narrow door at the rear of the room. To all appearances, the door to a closet; in reality, the door which connected to the chamber from which Servien could spy upon the cardinal's audiences whenever Richelieu so desired. Servien was one of the cardinal's handpicked special agents called *intendants*, and the one he relied upon for the most delicate work.

"You heard?" grunted Richelieu. Servien nodded.

Richelieu threw up his hands, as much with humor as exasperation.

"What a *formidable* woman!" Feeling a little tug on his robes, the cardinal gazed down at the kitten playing with the hem. The serene smile returned. He bent over, picked up the small creature, and deposited it in his lap. Then, as he petted the kitten, continued to speak.

"I never would have thought it possible, Etienne. A Sephardic Jewess—Doctor Balthazar Abrabanel's daughter, no less! That breed can talk for hours on end, ignoring hunger all the while. Philosophers and theologians, the lot. I'd expected to simply smile and let her fill my ears with information. Instead—"

He chuckled ruefully. "Not often *that* happens to me. I trust I didn't give away anything critical?"

Servien shrugged. "The Sephardic Jews also provide Europe and

the Ottoman Empire with most of its bankers, Your Eminence—
not a profession known for being loose-lipped. Moreover, while
he may be a doctor and a philosopher, Balthazar Abrabanel, as well
as his brother Uriel, are both experienced spies. *Also* not a trade
which favors blabbermouths. Then, to make things still worse,
Abrabanel's daughter Rebecca—by all accounts, including those of
her enemies—is extremely intelligent in her own right. She would
certainly have deduced, in any event, that France has not laid down
its arms. So . . . best to do as you did, I think. Beyond that, she
learned nothing. There was certainly no hint in your words of our
grand strategy."

" 'Grand strategy,' " echoed Richelieu. "*Which* grand strategy are
you referring to, Etienne? The greater, or the lesser?"

"Either of them, or both. I assure you, not even Satan himself
could have deduced our plans from anything you spoke. The
woman is intelligent, yes. But, as you said, not a witch."

The cardinal pondered silently for a moment, his lean face growing leaner still.

"Still, she is too intelligent," he pronounced at length. "I hope
she will accept my offer to provide her with an escort for a journey
overland to the Spanish Low Countries. That would enable us—
in a dozen different ways—to delay her travel long enough for our
purposes. But . . ."

He shook his head. "I doubt it. She will almost certainly deduce
as much, and choose to make her own arrangements for traveling by sea to Holland. And we simply *cannot* allow her such a close
examination of the ports. Not now, of all times!"

Servien pursed his lips. "I could certainly keep her away from Le
Havre, Your Eminence. Not *every* port on the Channel, of course—
that would be too obvious. But if she were forced to take ship from
one of the smaller ports, she might not notice enough—"

Richelieu interrupted him with a gesture which was almost angry.
"Desist, Etienne! I realize that you are trying to spare me the
necessity of making this decision. Which, the Lord knows, I find
distasteful in the extreme. But reasons of state have never been
forgiving of the kindlier sentiments." He sighed heavily. "Necessity
remains what it is. Do keep her from Le Havre, of course. One of
the smaller ports would be far better anyway, for . . . what is needed."

The cardinal looked down at the kitten, still playing with his
long forefinger. "And, who knows? Perhaps fortune will smile on
us—and her—and she will make a bad decision."

The gentle smile returned. "There are few enough of God's marvelous creatures in this world. Let us hope we will not have to destroy yet another one. On your way out, Etienne, be so kind as to summon my servant."

The dismissal was polite, but firm. Servien nodded and left the room.

A moment later, Desbournais entered the room. Desbournais was the cardinal's *valet de chambre,* and had entered Richelieu's service at the age of seventeen. Richelieu was popular with his servants, as he was with all of his allies and associates. However ruthless he might be in the service of France, the cardinal was invariably considerate and polite to those around him, no matter what their station. Very generous to them, as well. Richelieu repaid loyalty with loyalty of his own. That was as true of his kitchen help as Louis XIII, king of France.

The cardinal lifted the kitten and held it out to Desbournais. "Isn't he gorgeous? See to providing for him, Desbournais—and well, mind you."

After Desbournais left, Richelieu rose from the chair and went to the window in his chamber. The residence the cardinal used whenever he was in Paris—a palace in all but name—was a former hotel which he had purchased on the Rue St. Honoré near the Louvre. He'd also purchased the adjoining hotel in order, after having it razed, to provide him with a better view of the city.

As he stared out the window, all the kindliness and gentleness left his face. The cold, stern—even haughty—visage which stared down at the great city of Paris was the one that his enemies knew. For all his charm and grace, Richelieu could also be intimidating in the extreme. He was a tall man, whose slenderness was offset by the heavy and rich robes of office he always wore. His long face, with its high forehead, arched brows, and large brown eyes, was that of an intellectual, yes. But there was also the slightly curved nose and the strong chin, set off by the pointed and neatly barbered beard—those, the features of a very different sort of man.

Hernan Cortez would have understood that face. So would the duke of Alba. Any of the world's conquerors would have understood a face which had been shaped, for years, by iron resolve.

"So be it," murmured the cardinal. "God, in his mercy, creates enough marvelous creatures that we can afford to destroy those we must. Necessity remains."

❋          ❋          ❋

"Well, how'd it go?" asked Jeff Higgins cheerfully. Then, seeing the tight look on Rebecca's face, his smile thinned. "That bad? I thought the guy had a reputation for being—"

Rebecca shook her head. "He was gracious and polite. Which didn't stop him—not for a second—from issuing what amounted to a declaration of total war."

Sighing, she removed the scarf she had been wearing to fend off a typical Paris drizzle. Seeing it was merely a bit damp, she spread it out to dry over the back of one of the chairs in the sitting room of the house which the delegation from the United States had rented in Paris. Then, seeing Heinrich Schmidt entering the room from the kitchen, Rebecca smiled ruefully.

*Major* Heinrich Schmidt, as it happened. The officer who commanded the small detachment of U.S. Army soldiers who had accompanied Rebecca in her voyage, along with Jeff and Gretchen Higgins and Jimmy Andersen.

"I'm afraid—very much afraid—that you gentlemen may soon be earning your pay."

Heinrich shrugged. So did Jeff, who, although he had a special assignment on this mission, was—along with his friend Jimmy— also a soldier in the U.S. Army.

The next person to enter the room was Jeff's wife. "So what's happening?" she demanded, her German accent still there beneath the fluent and colloquial English.

Rebecca's smile widened. She always found the contrast between Jeff and Gretchen somewhat amusing, in an affectionate sort of way. What the Americans called an "odd couple," based on one of those electronic dramas which Rebecca still found fascinating, for all the hours she'd spent watching television—even hosting a TV show of her own.

Jeff Higgins, though he had been toughened considerably in the two years since his small American town had been deposited into the middle of war-torn central Europe in the year 1631, still exuded a certain air of what the Americans called a "geek" or a "nerd." He was tall, yes; but also overweight—still, for all the exercise he now got. Although Jeff had recently celebrated his twentieth birthday, his pudgy face looked like that of a teenager. A pug nose between an intellectual's eyes, peering near-sightedly through thick glasses. About as unromantic a figure as one could imagine.

His wife, on the other hand . . .

Gretchen, nee Richter, was two years older than Jeff. She was

not precisely "beautiful," not with that strong nose and that firm
jaw, even leaving aside her tall stature and shoulders broader than
those of most women. But, still, so good-looking that men's eyes
invariably followed her wherever she went. The fact that Gretchen
was, as the Americans put it, "well built," only added to the effect—
as did the long blond hair which cascaded over those square
shoulders.

Gretchen, unlike Jeff, was native-born. Like Rebecca herself, she
was one of the many 17th-century Europeans who had been swept
up by the Ring of Fire and cast their lot with the newly arrived
Americans. Including, as was true of Rebecca herself, marriage to
an American husband.

Regardless of her native origins, Gretchen had adopted the
attitudes and ideology of the Americans with the fervor and zeal
of a new convert. If almost all the Americans were devoted to their
concepts of democracy and social equality, Gretchen's devotion—
not surprisingly, given the horrors of her own life—tended to
frighten even them.

Rebecca was reminded of that again, as Gretchen idly played
with the edge of her vest. The blond woman's impressive bosom
disguised the thing perfectly, but Rebecca knew full well that
Gretchen was carrying her beloved 9mm automatic in a shoulder
holster. She had sometimes been tempted to ask Jeff if his wife
*slept* with the thing.

For the most part, however, Rebecca's smile was simply due to
the fact that she both liked and—very deeply—*approved* of Jeff
and Gretchen Higgins. In Jeff's case, if for no other reason, because
the young man had once saved Rebecca from certain murder at
the hands of Croat cavalrymen in the service of the Austrian
Habsburgs. In Gretchen's case, leaving aside their personal friendship, because Rebecca knew full well that Gretchen's near-fanaticism
was every bit as essential to the survival of the new society Rebecca
and her husband Mike were creating as anything else.

Gretchen might frighten others, but she never frightened Mike
Stearns. He did not always agree with her, true enough—and, even
when he did, often found her tactics deplorably crude. But, no
matter how high he had risen in this new world, Rebecca's husband
was still the same man he had always been—the leader of a trade
union of Appalachian coal miners, a folk which had its own long
and bitter memories of the abuses of the powerful and mighty.

"Don't kid yourself," Mike had once growled to Rebecca, on the one occasion where she had expressed some exasperation with Gretchen's zeal and disregard for the complexities of the political situation. They had just finished breakfast, and Mike was helping Rebecca with the dishes. For all that she had grown accustomed to it, Rebecca still thought there was something charming about having such a very masculine sort of husband working alongside her in kitchen chores.

"When push comes to shove, the only people I can *really* depend on—outside of my coal miners and the new trade unions, and probably Willie Ray's new farmers' granges—are Gretchen and her wild-ass kids." Mike finished wiping the last plate and put it in the cupboard. "Yeah, sure, right now we're in the good graces of the Swedes. Gustavus Adolphus is a friend of ours— so is even his chancellor Oxenstierna. But don't ever forget that he's a *king*, or that the *nobleman* Axel Oxenstierna is every bit as devoted to the aristocracy as Gretchen hates the bastards. If the tide turns . . ."

Staring out the kitchen window of their house in Grantville, he shook his head firmly. "As regretful as he might find the necessity, Gustav II Adolf will cut our throats in a heartbeat, under the right circumstances. Whereas without us, Gretchen and her radical democratic Committees of Correspondence are so much dog food—and she knows it perfectly well, don't think she doesn't. However often I may piss her off by my 'compromises with principle,' she knows she needs me as much as I need her."

When he turned away from the window, his blue eyes had been dancing with humor. "Besides, she's *so* handy to have around. You've read about the American civil rights movement, haven't you?"

Rebecca nodded. She'd devoured books on American history— *any* kind of history, actually, but American in particular—ever since Mike had rescued her and her father from marauding mercenaries. That had happened on the very same day as the Ring of Fire. Two years ago, now—and Rebecca was a very fast reader. She'd read a *lot* of books.

Mike smiled. "Well, there's a little anecdote that illustrates my point. Malcolm X once made the wisecrack that the reason the white establishment was willing to talk to the Reverend Martin Luther King, Jr., was because they *didn't* want to talk to him. And that's about the way it is with me and Gretchen."

A motion outside the window must have caught his eye, because

Mike turned away from her for a moment. Whatever he saw caused his smile to broaden into a grin.

"Speak of the devil . . . Come here, love—I'll show you another example of what I'm talking about."

When Rebecca had come to the window, she'd seen the figure of Harry Lefferts sauntering past on the street below. It was early in the morning, and from the somewhat self-satisfied look on his face, Rebecca suspected that Harry had spent the night with one of the girlfriends he seemed to attract like a magnet. Harry was a handsome young man, with the kind of daredevil self-confidence and easy humor which attracted a large number of young women.

She was a little puzzled. Harry's amatory prowess hardly seemed relevant to the discussion she was having with Mike. But then, seeing the little swagger in Harry's stride—nothing extravagant, just the subtle cockiness of a young man who was *very* sure of himself, Rebecca began to understand.

Whatever women might find attractive about Harry Lefferts, not all men did. Many, yes—those who hadn't chosen to cross him. Those who did cross him tended to discover very rapidly what the Americans meant by their expression "hard-ass." Harry was a muscular man, and his mind was every bit as "hard-ass" as his body. When he wanted to be, Harry Lefferts could be rather frightening.

"Did I ever tell you how I'd always use Harry in negotiations?" Mike murmured in her ear. "Back in my trade-union days?"

Rebecca shook her head—then, laughed, as Mike's murmur turned into a more intimate gesture involving a tongue and an ear.

"Stop it!" She pushed him away playfully. "Didn't you get enough last night?"

Mike grinned and sidled toward her. "Well, I'd always make sure that Harry was on the negotiating team when we met with the company representatives. His job was to sit in the corner and, whenever I'd start making noises about maybe agreeing to a compromise, start glaring at me and growling. Worked like a charm, nine times out of ten."

Rebecca laughed again, avoiding the sidle. Oddly, perhaps, by moving into a corner of the kitchen.

"I pretty much think of Gretchen the same way," Mike murmured. Sidling, sidling. The murmur was becoming a bit husky.

"The nobility of Europe hates my guts. But then they see Gretchen sitting in the corner . . . growling, growling . . ."

She was boxed in, now, trapped. Mike, never a stranger to tactics, swooped immediately.

"No," he said. "As it happens, I *didn't* get enough last night."

The memory of what had followed warmed Rebecca, at the same time as it brought its own frustrations. She envied Jeff and Gretchen for having been able to take this long journey together—never more so than when she heard the noises they made in an adjoining bedroom, and Rebecca found herself pining for her own bed back in Grantville. With Mike, and his warm and lovely body, in it.

But . . . there had been no way for Mike to come. He was the President of the United States, and his duties did not allow him to be absent for more than a few days.

Something in her face must have registered, for she saw Gretchen smiling in a way which was both self-satisfied and a little serene. However much they might seem like an "odd couple" to others, Rebecca knew, Gretchen and Jeff were every bit as devoted to each other as were she and Mike. And, judging from the noises they made in the night—*night after night, damnation!*—every bit as passionate.

But perhaps she was reading the wrong thing into that smile. If nothing else, Gretchen's fervent ideological beliefs often made her a bit self-satisfied and serene.

"What did you expect?" demanded the young German woman. "A cardinal! And the same stinking pig who tried to have our children massacred at the school last year, don't forget that either."

Rebecca hadn't forgotten. That memory, in fact, had been as much of a help as her husband's advice, during her interview with Richelieu. Charming and gracious the man might be. But Rebecca did not allow herself to forget that he was also perfectly capable of being as deadly as a viper—and just as cold-bloodedly merciless.

Still . . .

There would always be a certain difference in the way Rebecca Stearns, nee Abrabanel, would look at the world compared to Gretchen. For Rebecca, for the most part, the atrocities committed by Europe's rulers had always remained at arm's length. Not so, for Gretchen. Her father murdered before her eyes; she herself gang-raped by mercenaries and then dragooned into becoming their camp follower; her mother taken away years before by other mercenaries, to an unknown fate; half her family dead or otherwise destroyed—and all of it, all that horror, simply because Europe's nobility and princes had chosen to quarrel over their competing privileges. The fact that they would shatter Germany and slaughter a fourth of its population in the process did not bother them in the least.

Rebecca was an opponent of that aristocratic regime, true enough, and, along with her husband, had set herself the task of replacing it with a better one. But she simply never felt the sheer *hatred* that Gretchen did. And knew, perfectly well, that Gretchen would have found nothing charming or gracious about His Eminence, Cardinal Richelieu. She would have simply measured that long and aristocratic neck for a noose.

"Which," Rebecca muttered to herself, "is not perhaps such a bad idea, everything considered."

"What was that?" asked Heinrich.

The major's face exhibited its own serenity. For all his youth— Heinrich was only twenty-four—the former mercenary had already seen more of bloodshed and war's ruin than most soldiers, in most of history's eras, ever saw in a lifetime. Rebecca liked Heinrich, to be sure. But the man's indifference to suffering sometimes appalled her. Not the indifference itself, so much as the cause of it. Heinrich Schmidt was a rather warm-hearted man, by temperament. But the years he had spent in Tilly's army after being forcibly "recruited" at the age of fifteen had left him with a shell of iron. He had enrolled readily enough in the American army, when given the chance. And Rebecca was quite sure that, in his own way, Heinrich was as devoted to his new nation as she was. Still, when all was said and done, the man retained a mercenary's callous attitudes in most respects.

"Never mind," responded Rebecca. "I was just reminding myself"—here, a little nod to Gretchen—"that Richelieu is capable of anything."

She pulled out the chair over which she'd spread the scarf and sat down. "Which brings us directly to the subject at hand. There's no point in remaining in Paris any longer. So the question posed is: by what route do we try to reach Holland?"

A motion in the doorway drew her eyes. Jeff's young friend Jimmy Andersen had entered from the kitchen. Behind him, Rebecca could see the other five soldiers in Heinrich's detachment.

She waited until all of them had come into the room and were either perched somewhere or leaning against the walls. Rebecca suspected that her very nondictatorial habits would have astonished most ambassadors of history. She dealt with her entourage as colleagues, not as subordinates. But she didn't care. She was an intellectual herself, by temperament, and enjoyed the process of debate and discussion.

"Here's the choice," she explained, once all of them were listening. "We can take the land route or try to hire a coastal lugger. If the first, Richelieu has offered to provide us an escort to Spanish territory and assures me he can obtain the agreement of the Spanish to pass us along to the United Provinces."

Gretchen and Jeff were already shaking their heads. "It's a trap," snarled Gretchen. "He'll set up an ambush along the way."

Heinrich was also shaking his head, but the gesture was aimed immediately at Gretchen.

"Not a chance of that," he said firmly. "Richelieu's a *statesman,* Gretchen, not a street thug." He smiled thinly. "The difference isn't one of morality, you understand—if anything, I'd rather trust a footpad. But there is a difference in methods. If he has us murdered while we're clearly under his official protection, he'd ruin his reputation."

Gretchen was glaring at him, but Heinrich was unfazed. "Yes, he *would.* And stop glaring at me, silly girl! Hating your enemies is a fine and splendid thing, but not when it addles your wits."

"I agree with Heinrich," interjected Rebecca. "Not the least of the reasons for Richelieu's success is that people trust him. His word is his bond, and all that. It's *true,* Gretchen, don't think it isn't."

She reached back and pulled the scarf off the seat's backrest. It was dry enough, so she began folding it. "I have no doubt at all that our *safety* will be assured, if we accept Richelieu's offer. But I also have no doubt at all—"

Heinrich was chuckling softly. "We'd be 'enjoying' the longest damn trip anyone ever took to Holland from Paris. Not more than a few hundred miles—and I'll wager anything you want to bet it would take us *weeks.* Probably months."

Now that Gretchen's animosity had been given a new target, the woman's usual quick intelligence returned. "Yeah, easy enough. Broken axles every five miles. Lamed horses. Unexpected detours due to unexpected floods. Every other bridge washed out—and, how strange, nobody seems to know where the fords are. At least two weeks at the border, squabbling with Spanish officials. You name it, we'll get it."

Jeff, throughout, had been studying Rebecca. "So what's the problem with the alternative?"

Rebecca grimaced. "There's something happening in the ports of northern France that Richelieu doesn't want us to see. I don't know what it might be, but it's more than simply this alliance with the Dutch. I'm almost sure of it. That means"—she smiled at Heinrich—"and *I'll* offer this wager, that we'll never be allowed into Le Havre. Some excuse or other, but Richelieu will see to it."

"You're right," agreed Heinrich. "We'll have to take ship in one of the smaller and more distant ports."

The major, clearly enough, was thinking ahead. The man had a good and experienced soldier's instinctive grasp for terrain, to begin with. And, where Rebecca had spent the past two years devouring the books which Grantville had brought with it, Heinrich had been just as passionately devoted to the marvelous maps and atlases which the Americans possessed. By now, his knowledge of Europe's geography was well-nigh encyclopedic.

"I still don't see the problem," said Jeff. "So what if we add another two or three days to the trip? We'd still be able to make it to Holland within two weeks."

"Pirates," replied Heinrich and Rebecca, almost simultaneously. Rebecca smiled; then, nodding toward Heinrich, urged him to explain.

"The English Channel is infested with the bastards," growled the major. "Has been for centuries—and maybe never as badly as now, what with the French and Spanish preoccupied with their affairs on the Continent and that sorry-ass Charles on the throne in England."

Five of the six soldiers in the kitchen nodded. The sixth, Jimmy Andersen—who, except for Jeff, was the only native-born American in the group—was practically goggling.

*"Pirates?* In the *English* Channel?"

Rebecca found it hard not to laugh aloud. For all that they had been somewhat acclimatized in the two years since their arrival in 17th-century Europe, she had often found that Americans still tended to unconsciously lapse into old ways of thinking. For Americans, she knew, anything associated with "England" carried with it the connotations of "safe, secure, even stodgy." The idea of *pirates* in the English Channel ...

"Where do they come from?" demanded Jimmy.

"North Africa is where a lot of them are based," replied Heinrich. With a shrug: "Of course, they're not all Moors, by any means. The Spanish license 'privateers' operating out of Dunkirk and Ostend against Dutch shipping, and the Dunkirkers are none too picky about their targets. And even for the Moors, probably half the crews, at least, are from somewhere in Europe. The world's scavengers."

Jimmy was still shaking his head with bemusement. But Jeff, always quicker than his friend to adjust to reality, was giving Rebecca a knowing look.

"So what you're suggesting, in short, is that if we take the sea route ... how hard would it be for Richelieu to *arrange* a pirate attack?"

Rebecca wasn't sure herself. Neither, judging from his expression, was Heinrich.

Gretchen, of course, was.

"Of course he will!" she snapped. "The man's a spider. He has his web everywhere."

With Gretchen, as always, response was as certain as analysis. Sure enough, just as Rebecca had thought, the 9mm was in its place. A moment later, Gretchen had it in hand and was laying it firmly down on the table in front of her.

"Pirates it is," she pronounced, sweeping the room with a hard gaze. "Let's give them a taste of *rate of fire,* boys—what do you say?"

A harsh—and approving—laugh came from the soldiers. Rebecca looked at Heinrich.

He shrugged. "Seems as good a plan as any."

Rebecca now looked to Jeff and Jimmy. Jeff, not to her surprise, had a stubborn expression which showed clearly that he was standing with his wife. Jimmy ...

This time she *did* laugh. Befuddled, he might sometimes be, at the nature of his new world. But Jimmy Andersen, a teenager devoted to his games, adored the opportunities.

"Oh, how cool! We can try out the grenade launchers!"

# Chapter 3

Dr. James Nichols finished washing off his hands and turned away from the sink, fluttering his hands in the air in order to dry them. Even in the hospital, Mike knew, towels were in such short supply that James had decreed that medical personnel should use them as little as possible.

He braced himself for the inevitable complaint. But, other than scowling slightly, the doctor simply shook his head and walked over to the door.

"Let's get out of here and let the poor woman get some sleep."

Mike opened the door for the doctor, whose hands were still damp, and followed him out into the corridor. Wondering, a bit, how the sick woman was going to get much sleep with her entire family crowded around the bed.

A bit, not much. Mike himself would never get used to it personally, but he knew that Germans of the 17th century were accustomed to a level of population density in their living arrangements that would drive most Americans half-crazy. A good bed was valuable—why waste it on two people, when four would fit?

Once the door was closed, he cocked an eyebrow at Nichols. Trying, probably with not much success, to keep his worry hidden.

No success at all, apparently:

"It's not plague, if that's what you're worrying about." James' voice was more gravelly than usual. Nichols worked long hours as a matter of routine. But Mike knew that since Melissa had left Grantville, he practically lived at the hospital. Insofar as a black man's face could look gray with fatigue, James' did. His hard and rough features seemed a bit softer, not from warmth but simply from weariness.

"You need to get some sleep yourself," said Mike sternly.

James gave him a smile which was half-mocking. "Oh, really? And exactly how much sleep have *you* been getting, since Becky left?"

As they continued moving down the corridor toward Nichols' office, weaving their way through the packed halls of Grantville's only hospital, James' scowl returned in full force.

"What in God's name possessed us to send our womenfolk off into that howling wilderness?" he demanded. Indicating, with a sweep of the hand, everything in the world.

Mike snorted. "Paris and London hardly qualify as 'howling wilderness,' James. I'm sure James Fenimore Cooper would agree with me on that, once he gets born. So would George Armstrong Custer."

"Bullshit," came the immediate retort. "I'm not an 'injun-fighter,' dammit, I'm a doctor. Cities in this day and age are a microbe's paradise. It's bad enough even here in Grantville, with our—ha! what a joke!—so-called 'sanitary practices.'"

They'd reached the doctor's office and, once again, Mike opened for James. "Forget 'gay Paree,' Mike. In the year of our Lord 1633, the sophisticated Parisian's idea of 'sanitation' is to look out the window first before emptying the chamber pot."

The image made Mike grimace a little, but he didn't argue the point. He'd be arguing soon enough, anyway, he knew. James' wisecrack about Grantville's sanitation was bound to be the prelude to another of the doctor's frequent tirades on the subject of the lunacy of political leaders in general, and those of the Confederated Principalities of Europe in particular. Which, of course, included Mike himself.

Once they'd taken their seats—James behind the desk and Mike in front of it—he decided to intersect the tirade before it even started.

"Don't bother with the usual rant," he growled. His own voice sounded pretty gravelly itself, and he reminded himself firmly not to take his own grouchiness at Rebecca's absence out on Nichols. For all that the doctor's near-monomania on the subject of epidemics sometimes irritated Mike, he respected and admired Nichols as much as he did anyone he'd ever met. Even leaving aside the fact that James had become one of his best friends since the Ring of Fire, the doctor's skill and energy was all that had kept hundreds of people alive. Probably thousands, when you figured in the indirect effects of his work.

"What's she got?" he asked gruffly. "Another case of the flu?"

Nichols nodded. "Most likely. Could be something else—more precisely, *and* be something else. But I'd say it's just another case—out of God knows how many—where we Typhoid Mary Americans inflicted the helpless locals with our highly evolved strains of influenza." His thick lips twisted in a wry smile. "Of course, I'm sure they'll be getting their revenge soon enough, once smallpox hits us. Which it will, don't think it won't."

"Any luck with—"

James shrugged. "Jeff Adams thinks we'll have a vaccine ready to go within a month or so, in large enough quantities to make a difference. I just hope he's right that using cowpox will work. Me, I'm a little skeptical. But . . ."

Suddenly, he grinned. The expression came more naturally to James Nichols' face than did the scowl which usually graced it these days. "You'd think, wouldn't you, that a boy from the ghetto would be less fastidious than you white folks! But, I ain't. God, Mike, talk about the irony of life. I can remember the days when I used to complain, back in my ghetto clinic, that I was mired in the Dark Ages. And here I am—mired in the *real* Dark Ages."

"Don't ever let Melissa hear you say that," responded Mike, grinning himself. "Talk about a tirade!"

James sniffed. "Fine for her to lecture everybody on the upstanding qualities of people in all times and places. She was brought up a Boston Brahmin. Probably got fed political correctness with her formula. Me, I grew up in the streets of south Chicago, and I know the truth. Some people are just plain rotten, and most people are lazy. Careless, anyway."

He heaved himself erect from his weary sprawl in the chair, and leaned over the desk, supporting his weight on his arms. "Mike, I'm really *not* a monomaniac. You just don't have any idea what disease can do to us—the whole damn continent—living under these conditions. We've been lucky, thus far. A few flare-ups, here and there; nothing you could really call an epidemic. But it's just a matter of time."

He jerked a thumb toward the window. Beyond it lay the town of Grantville.

"What's the point of lecturing people every night on the TV programs about the need for personal sanitation—when most of them can't afford a change of clothes? What are they supposed to do—in the middle of Germany, in winter—walk around naked while they stand in line at the town's one and only public laundry worth talking about?"

There wasn't any trace of the grin left, now. "While we devote our precious resources to building more toys for that fucking king, instead of a textile and garment industry, the lice are having a field day. And I will *guarantee* you that disease and epidemic will kill more people—more of Gustav's own soldiers, the stupid bastard— than all the Habsburg or Bourbon armies in the world."

Mike sat up himself. The argument was back, and there was no point in trying to evade it. James Nichols was as stubborn and tenacious as he was intelligent and dedicated. The fact that Mike was at least half in agreement with the doctor just made him all the more stubborn in defending Gustavus Adolphus—and, of course, his own policies. The United States of which Mike Stearns was President was, on one level, just another of the many principalities which formed the Confederated Principalities of Europe under the rule of the king of Sweden. Even if, in practice, it enjoyed a status of near-sovereignty.

"James, you can't reduce this to simple arithmetic. I *know* disease—and hunger—are the real killers. But one year is not the same as the year after that, or the year after that. If we can stabilize the CPE and put a stop to the Thirty Years War, then we can start seriously planning for the future. But until that happens . . ."

He leaned back, sighing heavily. "What do you want me to do, James? For all his prejudices and quirks and godawful attitudes on a lot of questions, Gustavus Adolphus is the best ruler of the times. You don't doubt that any more than I do. Nor do you think, any more than I do, that Grantville could make it on its own— without devoting even *more* of its resources to purely military efforts. Being part of the CPE, whatever its drawbacks—and I think I understand those even better than you do—is our best option. But that means we don't have any choice except to do what we must to keep the CPE afloat."

He lurched to his feet and took three strides to the window.

There, he glowered down at the scene. Nichols' office was on the top floor of the three-story hospital, giving him a good view of the sprawling little city below.

And "sprawling" it was. Sprawling, and teeming with people. The sleepy little Appalachian town which had come through the Ring of Fire two years earlier was long gone, now. Mike could still see the relics of it, of course. Like most small towns in West Virginia, Grantville had suffered a population loss over the decades before the Ring of Fire. Downtown Grantville had some large and multi-story buildings left over from its salad days as a center of the gas and coal industry. On the day before the mysterious and still-unexplained cosmic disaster which had transplanted the town into 17th-century Europe, those buildings had been half vacant. Today, they were packed with people—and new buildings, well if crudely built, were rising up all over the place.

The sight caused him to relax some. Whatever else he had done, whatever mistakes he might have made, Mike Stearns and his policies had turned Grantville and the country surrounding it into one of the few areas in central Europe which were economically booming and had a growing population. A rapidly growing one, in fact. If Mike's insistence on supporting Gustav Adolf's armaments campaign would result in the death of many people—which it would; he didn't doubt that any more than Nichols did—it would keep many more alive. Alive, and prospering.

Such, at least, was his hope.

"What am I supposed to do, James?" he repeated, softly rather than angrily. "We're caught in a three-way vise—and only have two hands to fend off the jaws."

Without turning away from the window, he held up a finger.

"Jaw number one. Whether we like it or not, we're in the middle of one of the worst wars in European history. Worse, in a lot of ways, than either of the world wars of the twentieth century. With no sign that any of the great powers that surround us intend to make peace."

He heard a little throat-clearing sound behind him, and shook his head. "No, sorry, we haven't heard anything from Rita and Melissa yet. I'd be surprised if we had, since they and Julie and Alex were planning to sail from Hamburg. But I did get a radio message from Becky yesterday. She arrived in Paris a few days ago and is already leaving for Holland."

He heard James sigh. "Yeah, you got it. Richelieu was polite as could be, but hasn't budged an inch. In fact, Becky thinks he's planning some kind of new campaign. If she's right, knowing that canny son-of-a-bitch, it's going to be a doozy."

He looked toward the south. "Then, of course, we've still got the charming Austrian Habsburgs to deal with. Not to mention Maximilian of Bavaria. Not to mention that Wallenstein survived his wounds at the Alte Veste and God only knows what that man is really cooking up on his great estates in Bohemia. Not to mention that King Christian of Denmark—Protestant or not—is still determined to bring down the Swedes. Not to mention that most of Gustav's 'loyal princes'—Protestant or not—are the sorriest pack of treacherous scumbags you'll ever hope to meet in your life."

Mike started tapping his fingers on the pane. "So that's the first jaw. We're in a war, whether we like it or not. If anything, I think the war is starting to heat up again.

"Which brings us to 'jaw number two.' How should we fight it? The same way Gustav's been doing since he landed in northern Germany three years ago? With huge mercenary armies draining the countryside? Even leaving aside any outrages they commit on the civilian population—and they do, even with Gustav's disciplinary policies, don't think they don't—it's the stupidest waste of economic resources imaginable. It's already bled Sweden of too many able-bodied men, and left Gustav's treasury dry as a bone."

His fingers moved. Tap, tap, tap; like a drummer beating the march. "We can't keep borrowing money forever, James. The Abrabanels and the other Jewish financiers in Europe and Turkey who are backing us aren't really all *that* rich, when you get down to it. Not compared to the resources Richelieu and the Habsburgs can marshal. So that means more taxes and levies on our own population—and there are too many already."

He turned his head and returned James' glare with one of his own. "They won't be able to afford another change of clothes either, you know, with the taxes the way they are now. Levies on everything, once you go beyond the boundaries of the U.S. And, I hate to say it, but we've got too many levies going ourselves. We don't have any choice."

Nichols looked away, his face sagging a little. James was by no means stupid, however strongly he felt about his own concerns.

Mike drove on relentlessly. "So what's the alternative—besides John Simpson's 'new military policy'?"

The mention of Simpson brought a fierce scowl to Nichols' face. Mike barked a laugh—even though, as a rule, the name "John Simpson" usually brought a scowl to his own face.

"Yeah, sure. The man is an unmitigated ass. Arrogant, super-cilious, about as caring as a stone, you name it. What's that para-phrase from Gilbert and Sullivan that Melissa uses? 'The very picture of a modern CEO?' "

James nodded, chuckling. The doctor's lover despised John Simpson even more than he and Mike did.

Mike shrugged. "But whatever else he is, John Simpson is also the only experienced military officer in Grantville. On that level of experience, anyway. He *did* graduate from Annapolis and the Industrial College of the Armed Forces, you know. And however much ass-kissing the bastard did in his years in the Pentagon, he's the only one of us who has any real idea how to plan and coordinate something like this."

Mike planted his hands on the windowsill and pushed himself away. Then, went back and sat down again.

"Look, James, on this subject Simpson is right. That's why, grit-ting my teeth, I supported him from the day he first advanced the proposal. Not only supported him, but took the lead in con-vincing Gustav Adolf and his advisers and generals. We have *got* to shrink that damned army of his. It's become a giant tape-worm in the guts of the country. But the only way to do that—with the enemies we have surrounding us—is to replace quantity with quality. And *that* means devoting a huge percentage of our modern production facilities and skills here in Grantville to military work."

He sighed, and rubbed his face. "And that, of course, brings us right up against 'jaw number three.' Because those same resources being used to build Gustav's 'toys,' as you call them, aren't being used to develop other things. Such as really pushing a textile industry, or throwing the weight we ought to be throwing behind the small motor industry—farmers need a lot of little ten-horsepower engines, not a handful of diesel monsters driving a few ironclads—or damn near anything else you can think of."

For a moment, he and James stared at each other. Then, shrug-ging again, Mike added: "What the hell, look on the bright side. If nothing else, the economic and technical crunch is making everybody think for a change. Think, and *organize.*"

The word "organize," inevitably for a man brought up in the

trade-union movement, brought the first genuine smile to Mike's face. "Don't underestimate that, James, not for a minute. We may be a sorry lot of filthy disease-carriers, but I can guarantee you the population of the United States is rapidly becoming the best-organized group of people anywhere in the world. And *self*-organized, to boot, which is a hundred times better than anything that comes down from on high."

He waved his hand in a gesture which was as broadly encompassing as the one James had used earlier. But vigorous, where the doctor's had been despairing.

"You name it, we've got it. Trade unions spreading all over the place, farmers' granges, Willie Ray's kids in his Future Farmers of Europe spending as much time arguing politics as they do seeds, Gretchen's fireballs in the Committees of Correspondence. Damned if even the old boys' clubs aren't alive and kicking and talking about something other than their silly rituals. Henry Dreeson told me that his Lions club voted last week to start making a regular donation to the Freedom Arches Foundation."

James' eyes practically bulged. Somehow—to this day nobody knew exactly how she'd managed it—Gretchen had gotten the former McDonald's franchise hamburger stand in Grantville turned over to her Committees of Correspondence. (The manager of the restaurant, Andy Yost, swore he knew nothing about it—but he'd stayed on as manager, nonetheless, and—pure coincidence, perhaps—was on the Steering Committee of Gretchen's rapidly growing band of radicals.)

Gretchen had promptly renamed it the "Freedom Arches," and the former McDonald's had instantly become the 17th-century's equivalent of the famous bistros and coffee houses of the revolutionary Paris of a later era. Moving with their usual speed and energy, the Committees of Correspondence had begun creating other franchises patterned after it in every town in the United States—and beyond. A new "Freedom Arches" had been erected just outside the boundaries of Leipzig, the nearest big city in Saxony. Much to the displeasure of John George, the prince of Saxony, who had immediately complained to Gustav Adolf. But the king of Sweden, who was also the emperor of the Confederated Principalities of Europe, had refused to direct its dismantling. Gustav had his own reservations—to put it mildly—about the Committees of Correspondence. But he was no fool, and had learned the principle of keeping aristocrats under a tight rein from his own Vasa dynasty's history. The Committees made him nervous, true; but they terrified such men as John George of Saxony, which was even better.

The buildings in which the new "Freedom Arches" sprang up were themselves 17th-century construction, of course. But the two arches which prominently advertised them, even if they were painted wood instead of fancy modern construction, would have been recognized by any resident of the United States in the America which had been left behind. Granted, once they went through the doors, the average 21st-century American would have been puzzled by what they saw. The food served was more likely to be simple bread than anything else, with tea and beer for beverages instead of coffee. And they'd *certainly* be amazed to see a crude printing press occupying a place of honor in the "dining area," with—almost round the clock—youngsters cheerfully cranking out leaflets and broadsides.

"The *Lions*?" choked Nichols.

Mike grinned. "Yup. They're keeping it quiet, of course. Give them some credit, James. Sure, Gretchen and her firebrands make them twitchy, but even the town's stodgiest businessman knows we're in a fight for our lives. The Knights of Columbus aren't even trying to keep quiet about their own donations. As Catholics, they're determined to prove as publicly as possible that they're the most loyal citizens around."

James grunted. In the sometimes bizarre way that history works, the officially Protestant Confederated Principalities of Europe—in that portion of it under U.S. jurisdiction, with its rigorously applied principles of freedom of religion—had become a haven for central Europe's Catholics. By now, between the influx of immigrants and the incorporation of western Franconia after the victory of Gustav and his American allies over the Habsburgs at the battle of the Alte Veste, the majority of the population of the United States might well be Catholic. Catholics were certainly approaching parity with the Protestant population—and, typically, were even more devoted to its (by European standards of the day) radical political principles.

Mike spread his hands. "So, like I said, look on the bright side. We're buying time, James. I know as well as you do that we could get struck by an epidemic. But, if we do, we'll at least be able to deal with the crisis with a population that's alert, getting better organized by the day, and is probably already better educated than any other in Europe outside of maybe Holland."

"I still don't see the logic of devoting so much of our resources—military ones, I'm talking about—to those ironclads Simpson is gung-ho about," said James sourly. "Those things are a damn 'resource sink.' Leaving aside all the good steel we had to turn over—I can think of better things to do with miles of steel rails left over from the Ring of Fire than just using them for armor—we had to cannibalize several big diesel engines, the best pumps in the mine . . ."

He trailed off. "Okay, I grant you, I wasn't at the cabinet meeting where the decision was made, since I was in Weimar dealing with that little outbreak of dysentery—at least *that's* something we can deal with—but your summary explanation afterward never has made much sense to me."

Mike pursed his lips and stared out the window. He wasn't surprised his synopsis of the logic hadn't made a lot of sense to James, at the time. That was because it really *didn't* make much sense, in purely military terms, to build an American navy allied to Gustavus Adolphus which could only operate along the rivers of central Germany. It was a pure "brown water" navy, not even a coast guard.

Mike hesitated. He was reluctant to get into the subject, because the *real* reason involved such cold-blooded "Realpolitik" and Machiavellian thinking that he knew most of his American-born-and-bred cabinet members would choke on it. Melissa Mailey would have had a screaming fit. Fortunately, although she'd been at the cabinet meeting, Melissa generally found all military issues so vaguely distasteful that she hadn't really carefully examined this one on its own merits. For which Mike was thankful. Whenever the woman looked past her own biases and preconceptions, she had a fiendishly sharp mind.

Nichols, as a doctor—even leaving aside his romantic involvement with Melissa—would be just as likely to choke. Especially given that, unlike many doctors Mike had known in his life, James Nichols took his profession as a *healer* dead seriously. The Hippocratic oath was not something James Nichols had rattled off quickly just so he could get his license and start raking in the cash.

On the other hand . . .

Mike studied James for a moment. The rough-featured, very dark-skinned black man returned his gaze stonily, his hands clasped on the desk in front of him. There were scars on those hands which hadn't come from medical practice. Before Nichols turned his life around, he'd grown up as a street kid in one of the toughest ghettoes in Chicago. Blackstone Rangers territory that had been, in his youth.

*Screw it. If this damn job requires me to lie to one of my best friends, it's not worth it.*

"All right, James, I'll give it to you straight. The reason Gustav Adolf wants those ironclads is in order to secure his logistics routes in case the CPE is attacked from without. In this day and age, military supplies can be transported by water far more easily than any other way. If he can control the rivers—the Elbe, first and foremost, but also the smaller ones and the canals, especially as we keep improving them—then he's got a big edge against anyone trying to invade. But that's only part of it, and not the most important part."

He sat up straight. Harshly: "The more important reason is because he needs them—or, at least, thinks he might—in order to hold the CPE together in the first place."

Nichols' eyes widened slightly. Slightly, but . . . not much.

"Think about it, for Pete's sake," Mike continued. He waved his hand at the window. "The Confederated Principalities of Europe is the most ramshackle, patched-together, jury-rigged so-called *realm*"—the word dripped sarcasm—"the world's probably ever seen. A Swedish king ruling over a crazy quilt of German princedoms, independent imperial cities, an outright republic like ours founded by expatriate American 'up-timers'—you name it, we've got it. All of it riddled by religious bigotry and intolerance, not to mention the periodic outbursts of witch-hunting. It's something straight out of a fantasy, or a madhouse. And half of Gustav's semi-independent 'subjects'—let's start with John George of Saxony, who rules the most powerful of those princedoms—would stab him in the back in a heartbeat. While most of the rest of them—"

Nichols snorted. "Would take bets on how deep the stab wound went. And then start quarreling over who got to hold the money."

"Exactly. The whole thing could fly apart in an instant. So. Consider how the situation looks from the *emperor's* viewpoint. *If* he can improve the rivers enough, and *if* he can build new canals and upgrade the ones that exist, and *if* we can provide him with a handful of river-going ironclads which can hammer the living crap out of anybody within range, then the CPE starts looking like a viable proposition. At least, from the standpoint of naked *force*. Take a look at a map sometime—I can assure you Gustav Adolf has, because our surveying team provided him with the best there is today—and you'll see what I'm talking about. Consider the Elbe as the spinal cord and the aorta combined. Then look at all the branches—some rivers, some canals, some a combination of both—which tie everything together. Connects the Baltic Sea to Thuringia, Hesse-Kassel to Saxony and Brandenburg."

He smiled wolfishly. "Consider, for instance, the Finow canal which connects the Elbe and the Havel and the Oder—which, as you may know, is one of the ones Gustav has prioritized for rebuilding and upgrading. Second only, in fact, to the canals connecting the Elbe to the Baltic ports of Luebeck and Wismar. Consider what things will look like *then*—from the standpoint of the elector of Brandenburg, George William, who's almost as untrustworthy as the Elector of Saxony—as he contemplates one of Simpson's ironclads floating on the Havel in Berlin. With its ten-inch guns pointing at his palace."

"They could wreck the canals," protested James. "Destroy the locks, at least." But the protest was half-hearted.

Mike shrugged. "Easier said than done, James, and you know it as well as I do. With a good engineering corps—and Gustav has the best—they can be rebuilt. Besides, that all presupposes a bold and daring and well-coordinated uprising on the part of several princes acting in unison. Which—"

James was already chuckling. "*That* lot of greedy, bickering thieves? Not likely!"

Mike shared in the humor. Within a few seconds, though, James was no longer smiling. Instead, he was giving Mike a somewhat slit-eyed stare. "Are you *that* cold-blooded?" he murmured. "Hand Gustav that kind of power saw... knowing, of course, that the one part of his little empire he *couldn't* really use the blade against is us. Seeing as how, when you get down to it—for quite a while, at least—he's depending on us to make and man those ironclads."

Mike shrugged. "Yeah, I am. Like I said, James, I'm buying us time. And buying it for Gustav Adolf, too, because—for quite a while, at least—our fortunes are tied to his."

Nichols lowered his clasped hands into his lap, rocked back his chair, and gave Mike a thin smile. "You'd have probably done pretty good, you know, down there around Sixty-Third and Cottage Grove. Of course, your skin color would have been a handicap. But, if I know you, you'd have figured out some way around that too."

Mike's smile didn't waver. "Under the circumstances, I think I'll take that as a compliment."

Nichols snorted. "Under the circumstances, it *is* a compliment. The only difference between Chicago's street gang leaders and Germany's noblemen is that the gang leaders are generally smarter and the noblemen are generally more treacherous. A toss-up, which of them are more callous."

Silence fell in the room. James' face was still tight with concern, but, after a moment, Mike realized that the man's concern had moved from general affairs to the point nearest to his heart.

"I'll send word as soon as I hear from her," Mike said softly. "She'll be all right, James. I gave Rita and Melissa enough money to hire a *big* ship. And besides, with Tom Simpson and Julie along, any pirate who tries to attack that ship is in for a rude surprise."

James smiled. Julie Sims—Julie Mackay, now, since her marriage to a Scot cavalry officer in Gustav Adolf's army—was the best rifle shot anyone had ever met. And whatever James and Mike thought of John Simpson, both of them approved highly of Simpson's son Tom, who had married Mike's sister on the same day the Ring of Fire changed their entire world. Especially under these circumstances. Whatever other dangers James' lover Melissa and Mike's sister Rita would face in their diplomatic mission to England, they were hardly likely to be pestered by footpads. Tom Simpson was quite possibly one of the ten biggest men in the world. He'd been something of a giant even in 21st-century America, with the shoulders and physique you'd expect from a lineman on a top college football team.

But the doctor's smile faded soon enough. Mike knew he wasn't really worried—not much, anyway—about pirates and footpads. Melissa and Rita would be dealing with people a lot more dangerous than that.

"Kings and princes and cardinals and God-help-me dukes and fucking earls," grumbled Nichols. "Oughta shoot the whole lot of 'em."

Mike's grin was probably a little on the merciless side. He certainly intended it to be, seeing as how the doctor needed to be cheered up. "We might yet. A fair number of them, anyway. Like I said, look on the bright side. Simpson may be an asshole, but he knows his big guns."

# Chapter 4

The noise, as always, was appalling.

John Chandler Simpson had grown accustomed to it, although he doubted he was ever going to truly get used to it. Of course, there was a lot he wasn't going to get used to about the Year of Our Lord 1633.

He snorted sourly at the thought as he waded through another of the extensive mud puddles which made trips to the dockyard such an . . . adventure. There'd been a time when he would have walked around the obstacle, but that had been when he'd still had 21st-century shoes to worry about. And when he'd had the energy to waste on such concerns.

He snorted again, even more sourly. He supposed he ought to feel a certain satisfaction at the way that asshole Stearns had finally been forced to admit that he knew what he was talking about where *something* was concerned. And truth to tell, he did. But any satisfaction was alloyed by the fact that he'd had to worry about what Stearns thought in the first place. Taking orders from an Appalachian hillbilly "President" who'd never even graduated from college was hard for a man of Simpson's accomplishments to stomach.

Not that Stearns was a complete idiot, he admitted grudgingly. At least he'd had the good sense to recognize that Simpson was right about the need to "downsize" Gustavus Adolphus' motley mercenary army. Oh, how the President had choked on that verb!

It had almost been worth being forced to convince him of anything in the first place. And even though he'd accepted Simpson's argument, he hadn't wanted to accept the corollary—that if Gustavus Adolphus was going to downsize, it was up to the Americans to make up the difference in his combat power . . . even if that meant diverting resources from some of the President and his gang's pet industrialization projects.

Still, Simpson conceded, much as it irritated him to admit it, Stearns had been right about the need to increase their labor force if they were going to make it through that first winter. Which didn't mean he'd found the best way to do it, though, now did it?

Things had worked out better—so far, at least—than Simpson had feared they would when he realized where Stearns was headed with his new Constitution. There was no guarantee it would stay that way, of course. Under other circumstances, Simpson would probably have been amused watching Stearns trying to control the semi-anarchy he'd forged by bestowing the franchise over all of the local Germans and their immigrant cousins and in-laws as soon as they moved into the United States' territory. The locals simply didn't have the traditions and habits of thought to make the system work properly as it had back home. They thought they did, but the best of them were even more addicted to sprawling, pressure cooker bursts of unbridled enthusiasm than Stearns and his union blockheads. And the lunatic fringe among them—typified by Melissa Mailey's supporters and Gretchen Higgins' Committees of Correspondence—were even worse. There was no telling what kind of disaster they might still provoke. All of which could have been avoided if the hillbillies had just had the sense to limit the franchise to people who had demonstrated that they could handle it.

The familiar train of thought had carried him to the dockyard gate, and he looked up from picking his way through the mud as the double-barrel-shotgun-armed sentry came to attention and saluted. Like the vast majority of the United States Army's personnel, the sentry was a $17^{th}$-century German. Which was all to the good, Simpson reflected, as he returned his salute. The casual attitude the original Grantville population—beginning with "General" Jackson himself—brought to all things military was one of the many things Simpson detested about them. None of them seemed to appreciate the critical importance of things like military discipline, or the way in which the outward forms of military courtesy helped build it. The local recruits hadn't had much use for the niceties of formal military protocol, either, but at least any man who had survived in the howling chaos of a 17th-century battlefield understood the absolute necessity for iron discipline. Off the field, they might be rapists, murderers, and thieves; on the field was something else again entirely, and it was interesting how eagerly the 17th-century officers and noncoms had accepted the point Simpson's up-time compatriots seemed unable to grasp, however hard he hammered away at it. The habit of discipline had to be acquired and nurtured off the field as much as on it if you wanted to create a truly professional, reliable military force. That, at least, was one point upon which he and Gustavus Adolphus saw completely eye to eye.

He returned the sentry's salute and continued onward into the dockyard, then paused.

Behind him lay the city of Magdeburg, rising from the rubble of its destruction in a shroud of dust, smoke, smells, shouts, and general bedlam. Some of that construction was traditional Fachwerk or brick construction on plots for which heirs had been located; intermixed with balloon frames and curtain walls on lots that had escheated into city ownership. Before him lay the River Elbe and another realm of swarming activity. It was just as frenetic and even noisier than the chaotic reconstruction efforts at his back, but he surveyed it with a sense of proprietary pride whose strength surprised even him just a bit. Crude and improvised as it was compared to the industrial enterprises he had overseen back home, it belonged to him. And given what he had to work with, what it was accomplishing was at least as impressive as the construction of one of the Navy's *Nimitz*-class carriers would have been in his old world.

An earsplitting racket, coal smoke, and clouds of sawdust spewed from the steam-powered sawmill Nat Davis had designed and built. The vertical saw slabbed off planks with mechanical precision, and the sawmill crew heaved each plank up into the bed of a waiting wagon as it fell away from the blade. The sawmill was a recent arrival, because they had decided not to waste scarce resources on intermediate construction of a water- or windmill that would just end up being dismantled again. Only two weeks ago, the men stacking those planks had been working hip deep in cascading sawdust in an old-fashioned saw pit, laboriously producing each board by raw muscle power.

Beyond the sawmill, another crew labored at the rolling mill powered by the same steam engine. The mill wasn't much to look at compared to the massive fabricating units of a 21$^{st}$-century steel plant, but it was enough to do what was needed. Simpson watched approvingly as the crew withdrew another salvaged railroad rail from the open furnace and fed it into the rollers. The steel, still smoking and red hot from its stay in the furnace, emerged from the jaws of the mill crushed down into a plank approximately one inch thick and a little over twelve inches wide. As it slid down another set of inclined rollers, clouds of steam began rising from the quenching sprays. More workmen were carrying cooled steel planks to yet another open-fronted shed, where one of the precious gasoline-powered portable generators drove a drill press. The soft whine of the drill bit making bolt holes in the steel was lost in the general racket.

Simpson stood for a moment, watching, then nodded in satisfaction and continued toward his dockside office. It was nestled between two of the slipways, in the very shadow of the gaunt, slab-sided structures looming above it. They were ugly, unfinished, and raw, and even when they were completed, no one would ever call them graceful. But that was fine with John Simpson. Because once they were finished, they were going to be something far more important than graceful.

Another sentry guarded the office door and came to attention at his approach. Simpson returned his salute and stepped through the door, closing it behind him. The noise level dropped immediately, and his senior clerk started to come to his feet, but Simpson waved him back into his chair.

"Morning, Dietrich," he said.

"Good morning, Herr Admiral," the clerk replied.

"Anything important come up overnight?" Simpson asked.

"No, sir. But Herr Davis and Lieutenant Cantrell are here."

The clerk's tone held an edge of sympathy and Simpson grimaced. It wasn't something he would have let most of his subordinates see, whatever he might personally think of a visitation from that particular pair. Demonstrating any reservations he might nurse about them openly could only undermine the chain of command he'd taken such pains to create in the first place.

But Dietrich Schwanhausser was a special case. He might be yet another German, but he was worth his weight in gold when it came to administration. He'd also taken to the precious computer sitting on his desk like one of those crazed 21st-century teenagers . . . and without the attitude. That combination, especially with his added ability to intelligently anticipate what Simpson might need next, had made him an asset well worth cultivating and nurturing. Simpson had recognized that immediately, but he was a bit surprised by the comfort level of the relationship they had evolved.

"Thanks for the warning," he said wryly, and Schwanhausser's lips twitched on the edge of a smile. Simpson nodded to him and continued on into the inner office.

It was noisier than the outer office, because unlike Schwanhausser's space, it actually had a window, looking out over the river. The glass in that window wasn't very good, even by 17th-century standards, but it still admitted natural daylight as well as allowing him a view of his domain. And the subtle emphasis of the status it lent the man whose wall it graced was another point in its favor.

Two people were waiting when he stepped through the door. Nat Davis was a man in his forties, with blunt, competent workman's hands, a steadily growing bald spot fringed in what had once been dark brown hair, and glasses. Prior to the Ring of Fire, he'd been a tobacco chewer, although he'd gone cold turkey— involuntarily—since Grantville's arrival in Thuringia. That habit, coupled with a strong West Virginia accent and his tendency to speak slowly, choosing his words with care, had caused Simpson to underestimate his intelligence at first. The Easterner had learned better since, and he greeted the machinist with a much more respectful nod than he might once have bestowed upon him.

The young man waiting with Davis was an entirely different proposition. Eddie Cantrell was still a few months shy of his twentieth birthday, and he might have been intentionally designed as Davis' physical antithesis.

The older man was stocky and moved the same way he talked, with a sort of thought-out precision which seemed to preclude any possibility of spontaneity. That ponderous appearance, Simpson had discovered, could be as deceiving as the way he chose his words, but there was nothing at all deceptive about the sureness with which Davis moved from one objective to another.

Spontaneity, on the other hand, might have been Eddie Cantrell's middle name. He was red-haired and wiry, with that unfinished look of hands and feet that were still too large for the rest of him, and the entire concept of discipline was alien to his very nature.

Worse, he bubbled. No, he didn't just "bubble." He boiled. He *frothed*. He radiated enthusiasm and that absolute sense of assurance of which only inexperienced youth was capable. He had, in fact, in John Simpson's considered opinion, been intended as Mike Stearns' carefully devised revenge, assigned to the dockyard with malice aforethought. The fact that the entire project had originated with one of Eddie's bursts of unbridled enthusiasm had simply provided the President with the justification he required to inflict the youngster on him.

All of which made it even more surprising to Simpson that he'd actually come to *like* the insufferable young gadfly.

Not that he had any intention of telling him so.

"Good morning, gentlemen," he greeted them as he continued across the cramped office confines to his desk. He settled himself into his chair and tipped it back slightly, the better to regard them down the length of his nose. "To what do I owe the pleasure?"

Davis and Cantrell looked at one another for a moment. Then Davis shrugged, smiled faintly, and made a tiny waving motion with one hand.

"I guess I should go first . . . sir," the younger man said. The hesitation before the "sir" wasn't the deliberate pause it once might have been. Simpson was relatively confident of that. It was just one more indication of how foreign to Eddie's nature the ingrained habits of military courtesy truly were.

"Then I suggest you do so . . . Lieutenant." Simpson's pause *was* deliberate, and he noted Eddie's slight flush with satisfaction. He estimated that it would require no more than another three or four years of reminders for the young man to finally acquire the appropriate habits.

"Yes, sir." Eddie gave himself a little shake. "Matthias just reported in. He says that Freiherr von Bleckede is being, um, stubborn."

"I see." Simpson tipped his chair back a bit farther and frowned. Matthias Schaubach was one of the handful of Magdeburg's original burghers to have survived the massacre of the city's inhabitants by Tilly's mercenaries. Prior to that traumatic event, he'd been deeply involved in the salt trade up and down the Elbe from Hamburg, which had made him the Americans' logical point man on matters pertaining to transport along the river.

The Elbe, for all its size and importance to northern Germany, was little more than a third as long as the Mississippi. By the time it reached Magdeburg, over a hundred and sixty air-miles from Hamburg, whether or not it could truly be called "navigable" was a debatable point. Barge traffic was possible, but the barges in question averaged no more than forty feet in length, which was much smaller than anything the Americans would need to get downriver. Some improvements to navigation had been required even to get the barges through, and it was obvious to everyone that even more was going to be necessary shortly.

For the past several weeks, Schaubach had been traveling up and down the Elbe discussing that "even more" with the locals. The existing network of "*wehrluecken*" provided a starting point, but very little more than that. The *wehrluecken* were basically permanent dams built across the river with a central gap or spillway wider than the maximum beam of a barge. The dam raised the water level to a depth sufficient to float a barge, and the spillway allowed barges passage through the barrier of the dam. Unfortunately, none of the existing *wehrluecken* were going to suffice for Simpson's needs, and modifying them was going to be a herculean task. It was also going to severely hamper normal barge traffic while the work was in progress, and the owners of the current *wehrluecken* weren't particularly happy about that prospect. Nor, for that matter, was Gustavus Adolphus, for whose new empire in central Europe the Elbe River provided the critical spinal cord.

Most of the *wehrluecken* owners had decided to see reason when Schaubach approached them properly. Greed helped, after Schaubach finished describing the amount of traffic which would be moving up and down the river once the infrastructure had been improved and the Americans' river steamboats were in full production. Where that failed, a discreetly non-specific reference to the Swedish Army, coupled with the observation that Gustavus Adolphus would really appreciate their cooperation, tended to do the trick.

Some of them, however, were more stubborn than others. Like the petty baron Freiherr von Bleckede. A part of Simpson actually sympathized with the man, not that it made him any happier about Eddie's news.

"I take it Mr. Schaubach wouldn't have reported it if he thought he was going to be able to change Bleckede's mind?" he said after a moment.

"It doesn't sound like he's going to be able to," Eddie agreed. He made a face. "Sounds to me like von Bleckede doesn't much care for us. Or the Swedes, either."

"I'm not surprised," Simpson observed. "Hard to blame him, really." He smiled blandly as an expression of outrage flickered across Eddie's face. He considered enlarging upon his theme. It wouldn't do a bit of harm to remind Eddie that the pre-Ring of Fire establishment had a huge number of reasons to resent and fear the upheavals in the process of tearing the *status quo* apart. Except, of course, that whenever Eddie cared to think about it, he already understood that perfectly. He just didn't care. Or, more precisely, he was too concerned with blasting obstructions out of the way to worry about what motivated them. And if Simpson brought them up, it would only reinforce the young hothead's view of Simpson's own "reactionary" opinions.

"Well," Cantrell said more than a little impatiently, as if to prove Simpson's point for him, "whether we blame him for it or not, we still need to get clearance for the crews to go to work on his *wehrlueck*. That stretch isn't going to float one of the ironclads even if we completely empty the trim tanks."

"No, it isn't," Simpson agreed. He was careful not to let it show, but privately he felt a small flicker of pleasure at Eddie's reference to the trim tanks. The entire ironclad project had originated with Eddie's war-gaming hobby interest. He was the one who'd piled his reference books up on the corner of Mike Stearns' desk and sold him on the notion of armed river steamboats to police their communications along the rivers. Of course, his original wildly enthusiastic notions had required the input of a more adult perspective, but the initial concept when authorization of the project was first discussed had reflected his ideas of how best to update a design from the American Civil War. By Simpson's most conservative estimate, there hadn't been more than two or three dozen things wrong with it . . . which was only to be expected when a hobby enthusiast set out to transform his war-gaming information into reality.

Eddie's design, once Simpson and Greg Ferrara finished their displacement calculations, would have drawn at least twelve feet at minimum load. That draft would have been too deep even for the Mississippi, much less the Elbe. It also would have been armored to resist 19th-century artillery, like the Civil War's fifteen-inch smoothbores, rather than the much more anemic guns of the 17th century. Worse than that, Eddie had called for a single-screw design. His otherwise praiseworthy objective had been to save the huge bulk of a paddle wheel housing, which would not only have cut down on places to mount armament but required an even bigger investment in armor. Given that they'd had to fight people like Quentin Underwood tooth and nail for every salvaged rail-road rail dedicated to the project, that hadn't been an insignificant consideration.

Unfortunately, marine screw propellers were much more difficult to design properly than Eddie had imagined. Simpson knew that; his last assignment before the Pentagon had been as a member of the design group working on the propulsion systems for the *Seawolf*-class submarine. Moreover, an exposed prop and shaft would have been extremely vulnerable to damage in the event that one of the ships grounded, which was virtually certain to happen eventually to any heavy, clumsy armored vessel operating on inland rivers. And the provision of a single shaft would have meant that any damage to a propeller would leave one of the precious ironclads unable to move or maneuver in any way.

Which was why Simpson had bullied Stearns into letting him have the diesel power plants out of four of the huge coal trucks which had originally been used as armored personnel carriers. Fuel for the APC engines, though scarce, was still available, and once Underwood got the kinks out of his oil-field production, scarcity wouldn't be a problem. Not with the priority Stearns had agreed to assign to the Navy, at any rate.

With the engines figuratively speaking in hand, Simpson had created a highly modified version of Eddie's original concept— one which used powerful diesel-driven pumps scavenged from the Grantville coal mine to provide hydro-jet propulsion. The pumps were powerful enough to chew up most small debris without damage, and screens across the intakes protected them from anything larger. Using the diesels would increase the gunboats' logistic dependency on the Grantville industrial base, since it wouldn't be possible to fuel them with coal or wood in an emergency, as would have been possible with a steam-powered engineering plant. On the other hand, the diesel bunkers could be safely located below the water line, and at least if a freak hit managed somehow to penetrate to one of the ironclads' interiors, there would be no handy boiler full of live steam to boil a crew alive.

The other two things he'd done to Eddie's original design were to cut the armor thickness in half and add the trim tanks. Reducing the armor had let him squeeze an additional ship out of the rails allocated to the project, as well as saving displacement, but the tanks were at least as important. The original *Monitor* had been designed with minimum freeboard to reduce target area, but that wasn't going to be possible with this design. Since there was no practical way to design a proper turret at this point, they had no choice but to use a more or less traditional broadside scheme for their armament, which meant something that would look a lot more like the *Merrimack* . . . or, as Eddie was prone to correct in tones of exasperation, the *Virginia*. That explained the slabsided, ungainly appearance of the basic design. It also required a deeper draft than the "cheese box on a raft" *Monitor*'s design. Simpson had managed to minimize that to some extent by designing the ships to "flood down" for combat by filling the trim tanks built into them. That had allowed him to design a roughly five-hundred-ton vessel which drew less than four feet of water with the tanks pumped out and almost ten feet with the tanks filled. Which also, just incidentally, let him save about five feet worth of armored freeboard which would be protected by water when they flooded down.

At first, Eddie had been inclined to sulk when Simpson modified his basic design. To his credit, he'd recognized that the alterations were genuine improvements, and that was the reason Simpson (although he doubted that the young man was aware of it) had specifically requested that he be assigned to the Navy. Stearns had already sent him to Magdeburg to help oversee the project, after all, which meant Simpson couldn't have gotten rid of him, anyway. And the Navy was going to need officers who could actually *think*. Those were rarer than one might have thought, and from his own experience, Simpson recognized the mental flexibility involved in acknowledging that someone else had actually made one of your own brainchildren better. So he'd decided to make a virtue out of necessity . . . which was how both Eddie and his friend Larry Wild had abruptly become junior-grade lieutenants in John Simpson's Navy.

And if it had also let Simpson get the last laugh on Mike Stearns, so much the better.

"Fortunately," he went on after a moment, "convincing the freiherr to go along with our plans isn't really our concern. If Mr. Schaubach feels that he's unlikely to be able to get von Bleckede to see reason, refer him to Mr. Piazza." He smiled again, more blandly than ever, as Eddie frowned. Ed Piazza, the secretary of state, had been Stearns' choice to serve as his personal representative to all the various minor local potentates not worthy of the personal attention of the head of state.

"That will take time," Eddie began, "and—"

"That may be true," Simpson interrupted. "But it's the secretary of state's job to deal with things like this. Or let Gustav's chancellor Oxenstierna deal with it. We've got more to worry about than convincing one minor nobleman to see things our way. Besides, whether we like it or not, we've *got* time before we'll actually need to get that far down-river, now don't we?"

Eddie looked rebellious, but Simpson was accustomed to that. What mattered more to him was the fact that the youngster actually thought his way through it, then subsided with nothing more than one last grimace.

"Now," Simpson went on, "was there anything else you needed, Lieutenant?"

"No, I guess not . . . sir."

"Good." Simpson turned to Davis. "And what can I do for you, Mr. Davis?" he asked.

"Actually," Davis replied, "I just wanted to let you know that Ollie says he should have the first half dozen gun tubes ready to ship to us by the end of the week."

"Good!"

Simpson was unaware of the way in which his genuine enthusiasm transfigured his own expression. The change was brief, but Davis recognized it. It was a pity, he often thought, that Simpson had such a completely tone deaf "ear" where minor things like interpersonal relations were concerned. Personally, Davis still thought the man was a prick, especially as far as politics went, and he didn't much care for the "admiral's" obsession with matters of rank—social, as well as military—and the perquisites which went with it. But he'd come to recognize that however unpleasant Simpson's personality might be, the man undeniably had a brain. Quite a good one, as a matter of fact, when it could be pried away from things like his political disagreements with Mike Stearns.

However much Davis hated to admit it (and, as it happened, he hated it quite a bit), Simpson's experience as an officer in the up-time United States Navy really did show in the organization he was building here in Magdeburg. The up-timers under his command might carp and complain about "Mickey Mouse bullshit" and mutter balefully about "front office management pricks," but Davis had come to realize that there genuinely was a method to his madness. Of course, sometimes the machinist wondered how much of that method was due to the fact that Simpson had a clearer appreciation of what was needed than his fellow up-timers did and how much resulted from his own innate propensity for empire building. But whatever his reasoning, Simpson's Navy was much better disciplined and shaping up as a considerably more professional organization than Frank Jackson's Army.

Too many of Jackson's senior officers were still up-timers themselves, with a casual attitude toward him and toward each other which remained essentially civilian. That was fine as far as they themselves were concerned. They knew one another, and their relationships, however casual, worked. But the core of the Army had been the United Mine Workers of America. Davis wasn't certain how well the example of that attitude would serve as those from outside the original UMWA membership began attaining senior rank. And whatever might have been the case for the Army, Simpson didn't have that existing structure to build upon. He was creating the Navy out of whole cloth. Almost a hundred percent of its personnel were 17th-century Germans and Swedes, leavened with just enough up-timers to provide the technical skills the newly made Americans had not yet acquired. And that was another kettle of fish entirely.

It didn't make Davis like Simpson any more, but it had permitted him to at least appreciate that the man did have some worthwhile qualities. Which was why he thought it was such a pity that Simpson was so persistently unwilling—or unable—to demonstrate the enthusiasm Davis had come to realize he felt for his present task. Instead, Simpson was prone to giving the impression that he had taken on the "chore" as a matter of noblesse oblige, to save the uncouth Appalachian yokels from the results of their own ignorance. That, more than any real policy differences, explained the antagonism that Simpson had a positive genius for stirring up among the people in the U.S. government he dealt with.

*Thank God we're in Magdeburg,* Nat thought to himself wryly. *If we'd been based in Grantville, Simpson would be getting challenged to a duel every other Tuesday—the law be damned.*

"Are we going to use the wire-built design or bronze casting?" Cantrell asked. Simpson gave him a sharp glance for interrupting, but said nothing. Simpson, Davis had noticed, was prepared to cut the youngster a much greater degree of slack than he did for anyone else. He wondered if *Eddie* realized that?

"Wire-built, for the first half dozen, at least," Nat replied. "The power plant has more than enough Schedule 160 twelve-inch pipe for the liners for all sixteen of the rifled guns, and we've unlaid enough steel cable to provide plenty of wire."

Simpson and Eddie both nodded. Twelve-inch Schedule 160 pipe had an inside diameter of just over ten inches and a wall thickness of about one and a quarter inches. That was ample to provide the liner for a ten-inch artillery piece, and Grantville's machining capability was more than adequate for the task of providing it with rifling grooves. But that left the task of reinforcing it. The original Grantville power plant had run to relatively high steam pressures, but there was a world of difference between that and the pressures which would be exerted in the bore of a black-powder cannon!

Two competing solutions had been proposed. One was to reinforce the tubes by winding them in thick cocoons of steel wire, which just happened to be available in significant quantities once the spools of steel cable had been discovered at the coal mine. Unlaying the cables by hand to separate them into individual strands of steel wire had been a laborious and manpower-intensive task, but once the decision to support the ironclad project had been taken, the manpower had been made available.

The second solution had been to cast bronze reinforcements around the tubes. In some ways, that was a simpler approach. It would result in somewhat heavier guns, but the technology to accomplish it was already available to the 17th-century's metalworking industry. The finished guns would be somewhat heavier, and the tubes themselves might warp slightly in the casting process, but Davis doubted very much that the warping would present any insoluble difficulties. They were planning to do a final bore in all the gun tubes anyway, in order to bring them to a uniform size.

"The theory is that until we've got the on-site ability to do the casting here, they're going to have to ship the finished guns to us overland. The casting teams are pretty heavily committed to the field artillery and carronade projects right now, so coupled with the lighter weight for shipping considerations they decided to go with wire."

"As long as they make the delivery schedule, I don't really care which approach we use," Simpson observed.

"Yeah," Eddie agreed, but his expression was pouting. "I still say we could have produced a breech-loading design, though. Our rate of fire is going to suck."

"That decision has been made, Lieutenant," Simpson observed a bit coolly. Then he relented just a touch. "I'd obviously prefer breechloaders, myself," he said. "But the Allocations Committee was right. We don't have the resources to do everything we need to do, and muzzleloaders will do the job for us. Especially with the hydraulic recoil systems."

He shrugged, and while no one could have called Eddie's nod cheerful, there was no real disagreement in it.

"At least they'll recoil inboard so they can be reloaded under armor," he sighed.

"Especially in light of your suggestion to operate the port shutters with the same recoil system," Simpson agreed. Nat was aware that Eddie still considered himself an unabashed partisan of the Stearns administration and so, by definition, a natural enemy where John Chandler Simpson was concerned. Despite that, he noted a flicker of pleasure in the redhead's gray eyes at Simpson's acknowledgment of the youngster's contribution. One of his *many* contributions, to be sure—but Nat was still somewhat surprised that Simpson himself could recognize it, much less be willing to acknowledge it openly.

As he had sometimes before, Nat found himself wondering if the elder Simpson had found the personal rupture with his son Tom far more painful than he ever indicated in public. If so, it might be that in some odd way John Simpson was finding in brash young Eddie Cantrell—as well as his friend Larry Wild—something in the way of surrogate sons.

It was hard to know. Whatever John Simpson's other talents, "personal sensitivity" was very far down the list. Nat shook his head slightly and returned his concentration to the matter at hand.

The gun mount design Davis and Ollie Reardon had finally come up with was a far cry from anything the 21$^{st}$ century would have accepted, but it ought to be sufficient for their present purposes. It would permit the guns to recoil completely, then lock them there, with the muzzles well inboard while they were sponged out and reloaded, until the release lever was tripped and the hydraulic cylinders ran them back to battery. By adopting Eddie's suggestion and using top-opening armored shutters for the gun ports and an articulated rod between each shutter and the carriage of the gun it served, the same hydraulics would open and close the gun ports automatically as the weapon was served.

"What about the carronades for the wing mounts and the timberclads?" Simpson asked.

"They're coming along on schedule," Davis assured him. "And the team at Luebeck says that they'll be ready to begin casting Gustav's carronades on-site within another four to five weeks. We just got a radio message from them yesterday."

"As long as they don't distract resources from our project," Simpson grumbled sourly. "That monster Gustav demanded has already eaten up enough effort."

"I don't guess we should've been surprised," Eddie observed with a grin. "I did some research on seventeenth and eighteenth century navies for a war game a couple of years before the Ring of Fire, and it was only a few years ago Gustav built this really big galleon. Supposed to be the biggest and baddest warship in the entire Baltic. Named it for the Vasa dynasty."

"Really?" Davis looked at him and raised an eyebrow. "Should I assume from your expression that it was a less than completely successful design?"

"You could say that," Eddie chuckled. "Sucker sank right there in harbor. Seems they hadn't gotten the stability calculations just right."

"Wonderful," Simpson snorted. "Not exactly the best recommendation for his latest project, is it?"

"Oh, I expect they'll get it closer to right this time . . . sir." Eddie grinned again. "The king's naval architects just about *ate* my copies of Chapelle's books on American sailing ship designs. They don't show any ironclads, but the sloop of war design they settled on should carry the armor no sweat. Especially with the reduction in the weight of guns."

"I don't really doubt that the design is workable, Lieutenant," Simpson said. "Practical, now . . . That's something else again. It's a sailing ship. That means they're still going to have to have men on deck to trim the sails, which seems to me to leave a teeny-tiny chink in their protection."

"Guess so, at that," Eddie allowed. "Of course, the armored bulwarks oughta help some, even there."

"Some," Simpson acknowledged. "In the meantime, though, we're diverting the effort to build a *real* rolling mill at Luebeck."

"Maybe so," Davis said, "but it's going to be turning out iron, not steel. And the individual plates aren't going to be all that much bigger than ours, anyway." He grinned at Simpson. "Frankly, I'm just as happy to let him play with his own design while we get on with building ours."

"You may have a point," Simpson replied. He let his chair rock back and forth a few times while he considered what Eddie and Davis had reported. At least it didn't sound as if there'd been any more slippage in the construction schedule. He considered— again—suggesting that the timberclads be given a somewhat higher priority. True, they were going to be much smaller, armed only with relatively short-ranged carronades and protected only by extra thick, heavy timber "armor." In addition, they were going to be powered by paddle wheels between their catamaran hulls, and *their* power plants would be steam-driven. In every way that counted, they were going to be cruder, less capable designs. But they were also going to be available in greater numbers, and they were going to be shallower draft than the ironclads, even with the bigger ships' trim tanks.

He had a nagging suspicion that he ought to be pressing for their more rapid completion. After all, all they really needed was to be just good enough to do the job, not the best design that could possibly be produced. Surely he'd seen enough unhappy demonstrations during his original navy days of what happened when the service insisted on building in every possible bell and whistle!

He told his suspicion—again—to shut up. No doubt there was something to it, but there was also something to be said for building at least a few really capable units for the timberclads to back up. And if there was an element of the empire building Stearns was so contemptuous of (even while he was busy build- ing his own little political empire), then so be it.

"I think that will probably be all, gentlemen," he told them. "Mr. Davis, I would appreciate it if you would make it your business to check in with the local ironworkers. It looks to me like our next possible bottleneck is going to be bolt production. It won't do us any good to manufacture the armor if we can't attach it to the hulls! Please see what you can do to expedite that for us."

Davis nodded, and Simpson turned to Eddie.

"As for you, Lieutenant. According to Dietrich, there's a problem with the port gun mounts in Number Three. He's not certain what it is. I'd like you to check with the crew foreman and see what you can find out. If you can deal with it yourself, do so. If you need some additional assistance, I'm sure Mr. Davis would be happy to help out."

"Yes, sir," Eddie said. "I'll get right on it."

"Good. In that case, gentlemen, dismissed."

Davis nodded, and Eddie came to attention—or, at least, Simpson decided, closer to it than usual—and the two of them turned and headed for the door.

"Just a moment." His voice stopped them just before they left the office, and they turned back to look at him as he smiled slightly at Eddie. "I almost forgot. I thought you'd like to know, Lieutenant, that the President and Congress have accepted your recommendation for names for the ironclads."

"They have, sir? That's great!" Eddie grinned broadly.

"Indeed they have. Number One will be *Constitution*. Number Two will be *United States*. Number Three will be *President*, and Number Four will be *Monitor*. I trust this meets with your approval?"

"Oh, yeah!" Eddie said exuberantly. Then he shook himself. "I mean, it certainly does, sir."

"I am delighted to hear it," Simpson said dryly. "Dismissed, gentlemen."

# Chapter 5

"I have it!" Gustav Adolf suddenly exclaimed. "Let's pay them a visit!"

Standing next to him at the open window of the new palace overlooking the heart of Magdeburg, Axel Oxenstierna's eyes widened. He was staring at one of the new buildings which had been recently erected in the city. More precisely, he was glaring rather than simply staring; and doing so at the peculiar ornamentation of the building rather than the building itself.

The fact that the ornamentation was even newer than the building was not the cause of the Swedish chancellor's irritation. Almost every edifice in Magdeburg was new, or largely so. Two years earlier, in the single worst atrocity of a long war filled with atrocities, Tilly's Bavarian soldiers had sacked the city. Most of the inhabitants had been slaughtered—some twenty to thirty thousand people, depending on who told the story—and Magdeburg itself put to the torch. Between the damage caused by the siege and the sack, there had not been much left standing intact when Tilly's army withdrew.

For months now, starting with Gustav Adolf's decision the previous autumn to make Magdeburg the capital of his new imperial realm called the Confederated Principalities of Europe, Magdeburg had been a beehive of activity. No one knew the size of the population, but Oxenstierna was certain it had already exceeded thirty thousand. People from all over central Germany—

even beyond—were practically pouring into the city to take advantage of its prospects. New construction was going up everywhere, and of all kinds. New residences, of course—as well as the emperor's new palace in which Oxenstierna was standing. But also, along the banks of the river Elbe, the somewhat bizarre-looking new factories which Gustav's American subjects had designed. From where he stood, Axel could see the naval works where John Simpson and his men were building the new ironclad riverboats.

"*Subjects*," thought Oxenstierna sourly. *Like calling a wolf a "pet" because—for the moment—the wild beast has agreed to wear a collar. With a string for a leash, and no muzzle.*

"You must be joking," he growled. "Gustav, you *can't* be serious."

He twisted his head to look up at his ruler. Gustav II Adolf—Gustavus Adolphus, in the Latinized version of his name—had a personal size and stature to match his official one. The king of Sweden and emperor of the Confederated Principalities of Europe was a huge man. Standing more than six feet tall, he was wide in proportion and very muscular. The layers of fat which inevitably came to him whenever the king was not engaged in strenuous campaigning only added gravity to his figure.

"You must be joking," repeated the chancellor, more in a half-plea now than a growl.

Gustav shrugged. "Why should I be joking?" He lowered his heavy face, crowned with short blond hair and framed with a thick mustache and a goatee. The powerful beak of a nose seemed aimed at the offending structure below.

"They *are* my subjects, Axel, even if—" A little chuckle rumbled. "I admit, the rascals seem to wear their subordination lightly. But I remind you that not once—not *once*, Axel—have they done anything openly rebellious."

"Not *openly*, no," admitted the chancellor. Sourly, he studied the peculiar twin arches adorning the far-distant building. The arches had been painted a bright gold, which made them stand out amidst the gray buildings which surrounded them. All the more gray, in that most of those buildings were factories.

The color annoyed Oxenstierna perhaps more than anything else. Partly because its vividness, against the backdrop of the drab new factories and workshops, served to accentuate the awkward fact that these cursed Committees of Correspondence almost invariably found a receptive audience among the new class of workmen which was rapidly arising in central Germany. Nowhere more so than in Magdeburg.

But, mostly, he was annoyed because gold paint was *expensive*. The implications were disturbing to Oxenstierna. It was one thing for a realm to have a layer of its population filled with unrest and radical notions. There was nothing unusual in that. For two centuries, Europe had been plagued with periodic eruptions of mass discontent—even rebellion. The Comuneros had shaken even Charles V's Spanish kingdom to its foundations—the Dutch had thrown the Habsburgs out completely—and Germany itself had been convulsed, a century earlier, by the great Peasant War and the Anabaptist seizure of Münster. Even Sweden had had its share of domestic turbulence, now and then, such as the rebellion led by Nils Dacke a hundred years earlier.

But, for the most part, the rebellions had been easy enough to suppress. The rebels, as a rule, were a motley assortment of poor peasants and townsmen, many of them outright vagabonds, "led"— if such a term could be used at all—by a sprinkling of the lowest layers of the nobility. Poorly educated, as much in the realities of politics as anything else, with not much in the way of any guiding principles beyond extremist theology and sullen resentment at the exactions of the mighty. However large the "armies" such rebels could field—the peasants of central and southern Germany had put as many as 150,000 men into the fighting, at one time or another—properly led and organized regular armies could usually crush them within a year or two. Except for the Dutch, who enjoyed special advantages, none of the rebellions in Europe had lasted for very long.

This . . . was something different. The very fact that the Committees of Correspondence could always manage to raise enough money from their adherents to afford gold paint was a small, but vivid, indication of it.

"Curse that damn woman," Axel muttered. "I sometimes think . . ."

"Do *not* say it," commanded the king. "Do *not*, Axel. Not in my presence, not in anyone's." Gustav swiveled his head, bringing the predator's beak to bear on his chancellor. "I am not that English king—Henry the Second, wasn't it?—who is reputed to have said: 'will no one rid me of this priest?' "

The head swiveled back, resuming its scrutiny of the golden arches. "Besides, you worry too much. The very thing that frightens

you the most about Gretchen Richter and her malcontents is
actually the thing which reassures me. Those people are not ignorant villagers, Axel, never think it. I've read their pamphlets and
their broadsides. So have you, for that matter. Very thoughtful and
learned, they are, for all the shrillness of their tone. And do they
ever name *me* as their enemy?"

Oxenstierna tightened his jaws. "No," he admitted grudgingly.
"Not yet, at any rate. But I've met the woman—so have you—
and if you think for a moment she wouldn't just as soon—"

"Can you blame her?" grunted Gustav. "Tell me, nobleman—
had you undergone her personal history, would *you* be filled with
respect and admiration for your so-called 'betters'?"

Again, the swiveling beak. Accompanied, this time, by a laugh
rather than a frown. "I think not! You would do well to remember, Chancellor, that the simple fact that a man—or woman—who
has a grievance is of low birth does not make the grievance ille-
gitimate. Nor—"

The frown returned. "Nor should you forget that God does not
carry these distinctions all that far. Certainly not into Heaven,
whatever He may decree on this earth."

Oxenstierna suppressed a sigh. His king was a pious man, and
given to his own somewhat peculiar interpretation of Lutheranism.
Or perhaps, that was just the legacy of his family's traditions. The
Vasa dynasty had come to power in Sweden, as much as anything
else, because the great founder of it—Gustav Vasa, the grandfa-
ther of the man standing next to him—had always been willing
to side with the commoners against Sweden's aristocracy. Periodically, Gustavus Adolphus saw fit to remind all of his noblemen
of that fact.

"Enough!" exclaimed Gustav. There was a little tone of jollity
in the word. "I want to pay them a visit, Axel, and we will do so.
Today."

He turned away from the window and began lumbering toward
the door. "The more so since—you told me yourself, they're your
spies—this 'Spartacus' fellow is now residing in the city. I may as
well take his measure now. Your own spies tell us that he, more
than Gretchen Richter, is really the leader of the pack."

"They don't *have* a proper 'leader,'" grumbled Axel, following
after his king. "Richter is the most publicly visible and best known,
but there are at least half a dozen others who are as important
as she. Even if—"

The sourness came back to his voice, in full measure. The next words were spoken more like a complaint than a condemnation. "How in the name of Heaven did a *printer's daughter* learn to speak so well in public?"

They were in the hallway now. Gustav's lumber could hardly be described as a "stride," given the oxlike weight of his steps. But he covered ground very quickly.

"So tell me more of this 'Spartacus,'" he commanded over his shoulder.

"That's not his name, first of all. Just a silly affectation he uses on his pamphlets. His real name is Joachim Thierbach—or possibly *von* Thierbach—and he seems to be from some minor branch of the Saxon knighthood."

"If it's 'von' Thierbach, perhaps not so minor."

Axel twitched his head with irritation. "Saxons! All Germans, for that matter. Who can keep their complicated rankings straight? Not even they, I suspect."

They were at the entrance to the palace, now, the king almost bounding down the steps to the street below. Insofar as the muddy area could be called a "street" at all. Even here, in the imperial quarter, the workmen laying new cobblestones or repairing old ones were far behind the spreading growth of the reborn city.

A squad of the Scot mercenaries guarding the entrance began to form up around the king. Gustav Adolf waved them back to their posts.

"A diplomatic mistake, that, I think." As always, the mere prospect of being *bold* seemed to cheer up the Swedish monarch. "I think it would be wiser to make my entrance as *Captain General Gars.*"

He stopped and grinned back at Oxenstierna. "And would such an intrepid soldier require bodyguards?"

Axel, finally deciding to bow to the inevitable and get into the spirit of the thing, returned the grin.

"Certainly not." He eyed the sword belted onto Gustav, and placed a hand on the hilt of his own. "These are quite functional, after all, and we're experienced in their use. Students and artisans and street urchins! They'll cower before us!"

Gustav laughed. "Hardly that. But I suspect they'll be polite."

In the event, "Spartacus" was more than polite. He was downright gracious. And demonstrated, in his easy manners and relaxed if respectful demeanor, that Oxenstierna's suspicions were well-founded. "Von" Thierbach, almost certainly.

Gustav saw no reason not to find out. So, once he and Axel were seated at a table in the corner of the "Freedom Arches" of Magdeburg—the king, if not the chancellor, finding it hard not to burst into laughter at the sight of the small mob ogling them from every nook and cranny of the capacious central "dining room"—he went straight to the point.

"So which is it, young man? Joachim Thierbach? Or von Thierbach?"

Joachim smiled. The man seated across from the king and the chancellor could not be past his mid-twenties. He was slender in build, and on the tall side. The glasses perched on his nose, combined with a prematurely receding hairline, gave him a scholarly appearance.

"Von Thierbach, Your Majesty. My family is the aristocracy of a small town not far from Leipzig."

"An odd background, I should think, for someone of your— ah, shall I say, 'extreme opinions.'"

Thierbach shrugged. "Why so, Your Majesty? Why should I limit myself to the horizons of a petty Saxon nobleman?" The smile segued into a half-bitter, ironic grimace. "And 'petty' is the word, too. Squatting on a not-so-large estate, lording it over a not-so-large pack of dirty and half-literate peasants. Such is 'nobility.'"

Axel glared. Gustav smiled. "True, often enough," allowed the king.

Gustav waved his hand about, indicating the surroundings. The interior of the cavernous building which the Committees of Correspondence had obtained for their own in Magdeburg was kept very clean. Extremely so, compared to most buildings of the time. Cleanliness and personal hygiene were almost fetishized by the adherents of Gretchen Richter's political movement, simply because it was "modern" if for no other reason. Even Axel would admit, in private, that he appreciated that aspect of the Committees if nothing else about them.

Still, for all its size and cleanliness, the building's interior was spartan in the extreme. The furniture was cheap and crude, as were the stoves and ovens in the kitchen area of the building. The one exception was the new cast-iron "Franklin stove" situated in a corner of the main room. Gustav restrained himself from grinning. One of his Swedish courtiers, sourly, had recently remarked that the Committees of Correspondence had adopted the Franklin stove much as the early church had adopted the symbol of the crucifix.

The king glanced down at the platter of food which had been slid onto the table by one of the youngsters acting as a waiter. The platter contained some slices of an odd concoction of sauerkraut and cheese melted over what looked like crude bread. Gustav, despite having skipped his usual heavy lunch, was not even tempted to sample the food. It had obviously been made on the premises, by a none-too-skilled amateur baker, out of the cheapest materials available.

That, too, the king knew, was one of the things which fretted his chancellor. The combination of austerity in their personal habits and their all-too-evident skill at raising funds, bespoke a certain fanaticism in the members of the Committees of Correspondence. However much their ideology derived from their American mentors, the Committees filled that ideology with a fervor which Gustav suspected made even the Americans a bit nervous.

He understood Axel's concern. Potentially, the Committees were indeed quite dangerous. But . . .

*A war is a war, a campaign is a campaign, a battle is a battle, and a skirmish is a skirmish. Let us not confuse them, the one with the other.*

"Let me speak bluntly," he said. He hooked a thumb at the chancellor sitting next to him. "My friend and adviser Oxenstierna here is worried about your intentions. And the threat those intentions might pose to my rule."

Joachim studied Axel for a moment. There was something owl-like about the examination. Scholarly, yes—but owls are also predators.

"He's right to be worried," said the young man abruptly. "Not about our intentions, but about the logic of the situation. I will not lie, Your Majesty. The time might come—*might,* I say—when we find ourselves clashing. But—speaking for myself—I would much prefer to avoid such an eventuality."

The king grunted. *So. Even the most radical have factions. I thought as much.*

"Richter will be gone for some time," he commented mildly, probing.

Thierbach transferred the owl gaze to him. Again, he spoke bluntly. "Do not presuppose divisions in our ranks, Your Majesty.

Or, at least, do not read more into them than exists. It is true that Gretchen and I do not always agree. That is no secret, after all. We've each written pamphlets and given speeches where those differences are quite evident."

Gustav cocked an eye at Axel. The chancellor seemed to flush a bit. The king was torn between amusement and irritation. Clearly enough, to the aristocratic Oxenstierna, the subtle differences in the opinions of democratic radicals had been beneath notice.

*I need to set up my own network of spies,* thought the king. *Subtle ones, who understand what they are observing, instead of huffing with indignation. Unless I'm badly mistaken . . .*

He set the thought aside, for the moment. He was finding the subtleties of the young man seated across from him far too interesting to be diverted.

*. . . I will be dealing with Thierbach and Richter and their ilk for the rest of my life. Always best to know your enemies—and your friends, for that matter, since for a king the distinction is not always very clear.*

"Expand on that, if you would." For all the mildness of the words, it was a royal command.

Young Thierbach did not bridle. A fact which was also interesting. Most hotheaded youngsters would have, in Gustav's experience.

"The differences between Gretchen and me are not so much differences of opinion, Your Majesty—certainly not differences over principles—as they are simply the natural differences which derive from our differing activities. Gretchen is . . ." He didn't seem to be groping for words so much as simply trying to find the most precise. "Call her our 'guiding spirit,' if you will. She is fearless, bold—the one who will always lead the charge into the breach."

Gustav nodded. He'd met the young woman—and the first time, while she was standing with a smoking pistol over the bodies of Croat cavalrymen in the service of the Habsburg emperor. Some of whom she'd slain personally.

Joachim smiled, adjusted his glasses, and ran fingers over his balding forehead. "I like to think I would not flinch at that breach myself, you understand. But I'm hardly cut from the same cloth. I am more of what you might call the organizer of our Committees. The one who comes behind and makes sure that the fearless ones in front don't fall over in a faint from lack of food." The smile widened. "The Americans have a crude expression for it. They abbreviate it as 'REMF.' "

Gustav grinned. Oxenstierna laughed outright. For all his snobbery, the chancellor was not a prig—and he'd led troops himself in battle. "Rear echelon motherfuckers," he chuckled. He glanced sidelong at his monarch and added: "Which is the role Gustavus Adolphus usually bestows on *me*, you know."

Oxenstierna's eyes moved back to the young political radical at the table, and, for the first time, Gustav saw something beyond blank incomprehension and veiled disdain in that gaze.

*Thank God. I could use your intelligence for a change, Axel. Your prejudices are no good to me at all.*

"Please continue," said the chancellor. For a wonder, the tone was as polite as the words themselves.

"The point I'm trying to make is simply that Gretchen, because of her position at the front, often ignores what you might call the political logistics of the campaign." Joachim's face seemed suddenly that of a much older man. "I am not oblivious, King and Chancellor, to the *cost* of a revolution as well as its benefits. I've studied the same history books the Americans brought with them—as I'm sure you have. And while those books played a great role in leading me to the conclusions which I have reached, they have also—more than they did with Gretchen, perhaps—cautioned me about the possible dangers. So, personally, I would prefer a slower campaign."

The owlish gaze was back—and, this time, very much that of a raptor. "Sieges can be won in many ways, after all. A furious battle at the breach, followed by a sack, is only one of them—and not, all things considered, usually the ideal resolution."

Gustav II Adolf, king of Sweden, emperor of the Confederated Principalities of Europe, returned the raptor gaze with one of his own. Given that he was almost universally acknowledged as the greatest soldier of his time, it was an impressive stare. The great beak of a nose helped, of course.

Still, the young owl did not flinch from the eyes of the eagle in his prime. For some odd reason, Gustav found that reassuring.

"True," he said abruptly. "I've fought and won many sieges, you know—more, perhaps, than any man of my time. The best way to resolve a siege is for the defenders to surrender. And, in my experience, that's always helped greatly if they are allowed to surrender with honor and dignity, and march out of the town still carrying their colors and arms. Best of all, if they then take service in your own ranks."

Finally, Thierbach seemed to be what he was—a very young man, confronting an older and much more powerful one. His expression was . . . not abashed, no, not even nervous—but perhaps a bit uncertain.

"So I believe also," he said softly. "I have no love for bloodshed, Your Majesty. Neither does Gretchen, for that matter, whatever others might think."

A very young man, now. His eyes were worried. "How is she, by the way? Have you heard anything?" He made a little gesture toward the crowd of people in the room. "We're all worried about her. Things in France seem . . . not good."

Gustav barked a laugh. "Isn't that why you sent her there in the first place? 'Not good,' indeed! The perfect place for a trouble-maker."

Joachim managed a smile, but the worry was still evident.

The king waved his hand heavily. "I have not heard anything, no. But—"

Afterward, Axel would chide and scold him. For hours, and days, dribbling on into weeks and months. But Gustavus Adolphus had always been a decisive man. Convinced, since he was sixteen, a teenage prince leading his father's troops in the capture of a Danish fortress, that hesitation lost far more battles—and wars—than mistakes ever did.

"Done," he said firmly. "Whatever I can do to help your fire-brand lady, if it proves necessary, I will do. You have my word on it. For my part—if it proves necessary—I will expect your full support against my own enemies. Things in France, as you say, do not look good."

"*Richelieu*," hissed Joachim. Gustav was gratified to hear the hiss echoed throughout the room.

The young radical straightened. "Richelieu, the Habsburgs—all that carrion—against *them*, Your Highness, the Committees of Correspondence stand firmly at your side."

Again, the murmur rippling through the crowd indicated that young Thierbach spoke for all of them. Gustav nodded his head.

"Good. And now, before I leave, is there anything further you wish to discuss?"

Joachim studied him with those solemn, owlish eyes. Then, a

bit abruptly: " 'Discuss' is not perhaps the right term, Your Majesty. 'Illustrate a point,' might be better."

He swiveled in his chair and pointed to one of the young men standing toward the front of the crowd. A stripling, perhaps seventeen years old, short and skinny. "That's Friedrich Gulda. He comes from Mecklenburg. He's an orphan now. Has been for five years, since Wallenstein passed through the area. He managed to hide in the fields while his family was destroyed. He was there for hours, listening to it all. Wallenstein's soldiers took their time about it."

He allowed Gustav Adolf and Oxenstierna to flesh out in their own minds the details concerning what 'took their time about it' meant. Being very experienced soldiers, neither of them had any difficulty doing so. Joachim's finger moved on.

"That girl is Hannelore. She's sixteen years old. She's from Brandenburg. A similar story, except her older brother survived also and their people were killed by Danish troops. They think, at least. Might have been some of Mansfeld's men. Who knows? To commoners, especially peasants, mercenary armies are hard to tell apart."

Gustav Adolf's jaws tightened. *Hard to tell apart for their own supposed "commanders," too. Not the least of the reasons I agreed with Stearns' proposal. Or Simpson's, as I think it really emerged.*

The finger moved on, centering on a hard-faced man in his mid-twenties. The expression on the man's face was . . . implacable.

"That's her older brother, in fact. Gunther Achterhof." Joachim's lips twisted. "When Gunther first arrived here he had some ears and noses wrapped up in a cloth. Horrid withered things. It took me a week to convince him to throw them away. Fortunately, he'd already thrown away the private parts."

He gave king and chancellor a glance which was every bit as hard as Achterhof's face. "He and his cousin and some neighbors, you see, caught two of the soldiers afterward. Stragglers. Probably not the soldiers who murdered his family, but Gunther doesn't care much. Not at all, in fact. A mercenary soldier is a mercenary soldier. And . . ."

If anything, Joachim's face was now even harder than Achterhof's. "As far as he's concerned, the prince who hired the soldier is simply another prince. Gunther Achterhof is no longer interested very much—if at all—in making fine distinctions. Neither is his cousin Ludwig, who is the tall man standing over there in the corner."

The inexorable finger moved on. "That red-headed man is Franz Heidbreder. He comes from Mecklenburg also. Most of his family survived, fortunately. In fact"—the finger slid sidewise—"that's his brother Friedrich and over there are his cousins Moritz and Agnes. Their farms were destroyed three years ago when your own Swedish army arrived in Germany. All the sheep were requisitioned, along with just about everything else. True, they were paid for the sheep. But you have debased your currency so many times that Swedish coin isn't accepted by most merchants."

Gustav's heavy jaws tightened still further, but he did not argue the point. He *had* debased his currency, trying to cover the huge expenses of his expedition to Germany.

Softly, but in a tone as unyielding as granite, Joachim continued. "Franz's mother died that first winter, from disease brought on by hunger. His youngest brother died in the spring. After the whole family left Mecklenburg to try to find shelter elsewhere, one of his cousins and an aunt died on the road. Again, disease; again, because they were weakened by hunger and had no shelter. When Franz found his aunt's body, she had a handful of grass stuffed in her mouth. At the end, apparently, she tried to eat it."

By now, Oxenstierna's face was pinched. Gustav's was simply impassive. The chancellor began to say something but the king laid a firm hand on his arm.

Meanwhile, Joachim's finger had moved on. The young Saxon nobleman's face seemed to soften a bit. "That girl there is Mathilde Wiegert. She was the one who introduced me to Gretchen Richter, as it happens. She's from the Palatinate, also driven into exile when the war struck. I met Mathilde herself when I was a student at Jena. She and her cousin Inga had become prostitutes by then, in order to support themselves and the younger girls with them."

The pretty young woman named Mathilde gave Gustav Adolf a little smile. Hers was the only smiling face in the room. But the king understood that the smile was not really directed at him. It was directed at the young man who was giving the king a none-too-subtle "illustration."

Joachim swiveled back in his chair, to face Gustav and Oxenstierna squarely. "As it happens, also, Mathilde is the immediate cause of my estrangement from my family. My noble father had no objection at all to my having mounted a commoner prostitute—in fact, he encouraged me to do so as part of my education—but he was outraged when I told him I plan to marry her once the laws have been changed here in Magdeburg to match the laws of the United States."

*Once* the laws have been changed. Not *if.* There, too, was a point being made.

"Such is the piety of aristocracy, King and Chancellor. Such is what—nothing more—all of your fine distinctions between Lutheran and Calvinist and Catholic come to in the end. Which nobleman gets to plunder and abuse which commoner at his convenience."

"Enough!" barked Oxenstierna.

A little growl rumbled through the cavernous room. Joachim fixed Oxenstierna with a stony gaze. "Yes, indeed, Chancellor. Precisely my point. *Enough.*"

Oxenstierna started to rise, angrily. But Gustav's hand, this time, was more than "firm." The king of Sweden was an immensely powerful man. He simply seized Oxenstierna by the shoulder and drove him back down into his chair.

"You *will* listen to my people, Chancellor," he hissed. "I will not lose my dynasty because of the folly of nobility." He gave Oxenstierna his own version of a stony gaze; which, if it had none of the fervor of Joachim's, made up for the lack by sheer self-confidence. "*Vasa.* Do not forget."

He turned back to Joachim, sensing the crowd settling down a bit. For a moment, the king and the revolutionary studied each other. Then Gustav Adolf nodded, and came to another decision. It would not be the first time, after all, that the king of Sweden had found it necessary to burn a bridge while on campaign. Some of those bridges had been behind him.

"I have decided to bring my family from Sweden here to Magdeburg. My daughter, at least. Kristina, as you may know, is quite young. Seven years old."

He glanced around the room. From their appearance, most of the crowd consisted of teenagers and people in their twenties. But, sprinkled here and there, he could see a few older ones—and a handful of children.

"Palaces are stodgy places. Very boring, for a spirited young girl. I think she would enjoy an occasional outing here."

He brought his eyes back to Thierbach. The young man seemed paralyzed for a moment. Then, astonished; then . . .

His thin shoulders squared. "She would have to learn how to

bake," he said firmly, in a voice which had barely a trace of a quiver. "It's the rule."

Axel looked like he might be on the verge of apoplexy. Gustav burst into laughter.

"Splendid!" he said, slapping the table with a meaty hand. "Her mother—my wife—will have a fit, of course. So would my own mother. But my grandmother, on the other hand—the wife of the great Gustav Vasa—is reputed to have been quite an accomplished baker. I see no reason not to restore that skill to the family."

Oxenstierna began expostulating his protests the moment they left the building. But Gustav waved him down impatiently.

"Later, Axel, later. You know as well as I do that my wife is unfit to bring up my daughter. She's a sweet woman, but . . . weak. How much trouble has she caused us already, by her susceptibility to flattering courtiers?"

He stopped, boots planted firmly in the muddy street, and glared down at his chancellor. "And you *also* know—you've read the histories, the same as I have—what happened to Kristina. In the end, for all her obvious brains and talents and spirit, she converted to Catholicism and abdicated the throne. I won't have it!"

"You were *dead* in that—" Axel's hand groped in midair. "Other history. You're alive in this one."

The king shrugged. "True. She still needs to be brought up among women. Part of the time, at least." He jerked his head toward the Freedom Arches. "Say whatever else you will about Gretchen Richter and her cohorts, they are not *weak.*"

Axel's face was almost red. Gustav decided to relent. He placed a hand on his chancellor's shoulder and began guiding him back toward the palace. "Oh, do relax. I don't plan to have Kristina spend much time with that radical lot, I assure you. No, no. I'll find some suitable noblewoman to serve as her—what do the Americans call it? 'Role model,' as I recall."

Oxenstierna seemed mollified. Gustav, looking ahead to a day filled with contentious meetings, decided to leave it at that. No reason to mention the *precise* noblewoman he had in mind, after all.

Alas, despite his often unthinking prejudices, Oxenstierna's own brains were excellent. Within ten paces, the chancellor was scowling fiercely again.

"Don't tell me. Gustav! You *can't* be thinking—"

"And why not?" demanded the king. "I think my newest—and youngest—baroness would make a splendid companion for Kristina."

He held up a finger. "Given the nature of the times, Kristina should learn how to shoot." Held up another. "And, in reverse, Julie Mackay rides a horse like a sack. Kristina's already an excellent rider, so she can teach the baroness that skill—which, I'm sure you'll agree, is essential for a proper and respectable Swedish noblewoman."

"Julie Mackay is in England," grumbled Oxenstierna. "Maybe even Scotland, by now."

"So? She'll be back."

"Things in England also do not 'look good.'"

"So?" repeated Gustav. He jerked a thumb over his shoulder, pointing back to the Freedom Arches. "If I wind up having to rescue one contentious young woman, why not two?"

They plodded on in silence for a bit. Then, Axel sighed. "Or three, or four. I never thought the day would come I'd say this, but I wish Rebecca Stearns were back in our midst. I . . . miss her advice. She is very shrewd, and easy to work with."

Gustav chuckled heavily. "Indeed. It's a bit amazing, isn't it, the way it works. Having Gretchen Richter—or Julie Mackay—as a frame for the portrait, Rebecca Stearns suddenly looks like the wisest woman in the world."

# Chapter 6

"Remember, Julie," said Melissa sternly, "that you don't have any antibiotics. So—"

"Will you cut it out?" interrupted Julie crossly. She folded another corner of the blanket around her baby's head. "If I have to listen to one more lecture about this, I think I'll scream." She gave her husband a sour glance. "Alex chews on my ear about it ten times a day."

Julie's Scot husband flushed. With his fair complexion and redhead freckles, a "flush" was fairly dramatic. "Damnation, lass," he growled, "'tis no joking matter. I shouldna allowed you to come on this trip at all, much less bring the child."

For a moment, Julie's lips parted. Melissa almost winced, imagining the retort. *And how the hell do you propose to have STOPPED me from coming? You—!*

Fortunately, Julie reined in the impulse. Whatever the realities of their personal relationship, Julie had learned to accommodate her husband's need to maintain, at least in public, the façade of being the "man of the house." That—just as his willingness, however reluctant, to allow her and their infant daughter Alexi to accompany him on his sudden emergency trip to Scotland—was one of many compromises the two young people had learned to make in order to keep their marriage a going concern.

It had not always been easy for them, Melissa knew. The clash of cultural attitudes between a 17th-century Scot cavalryman and a 21$^{st}$-century American woman was . . . awesome, at times. That wasn't helped by the fact that, on one side, Alex Mackay was a Scot nobleman—born under the bar sinister, true, but still with a nobleman's attitudes. And, on the other . . . Melissa had to force herself not to laugh. To describe Julie Mackay as "stubborn and strong-willed" would have been much like describing the ocean as "wet and salty." A given; a fact of nature. As well command the tides to roll back as expect her to be meek and demure.

Then, too, they were both very young. Alex in his early twenties; Julie still months away from her twentieth birthday. With all the advantages of being in late middle age, and separated by far less in the way of a culture gap, it was not as if Melissa herself and James Nichols hadn't had their share of domestic quarrels.

Feeling a little guilty that she'd occasioned this latest clash, Melissa groped for words to soothe the situation. *Dammit, woman, you're supposed to be a* peacemaker *on this mission. You're not a '60s college radical any longer, cheerfully poking the establishment.*

Grope, grope. The truth was that Melissa found agitation and troublemaking a lot more natural than being a diplomat. She couldn't find the words.

Fortunately, Julie had other characteristics than stubbornness. One of them—quite pronounced, in fact—was affection. So Melissa was spared the need to play the role of peacemaker. Julie suddenly smiled, slid an arm around her husband's waist, and drew him close. A wet and enthusiastic kiss on the cheek drained the flush right out of Alex's face. And immediately put another one in its place, of course. But that was a flush of pleasure, not anger.

Nor embarrassment, even though Julie's display of affection was quite public. They were all standing on the quays where the ship from Hamburg was moored. The Pool of London was crowded with stevedores and sailors and people waiting to embark on other ships. But Alex was not disturbed. Not at all, judging from the way his own lips sought Julie's.

One of the things Melissa had learned, in the two years since the Ring of Fire, was that people of the 17$^{th}$ century were far removed from the prim and proper attitudes of that later era usually labeled as "Victorian." That had surprised her, even though she was a history teacher by profession. Without ever having thought much about it, Melissa had assumed that European culture got progressively more "Victorian" the further back you went in time. She *certainly* would have expected the early 17$^{th}$ century—

the heyday of religious zeal; the era of "Puritanism"—to have been one characterized by tight-lipped reserve on all subjects, and sex in particular.

The reality was quite otherwise. The primness of social customs in the 19th century had been a recent development, occasioned by the Wesleyan Methodist response to the horrors of 18th-century English city life, and its spread onto the Continent through the Pietist movement. Melissa had discovered that people of the 17th century were actually quite earthy—even bawdy. If the Scot cavalrymen who stumbled onto Grantville soon after the Ring of Fire had found the clothing of American women rather scandalous, they hadn't thought their "modern" casualness about sex to be peculiar at all. They themselves, like most people of 17th-century Europe, had a relaxed attitude about sex which had far more in common with the mores of late 20th- and early 21st-century America than either did with the Victorian era.

More so, in some ways; even incredibly so, to someone with Melissa's upbringing and attitudes. She could still remember the shock she had felt when she discovered that one of the widowed farm women near Grantville had sued one of her employees because the man, coming upon her bent over in her vegetable garden, had cheerfully taken the opportunity—as the euphemism of a later era would put it—"to have his way with her" despite her vehement protests.

The shock hadn't been at the fact of rape. Melissa was no sheltered girl, and rape was common enough in 21st-century America. It had been the attitude of the woman herself which had appalled her. True, the farm woman had been furious at the man, for acting like such an oaf. But she had not filed criminal charges of *rape*. She'd simply stormed into the courthouse to demand that the crummy SOB be placed under a bastardy bond to provide child support in case he'd gotten her pregnant.

The case had been quite notorious in Grantville, at the time, because it had caused something of a firestorm in the already-turbulent attempt to forge a unitary legal code for the new society being constructed. On this question, as on many others, where modern Americans tended to see things in terms of personal rights, 17th-century Germans tended to see them in terms of property and its obligations. The fact that the man had violated the woman herself was a matter for anger, to be sure. But the *real* outrage was that he had endangered her *property*—by, possibly, begetting an unwanted child on her which would be a continual drain on her none-too-substantial resources. Even the culprit himself had seen it in those terms. On the stand, he'd admitted quite freely that he'd been hoping to embarrass his employer into marrying him and thus giving him a secure lifetime interest in the farm.

In the end, the case had been settled on the woman's terms. And, while Melissa had been angry at the time, in retrospect she wasn't sure the lout of a handyman wouldn't have been better off spending a few years in an American prison—with time off for good behavior—than being stripped of every penny and possibly locked into what amounted to a condition of involuntary servitude for two decades.

Remembering that episode as she watched Julie's kiss turn into something very demonstrative—Alex's face was almost beet red, now, but he was returning the kiss with enthusiasm—Melissa found herself fighting down a laugh again. *O brave new world, that hath such people in it!* There were things she detested about 17th-century society; others, which she had found herself coming to treasure, almost despite herself.

Disease, however, was not one of them. And the fact was that Julie was taking a real risk in bringing her child on this voyage. As a rule, people of the time left their children behind—especially infants—whenever they traveled anywhere beyond their immediate vicinity. Rebecca and Gretchen hadn't even considered bringing their babies along on their own mission. Leaving aside the very real danger of piracy and highway robbery, there was the ever-present risk of disease whenever a child was exposed to strange populations. Even without travel and unnecessary exposure, a third of all children born alive did not survive their first year; fully half died before the age of five.

Hearing a clatter of hooves, Melissa turned away from Alex and Julie. A small party of cavalrymen was trotting onto the quays, some fifty yards away. They were using the weight of their mounts to brush aside the stevedores and sailors, exhibiting all the arrogance of soldiers toward civilians that was another of the characteristics of the time which Melissa despised. *Move or be trampled, damn you.*

Her lips tightened. The officer at the head of the troop was scanning the area, obviously looking for someone. Which, she had little doubt, was Melissa herself. Or her party, rather. Although the cavalrymen weren't wearing uniforms as such—which were still

uncommon in this day and age—the similar buff coats and knee
boots and gauntlets and plumed hats amounted to the same thing.
Only royal troops would be so accoutered in this area.

*An official escort. I'm not sure whether to be pleased or not.*

She felt a looming presence behind her. She didn't have to
turn her head to know that was Tom Simpson. Rita's husband
had a personality which was diametrically opposite that of the
haughty officer coming toward her. Melissa had seen Tom
Simpson step aside for almost everyone he encountered. But the
man's sheer size was enough to make him "loom" just by being
in the vicinity. That wasn't due to any great height—Tom was
not much over six feet tall—but simply to his bulk. All of
which, she knew, was bone and muscle. Tom Simpson hadn't
been out of shape as a nose guard for West Virginia University's
varsity football team. The time since, most of it spent as an
officer in the army of the new little United States, had kept him
in even better shape.

She found that presence comforting, the more so as the officer
and his cavalrymen approached. Melissa had learned, in the two
years since the Ring of Fire, to dismiss her long-standing prejudice against soldiers for what it was: prejudice. But if there were
Alex Mackays and Tom Simpsons and Heinrich Schmidts in the
world's armies, there were also officers she wouldn't have trusted
any more than she would a rattlesnake. Quite a bit less, in fact—
no one had ever accused a rattlesnake of committing "atrocities."

The officer in charge of this party . . . didn't look promising.
Plumed like a peacock, staring at everyone in a haughty manner
which was almost a parody from a movie, his long nose tight with
what seemed a perpetual sniff.

*Not, I admit, that this place doesn't stink.* Whatever else Melissa liked about the 17th century, the smell of its cities and towns
was not one of them.

"That's got to be for us," murmured Tom. "I'll get Rita."

Melissa nodded. Rita Simpson was the *official* ambassador to
King Charles I. To all the Americans in Grantville—including the
woman herself, all of twenty-three years old—that seemed a little
ridiculous. But, following the advice of Balthazar and Rebecca, and
Francisco Nasi—and Gustav's chancellor Oxenstierna, for that
matter—Mike had given his kid sister the assignment. For 17th-
century Europeans, "diplomacy"—in the sense of crucial, binding,
negotiations rather than routine matters—was not something

conducted by professional ambassadors. The distances involved were simply too great, and transport and communications too poorly developed, for nations to oversee closely their own envoys. As a result, it was the common practice for ambassadors to be relatives of the rulers involved, because only they could be presumed to speak with real authority.

Granted, Mike Stearns was not a king. But he was the closest thing the United States had; and so, willy-nilly, the embassies to France and Holland and England were being officially headed up by his wife and his sister.

In the case of Rebecca's mission, formality and reality matched. Everyone, except possibly herself, had full confidence in Rebecca's ability to handle the task. Indeed, she had been given the more difficult and critical mission—to make peace with France, if at all possible, and forge an alliance with Holland.

With the mission to England, the situation was different. There was nothing *wrong* with Rita. Melissa thought she was a splendid example of an American young woman, sane of mind and sound in body. But nobody, certainly not Rita herself, thought she had the same brilliance which Rebecca had demonstrated many times over.

Thus, despite her own wishes, Melissa Mailey had been dragooned into serving as Rita's "adviser"—in truth, the real head of the delegation.

*Damn it, I'm closing in on sixty! I'm too old and decrepit for these adventures. And I miss my bed at home, with James in it. And my little creature comforts and habits. I even miss the squeaky hinge on the kitchen door that James swears he'll get fixed some day.*

The oncoming officer still hadn't spotted them. Moved by an impulse, Melissa turned back to Alex and Julie.

"We should part company. Now. There's no reason to think . . ." She hesitated. "Still—"

Alex nodded. "In case of trouble, best there be no known connection between us." He put his arm around Julie's shoulders and began to turn her away. Then, with a little smile: "Of course, there *will* be spies. But by the time they finish squabbling with Charles' tight-fisted paymasters over the price for the information, we'll be halfway to Edinburgh."

Melissa could see Julie starting to rebel, a bit. The young woman obviously wanted to give her a parting hug. But Julie was stubborn, not stupid. So, after a moment, she satisfied herself with a warm smile and a whisper: "Don't forget to stay in touch with the radio. I'll listen every day, just like we planned."

Melissa nodded. Since her head was turned away from the officer, she blew Julie a kiss. Then, firmly—and not easily; Julie had become something of an adopted daughter to her, since the Ring of Fire—she turned her back on them.

Turned her back, straightened her shoulders, reared her head as high as her long neck allowed; then, bestowed upon the approaching officer a nose which—truth be told—was every bit as aristocratic as his and a gaze whose haughtiness would have graced an empress. Not for nothing had Melissa Mailey spent years as a schoolteacher staring down youthful insolence.

The officer spotted her, then. And, a moment later, Tom and Rita Simpson standing next to her. Behind them, Darryl McCarthy and Gayle Mason and Friedrich and Nelly Bruch were standing next to the party's luggage. The two couples—true couple with the Bruchs, faked with Darryl and Gayle—were the "servants" for the mission. All embassies of the time would bring their own servants. Whose tasks, cheerfully enough, all of them would carry out—even if Darryl and Gayle could be counted on to make sarcastic remarks about it in private. But their real reasons for being there were to maintain the radio communications, in the case of Gayle; provide Tom with whatever he needed in the way of physical security, in the case of Darryl and Friedrich; and, since Friedrich's wife was a native Londoner and he was familiar with the city himself, whatever local intelligence might be needed.

Melissa saw the officer's eyes widen a bit. His nose seemed to narrow still further.

*Sorry, jackass. I don't wear feathers and plumes. Low-class we may be, but this is the official delegation from the United States.*

That was a bit unfair. She *had*, after all, tried to talk Rita into wearing a very elaborate outfit, complete with plumed hat. But that had been too much for Rita's ingrained Appalachian modesty.

The officer's eyes fell on Tom. Melissa found herself chuckling softly at the subtle change in the man's arrogant expression. Even sitting astride a horse, the officer was obviously pondering the very real possibility that Tom could bring the horse down with one hand while he plucked the officer off with the other. Judging from his squint, Melissa suspected the man was now considering what might *follow.*

Too horrible to contemplate, apparently. The officer forced a
smile on his face and trotted up.

"Ah. Lady Stearns, I presume?"

Melissa had managed to coach Rita well enough that she didn't
blurt out what would normally have been her response. *You've gotta
be kidding. Besides, I'm Mrs. Simpson now—this big fella is my
hubby.* Instead, Rita simply nodded graciously and gestured to the
others. "And my party," she said.

*A bit too softly*, thought Melissa. *But . . . not bad. Hey, what the
hell. As long as I'm here, I may as well enjoy it.*

Some time later, as their coach and its cavalry escort approached
their destination, Melissa was not enjoying herself at all. She recognized the place, as it happened, having visited it as a tourist three
times in her life.

"What's the matter?" asked Rita softly. "You look like you just
ate a lemon."

Melissa pointed a finger out the window. "*That's* the matter.
Where we're going. I thought they'd take us to Whitehall Palace,
which is the royal residence in this period of English history."

Tom leaned over and peered out the window. A moment later,
he grimaced. Melissa was not surprised to see that he recognized
their destination, even though, unlike her, he'd never been to
England. Tom had grown up in Pittsburgh, not a small town in
West Virginia, and his parents had been very wealthy. The kind
of parents who got mail from all over the world.

The place whose gates they were approaching was quite famous,
after all. Its distinctive outline graced millions of postcards.

"Oh, lovely," he muttered. "The Tower of London."

# Chapter 7

"It's not as bad as it sounds, Rita," said Melissa, looking around the room the officer and the escort had led them to. Rita's face had been tight with apprehension since being told of their destination.

"Being 'tossed into the Tower' isn't actually the same thing as being tossed into a dungeon. Mind you, there *are* some real dungeons in this place—plenty of them—but, for the most part, the Tower is where the British monarchs keep important people they want to more or less 'lock up' in comfort."

She made a little motion with her hand, indicating their surroundings. "I mean—*look* at it. Sure, the underlying construction is medieval, and the less we think about the toilet situation the better. But, other than that, these rooms and their furnishings are fit for a king. Quite literally, as a matter of fact. This is St. Thomas' Tower, where at least one medieval king of England actually lived. One of the Edwards, if I remember right."

Melissa moved over to one of the windows on the side opposite the Thames. The glass, she noticed, was almost as clear as modern glass would have been. Below, a narrow cobblestoned street separated the outer wall of the Tower, of which St. Thomas' Tower was a part, from the inner wall of the fortress. She pointed at the mass of stone buildings which formed most of the construction of the inner wall in this portion of the Tower of London.

"That's where they kept Sir Walter Raleigh, you know, for some twelve years—and not all that long ago. In considerable comfort."

She decided, under the circumstances, that there was no need to mention that the nickname for Raleigh's tower was "the Bloody Tower." That was legend, anyway. Who really knew if Richard III had murdered his nephews in the first place—much less done it there? She also decided there was no reason to mention the open plot of ground somewhere on the other side of the Bloody Tower—you couldn't see it, from their vantage point—where Henry VIII had had Anne Boleyn's head chopped off.

Rita seemed to relax a little. "So what you're saying, in a nutshell, is that we're under 'house arrest.' And they've provided us with the nicest house they have for the purpose."

Melissa nodded. She was about to elaborate when Darryl McCarthy appeared through a door on the far end of the connected rooms they'd been led into—what Melissa was already thinking of as "the ambassadorial suite." The young coal-miner-turned-soldier was shaking his head, but the gesture was more one of bemusement than disapproval.

"Fancy digs, that's for sure, except for the—ah—I guess we can call it a 'toilet.' But—" He gestured over his shoulder with a thumb. "They've got guards posted at a walkway that leads over to the other side of the street, and they made real clear that I wasn't allowed to go across. Said we had to wait until some muckety-muck—I didn't catch the name—showed up."

From the idle way he rubbed his chest, Melissa suspected that "real clear" had involved the point of a partisan when Darryl tried to push the issue. Probably two or three partisans, held in the hands of a squad. Like his friend Harry Lefferts, Darryl was brash and bold. The sort of Appalachian lad who had, throughout American history, provided a disproportionate share of its gunslingers and desperadoes—and, for that matter, test pilots.

Melissa had often found that hillbilly machismo rather aggravating. But . . .

*Different times, different places. God, I'm glad Darryl's here. Worse comes to worst, at least we won't go gently into that good night. I even miss Harry Lefferts. Well . . . sorta. I can probably keep Darryl from doing anything really nuts. But if Harry were here with him . . . Eek.*

She smiled, remembering times past—before the Ring of Fire—when, as a schoolteacher, she'd often enough been ready to throttle

two rambunctious teenagers. When Harry and Darryl finally graduated from high school and went to work in the mines, Ed Piazza,
the principal of the high school, had invited Melissa and several
other teachers into his private office for a surreptitious drink from
a half pint of Jack Daniels he had stashed away in a drawer of
his desk.

"Now that *those* two are gone," he'd said, examining the empty
bottle—it had been emptied very quickly—"maybe I can start
following my own rules about no alcoholic beverages on the
premises."

"I doubt it," grunted Greg Ferrara, the science teacher. He eyed
the empty bottle regretfully. "Don't forget we've still got—"

"Shuddup," growled Piazza. "Just shuddup."

*Different times, different places.*

Hearing the clump of feet coming up the staircase which led
to St. Thomas' Tower, Melissa turned away from the window. From
some subtlety in the noise, she knew that whoever was coming
up was no mere guard. The footsteps had that vaguely ponderous feel to them—dignity rather than simple force—which signified
the arrival of a "man of substance."

And, sure enough, the man who came through the entry into
the suite was very finely dressed. He was quite an imposing man,
besides, even leaving aside the garments. Tall, lean, strong-featured
if not handsome; thick dark hair and brown eyes contrasting rather
sharply with the pale complexion. His expression was grave and
solemn. Melissa had the impression this was more because of
practiced habit than natural temperament. The quick flashing smile
which suddenly appeared, quite at odds with the formal dignity
of his stance, lent support to that suspicion.

"May I bid you all greetings," the man said. "On my behalf, as
well as that of King Charles. I am Sir Thomas Wentworth—"

He broke off, briefly, an odd look coming over his face. It was
a subtle thing. Half-surprise; half-delight—the look of a man who
has suddenly remembered a recent and very unexpected stroke of
good fortune.

"The earl of Strafford, actually. The king saw fit to bestow the
title upon me recently." He cleared his throat. "I'm afraid the king
himself is indisposed at the moment. The queen is quite ill, and
between his concern for her and the press of state affairs, His
Majesty asked me to greet you on his behalf. He also asked me"—

another clearing of the throat; louder, this one—"to extend his apologies for not providing you with lodgings at Whitehall. Alas, the queen's illness is shared by many of the courtiers and servants, and the king fears for your safety should you be installed in what has, sadly, become a palace rife with disease."

He got that out quite nicely, thought Melissa, given that she was almost certain it was a straight-up lie. Strafford bestowed that quick smile upon them again. It was quite a striking expression—as much due to its brevity as its gleam. As if the man who made it distrusted his own tendency toward warmth.

"To be perfectly honest—I've stayed in Whitehall myself, at times—you'll be more comfortable here anyway. The royal palace is a madhouse, half the time, and so crowded we'd have been forced to cram you all into one or two tiny rooms. Whereas here—"

His hand, in a slow-moving regal gesture, indicated the charms of their surroundings. "Separate rooms—good quarters for the servants, even—one of the finest fireplaces in all England, and quite possibly the best beds this side of the queen's chambers in Whitehall. Much better."

That much was probably true, Melissa suspected. She'd barely recognized St. Thomas' Tower when they'd been led into it. From the outside, it looked not too different from the way it had looked when she'd visited the Tower in the late 20th century. But the inside, on her tours, had been barren. More than that, really, because the people who managed the Tower had deliberately left some of the old architecture exposed so that tourists could see the way in which the Tower had been constructed in layers, century after century. Today, she was seeing the place the way it would have actually been used in those long-gone centuries. Carpets, rich tapestries, linens on the beds and the fine upholstery of the furniture looking as if it had been used recently. Most impressive of all, to her, was the great fireplace which dominated the suite. She remembered the thing, from her visits as a tourist. But there was a great difference between the cold if majestic structure she remembered, and this fireplace warm with ashes and half-burned logs.

*Of course, I could have done without the authentic smell.*

But even that was something wafted in through the open windows on the Thames side of the suite. Most of it came from the still waters of the moat, which was, for all intents and purposes, an open-air sewer. The rooms in St. Thomas' Tower themselves were immaculately clean.

Melissa was about to say something when Rita spoke. "I thank you, Lord Strafford. And please convey my appreciation to His Majesty. But when, may I ask, will we be able to meet the king himself?"

Strafford clasped his hands behind his back and leaned forward a bit. "I'm afraid I can't say. The press of affairs really *is* frightful at the moment—and was, even before the queen took ill. And with that coming on top of it all . . ."

Strafford's expression was a diplomatic marvel. Melissa almost laughed. It conveyed the subtleties of a man who, moved by bonhomie and good will, would impart a confidence to strangers in whom he had taken a sudden trust and liking. False to the core, but—well done. Oh, very well done indeed.

"If I may say so, the king perhaps dotes a bit too much on the queen. Personally, I think the accusations that he is besotted with her are quite false—even slanderous. But there's no doubt the man treasures her deeply. When she's ill . . . it's difficult to tear him away from her side, and then only for the most immediate and urgent matters."

Melissa decided Rita was handling the situation well, and let her continue. However nervous the young woman might be at the role she had been called upon to play, it was a role she would have to learn. No way to do that, after all, other than to just do it.

"I see. Well, let's hope for Her Majesty's quick recovery, then. In the meantime . . ." Rita glanced toward the window overlooking the rest of the Tower of London. The aplomb she'd managed to retain thus far seemed to desert her a bit.

Perhaps sensing the awkwardness, Strafford intervened smoothly. "Your servants, of course, will be quite free to move about the Tower in order to obtain whatever you need." He gave Darryl a quick, skeptical glance, but left it at that. "They will not, however, be able to leave the Tower itself. And I'm afraid I must ask you, Lady Stearns, as well as your husband and—ah—"

He was looking at Melissa. Like Rita herself, Melissa had not quite been able to force herself to wear the plumage of a noblewoman of the times. But, also like Rita, she was clothed in garments which were considerably finer than those worn by the Bruchs or Darryl and Gayle.

"Melissa Mailey," she announced.

Strafford frowned slightly, as if searching his memory. Melissa was struck by how rapidly the frown vanished. "Ah, yes. You are one of the members of—what's the term?—yes, 'the cabinet,' I believe, of your government." He nodded graciously, extending a personal welcome. "And yourself as well, then. Please do remain in your quarters."

Rita seemed unable to think of the right words with which to register a protest. Neither could Melissa, for the simple reason that she was in something of a state of shock.

Not at the restriction to quarters—she'd been expecting that; it was standard practice for important "guests" in the Tower—but at the simple fact that Strafford knew who she was.

*God in Heaven, the man can't have arrived in London but recently. And he's already learned this much about us?*

As suavely as ever, Strafford glided on. "The restriction is for your own safety, do please understand that." He turned his head, scowling at the river visible beyond the southern windows. "I'm afraid there's been some turbulence in the kingdom recently. No way to know how much of the sedition may have spread into the Tower itself, and who knows what madmen might think to do?"

He straightened a bit, bowed. The gesture—very well done, as everything the man did—conveyed, simultaneously, regrets and cordiality and firm resolve and . . . *I've done what I had to do and I'm getting out of here. Adios, amigos—and don't even think of messing with me.*

A few murmured words of polite departure, and he was off. Moving more quickly than he had arrived, perhaps, but still with that same, solid, dignified tread.

When he was gone, and clearly beyond hearing, Melissa blew out a breath and stifled a curse.

More or less. "Damnation. *Wentworth!* And they've already made him an earl!"

*Shit-shit-shit.* But she kept that vulgarity to herself, from the lifelong habits of a schoolteacher.

Everyone was staring at her. Melissa turned to Gayle. "Can anyone hear us?"

The stocky woman shook her head. "Nope. While Darryl was busy playing macho-man with the guards, I checked everything. So did Friedrich. There's no place for hidey-holes or listening posts, and the guards outside can't possibly hear anything in here short of a shout or a scream. Or a gunshot."

Melissa nodded. "All right, then." She moved over to a nearby armchair and plopped herself into it. Very plush and comfortable, it was. "Gather round, folks. Let me explain the situation—as near as I can figure it out, anyway."

When they were clustered about, Rita and Tom perched together on a small couch and the rest standing, Melissa pointed a finger at the entryway through which Wentworth had departed.

"That man is probably the most dangerous man in England. For us, anyway. Sir Thomas Wentworth, later to become the earl of Strafford. Except in *our* universe, the king didn't make him an earl until . . ." She groped in her memory. "I can't remember the exact year, but it sure as hell wasn't as early as 1633. He's *supposed* to be on his way to Ireland right now. Just recently appointed Lord Deputy of the island."

The name finally registered on Darryl McCarthy. Melissa had been wondering when it would. For all that Darryl had the typical Appalachian working-class boy's indifference to history, there was one subject on which he didn't. Darryl's father Michael had been a long-time supporter of NORAID, the Irish Northern Aid Committee, and the whole McCarthy clan were rabid Irish-American nationalists.

"Black Tom Tyrant!" he snarled. "The fucking bastard! He's the one who killed the Men of '98!"

Melissa sighed. And, as usual, he had his history all jumbled up. She could remember a test question, years before, which Darryl had answered: "George III, first president of the United States."

"He's forty years old, Darryl!" she snapped. "So he'd have been five years old when he 'killed the Men of '98'—assuming, of course, that those had been the men of *fifteen* ninety-eight instead of 1798, which is when the rebellion actually happened. You're almost two centuries off."

Darryl was glowering. Not at the reproof—water off his back, that; always had been—but with the glower of a man who knew what he knew, dammit, and don't confuse him with the facts.

Melissa rubbed her face, reminding herself that she was a diplomat these days, not a schoolteacher. No point in trying to correct Darryl's grasp of history. For whatever reason the young man detested Strafford, the detestation was probably good enough. She wasn't certain yet, but all the signs pointed to an England which was already lost to them. She'd come here looking for peace—even, possibly, an alliance—but with Strafford now an earl, and all the rest she'd seen . . .

"The point's this, people. Wentworth was always—by far—the best adviser and official King Charles ever had. But, in the world we came from, Charles never much cared for the man. Basically, because Wentworth was too smart and too capable and too efficient."

"Didn't trust him, huh?" grunted Tom.

Melissa shook her head. "No, it wasn't that. Wentworth—Strafford—was loyal to the bone. When the time finally came, oh, when was it? In 1641, I think, give or take a year. When the time came when the English revolution demanded Strafford's head, King Charles let them have him—even though he'd sworn to Strafford that he would stand by him no matter what."

Melissa, unlike Darryl, had a sense for the grayness of history. Heroes were rarely simply heroes, nor villains always "villainous." Strafford, like Richelieu—like Wallenstein, even—was a man of many parts. Some of which could only be admired, however much the men themselves might be enemies of what she stood for now, in this time and place.

"Strafford's quite a guy, actually," she said softly. "He sent—would send, years from now, in that other universe—a letter to the king absolving him of his vow. And by all accounts, even those of his enemies, went to his death with great courage and dignity—and not a murmur of complaint about his—"

There was no reason to be diplomatic. "His worthless, treacherous, useless, incompetent, feckless, *shithead* of a king."

*There! I feel better.*

Darryl was grinning at her use of the vulgar term. *Miz Mailey!*

Everyone in the room chuckled. Melissa grinned herself.

"King Charles the First was—is—one of the dumbest kings the English ever saddled themselves with. Well . . . 'dumb' isn't exactly the right word. Frankly, that's giving him too much credit. He was—is—probably smart enough. So he doesn't even have that excuse. But he's got the temperament of a child. He sulks, he pouts, he always wants to have his cake and eat it too. For years he neglected his French Catholic wife, in favor of his infatuation with his favorite courtier, the duke of Buckingham—who was an even bigger jackass than he is. Buckingham was assassinated in 1628. That's happened in this universe too, because it was before the Ring of Fire. Since then, Charles has been doting on his wife. And—never fails!—Henrietta Maria is *another* royal twit. She's Louis XIII's sister, and she's pretty much cut from the same cloth as her brother.

If Louis didn't have Richelieu running France for him—at least *he's* smart enough to know talent when he sees it—he'd be in a mess."

Tom chuckled heavily. "Are there *any* kings or queens who can tie their own shoes, in this day and age? Outside of Gustav Adolf, of course."

"Several, as a matter of fact. King Christian of Denmark is quite an impressive monarch. The biggest problem he always had was trying to bite off more than he could chew. But—capable, no doubt about it, even if he is drunk half the time. And if the current rulers of Spain and Austria aren't anything to write home about, their *younger* relatives are something else. Don Fernando of Spain—they'll already be calling him the 'cardinal-infante,' I imagine—is just about to start his impressive military career. That's the Spanish Habsburgs. On the Austrian side of the family, Emperor Ferdinand's son the King of Hungary is also on the eve of coming into his own."

She twirled her fingers in the air, trying to depict the confused workings of space and time. "In the universe that was—would have been; hell, probably is somewhere else—the cardinal-infante and the king of Hungary would lead the Habsburg armies that defeated the Swedes at Nordlingen in 1634. Of course," she added, comforting herself, "they didn't have to face Gustav Adolf himself, since he died at Lützen."

Tom Simpson, if nothing else, knew his military history. "November of last year, that would have been." His thick chest rumbled a little laugh. "Not in *this* universe, though. We pretty well put the kibosh on that at the Alte Veste."

Rita shushed him with a hand on his arm. "Keep talking, Melissa."

"The point is this," she repeated. "The reason Charles didn't like Wentworth—and his queen Henrietta Maria disliked him even more—is because the man *pestered* him. 'Do this, do that.' The fact that he was unquestionably loyal and his advice was generally good didn't matter to Charles. He just found the man tiresome, that's all. Wentworth distracted him—tried to, anyway—from his beloved round of masques and the flattery of that pack of toadying courtiers he and the queen always had around them."

She snorted. "Earl of Strafford! Wentworth didn't come from the nobility, he came from the gentry. Like any capable and ambitious man of his time—this time—he wanted honors and recognition. For *years,* hard years in which he served the king ably and even brilliantly, he petitioned Charles to make him an earl. And, naturally, Charles—God, what a sorry man he was—*is*— rewarded him with indifference. He showered earldoms on every twit of a courtier who gained his or Henrietta Maria's favor, but nothing for Wentworth. Nothing except another assignment. Not until almost the very end, when England started to blow up under his feet, did Charles finally make Wentworth the earl of Strafford. Years from now, that should have happened. Right *now,* Wentworth is supposed to have just arrived in Ireland—where he'd spend years hammering that place into shape for the English."

Darryl scowled but, thankfully, kept quiet.

"Do you see what I'm getting at, people?" She pointed again at the entryway. "In *this* time and place, Charles has already made him the earl of Strafford. And you can be sure it isn't because Charles is any brighter or less of a jerk. So what does that tell us?"

"They *know* what's going to happen," said Tom immediately. "Of course, we were already pretty sure of that, once Rebecca found out that Doctor Harvey took some copies of pages from that history book he ran into while he was visiting Grantville. But knowing is one thing, figuring stuff out is another."

He rose, and went to the window overlooking the street between St. Thomas' Tower and the inner wall of the Tower of London. "The shit's hitting the fan, isn't it? That's what you're telling us, Melissa."

"Well, I wouldn't put it quite like that," she said primly—until the laugh which swept the room reminded her that she'd use the vulgar term herself, not minutes past. Then, smiling a bit sheepishly, she continued:

"But, yes, that's the gist of it. Charles obviously knows there's a revolution coming and the 'historical agenda' has him scheduled for the chopping block. It's like Samuel Johnson said: 'Depend upon it, sir, when a man knows he is to be hanged in a fortnight, it concentrates his mind wonderfully.' Not even Charles is silly enough to let his petty irritation with Wentworth stand in the way of staying alive and staying in power. So he must have called him back from Ireland and given the task of stopping the revolution before it even starts into his very capable hands."

She nodded toward the window overlooking the Thames. "We all noticed that the shipping pattern in the Channel was odd."

Then, nodded toward Bruch. "To be precise, Friedrich told us it was." In years gone by, Friedrich had served as a sailor on one of the Hanseatic League's ships. "And then, how busy the river traffic on the Thames seemed to be. Remember that most so-called 'warships' in this day and age are just armed merchantmen. At a guess, I'd say the English are preparing some kind of naval expedition."

"What for?" asked Rita, her face creased with a frown. "I'd think that if Charles was worried about revolution at home, that he'd be keeping his attention on *that*. Not playing games with military adventures somewhere else."

"I don't know myself, Rita. But . . ." Melissa tried to figure out a quick and simple way to explain the complexities.

"Look, we've been hearing about the new Spanish expedition against Holland for months now. And about France's reaction to it. Well, the English aren't all that fond of the Dutch themselves at the moment. In our own history, Charles and the court actually favored the Spaniards over the Dutch, despite all the English pride in having defeated the Armada. Of course, *our* Spain didn't get around to launching its 'Second Armada' until several years from now in our history, so the fact that they're planning one now seems to indicate that they've been doing a little future research of their own.

"But my point is that even though 'official England' favored Spain then, there's no way Charles would have actually *helped* the Spaniards. However much he disliked Holland, he recognized a certain commonality of interest with them. And he knew Richelieu's policy was always directed at defeating Habsburg power, so siding with Spain against the Dutch would have made him France's enemy, as well. That's why he stayed neutral in this particular little conflict in our own past.

"But if he's preparing a naval expedition now, then that suggests he doesn't plan on sitting this one out this time around. I can't believe he'd openly support Spain—not with the potential for pissing off Richelieu, and especially not in light of the fact that there's nothing in particular Spain could give him to make it worth his while. But if not Spain, then he has to be planning on siding with the Dutch, instead, and that doesn't make any sense either. Unless Richelieu is involved somehow."

"But why would he want to help Richelieu?" Rita asked with a frown.

"It all comes down to *money*, in the end," Melissa replied.

"Charles hasn't summoned a Parliament in years, now—not since the Parliament of 1628 which infuriated him. But without a Parliament, his means of raising funds are pretty limited. That was always what hamstrung the English monarchy, you know. It's the reason that England has a much smaller army than most countries of this day and age. The crown doesn't have much of a war chest without getting Parliament's approval. And summoning a new Parliament is the one thing Charles is not going to do, for sure. The last one had already become a hotbed of Puritan dissent."

Not to her surprise, Tom's mind was already ranging ahead. If the huge soldier didn't have his father's temperament, he had inherited the man's brains. "He needs money to crush revolution at home, so he's getting it from abroad. Why not France? His wife's the French king's sister, after all. But wherever he gets it, he'll have to pay a price for it. So, yeah, that could be by supporting somebody *else's* military adventures—like Richelieu's bid to stop the Spanish Habsburgs from regaining control of Holland."

He cocked his head away from the window, looking at Melissa. "Makes sense, I suppose. But it also seems a bit fancy, though—far-thinking, let's call it—for a king as goofy as you've described Charles."

"It is. But Wentworth's capable of thinking that far ahead. And, as I said, he's been made the earl of Strafford . . ."

"Way ahead of schedule," Tom concluded, turning back to the window. A moment later, he seemed to stiffen.

"And here's something else." He pointed down at the street below. "Dunno what it means, Melissa, but they're hauling somebody else into this joint. And I'd say, going by the chains they've got all over him, that he's *not* going to be getting the 'royal treatment' we are."

Melissa rose hurriedly and came to the window. Looking out and down, she saw a man being frog-marched past on the street below. Each of his arms was firmly held by a guard, with more guards marching ahead and behind. The precautions seemed a bit ludicrous. As Tom said, the man's wrists and ankles were manacled, with chains connecting to a heavy leather belt cinched around his waist.

For a moment, his eye perhaps caught by the motion in the window, the man looked up at her. There was no expression on his face, beyond stolidity. It was the face of a man who was determined to show neither fear nor favor to fortune. *Come what may, 'tis all God's will. I am who I am.*

Then he looked away, giving her a view of his profile.

"Oh, Jesus," she whispered. The face was younger, of course. But she recognized it easily enough. It was a distinctive face. The same one she'd seen on portraits, in every book in Grantville which discussed the English Revolution of 1640.

Darryl was at another window, by now, and he recognized the face almost as quickly as she did.

"That son-of-a-bitch!" he snarled. Then, almost shouting through the heavy panes of the window: "I hope they draw and quarter you, you stinking—"

Melissa spun away from her own window. *"I've had quite enough from you, young man!"*

That was the True Voice. *The schoolmarm in full fury.* Darryl fell silent as instantly as he had in years gone by. He even cringed a bit.

She glared at him. Then, looking at Tom, pointed a stiff finger at McCarthy. "You *will* maintain discipline with your subordinate. You *will* see to it that the lout—the cretin—the wet-behind-the-ears—"

Tom grinned. "Not to worry, ma'am." Then, flexed his shoulders. Even Darryl, clearly enough, found *that* intimidating. He cringed still further.

Melissa smiled thinly. "Excellent." She bestowed a look upon McCarthy which did not bode any better for his future than that same look, in times past, had boded for his grades and chances for advancement.

"I will save the history lesson for another time, young man. But for the moment, we have business to deal with. And you *will* obey me."

Darryl almost gulped. He did nod hastily.

"Splendid." She turned now to Friedrich and Nelly. Like everyone in the party, the Bruchs were now standing at one of the windows which overlooked the street. "You'll be able to move around more easily than any of us, and you don't have Gayle's odd accent. So you'll be our spies."

She glanced out the window. The man being marched under guard was now being taken through a doorway farther down. The kind of doorway which practically shrieked: *This way to the dungeons!*

"Will you be able to recognize him again?" The Bruchs nodded.

"Try to find out exactly where they've taken him and, if you can, what they plan to do with him."

Nelly opened her mouth to say something, but Melissa was driving on. "Tom—you too, Darryl—we need to start planning an escape. Nothing immediate, and I hope it won't come to that. But we need to be ready, if necessary."

That statement immediately brought back Darryl's usual insouciance. As Tom started scrutinizing the rooms, calculating the possibilities, Darryl was opening one of the great trunks they'd brought with them. It didn't take him more than a few seconds to work his way under the mass of clothing and start retrieving the items secreted there. Over Melissa's objections, Mike Stearns had insisted they bring those items. *Just in case,* as he'd put it.

"I can't believe they were dumb enough not to search us," Darryl said gaily. *Thump, thump.* Two automatic pistols materialized on the low table next to him. *Thump.* A box of ammunition.

"That would have been *most* undiplomatic," said Melissa. "I was almost certain they wouldn't."

*Thump, thump, thump.* Three sticks of dynamite. *Clink.* Melissa recognized some blasting caps.

*Thrump.* She was pretty sure that was what they called "prima-cord." Not positive, of course—she knew very little about explosives, beyond the primitive incendiary bombs an anarchist boyfriend of hers had once fiddled with in his attic, in the long ago and heady days of the 60s. But she hadn't stayed with him very long. Even in her radical youth, Melissa had frowned on violence.

*THUMP.* A battery, that was. She could imagine its purpose. She sighed, remembering those innocent days.

"Besides," she added, "people in this day and age think of firearms as big and clumsy things, which take forever to reload."

"Yup," said Darryl cheerfully. "Betcha we can find plenty of places to hide these little-bitty eeny-weeny itsy-bitsy Smith and Wessons." He glanced up at one of the heavy shelves along a wall. "And the dynamite's a gimme. Just smear a little dust on 'em and hide them up there with all the rest of the candles. Just like Harry and me once—"

He broke off, glancing guiltily at Melissa, and busied himself with something heavier at the bottom of the trunk. Then, heaving:

*WHUMP.*

"Jesus, Darryl!" chuckled Rita. "We're not going to be climbing a *mountain.*"

Darryl shook his head firmly. "You can't ever have too much rope. And this is nylon, too. We've got enough—ha! I remember that time Harry and me almost got caught, because—"

Again, his eyes avoided Melissa's, and he went back to his rummaging. "Well, never mind. Dammit, where's the smoke bombs?"

Melissa didn't know whether to laugh or scream. *Well, at least this time the rascal is on my side. I hope.*

Nelly came up to her.

"Oh, sorry, I think I interrupted you earlier. You were going to ask me something?"

Nelly nodded; then, transferred the nod toward the distant doorway where the prisoner had been taken.

"What's his name?"

Before Melissa could answer, Darryl did it for her. "Oliver Cromwell. The rotten bastard, may he burn in eternal hellfire." But he said it quietly, and kept his eyes away from Melissa while he continued his rummaging. Not, of course, without adding: "The butcher of Ireland. The tyrant—" The rest trailed off into a murmur.

Melissa tighten her lips. "On some other occasion, Darryl McCarthy, I will explain—*attempt*, I should say—the complexities of the matter. But, for the moment . . ."

Her eyes swept the room, taking in everyone.

"For the moment, here is what *matters*. In this day and age, *that man* is simply country gentry. A man in his mid-thirties; a relatively unknown member of Parliament. In his own district, however—in East Anglia, near Cambridge—he's rather famous."

She gave Darryl's back a sharp look. " 'The Lord of the Fens,' they call him. That's because, for a few years now, he's been the leader of the poor farmers in East Anglia trying to resist the encroachment upon their lands of their rich neighbors."

Darryl's shoulders twitched and his head popped up. He gave Melissa a puzzled look. "I didn't know that."

Melissa almost laughed. Whatever his Irish-American attitudes on other subjects, Darryl was also a fervent union man. Like all members of the United Mine Workers of America, he tended to divide the world into simple class categories: hard-working stiff, good; rich gouger, bad. And now he found himself caught in one of history's multitude of contradictions.

"There are a great *many* things you don't know, young man," snapped Melissa. "As I recall saying to you—quite often—in times past."

Tom finished the history lesson for the day. "I didn't know that, either. But I *do* know what he became later." He seemed to have little, if any, of Darryl's ambivalence. Even though, as the scion of a family which traced its own roots back to English nobility, the name of *Oliver Cromwell* could hardly have been passed on with favor.

" 'Old Ironsides' himself," said Tom, seeming to relish the words. "In the flesh, by God. The man who created the New Model Army which overthrew the English crown. Except for Gustav Adolf, and maybe that young Turenne fellow who's just getting started in France, the best general of the era. Lord Protector of England, eventually."

He grinned down at McCarthy. "Of course, that came a bit later. After he separated King Charles from his head. Which, from what I hear, was no great loss."

Darryl stared up at him. Outside of Irish history, what Darryl knew of any other could easily be inscribed on the head of a pin. "I didn't know that."

"Yup," said Tom cheerfully. The edge of a huge hand slammed into the palm of another. "*Chop.* Cut the sucker right off. Oliver Cromwell. One serious hard-ass, even by hillbilly standards."

# Chapter 8

The cell was dank, and, sunset now past, lit only by the taper in Strafford's hand. The light was just enough to make out the figure of the man squatting against one of the stone walls. The dim light glinted off the manacles on the man's wrists and ankles, but the earl could make out few details of the face beyond that distinctively strong nose.

Strafford resisted the impulse to order the chains and manacles removed from the prisoner. His sudden elevation to royal favor was too recent for Strafford to risk incurring the king's displeasure for such a small matter. And it would be hypocritical anyway, since Strafford was doing his best to convince King Charles to have the man executed outright.

A husky voice came out of the darkness. "You're looking prosperous, Thomas."

The tone in the voice was filled more with harsh, bitter humor than anything in the way of real anger. It had been five years since the earl and the prisoner had last seen each other, but the man's composure did not surprise him. Strafford—Thomas Wentworth, as he'd been then—had spent some time in the private company of his fellow young member of Parliament. The two men had taken something of a liking to each other. Perhaps that was because they came from similar backgrounds, gentry families rather than nobility, striving to gain a place in the sun. Or, perhaps, it was simply a matter of temperament.

"I only found out two days ago, Oliver, when I arrived in London." Strafford cleared his throat. "I *am* sorry about Elizabeth. The men had no orders to harm your wife."

"Soldiers. What did you expect?" Again, that harsh, bitter humor. "But you were always adept at washing your hands, as I remember."

Any trace of humor left, then. All that was left was raw and bitter pain. "They shot her like a mad dog, Thomas. And she never laid so much as a hand on one of them. Just denounced them for a pack of mongrels. Then shot my son Richard, when he cursed them for it. Killed both of them in front of my eyes, with me already chained and helpless."

Strafford winced. He began to utter harsh words of his own, vowing to see the culprits brought to justice. But the phrases died in his throat. The earl would have neither the time nor the opportunity to see to the punishment of undisciplined soldiers.

And Cromwell knew it. A harsh chuckle came from the corner where he squatted. "Good for you. Whatever else, at least you've not become a liar."

"I've never been a liar," grated Strafford.

"No, you've not. Other things, but not that. So tell me then, honest Tom—*why?*"

Cromwell thrust his face forward, further into the dim lighting thrown out by the taper. Strafford could now see the man's mouth as well as his nose. He'd forgotten the prominent wart on Cromwell's lower lip.

"*Why?*"

The sight of the wart froze Strafford for a moment. His thoughts veered aside, remembering a portrait of Cromwell he'd seen in a book which the king had shown him. That had been one of the history books which Richelieu's men had obtained from Grantville, and presented to the king of England as a gift.

There had been a portrait of Oliver Cromwell in it, made when he was much older than the man chained and manacled in the cell. A man in his fifties, not one in his mid-thirties. A portrait of the "Lord Protector of England," regicide and ruler of the island, not a prisoner in the Tower.

Much was different, but the wart had been in the portrait also. That would have been like Cromwell, Strafford knew. Most powerful men ordered their portraits idealized. This man would not have done so.

Strafford took a deep breath and let it out. Had God willed it so, he would have far rather been the minister for King Oliver than King Charles. But . . . things were as they were. Charles, for good or ill, was the legitimate monarch of England. And Oliver Cromwell, however much Strafford might admire and respect the man, was not. He was simply a rebel and a traitor in the making, and Strafford had seen enough of the lunacies of parliaments to know what havoc and ruin rebellion would bring in its train.

"Why?" demanded Cromwell again.

"You didn't know? They didn't tell you?"

Silence.

Strafford sighed. *No, they wouldn't have. Just had the soldiers murder his wife and one of his sons and drag him here in chains.*

"You've heard of this new place on the continent, in Germany? This town called Grantville, delivered here from the future."

"Wild rumors. The fens are full of superstition."

"No superstition," replied Strafford, shaking his head. "It is true enough, Oliver. Believe it true. They broke the Spanish at Eisenach, and the imperials at the Alte Veste. 'Tis said one of their women shot Wallenstein himself, across a distance of a mile, with one of their fiendish guns."

The prisoner's eyes widened. "So what does that have to do with *me?*"

The earl stared at him for a moment. "They brought other things than guns with them from the future, Oliver. Histories, for one. The cardinal of France—Richelieu, that is—saw to it that several such books were given to King Charles. In the future—"

He cleared his throat. "The future that *would* have been, I should say. There would be a revolution here in England. Starting not many years from now. By the end of it, you would rule the country—and have the king's head on a chopping block."

The face drew back, now shadowed again. Only the nose still showed in the candlelight. "You are something of a Puritan yourself, Thomas, as I recall. Predestination, is it?" A wintry chuckle came from the corner of the cell. "Leave it to King Charles to kill a regicide's wife and son, and leave the regicide alive. I advise you to have me executed. For I will do my best, I can assure you, to see that God's will is not thwarted."

Strafford tightened his jaws. *Never a liar.* "Indeed. I so advised His Majesty yesterday."

Silence again. Then Cromwell asked: "And you, Thomas? In that future world."

"I was executed as well. Before the king." He saw no reason to tell Cromwell of the shameful manner of the king's behavior. Even Charles had had the grace to look away, embarrassed, when Strafford came to that portion of the history in his reading.

Cromwell was not fooled. "Threw you to the wolves, did he? That would be just like the man. And you, Thomas—how did you manage the affair?"

The earl of Strafford straightened a bit. "I died well. Even my enemies said so."

"Oh, I am not surprised. Remember it, Thomas Wentworth." The face withdrew completely into the darkness. "Best you be off, now. The king will have more chores for you. And I have grieving to do."

Laud was waiting for him in Strafford's chambers in Whitehall. The bishop of London was pacing back and forth, obviously agitated.

"What's this nonsense His Majesty's been telling me?" he demanded, as soon as he caught sight of Strafford.

The earl restrained his temper. A part of him wanted nothing so much as to throttle the bishop, but . . . when all was said and done, Laud was a friend of his—and Strafford suspected he had few friends left, these days. Nor did he have any doubt that as soon as the current archbishop of Canterbury died—and Abbot was by all accounts on death's doorstep—Laud would succeed him. So had it happened in "the other world"; so it would happen here. King Charles approved of Laud.

Not throttling the man, however, did not mean being delicate with him. Strafford had been expecting this quarrel, and was ready for it.

"Don't be an imbecile, William. Even *you* must understand that the new situation requires us to set aside your plans for reforming the church. Plans which, I might add, were the single most prominent cause of the revolution which took place"—his hand groped in midair—"in that other history."

He matched the bishop's glare with one of his own. "Damn all zealots, anyway! You and your meddling with the Scots once you became archbishop—ruin, that's what it brought. *Would* have brought, but not now. And I so told the king, and told him firmly."

He stalked over to a chair and threw himself into it. "And His Majesty agrees, so there's an end to it. There will be no meddling with the Scots and their Presbyterian obsessions. Leave them *alone*, William. Leave those thick-headed half-barbarous clansmen to their own quarrels and feuds. Stir them up—as you did, in another time—and they'll become the hammer to the Puritan anvil."

*May as well get all of it over with,* he told himself firmly. He was expecting a complete rupture with Laud. That would sadden him, personally, but—so what? It had saddened him to see such a man as Oliver Cromwell rotting in a dungeon also. The needs of the state remained.

"And the same for Ireland. Leave the Old English there in peace with their papist idolatries, and Ireland will be a bastion for royalism. Stir them up, and we'll have another rebellion to contend with."

Laud was starting to splutter, but Strafford's strong voice overrode his protests.

"Damnation, William! Is it *impossible* for you to see your hand in front of your face? Did you *read* the books?"

"And why should we trust them?" shrilled Laud. "For all we know, those books were created by the Satanists themselves—or they're French forgeries." The bishop's eyes narrowed. "You met the witch yourself, earlier this day. Surely you could smell the stench of abomination."

Strafford burst out laughing. "The 'witch?' Which one, William? The one by the name of Melissa—who, I must tell you, is as fine looking an older woman as any duchess in Europe? Or the young one by the name of Rita? Who is as obviously a prince's young sister, uncertain of her role but determined to carry it out, as any infanta of Spain?"

He sat up straight, shaking his head. "There was no stench, William. Put that aside, man. You don't even believe it yourself—the whole notion smacks of village superstition. Is Satan so powerful he can create a new universe? Nonsense. Wherever these people came from, it was not the Pit. On that issue, if nothing else, I am inclined to agree with Richelieu. They are not *personally* evil. Indeed, it is that very lack of personal wickedness which drives home all the more strongly God's warning to us: let this madness unfold, and even the best will be encompassed in the ruin."

As always, theological questions were able to distract Laud as nothing else could. The bishop's scowl remained, but it became more one of thought than simple outrage. "You cannot trust a papist cardinal to reason properly, Thomas, never think it. Ours, here in England, is the only *true* catholic church. Still . . ."

He resumed his pacing. "I will admit that Richelieu's reasoning—in this instance—has substance to it. Still . . ."

He stopped his pacing, spun around, and extended a beseeching hand. "Can't you see what you're doing? For all intents and purposes, you are adopting the policies of—of—*them*." His lips pursed, as if he'd eaten a lemon. "Religious toleration. Let every fool in the land set himself up as if he were a bishop."

Strafford laughed again. " 'Them?' The colonial Satanists, you mean?"

Laud seemed to have calmed down enough for Strafford to have hopes of preventing a complete rupture. He arose, went over to his old friend, and put an arm around the smaller man's shoulder.

"I did not say we must *forever* abandon our plans for reform of the church, William. Nor, I can assure you, do I share the foolish belief of these 'Americans' that religious toleration is some kind of principle."

*Not,* he added sourly to himself, *that a heavy dose of it wouldn't be of benefit to the world's statesmen. Idiots!*

"But even the Son of God required three days to return from the dead, after all. We can't do everything at once, William. Without a king to serve as the anchor, an established church is impossible—you know that as well as I do. So will you allow me the freedom to do as I must to ensure the survival of the throne? Or—"

His tone hardened, as did the grip of the large hand on the bishop's shoulder. "Or will you enroll yourself in the ranks of my enemies? Choose, William. Choose *now*. His Majesty has seen fit to bestow the task upon me, and I will not shirk from the duty. Not for anything, including friendship or personal sentiment."

Laud's shoulder stiffened. Then, slumped.

"Oh, not that, Thomas. An 'enemy'? Never that."

"Good." Strafford used the hand on the shoulder to steer Laud into a nearby chair. "That settled, old friend, I *could* use your advice and guidance. The Lord knows I could use your energy and discipline."

After both men were settled, Strafford pushed the advantage. "Besides, look at all the bright spots. With the money the French are showering on us, I can afford to hire some real soldiers. For once, the king of England will be able to bare some real teeth."

"Not *French* soldiers," hissed Laud. "Let those swine onto the island . . ."

Strafford laughed. "Was I born yesterday? The cardinal's envoy made the offer, of course—indeed, he even raised the possibility of Spanish troops, if you can believe it."

Laud's face turned bright red. "*Spanish troops!*" he screeched.

Strafford, still chuckling, waved his hand. "Rest easy, William. There's this much good came out of the madness on the Continent. After fifteen years of warfare, there are thousands—tens of thousands—of experienced English mercenaries, any of whom would be delighted to return to England and serve under their own king's colors."

Laud was not quite done with his glowering. "A scandalous lot. Soldiers-for-hire. Sinners."

Wentworth shrugged. "Frankly, all the better. They'll hardly care about the fine sentiments of Parliament, now will they?"

He rose and went to a window, overlooking the great city. Then, completed his conversion of the bishop.

"They'll certainly not be given to tenderness dealing with the Trained Bands of London."

Mention of the militia of England's capital, that body of artisans and apprentices who had caused so much grief and disturbance over the years to England's monarchs and bishops, brought Laud to his own feet.

"Crush the rabble!"

Strafford clasped his hands behind his back, and straightened his shoulders. Then, gazing serenely down at the dark streets of London:

"Oh, I intend to. Be sure of it, William."

Some time later, over a much more convivial meal, Laud inquired as to the fate of the new prisoner in the Tower.

Strafford's face darkened a bit. "Tomorrow, I shall try again to convince the king to have Cromwell beheaded. Pym, too, once the soldiers bring him to the Tower. And Hampden, if we can catch him. But . . ."

"He's an indecisive man by nature, Thomas."

The king's new prime-minister-in-all-but-name shook his head glumly, thinking about the king he served. "Worse than that, really. Indecisive in big things, stubborn in small ones. I think he has vague notions—probably put there by his wife—of having some sort of grand spectacle of a trial at a later date. When he can haul all of his enemies out of the Tower and put them up for display."

"In front of *whom?*" demanded Laud. "Not Parliament, surely!"

Strafford shrugged. "That will be up to us, I suppose. Create some suitable body to replace Parliament, I mean. On that, it occurs to me—please take no offense!—there's something to be said for the French system—"

The argument which erupted thereafter was fierce enough, in its own way. But it was the ferocity of an argument between friends, enjoying the dispute, not that of a quarrel between enemies.

And so Thomas Wentworth, the earl of Strafford, was able to end the day on a better note than it began. And was able to carry with him to his bed the memory of a friendship retained, to blunt the sorrow of seeing a man he much admired fester in a dungeon, grieving a murdered wife and son.

Duty, of course, remained.

*First thing tomorrow—I'll do my best to convince Charles to remove his head. Oliver is dangerous. If he ever gets out . . .*

He drifted off to sleep, comforted by thoughts of the thick walls of the Tower. True, men had escaped from the Tower, in times past. But never men immured in the dungeons.

Strafford would have been less relaxed—considerably less—had he witnessed what a young man named Darryl McCarthy was doing at the very moment he fell asleep. For all his brilliance, the earl of Strafford—like Richelieu—had not fully grasped the nature of the new American technology. He could accept, readily enough, guns which fired across half a mile with uncanny accuracy. But still, he—like Richelieu—had the ingrained habits of men born and bred in the 17th century. An impressive machine or device, they could accept, yes. But, without even thinking about it, they assumed that such a machine or device would *look* impressive.

A cannon which can destroy a stone wall does, after all. A great, big, brute of a thing.

"That's it," said Darryl softly, turning his head and smiling up at Melissa. "You just give the word, ma'am, that fancy wall is so much rubble and we're outa here. Assuming you can scrounge us up some transportation, of course." He gave a skeptical glance out the window at the moat and the Thames beyond. He couldn't see the water, in the darkness of the night, but he could smell it. "Can't say I much want to swim in that stinking river, much less the moat, even if I could make it across in the first place."

Melissa winced. "I can't quite believe I might destroy . . . I mean, *the Tower of London*, for God's sake. It's a world historical monument."

"Not here, it isn't," said Tom Simpson. "Here, it's just another damn prison."

Melissa nodded. She eyed the little hole in the wall which Darryl was now disguising with mud smeared over bits of stone. Once the mud dried and a little dust was spread over it, there would be nothing to indicate an explosive charge except a thin wire leading off. The wire would be disguised behind furniture—a heavy couch that Darryl and Tom said would help direct the blast—and, in any event, wasn't something that a 17th-century guard would recognize anyway.

"Doesn't look like much, does it?" chuckled Tom.

"That's what I'm counting on." Melissa turned away firmly. If nothing else, over the past two years, she'd learned to discipline her own "finer sentiments." World historical monument or not, if the time came she *would* have that wall destroyed. Let the middle ages and its architecture take care of itself. She had living people to answer for.

"How's the radio coming?" she asked.

Gayle looked up from where she was squatting on the floor. "I've got the generator assembled, Friedrich's screwing the pedals down next to the loveseat, and Nelly's stringing the antenna. It's a good thing the guards can't see us or they'd think we're insane."

Melissa made a face. "I'm not sure they wouldn't be right."

# Chapter 9

On his way home, moved by a sudden impulse, Mike swung away from his normal route and walked past the complex of trailers where, the year before, Gretchen's somewhat peculiar extended family had lived. "Officially"—which really meant whatever the rather fearsome Gramma Richter said—it had been known as the "Higgins residence." Jeff had married Gretchen Richter, very shortly after the Ring of Fire, and her grandmother Veronica had insisted on the proper marital protocol. Proper, at least, by American standards if not her own. The fact that Gramma herself thought Jeff was much too young to be a husband had been neither here nor there.

Privately, Mike—like most people in Grantville—had thought of it otherwise. Depending on the circumstances, either as "the boys' place," since Jeff's friend Larry Wild owned one of the trailers and his other two best friends Eddie Cantrell and Jimmy Andersen lived there also; or "the Richter place," since Gretchen and Gramma Richter's huge collection of relatives and unofficially adopted orphans had moved in after the wedding. Since Jeff and Gretchen's wedding, the confusion had deepened. To native-born Americans, Gretchen was now "Gretchen Higgins" and that made it the "Higgins' place." But 17th-century Germans did not follow the custom of a woman assuming her husband's last name, so for them it was still "Richter."

Mike couldn't help but chuckle. There had been plenty of time he'd thought of the place simply as "Gretchen's Lair." If ever Mike had met a tigress in human form, it was that young woman.

He stopped for a moment, and stared at the trailer complex. Everything had changed since then, and Mike wasn't entirely sure how he felt about it. Granted, the changes had all been positive ones—the inevitable transformations brought into peoples' lives by marriages, childbirths, and other duties and obligations. Still, he found himself missing the rambunctious energy the place had had in the days immediately after the Ring of Fire. Perhaps more than any other place in Grantville, he'd always thought that trailer complex was the brightest symbol of a hopeful future.

But . . . things change.

Call them the Higginses or the Richters, they were all gone now. The trailers themselves were still full of people, but these were tenants. Several related German families, as Mike understood what Gramma Richter told him. He didn't know them personally.

Again, he chuckled. Gramma now managed the complex for Jeff and Larry, in their absence. Knowing Veronica, Mike was quite sure the new tenants paid the rent promptly, and in full. It would be unfair to label the woman a "scrooge," but . . . she had a proper and thoroughly Teutonic notion of the value of property.

He glanced at his watch and saw that he was coming home a bit earlier than usual. So, moved by another impulse, he walked across the street and turned down another. He was heading in the opposite direction from his own house, now, but he didn't have far to go.

Less than a minute later, he was standing in front of the very large two-story house owned by Grantville's mayor, Henry Dreeson. The house was on a corner, and the new gas lamp situated there had already been fired up.

Mike studied the lamp for a moment. He had mixed feelings about that also. On the one hand, he understood and agreed with the logic of moving away from Grantville's profligate use of electric lighting. The problem wasn't the power supply, as such, which would last indefinitely. The problem was much simpler, and somewhat maddening—as most of Mike's problems were. Sure, there was plenty of *power*. But power doesn't do you any good once you run out of lightbulbs—and those, like so many "small" things 21st-century Americans had taken for granted, were now in very short supply and very difficult to replace.

On the other hand . . . it also seemed stupid to have to fall back on 19^th^-century technology when they knew everything they really needed to know in order to *make* such things as lightbulbs and other types of lighting fixtures. But, that was the reality. It was the old, well-known if not always accepted, distinction between science and engineering. The simple fact that you understand the scientific principles involved doesn't necessarily mean that you have the technology or the economic resources to do anything about it.

So the decision had been made to start switching over to gas lighting; and Henry Dreeson, being the mayor of the town, had taken the lead in having the first new gas lamp installed in front of his own house.

Mike heard the door open and swung his eyes toward it. Henry Dreeson himself was emerging and coming down the stairs toward him.

"Hi, Mike!" The elderly man saw what Mike had been examining, and smiled. "Oh, stop fretting. The next thing you know, you'll be wallowing in the classic problem—toilet paper."

Mike grimaced. "Don't remind me."

Henry was still smiling, but there was a trace of apprehension in the thing. "Is there any news? I mean—"

Mike shook his head. "Nothing bad, Henry. So far as I know, Gretchen and the boys—and Becky and Rita and Melissa and everybody else—are fine. That's not why I came over. I just . . . I don't know. I guess I wanted to see you, and Ronnie, and the kids. It's nothing pressing, if you're busy."

But before he'd even finished, Dreeson had him by the elbow and was marching him up the stairs.

"No, no! Come in! Ronnie'll be glad to see you. Of course, you won't know it, from the way she'll fuss at you about letting those 'innocent babes' wander around loose all over war-torn Europe, but—"

The old man grinned. "Hey, what can I say? I'm crazy about the lady, but I'll be the first one to admit my new wife's something of a harridan."

"Oh hell, Henry, I wouldn't call her a *harridan*, exactly, just—"

But now Veronica Dreeson was standing in the doorway herself, hands planted firmly on her hips, and glaring down at the two men coming up the stairs.

"So! They are all dead, yes? I warned you!"

"Not *exactly* a harridan," muttered Mike. "Just . . . close."

Henry grinned up at his wife. "Now, sweetheart—everybody's fine. Mike just told me so."

Veronica Dreeson was not to be mollified so easily. She sniffed, imparting to the sound a lifetime's worth of bitter experience. *Men and their lies.*

"And how does *he* know what's happened to the children?" Somewhat grudgingly, she stepped aside and waved Mike into the house. As he passed by her, she continued to scold. "They are probably lying in a ditch somewhere. *Tot—alle!* All dead. Maybe the girls are still alive. Ravished, of course, and turned into camp women."

Mike winced. He was tempted to argue with the old woman, but . . .

The fact was that the horrors she was depicting were all too real. Veronica Dreeson, in the years since the Thirty Years War erupted, had seen all of them happen—and to her own family.

Fortunately, someone else came to the rescue. Gretchen's younger brother Hans was sitting on the couch in the living room, next to James Nichols' daughter Sharon. The young man sprang up with his usual energy and extended a hand of greeting.

"Welcome to our house, President of the nation!" He gave his grandmother a stern look of reproof. Which, needless to say, bounced like a pebble off a stone wall. Veronica didn't even bother to sniff.

Sharon's greeting was considerably less formal. "Hi, Mike."

Mike gave her a smile and a nod. And made a silent vow not to mention Sharon's presence here to her father. James Nichols, perhaps because of his own ghetto childhood and youth, was more inclined toward paternalistic intervention in his daughter's romantic affairs than most American men with a twenty-three-old daughter would dare to be. Mike didn't want to get an earful. *Another* earful.

The problem wasn't that James Nichols didn't approve of Hans personally—at least, leaving aside the young German's recklessness when driving the American motor vehicles Hans adored. The problem was simply that, first, Hans was three years younger than Sharon and James had his doubts whether the age and educational gap between the two young people wasn't simply insurmountable. So did Mike, for that matter, if not as much.

The other problem was even simpler. In James Nichols' eyes, the young man for whom his daughter had developed an affection suffered from a character trait which placed him in the legions of Satan.

*He's a young man, dammit! I remember what I was like at that age! And lemme tell you—only one thought on his mind—*

"And *don't* tell Daddy I've been here," she added. "I don't want to get another lecture."

As ever, Veronica was not bashful about her own opinion. "If Hans started courting you properly, your father would not object." Sniff. "*I* would, of course, because Hans is much too young to be courting anyone. But—"

She heaved a sigh which contained the grief of the ages, and plumped herself into her favorite armchair. "So be it. Americans are all mad—even my Henry—and I have given up. Do as you will."

Mike smiled down on her. He was quite fond of Veronica Dreeson. Sure, sure, she was a tough old biddy. So what? Mike approved of "tough old biddies"—in the new world created by the Ring of Fire even more than in the one they had left behind. One of the reasons he hadn't been quite as concerned as he would normally have been at the fact that Rebecca and Gretchen were leaving their infants for a few months was because Gramma Richter had immediately volunteered to make sure they were looked after properly. Which, indeed, she had. Directly, in the case of Gretchen and Jeff's two children, who were now living in the Dreeson household. Indirectly, in the case of Mike and Rebecca's daughter Sephie, for whom she had found a young German couple who could serve as Sephie's live-in nannies while Mike was absent during the day. Mike had trusted the old woman's judgment, and had not found reason to regret doing so.

*Old woman.* She wasn't, really. Veronica was still short of sixty—almost the same age as Melissa Mailey. If she'd been a 21st-century American, people would have thought of her as being in late middle age. But the rigors of her time and her life made her appear much older than Melissa; older, even, than her husband Henry, who was pushing seventy.

Still . . .

"You're looking good, Ronnie," he announced. And, in truth, she was. The withered crone who had appeared in Grantville two years earlier, as part of the family Jeff and his friends had rescued from mercenaries, was long gone. Now, Veronica just looked "weathered by experience." She'd gained her normal weight back, for one thing, and for another—

"It is my new teeth," announced Veronica with satisfaction, opening her mouth to display the marvelous dentures. The teeth clacked shut firmly. "Other than that—no difference. Just a feeble old woman."

Mike and Henry both started assuring her that there was no truth whatsoever to that self-assessment—which there certainly *wasn't* when it came to the "feeble" business—but were interrupted in mid-peroration. Gretchen's younger sister Annalise more or less barreled into the living room, holding Jeff and Gretchen's son Joseph.

"Are they all right?" she demanded breathlessly. Not waiting for an answer, plunged on to the *real* question which preoccupied a sixteen-year-old girl nursing her first serious crush: "Has anything happened to Heinrich?"

Then, glancing guiltily at her grandmother: "I mean, Major Schmidt."

Mike suppressed a grin. The glare Veronica was bestowing on her granddaughter Annalise was truly a wonder. Entire legions of vagabond hoydens might have crisped like bacon in that basilisk gaze.

Veronica had firm opinions on the subject of romance, and they were the opinions of most Germans of the era. Rather to Mike's surprise, he had discovered that people in northern Europe in the $17^{th}$ century did *not* typically marry at a young age. Quite the opposite, in fact. Most men didn't marry until they were in their late twenties, and women not until they were in their mid-twenties.

The reason was simple, and economic. Unlike a modern industrial society, where men and women could find jobs which could support a family at a young age, northern Europeans—unless they were of the nobility or rich—had to spend years accumulating the capital necessary to do so. In the case of young men, usually by learning a trade or establishing themselves as a farmer; in the case of young women, often, by working as a servant.

So, there was not much of an age gap, either, between groom and bride. Certainly not the eight-year gap which existed between Heinrich and Annalise—even assuming Heinrich was interested in the first place, which Mike rather doubted. He knew the young German officer was aware of Annalise's enthusiasm, but so far as Mike knew Heinrich did not return it. Judging, at least, from veiled comments the man had made to him before he left with Rebecca on their diplomatic mission. (With some relief, from what Mike could tell—Annalise was not exactly subtle about the whole thing.)

It wasn't that Heinrich didn't find Annalise attractive, of course— no healthy man his age *wouldn't* have found her attractive. At the age of sixteen, it was now evident that Annalise was going to be even better looking than her older sister, and her personality was considerably sunnier than Gretchen's. But Heinrich shared Veronica's traditional German view of such things: marriage was something which was a matter of practicality, not "romance" in the American sense of the term. And while the handsome young officer might have been willing to engage in a casual dalliance with an eager teenage girl—

Doing so with *Gretchen's* younger sister was not something even the boldest soldier would undertake lightly, even leaving the doughty grandmother out of the equation. Although it had never been proved, the story that Gretchen had once dealt with a mercenary lusting after Annalise by cutting his throat—and scrambling the thug's brains with a knife through the ear for good measure—was accepted throughout the area as Established Truth. Indeed, the story had become rolled into the ever-growing "Gretchen legend."

Hans, as it happened, was one of the exceptions to the rule that Germans viewed romance differently from Americans. Perhaps because of his own situation with Sharon, or simply his age, he had acculturated on this issue more than most. So, seeing that Veronica's glare at Annalise bid fair to become fixed in stone, the young man demonstratively moved to stand by his younger sister.

"He is a respectable officer, Gramma," he stated forcefully, "and in a *real* army. The *United States* Army. *Not* a typical mercenary! Furthermore—"

Mike decided to intervene, before what had started as an impromptu social visit turned into a family brawl he wanted no part of. So he took a few hasty steps forward and bent to examine the infant.

"And how's Joseph?" he asked the baby himself. Joseph stared up, with what seemed to be a slight look of alarm at the very large man looming over him. Belatedly, Mike remembered that the baby was now old enough to start feeling "stranger anxiety." And while Mike wasn't precisely a stranger, he wasn't often in the baby's presence because of the press of his own responsibilities.

But it was enough to break the moment's tension. Annalise smiled and kissed Joseph's fuzz-covered scalp. "He's fine. So's Willi. Although I think Willi's old enough to miss his parents. But this one—" She laughed softly. "At his age, I really don't think it matters much that they're gone for a while."

Silently, Mike hoped she was right. So far as he could tell, his own daughter Sephie wasn't showing any real ill effects from the total absence of her mother and the frequent absence of her father. But it was hard to know, for sure, and he often worried about it.

And now it was Gramma's turn to intervene, and she did so in a manner which Mike found very relieving. Acculturation worked both ways, after all, and on some subjects he'd come to the conclusion that $17^{th}$-century German stoicism was superior to $21^{st}$-century American . . .

*Psychobabble, let's call it that.*

"Of course the baby is fine!" snapped Veronica, sounding quite peeved. "Why would he not be? He is well fed, warm, properly taken care of." Her glare at her granddaughter softened a bit; or, at least, eased onto a different focus. "The biggest problem Joseph has is that Annalise spoils him constantly."

And now Wilhelm, Gretchen's older son, was toddling into the room, his hand being held by one of the young women who were part of the Richter family. Mike couldn't remember the girl's name—she was so shy he'd never heard her talk—although he recognized her. Like most of the members of the "Richter family," she wasn't actually related to Veronica and Gretchen. The girl had been one of the few survivors of a farming family ravaged by Tilly's mercenaries, and Gretchen had taken her under her wing shortly before those same mercenaries got chewed to shreds when they attacked Grantville.

"Willi's certainly looking good," said Mike. And, indeed, he was. His father, now dead—killed in that same battle outside Grantville—had been one of Tilly's mercenaries who had taken Gretchen for a concubine after her own town was overrun. By all accounts, the man had been a sheer brute. But other than sharing his father's blond hair and—it was already obvious—his large size, Wilhelm's temperament seemed to derive far more from his stepfather. Like Jeff, who was also large, Willi seemed to be studious and solemn by nature.

Of course, at his age, it was hard to assess Willi's personality all that well. But the boy was staring up at Mike with interest and curiosity, much as Mike had often seen Jeff pondering some new aspect of the universe which he'd suddenly discovered.

"Why'd you drop by, Mike?" asked Henry Dreeson. "Not that you aren't always welcome, of course."

Mike had wondered a bit himself, standing outside the door. And now, the answer coming to him with the force of a hurricane, felt himself fighting off tears. Tears not brought on by grief, or sorrow, but simply a sense of satisfaction so deep and profound that it seemed to shake his soul like a tree in the wind.

Slowly, his eyes scanned the room—now crowded, as more and more of the "family" came to see who the visitor was.

Henry Dreeson's kindly old face, smiling at him. A man Mike had known all his life, the mayor of what had once been nothing more than a small coal-mining town in West Virginia. The tough, almost hard, face of his new German wife, a refugee blown into their midst by the holocaust sweeping central Europe.

The face of her blond granddaughter, a face that was as sunny as it was beautiful despite the hardships she had been through herself as a young girl. Next to her, the wiry figure of her brother, almost— but not quite—comical in the way he exuded *youthful vigor!* To one side, still sitting and gazing warmly on her young German boyfriend, the dark face of James Nichols' daughter Sharon.

Children, everywhere. Healthy, all of them. A mixture of disparate people which had somehow, in some way, managed to begin the process of blending themselves into a new and genuine nation. And if there was a goodly share of hardness in that room—more, really, in the tough old biddy of a grandmother than the valiant youth—there was far more in the way of love, and caring, and acceptance, and a quiet resolve to make the best of things.

So the trailer complex was not gone, really. It had simply moved into somewhat more spacious and comfortable quarters.

"Oh, nothing, really," he murmured softly. "Just . . . touching base, let's call it."

He glanced at his watch. "And now I've really got to go. I like to tell myself, anyway, that my little girl Sephie expects me to be on time and gets upset if I'm not."

He departed, with Henry ushering him out the door and Gramma's tough old biddy wisdom following.

"Nonsense," sniffed Veronica. "Your daughter is a baby. The world begins with a tit and ends with a tit. So easy! Later, of course, she will give you plenty of grief."

He hurried home, down streets which were now dark. Perhaps because of that darkness, Mike allowed his steps to have more of a swagger than he usually did, now that he was a man well into his thirties and enjoyed the august title of President of the United States. The same cocky swagger with which years earlier, as a young professional boxer, he had entered the ring.

*Go ahead, Richelieu. Start something, if you're stupid enough. But you'd do better to listen to my wife.*

# Part II

*O sages standing*

# Chapter 10

"What does he say?" Jeff Higgins asked, glancing at the captain of the coastal lugger.

Rebecca made a little face. "Not much, and most of that—if I am not mistaken—are Flemish profanities."

She glanced herself at the man in question, who was leaning over the rail of their little ship and glaring toward the stern. Two or three miles behind them, another ship could be seen following them.

"Most of those curse words, I suspect, were addressed at me. He seems to be having second thoughts about conveying us to the Low Countries."

"As much as he's charging us?" snorted Jeff. In a gesture which was not quite idle, his large hand caressed the stock of the shotgun slung over his shoulder. That shotgun, along with the other firearms carried by Rebecca's escort, had been the subject of a number of sidelong examinations by the lugger's captain and his seamen. The weapons bore little resemblance to the arquebuses and wheel-lock pistols with which they were familiar. But Rebecca didn't wonder at their reaction to it. She could remember the first time she had seen an American firearm; and how, even for someone as inexperienced as she had been then, the things had practically shrieked: *deadly*.

"Do you expect any trouble?" Jeff jerked his head an inch or two in the direction of the captain. "From him, I mean, and his crew."

Rebecca considered the question. "Hard to say," she replied after a few seconds. "On the one hand, they will not be eager—not in the least—to get into a confrontation with you and your soldiers. On the other hand..."

She resumed her study of the distant ship in their wake, her face tightening. "On the other hand, it seems increasingly clear that we *are* being followed by a pirate vessel. Given the savage reputation of pirates in these waters, the captain and his crew will be wanting to make port anywhere they can before we are overtaken."

"Which would put us back on French soil," concluded Jeff, his head swiveling to starboard. The coast was not far distant. "Exactly where we don't want to be."

Heinrich came up to stand beside them. "There's going to be trouble," he murmured. "The crew—three of them, in the bow— are fiddling with a locker. I'm quite sure it contains weapons." He smiled grimly. "And from what I overheard, I do not think they intend to shoot fish."

Rebecca eyed him. "How good is your Flemish?"

"Good enough," answered Heinrich, shrugging slightly. "Most of it was curse words."

"That's it, then," said Jeff. He straightened and looked down at Rebecca. "It's your call, of course, but I'm assuming you don't want to return to Richelieu's 'hospitality.'"

Rebecca shook her head, but the gesture was half-uncertain. "No, but... *Can* we fend off pirates, if need be?"

The only answer was a grin from Heinrich, and a faint sound from Jeff's nostrils. It might have been a sniff of derision.

A moment later, Heinrich was moving toward the captain, with Rebecca and Gretchen following in his wake. Jeff turned his head toward Jimmy and the other soldiers of the escort. "Jimmy, stay here with the ammunition. One of you give him a hand if he needs it. The rest of you come with me. I need to explain the facts of life to those twits up front."

The soldiers had been half-expecting the command. In an instant, their shotguns were unlimbered and four of them were following Jeff toward the bow. Jeff's own shotgun was still slung over his shoulder. The seamen working at the locker had just managed to open it when the sound of shotgun shells being jacked into chambers came to them. They looked up into four barrels aimed at their heads, and froze. Unfamiliar or not, the weapons looked . . . *deadly.*

Jeff motioned at them to step back. Hastily they did so. He came forward, making sure not to interpose himself between the shot-guns and their targets. Then, after glancing into the locker, slammed the lid back down.

"You won't be needing those, fellas. Buncha junk, anyway." He grinned at the sailors cheerfully. "Just tend to your sails—whatever—and we'll handle the rest of it."

Clearly enough, the sailors didn't understand English. Jeff repeated the words in German. Then, when they didn't seem to understand that either, in his rusty high school Spanish.

Spanish, they did understand, even 21$^{st}$-century Mexican-style Spanish spoken poorly and with an American accent. Well enough, at least. Their eyes moved nervously back and forth between the American soldiers holding them at gunpoint and the pirate ship two miles behind.

After a few seconds, one of the sailors muttered something to the others. Jeff didn't understand what he said, but gist of it was clear: *devil and the deep blue sea, but the devil's right here.* Words to that effect, at any rate. A moment later, the sailors sidled away from the locker and went back to their duties.

Jeff cocked his head and hollered: "Everything's clear here!"

By the time Heinrich got the word, everything in the stern was "clear" also. Crystal clear, in fact. Heinrich's command of Flem-ish might have been imperfect, but it was good enough for the purpose. The face of the lugger's captain was a mottled red and white. Red, with fury at Heinrich's insults; white, because the tough young German officer had been extremely explicit in his expla-nation of the consequences of disobedience. Even broken Flem-ish is good enough to explain mangled fingers, wrists, arms, heads, practically every body part in existence.

Rebecca's own face was a bit pale. Heinrich was normally such a pleasant fellow that she tended to forget just how savage he could be when he thought it necessary. She had no more doubt than the lugger's captain that the threats had not been idle ones.

Neither did Gretchen. The young German woman hadn't even bothered to draw her pistol. She'd known Heinrich for years, after all.

"That's that, then," she said with satisfaction. "Now we just have to deal with the pirates." She started to express her own opinion on the proper way to manage that task, when the scowl on Heinrich's face cut the words short.

"Never mind," she said, smiling sweetly. "Far be it from me to meddle in such manly and soldierly matters."

Heinrich's scowl faded into a half-grin. Then, after exchanging a glance with Rebecca, the major shrugged.

"Let him have his fun, why not? Besides, he's probably right."

Heinrich nodded at Jimmy Andersen, who had been watching them eagerly. Jimmy already had the trunk containing the rifle grenades open. An instant later, he was pulling out the first of them and, with the help of another soldier, starting to position them on the deck.

Jeff and two of the soldiers at the bow came trotting back, leaving the other two to keep standing guard over the sailors. Jeff unlimbered his shotgun and began removing the rounds of buckshot so that they could be replaced with the special rounds for the grenades. Jimmy gave him a bit of a cold eye, but didn't try to argue the point. Jimmy loved the new rifle grenades. But Jeff was much more accurate with them than he was, and they didn't really have that many to spare.

As he took the special rounds from Jimmy and began reloading the shotgun, Jeff studied the ship pursuing them. That it *was* pursuing them was no longer subject to doubt, so much was obvious. The faster pirate vessel had been steadily overtaking them, and was now not much more than a mile astern. No honest ship would have approached that closely in these waters. The English Channel was still wide enough here to make a close approach unnecessary, especially since it was bound to be interpreted as a threatening gesture.

"Be a while yet," he pronounced calmly. Rebecca, watching him, was struck by the change in the young man in the two years since she had first met him. She could still see traces of "Jeff the nerd" in his youthful, pudgy features and thick eyeglasses. But the traces were faint, now. The large body had lost most of its adolescent softness, even more than the face. True, Jeff would probably be overweight all his life. But so is a boar, when you get down to it. And no one now, watching the young soldier calmly scrutinizing his approaching enemy, could have any doubt that the green eyes magnified by those spectacles were those of an experienced killer.

Rebecca didn't entirely like the change, but . . . She shrugged off the sentiment almost with irritation. Had the change not happened, after all, she would herself have been dead some time ago. And she couldn't deny that it amused her, a bit, to see the way Gretchen's hand idly stroked Jeff's broad back. Gretchen, of course, had never had any trouble accepting the transformation in her husband. Indeed, she was in good part responsible for it herself.

Jeff's superior officer came up to stand next to him at the stern. Gretchen, a bit reluctantly, moved aside. Her accommodation with military discipline, as always, was grudging.

"You're the expert," said Heinrich. "You want to handle it yourself, or with a volley?"

Jeff's heavy lips pursed. "Just myself, I think." Then, as if suddenly remembering that they *were* in a military situation: "Sir. We don't have that many of the grenades, when you get down to it. Besides, having to use manual arming pins like we do . . ."

He and Heinrich both winced. The idea of an armed grenade let slip from someone's hand, rolling around on a ship's deck, was the stuff of nightmares. Part of the reason Jeff was steadier and more accurate than anyone else with the weapons was simply because he was large and solidly built. Fired from a shotgun, the heavy grenades made for a vicious recoil. A lighter man, on the somewhat unsteady footing provided by a ship at sea, might well be knocked off his feet.

Jeff was back to studying the pirate vessel. "Do you know any more about ships than I do, sir?"

Heinrich smiled at the military formality. In the weeks since they'd left Grantville, Rebecca's escort had slid into a rather informal style of operation.

"I'm fairly certain that my aunt's old cow understands more about ships than you do, Sergeant." He swelled out his chest. "I, on the other hand—officer-grade material, even as a lad—could always stump the beast."

He fell silent for a few seconds, looking at the pirate ship. "I assume what you're wondering is if they'll have a bow chaser?"

Jeff nodded. Heinrich scratched his chest idly. "To be honest, I don't know. But, I wouldn't worry about it, either, not given how accurate naval gunnery usually is, anyway." He glanced at the sea around them. "The seas aren't that heavy, yeah, but if they really want to hit us they'll have to turn for a broadside."

"I don't think 'turn' is what you're supposed to call it. Sir."

Heinrich curled his lip. "Sailors and their damn jargon. And stop trying to pretend you're a—what's that American expression? 'Old salt,' isn't it, Jeff? Excuse me, *Sergeant*. You and me are foot soldiers."

He pointed a finger at the pirate ship. "So they'll have to *turn*, and if they do they'll lose too much ground. Water. Whatever you call it. Add to which, this pissant little tub carries exactly four swivels." He pointed at the small, one-pounder guns mounted on the bulwarks. "They're not going to be too worried about *those*, which means they'll keep following us until they can pull alongside and board us. Why waste time with guns when they can just swamp us with men? And if you can't hit them sooner than any gun they've got aboard can hit us—"

"I'll fire the first grenade at a hundred and fifty yards. Probably miss, but it'll give me a feel for it." He looked down between his feet at the deck; then, at the sea surging up and down with the vessel's motion. "Good thing I don't get seasick."

"Contact or timed fuse?" asked Jimmy eagerly. "Antipersonnel or incendiary?"

"Contact," growled Jeff. "You never know. I might *get* seasick, and if I do I'm damned if I wanna be fiddling around with a lit fuse. And let's save the incendiaries for close range if we need it. We've only got five of them."

"Contact it is. Hand me your shotgun."

The first grenade missed. One hundred and fifty yards, Jeff discovered, was too far to properly gauge the effect of the lugger's roll on the missile's trajectory. The grenade fell short. But its white waterspout showed he'd fired it in line, dead true.

"Just wait a bit," he said casually. Rebecca wasn't sure whether to laugh or cry.

At a hundred yards, he fired again. The second grenade landed in the pirate's rigging. The explosion didn't break the mast, but it did do a fine job of shredding the vessel's foresail yard. The big oblong of weather-stained canvas spilled down like an ungainly, dying bird, draping itself over the foredeck in a huge, untidy heap. Unfortunately—bad luck, here—neither the sail nor the highly inflammable rigging caught fire, but the ship's speed fell off noticeably.

Judging from the sudden bustle of activity on its deck, the grenade had shredded a lot of the pirate crew's self-confidence, too. They crew got the foretopsail set quickly enough, regaining most of their lost speed, but it took them almost five minutes to clear the foredeck of its enshrouding canvas. Soon thereafter, however, a cloud of smoke covered the pirate's bow. They *did* have a bow chaser, after all.

And it was just as inaccurate as Heinrich had guessed. The cannonball splashed into the water fifteen yards astern and as many yards to starboard.

Before the ball hit the water, Jeff had sent the third grenade on its way, and this one didn't waste any time on sails. It landed almost directly amidships, and from the sound of things, the pirates had been just a little careless with their own ammunition handling arrangements. The grenade obviously hadn't found the brig's magazine, but the initial explosion was followed by at least two more as ready charges for the broadside guns went up. The series of blasts threw up a thick cloud of dirty, gray-white smoke . . . and cut away the mainmast shrouds on the windward side. They may have damaged the mast itself, as well, or perhaps it was simply the loss of the shrouds' support. Neither Jeff nor Heinrich could tell, and the precise mechanics didn't really matter, anyway.

The brig's mainmast seemed to bend in the middle. Then the topmast and topgallant mast broke off and tumbled messily to leeward. The fore topgallant followed in a twanging forest of parting cordage, and the pirate ship staggered as its rigging was reduced to ruin. Judging from the faint sounds coming across the water, the grenade had also killed or injured several of the pirates themselves. And, within a few seconds, Jeff and Heinrich could see wisps of smoke. Apparently, the grenade had also started some fires aboard the enemy vessel.

"One more," commanded Heinrich.

The pirate had fallen off, turning broadside-on to the lugger. Not from intent, but simply from the effect of suddenly losing two-thirds of its masts. The fourth shot almost over-ranged completely, but struck the far rail on the pirate's deck. There probably wasn't much damage done, or casualties inflicted, but the screams coming from its crew seemed much louder.

"That should do it," said Heinrich. "I think they've probably had enough. They'll be scrambling around for a while, anyway, trying to put the fires out. Besides," he grinned nastily, "they can't possibly catch us with most of their spars turned into toothpicks. May as well save the ammunition."

✳        ✳        ✳

So it proved. Within a few more minutes, the lugger had increased the distance between the two vessels by several hundred yards. And, from what they could tell, the pirate's crew was now simply trying to jury-rig a new sail and depart the scene. Luckily for them, whatever fires had been started by the grenade hadn't spread to what was left of the rigging.

By mid-afternoon, the pirate had fallen out of sight altogether.

"Good enough," pronounced Heinrich. He gave the lugger's captain a friendly smile. "See? Nothing to worry about."

The captain's returning smile was not as sickly as it might have been. True, the man was probably still resentful of Heinrich's peremptory ways. On the other hand, he *had* been paid a rather munificent sum—and, clear enough, he wouldn't have much to worry about from pirates on *this* voyage. Moreover, Rebecca was quite certain that the man would turn another tidy profit by selling his account of this incident to one of Richelieu's agents. Or, possibly, the Spanish; or, most likely of all, the French and Spanish both.

The pirate vessel's captain, on the other hand, was purely livid. When his battered ship finally moored at the dock in the nearby small port from which it had sailed, he stormed ashore and into one of the town's many taverns.

The man he was expecting to see there was seated at a table in the rear of the grimy room. The pirate captain slid into a chair across from him, leaned heavy arms on the table, and hissed angrily:

"Servien, you *bastard*. You never said—"

The cardinal's *intendant* cut him off with a peremptory gesture. "I told you they were dangerous. You laughed, as I recall, and only wanted to talk about the women." Servien shrugged. "Give me a full report, at least. I'll pay for that."

After the pirate captain had finished, Servien pulled out a heavy purse. Then, spilled a few coins onto the table. The casualness of the gesture—the apparent lack of concern for the danger of any lurking footpads who might be watching—indicated more than anything else the cardinal's subtle power. Not even a pirate-harbor footpad was crazy enough to try to rob one of Richelieu's special agents.

Sourly, the pirate captain swept the coins off the table and into his own purse. "Won't even cover the rigging, much less the spars."

Servien gave him a cold, reptilian stare. "You failed. Be glad I gave you that much."

With no further words, Servien rose from the table and stalked out of the tavern. After he'd taken three steps onto the muddy street beyond, he was joined by two other men. Both of them were considerably larger than the *intendant* who walked between them, and obviously soldiers. Officers, in fact, from the casual arrogance of their stride and the fine workmanship of the swords they carried.

"You will recognize him?" asked Servien. "And his ship?"

One of the officers grunted. The other murmured sarcastically, "If you can call that thing a 'ship' to begin with."

Servien nodded. "By tomorrow morning, at the latest, I want the captain dead. He'll be drunk within two hours and you should manage it easily. You can keep the money he carries." The *intendant* glanced toward the harbor. "Then rejoin your vessel and tell Captain de Hautforte to maintain a watch on this harbor. The next time that ship leaves, see to it that it is destroyed. And all the crew executed."

"Pirates," grunted the first officer.

"Under sentence of death whenever captured," added the other.

Servien said nothing further, plodding on grimly through the mud. He hadn't really expected this ploy to work, truth to tell. The cardinal, he'd found, still tended to underestimate the damnable new American technology. The problem was that it wasn't necessarily *big*. That made it hard to gauge what havoc might be contained in a few innocuous-looking trunks and valises.

Even worse was the fact that the Americans didn't seem prone to making the standard mistakes of foreign conquistadores. Instead of sneering at the "natives" and ignoring their advice, they seemed to have a positive genius for winning them over. The Jewess who headed the diplomatic mission was shrewd, for all her youth. And Servien had caught enough glimpses of the German mercenary who headed her military escort to recognize the type. Men like that, steeled in years of the warfare which had swept the continent since 1618, were as ruthless as any of the cardinal's agents.

Servien sighed. The sound was as heavy as his mud-laden feet. Then, there was the damn German *woman*. Servien had no doubt at all that, upon his return to Paris, he would be spending a fair amount of his time trying to ferret out the treasonous little cells of students and artisans she would have left behind her.

"*Merde, alors!*" he suddenly exclaimed.

One of the officers grunted again. The other glanced at his boots and grimaced. "Yes, that too. It'll take my servant an hour to clean them properly."

# Chapter 11

"Clear!"

Joseph "Jesse" Wood looked to the left and right, crossed the fingers of his throttle hand, and turned the screwdriver. Stuck in the salvaged ignition switch, replacing a long-lost key, the screwdriver completed the connection and the VW engine turned over, caught, and roared to life. The propeller whirled in front of him.

He grinned involuntarily and looked to the left where Kathy stood, shading her eyes against the early sun. She saw his glance and waved. He gave her a smile and a gloved thumbs-up. Then he looked at Hans Richter, waiting at the wingtip, and gave him the signal for chocks out. Hans grinned, ducked under the wing, and returned into view, holding the wooden chocks. Jesse turned his attention back inside the cockpit.

Not that there was much to look at. The tach indicated idle RPMs, oil pressure was good, battery the same. The airspeed indicator, altimeter, and vertical velocity indicator motionless, while the bubble in the homemade turn and slip vibrated slightly. The whiskey compass shook when he tapped it. The four inches of string attached by a screw in front of the windscreen flapped wildly at him. He wound the small clock, noting the time.

Cockpit check done. A 747 it was not.

*You're wasting gas.* Carefully, he moved the stick to the stops— left, right, while watching the ailerons. Then forward and back, looking at the elevator through the little mirror he had fixed slightly above eye level on the windscreen, aligned with the small Plexiglas window installed on the centerline behind the main spar above his head. He moved the rudder pedals deliberately, stop to stop. *So far, so good.* Before take-off check complete.

He had no brakes, which worried him some, but the plane stayed motionless, vibrating only a bit. He tightened the homemade harness. Advancing the throttle in its slot with his left hand, he felt the plane move forward over the grass. Just as he had during the taxi tests, he advanced the throttle, letting the craft gather speed, working the rudders nervously until he could feel the rudder bite. He was already pointed into the slight wind.

Moving faster now, he suddenly realized he was mentally behind the action, unready for what came next, despite the countless hours spent running it through his mind. He hadn't flown for over two years. He stared uncomprehendingly at the instruments, fighting down a slight panic. He concentrated on the tach. Engine revs good. Just as before, the salvaged motorscooter tires bumped along smoothly enough and he realized he was nearing flying speed, though the instruments still seemed mostly mysteries. Sweat rolled down his face, despite the cool morning. He pushed the stick forward slightly, lifting the tail, and before he realized what was happening, the wheel noise ceased. Pulling the stick back past neutral, he was climbing. Airborne.

Feeling the familiar rush, he caught himself. "You're behind the airplane, damn it. Get your head out!"

The sound of his own voice calmed him. The engine was still howling at full revs. Chagrined, he reduced throttle and looked around as the wind roared past the paneless window. He was already high above the trees and still climbing. The controls worked fine, though the ailerons were a bit slow, a little mushy. He made a mental note to tighten the cables and looked at the altimeter, watching it move quickly past 500 feet. That looked about right. The VVI wasn't working properly, though, as it showed first no climb, then a dive, then an impossible 4000 feet per minute rate of climb. *Oh, wonderful,* he thought sarcastically. Watching the altimeter, he did a quick calculation. About 500 feet per minute.

"Not bad," he said, tapping the dial. He looked at the airspeed and knew he had another problem. It, too, was operating erratically, showing only 25 knots of airspeed, then 40. He glanced at the string, his poor man's attitude indicator and angle of attack gauge. It was streaming straight back toward him, the last inch or so twitching a bit above the cowling surface. He crosschecked the angle of attack with the reference marks he had drawn on the windscreen.

"It's okay, Jesse. Settle down," he told himself. "You're about four or five degrees nose high. You gotta be doing about sixty knots." He thought about the airspeed indicator. *Installation error, probably. The pitot tube must be cocked a little.*

He leveled the small high-wing monoplane at 2000 feet—*give or take*, he reminded himself—and noticed an increase in speed. The airspeed indicator gradually caught up and showed a steady 85 knots. The string was now straight and flat against the cowling. Throttling back further, he relaxed a bit and took stock of where he was. Looking down past the strut to his left, he saw nothing but the expected forest, since his takeoff had taken him away from Grantville toward the Thuringenwald. He banked slightly to the right, holding top rudder to stay on course, and looked past the right seat. More trees.

Fine, he needed privacy, anyway. Checking the compass and the clock, he was surprised to see he had been airborne only five minutes. Keeping his course, he flew on for several minutes, experimenting with the controls. Aside from the sloppy ailerons, the craft handled just fine. He began to enjoy the clear morning as he tried a few basic flight maneuvers.

"Damn, I'm good!" He grinned ironically as he finished off with a rather timid cloverleaf. The sun glinted off the angled, glossy skin of the fuselage and cowling as he leveled off.

Jesse squinted at the glare off the shiny cowling. *Shoulda painted it flat black or something. Well, you can't think of everything. I got most of it right, anyway.*

He took a few minutes to admire his own handiwork. There was very little vibration, a testament to the care with which the engine had been braced on its welded steel cradle. That assembly had been likewise well joined to the four angled, light steel tubes that served as the base of the fuselage, converging at the tail and to which the castering tailwheel, salvaged from a garbage Dumpster, had been affixed. More steel tubing overhead anchored the main spar, to which the wings were joined. Vertical pieces bracketed the cockpit space, further braced with half-inch plywood, secured with screws. The cockpit floor was a single cut sheet of three-quarter-inch plywood, perhaps more than needed, but solid and giving a firm base for the seats.

Jesse glanced behind him at the thin wooden strips that formed the remaining longerons for the fuselage, looking for gaps or vibrations where the semi-rigid skin had been secured. He could see none, though he'd thought he should have used more wood screws.

*Tight,* he thought. *Well, we'll see when it rains. Maybe I can liberate a tube of bathroom caulk or something.*

He ran his fingers over the rough interior side of the door, made of the same material as the fuselage and cowling sections.

*Best use of pink kitchen Formica anyone ever came up with,* he thought smugly. *Especially when you're short of lacquer.*

He had found a room almost half full of sheets of the stuff at his father's place, undoubtedly acquired at some ridiculously low price when it had gone out of style. Heavier than prepared cloth, the Formica, while too inflexible for the wings, served to stiffen the fuselage construction admirably. Jesse had always preferred a stout design and he suspected the smooth surface would cut down on drag.

With a glance at the cloth-covered wing, traditionally braced from the spar above to below the door, he turned his attention back to flying.

The last part of his flight profile was the most critical, especially with a balky airspeed indicator. Before attempting a landing, he wanted to know how the aircraft felt as it approached stall speed. He deliberately went into his instructor mode, talking himself through the procedure.

"Okay, Jesse," he told himself, "take it slow and easy. Straight and level at three thousand feet—no, better make it five thousand." He whistled as the aircraft climbed and leveled at the higher altitude. "Okay now, slowly pull off some throttle. Try to keep it level as it slows. Pull off some more. A little more."

Working off the altimeter, he followed his own instructions, hands more sure now, feeling the aircraft slow and raising the nose as it did so. The controls became less effective and it became harder to keep the nose up. His experience made him confident he could sense the stall approaching. He made a quick note of the power setting and angle of attack. The aircraft felt steady.

The string blew out at an increasing angle from the cowling and then fluttered wildly. As the aircraft slid past fifteen degrees nose high and slowed even further, it suddenly fell off in a stall, snapping over to the left, plunging toward the ground, departing controlled flight as it whirled into a tight, nose-down spiral. Despite his earlier confidence, he was completely surprised. Negative G forced his body up against the straps and his head struck the low cockpit ceiling, stunning him.

"Jesus! Shit!" he yelled, disoriented and scared, as he looked out the windscreen at the blurring trees. He churned the stick with no result. His heart raced. The instruments were crazy.

*No they're not, Jesse,* he thought. *You're in a spin.* He shook his head and checked again. The bubble in the turn and slip was in the far right of the curved tube and the altimeter was unwinding past 2600 feet.

"Okay, okay," he panted, as his training took over. His hands went through the recovery procedure learned thirty years earlier and a world away, his mind seeing the boldface words from the manual. CONTROLS NEUTRAL. STICK ABRUPTLY FULL AFT AND HOLD. He pulled the stick into his stomach. DETERMINE DIRECTION OF SPIN. *Left.* FULL RUDDER AGAINST THE SPIN UNTIL ROTATION STOPS. He stomped right rudder and the world slowed. STICK FULL FORWARD TO BREAK THE STALL. He slammed the stick forward and the nose pitched over even more. He felt the controls start to bite. RECOVER FROM THE ENSUING DIVE. The engine roared as he firewalled the throttle and eased back on the stick.

Flying again.

He wiped the sweat from his eyes as his breathing slowed back to normal. He noted the altitude. 1200 feet. The tree-covered hills were no more than 700 or 800 feet below, and ahead of him he could see Grantville looming up, with the unmistakable outline of the power plant beyond it.

*Yep. Five thousand feet was a good idea. You were a little rusty there, Slick.*

He needed to know what had gone wrong, why he had been surprised. It came to him almost immediately. "No stick shaker, you dummy," he told himself, referring to the artificial device installed in most aircraft to give the pilot a critical three or four knots warning of a stall. "A little something to remember."

Fifteen minutes later, he had completed three uneventful approaches to stall with no problem and was headed home. The sky was an achingly beautiful blue, with small cumulus clouds near his altitude. A flood of memories from a carefree time rushed at him as he slalomed between the white clouds, practicing coordinated turns with a grin plastered on his face. He took his own dare and punched right through a small puffy, reveling in the sudden dimness, the cool mist flowing through the window, and the blinding brightness as he burst out the other side. He had to stifle the urge to do a victory roll. *You're flying an experimental, Jesse.*

All too soon, he was approaching the field and it was time to concentrate again. He set up in a downwind at a thousand feet and throttled back as he checked his spacing before turning final. For the first time, he noticed people on the ground—a lot more than had been there when he took off—farmers working with horses in a small field, staring up at him, shading their eyes. A pickup truck was highballing it from town toward his place, raising dust on the gravel road, followed not too far behind by one of the town's buses. He recognized the pickup as the one set aside for the use of the President of the United States.

*Well, shit.*

Back in instructor mode. *Okay now, Jesse, nice and easy. Let's make this a good one. Low and drug in, with lots of power. A real bomber pattern. Mind your speed. No other traffic.* He grinned at the last thought.

He pulled off power and turned ninety degrees, descending, leveled the wings for a few seconds and turned to final, rolling out of the turn about one mile from the field at 400 feet, right over the Sterling house.

"Falcon 01 on final, gear down and welded," he made the old joke aloud, as he lined up on the intended touchdown point, coming in twenty feet over the small trees at the edge of the field. Lower, straight into the wind, the grass racing beneath the wheels. He glanced at the string, now slightly separated from the cowling surface. He tweaked the throttle back and felt for the ground with a small flair. Feeling the wheels touch, he let the machine settle, pulled the throttle to idle, and let her roll to a stop. Engine off. He'd waste no fuel taxiing.

Joseph Jesse Wood was down, back in the world of people and trouble, in the Year of our Lord 1633. And, judging from the way Mike Stearns brought his pickup skidding to a halt on the edge of the field, was about to catch his full share of that trouble.

※          ※          ※

Fortunately, Jesse's partner Hal Smith intercepted Mike before the obviously irate President had taken three steps from his pickup. By the time Jesse clambered out of the cockpit and started securing the plane, with Hans and Kathy's help, Hal seemed to have gotten Mike to simmer down a little.

Jesse gave silent thanks. The retired aeronautical engineer had a far more placid temperament than Jesse did himself. If he'd caught the first sharp edge of Mike's displeasure, instead of Hal, the thing probably would have escalated immediately.

Still, the inevitable could only be postponed for so long. "Finish it up for me, would you," Jesse whispered to Kathy. She gave him a quick sympathetic smile and he straightened up.

"—dammit, Hal, you both *swore* to me you wouldn't pull a stunt like this," Mike was half-bellowing. "I've got enough grief to deal with as it is, without people climbing all over me with *another* accusation that I'm presenting them with *another* high-handed and unilateral policy decision. Damnation—"

As Jesse walked slowly toward the arguing pair, he winced a bit. The accusation, applied to himself instead of Mike, wasn't too far from the truth. They *had* decided to launch this first, unauthorized flight, as a way of forcing the issue. Mike had supported them from the start, but there were plenty of people in the new government who hadn't been enthusiastic about the "harebrained" notion of restoring manned flight to the "new world"—not to mention a large pack of budding industrialists and entrepreneurs who'd resent the diversion of resources from their own pet projects.

Mike was glaring at him, now. "And you! What the hell's the idea of risking yourself—the only damn real pilot we've got except—"

Catching sight of Hans, who was practically grinning from ear to ear, Mike broke off. Then, sighed. Then, wiped his face with his hand.

"Oh, don't tell me," he groaned softly.

Jesse shrugged. "Sure, who else? But I couldn't very well let *him* take it up the first time. He's never flown before, Mike. Nobody around here has, except Lannie and the Kitt brothers and Bob Kelly and, uh, Bob's wife." As always, *that woman* was "Bob's wife." Jesse never used her actual name to refer to her. It wasn't that he had any particular prejudice against women flying, it was just that he completely, thoroughly and utterly detested the woman.

"And the Kitts and the Kellys are working on their own designs," added Hal, "so we could hardly ask *them*. And Lannie, well . . ."

"He's plastered half the time," concluded Mike glumly. His hand was still rubbing the lower half of his face, as his eyes remained on Hans Richter. "Not," he muttered, "that I don't wonder if a drunk wouldn't do better than *him*. Christ, the kid could wreck a toy wagon taking corners."

Jesse felt compelled to rise to his young German assistant's defense. "That's not fair, Mike. I won't really know whether he'll make a pilot until I get him in the air, of course. But the fact is Hans has got very good reflexes, and he keeps his cool pretty well when things get dicey—"

Jesse broke off. He was speaking from experience, to be sure, but he decided to skip over that particular episode. There was no reason to delve into the awkward fact that if Hans hadn't been driving like a maniac to begin with the pickup would never have fishtailed, even if the kid *had* pulled out of it with style and verve.

"I've driven with him too, y'know," Mike muttered between his fingers. He lowered his hand, and Jesse was relieved to see the hint of a smile on his face. "Okay, 'wreck' it, maybe not. Just put a zillion dents in it. And how many dents can an airplane stand, anyway?"

By now, the bus which had been following Mike had arrived, and started disgorging its passengers. With a sinking stomach, Jesse saw what seemed like half the government of the United States unloading—the executive branch, anyway. Not too many of whom seemed any too pleased, either.

Mike glanced over his shoulder. "We were in the middle of a cabinet meeting when you flew over the town. Nice timing."

Luckily, the first one up was Frank Jackson. Frank wore a lot of hats, one of which was "Mike's good buddy" and another was "Vice-President of the United States." Rather more to the immediate point, however, was a third one: "General." His precise title had still never been decided, but what it amounted to in practice was that Frank was the "Chairman of the Joint Chiefs of Staff"—on a "staff" which had exactly one member. Himself.

Best of all, Frank and Jesse liked each other, and Frank had been supportive from the beginning also—more even than Mike, in fact.

Frank's first words, however, caused Jesse's stomach to plummet.

"Congratulations!" he boomed. " 'Greetings' and all that. You're recalled to service, Jesse. Pick your own title, as long as it's not too fancy. But call it whatever—I'd recommend a simple 'general'—

you're now in charge of the U.S. Air Force." He grinned wickedly. "And the 'chiefs' are now actually joint."

Jesse started to protest, but one look at Mike's face squelched that idea. He was, after all, still a reserve officer in the U.S. Air Force, even if *that* 'United States' was gone somewhere, in some other universe. And he'd been half-expecting this development, anyway, if he could prove that manned flight was practical.

So, he decided to make the best of it. "From major to general overnight, huh? Hell of a promotion. Too much. It's silly, having a general in charge of a one-plane air 'force.' Colonel will do fine. Modest Joe Jesse, that's me."

He ran fingers through thinning hair. "You going to let me have a separate Air Force, then? Or are we going to have to go through that silly 'Army Air Corps' crap again?"

Frank's grin seemed permanently fixed. "Won't be a problem with me. But the Chief of Naval Operations might have a different opinion. Once he gets appointed."

It took a moment for the meaning of that to register on Jesse. Once it did, his stomach felt like it was trying to dig a well.

"Oh, Christ," he groaned. "Don't tell me . . ."

Mike was now grinning himself. "Two birds with one stone. As long as you've handed me this headache, I may as well make the best of it. Simpson's been hounding me for weeks. You know how he loves his titles. It'll give me, oh, maybe a week's worth of peace and quiet, before he starts bitching about something else."

Jesse couldn't help but chuckle. His own occasional encounters with John Simpson hadn't endeared the man to him. "Almost a shame we couldn't pretend we didn't have radio, isn't it? With couriers, it'd take Simpson forever to send complaints all the way from Magdeburg."

The word "Magdeburg" consoled Jesse, a little. At least he wouldn't have to deal with Simpson directly. Not for many months, at any rate. The dictates of simple geography meant that the "U.S. Navy" coming into existence was going to be based at Magdeburg on the Elbe.

But that was all grief for later. For the moment, he was suddenly deluged, as the rest of the cabinet—and what seemed like half the town, by now—surrounded him. What followed was a veritable Niagara of words. A lot of them questions, a lot of them gripes, but most of them . . . simply the sounds of acclaim.

Somewhere in the middle of it, he caught a glimpse of Mike's face. The President had eased himself back, away from the crowd clustered immediately around Jesse. He seemed to have a sly little smile on his face. It didn't take Jesse long to understand it.

Arguments over policy were one thing. Success was another. And no matter what they felt about the complicated economic issues which surrounded the question, there was not a single American in Grantville—and precious few Germans—who hadn't found the sight of that airplane flying over the capital of the new United States a lift to their spirits.

Yeah, sure, it was a home-built contraption, jury-rigged from top to bottom. Even World War I era pilots would have sneered at it. But in this world, it was the *only* airplane in existence.

*Eat* that, *Richelieu. You too, Emperor Ferdinand II and Maximilian of Bavaria. As for you, King Philip IV of Spain—*

Grantville, in the two years since the Ring of Fire, had developed no fewer than three newspapers—and had stringers from newspapers springing up in all the major cities of the United States. However inexperienced most of those reporters might be, by now they'd all learned to elbow their way through a crowd. So, soon enough, the questions started getting more pointed.

"—many more, do you think?"

Jesse pondered the question, glancing at Hal for assistance. His partner, smiling, held up one finger, then three.

"We figure we can build another about like this, then three more with a larger load capability. All of them will be two-seaters, although we'd maybe go with tandem seating in the bigger ones. That's 'cause—"

"—many bombs?"

He shook his head. "Folks, don't get carried away." He jerked at thumb toward the aircraft. "This one'll carry two people—figure three hundred and fifty pounds—plus maybe another hundred pounds in the way of a load, and with a thirty-two gallon tank weighing, say, another sixty-five pounds or so. We aren't talking B-52 here, we're talking early days. Even the bigger ones—"

"—machine guns?"

"Forget it! D'you have any idea how tricky—"

"—oughta be something the machine shops could—"

"—not to mention the weight of the ammunition. So forget it. Early days, I said."

"—fuel?"

He nodded. "That's one of the problems, of course. We're looking into the possibility of using a converted natural gas engine—"

He could see Hal wincing, and had a hard time not doing so himself. Flying a plane, especially under combat conditions, was dangerous enough under any circumstances. With a natural gas tank in the middle of it . . . just waiting for any stray round . . .

He *did* wince. But the reporters bombarding him with questions didn't seem to notice. Or maybe it was just that they didn't care. They tore at the fuel problem like sharks in a feeding frenzy.

"—*very* limited. What's the point of building the things if they're all grounded a month later because we're out of fuel?"

He tried to fumble his way through, mouthing vague generalities about the new Wietze oil field coming on-line near the town of Celle and the likely success of the methanol project. But, in truth, this was not something he was especially knowledgeable about. Jesse had never worried about the fuel shortage much, because he was firmly of the opinion that if you made something *necessary*, some smart fellow would figure out how to do it.

Fortunately, the reporters let it drop after a bit. Jesse could see that Mike's sly little smile was gone. No doubt they'd be pestering *him* on the subject before the sun was down.

Finally, he'd had enough. "One last question, that's it."

There was a moment's pause. Then: "What'd you name the aircraft?"

He stared at the reporter who'd asked the question. Dumbfounded, for a moment. *Name?* Jesse was the product of Purdue ROTC and the U.S. Air Force of the late 20$^{th}$ century, before he'd retired. A tanker pilot, fer Chrissake. Who the hell *named* a KC-135?

Another face, far back in the crowd, swam in front of him. A face he'd seen for the first time after the Ring of Fire, when the turbulence of a new society had brought a retired Air Force officer to a community dance—first one he'd ever attended in his life—where he'd met a woman whose own drifting life had brought her through a small West Virginia town for a few months. It wasn't a particularly beautiful face. Middle-aged, careworn under the dark blond hair. There was still more than a trace of a pretty young girl there, to be sure. But the truth was, he'd been more attracted by the lines that time and travails had added to it.

"The *Las Vegas Belle!*" he boomed loudly. And then, seeing Kathy's face light up, he felt his heart lifting.

❊          ❊          ❊

He liked the feeling. So, some time later, as they walked back toward the hangar—a converted barn, jury-rigged like everything else—he finally got up the nerve to ask the question he'd been mulling over for several weeks.

"Will you marry me?"

"Sure," responded Kathy immediately, her arm tightening around his waist. "Makes perfect sense. I've been working toward this my whole life. Small-town girl from the boondocks of northern California, Las Vegas showgirl, piano bar singer—God, they missed a bet there, those music industry dummies—cocktail waitress, greasy spoon waitress—the trajectory's obvious, isn't it? Where else would I wind up except as Mrs. Strategic Air Command?"

"You'll need an official driver!" piped up Hans from behind them. "Me, of course!"

Kathy turned pale.

# Chapter 12

Frank rode with Mike on the way back, since Mike had decided to adjourn the cabinet meeting until the next day. The excitement at the airfield had wound up using most of the afternoon, and Mike said he had an important appointment that evening he didn't want to postpone.

"You pissed at me?" asked Frank, as soon as the truck started driving off. Mike had a fairly ferocious frown on his face. "I guess I should have asked you before—"

"Nah, forget it," said Mike, shaking his head. "We'd talked about putting Jesse in charge, once before, if he ever got that contraption off the ground. It made sense to me then, makes sense now. That's not the problem. It's the damn oil."

Frank's eyebrows went up. "I thought things were going pretty well up there. The last report you gave from Quentin sounded good."

Mike's frown deepened, became almost a scowl. "Yeah, sure. Quentin's a hard-driving manager, about as capable as they get, and you know as well as I do that he'd get that oil field up and working faster than anyone. So I'm sure his report was accurate. He's *also* got about the worst case of tunnel vision I've ever met in my life. Or have you forgotten?"

Frank smiled. In the days before the Ring of Fire, he and Mike had been coal miners working *for* Quentin Underwood, who had then been the manager of the coal mine they'd worked at. No one had ever questioned Quentin's managerial competence, to be sure, but . . . damn near everything else about the man had tended to drive his employees nuts.

"So, naturally, Quentin hasn't given a bit of thought to how we're going to *haul* the oil, once he's got the refinery running. That's my problem, I guess, not his."

"That's Quentin Underwood, all right. He's probably assuming a pipeline will materialize out of nowhere. Made out of what, I wonder, and by who? A cast-iron industry that's just got up to cranking out potbellied stoves a few months ago?"

Mike shook his head. "Not to mention that Quentin doesn't seem to have the slightest understanding of what the term 'conflict of interest' means. According to Uriel, he's already gotten himself a partnership with the Germans who put up most of the money for the operation. So I'll have to bring the hammer down. Again."

Frank made a face. Quentin had gone out to Celle to oversee the establishment of an extraction and refining operation at the nearby Wietze oil fields in his capacity as the United States' secretary of the interior—*not* as a private entrepreneur. But, as had been true several times already, the man seemed unable to grasp that there was anything wrong with using his official position to further his own personal interests. As long as he didn't steal anything, of course. Quentin Underwood would have been more outraged than anyone at the suggestion that he was a *thief*.

*My books are good, dammit!*

*Yeah, fine, Quentin—but they're not supposed to BE your books in the first place.*

Mike continued grumbling. "How the hell did two good union men like you and me wind up in charge of a pack of robber barons anyway? I swear to God, Frank . . ."

He broke off, sighing.

Frank shrugged. "It's not that bad, really. Stuff like this is bound to happen, Mike, under the circumstances. Everything's busting wide open and everybody wants to grab a piece of it. Hell, half the guys in the UMWA have got businesses on the side now. No way to stop it—even if you wanted to anyway, which you don't. However messy it is, we need that economic growth badly.

"I grant you," he added, "it'll make for some nasty situations down the road. But don't forget that we *do* have a powerful trade union movement also. So . . ."

He scratched his head. "Becky probably knows more American labor history by now than I do, but I do know *this* much—when the old-style robber barons were cutting loose in the 19th century they had all the advantages of labor legislation—if you can even call it that!—that was nowhere near as good as we've got. Not to mention—"

Frank cleared his throat. "I hate to be crude about it, Mike, but let's not forget that this time around *we've* got the army instead of them. So there won't be any federal troops being sent in to stop any big strikes, like the bastards did at Blair Mountain or that railroad strike in, when was it? The 1870s, I think. *No goddam way.* And just let those fucking rich boys try to get tough using nothin' but hired goons. Hah!"

For a moment, the cab of the pickup was illuminated by the righteous scowls of two lifelong union men, glaring at the world around them as if *daring* any new would-be robber barons—

*Go ahead! Try it!*

Suddenly, the scowls dissolved into laughter.

"True, true," admitted Mike, shaking his head, still chuckling. "Lord, aren't we a pair of good old-style hillbillies! Just goes to show: you can take the man out of the shack, but you can't take the shack out of the man."

By now, they'd reached the town itself and Mike slowed down. By the summer of 1633, Grantville had become almost as densely populated as Manhattan and—except for buses and the occasional official vehicle—the streets were given over entirely to pedestrian traffic. Well . . .

Not quite. Now and then, a newcomer to the town not aware of the city's ordinances would try to take his horse onto the streets. And, beginning a month earlier, the first products of the recently formed Jennings, Reich and Kuhn company had started showing up on the streets. The new bicycles were crude things, compared to the few modern ones which had come through the Ring of Fire. But they worked, and they were priced in a range which a family with a decent income could afford.

"Damn!" exclaimed Frank, his eye caught by something moving along one of the side streets. "D'you see that?"

"What?" Mike's eyes had been on the road ahead, picking a way through the crowd.

"It was like—I dunno. A rickshaw, I guess you could call it, except it was being hauled by a guy on a bike. Two people sitting in the back. Reminded me of Saigon, for a moment."

Mike grunted. "Steve Jennings told me, a while back, that they were thinking of introducing a line of 'cabs.' "

"He's gotta be doing well, these days."

"I'd imagine," agreed Mike. His frown was back.

"What's the matter? Steve's a good guy, and after that tough run of luck he had some years back, I sure as hell don't begrudge it to him."

"Neither do I, Frank. But the problem is . . ." Mike was silent for a bit, as he slowly worked his way through the town's main intersection. Then: "The problem isn't Steve personally, and it's a long-term problem."

He waved his hand around, indicating the town itself. "Give it a few years, Frank, and everything'll change. It's bound to. The truth is, when the dust finally settles—at a guess—I'd say at least half the original Americans who came through the Ring of Fire will be richer than they ever were. *Way* richer. Sure as hell in relative terms to everybody else, even if they miss their fancy toilet paper. Any high school kid with half a brain can figure out a way to apply his knowledge to something that'll turn a profit. And if he can't, some eager German partner of his will."

He swiveled his head and gave Frank a considering look. "And then what? How solid is a commitment to democracy and equality going to remain—in *this* world—when most of the people who brought it with them are part of the upper crust? Huh?"

Frank pursed his lips. Then, somewhat uncomfortably: "Hell, Mike—*I* went from 'coal miner' to 'head of the army.' You did even better than that. But I can't say I think my—what would you call it?—'political moral fiber' has declined any."

Mike smiled. "Mine, either. But that's not really what I'm talking about, Frank. I don't expect anybody—well, not more than a handful anyway—to start making paeans of praise to aristocratic rule. It'll be a lot more subtle than that. But it'll start happening, soon enough, don't think it won't. People on top always see the world from their angle, don't ever think they don't. We're no exceptions to the rule. Nobody is, really, except a few individuals here and there. And, by themselves, a few individuals aren't enough to make a difference. Not unless they have a mass base."

They had reached Frank's house and Mike pulled up the truck. Quietly, he added: "We're in a race against time, Frank, is what it is. So far we've been able to run a long way with the initial edge we had. But it won't last—not any of it, including the politics and the ideals. Not unless we convert, if I can use the term, enough of the people in *this* world so that they can pick up the slack after most of the original Americans have slacked off. Or it'll all start coming apart."

Frank studied him for a moment. "You've been listening to Becky, haven't you?"

"Yes. And, God, do I miss her."

"Yeah, me too. Although that stuff sounds gloomier than she usually does."

Mike shrugged. "I'm not actually 'gloomy' about it, Frank. Neither's Becky, for that matter. I'm just trying to be realistic, so I don't get caught by surprise when the time comes. And, what's probably way more important, don't screw up ahead of time and fail to take steps that'll make it easier."

Frank's eyes narrowed a little. Mike grinned.

"No, dammit! I'm *not* thinking of coups d'état and all that other banana republic bullshit."

Frank didn't quite heave a sigh of relief. Not quite. "Well, that's good. We've been friends a long time and I'd really hate to see it hit the rocks. Which it would if . . . ah, hell. Yeah, there's no way I'd let my troops get used to break strikes, sure—my resignation's on the table the first time anybody asks. But that's not the same thing as, you know, military rule and all that."

Mike was still grinning. "I said I'd been listening to *Becky,* Frank. Not Otto von Bismarck."

"Who?"

The grin widened. "It's no wonder you flunked history."

"I got a D, dammit. I didn't flunk." Frank opened the door and started to get out. "I'll admit, I think Mr. Pierce only gave me the D 'cause he wanted to get me out of his class. Still, I didn't *flunk.* Says so right on the high school transcript."

Once out of the car, he closed the door and leaned through the open window. "So where you off to now? And what *is* this mysterious meeting you said you couldn't miss?"

Mike grin faded some, but didn't vanish entirely. "Oh, hard to explain. Let's just say I hope to take one of those little precautionary steps I was talking about."

Frank leaned away from the truck, shaking his head. "Glad I'm just a grunt. Even if nowadays I do wear a fancy—hey, now that

I think about it, we never did get around to designing a suitable uniform for—*harumph!*—the Army Chief of Staff. How much gold braid d'you think I ought to insist on? Two pounds? Three?"

Mike drove off.

"Geez," complained Frank, "you didn't hafta peel rubber . . . We ain't got much rubber left, y'know!" he yelled after the truck.

Smiling, Frank walked toward his house. His wife Diane was already opening the door.

"That boy worries too much," he announced.

Diane shook her head solemnly. "Not enough," she pronounced. Looking down on her, less than five feet tall, Frank was suddenly reminded that she came from a country named Vietnam.

"Maybe you're right," he allowed.

The meeting was held on "neutral ground," insofar as that term meant anything in Grantville. Whatever the future might bring, for the moment Grantville was still solidly in the hands of Mike Stearns and his supporters. But, in the year and a half since it had opened, the Thuringen Gardens had become such a famous landmark of the town that almost everyone would accept it as a suitable place for an informal meeting.

Even the man who had, once, been the duke of the region.

"You're looking good, Wilhelm," said Mike, shaking the hand held out to him.

Wilhelm of Saxe-Weimar smiled and, with the same hand, invited Mike to sit at the small table in the booth. "Does a booth suit you? I thought it would be quieter than trying to speak in the main room."

Mike grimaced. Trying to have an actual conversation in the main room of the Gardens on a Friday night—any night of the week, actually—would have taxed the lungs of an ox. "No, this is fine. In fact, let's draw the curtains."

He reached behind him and did so. When he turned back, Wilhelm was already seated. Next to him was a man who bore a close resemblance.

"I trust you will not object if my brother Albrecht stays. I would have asked Ernst to come also, but—as I believe you know—he is campaigning with General Banér against the Bavarians."

Mike shook his head. "Not at all. In fact, I should have asked you to bring him myself."

They made small talk until a waitress appeared with a pitcher of beer and three mugs. Then, after taking a sip and smacking his lips appreciatively, Wilhelm set down the mug and folded his hands on the table.

"So, Michael. Why did you ask me here?"

Mike studied him for a moment. The four Saxe-Weimar brothers—Wilhelm, Albrecht, Ernst and Bernhard—still constituted the official ruling aristocracy of the region. Wilhelm, the oldest and senior of the Saxe-Weimar dukes, was a slender man in his mid-thirties—just about Mike's own age. His brown eyes were those of an intellectual, though, not a cavalier. The more so as they peered at Mike through a pair of American-made spectacles. The fact that Wilhelm's command of English had become excellent and almost unaccented, in a relatively short time, was just one indication of the man's intelligence. Truth be told, Wilhelm's English was better than Mike's German—and Mike had concentrated on learning that language.

An intellectual's eyes, yes. But still, at the same time, those of a man accustomed to wielding authority and moving easily in the corridors of power. The eyes of a dean, perhaps, or a college president—and of a major and prestigious university, at that—not an absentminded associate professor still unsure of gaining tenure. Mike had never allowed himself to forget that the man sitting across from him was one of Gustav Adolf's most trusted German allies and advisers.

"I wanted to offer you a position on the Supreme Court," Mike said abruptly. "Not Chief Justice—I'm going to be renominating Chuck Riddle for that—but the next nomination I'll be sending to the Congress. I can't make any guarantees, of course, but I don't imagine there'll be much in the way of opposition."

Wilhelm studied him for a moment, his eyes indicating nothing beyond calm calculation. Then:

"You've decided to move quickly, I take it. You are not required by law to make permanent nominations until the 'emergency period' is over. Which is not for several more months."

Mike lifted his shoulders. The gesture was not so much a shrug as the movement of a man shedding a load.

"Why wait? Damn the formalities. The only legitimate purpose of the emergency period was to give the new government a bit of breathing space right after being formed. Which we don't need any longer. If you start getting into the habit of stretching things like this . . . it gets to be a habit."

There was a moment's silence as Wilhelm continued his calm scrutiny. "Good for you," he said quietly. "But will you extend that across the gamut? Or is it just to be with the judicial structure?" Wilhelm took another sip of his beer. "I feel obliged to give you fair warning. If I take a seat on the Supreme Court, I will rule favorably on any challenge to having Frank Jackson remain Vice-President while he continues to serve as head of the Army. One or the other, Michael, but not both."

Mike inclined his head, combining a nod with lifting his own tankard. "It's a moot point, Wilhelm—or will be soon, at any rate. Frank's going to resign as Vice-President, as soon as I announce that the government considers the emergency period at an end."

Wilhelm's eyes crinkled a little, as he watched Mike drain half his tankard in one swallow. "Ah, to be so vigorous! And, I think your assessment is correct—I would retain Frank in the Army also, in your position. I do not expect there will be any serious opposition."

Mike lowered the mug and cocked his head. "No? I'd think people might be cranky about it. Being as how it makes it pretty obvious where I think the real power lies."

For the first time, Albrecht spoke up. "Please! No ruler with any sense would relinquish control of the army. Especially not in order to retain that—you will pardon the discourtesy—silly and useless post of 'Vice-President' you insisted on placing into the Constitution."

Wilhelm shook his head. "Not so silly, Albrecht. True, the post itself is a—what do Americans call it?—yes, a 'fifth wheel.' But it does provide a clear and established line of succession." He gave his younger brother a sharp glance. "Something which, you may have noticed, we Germans have mismanaged approximately ten thousand times in the past century alone."

Albrecht took the reproof in good nature. "Always the scold! You see, Michael, what we poor brothers have had to put up with over the years?"

Mike bit off the comment which immediately came to him: *your brother Bernhard didn't!* That would be . . . impolitic. Since Bernhard's treacherous switch of allegiance from Gustav Adolf to the French, the other three Saxe-Weimar brothers never spoke of him in public. To their credit, Mike would admit. Wilhelm and Ernst, in particular, had thrown their considerable talents into the task of forging the CPE.

Wilhelm was back to studying Mike. Again, there was a moment's silence, while he sipped his beer.

"Let us approach the question from a different perspective," he said. "Rather than making me an offer, Michael, why don't you give me your *advice*. If you were in my position, would you accept the offer?"

"No," said Mike immediately. "It's a trap, really. A very well-baited one, sure. You'd have quite a bit of authority, even some real power. Lots of prestige, of course. And . . .

"You'd do well at it, too. I'm not making the offer lightly, Wilhelm. I think you *would* make a good Supreme Court justice. Even if"—here, a smile took off the sting—"I'm also sure I'd be cursing your name more often than not."

Albrecht stirred in his seat, as if he wanted to say something but somehow sensed he would be making a fool of himself. Gently, his older brother laid a hand on his arm.

"Just listen, Albrecht. I've told you before—do not assume these Americans are naïve simply because their manners seem unpolished. I've studied the histories; you haven't. Not enough, at any rate. They managed to govern a realm the size of a continent for over two centuries, without more than one civil war. Compare that to our own European history."

Albrecht frowned, still obviously not sure of the point. Wilhelm smiled. "Their concept of 'power' is more subtle than ours, brother. To us, power comes directly from the sword, or the law. So just listen, and learn a bit."

He nodded at Mike. "Please continue."

"The most you can do as a judge is interpret the law. To a point, of course, interpretation can shape it. Sure. But it can't create it in the first place, or change it beyond certain limits. For that, you need to be in Congress."

Albrecht couldn't restrain himself. "That silly House of Lords you allowed us has the teeth of a puppy! You only agreed to it because the emperor and his Swedish advisers insisted. I've tried—"

"*Listen*, I said." This time, Wilhelm's admonition had an edge to it. His younger brother shrank back a bit.

"Continue, Michael." Wilhelm was still smiling, but his eyes had narrowed. "I think we are about to get to the real point of this meeting."

Mike drained the rest of the tankard and placed it solidly back on the table. Almost, not quite, slamming it down.

"Take yourself seriously, for God's sake! Wilhelm, I've been watching you for over a year now. I'd call it 'spying' except I haven't actually violated any of your personal and civil rights. But I know you've been doing a lot more than just having private meetings with every big shot in Thuringia or Franconia who's got a beef with me."

"And you discovered . . . what, exactly?"

"For starters, the library records show you've checked out— usually several times over—every single book relevant to early American history and political theory there is. And British. One book in particular, which you kept renewing for three months."

Wilhelm leaned back. "Surely you are not accusing me—"

Mike waved his hand impatiently. "Oh, don't be stupid. What the hell use would Richelieu—much less that bastard Ferdinand— have for *those* books?"

"Ah." The duke's eyes suddenly widened.

"Bingo," said Mike. "And it's about time. Wilhelm, the day is going to come—I don't know when, but it will, sure as sunrise— when I'm going to need another *real* Edmund Burke. More precisely, when the country's going to need it. Not some useless nobleman who's read *Reflections on the Revolution in France* eighteen times over because he had nothing better to do."

Wilhelm's eyes were very wide, now. His brother was staring at him, puzzled. Clearly enough, Albrecht had not often seen his older brother so completely taken off guard.

"Stupid," growled Mike. "Damn stupid, petty, meaningless privileges. Do you really *care*, Wilhelm?"

Slowly, the duke began to shake his head.

"Good. Didn't think so, once someone pointed out the obvious to you."

"Why are you doing this?" asked Wilhelm, almost in a whisper.

Mike rubbed his large hand over his head, smiling a bit slyly. "Hey, will you look at that? Not even a trace of baldness yet. Won't last, of course. My daddy looked like a monk by the time he died. But I'd just as soon keep as much of it as I can, as long as I can."

He placed the hand on the table and spread the fingers, leaning his weight on the table. "Wilhelm, there is *going* to be an opposition. Hell, it's already there, and plenty of it. But, so far, it's had no clear pole around which to organize. Simpson's still discredited among the Germans because of that racist crap he pulled in the last election. The existing aristocracy, with a handful of exceptions—you're one; I think Wilhelm of Hesse-Kassel might be another—has the political vision of a pack of hyenas. No offense and all that, I'm just being my usual crude, uncouth self." He gave Albrecht a brief little nod, as if (conditionally) exempting him from the blanket charge also.

"Figure it out, Wilhelm. The meat of the opposition—the real driving force of it—is going to come from the rising new men. People like Troelke, among the Germans, and Quentin Underwood among the up-timers."

"Underwood's a member of your own party," countered Wilhelm. But the riposte was almost feeble.

Again, Mike waved his hand impatiently. "That won't last forever, and you know it as well as I do. The 'Fourth of July Party' is a coalition, and Quentin's never really been that comfortable in it. If he sees a viable alternative, he'll jump at it."

"Then why should he not create it himself?"

Mike said nothing; simply stared at the duke. After a moment, Wilhelm took a deep breath and looked away.

"Ah, yes. But . . . 'new men,' as you say. Without, really, any more in the way of a vision than the aristocracy."

"Yeah. More energy, sure. Vision? Probably even less. *Gimme.* That's about the sum and substance of whatever program they'd come up with."

Again, there was silence for a moment. Lost in confusion, Albrecht used the opportunity to refill everyone's tankards. Mike drained half of his immediately, never taking that cold, challenging stare from the duke's face. Wilhelm, for his part, sipped slowly and thoughtfully. Not avoiding Mike's eyes, exactly, but not quite meeting the gaze either.

Suddenly, the duke laughed. "God, has the world ever seen such a political adventurer!" He bestowed on Mike a look of approval, mixed with wonder and a bit of derision. The sort of look a man gives another who is walking a tightrope across a chasm, for no better reason than to prove to the world that he can do it. "I must inform you that Machiavelli would disapprove of you most strenuously." He finished another sip and gently placed the tankard on the table. "Or, perhaps, might hail you as his ultimate student."

Albrecht couldn't restrain himself any longer. "What are the two of you *talking* about?"

Wilhelm glanced at his younger brother, smiled serenely, and then brought his intellectual's eyes back to Mike. "This crude and uncouth fellow across the table from me is trying to engineer the best opposition he can think of. Because, *given* such an opposition, he might someday be able to relinquish power. For a time, at least. Instead of having to fight a civil war. You might say he wants a Jefferson to his Washington. A Burke, as well as a Pitt."

Albrecht was still frowning. "But there's no way . . . Sorry, Wilhelm, I think you're the smartest—certainly the most knowledgeable—political thinker I know." He gave Mike a glance which was almost angry. "But the way they created this new realm, there's simply no way you can lead anything. I *know*, Wilhelm. Unlike you, I've sat in most of the sessions of the House of Lords. I'm telling you—"

"You and Ernst will have to decide," said Wilhelm quietly. "Which of you succeeds me, I mean, after I abdicate."

"I'll drink to that!" boomed Mike, refilling the tankards and holding his up. "To the new contender for the post of Representative, District 14."

"The *Commons*?" choked Albrecht.

"Mind you," added Mike, slurping cheerfully at his mug, "it won't be a pushover. I'll see to it you have to run a vigorous campaign. If I didn't, people would wonder."

He and Wilhelm clinked mugs. For the first time, the duke drank deeply.

"Now that I'll be a plebeian," he explained, "I can afford to be uncouth."

# Chapter 13

"There's no way we can get in to talk to him, Melissa," said Tom. "Not a chance, according to Nelly. The cell they've got him in can only be reached through a single entrance, and there are always no fewer than three guards there. Yeoman Warders, at that, not run-of-the-mill goons."

Melissa nodded. One of the things which had become obvious in the weeks since they'd arrived in the Tower of London was that the Yeoman Warders of this era were not the friendly, relaxed, tour-guides-in-all-but-name of the "Beefeaters" she'd encountered as a tourist in the late 20th century. These were elite soldiers, well-disciplined and organized. And they considered themselves very much "the king's men," not mercenaries simply passing through. It might be possible to bribe one of them, but not a squad of three or more. Unless—

Tom cut that idea off immediately. "And before you ask, no, they rotate the personnel constantly. It's never the same three or four men, more than a couple of days in a row. Apparently that's an order direct from Strafford himself. He's not taking any chances with Cromwell."

"Because he knows, probably even better than we do," sighed Melissa, "that almost every escape from the Tower depended on subverting people on the inside." She planted her hands on knees, and levered herself upright. "Damn, I'm too old for this. At my age—planning a jailbreak!"

Tom gave her a sly look. "I'd have thought—years ago, you know—that you must have spent hours planning jailbreaks."

"Please," sniffed Melissa. "I was a *protester,* not a common criminal. Much less a foreign adventuress. I was *trying* to get arrested, to make a point. It would have undercut the whole gesture terribly to have then taken it on the lam." Another sniff. "I mean, that would have implied that I was *guilty* of something. Instead of being, as I was—and remain, dammit!—an advocate of civilized common sense."

Darryl McCarthy had been listening in on the conversation, lounging against a nearby wall. As always when the subject of Oliver Cromwell was being discussed, his young face was tight with disapproval. Now, disapproval was replaced by alarm. He thrust himself erect.

"Hey, Melissa—I mean . . . Come *on.* That 'civil disobedience' crap—uh, idea—I mean, it *ain't* gonna work in the here and now. No way!" A bit wildly, his eyes ranged toward the far door leading to the main complex of the Tower where, although they couldn't be seen, he knew Yeoman Warders were standing guard on the U.S. delegation. "Jeez, you try chaining yourself to a gate *here* . . . They ain't gonna bother with getting a blacksmith. They'll just whack your hands off at the wrist. Laugh while you bleed to death. Mop up the blood for sausage. I mean—"

"Oh—cease and desist!" Melissa tried to accompany the admonition with a fierce frown, but failed miserably. The word "desist" was followed immediately by a laugh.

Tom and Rita were laughing also. Gayle, sitting on a chair, was grinning.

"Whazza matter, Darryl?" she demanded. "I think you'd look cute marching into Whitehall and sitting at the lunch counter next to the king and queen. Make your mark on history."

Darryl glared at her. Unlike Melissa, Gayle Mason didn't intimidate him. Well, not much. Gayle was combative enough to intimidate any man who really tried to push her around, true. But she was in her mid-thirties, not nearing sixty—and, more to the point, she'd never been Darryl's schoolteacher. So his relationship with her was more that of a younger brother to an older sister.

"Very funny!" he snapped.

Melissa waved a hand weakly. "Enough, you two. Darryl, I'm not stupid. I am quite well aware that anyone trying to emulate Mahatma Gandhi or the Reverend Martin Luther King in this day and age is guaranteed a short life." She grimaced. "Short and painful life. Drawn and quartered first, the rack, God knows what else."

She moved over to the nearest window and studied the Thames. For a moment, she felt awash in a sadness as broad as the river. "Civilized common sense," she murmured softly to herself. "But what does that mean, in a 'civilization' which thinks thumbscrews are a source of justice?"

Rita came over to stand next to her. The young woman seemed to understand her mood. "It's not your fault, Melissa. I mean, *really* it's not."

The concern evident in Rita's tone caused Melissa to smile. And, with the smile, her vague sorrow faded away. There was much to console her in this callous new world, after all. In the old one, as "civilized" as it might have been, Melissa Mailey had been alone. Respected, yes; even admired, by many. But alone. She'd often thought, sometimes, that her identity began and ended with *schoolmarm; radical*—and, increasingly, behind her back if not to her face: *spinster; no children of her own, that's why she's such a pissant.*

Now . . . she had a lover, a husband in all but name. And, in all but name, a multitude of children.

She turned to face Rita. *Especially daughters.*

That thought cheered her immensely. She turned now to Gayle. "Do you think you've made contact with Julie and Alex yet?"

Gayle shrugged. "No way to be sure, of course, since they're only set up to receive. But I doubt it. Until they reach Scotland, Julie won't really be able to set up her radio very well. It's just an off-the-shelf Radio Shack DX-398. Hell of a nice radio, mind you, for what it is, but—" Her voice swelled with a touch of pride. "It's nothing like the special rig I brought, or that Becky has. Even then, I'm pretty sure we're going to have to relay to Scotland through Holland."

Melissa nodded. Gayle was one of Grantville's three "Amateur Extra class" hams, and had played a major role in designing the radio equipment all the diplomatic missions had taken with them. She was the specialist in their party on radio, just as Jimmy Andersen—a "General class" ham—was for Rebecca's. "And nothing from Becky either. To be honest, I'm getting a little worried about that."

"It's too complicated to figure out, Melissa, without knowing enough facts." Gayle glanced at the trunk where the radio was kept out of sight. "With this equipment, we'll be able to reach Jimmy once he gets set up in Holland, no sweat. But until he does . . ."

She shrugged. "It's that freakin' Maunder Minimum. From a ham's point of view, we came to Europe at just the wrong time. Officially, it doesn't start until 1645, but in the real world it's more complicated than that. The sunspot count is already plunging—"

"Dammit, Gayle," growled Darryl, "I *don't* want to hear it again. Bad enough I gotta listen to history lectures from Melissa every day, without you gettin' in on the act. Especially the history of sunspot cycles and how they screw up—or don't, I can't remember—radio transmission!" Sullenly: "I mean, *Jesus*. I had a hard enough time keeping the Roosevelts straight."

A little chuckle went through the room. Melissa's was more prolonged than anyone's. "You didn't, as a matter of fact." She gave Darryl a smile that was a lot friendlier than the scowl she'd given him at the time. "Oh, yes, I can still remember it. I'll say this, Darryl McCarthy—your answers to test questions were always, ah, unique."

Her voice slid into a slight singsong. " 'Teddy Roosevelt. Led the Rough Riders against the Japanese at Pearl Harbor.' "

Tom burst out laughing. "He didn't—really?" Darryl flushed.

Melissa nodded cheerfully. "Oh, yes. Then there was 'George III, first President of the United States.' "

Rita joined her husband's laughter. So did Gayle. Darryl's face was now bright pink.

Melissa decided to relent. Or, at least, slide off. "But I will say, in Darryl's defense, that Harry Lefferts could always top him. I remember one test question which Harry answered: 'Abraham Lincoln. Invented the Continental for George Washington.' And then there was the little essay he wrote explaining how the ancient Greeks conquered the Romans because they were mad at the Romans for giving them all lead poisoning when Mount St. Helens erupted."

Tom was laughing so hard now that he had to sit down before he collapsed. Gayle wasn't doing much better; neither was Rita.

Darryl, on the other hand, apparently decided he'd gone so far beyond "embarrassment" that he might as well join the fun. So he, too, started laughing.

"Hey, ease up. Me and Harry were too busy rebuilding cars to worry about history. I mean, whaddaya really need to know beyond the fact that President Ford invented the automobile?" He frowned.

"I mean, the *first* President Ford, of course. Not the guy who couldn't cut it in football."

Tom fell off the chair.

Outside, standing on the walkway which led from St. Thomas' Tower to the inner complex, the two Yeoman Warders on guard listened to the riotous laughter. Then, looked at each other.

"Jolly lot, I'll say that."

His comrade nodded, smiling. "Aye. I think the earl is worrying himself too much." He jerked his head a little, indicating the unseen occupants. "Hardly the sound of a new Gunpowder Plot in the making, eh?"

Silence followed, for a minute or so. Then, after glancing around, one Warder spoke in a lower tone. " 'Tis said they're rich."

"Said truly too. I've seen the silver meself."

Again, a period of silence. Longer, this time. Finally, the one who'd seen the silver spoke again in a half-whisper. "Can't see any harm in it, Andrew. Not to the king, not to us, not to anyone."

His comrade, nodding, slid into the status of *partner*. "Aye. Even split then, Will? Whichever of us is on duty?"

"Done. All the woman wants, she says—the one who showed me the silver—is to have packages brought and delivered."

Andrew frowned. "Small packages only." For a moment, leaning the partisan against a shoulder, his hands made quick motions indicating the acceptable size.

"Oh, to be sure. Anything else's too risky." Will shrugged. "But I think that's all they want anyway. Just luxuries, you know."

"No harm in that."

"—see the harm in His Majesty's, ah, foible," concluded Laud. The bishop of London shifted in his seat. "So leave it alone, Thomas, it's not worth irritating the king over any longer. If it pleases Charles to think of Oliver Cromwell rotting in his dungeon instead of a grave, what of it?"

Strafford started to argue the point; then, pressed his lips shut and satisfied himself with glaring down at London from the vantage point of his chambers in Whitehall Palace.

"I suppose," he growled, after a few seconds of silence. "With Pym now dead—God, what possessed the man, anyway? Fighting off soldiers, at his age! What was he, fifty?"

Laud's face seemed to tighten, as if he'd bitten into a lemon.

The earl had to restrain himself from laughing aloud. For the bishop, clearly enough, knowing the age of a rebellious parliamentarian was as foreign to his nature as knowing the inside of an Ottoman harem.

The momentary amusement lifted his annoyance at the king's stubbornness. "Well, perhaps you're right. True, Hampden slipped through our fingers. But he's certainly off the island by now, and I can't really see what harm he can do us from the Continent. Oliver was—would have been—the soldier amongst them."

"There's Monck."

Strafford's smile was not quite a sneer. "Ah, yes. The estimable George Monck. There's a piece of work."

"You've spoken to him, then?"

"Two days ago. I sat him down, showed him the relevant portions of the history, and brought him to the light of reason in less than half an hour. What's the point of it all, I asked him? He'd start as a Royalist, switch sides halfway through—and then, in the end, wind up putting the Prince of Wales on the throne after Cromwell's death. So why not eliminate all the mess and confusion?"

Laud looked slightly alarmed. "I trust you didn't—"

"Certainly not!" Strafford laughed. "I took the book from him before he could turn the page and see that Charles the Second would reward him with a dukedom. That man is quite ambitious enough, thank you!"

Strafford's face, for a moment, looked as lemon-sour as Laud's had done. *He* had no chance at a dukedom, he knew full well. When all was said and done, the king depended on Strafford . . . but didn't like him, and never would.

" 'Duke of Albemarle,' " muttered the earl. "Granted a large pension and made Master of the Horse, to boot. Died of old age, rich as Croesus, in his bed. While I went to the block. So did you, not long after."

Silence fell on the room. Both the earl and the bishop had studied the history books brought to England by Richelieu's agent, as well as the copies of pages from another brought back by the king's physician. William Harvey, that was, who had been given something of a hero's welcome when he visited the Americans at their capital in Grantville the year before. It seemed he would become famous also, in the future.

The bitterness in that silence was almost palpable. In *that* history, the king had handed the faithful earl over to his enemies. Then, after doing the same with the archbishop, Charles had pronounced that Laud's execution at the hands of Parliament would be viewed by God as the king's atonement for betraying Strafford.

The logic was . . . something only a man like Charles I could follow.

"We mustn't be filled with rancor," admonished the bishop. "It borders on sin."

Strafford shifted his shoulders, and clasped hands behind his back. "No . . . you're right, of course. But that doesn't require me to *like* the man." It was unclear, even to himself, which man he was talking about—the future duke of Albemarle, or the present king of England.

He decided that was a thought best left unpursued. Turning his head a bit, he added: "In any event, I saw no reason for George Monck, son of a minor landowner in Devonshire, to become a duke in *this* . . . what would you call it, William? History? World? Universe?"

Laud shrugged, somewhat uncomfortably. "That's for God alone to understand. Fully, at least. I simply think of it—" He made a little gesture with his hand, indicating everything around him. "This world, that is, as the *true* one. That other, as God's image to us of falseness."

Strafford barked a laugh. "Easy for you to say! *You* aren't the one who meets with Lady Mailey and tries to explain to her exactly how their stay in the Tower is a 'courtesy.' I assure you, William, if the lady herself is false, her brains certainly aren't."

"She's not a 'lady!' " snapped Laud. "Nothing but a commoner." The little bishop's face, habitually red to begin with, was flushed brighter than usual. Like many people born to common stock—Laud's father had been a draper—he tended to be even more sensitive than noblemen on the subject of "good breeding."

Strafford started to make a retort, but held it back. They were now verging on a subject which was one of the few—perhaps the only one—that Thomas Wentworth could not discuss with William Laud, for all that they were good friends. William, and Bishop Laud, were one and the same man. The earl of Strafford, and Thomas Wentworth, were . . . not quite.

His eyes moved toward the Tower, which, though he could not see it directly, he could imagine in his mind.

*No, William—she* is *a 'lady.' If that name means anything beyond a mere title. I've met her; you haven't. She has a poise, a self-confidence, a sureness of self, that would be the envy of any duchess.*

The image of Queen Henrietta Maria came to him, a giddy Frenchwoman married to an English king who, in his own way, was perhaps even giddier. *Or a queen, for that matter. And the young sister of her ruler who came with her bids fair to do the same, if I don't miss my guess.*

"How do they do it?" he murmured.

"What was that?"

Strafford shook his head. "Nothing, William. Just talking to myself."

The bishop chuckled. "Bad habit, that. Best you rein in it before it takes you over."

"Aye." Wentworth—no, the earl of Strafford—tightened his clasped hands. *"Aye.* Our course is clear."

He turned away from the window then. But not before, in a last flash of imagery, seeing the figure of Oliver Cromwell huddled in a cell. And remembering something else he'd read in those books. A line from a letter which would have once been written by that same prisoner, appealing to his opponents.

*I beseech you in the bowels of Christ—think it possible you may be mistaken.*

"You made a mistake!" squealed Nan, clapping her hands. "Look, everyone—Papa made a mistake! He played the wrong card!"

"Hush, child," scolded Wentworth's wife Elizabeth. "Your father's just preoccupied with affairs of state, that's why he made the mistake." The young woman—at nineteen, barely more than a girl—smiled shyly at her new forty-year-old husband. "He's a very important man, you know."

Strafford returned the smile. And genuinely, not simply as a matter of courtesy. He was pleased to see that his daughter Nan had accepted the reproof in good spirits. Indeed, she was smiling fondly at her stepmother. Elizabeth, as he had hoped, was proving to be very good with the children.

That thought brought sadness, for a moment. He was fond of his new wife, true enough. But he knew she would never be able to replace Arabella in his affections. His former wife had been . . . special.

A flash of memory came to him. That horrible time in York,

less than two years ago, when Arabella had died. They'd gone there to escape the plague which had been ravaging England in the summer of 1631. He could still remember—he thought he'd never be able to forget—the moment when it all happened.

*Arabella, pregnant with their fifth child, rising to greet him with a smile as he came in from the garden . . . brushing an insect off her clothing . . . the creature suddenly spreading its wings and flying in her face . . . she tripped, fell, he couldn't reach her in time . . .*

She'd died soon after. October 5, 1631, a date he would always hate with a passion.

"Why are you so sad all of sudden, Papa?" asked Nan. "It wasn't really a *bad* mistake. And it's just a game anyway."

He forced the melancholy into a corner of his mind, and bestowed a reassuring smile upon his family gathered about the table. More for Elizabeth's sake, really, than his daughter's. Nan had been too young to really remember her mother—not more than four, when she died. Will, not much older.

His young wife Elizabeth, on the other hand, was painfully aware that she was trying to take the place of a woman for whom Thomas Wentworth, now earl of Strafford, had felt a deep and passionate love. And however much Strafford sometimes found Arabella's memory overwhelming, he was determined not to inflict that grief upon Elizabeth. True, the girl had little of Arabella's gaiety and quick intelligence. Elizabeth was, in every respect, a typical daughter of a country squire, with little of his former wife's sophistication. But he'd married her so soon after Arabella's death for the sake of the children, and Elizabeth had proven as good a stepmother as he could have asked for. He owed her kindness and consideration, at the very least.

"It's as your mother said," he explained. "I'm just a bit distracted by . . . problems of government." The last three words were accompanied by a vague wave of the hand.

"You should just do the right thing," his five-year-old daughter stated firmly. Nan, as always, made her proclamations with the surety of an empress. "Then you won't be sad, no matter what else. That's what you always say to me."

Strafford chuckled. "Oh, and aren't you the little tyrant? I can remember how you used to drive the workmen half-mad, marching up and down the planks while they were adding the new wing to the house. 'Do this, do that.' Four years old, you were."

Nan looked as dignified as a girl still short of her sixth birthday could possibly manage. "They were slacking off, now and then," she proclaimed. "People should do the right thing."

Later that evening, after the children had been taken to bed, Elizabeth rose from the table. Somewhat timidly, she asked: "Are you retiring for the night, husband?"

Abruptly, Strafford shook his head. "No, dearest. I was planning to, but . . . there's a matter I must attend to. Now. It'll keep me awake through the night if I don't."

He rose, then hesitated. "Don't wait up for me. I won't be back for hours. It's a ways to the Tower."

"Have the cell cleaned thoroughly. Provide him with some decent bedding. Good rations. Exercise, once a day. Keep him chained and manacled whenever he's outside the cell, but remove the fetters while he's in it."

The Yeoman Warder in charge of the detail nodded. "Aye, sir."

Strafford gave him a stony look. "No slacking off, mind. I want him guarded more closely than ever."

"Aye, sir."

"Leave, then. I want a moment alone with the prisoner."

"Aye, sir." The Yeoman Warder bowed and backed out of the cell. Strafford turned toward the dark shape in the corner and lifted his taper. A strong nose came into the light.

"I did my best to convince His Majesty to have you beheaded," he said abruptly. "But he declines, for whatever reason. I'll press the matter no further."

There came a little rasping laugh. "Hunger and disease'll do the trick too, Thomas. Why not just wait and let winter take care of the chore?"

Strafford's lips tightened. "That's an injustice to me, Oliver."

A moment's silence. The nose faded from view, as if the half-seen head were lowered for a moment. Then: "True enough. My apologies."

"I'll kill a man, if I think it needed. But I'll kill him as a man, not a dog or a rat."

Strafford cleared his throat. "I did try to find out what happened to your children, Oliver. But they seem to have vanished."

The nose returned. "Oh, I'm not surprised. You know the fen people, Thomas. Someone will have taken them in, kept them hidden. No soldiers blundering about will find them."

Strafford nodded. He did not have Cromwell's intimate knowledge of the great fens of Norfolk, but he knew the realities of fen life well enough. When he'd been appointed Lord President of the North, at the end of the year 1628, the traditionally overbearing great landowners of northern England had been shocked by the newly powerful Thomas Wentworth's actions in frequently supporting the poor of the region against them. He'd forced the powerful and influential Dutchman Vermuyden, brought over from Holland to drain the fens of Hatfield Chase, to give up large shares of land he'd taken away—*and* pay for repairing the damage he'd done to poor villages in the area.

The same Vermuyden, disgruntled, had then moved his operations to Norfolk. Where, with a more powerful band of shareholders supporting him—and *without* having to face fenmen championed by Wentworth—he'd had a free rein. Only a handful of local squires, led by Oliver Cromwell, had tried to oppose him.

The former Lord President of the North and the former "Lord of the Fens" stared at each other, for a moment. Now, the one was the most powerful man in England except for the king himself, and the other was his prisoner. Two men who had once been something in the way of allies.

"What do you think of predestination?" Strafford suddenly asked. "Truly, I mean."

Cromwell's chuckle was a raspy thing. Strafford couldn't see him well, in the darkness of the cell, but he had no doubt the man was feeling the effects of several weeks' imprisonment in a dungeon. He made a silent decision to instruct the Yeoman Warders to have a physician look at him.

"I was never much of a theologian, Thomas. But it always seemed to me that the heart of the matter involved the nature of a man's soul, not his history—past, present, or future." Dryly: "No doubt your Arminian friend Bishop Laud would disagree."

Strafford was silent, for a moment. Then, almost in a whisper: "It's all gotten . . . very complicated. It's these Americans."

"They're real, then? I wasn't sure. It didn't seem like your methods, but . . . I thought the whole business might just be a ploy. Though why the king should want me imprisoned remained a mystery, I admit." The harsh, rasping chuckle filled the cell again. "It's not as if that grand-sounding 'Lord of the Fens' meant anything outside Norfolk."

Strafford's eyes widened. *"Real?"* he choked. His head swiveled. "For God's sake, Oliver, they're *here*. A delegation of the creatures, sitting right there in St. Thomas' Tower. Ambassadors. The sister of their ruler is the head of it."

Abruptly, he shook his head. *Why am I discussing this with a prisoner?*

The reality of the present returned, pushing aside all thoughts of other pasts and futures. "Pym's dead," he said coldly. "Hampden's gone into exile. Monck's given his allegiance to the crown. And you are here in the Tower. So there's an end to it."

Cromwell's form shifted, as if he'd made a shrug. "I don't know any of those men, Thomas, other than by sight. Not even that, with whoever 'Monck' is. I recall exchanging a pleasantry, once, with Hampden. At the last parliament, that was."

There seemed nothing to say. Strafford turned to leave. Cromwell's low voice stopped him.

"When the news came to the fens, Thomas, I was deeply grieved to hear it. About Arabella, I mean. I never met the lady, but I knew you were most attached to her. You spoke of her, you may recall. You were a man I much admired, once, and even if you weren't, I'd not wish that ill on any man."

The raw sound of a grieving widower lurked under the words. Strafford stared at the dark figure crouched in the cell.

*That, too, we have in common.*

But he said nothing in response. Simply turned, and left.

*And what of it? King's deputy. Prisoner in the Tower. So it is.*

# Chapter 14

The earl of Strafford was not the only man in the world who was contemplating the general subject of predestination. The next day, in the sky over central Germany, Jesse Wood was doing much the same thing.

"Try it again, Jim."

Jesse looked to the right at his sweating student. He hadn't yet reached the comfort level where he would allow this student to sit in the left seat with the only throttle. It mattered little here in the patch of sky north of town that he had designated the high training area, but the young man's touch was even more ham-fisted near the ground.

He set the power near maximum and unconsciously cleared left as Jim Horton began another sloppy cloverleaf. Jesse felt the rudder pedals moving erratically beneath his feet and knew the student was already having trouble making the first coordinated climbing turn in the simple maneuver. Jesse felt the aircraft skid and noted far too much variance in the bank angle.

"Crosscheck with your turn and slip, if you have to," he advised. "Keep steady back pressure on the stick and gradually let the bank angle increase to ninety degrees as you reach the top."

Instead, what he saw disappointed him again. As the aircraft neared the top of the climb, he felt the student relax back pressure and slide around the turn, never approaching the vertical. The instructor remained silent as the struggling student finished the other three sections of the cloverleaf and looked over for approval.

"That was better, wasn't it, sir?" Jim asked hopefully.

"A bit, Jim," Jesse admitted, though he noted to himself that the aircraft was pointed at least thirty degrees off where it should have emerged from the last turn, had lost a thousand feet, and was somehow twenty knots slower than what it should have been. He was certain that all of his other students had done better on only their second flights. In the case of his best students—Hans, Woody, and Alice—maybe even on their first.

"Let's take her home, huh?"

Jesse took refuge in his notes as he sat reviewing the just-finished training flight with Jim. They were seated in two of the torn and broken overstuffed chairs the students had scrounged from somewhere and placed in the grass below the control tower, giving a fine view of the entire airfield on the warm afternoon. He listened as Jim gave his version of how the second touch and go landing had gone wrong, forcing the instructor to take over to avoid a crash. Jesse knew exactly what error had been made. And what he had to do now.

*If only he weren't so damned eager and dedicated,* he thought. *Well, tell him, damn it. Don't leave him hanging. Be businesslike.*

Jesse closed the training folder and sat up in the chair, as the cadet's explanation trailed off.

"Jim, I am removing you from the flight portion of your training." He watched the news strike the young man like a blow and plowed on. "You have an excellent grasp of aeronautical theory and you have the best study habits of all our students. None of the others can match your knowledge of the aircraft systems and construction. However, in my professional opinion, you will not advance in flight training to a successful solo. I'm sorry."

Jesse saw tears well up in Jim's eyes as the cadet struggled to speak.

"How about one more chance, sir. Just one more flight. Please, sir?"

Jesse steeled himself. "No, son, I'm sorry. Maybe under different circumstances, a different time . . . But we don't have the luxury of time and I'm telling you straight—you don't have the aptitude."

Jim's eyes tightened. "Yes, sir. With your permission, then, I will remove my things from cadet quarters and move back into town tonight." He began to lever himself out of the chair.

Jesse touched the young man's arm. "Not so fast, Jim. Sit back down. I've got something else in mind."

Jaw set and trembling a little, Jim sank back into the chair.

"Jim, look around and tell me what you see."

"An airfield, sir."

Jesse snorted. "No, what you see is a poorly mowed pasture, getting ruts in it. You see a half-assed 'control tower' which doesn't control anything. You see one airplane, a windsock, a barn serving as a hangar and aircraft production line, and maybe the world's sorriest set of shacks passing themselves off as 'quarters' on a so-called 'air force base.' "

He scowled at the world in general. "In short, you see a disaster waiting to happen. At least, that's what I'm seeing."

He caught Jim's eye. "We need organization, Jim. More specifically, our ground operations need it. I can't do it alone, not while flying a full training schedule and helping with aircraft design. And I can't keep relying on Kathy without telling Mike he's got to draft her into the service, and—" He winced. "That's *not* going to make for marital harmony in my life, leave 'bliss' out of it altogether."

He glanced at the reconverted nearby barn. "Speaking of which— aircraft design, I mean—Hal Smith needs a full-time assistant himself. He's got his German helpers and the mechanics from town, when they have the time, and he's got me. But that's not enough. He's falling behind on just about everything."

Jesse watched a look of curiosity and speculation come into Jim's eyes.

"What's that got to do with me, sir? I just washed out."

"It's got everything to do with you, Jim. Back in the other U.S., the Air Force had over eighty thousand officers. How many of them do you think were pilots? I'll tell you—less than twenty-five thousand. And more than half of them were always in nonflying jobs, because many support functions needed someone with flying experience. Running an air force takes more than some idiots whose only desire is to 'kick the tire and light the fire.' It takes dedicated support. I want you to organize that support. To be more precise, I'm hoping you'll *lead* that work."

Jim was listening intently now, so Jesse plunged on.

"Jim, this here 'Air Farce' needs a ground operations officer. We don't need an aide-de-camp, or a public affairs officer, or an adjutant." *Not yet, anyway, but the paperwork is starting to grow, damn it.* "What we *do* need is someone who can take those day workers out there by the fence and turn them into airmen. Someone to keep the field mowed and smooth, to care for the aircraft, and to change that friggin' ramshackle fuel storage and refueling area back there into something that won't explode if someone makes a mistake. We need someone to organize a weather service and eventually teach air traffic control. And finally, we'll need someone who can go out on his own and create the whole thing all over again somewhere else."

Jesse paused. "You're about twenty-four, aren't you? Got some college before the Ring of Fire? ROTC?"

"I'll be twenty-four next month. Yes, sir. Two years at WVU." Jim sat up straighter now.

Jesse nodded. "Thought so. You're a few years older than the other cadets. I know you're more mature and smarter than hell. I think you can handle a man's job. Wanna take a swing at it?"

Jim jumped to his feet and came to attention. "Yes, sir!"

Jesse painfully pulled his sore back out of his chair.

"Okay, then. As of now, you are the ground operations officer for the First Air Squadron. Also base commander. And to make those cadets pay attention to you, you are now a captain. Congratulations, Captain Horton. You will immediately remove your things from the cadet area and move into the spare room in the house with Kathy and me. For the time being, anyway. We'll talk again later."

"Yes, sir!" Jim smiled and snapped a salute.

Predestination was on Rebecca's mind also, that day. In her case, spoken with a curse.

"They will not listen to me," snapped Rebecca, the moment she came through the front door of the house they'd rented in The Hague. "There is no point in trying any longer. Is the radio working?"

She stormed across the room, heading for the staircase leading to the upper floor. Behind her, Jeff gingerly closed the door, as if he were afraid the sound itself would send Rebecca's temper soaring higher still. He and Gretchen exchanged a glance. His wife shrugged and rose from the couch she'd been sitting on.

Gretchen had never entertained any great hopes that Holland's complacent oligarchs would listen to warnings brought to them by a young woman, the wife of the "President of the United States" or not—especially one who was a Jewess to boot, and whose father had even managed to fall afoul of Amsterdam's Jewish community. Three days after they'd arrived in The Hague, Holland's capital city, the normally even-tempered Rebecca was like a cat spitting fury. The treatment she'd received from Holland's powers-that-be had ranged from bureaucratic indifference to paternalistic condescension to—often enough—barely veiled outright hostility.

Gretchen, on the other hand, had the complacence of someone who could at least take comfort in the fact that the bad news was something she had firmly predicted. *Fat burghers. Pigs in a trough— and you're trying to warn them the slop is about to run out. They don't want to hear it, simple as that.*

As Gretchen headed for the stairs, she could hear Rebecca's voice coming from the landing above.

"Stupid!" That was almost a shout. Gretchen tried to remember if she'd *ever* heard Rebecca shouting.

No, she couldn't. Not once.

"*Stupid!*" That *was* a shout. The words which followed declined some in sheer volume, as Rebecca continued stamping up the stairs, but the tone remained furious.

" 'The French have always been our allies,' " she added in a singsong. " 'It is in their own interests to oppose the Spanish. Why would they change that long-standing policy?' "

When Gretchen reached the landing on the third floor, she saw that Rebecca was talking with Heinrich. More precisely, was using Heinrich as a sounding board for her snarls.

Rebecca, hearing Gretchen's footsteps, glanced back. "It is just as Gretchen said it would be. Fat stupid burghers! Pigs in a trough. Except not even pigs are that stupid."

"Quite intelligent animals, actually," said Heinrich mildly. "But it's true that a pig in a trough usually can't think of anything beyond his slops."

Rebecca was starting to simmer down. From the experience of the past few days, Gretchen knew that the young Sephardic woman would be her normal calm self within a few minutes. Rebecca could not hold a grudge for very long. Unlike Gretchen herself, who could hold one for eternity.

Heinrich's next words helped. "As it happens, Jimmy finally got the radio working tonight. Not more than an hour ago, in fact."

He smiled sweetly. "There's a message to you from your husband. He and the baby are fine. He sends you—"

But Rebecca was not listening. She was already through the door leading to the radio room. Heinrich transferred the smile to Gretchen.

"So impatient. It's this 'true love' nonsense the Americans talk about."

Gretchen returned his smile with one that was even sweeter. "Be careful, Heinrich. Annalise reads at least two American romance novels a week. One a day, I bet, now that summer's here and she's out of school. I think she's already gone through half the stock in the libraries."

*That* wiped the smile from his face. Gretchen couldn't resist the impulse to rub it in. She slid from the "Germanized English" which had become the lingua franca of the United States into the colloquial Oberpfalz-accented German which was the tongue she and Heinrich had both grown up with. "And there won't be any letup once she does, either. Just before we left, she paid the two dollars to join the romance readers' club."

Heinrich rolled his eyes. "'Letup,'" he muttered. "Even our good stout Oberpfalz German is getting corrupted by these newfangled terms and notions. Whatever happened to the idea that reading begins and ends with the Bible? Not even the damn Protestants tried to claim you needed more than that. Now—romance readers' clubs!'"

Gretchen grinned at him. "You should see what my husband belongs to. Something called a 'science fiction readers' club.'"

She and Heinrich had been born and raised in nearby towns in that part of the Palatinate known as the Oberpfalz. Although both of them were usually considered "Catholics" by most Americans in Grantville, the reality was far more complex. In the year 1555, in the so-called "Peace of Augsburg," the German princes had established the principle known as *cuius regio, eius religio,* according to which the religion of a territory was determined by the faith of the prince who ruled it. In some areas of Germany— the Palatinate being one of the most flagrant examples—what followed were decades of constant changes in official religious affiliation. In their short lives, Gretchen and Heinrich had gone from Lutheran to Calvinist to Catholic—and Gretchen's grandmother Veronica had gone through three more such switches before they'd even been born.

By the time they'd actually met, he as a mercenary and she as another mercenary's camp woman in Tilly's army, neither of them had much left in the way of practicing faith. In their day and age, before the Americans arrived and started turning everything upside down, "agnosticism" was a meaningless word. But now, it was an accurate enough description of both of them—Gretchen openly, Heinrich less so.

Still, both of them tended to retain a number of German attitudes on many questions. Neither of them, for instance, had any use for the silly namby-pamby American notions about the "evil of corporal punishment applied to children." One exception, however, was the subject of "romantic love." On *that* question, Gretchen had been thoroughly converted. Not by books or theory, but by the simple fact of her young American husband's own love for her. Beginning with their wedding night, Jeff's uncomplicated passion had washed her level-headed German practicality aside.

Not so Heinrich. He regarded Gretchen's younger sister's infatuation with him exactly the way Annalise's grandmother did: silliness; unpractical; *Heinrich* was still too young to be married, much less a sixteen-year-old girl with no property.

Gretchen patted him on the cheek and passed by him into the radio room. "Poor Heinrich," she murmured. "Like a piglet being led to slaughter."

Inside the room, she found Rebecca sitting on a chair, holding a piece of paper in her hands and reading it by the light of an oil lamp. Seeing the slump in her shoulders, Gretchen was alarmed for an instant. Then, as Rebecca raised a smiling face toward her, she realized that the slump had been simply one of relief.

"All is well," Rebecca announced. "Although I *so* miss them. Bad enough to be absent from Michael. Not being able to see my little daughter every day is even worse."

Gretchen came over to her and laid a reassuring hand on Rebecca's shoulder. "Sephie will be fine. I raised little Willi in an army camp, and he did well enough. Children are much tougher than you think, as long as they don't become ill."

Rebecca stared up at her. Gretchen knew that Rebecca found her own calm attitude about leaving her and Jeff's children behind somewhat puzzling. But it was probably impossible to explain. Though she was a 17th-century woman herself, Rebecca had been born and raised in a rather sheltered environment. Gretchen's had been also, in truth, until she was sixteen. Then . . . Tilly's soldiers arrived in their town, plundered their house, murdered their father, subjected her to gang rape—Annalise, thank God, had still been too young for that—and took what was left of the family to become camp followers. In the two years that followed, Gretchen had given birth to a son of her own and become the unofficial mother of a number of others. The experience, when it came to the subject of child-rearing, had left her with a very "stripped down" attitude on the subject. *Feed them; care for them; above all, make sure they don't get sick. They'll survive anything else, well enough.*

Suddenly, Rebecca's face looked a bit guilty and she glanced back at the paper in her hands. "Oh, I forgot. Michael asked me to tell you and Jeff that Willi and Joseph are doing well also. So is your grandmother. And Annalise."

Gretchen nodded. "Any other news?"

"Not really. Michael senses that something is—'in the air,' as he puts it. But neither he nor Gustav Adolf can quite determine what Richelieu is up to. He does say—this came from Axel Oxenstierna—that the Danes have been acting especially hostile lately. There have been some minor clashes in the Baltic."

By the time she finished, Rebecca was tense again. Gretchen turned her head and stared out the window. That window, as it happened, looked to the north. Denmark was somewhere beyond that horizon, and . . .

*Increasing Danish hostility.*

In the two years since she and her family had been rescued by the Americans, Gretchen's own political sophistication and knowledge of the world had grown rapidly. So she was almost as quick as Rebecca in making the connection.

"Oh, God," she hissed. "If Richelieu's managed—"

"I think he has," said Rebecca firmly. "It all makes sense, Gretchen. Everything fits together now. Except . . . I wonder why he didn't want us to see what sort of preparations the French ports are making?"

"But everyone knows the French and Dutch are preparing to fight the Spanish," Gretchen protested, less because she thought Rebecca was wrong than because she so badly *wanted* her to be. "Why should he try to hide that from us?"

"Of course everyone knows about the Dutch alliance," Rebecca agreed grimly. "And he's gone to some lengths to see to it that they do. But there had to be *something* he wanted to hide from us. Something besides the fact that he's impressing merchantmen."

"Everyone's impressing them, Becky."

"Yes," said Rebecca, nodding. In the 17$^{th}$ century, during time of war, "navies" were mainly made up of armed merchantmen. Naval mobilization consisted largely of impressing the ships into military service and adding them to a core of vessels which had been specifically designed as warships. "But to what end?" She smiled with absolutely no humor. "I know we all thought we knew the answer to that question, but now . . ."

Gretchen went over to the window and pressed her nose against the pane. The glass, as was usually the case except in the richest homes, was not as clear as the glass she'd become accustomed to in Grantville. Leaving aside minor imperfections, the "flat" panes were almost always wavy, producing a certain distortion in the view. But it wouldn't have mattered, even if the glass had been perfect and it had still been daylight. There would have been nothing to see beyond the houses of The Hague, anyway, except Holland's flat terrain to the north. And then, beyond that, the Frisian islands and the North Sea and, eventually, Denmark.

"If the Danes have secretly allied with the French," she said softly, "which would make sense from their viewpoint, of course—"

She heard Rebecca's little murmur of agreement. For all that Denmark and Sweden were both Lutheran nations, they had been enemies for decades. As was usually the case in the Thirty Years War, political and dynastic ambitions overrode religious affiliation. Until Gustav Adolf's stunning victories at Breitenfeld and the Alte Veste, France had been the Swedes' principal supporter. Religion be damned. Catholic France had always been far more concerned about the ambitions of the Catholic Habsburg dynasty which ruled Austria and Spain than they were about heresy.

Since Gustav's power had grown so unexpectedly, largely due to his alliance with the newly arrived Americans, France had become hostile. So an alliance with the Danes was now quite logical. Still, that left Spain as France's traditional enemy. If the history of *this* universe remained true to that from which the Americans had come, France and Spain were "scheduled" to start a war in the year 1635.

That war would last for a quarter of a century, have no conclusive result, and leave both countries exhausted and Spain half-shattered. The Portuguese would revolt successfully in 1640, the Catalans unsuccessfully. Both revolts would be brought on by the stresses of the war and the exactions of the Spanish crown. The

French would come out of it in somewhat better shape than Spain, but not much. They would gain a few piddling little territories—Artois, Gravelines, Roussillon and Cerdagne—at an enormous cost in blood and treasure.

"Richelieu's read the history books too," Gretchen murmured. "And the man is not stupid."

She turned to look at Rebecca, and saw in the vigorously nodding head a confirmation of her own thoughts.

"There is really no *great* reason for France and Spain to go to war," Rebecca stated firmly. "In—" Her left hand made that little vague motion which people often did when trying to indicate *that other universe that would have been, or might be somewhere else.* "In *that* universe, the war was brought on by nothing more than the usual stupid reasons. Petty dynastic quarrels over petty towns and statelets. And nothing came of it worth the cost."

"A grand alliance, then," said Gretchen. "France and Denmark and Spain—and *that,* in turn, will require the French to end their long support of the United Provinces. That would be the Spanish price." She hesitated. "But I still don't really see what France gets out of it, other than striking against us."

Rebecca's eyes seemed a bit unfocused, as they often did when she was thinking. "True. At first glance, at least. Richelieu can be subtle, though. And let us not forget how critical the Baltic is to any nation with maritime pretensions. Timber, pitch, iron, copper . . . the list is endless, all of it the sinews of naval power. The fact that Gustavus is poised to cut all of Europe off from those supplies—or, at least, to grant access solely on his own terms—gives him enormous additional influence. Indeed, over the next few years, Dutch foreign policy will—or would have—walked a careful line designed to play Swede off against Dane to insure that *no one* was ever in the position Gustavus now holds."

"You think that accounts for all of this?" Gretchen asked skeptically, and Rebecca snorted.

"Of course not. Oh, I feel sure it forms part of the . . . subtext, let us say, but it is scarcely the major factor. Not for France, at any rate."

She frowned, obviously thinking hard.

"It seems clear enough for everyone else," she murmured, as much to herself as to Gretchen. "The Danes would get the strength they'd need to attack Sweden in the Baltic and reestablish Danish control over it. The Spanish would get another chance to reconquer the rebellious provinces in the Low Countries—and a better one than they've had in decades, without the French army to threaten them from the southwest."

"Still have to defeat the Dutch navy, which is the strongest in the world," Gretchen pointed out.

Rebecca made a face. "With a French betrayal, Gretchen, that becomes possible. *Especially*"—the next words were almost hissed—"when the stupid Dutch won't listen to my warnings."

She rose abruptly and began pacing around. "I *knew* there was something wrong. But it was hard to explain it to those stupid fat burghers just based on my impressions of Richelieu's demeanor in a private meeting."

"Hard to blame them for being skeptical, in some ways," Gretchen said unwillingly. Rebecca looked a question at her, and she shrugged. "The one constant point of Richelieu's foreign policy, the single goal from which he has *never* wavered, has always been to resist and beat back Habsburg power," she pointed out. "Why should he change that now? If *we* can see no advantage for him in such a betrayal, then why should the Dutch? He's told the entire world he intends to support them against any fresh Spanish aggression, and we've seen no true evidence to prove he's lied. If I were the Dutch, I wouldn't believe he had, either. Not without some sort of hard proof, at any rate."

"Well, then," Rebecca said, holding up the radio message in her hands, "perhaps with this—"

"Don't be silly, Rebecca. All that contains is a Swedish chancellor's *impressions* of the Danes. Of course Oxenstierna will suspect King Christian of all manner of dark designs upon Sweden and the Baltic! The Dutch will just say it's the usual Swedish-Danish rancor at work."

Rebecca's hand fell to her side. "True," she sighed. "Damn those complacent Dutchmen."

"Danish, Spanish, and French," Gretchen murmured to herself, then looked back at Rebecca and raised an eyebrow. "That accounts for everyone but the English," she observed. "Where do you think *they* fit into all this?"

Rebecca shrugged.

"At this point, I don't have the least notion," she acknowledged. "They have a much greater interest in the Baltic's naval stores than the French, and I would think they would be unlikely to support anyone who threatened to monopolize access to them. That should mean they would be as opposed to giving the Danes dominance of the Baltic as to leaving it with Gustavus, so perhaps they intend to remain neutral in all this. God knows the rumors suggest Charles faces troubles enough domestically without borrowing still more in foreign adventures! But what matters most is the French. The French . . . and the Spanish."

She shook her head decisively and moved over to the table where Jimmy had set up the radio equipment. To his right, sticking out of the third-story window, was a hexagonal thing with a coil in the middle on the end of a stick. Even to Rebecca, who was not very familiar with radio, the antenna looked bizarre. It was large in cross-section, too—almost three feet across in its widest dimension.

Gayle Mason and the two other Extra-class hams in Grantville had built the thing, along with an identical one carried by the mission to London. They called it an "isotron design," and had chosen it because it could be packed up to fit easily in a trunk and didn't require a tall antenna.

Jimmy was fiddling with the radio, which was getting nothing but static. To his left, sitting on a nearby chair, one of the German soldiers was stoically pedaling away at a small contraption which they'd bolted to the floor. That provided the power source for the radio, and had also been designed by Gayle and her cohorts. Jimmy had told Gretchen that it was modeled on a device first pioneered in the early 20th century by people in the Australian outback.

For a moment, Gretchen was almost overwhelmed by an urge to laugh. There was something peculiarly comical about her situation. There she was, in a house in Holland, a girl born in 17th-century central Germany, consorting with Americans from centuries in the future, who, in turn, were relying on a gadget which had been designed in a country which didn't exist yet—on a continent which had only recently been discovered by Europeans.

She saw Rebecca giving her a cocked eye, with a smile on her face.

"Yes," murmured the young Sephardic woman. "It *is* all a bit . . . twisted."

Rebecca turned to Jimmy and laid a hand on his shoulder. "No luck with England?"

His long, half-muttered reply meant very little to Gretchen. Not because his voice was too low but simply because the words themselves were meaningless. To anyone, at least, except someone who shared his technical jargon.

"There's a lot of static, but the bands are clean, since we're the only folks on the air. So there's no QRM, and the QRN ain't too bad—probably some thunderstorms causing that—and it wasn't any real problem making the QSO earlier with SK-1."

Rebecca rolled her eyes. Jimmy plowed on: "But if they're having any kinda problem in London getting that antenna outside—like maybe they've gotta keep it hidden in a room—bad business that, you don't want to get too close to an operating antenna with them kinda voltages—so—"

"Jimmy!" exclaimed Rebecca. "Could you please translate all that into *English*?"

The youngster started in his chair. "Oh. Sorry. What I mean is . . ." The effort of abandoning his beloved acronyms was obvious on his furrowed brow. "'QRM' is interference caused by other radio stations. In the here and now, that's not gonna be a problem. Not for a while, anyway. 'QRN' means noise caused by . . . uh, God, basically. You know, bad weather, that kinda thing. 'QSO' just means 'contact made.'"

"Three syllables saved by using three other syllables," chuckled Rebecca. "Sometimes I think Americans suffer from a bizarre form of dementia that manifests itself in a compulsive urge to use acronyms."

Jimmy stared up at her, confused. Rebecca smiled sweetly. "Never mind. And what does 'SK-1' stand for?"

"Oh. That's a station call sign. Gotta have 'em."

"*Why?*" mumbled Gretchen. But—perhaps fortunately—Jimmy didn't hear her.

"'SK-1' is Magdeburg. Chester'll be guarding the sked there. Uh . . . that means he's monitoring the frequency at scheduled times. Which, for him, means pretty much the first four hours after nightfall."

"'SK-1.'" Rebecca rolled the syllables over her tongue, smiling. "Again, three syllables for three. I admit the logic escapes me."

Jimmy was frowning. "You *gotta* have call signs, Becky! It's—it's—just the way it's done, that's all. Grantville's 'W-1.' People got 'em too. I'm 'NØOXF'—"

"Instead of the two-syllable 'Jimmy,'" murmured Rebecca.

"—and Gayle's 'KC6EU'—"

"Instead of the one-syllable 'Gayle.'"

"—you just don't *understand!*" The last was practically a wail.

"Never mind, Jimmy," soothed Rebecca, patting his shoulder. "I am quite sure I am mistaken and being obstreperous. 'NØOXF' it is. It is quite a nice name, by the way. It suits you, I think."

Jimmy looked somewhat mollified. "Had it since I was—"

Suddenly the radio burst into noise. Interposed over the static came a series of beeps and whoops. That, at least, was what it sounded like to Gretchen.

Jimmy almost jumped in his seat. "That's her! That's her! That's Gayle!" He grabbed his pencil and began scribbling, translating the noises as he went.

" 'CQ CQ DE KC6EY CQ CQ'—jeez, why is she CQ-ing? That means 'call for anyone out there.'" He sounded aggrieved. "Who the hell else would be out there except *me?* She can't reach SK-1 or W-1 directly, not with this gear."

He started tapping away at his own key, muttering the words aloud as he transmitted them.

" '—KC6EY HC6EY KC6EY DE NØOXF'—that's the way she *shoulda* done it except the other way around—'reading you 559'— that means . . . never mind, it's too complicated. But it's good, especially the tone."

A moment later, the whoops-and-beeps returned and continued. And continued. Jimmy was now scribbling furiously. "I ain't gonna be able to translate for a while—this is gonna be a long message, I can tell—"

Slowly, Rebecca lowered herself into a nearby chair and perched herself on the edge of the seat. Her hands were clasped tightly in her lap. Gretchen, too tense to sit, went back to the window and pressed her nose against the pane again. Below, she could see lights in the windows of The Hague's nearby houses. The lights were steady, not flickering. Not much, at any rate. Holland was a wealthy country—the wealthiest in Europe, in all likelihood—and even common burghers could afford the best lamps and tapers.

—*BEEP BEEP BEEEEEP WHOOP BEEP BEEEEP*—

Somehow, those odd noises seemed ominous. Gretchen suddenly found herself wondering how much longer Holland's complacent citizens would be able to enjoy good lighting in their homes.

*Not long, unless I miss my guess. I think—as my husband would put it—all hell is about to break loose.*

—*BEEEEEP WHOOP BEEP BEEP WHOOP*—

"I think all hell's gonna break loose," muttered Jimmy. He pushed the first completed sheet across the table toward Rebecca. She picked it up and began to read. "Things don't sound good in England neither." *WHOOP BEEEEEP WHOOP BEEP BEEP BEEP.* "I can't believe the bastards locked 'em up!"

Gretchen turned from the window and looked at Rebecca. The beautiful face was growing tighter as her eyes moved down the page. Her lips seemed to thin with every sentence.

A motion in the doorway caught Gretchen's eye. Jeff was standing there, gazing at her. "Bad?" he asked.

She shrugged. "Not sure yet, but—I think so."

He nodded, not seeming overly concerned. "So be it. Our kids'll be safe enough."

For a moment, husband and wife exchanged simple looks of love. Then, looked to Rebecca. Jimmy had handed her a second page, which she was studying as he kept transcribing yet another.

"Yes, bad," she said. "Rita and Melissa—the whole delegation— is essentially imprisoned. Wentworth's in charge—Strafford, rather, and that's a sign in itself. From everything they can tell, the English fleet *is* moving. A foreign adventure of some kind. They don't know much."

She and Gretchen looked at one another, two pairs of brown eyes filled with the same bitter surmise.

Jimmy finished, and pushed the third page over. Then, after keying a few short phrases which Gretchen assumed were some kind of "sign off" message, swiveled in his chair.

"You got anything you want to sent to SK-1?"

Rebecca sighed. "Oh, yes. But stretch a moment, Jimmy. Get a glass of water, whatever you need. It is going to be a long message."

Which, indeed, it was. But it began with only three syllables.

*War again.*

# Chapter 15

Jesse waited patiently for Hans to recognize the situation and react. *Come on, Hans, get your head out,* he thought to himself, as he watched the student pilot in the left seat level off and enter downwind.

Jesse had always been a mild-mannered instructor, a reaction to one of the flight instructors all the way back at Purdue. That worthy had been a real "screamer," seeming to take delight in making an already nervous student miserable and prone to even more mistakes. Jesse thought the method was stupid. He preferred a more calm approach, giving students plenty of time to catch errors on their own. But he'd seen enough. Hans was obviously pleased with his earlier performance on this, his fifth training flight, and hadn't noticed his potentially fatal error.

"Hans! Airspeed!" Jesse said sharply.

Hans jerked his eyes back into the cockpit where the airspeed indicator was slowing below fifty knots. The throttle lever was back at idle where he'd placed it for the long descent to traffic pattern altitude.

Hans gasped, and cobbed power to the dependable VW engine. The monoplane gained speed quickly and Jesse noted with satisfaction that Hans, despite his surprise, hadn't throttle burst or lost altitude control.

He had, however, by now flown considerably past the final turn point. Jesse tapped the young German on the arm.

"Son, I believe the airfield is back thataway," he said with a jerk of the thumb, as his student searched for the large tree, now far behind, that marked the normal spot to "come off the perch."

"Uh," Hans grunted and banked left, pulling off the power he had added only a few seconds earlier. Descending quickly, he looked at the field and made his turn to final, using too much bank and failing to compensate for the additional distance to the field. As a consequence, the aircraft, though safe, was lower than it should have been, giving Hans a flatter than normal approach and an unusually shallow view of the landing zone.

Jesse, knowing what was coming, waited patiently for his student to make one of the two usual rookie mistakes. He nodded as Hans avoided the first by not descending at the usual rate and compounding his error.

"That's right, Hans. Level off and catch the normal glide path. Put your touchdown point about one third up the windscreen, just like always. Give it a touch more power."

The young man followed instructions and, momentarily swapping hands on the stick, wiped his sweaty right hand on his jacket. The feeling of well-being that had been with him only two minutes ago was obviously long gone and, in his nervousness, he committed the second mistake Jesse was expecting. Approaching the field from an unfamiliar angle, at a higher than normal power setting, he failed to catch the proper glide path. Suddenly, he was too high as he crossed over the small trees at the field boundary.

"Gott!" Hans exclaimed, as he pulled the throttle to idle and dove for the grass beneath him.

"Easy, easy," Jesse said. "Let it settle. Put some power in." Not for the first time, he regretted not installing dual throttles. While he could just reach the throttle across the narrow cockpit, now wasn't the time to stretch across his student to do so.

Hans flared too early, twenty feet or so above the ground. The aircraft slowed as he raised the nose and felt for touchdown.

"Too high! Lower the nose. Power!" Jesse pushed the heel of his palm against the back of the stick in front of him.

Feeling the instructor's pressure against the stick, Hans obeyed, adding power and leveling off ten feet in the air.

"Copilot's aircraft," Jesse said as he shook the stick and took control. "Set climb power."

Hans shakily set the throttle and sank glumly back in his seat.

"Not so good." He grimaced at his mentor.

"No, not very good," Jesse agreed. "Take a rest for a minute, Hans, and let me fly for a while. Tell me what you did wrong."

Jesse studied his student as he methodically recounted his own errors. Jesse was pleased to see that Hans knew exactly where he had erred, explaining what he should have done at each misstep. By the time he finished, Hans was calm and ready to try again.

"Okay, pilot's aircraft. Take it in for a full stop landing." Jesse smiled at his student. "We'll talk more about it on the ground. This time, try not to screw the pooch."

His student smiled back. "Roger that, no screwing of the pooch."

Once on the ground, and the airplane secured, Jesse and Hans walked toward the control tower. The structure had been erected hastily as soon as Mike Stearns had rammed through the new aircraft production policy after Jesse's first successful flight. There hadn't been much opposition, once the people backing the two alternate designs were assured that they'd get some of the funds being allotted.

Jesse smiled, as he did almost every time he looked at the control tower. "That has *got* to be the only log cabin control tower ever made," he chuckled. "And those old timers used to brag about their Quonset huts."

"What is a Konset hut?"

"Stick around, Hans. In a couple of years or so—advance of progress, all that—you'll probably be seeing 'em popping up all over the place. Maybe sooner, if Jerry Wright and his partners can make good on their boasts about sheet metal."

Jesse started to explain the design, but broke off when he saw that Hans' attention had suddenly become completely distracted.

Sharon Nichols had emerged from the door leading to the upper floor of the control tower and was striding toward them. Behind her came Mike Stearns.

"I didn't know *she* was here," exclaimed Hans. Jesse was amused by the expression on his face. Clearly enough, Hans was both delighted and chagrined to see that Sharon had witnessed the training flight. Delighted, simply because she was here; chagrined, because the flight itself had not exactly shown him in the best light.

As she drew nearer, and the expression on Sharon's own face became clear, Hans' pleasure vanished. Sharon seemed both angry and apprehensive.

"I didn't think it was *that* bad," Jesse heard the young man mutter.

But Jesse had been watching Mike, as he approached, and suddenly realized that Sharon's expression had nothing to do with the flight.

"The shit's hitting the fan, Hans. If I don't miss my guess."

Mike's first words were: "How soon can you have combat airplanes ready? And how soon can you have the pilots for them?"

Sharon didn't say anything. She just clutched Hans, her eyes wet, and started whispering something to him. "I don't want you to *do* this," was the only part of it Jesse overheard.

Jesse took a deep, almost shuddering breath. "Four to six months, for the planes. That's the test flight, you understand. We'll probably need some more time after that to work out the bugs and get all the other equipment up to snuff." He glanced at the young couple embracing next to him; then moved his eyes away, took Mike by the elbow and led him off a few paces.

"The pilots'll be ready by then. Hans, sooner than the rest of them."

Mike nodded, glanced at Hans and Sharon himself. Then, like Jesse, looked away.

"What were the casualty rates for pilots in World War I?" he asked softly.

Jesse shrugged. "I don't know, exactly. High. Real high, Mike. I saw the graveyard at Camp Talliaferro once, where British Royal Flying Corps instructors trained American pilots from 1917 to 1918. During the months British and Canadian troops were stationed in Fort Worth, there were something like forty officers and cadets killed during flight training. Eleven of them were buried there. And that was before they even went into combat. I do know that during the worst stretches, the life expectancy of a British pilot newly arrived in the combat zone was measured in days."

Mike's expression was grim. Jesse tried to find words of reassurance.

"Mind you, it shouldn't be that bad for *us*. We're not going to be sending newbies up against the likes of Baron von Richthofen, after all. And during World War I they really rushed people through flight training. We can—"

He broke off. "Well, I think we can, anyway. Just how much time *do* we have, Mike? And what exactly is happening?"

Mike ran fingers through his hair. "I can't answer your second question all that precisely, Jesse. The truth is, we still don't know much. But I got a message from Becky last night—the first one that's come over the radio—and she's just about dead certain the war is blowing wide open again."

He paused, his eyes moving back toward Hans and Sharon. Jesse followed his gaze. The two young people were kissing now. Despite the gravity of the moment, Jesse almost laughed. Sharon, clearly enough, was swept up in the passion of the moment. Hans, too, yes. But from the expression on his face, Jesse suspected he was mostly just astonished—and ecstatic—at the fierceness of the kiss.

Jesse wasn't positive, but he suspected that Hans and Sharon's relationship up till now had remained—technically, at least—short of what Americans called "going all the way." Hans was a proper German lad, for all the horrors he'd experienced in his two years as a mercenary. It wouldn't surprise Jesse a bit if he were still a virgin. Germans of the time were far from prudes, when it came to sex. But intercourse was still considered improper until a couple was officially betrothed. Then, typically enough, they wouldn't wait for the actual wedding. A good third of the German girls he'd seen getting married since the Ring of Fire had been visibly pregnant at the altar. As long as they'd been engaged, however, the families didn't seem to care. By their lights, according to traditional German law, a betrothal was legally binding—it couldn't be dissolved short of a court ruling, and dissolution of a betrothal required the same grounds as a divorce.

Jesse knew the whole issue was one of many which were causing the new courts established since the founding of the United States a passel of grief, since, obviously, American traditions on the matter were quite different. But, however the courts finally ruled, the customary attitudes remained—and Jesse had started noticing that more and more Americans were starting to look on "engagement" as something a lot more solemn than simply buying a diamond ring.

*He'll get laid tonight, I bet. Proper engagement or not, Sharon ain't gonna take "no" for an answer.*

The thought cheered him up. Quite a lot.

Mike, too, it seemed, judging from the little smile on his face as he watched the young couple.

"Screw it," Jesse heard him murmur. "It'll be good for James to have something else to worry about."

Mike turned back to Jesse. When he spoke again, his voice was firm and harsh. "But I *can* answer the first question. You've got as much time as you think it takes to train a pilot properly." The broad shoulders shifted, and Jesse was reminded that in his youth Mike Stearns had been one hell of a boxer. "I will be good goddamned if I'll send any half-trained kids up in a crate to go fight a war. Train 'em, Jesse. Train 'em till they're ready."

When James Nichols returned from the hospital that night, he found his daughter and Hans Richter sitting together on the couch in the living room. Side by side, holding hands. It was obvious they'd been waiting for him. Hans' face looked very pale and apprehensive. Sharon's dark face, simply stubborn.

He hadn't taken more than two steps into the room when Sharon spoke.

"Hans and I got engaged this afternoon." She lifted her hand, Hans' still clasped in it, to show him a ring.

"It belonged to my mother," Hans said, his voice almost trembling with nervousness. "I managed to save it, all these years since— since soldiers took her away when I was a boy. I kept it hidden."

Nichols was paralyzed, for a moment. He knew the history of the Richter family. Staring at that pale, tightly drawn, twenty-year-old face, he was suddenly reminded that there were worse things in the world—much worse—than gaps in age and education and race.

"Hans is spending the night, Daddy," continued Sharon. "With me." The tone of her voice now verged on sheer belligerence. "Don't give me a hard time about it. It's a good German custom, once you're engaged. They even have a name for it."

A bit wildly, Nichols' mind veered aside. He was familiar with the term, as it happened. *Fenstering*, the Germans called it— literally from the boy coming in through the window, but with the knowledge and consent of the girl's parents. Melissa had once explained the custom to him. *Makes perfect sense, James. You know they don't usually get married until they're in their mid-late twenties, because it takes that long to put together the capital to form a household. So they get engaged way ahead of time and then . . . what the hell—*

He remembered the impish smile she'd given him, and felt a

sudden longing for her presence. An even deeper longing than usual. Melissa would have known how to handle this.

*—it beats outright fornication, doesn't it?*

Even more suddenly, the realization of what must have triggered this act of defiance on his daughter's part came crashing down upon him. "Oh, Jesus," he whispered. There was a chair nearby. He took a step, pulled it under him, and more or less collapsed onto it.

For a moment, he stared at the two youngsters on the couch. Then, not being able to find any words, simply nodded his head. It was not . . . quite a blessing. More in the way of a simple acknowledgment of reality. If nothing else, James was too damn old to be staying up every night watching the windows.

The beaming smile which came to his daughter's face warmed him. Even more so, oddly enough, did the look of relief which washed over her fiancé's. Whatever reservations James had about the relationship, he had none at all about Hans himself. Outside of his reckless way behind a wheel, at any rate. He was a sweet kid, truth to tell. And the boy had had enough grief in his short life, without James Nichols adding any further to it.

The doctor cleared his throat. "I managed to get some eggs yesterday. May as well use 'em up for breakfast tomorrow. Sharon likes hers scrambled, Hans. How about you?"

After they'd gone up the stairs, James sighed and levered himself out of the chair. Feeling like an old man, he went over to the telephone and dialed a number.

"Mike? James here. Is it as bad as I think it is?"

Three minutes later, he hung up the phone and dialed another number.

"Stoner? James here. Look, I'm sorry, but I'm going to have to ask you to break off on the chloramphenicol project. You've already got production started anyway, so you can leave the rest to Sally. You're just fine-tuning now, trying to improve the yields."

He winced at the immediate eruption of protest and moved the phone an inch away from his ear. When the angry words died down, he spoke again.

"Yeah, I understand that it's our best bet against epidemics. But that's tomorrow, and today is today." He drew in a deep breath. "I'm going to need more sulfa drugs pretty soon, Tom. Lots of the stuff. We're going to have wounds to deal with before much longer."

For a moment, there was silence on the other end of the telephone. Then, simply: *Shit.*

"Shit is right," concurred Dr. James Nichols. "Sorry, Tom, but it doesn't look as if this century's going to be any kinder to hippies and flower children than the one we came from. Not even over-aged ones like you. Less, looks like. You're still the best pharmacist and—ah—" His lips quirked. "—drug chemist we've got."

*Shit.*

"Hey, Stoner, look on the bright side. At least your main crop's legal in this day and age—and, by the way, I'm going to be needing plenty of that, too. It's still the best analgesic we've got, in any quantity."

# Chapter 16

When Richelieu was finished, he had to struggle mightily not to burst out into laughter. The young French officer standing in front of the cardinal's desk seemed paralyzed by shock. His jaw, sagging; his eyes, as wide open as human eyes could get.

After a moment, Richelieu did allow himself a single laugh.

"Oh, please! I like to think of this as confirmation of the principles of aristocracy. You *do*, after all, have as distinguished a military pedigree as any man alive. Grandson, through your mother Elizabeth, of William the Silent himself. Mauritz of Nassau and Frederik Hendrik—both renowned soldiers of the day—as uncles. So why should the king's decision come as such a surprise, Henri de la Tour d'Auvergne? Or, to use the new title which His Most Christian Majesty has chosen to bestow upon you, Vicomte de Turenne."

The young man's eyes were still practically bulging. Richelieu decided to relent a bit. De la Tour d'Auvergne—no, Turenne—*was* a very young man, after all. Still short of his twenty-second birthday, and just now informed that he had been appointed to high military command as well as having been made a vicomte.

"I have never been harsh toward Protestants, you know," the cardinal said softly, "so long as they remain loyal to the king and France. Nor have I inquired—nor will I, young Henri—as to your own faith, despite the fact that your father the duc de Bouillon is a Huguenot and your mother a Dutch Protestant."

Richelieu laid a long-fingered hand atop the stack of books and manuscripts on his desk. "It is all here, young Henri. Not in the detail I would have preferred, of course—sadly, the Americans seem to have little interest in French history, judging from their libraries. But . . . there's enough. Certainly for *this* decision. History will record that Henri de la Tour d'Auvergne, later vicomte de Turenne, was one of the greatest generals ever produced by France. From his early career through his death in battle at the age of sixty-four, the record is clear. Brilliance, combined with unswerving loyalty. More than that, neither I nor any man can ask. And the king agrees. So why should we waste the next few years while you prove it? We may not have the luxury of those few years. France needs you *now.*"

The last sentence seemed, finally, to break through the young man's shock. Turenne closed his mouth, almost with a snap, and his eyes narrowed.

"Yes, Your Eminence. I will certainly do my best." He glanced at the stack of books and manuscripts. "May I take those to study?"

Richelieu lifted his hand and nodded. "By all means. That is why I had them brought here."

Turenne began to reach for them, but drew back his hand. His jaw was no longer loose at all; indeed, it was very tight. "If I am to do this, Your Eminence, I must insist—*insist*—on the right to select my own staff. And I will require—"

"Whatever you need, Henri. I assure you, the king's confidence in you is absolute. Mine also."

Turenne stared at him for a moment. Then, his shoulders slumping a little, bent over and picked up the stack of books and manuscripts. "I shall do my very best, Your Eminence."

Less than five minutes after Turenne left the cardinal's chamber, another man was ushered in. No youngster, this—Samuel Champlain was now in his mid-sixties.

Champlain advanced to the center of the room and bowed deeply. "I thank Your Eminence. From the bottom of my heart. This is a life's dream fulfilled."

Richelieu waved his hand languidly. "I always assured you that I supported your ambitions. But, in times past, my support was constrained by . . . ah, well, you understand."

Champlain nodded stiffly. "That damned treacherous Gaston. You ought to—"

"Samuel!" cautioned the cardinal. "Say no more. Monsieur Gaston, after all, *is* the king's brother. And also, I would remind you, the heir to the French throne. Since the king has no children of his own."

The last few words caused Champlain's lips to tighten. In truth, the cardinal had to fight not to let the same sour sentiments show on his own face. Louis XIII, unfortunately, was . . . ah . . .

Even in his own mind, the cardinal shied away from the thought. It was enough that the king had not sired an heir upon his wife, Anne of Austria. Had not, so far as Richelieu could determine, even had conjugal relations with her for many years. For all those years, since Richelieu had been appointed head of the Royal Council, the king's childlessness had hovered over the cardinal like the proverbial Sword of Damocles. The king's younger brother and his entourage of courtiers hated and despised Richelieu. Should Louis XIII die, with no children . . .

Then Gaston, the duc d'Orleans, would become the new king of France. No one had any doubt—Richelieu least of all—that on the morrow, the cardinal's head would roll from the executioner's block.

For years, now, the cardinal had outmaneuvered Gaston and his pack of toadies, as he had all the rest of his enemies within France. Fortunately, both the heir apparent and the followers he drew around him were prone to hotheaded and reckless schemes. Because of his position, of course, Richelieu could not touch the duc d'Orleans himself. But he had executed or imprisoned or sent into exile a goodly number of Gaston's supporters, whenever they made one of their frequent missteps. And in the famous "Day of Dupes" in November 1630, Richelieu had even finally managed to dislodge the king's mother, Marie de Medici, from her position of power and influence. As well as punish a fair number of *her* courtiers—the marshall de Marillac, for instance, who had been executed and his brother tossed into the prison where he died soon after.

Still, while Richelieu had always triumphed in these savage factional struggles, the struggle itself had often diverted his attention from pressing affairs of state, as well as set limits upon his freedom of maneuver. Now, however—if nothing else, the Ring of Fire and the arrival of the Americans had accomplished *this* much—Louis XIII seemed willing to give Richelieu *carte blanche* on everything. And, in any event, most of the cardinal's enemies were either crushed or hiding in their mouseholes.

Which meant, among other things, that a certain Samuel Champlain was going to finally get the support he had long pleaded for—and then some.

"Let us not speak of unpleasant matters, Samuel, when the news I have for you is so good. Not only have the English released you from captivity, but they have agreed to return all of our properties in New France."

"Quebec too?" asked Champlain eagerly. He had founded that town himself, in 1608, and was especially attached to it.

"Everything." Richelieu smiled. "More than that, in fact. The new secret treaty I have signed with the English transfers all of *their* properties in the New World to us as well. Plymouth and Jamestown, everything. Henceforth, all of America north of the Spanish possessions belongs to the crown of France."

Now Richelieu had an old man's sagging jaw and wide eyes staring at him, as he had had those of a youngster earlier. Again, the cardinal laughed.

"Oh, yes—all of it, Samuel! When you return to New France— the greatly *expanded* New France—your title of 'lieutenant-general' will match the reality. I am sure you will rise to the challenge."

"Indeed, Your Eminence!" Champlain squared his shoulders, as best he could given an old man's stoop. "I shall do my best!"

Five minutes after Champlain was ushered out, a man in early middle age was ushered in. He found the cardinal staring out the window, not seated in his chair.

"Let him live out what days remain to him in peace, Michel," murmured Richelieu. "As best you can, at any rate. He deserves that much, for his long years of service to the crown.

"Champlain will be dead in two years anyway, and, in the meantime, the prestige of his name will help me to raise the funds needed here in France. The backers of the Compagnie des Cent Associes are already ecstatic over our new policy, of course, but I think I can open their coffers a bit more. Quite a bit more, actually—and those are very big coffers." Richelieu turned away from the window. "You, of course, will be the real governor of the new territories. But do try not to clash with the old man unless it is absolutely necessary. Loyalty should be repaid in kind."

Michel Mousnier shrugged. "After Champlain's experiences, I doubt he'll protest much if I need to be firm with the English settlers. Not sure how he'll react to our plans for New Amsterdam and the Dutch forts at Orange and Nassau, though."

"It hardly matters. Keep him in Virginia, Michel, where we'll be landing most of the new French settlers. We'll need a new name for that province, by the way. Champlain is quite good at founding new towns, it seems, so why aggravate the old man with the harsh realities of conquering established ones?"

The cardinal glanced at a nearby cabinet. "Dead in two years, as I said." In that cabinet were kept other manuscripts and books, ones which he had not bothered to copy for Turenne. "I don't know the exact date. But it will be sometime in the year 1635. After which, Michel, you will assume the title as well as the real authority."

"I will do my best, Your Eminence."

"Oh, I have no doubt of that at all."

As Don Fernando strode toward the door of her chambers, being opened for him by his aide, Isabella called him back.

For a moment, Fernando considered pretending he had not heard her, so avid was the prince of Spain to launch himself into a life of martial glory. But . . .

She *was* the Infanta Isabella, after all. Archduchess and governess of the Netherlands, daughter of the great Philip II, and a woman whose life had been illustrious and renowned in its own right. Even now, on her deathbed, no man could dismiss her lightly. Not even the king of Spain's younger brother.

The prince's aide, certainly, was not inclined to rebellion. Miguel de Manrique had the door closed before the prince even came to a halt.

When Don Fernando turned around, Isabella croaked a laugh at the look on his face. "Oh, my dear boy! It's not so bad as all that! Wasn't I the one, after all, who told you to leave off all those damned ecclesiastical robes and start wearing a soldier's apparel?"

Grudgingly, Fernando nodded. Then, not so grudgingly, gave his elderly great-aunt a genuine smile. Don Fernando had not been pleased, to put it mildly, when the needs of state and his brother's will had forced him to become a cardinal of the church. Fernando had wanted a soldier's name and titles, not "cardinal-infante." But, he had been a dutiful son of Spain, for all that he had chafed under the necessity.

Once he arrived to take up his new duties in Brussels, however, his great-aunt had urged him to cease wearing churchly raiment.

As she had for decades, Isabella was trying to bring a final peace to the Netherlands. Catholic regalia, she'd informed the cardinal-infante, would just inflame many of his subjects. Whereas even the most Calvinist Dutchman could respect a soldier, especially one who followed the policies of the duke of Parma and Spinola.

Don Fernando had needed no further urging. In truth, he was basically inclined to heed Isabella's advice. Still, he was a young prince on the very eve of his first great test in battle, and the last thing he really wanted to listen to was more of the cautions of a very ill and elderly lady.

"Please, Fernando," whispered the old woman, the tears of a lifetime beginning to leak into her eyes. "I will be gone soon, and can do no more. *Please*. If you triumph, follow the legacy of Spinola. My legacy, also. Give peace to this long-tortured land."

Not even a brash young prince could remain indifferent to the appeal in those old eyes. He lowered his head. "I promise, *Tia* Isabella. I gave you my word, and I will keep it. There will be no 'Spanish Fury.' The duke of Alva is dead and buried. Let the savage old man remain in his grave."

"Not enough!" Tired and sick, the voice was, and quavering with age. But, at least for a moment, it was still a voice sired by Philip the Second. "Not enough! I want your word on the settlement."

The cardinal-infante hesitated. He planned to conquer, after all, not to "settle." And what self-respecting conqueror in history would settle for the same terms which his opponent had turned down in negotiations? Why give back what has been *taken*?

But . . . whatever he thought of his great-aunt's wisdom, he could not face those ancient eyes. And perhaps she was right, anyway. She was wise, still, even on her deathbed.

"Agreed," he said softly. Then, more firmly: "I swear, on my honor. Blood of Spain. Even if I win—*after* I win—I will impose the terms we advanced in The Hague. Nothing more."

A last spark of rebelliousness drove him to add: "Nothing *less*, either, you understand."

Isabella smiled. "Oh, to be sure. I am really no fonder of Calvinists than you are, nephew. Especially not those foul Counter-Remonstrants." Firmly: "I certainly see no reason that our own faith should not be practiced freely in towns with Spanish garrisons!"

The smile faded. "But keep that stinki—the Inquisition. On a *leash*, Fernando!"

On *that* subject, nephew and aunt were in full agreement. The young eyes which met old ones were bred by the same family. The Spanish branch of the Habsburgs had often been accused of intolerance; they had never once been accused of lacking royal will.

"The Spanish Inquisition serves at the discretion of the Spanish crown," growled Fernando. "And I *am* a prince of Spain as well as a cardinal. I will keep them on a leash. A very *short* leash, as a matter of fact."

Isabella closed her eyes, nodding. Then, waved her hand. "Go, go. Glorious youth, all that. Do try not to get yourself killed."

Outside, as they walked side by side down the corridor of the palace, Fernando glanced at Miguel. "Your job, that. Keep them on a leash, Miguel. Muzzle them, if you have to. I will support you in every particular."

"Be my pleasure." De Manrique's growl was that of a man in middle age, not a youth. Different in timbre; different, even more, in the depth of the gravel. "Damn them, anyway. The grief they caused us, everywhere we went. Ha!" His rough, scarred face broke into a narrow grin. "I'll say this for those cursed Americans. When the Inquisitors in the Wartburg tried to drive the soldiers back to the walls, their sharpshooters singled them out for the killing."

But the grin faded, within three steps. De Manrique had been the commander of the Spanish army shattered outside Eisenach and then trapped in the Wartburg. One of the worst defeats in Spanish history, that had been. Precious few times in history had an entire Spanish army surrendered, especially to a smaller force. De Manrique had been lucky, afterward, to have been simply disgraced instead of imprisoned. As it was, he had spent several weeks in the tender graces of the Inquisition, being tested to see if his failure reflected a deeper evil.

The cardinal-infante had saved him, then—just as Don Fernando had been the man who insisted on adding Miguel to his staff for the expedition to the Netherlands. In the months since, the veteran general had come to have a great deal of respect for the young prince of Spain. Headstrong he might be—and no "might be" about it. Rash, reckless, given to taking chances . . . yes, yes, certainly. But he *listened*. And, if nothing else, did not share the automatic assumption of most Spanish hidalgos that they already knew all the secrets of the ancient art of war.

The corridors of the palace were a bit chilly, despite the season. But it was not the chill of the evening which caused a momentary shiver in Miguel's shoulders. He—not self-satisfied hidalgos on their estates in Castile—had been the one who saw the inferno which the Americans had unleashed on the Wartburg. Some kind of hideous flame-weapon worse than any legends of Greek fire. And he—not them—had seen the brains of his soldiers splashed out of their skulls by muskets fired at an impossible range.

The shiver came, and went. Miguel de Manrique was a soldier, after all. And he *did* have the pleasant memory of seeing the brains of arrogant Inquisitors being splashed as well.

"On a leash," he repeated. "Leashed, and muzzled."

# Chapter 17

Halfway across Europe, another middle-aged face was creased by a scowl.

"Goddammit, Mike, there are *laws.*"

Mike Stearns returned the glare of Grantville's former police chief with an expression which did not even strive for innocence. Just . . . mild-mannered.

"I'm aware of that, Dan. I'm also aware that I can't slide around you the way I used to do—now and then—by arguing it was out of your jurisdiction."

"Not hardly!" snapped Dan Frost. Frost was now head of the national police force of the entire United States—which, for all that its powers were constrained, had much greater authority than the Federal Bureau of Investigation in the U.S. of another universe. Mike Stearns had insisted on that, just as he had insisted on Dan's appointment to the post. With the crazy quilt of legal jurisdictions that still made up the newly formed United States, he wanted no chance of allowing some arrogant little German princeling to flaunt new laws on the grounds that his domain of a few hundred acres was "beyond national jurisdiction."

Still, the U.S. Police Force was hardly unrestrained by legal limits. The Constitution of the new U.S. had the same Bill of Rights as that of the old one. And—what was more to the point, in the current discussion—was based on the same fundamental legal principles.

One of which—*very* basic—was that if a man breaks the law he gets arrested and charged in a court. He does *not* get subjected to the secret and essentially private justice of the executive branch of government.

"Dammit, there are *laws*," repeated Frost. The police chief cast a sour glance at one of the other occupants of the greenhouse where this little impromptu meeting was being held. Harry Lefferts, that was, lounging casually against a nearby planter. The young soldier, formerly a coal miner, had a rather peculiar position in the hierarchy of the new U.S. Army. Officially, he was "Captain Lefferts." In practice, he amounted to Mike Stearns' personal little one-man combination of the old OSS—in its woolliest World War II days—and what militant trade unions like the UMWA sometimes euphemized as the "education committee."

"Especially with *him* around," gruffed Dan, jerking his thumb at Harry. "Or are you going to tell me you brought him to 'reason' with Freddie?"

Harry just smiled. Mike shook his head. "Dan, if I *hadn't* brought Harry, you'd be giving me a hard time for risking myself—not much of a risk, bracing Freddie—in my august capacity as Mister President. You can't have it both ways."

Suddenly, unexpectedly, the owner of the greenhouse spoke up. Until now, Tom Stone—"Stoner" to everyone—had kept silent. Clearly enough, the whole situation made him very uncomfortable to begin with. Mike had been tipped off about Freddie Congden's treason by Tom himself, who was the man's nearest neighbor. Given Stone's history and general attitudes, it was well-nigh miraculous—and something of an indication of his personal trust in Mike—that he had done so at all. The nickname "Stoner" was no accident, and Tom had the usual attitude toward "snitching" that any longtime hippie and enthusiast for what he liked to call "alternate reality" normally had. It was crime which ranked almost on a par with arson or armed robbery.

Still . . . he *did* trust Mike, and his marriage to a German woman the year before had given him a somewhat different perspective on things. His wife Magdalena's definition of "atrocity" was a lot more material than Stoner's. Just as her definition of a "bad trip" was a journey across her war-torn homeland.

"Let me ask you something, Dan," Stoner said abruptly. "Seeing as how you're making such a fuss over the official rules and regulations. How come, all those years, you never busted me? Back when you were the town's police chief." A nod of Stoner's head indicated the marijuana plants growing in the adjoining greenhouse. "Sure, *now* that stuff's nice and legal—even a prized crop, seeing as how we haven't got anything better in the way of an analgesic. Not in the kind of quantity I can produce, anyway. But it sure as hell wasn't legal in the old days."

He glanced proudly at the vigorously growing, healthy plants. A special strain, those were, that he'd carefully cultivated over the years, and which produced a variety of the drug that all the area's medical and dental practitioners had come to prize highly. "And— yeah, sure—in the old days I didn't grow the stuff in the open like this. But don't tell me you never had any idea what I was doing."

Dan Frost looked uncomfortable. Then, looked away, staring at a nearby patch of herbs. Mike had a hard time not laughing. Clearly enough, Dan was trying to figure out which plants in *that* batch might have been illegal substances before the Ring of Fire.

It was hard to know. Tom Stone was as good a greenhouse grower as he was an "informal pharmacist." Since he'd left Purdue as a pharmaceutical graduate student in the late 70s, he'd spent most of his time in Grantville running his own commune of sorts. There probably wasn't much of *anything* he couldn't grow, if he wanted to. Mike had noticed Dan giving the mushrooms in another adjoining greenhouse something of a stony look.

"Ah, hell," muttered the police chief. "Yeah, sure, I knew what you were doing. But . . . I never got a whiff of you messing around with cocaine or heroin, and I knew you weren't selling any of your pot to the kids in town." He shifted his seat on the bench, still looking uncomfortable. "And . . . you looked to be raising those three kids of your own okay. I knew they were doing well in school. I checked. So. You know. What was I supposed to do? If I busted you, who was going to take care of the kids?"

He took a deep breath and scowled at nothing in particular. "Truth is, I always thought that damn 'War on Drugs' was friggin' stupid anyway. At least, the way it was being done. And I had other things to worry about. Small stuff, like a guy beating his wife half to death or drunk drivers or grand theft auto or a brawl every other night in the Club 250. So . . . Fuck it. I just looked the other way."

"Broke the rules, in other words," said Stone.

Frost's face tightened. "Dammit, it's *not* the same thing."

Mike was tempted to intervene, but decided to let Tom keep handling it. As much as anything else, because James Nichols had given him firm instructions to do anything possible to keep advancing Stoner's slowly developing sense of "civic responsibility." The ex-hippie and drop-out was proving to be one of the most valuable members of their new society, as far as the good doctor was concerned.

Besides, there was just something quietly hilarious about watching Tom Stone lecturing Dan Frost on the fine points of police ethics. Mike could see Harry Lefferts, standing far enough behind Dan Frost to be out of sight, grinning widely. Mike didn't have any doubt at all that Harry and his friend Darryl had been among Stoner's regular customers in the days before the Ring of Fire.

"Yeah, it is, Dan. If you think about it, what Mike's proposing to do is to *not* bust Freddie. So there's no issue here about Star Chambers and secret prisons and gulags and torture cells. He just wants to quietly let the situation continue . . . just . . . you know. What you might call under new management. I mean, what the hell. How can you accuse him of wanting to violate Freddie's 'rights' when he *could* have him pitched in jail forever or even—" Stoner scowled. "Dammit, why the hell we had to keep that stinking death penalty is a mystery to me, but we do have it even if it's never been used. And don't think once people found out what Freddie's been doing they wouldn't be hollering for the hangman."

Mike said nothing. Personally, although he'd never fully made up his mind, he tended to lean heavily against having a death penalty. But . . .

One battle at a time. Most of the "old Americans," even, were in favor of the death penalty. 17th-century Germans already tended to think he was crazy enough, without tossing *that* issue into the soup. To them, having a death penalty was as much of a given as dew in the morning.

"So the point is," Stoner continued, "you can't hardly accuse Mike of wanting to do anything to Freddie secretly that he couldn't do ten times worse right out in the open. And there's another advantage to his approach, you ask me, which is that . . ."

Stoner eyed the police chief aslant, clearly a bit wary of his next words. "Look, Dan, I hate to be the one to tell you this—you being a cop your whole life and all—but *too much* law can be even worse than not enough."

Suddenly, Dan Frost burst out laughing. "You're telling *me*? Christ, Stoner, sometime I oughta make *you* fill out one of those old forms I used to have to use."

The mood had lightened enough, Mike decided. It was time to "close the deal."

"Look, Dan, I *know* I'll be bending the rules. But, dammit, Stoner's right. Leave aside whether they'd hang the bastard or not. Frankly, I can't say I'd lose much sleep over that, anyway. On the best day of his life, Freddie Congden was a flaming asshole. You know it as well as I do. I never could figure out why Anita took as long as she did to pack up her bags and leave the guy."

" 'Fraid he'd kill her," grunted Dan. "Took me months to convince her I'd see to it he didn't. Which, ah—" He looked away. "I did."

Harry's grin was even wider than before. "Broke the rules again, huh? Hell, Dan, you should've kept your own hands clean and just quietly passed the word to me and Darryl. We'd've seen to it good old Freddie didn't lay a hand on Anita. Hard for a man to beat his wife when he can't catch her. Which I'll gua-ran-tee Freddie couldn't have done, not after Darryl and I reasoned with him. Amazing, the persuasive powers of a two-pound ball-peen hammer applied to a kneecap."

Dan scowled, but said nothing. Mike continued smoothly.

"And you know what else will happen, Dan. Every old maid in the country—most of 'em pot-bellied men—will set up a howl and a shriek for every book in sight to be put under lock and key. Before you know it, it'll be harder to get into a library than Fort Knox. Leaving aside the damage to *real* civil liberties, that'll cause ten times worse damage to our own technical development than any amount of spying could do. I mean, face it. Do you *really* want to see all books published in the old universe declared 'items of national security'?"

Mike glanced at the marijuana plants. "If you thought the 'War on Drugs' was stupid, how's about the 'War on Unauthorized Reading?' "

Dan grimaced. Then, held up his hand in a gesture of peacemaking. "All right, all right. But—" He turned his head and studied the final member of the little group, who had kept silent throughout. The only one of them, as it happened, who had been born in the 17th century—and had the elegant and aristocratic apparel to prove it.

"*But*," he repeated, "I want you to stay out of it personally. Let Francisco handle it. Him, at least, I trust to be reasonably judicious. And if the word ever gets out, it'll look better anyway having a well-regarded banker being the one who did the, ah, 'negotiations.' At least he's not a union strong-arm boy or a former professional boxer."

"Sure, no sweat," said Mike. Francisco Nasi, formerly a high courtier in the Ottoman Empire, a shaker-and-mover among the widespread and influential Abrabanel family, and now perhaps Grantville's most highly esteemed banker, was a man of many parts. Mike had high hopes that the young Sephardic Jew would prove to be as good a head of his new intelligence and counter-intelligence service as he had been at everything else in his life. Especially with Uriel and Balthazar Abrabanel to serve as his advisers, since they were too old to serve as functioning spies any longer.

But he left all that unspoken. He saw no reason to start *another* long argument with Dan Frost. Seeing as how his new intelligence service was completely informal and had—mentally, Mike cleared his throat—ah, never actually been approved by Congress or anybody else except Mike himself.

Francisco let Harry handle the introductory negotiations. By the time he walked through the smashed-open door of Freddie Congden's shabby trailer, the introduction was pretty much over.

Freddie, his eyes looking a bit dazed and his hand covering a bleeding mouth, was looking sideways at the drawer of a nightstand next to the filthy couch on which he apparently slept most nights. Judging, at least, from the number of empty beer containers perched on the nightstand, he wasn't in the habit of reading himself to sleep—whatever other use he had for the books he owned.

"Do it," said Harry cheerfully, the butt of the heavy revolver he'd used to split Freddie's lip now curled back into his fist. "Go for it, you piece of shit. Betcha anything you want I can blow your spine into four separate pieces before you even get that drawer open. And what good would it do you, even if you could get it open? When was the last time you fired it, anyway? Much less cleaned it? Huh?"

Almost casually, his boot lashed out and drove Freddie down onto the couch. "Fuck you, asshole." Harry leaned over, pulled the drawer completely out of the nightstand, and slid it onto a nearby formica table. The trailer's dining table, that was, insofar as the term could be used to refer to a piece of furniture which was so completely covered with debris that even a cup couldn't have been set down on it. In the course of sliding the drawer onto the table, Harry sent a small landslide of rubbish tumbling to the floor.

He glanced, very briefly, into the drawer. "Where the hell did you get that piece of crap, anyway? Musta bought it from some guy standing by the road with a placard that said: 'Will sell Saturday Night Special for food.'"

He shook his head. "Jesus. You were a cheapskate about everything, weren't you? What I can't figure out is how you ever came to own any books in the first place."

Finally, Freddie spoke. "Jeez! Hey, Harry, I'm in the *union*."

"Freddie, you were the sorriest damn member the United Mine Workers ever had. And if you're smart, you *won't* remind me about it." Harry stepped forward a pace or two. "And answer my question. Where in the hell *did* you get all the books you've been selling? I didn't think you'd read anything since you dropped out of high school—not even a newspaper."

"I don't know what you're talk—" Harry's boot drove him back into the couch, leaving a muddy print on his chest. Freddie gasped for breath.

"You get one lie, Freddie," said Harry softly. "You just had it." He nodded toward Nasi. "You either do it the man's way—or you'll do it *my* way. Personally, I'd suggest you throw yourself on the mercy of the banker. That's sorta what you might call a 'strong recommendation' kind of suggestion."

Another man might have accompanied those words with some sort of threatening physical gesture. The fact that Harry said the words without moving a muscle beyond those needed to speak made the implied threat . . . frightening. Francisco Nasi was a little taken aback. He realized that he still had a tendency to think of Harry the way the up-timers did: as the often-reckless and always pugnacious youngster he'd always been, but one who, nevertheless, was basically quite decent. Decent, Harry Lefferts still was—Francisco was quite sure of that. But he too had been subtly transformed in the two years since the Ring of Fire. This was no "kid," any longer. This was a very, very dangerous man.

Freddie, obviously, had no doubt about it at all. He looked away, blood still oozing from the gash on his lip. "What the hell," he mumbled. "Was just books, fer Chrissake, and I needed the money. Only fair, dammit, all the money I wasted on that rotten kid."

Francisco had already started searching the trailer. Behind him, he heard Harry's cold answer. "Call your kid George 'rotten' again, fuckhead, and you'll spit teeth. I remember the little guy, y'know. He always seemed beaten down, scared to death by everything. With a father like you, that ain't hard to understand."

Nasi opened one of the interior doors of the trailer and entered the small room beyond. After taking two steps, he came to a halt. The room was . . . impressive.

The room was clean, for a start—certainly by the standards of the rest of the trailer. Francisco suspected that was because the son George had kept it clean when he lived there, and Freddie had never entered it since except to steal his own son's possessions for the sake of treason.

"That poor boy," he murmured.

The room was practically a library in its own right. Outside of a narrow bed, every wall except one was covered with shelving. Cheap shelving, naturally—Freddie wouldn't have allowed anything else. But the books resting on those shelves weren't particularly cheap. No fancy first editions, of course, and only a few of them were hardcovers. But every shelf was packed with paperbacks of all kinds, ranging from children's books George must have gotten as a little boy all the way through dog-eared copies of a history of the American civil war by someone named Foote and a thick volume on the principles of astronomy.

Nasi's eyes moved to the one wall which was bare of shelves. From the ceiling, suspended by a string over the bed, hung a plastic model of some sort of spacecraft. Francisco wasn't positive, but he thought it was a replica of what the up-timers called an "Apollo." He'd seen pictures of them. Behind it, covering most of the wall, was a very large stellar map showing the galaxy. In a corner inset, the Solar System was displayed.

For a moment, Nasi felt a pang of sorrow. He could imagine the life of young George Congden, with a sullen brute of a father and a terrified mouse of a mother. Trying to carve out for himself, in the one little room which belonged to him, a world of his own imagination. Quietly but stubbornly fighting his father for every dime he could get, to buy another precious book or a map of another universe.

*Another universe.* "Good luck to you, George, wherever you are,"

Francisco murmured. "At least you won't have your father to worry about any more."

By then, Harry had come over and peeked in. "Jesus," he said.

Francisco glanced at him, shaking his head. "Why did they leave it all behind them?" he wondered. "I'm sure the boy must have been heartbroken."

Harry's head-shake was one of anger, not puzzlement. "I didn't see her leave, myself, but I heard about it. All Anita had—the only thing she owned except maybe a suitcase or two of clothes for her and the boy—was a beat-up old Fiesta. There'd have been no way to fit this stuff into it." His jaws tightened, making him looking scarier than ever. "But I'll tell you this for sure, Francisco. However heartbroken George might have been at leaving his books behind, he'd have done that in a minute to get away from *his* father. Any kid this side of an insane asylum would. Freddie Congden is a real piece of work."

Harry turned on his heel and walked back into the main compartment of the trailer. In seconds, he was standing in front of Freddie again, with Francisco a step or two behind him. Freddie himself was still on the couch, dabbing at his lip with a grimy rag of some kind.

"Okay, Freddie, here's how it's gonna work. If we wanted to, we could have you arrested. I'm not sure we could get an actual charge of treason to stick, since I think—I'm no lawyer, y'know, so I'm guessing a little—that 'treason' has a lot of fancy curlicues and quibbles that your case might not exactly match. But it doesn't matter. I'm not a lawyer, but Mike Stearns has the best one in town as his attorney general. 'Trafficking with the enemy,' whatever— we'd make enough charges stick to put you away forever. If you were lucky, that is. Keep in mind the jury'd be mostly German, and those folks'd have no trouble at all voting for the noose. Don't doubt it for a minute."

Freddie left off dabbing his lip, his face growing pale. "Hey, what the hell! We're just talking about *kids' books*—and they were my own property to begin with!"

Harry smiled thinly, put his left hand around his throat, and mimicked a man strangling to death. Then, after lowering the hand:

"Save your breath, Freddie—especially since you haven't got all that many breaths left to spare. I can just see you trying that argument on the jury. Buncha primitive Krauts, y'know—most of 'em holding a lot of silly grudges on account of how the people

you've been selling your books to have been murdering and rap-
ing and looting and butchering and burning out their families for
the past fifteen years or so."

Freddie's face was very pale, now. "Yeah, that's the way it is,
Congden," said Harry coldly. "If you want to try your luck, go
ahead. But I suggest you consider my alternative."

Freddie's swallowed. "What alternative?"

"From now on, you work for us. You'll keep living here, just
like you have been. And you keep selling your kid's books and stuff.
Except you'll tell your customers you're starting to run a little low
on your stock, so from now on you'll have to sell them *copies* of
the books." Harry glanced at the littered dining room table. "You'll
have to clean that off, since you'll be spending most your time
from now on sitting at that table, hand-copying the books we tell
you to copy—*with* certain adjustments in the text."

He hooked a thumb at Nasi. "Francisco here will tell you what
adjustments he wants. I think the real spy types would call him
a 'control officer.' But you and me are coal miners—even if you
were the sorriest bastard ever went down in a mine—so you can
just think of him as your boss. From now on, Freddie, you'll do
whatever Francisco tells you to do. Understand?"

Freddie's eyes flicked at Francisco, then back. His lips twisted
a bit. "Get somebody else. I ain't taking orders from no kike.
Anybod—"

This time, Harry's boot drove into his belly. Freddie lurched
forward on the couch, clutching his stomach, his mouth gasping
for breath.

An instant later, the gasp turned into a gag. Harry had the barrel
of his revolver pressed against the back of Freddie's throat. Freddie
was literally cross-eyed, staring at the gunbarrel in his mouth. The
eyes grew round as well as crossed when he saw—and heard—
Harry cock the hammer.

"This is a .357, did I mention that?" Harry's tone of voice was
light-hearted. "And I *do* want to thank you, Freddie, since you're
gonna make it possible for me to win an old argument with Darryl,
whenever I see him next. Him and me had an argument about
it, way back when. Darryl claims if you blow a man's head off with
your gun shoved all the way down his throat—handgun, that is,
major caliber, magnum round—you'll blow your own hand apart
along with it. 'Hydrostatic shock,' somethin' like that—Darryl always
did fancy himself with big words."

Harry grinned. Watching, Francisco thought it was the coldest and most savage grin he'd ever seen in his life.

"Me," continued Harry, "I think Darryl's full of shit. I bet I can blow your brains right out of the back of your head without getting worse than maybe a split thumb. 'Course, I admit, Darryl's bound to claim the experiment was no good—on account of you got no brains to begin with—but I can't say I really give a damn. I'd like to do it anyway, just 'cause I despise your sorry ass."

For a moment, Nasi thought Freddie might faint. Then, seeing the man's eyes rolling wildly at him, Nasi patted Lefferts on the shoulder.

"I think he's seen the light of day, Harry."

Harry withdrew the gunbarrel, tilted it away, and lowered the hammer. Then, made a face at it and stepped over to the dining table. He plucked a rag of some kind from the debris—a towel, perhaps; it was hard to tell—and started hurriedly wiping off the barrel. "Damn," Harry muttered. "Your saliva's worse than acid. My favorite piece, too."

Harry lifted his eyes from the task and gave Freddie a look of sheer menace. "You *will* take orders from your boss, shithead—that's *Mister Nasi*, to you—or you won't have to worry about a German jury. I'll just kill you myself. Save the taxpayers some money."

"Okay," croaked Freddie.


When they returned to Stoner's place, where Mike had waited for them, Harry made an announcement. "I think I've got the knack for this Double-O-Seven stuff. All I gotta do now is learn that fancy game. Whazzit called? Shummin-de-fur, or something. Y'know, what they play in Monaco."

Nasi seemed to choke a little. Mike shook his head firmly.

"Not a chance, Harry. You'd have to give up your boilermakers and learn to drink dry martinis. Shaken, not stirred."

Harry scowled. "Well, forget it then. I guess I'll just have to learn to be a country-boy roughneck instead."

# Part III

*Those mackerel-crowded seas*

# Chapter 18

The English Channel was brisker than usual, even for September. Despite the bright sunlight, the temperature hovered around no more than fifty degrees, and the wind blowing out of the northeast had teeth to it. It put a lively chop on the Channel's blue water and whined in the rigging, and Maarten Harpentzoon van Tromp, lieutenant-admiral of Holland, drew its freshness deep into his lungs as he stood on the quarterdeck of his flagship and gazed astern at the other ships of his fleet.

"They make a goodly sight," the man standing beside him said, and Tromp glanced at him. At thirty-four, Vice-Admiral Cornelisz Witte de With was two years younger than Tromp, which made both of them very young indeed for the posts they held. But there seemed to be a lot of that going around lately, Tromp told himself with a small, crooked smile.

"That they do," he agreed, turning his eyes back to the weather-stained canvas of the ships forging along in *Amelia*'s wake. Their formation keeping was indifferent, to say the very least. But that was typical of a Dutch fleet, and even from here he could almost taste the confidence, born of forty years of victory at sea, which filled their crews. "I'd like it better if more of them were regular Navy ships," he added after a moment, and de With chuckled.

"Wouldn't any of us?" he responded. "But the States General is doing well to keep forty ships in commission. There's not much left, even with the French subsidy, after they pay for the Army and the border fortresses' upkeep. And it isn't as if we're not used to it!"

"No. No, it isn't." Tromp shook his head and thought about the purloined pages he'd been shown by Constantjin Huygens, Prince Frederik Hendrik's secretary. They'd been frustratingly vague, not to mention fragmentary and incomplete, but they'd also been fascinating, especially with their hints of how countries of the future would maintain their fleets. Still, he wasn't sure he approved of the notion of a nation which maintained hundreds of state-owned naval vessels. The expense must be staggering, if nothing else. Besides, the long-standing practice of hiring and impressing armed merchant ships in time of war favored a nation like the United Provinces. The Dutch bred the finest seamen in the world, which turned the Republic's enormous merchant marine into one vast naval reserve. His present command boasted only twenty-seven regular warships, but they were supported by eleven more vessels of the East India Company's fleet and another thirty-six well-armed, well-found merchantmen.

Most of them were smaller than his own *Amelia*'s fifty-six guns, and all of them were built for the shallow waters of the North Sea and the Baltic. Other countries—like Spain—might build larger, more heavily armed ships. There were rumors that Charles Stuart had recently decided to lay down a ship which would mount over a hundred guns, although the current restiveness in England might disorder his plans. But no one built handier ones than the Dutch. Or put finer crews aboard them. And the Dutch Navy had the first officer corps of professional seamen in European history, as well.

Seventy-four ships. Cornelisz was right; they *did* make a goodly sight, and he allowed himself a moment of unalloyed pleasure as he surveyed it. But the moment was brief, and he turned back to de With with a frown.

"Tell me honestly, Cornelisz," he said, his voice half-buried in the sound of wind and wave. "What do you think?"

"About what?" The taller de With looked down his proud prow of a nose with an expression of artful innocence, and Tromp grimaced.

"You know perfectly well what," he growled, and waved a hand at the ships trailing along behind *Amelia*, including de With's own flagship, the *Brederode*. "This—all of this. You and I, Richelieu and Oquendo. And these 'Americans'!"

"I think we live in wondrous times," de With replied after a moment. "Beyond that, I don't begin to understand . . . and God hasn't gotten around to explaining it to me yet."

Tromp barked a laugh and reached out to slap de With on the biceps.

"Perhaps He's decided explaining doesn't do much good, given the way the lot of us have been squabbling over the things He specifically told us about in Holy Scripture," he suggested. "Maybe He thinks he can distract us from killing one another in His name if He gives us something so obscure we spend all our time puzzling about it instead of fighting about doctrine!"

De With considered the proposition, then shook his head.

"You could be right. And if that's what He's thinking, I suppose we have no choice but to accept it. For myself, I could wish He'd chosen to be just a bit less mysterious. Or confusing, at any rate."

"I can't argue with you there," Tromp murmured, and scratched the tip of his own equally proud but sharper nose while he frowned pensively. "Still, I suppose He expects us to do the best we can. So tell me what you think about the 'Americans.'"

"I think they're dangerous," de With said quietly, and there was no more humor in his voice. "I think they're probably the most dangerous thing to be introduced into the world since Jan Huss first twisted the pope's nose. The only thing I haven't been able to decide is who they're most dangerous to."

"You don't think the fact that they're a republic makes them our natural allies?" Tromp asked, and de With snorted.

"I don't believe in 'natural allies,'" he said. "If there were any such thing, Catholic France wouldn't have to bribe Protestant England into siding with us against Catholic Spain!"

"And Protestant Holland wouldn't be worried over the threat posed by its 'natural ally' Protestant Sweden, either," Tromp agreed. "Even so, wouldn't you say two republics have a certain . . . commonality of interest with one another? Especially when they're both surrounded by monarchies?"

"Not when the other one seems to be a *true* republic," de With said bluntly. Tromp looked around quickly, but no one else was in earshot, and de With smiled thinly at him. "From all I've been able to discover—which isn't much, granted—these 'Americans' seem to have very little use for *jonkers*. Or for princes. And this 'Congress' of theirs seems to be far more accountable to their citizens. Not to mention their bizarre notion of a 'universal franchise' and enough religious toleration to make a Remonstrant dizzy!" He shook his head. "I have a feeling our own government would find notions like that far more threatening than any monarchy."

"That sort of blunt spokenness can be risky," Tromp cautioned.

"Of course it can. But that doesn't mean I'm wrong, does it?" de With chuckled harshly. "Or was there another reason you were about to resign before they offered you this command?"

Tromp grimaced, but he didn't disagree. He couldn't. He and De With had known one another too long, and de With knew all about his own long-standing feud with Filips van Dorp.

Dorp was an imbecile. He was also more venal than most, and inept to the point of total ineffectualness. He'd demonstrated that convincingly enough to be dismissed from his post as lieutenant-admiral of Zeeland, but he was also the son of *jonker* Frederik van Dorp, one of the Sea-Beggar captains who'd won his own barony serving William the Silent. Which meant that even though Zeeland had gotten rid of Filips, the States of Holland had seen fit to make him Holland's lieutenant-admiral. It was a decision which had inevitably brought him and Tromp into bitter conflict. The Navy was too important to allow an idiot to ruin it through mismanagement, and the man's total inability to deal with the Dunkirker privateers only underscored his basic incompetence. Unfortunately, the States—and Prince Frederik Hendrik— had believed a nobleman would somehow exercise more natural authority than a man of humbler origins . . . like Maarten Tromp.

To be honest, things had always been that way. Personal alliances and patronage were the way of the world everywhere, Tromp supposed. Even in the Dutch republic, those noble families known collectively as the *ridderschap* dominated the top military and naval posts. And the situation had become even worse in the fifteen years since Prince Mauritz organized the downfall of Johan van Oldenbarnevelt to break the primacy of the States of Holland and reassert the House of Orange's control of the Republic.

"I still hadn't actually made up my mind to resign," he said after a moment, and de With snorted in splendid derision. "All right—all right!" Tromp admitted. "I was going to. There. Are you satisfied?"

"That you didn't? Of course I am. But, you know, it's all the Americans' fault that you changed your mind. Or, rather, that the stadtholder changed *his* mind about Dorp."

"It wasn't just the Americans," Tromp said a bit somberly. "Richelieu had a little something to do with it, too."

"I know. And that does tend to make one wonder where the advantage lies for him in getting rid of Dorp, doesn't it?"

Tromp made a wordless sound of agreement and folded his hands behind himself. He rocked up and down on the balls of his feet, eyes distant as he gazed once again—this time unseeingly— at the sails of his fleet. The fact that Richelieu had intervened so directly was, as Cornelisz had just intimated, enough to make anyone nervous. The only thing more certain about Richelieu than his brilliance was his deviousness. He always had at least three different motives for anything he did, and Tromp was far from happy knowing that it was he who had delivered the pages, stolen from one of the Americans' history books, that had prompted Frederik Hendrik to summarily demand Dorp's dismissal and Tromp's own appointment in his place.

The mere fact that those pages had described a "history" which hadn't happened yet—and which never would, now—was enough to make any good Calvinist uneasy. In his own thinking, Tromp was much closer to Arminianism's toleration of individual conscience than he ever allowed most people to realize. He found Simon Episcopius' argument that different perspectives on Scripture could only enhance the fullness and richness of Man's understanding of the Almighty convincing. Just as, privately, he thought the unyielding insistence on the doctrine of predestination of the strict Calvinists seemed to devalue and deny human freedom of will. But despite any secret religious liberalness he might entertain, this tinkering with the life he'd been "destined" to live before the Americans arrived to turn the entire world topsy-turvy still smacked of the supernatural . . . or something worse.

Yet what worried him more at the moment than theological questions was the fact that the American embassy to Amsterdam and the one from Richelieu carried such different warnings. Left to his own devices, his natural instinct would have been to pay close heed to anyone who disagreed with Richelieu. Unfortunately, he knew enough of this so-called "United States'" situation to recognize its desperation. Powerful as the protection of a king like Gustavus Adolphus might be, the new republic was surrounded by implacable, unyielding enemies. The threats it faced were at least as great as those the United Provinces had faced in their long war with Spain, but without the natural frontiers which had been

Holland's salvation. For all of the reputed wonders of their crafts-men, all the deadliness of their weapons and their other marvel-ous devices, the odds against the Americans' survival were high, even with Gustavus' protection.

Under those circumstances, anything they said must be consid-ered as carefully as if it had come from Richelieu himself. Tromp had never personally met any of the Americans, but he'd spoken to those who had, and even the most jaded of them had spoken glowingly of the beauty and brilliance of the Jewess who repre-sented them. Even the most intolerant of Counter-Remonstrants had been impressed by her, although, of course, as a Jew, anything she said was automatically suspect in their eyes.

Tromp himself was unconcerned by her origins or religious beliefs, but his awareness of how the multitude of threats her new coun-try faced must shape her message was something else. And yet . . .

He shook his head impatiently. If only they had more infor-mation! The pages Richelieu had sent with his ambassador offered a frustratingly incomplete glimpse of the future which would have been. The paper on which they were printed, and the printing itself, not to mention the breathtakingly lifelike illustrations, had been proof enough of their authenticity. No printer of this time and place could possibly have produced them, or the strange English in which they were written. No doubt that was the exact reason Richelieu had sent them rather than a transcript. But there were less than a dozen sheets of paper, which seemed all too frail a basis upon which to decide the course of a nation's foreign policy, even if they had come from three and a half centuries in the future.

"It wasn't just the Americans' 'history,' you know," he muttered to de With. "Oh—" he looked up at the taller man "—that was what caused the stadtholder and the States General to sack Dorp and give me the command. And I'm none too happy, just between us, to know I've been given my job on the basis of how well I *would* have performed in battles that will never be fought now! But the decision to accept Richelieu's new anti-Habsburg alliance wasn't made solely on that basis."

"Of course it wasn't," de With acknowledged. "But I can't quite free myself of the suspicion that the pages he chose to send us served his purposes damnably well."

"Oh, come now, Cornelisz!" Tromp chuckled. "It would be expecting a bit much of any man—much less Richelieu—for him to have sent us anything that *wouldn't* have served his purposes!"

"I know. I know. I'm just . . . uneasy. Especially with the Americans, who obviously had the entire book he sent us pages from, telling us not to trust him."

"We hardly needed them to warn us about that," Tromp said dryly. "And according to Frederik Hendrik, nothing in the books they showed his representatives disagreed with the pages Richelieu had sent."

"The prince saw their complete history books?" De With's bold eyebrows rose in surprise.

"Not their 'complete' history. From all accounts, they could fill a couple of galleons with their books, without half trying. But they did allow us to examine a short history of the Republic." De With was staring at him, and Tromp shrugged irritably. "I don't know what it said. No one told me. And, frankly, I'd sooner not know. But the key point is that nothing in it contradicted the information from Richelieu."

"Did they realize we had anything to check it against, I wonder?" de With murmured thoughtfully, and Tromp shrugged again.

"I can assure you that *we* didn't tell them," he said even more dryly. "On the other hand, I'd be very surprised if they were such fools as not to suspect the possibility, at least."

"So both sides are busy giving us glimpses of the future—or, at least, *a* future—to convince us that they're right." De With laughed with very little humor. "Life was so much simpler when no one was trying to be quite so helpful to us!"

"I know what you mean." Tromp bounced on his toes a few more times, then shook his head. "Only a fool would believe that Richelieu would help anyone simply out of the kindness of his heart. In some ways, I actually prefer someone who thinks like that. At least we know he'll do whatever he decides is in his own best interests. And he was clever enough to make that very point to us, you know."

"He was?"

"Oh, he most certainly was!" Tromp chuckled. "And he pointed out that the Americans will do the same—that they have no choice but to do the same, any more than our own Republic, if they intend to survive."

"Are you in favor of their surviving?" de With asked quietly.

"I don't know," Tromp admitted, and pursed his lips thoughtfully. "There's much about them which I find admirable, even on the basis of the limited information I've been given. But Richelieu is right. Terrible as the war in Germany has already been, or as our own wars with Spain have been, the conflict this new United States will provoke will dwarf all of them. Unless it's crushed immediately, of course, and somehow I don't think that will be as easy as its enemies believe."

"Do they really believe that? Or is it simply that they need to believe it?" De With's expression was troubled. "If the reports about what the Americans managed to do at the Wartburg and the Alte Veste are accurate, then coupled with Gustavus' Swedes . . ."

His voice trailed off, and Tromp frowned.

"From all reports, the Habsburgs—both branches of them—are terrified of exactly that combination. But I think Richelieu's estimate is probably more accurate."

"Richelieu's?"

"Oh, he hasn't shared it with us in so many words," Tromp admitted. "But if he weren't convinced that the Americans can be dealt with, then I feel certain he'd be looking for some way to enmesh them in his coils, not urging us to reflect upon the danger they represent to us. He sees them as a threat, yes. As a very serious threat, in fact. But if he thought they were impossible to defeat, he would be seeking some sort of accommodation with them rather than looking to conclude alliances against them."

"So he *is* shoring up his defenses against them? And, of course, urging us to follow his example?"

"He is. And I wish I knew whether or not we should take his advice. One thing I'm certain of, though; the Swedes and the Americans won't go easily. What's already happened in Germany is nothing compared to what it will cost the emperor yet to crush this threat. And a war on that scale has a nasty habit of spilling over onto other people's territory. That's where the real danger to us lies, I think. We're not that far from Thuringia and Franconia, Cornelisz, and in the end, it's not just the Habsburgs who will be lining up to crush the Americans. Denmark, Spain, the Empire, even France. I won't be surprised to see the Poles and Russians getting involved! None of their 'neighbors' can stand the threat of all of their knowledge and marvels in the service of a new Swedish empire. And if they're truly as serious as they seem to be about building their style of republic, then they're a greater danger to Europe as a whole than even a Sweden which entirely dominates the Baltic and Northern Germany.

"So, much as I may distrust Richelieu, I understand his logic.

Best to go ahead and deal with the Spanish branch of the Habsburgs while we can. Remove at least one threat and protect our
backs before we find ourselves forced to deal with the multitude of new threats these Americans and their 'Ring of Fire'
are going to bring to us all. Besides—" he shrugged with a
chuckle, "—according to the history books, you and I 'already'
smashed Oquendo's fleet at The Downs in 1639. As a matter of
fact, Richelieu seems quite put out with Philip IV for moving early
this way. I don't know if Olivares' spies have been as good as
Richelieu's, but it seems apparent that *something's* gotten Philip
moving faster than he did in the future the Americans came from.
From what Huygens told me, it sounds as if Richelieu tried approaching the Spaniards with the notion of an anti-American
alliance only to discover that Philip prefers to seek a military victory
and impose terms on both us and the French in order to free his
own hands to deal with the Americans directly.

"So all we're really doing is moving The Downs up by five or
six years. And at least this time, as you say, Richelieu has managed to bribe the English into being on our side instead of standing
to one side and cheering for the papists!"

"Which papists?" de With asked. "Our noble French papist allies?
Or our mortal enemies, the servants of Satan Spanish papists?"

"I think we'd best settle for dealing with one set of enemies at
a time," Tromp told him. "And—"

De With never learned what Tromp had been about to say, for
a lookout's shout interrupted the lieutenant-admiral. Both men
looked up, listening to the report, and then, as one, stepped to
the rail and peered to the west. Landsmen's eyes might have
mistaken the slivers of white on the horizon for more of the
Channel's whitecaps, but Tromp and de With had spent too many
years at sea to make that mistake.

"And so it begins," de With said, so softly Tromp felt certain
he was speaking to himself.

"So it does," he responded anyway. "And whatever else, I'm glad
to see them."

"True enough," de With agreed.

The combined French and English squadrons numbered little
more than half as many ships as the Dutch fleet by itself, but if
their spies' reports were as accurate as usual, Oquendo was headed
to meet them with over a hundred Spanish and Portuguese vessels. It was a smaller fleet than the one Medina Sidonia had led

against England half a century before, but not by very much ... and Oquendo was no Medina Sidonia. He'd demonstrated that in 1621, at the end of the Twelve Years Truce with Holland, when he broke the Dutch blockade of the Channel ports. Even with the assistance of his allies, Tromp's combined force would have only the thinnest margin of superiority, and many of the Spanish vessels were larger and better armed than anything in his own fleet.

"I only hope they can carry their own weight when it comes down to the melee," de With murmured, still gazing at their allies' topsails.

"Well, I suppose we'll find out soon enough," Tromp replied. "One way or the other."

# Chapter 19

In very many ways, the officers gathered in *Santiago*'s great cabin were completely typical of their class. Hidalgos, one and all, with fiercely trimmed mustachios and beards, strong Spanish noses, and rich clothing, bright with embroidery and gems. They stood with that complete and total confidence, that arrogance, handed down from the conquistadors who had conquered empires and squeezed the gold of Mexico and the Andes into the coffers of Spain like Incan tears. They carried the legacy of Don John, the victor of Lepanto, of Gonzalvo de Cordoba, father of the invincible tercios, and of Cortes, the conqueror of Montezuma and Cuauhtemoc. Any trifling defeats they might have suffered along the way, like the minor mishap which had befallen Medina Sidonia and his Armada, were powerless to breach the armor of that assurance.

Don Antonio de Oquendo understood that. Their background was his, as well, after all. But he also understood that Spain could not afford that blind arrogance. Not any longer.

The waiting officers broke off their side conversations as he and the cardinal-infante entered the cabin, and there was more than a hint of wariness in some of the faces they turned toward him. Which was as it should be. The fragmentary glimpses of the future Oquendo had been granted in the books the duke of Olivares' spies had acquired left him with no illusions. Incomplete as that glimpse might have been, its message had been clear enough. More than anything else, it had been the hollow arrogance of hidalgos choosing to live in the glories of the past, rather than acknowledge the defeats of the present, which had doomed Spain to decline and impotence in that other future. And so he had made it his business to bring his officers ruthlessly to heel.

In that, if nothing else, he and the prince at his side were in full agreement. Oquendo was still not certain of Don Fernando's character as a whole. But even in the short time since he and the cardinal-infante had begun working together to shape the campaign they were about to launch, Don Antonio had been reassured by the young prince's attitude. Despite his youth—or perhaps, *because* of his youth—the king's younger brother seemed to understand that Spain's greatness had not been created by unthinking arrogance. However bold the long line of Castilian rulers had been who, over the centuries, carried through the *Reconquista* and the unification of Spain, they had been neither stupid nor prone to under-estimating their enemies.

As he surveyed his assembled officers, Oquendo knew how greatly his record of success at sea had helped him in breaking *their* stupidity, as well. Arrogant and contemptuous of their foes though they might be, even his subordinates recognized that for forty years the accursed Hollanders and English had humiliated and humbled proud Spain upon the waters of the world. Whatever triumphs the Crown's tercios might have attained on land, naval victories— especially beyond the confines of the Mediterranean—were few and far between, which meant his own accomplishments lent him a special aura when he . . . admonished them.

The severity of his habitually stern expression threatened to falter for just a moment as he recalled some of the councils of war in which he had accomplished that admonition. But he suppressed the smile as he made his way to the head of the waiting table, accompanied by Don Fernando.

"I see we're all here," he observed dryly as he and the cardinal-infante seated themselves in the waiting chairs. He waved for the others to find seats where they could. Despite the relatively generous dimensions of the great cabin, space was at a premium. There were far too few chairs to go around, and the silent assertions of precedence which raged as eye met eye until the seating had been apportioned reminded him of a cabin full of tomcats.

*Strange,* he reflected. *That's an image which would never have occurred to me before I read those pages from the Americans' books.*

He brushed the thought aside and straightened in his own chair as the officers—seated and standing, alike—settled once more about the table.

"I will not keep you long, gentlemen," he assured them, letting his gaze sweep the circle of their faces. "All of you know our purpose and our plans. This morning, Don Mateo—" a courteous gesture indicated Don Mateo de Montalva, captain of the *Princessa* "—spoke with an English merchant out of London. Her master confirms that Tromp and de With have indeed reestablished their blockade of Dunkirk and Ostend.

"They seem to be making no effort to find us. No doubt they feel confident that I will move promptly to break the blockade once more . . . at which point, they and their allies will fall upon us like wolves. Under the circumstances—" he smiled thinly, and something like the soft, satisfied snarl of a wolf pack, indeed, ran around the cabin "—I see no reason we should disappoint them."

"Your pardon, Don Antonio," one of his senior captains said respectfully, "but may we assume from your words that all continues to proceed as planned?"

"You may," Oquendo replied. A part of him wondered caustically exactly what else anyone might have been expected to conclude from what he'd just said. But he allowed no trace of the thought to touch his expression or his tone. After all, he'd worked hard to ensure that his subordinates would risk their precious dignities by asking precisely that sort of question if there was any doubt in their minds.

"There is no way to be absolutely certain that all will continue to unfold according to our plans, of course," he continued. "But at this point, it would appear God is being good to us. Now it becomes our part to ensure that we do not waste the opportunity He has granted us."

"Well, at least Don Antonio is prompt," Maarten Tromp observed wryly to Captain Mastenbroek.

He stood on his flagship's poop deck beside *Amelia*'s captain and gazed through a telescope at the approaching Spanish fleet. The telescope's brass barrel was heavy and awkward in his hands. He managed it anyway, with the ease of long practice, but even now a corner of his brain enviously recalled the "binoculars" the Americans had presented to Frederik Hendrik. (*Tried* to present, rather. The prince, mindful of the need to keep a certain distance from the Americans due to the exigencies of Dutch factionalism, had accepted them only through an intermediary.) Huygens had allowed him to examine the optical device at the same time the secretary had shown him the pages Richelieu had sent. The stunning visual clarity, featherlight weight, and exquisite craftsmanship of the binoculars had been convincing evidence of the marvels of which American artisans were capable.

Tromp's eye ached from staring through the glass, but he continued his examination until he was completely satisfied. The Spaniards were advancing boldly, their squadrons in line abreast. Their sail handling was no more than indifferent by Dutch standards, but their formation was better than his own ships were likely to maintain. That was impressive, but not really any less than he'd expected from Oquendo. And neatness of formation wasn't everything. In fact, it wasn't even close to everything.

"They look confident enough," Mastenbroek remarked, and Tromp snorted. The captain sounded downright complacent as he regarded the oncoming enemy fleet, like a lion debating which antelope he might dine upon. And well he might. That tidy alignment wasn't going to help the Spaniards much once Tromp's sea wolves got to grips with them!

He felt no need to waste precious time trying to pass any additional orders. Sending messengers by boat would have taken far too long, and time was the most precious commodity any naval commander could possess. Besides, all of his captains and crews, from Cornelisz down, knew precisely what they were supposed to do, and so he simply nodded to Mastenbroek.

"Indeed," he said. "They do look confident. I believe it's time we did something about that, Captain. Be good enough to get underway, if you please."

Mastenbroek nodded and turned to begin bellowing orders. In most navies, that would have been the task of the sailing master, not the ship's captain. But that was because most "navies" assigned command to men whose only trade was war—professional soldiers, rather than professional sailors. Such men might be extremely capable at fighting battles, but they had never acquired the expertise to actually manage a ship under sail. That was a task sufficiently difficult to require a lifetime's study in its own right, after all.

But the Dutch Navy was different. It, even more than the Army, was the real reason Holland had been able to win its freedom from Spain and keep it, and in the process, it had thrown up a new breed of naval officer. Men who were both professional warriors *and* professional seamen. Men like Captain Jan Mastenbroek, or Maartin Tromp himself.

Now men swarmed up the ratlines at Mastenbroek's orders. They scurried out along the yards to set more sail, and *Amelia* heeled slightly under the press of the additional canvas as she headed directly for the enemy.

The rest of the Dutch ships followed her promptly. Indeed, several of her consorts began to jockey for position, trying hard to steal the flagship's lead and reach the Spaniards first.

"We can't have that, Captain!" Tromp said, pointing at the sixty-gun *Dordrecht* as the other ship began to overtake and pass *Amelia*. Mastenbroek scowled at *Dordrecht* and snapped orders at his own crew, and additional canvas blossomed as *Amelia* set her topgallants and began to forge ahead once more.

Tromp nodded in satisfaction. *Dordrecht*'s captain was just as eager as he was to get to grips with the enemy. His confidence boded well, and Tromp was delighted to see it, but that didn't mean he was prepared to allow *Dordrecht* to win the race. The lieutenant-admiral wasn't blind to the irony inherent in otherwise rational men racing to see which of them could expose themselves to hostile cannon fire first, yet it was that eagerness, that impetuous drive to fling themselves bodily upon their foe, which made the Dutch so dangerous at sea. Tromp could recognize and admire the discipline with which Oquendo's ships held their formation even as the Allies sailed down upon them, but time and again the men of the United Provinces had demonstrated that discipline alone was not enough.

No formation, however disciplined, could be maintained against the savage, unrelenting onslaught that was Holland's stock in trade. Supremely confident in the quality and experience of his captains and crews, Tromp intended to bring on a general melee as quickly as possible. It was the sort of fight at which the Dutch were best, closing in on their more massive Spanish opponents in twos and threes in brutal, close-range hammering matches. Not close enough to let the Spanish board and use their traditional advantages in manpower in hand-to-hand combat. No, Tromp and his captains would take a page from Lord Effingham's book. They would pound the Spaniards with artillery fire, as Effingham had, but their guns were far heavier than anything Queen Elizabeth's navy had been able to bring to bear against Medina Sidonia. And so, where Effingham had been forced to hit and run, the Dutch would hit and stand, smashing away until *this* armada was destroyed out-right.

Tromp had discussed his plans, not just with de With and his own captains, but with the commanders of their French and English allies, as well. The compte de Martignac, the French admiral, had looked a bit dubious, but Tromp had expected that. And truth to tell, that was the real reason he'd organized the fleet as he had. The Dutch would lead the attack, charging down upon the Spanish fleet which had been obliging enough to present itself from leeward, while the French and English followed in their wakes. Officially, that would permit his allies to bring their weight to bear most advantageously once they had seen how the action was developing. In fact, he was less than completely confident of their stomach for the sort of brutal, short-range action he intended to bring on. If they were going to hesitate to engage, he wanted them behind him rather than in front.

He was probably doing them an injustice by doubting their determination in the first place, of course. Sir John Tobias, the English commander, obviously would have preferred to be some-place else. He'd been subdued, almost distant, in his two private meetings with Tromp. But the lieutenant-admiral suspected that any reluctance on Tobias' part reflected his monarch's prejudice against the Dutch rather than any lack of courage.

The range dropped steadily but scarcely quickly. Even under optimum conditions, a ship did well to make good a speed as high as eight knots. Under present sea and wind conditions, the Allied fleet was able to close with the Spaniards at no more than three or four, and the approach seemed to take forever. *Amelia*, at the head of the jostling, elbowing Dutch as they jockeyed for posi-tion in their efforts to reach the enemy first, had already entered the theoretical maximum range of the Spaniards' guns. But what-ever a cannon might be capable of ashore, no naval gunner—and especially no *Spanish* naval gunner—was going to hit a target from the deck of a moving ship at two thousand yards. Besides, the crushing moral effect of the first, carefully aimed broadsides was too precious to fritter away at anything beyond point-blank range . . . and point-blank range was no more than a tenth of maximum.

With *Amelia* closing at perhaps a hundred yards a minute, she would require over a quarter-hour to reach point-blank range from the closest enemy ship. That slow, steady approach to carnage was always the hardest part for Maarten Tromp. He'd experienced it too often, and memory and his active, acute imagination replayed every one of those other battles, all the sights and sounds and horror, as his ship carried him inexorably into their midst once again. But those memories and imaginings, like the experiences which spawned them, were something Tromp had learned to deal with long ago, and he turned his thoughts resolutely away from them.

He looked astern, instead, and nodded in satisfaction. A sizable gap had opened between his own ships and his allies, but that was only to be expected. The French and English squadrons didn't share his own captains' instinctive awareness of the way his mind worked, and they'd been a bit slower off the mark when he bore down upon Oquendo. Coupled with their starting positions, farthest up to windward of any of the Allied squadrons, that meant they were at least forty or fifty minutes behind *Amelia*. But they were working hard to catch up, and Tobias was actually taking the lead away from the French. The Englishman obviously intended to be in the thick of things after all, whether he liked Dutchmen or not!

Tromp grinned at the thought, but then the dull thud of cannon fire brought his attention back to business. He turned to look forward once again, and found himself torn between a scowl and a laugh as he realized *Dordrecht* had somehow stolen the advantage from *Amelia* after all. The other ship was shortening sail now, slowing her speed once more but reducing vulnerable target area aloft, even as she exchanged fire with the lead Spaniard. He could hear her crew cheering in the intervals between the crashing discharges.

Captain Mastenbroek was bellowing orders of his own, and the courses on main and fore disappeared as if by magic, brailed up to the yards as *Amelia*, like *Dordrecht*, stripped down to her topsails. Her speed dropped, and the deck vibrated and quivered, shivering under Tromp's feet like a living creature, as the guns ran out in a savage squeal of wooden gun trucks.

"There!" he shouted, pitching his voice to cut through the bedlam, and Mastenbroek turned to look at him. "There!" the lieutenant-admiral shouted again, pointing across the water at a galleon in the middle of the Spaniards' second squadron. "That's your target, Captain!"

Mastenbroek followed the direction of his hand, then grinned savagely as he recognized the standard of the king of Spain flying at the head of the galleon's mainmast. He nodded in understanding, and turned back to his helmsman, gesturing and pointing himself. Tromp watched him for a moment, then grunted in satisfaction as *Amelia* altered course slightly to bear directly down on Oquendo's flagship.

More cannon fire thundered and bellowed as the *Breda* followed *Dordrecht* into the teeth of the Spanish squadrons, and then—finally—it was *Amelia*'s turn.

The flagship had closed to less than two hundred yards from *Santiago*. The wooden deck planking seemed to leap up and hit the soles of Tromp's shoes like a hammer as her own guns roared. *Amelia* carried twenty-two twenty-four-pounder cannon on her lowest deck, with twenty-four twelve-pounders on the upper gundeck, and her starboard side vanished in a cloud of spurting flame and choking powder smoke. Before the rising smoke could obscure his vision, Tromp saw the heavy roundshot smashing into *Santiago*'s side. At such a short range, the twenty-four-pounders' shot hammered straight through even the Spanish ship's massive timbers. The jagged holes in *Santiago*'s outer planking looked deceptively small, but Tromp's experienced mind pictured the horror and carnage on the Spaniard's packed gundeck as the five-and-a-half-inch balls erupted into the gun crews amid a spreading hail of lethal splinters . . . if hull fragments which might be six feet long and as thick as a man's wrist could be called by a name as innocuous as "splinters." Then the blinding, lung-choking billow of powder smoke blotted away the sight and went rolling downwind towards the target of *Amelia*'s rage.

The obscuring cloud seemed to lift suddenly, flashing with a deadly fury, as *Santiago*'s broadside hurled back defiance. *Amelia* shuddered and bucked as Spanish roundshot blasted into her, but *Santiago*'s gunners were less experienced than their Dutch opponents, and their fire was less accurate. No more than half a dozen of the thirty or forty balls they fired managed to hit *Amelia,* even at such short range. Most of the misses went high, whimpering and wailing overhead like damned souls, lost and terrified in the smoke. One of them punched through the lateen mizzen sail above Tromp's head with the sudden slapping sound of a fist, others cut away rigging like an ax through spiderwebs, and one carved a divot out of the starboard bulwark barely twenty feet from him. A cloud of splinters hummed across the upper deck, and a gunner at one of the swivel-mounted serpentines atop the rail shrieked and

stumbled back, clutching his face in both hands. The butt end of
a splinter thicker than one of his own thumbs protruded between
his fingers, and then he slumped to the deck. His hands slipped
from his face as he thudded to the planks, the jagged splinter
protruding from his ruined eye socket.

More screams came from underfoot as the Spanish roundshot
which had found their mark crashed into *Amelia*'s side. The shrieks
rose like the Devil's own chorus, but Tromp's was an experienced
ear. Terrible as the sounds were, they were far less terrible than
they might have been, and he knew *Amelia*'s fire had hurt *Santiago*
far more than she had been injured herself.

Mastenbroek knew it, too. The flagship's captain strode back and
forth across his deck, waving his hat to encourage his crew even
as he shouted the orders that edged *Amelia* still closer to her target.
The Dutch ship turned on her heel, ranging up directly alongside
the Spanish flagship to run parallel at a range of barely a hundred yards. Her port broadside belched fresh fury, and *Santiago*
fired back, barely visible even at this range, a poorly seen ghost
in the rolling bank of gun smoke. Tromp waved his own hat, adding his encouragement to Mastenbroek's while the gun crews bent
to their pieces like damned souls laboring in the flames and stench
of Hell itself.

The firing became increasingly ragged on both sides. The precisely coordinated, concentrated blows of the initial broadsides gave
way to a fierce pounding match, crews firing independently, as
quickly as they could serve their guns. The concussions of scores
of guns—hundreds of them, as more and more of Tromp's fleet
scrambled into action—hammered the ear like mallets, and in the
fleeting intervals between them, the lieutenant-admiral could hear
the cheers—and screams—from other ships.

Two more Dutch ships, *Joshua* and *Halve Maan*, came charging in to support Amelia against *Santiago*. The Spanish *Argonauta*
intercepted *Joshua*, and the two of them squared off in a furious
duel of their own, but *Halve Maan* took station just astern of
Amelia and began hammering away at *Santiago*'s starboard quarter.
The Spaniard fired back at both her foes with the courage and
determination only to be expected of Oquendo's flagship, but even
that stouthearted ship found herself in increasingly desperate straits
as the two Dutchmen pounded her.

Tromp dragged his concentration away from *Santiago* by sheer
force of will and made himself look up at the sun. It seemed

incredible, but the two fleets had already been engaged for the better part of an hour, and their units had become hopelessly intermingled, smashing away at one another as they stood literally yardarm-to-yardarm. *Santiago* was barely twenty yards clear of Amelia's side now, and *still* the guns bellowed their hate back and forth.

He shook himself like a drunken man and then turned to stare up to windward, searching for his allies. The rolling pall of smoke to port was all but impenetrable, but looking to starboard he could see both the French and English squadrons, still out of action but closing rapidly now. The French seemed to have fallen a bit further astern of the English, but they were making up for it now, crowding on sail with an almost Dutch-like eagerness. Indeed, he was surprised and more impressed than he might have cared to admit by the way the two squadrons were massing together. They might not yet have come into action, but that was about to change, and when they hit it would be as a concentrated fist, punching into the center of the Spanish formation almost directly behind *Amelia*.

He nodded in satisfaction and turned back to the battle, squinting as he peered through the smoke, trying to make out details even though an admiral of his experience knew how futile the effort must be. As always in a sea action, the universe of each combatant shrank to the world of his own ship, or perhaps two or three more on either side. It was literally impossible to see any more than that in a fight this close and furious, but he could just barely make out de With's *Brederode*, locked in a brutal close-ranged hammering match with the *San Nicolas*. *Brederode* seemed to be beating down the Spaniard's fire, but she'd lost her own mainmast in the process. Other ships on both sides had taken damage aloft, as well. Indeed, it seemed to Tromp—although he couldn't be positive, under the circumstances—that even more than usual of the Spanish fire had gone high. *Amelia*'s own spars had taken relatively little damage, although strands of severed rigging blew out in the smoke and her topsails seemed to be almost more hole than canvas, but *Brederode* was far from the only Dutchman to have lost a mast.

Yet whatever rigging damage Tromp's ships might have suffered, the Spaniards were in far worse condition. While their fire was going high, punching through canvas and severing cordage, the Dutch guns were lacerating their hulls and massacring their crews. The Dutch ships might be becoming progressively less manageable, but that wasn't going to be enough to save Oquendo's fleet. Here and there an individual Dutchman, especially among the armed merchantmen, was hard pressed, but the tide of battle was setting strongly in Tromp's favor. He could feel it, sense the pulse and rhythm, the steady decline in the weight of Spanish fire as his own gunners beat it down. Frankly, he was amazed at the way the Spaniards continued to stand and fight; under similar conditions in other fights Oquendo's fleet would have been shedding entire handfuls of ships by now. But not today. Today, they stood to their guns, pounding back with a determination that fully matched the Dutchmen's own.

Which was going to make their ultimate defeat even more crushing, Tromp realized. His fleet might have been brutally hammered, but the Spanish had taken even more damage, and even those which might have escaped from his own lamed ships were too damaged themselves to escape the French and English now beginning to thrust vengefully into the fringes of the battle.

*Santiago*'s fire finally began to falter, and he peered at her. *Amelia*'s deck was littered with bodies, screaming wounded, severed limbs, broken cordage, and huge bloodstains. Her bulwarks were holed and feathered with splinters where enemy roundshot had chewed pieces from them, and he heard the doleful clank of the pumps in the fleeting instants between gunshots. But as the smoke thinned slightly he could see that the Spanish flagship was in a far worse state. Her starboard side seemed to have been beaten in with hammers—indeed, it was so badly damaged that three of her upper gundeck ports had been smashed into a single, gaping wound—and he could see thick, glistening tendrils of blood seeping from her scuppers, as if the ship herself was leaking away her life. Bodies were heaped at the feet of her masts, heaved there by the surviving members of her crew in order to clear the recoil of her deck guns, and at least half a dozen of those guns had been dismounted by *Amelia*'s fire. Tromp could make out officers moving amidst the carnage and confusion, fighting to impose some order upon it, and one officer—he rather thought it was Oquendo himself—clung to the shattered poop deck rail, supporting himself while blood streamed steadily down one of his legs.

It was obvious to Tromp that even that stoutly fought ship had no option but to surrender. It might take a little longer, cost a few more Spanish lives, but *Santiago* was too badly wounded to run and her crew was too savagely maimed to continue the fight.

He turned away from her once more, listening to the howling bedlam of the battle, and looked back at *Brederode* as *Revenge*, Tobias' flagship, altered course very slightly in order to cross astern of de With. Obviously, Tobias intended to rake *San Nicolas* as he crossed her stern, then range up on the Spaniard's disengaged side and smash the already crippled ship into submission.

The Englishman's bowsprit was no more than sixty or seventy feet clear of *Brederode's* high, ornate poop as *Revenge* started across her wake . . .

And then Maarten Harpentzoon van Tromp's face went bone-white under the soot and grime of powder smoke coating it, as the English flagship poured a deadly broadside through *Brederode's* stern.

For perhaps two heartbeats, Tromp told himself it had to be an accident. A colossal blunder. But no "accident" would have been that accurate. The Englishman's guns fired two by two, upper and lower deck together, carefully aimed, and the impact of those deadly shots turned *Brederode's* stern windows into the gaping cavern mouth of an abattoir.

De With's flagship was over four hundred yards from *Amelia*, but even at that range Tromp could hear the English roundshot hammering home, crashing the full length of her hull in maiming, mangling fury. An entire twenty-four pounder slammed forward, flung two-thirds of the way out its port as a screaming roundshot dismounted it and shattered its carriage. Even as Tromp realized in horror that the attack was deliberate, *Brederode's* foremast toppled like a weary tree. It pitched over the side while the ship wallowed in agony, and Tromp heard English voices baying in triumph.

*The Americans were right,* a small, numb corner of his brain told him. *Richelieu's offer was too good to be true.*

He spun around as fresh, concentrated broadsides thundered, and his belly knotted as more of his "allies" poured fire into his own ships. The French flagship surged past *Dordrecht*, firing as she went, and *Dordrecht* staggered. Her already damaged mizzen mast toppled into the smoke, splinters flew from her "disengaged" side, and she began to fall away to leeward as the French fire killed her helmsman and smashed her wheel.

From triumph to despair. The transformation required no more than a minute—two, at the most. That was how long it took Maarten Tromp to realize that the Dutch Navy had just been destroyed. It might take some time still to accomplish that, but the outcome was inevitable, and he knew it. Everywhere he looked, as far as he could see through the smoke and spray and splinters, French and English warships vomited flame and fury as their fresh, carefully aimed broadsides crashed into his weary, already damaged vessels. And he understood now why the Spanish fire had been so "badly aimed." With their rigging mangled and crippled by Oquendo's gunners, his ships would be unable to outrun their undamaged "allies."

Fresh cheers went up, this time from the Spaniards' bloodsoaked decks as they saw the trap they had paid so much in life and limb to bait spring. And then Tromp flinched in shocked disbelief as *Revenge*'s fire found *Brederode*'s magazine and de With's flagship vanished in a single, terrible explosion.

The explosion, and the sudden blow of realizing his friend and *Brederode*'s entire crew had just died, shocked Tromp out of his immobility. He shook himself savagely and spun away from the horrible vision while broken fragments of *Brederode*'s hull were still rising in lazy arcs above her fireball death. Mastenbroek stood no more than fifteen feet from him, but *Amelia*'s captain was frozen, mesmerized by the spectacle of *Brederode*'s destruction. He didn't seem to hear the lieutenant-admiral when Tromp shouted at him, didn't even blink until Tromp seized him and shook him brutally.

"Get under way!" Tromp barked.

Mastenbroek shook his head, fighting his way up out of his own confusion.

"Make more sail—now!" Tromp commanded harshly. Mastenbroek stared at him for a moment longer, and Tromp flung out an arm, sweeping it in an arc which indicated the ruin encompassing their fleet. "All we can do is try to run for it," he grated. "So make sail, Captain! Make sail *now!*"

# Chapter 20

"And so, while the final reports have yet to come in, I have no doubt what they will tell us." Armand Demerville, comte de Martignac, smiled thinly at Don Antonio Oquendo. "So far, over sixty of the enemy have been definitely accounted for."

"I see." Oquendo sat on *Santiago*'s poop deck in the only one of his chairs to have survived the action intact. Well, not entirely intact, he reminded himself, his face taut with pain. Its cushioned leather back was split in three places, and one arm had been entirely removed. Which made it an appropriate seat for him at the moment, since the surgeons seemed so eager to amputate his own left leg at the knee.

Of course, that decision would be his.

It was hard to believe, even now, that they had truly gotten away with it, he thought. The trap had required that the Hollanders suspect nothing until the moment it actually sprang, and that had been impossible on the face of it. Even assuming that none of the French or English officers had been in the pay of the Dutch—or Swedes—there were the crews to consider. However bloodthirsty the threats intended to keep them from letting the secret slip, they would have failed. No navy could keep its men from drunkenness once they went ashore, and all it would have required was a single drink-addled seaman—or a sober one, boasting to a whore—to alert the Dutch beforehand.

But Richelieu had had an answer for that, as well. "Sealed orders," he'd called them—another notion borrowed from the future. No one in the Franco-English force, except for the fleet commanders themselves and one or two of their most senior, most trusted captains, had known a thing about the true plan. All the others had discovered what was going to happen only when Oquendo's ships actually came into sight and they opened their sealed orders as they had been instructed to do when that moment came.

And so it had worked, he told himself grimly . . . however much it had cost.

"And your own losses?" he asked Martignac after a moment.

"None," the Frenchman assured him, then made a small throwing-away gesture with one hand. "Oh, we've lost a few dozen men, but nothing of significance."

"Would that we could say the same," Oquendo said flatly, and even Martignac had the grace to look briefly abashed.

All of Oquendo's ships had survived the battle, but five of them were so savagely damaged that he had already ordered them abandoned and burned, and he would be extremely surprised to discover that even a dozen of the others remained fit for further action. When the Dutch had realized what was happening, many had been too damaged—or too enraged—to even attempt to disengage. Instead, they'd set their teeth in their foes' throats like wounded wolves and continued to hammer their enemies until they were literally overwhelmed. Their casualties had been horrendous . . . and Oquendo's were little better.

*The Hollanders and we have paid a bitter price for your master's plans, my friend,* he told Martignac silently from behind his expressionless mask. The Frenchman's ship had taken no more than a half dozen hits as he and his English allies crushed the Dutch from behind, and his clean clothing and perfect grooming stood out against the wreckage and bodies littering *Santiago's* battered decks like some alien creature from an undamaged world. *I hope it was worth it.*

Maarten van Tromp slumped in the chair at the head of the table. Darkness pressed close and hard on the shattered glass of the cabin windows, but the lamplight was more than sufficient to show the smoke stains on the overhead deck beams . . . and the wide, dried bloodstain under his chair.

Five other men sat with him, their faces gray and stunned, overwhelmed by the disaster which had engulfed them. They were the captains of every ship he knew—so far, at least—to have escaped Richelieu's trap. Mastenbroek wasn't one of them; *Amelia*'s captain had been turned into so much mangled meat by an eighteen-pound shot as Tromp's flagship clawed her way free of the crippled Spaniards, and Tromp had taken command in Mastenbroek's place with something very like gratitude. Desperate as *Amelia*'s predicament had been, grappling with cutting her way out of it had been almost a relief from thinking about the catastrophe which had devastated his fleet.

Now he could no longer avoid those thoughts, and his jaw clenched as his memory replayed *Brederode*'s apocalyptic end.

He lifted his head to survey the other five men at the table. Five ships—six, counting *Amelia*—out of seventy-four. It was possible, even probable, that there were at least a few other escapees, but there couldn't have been many of them. He supposed it would be called the Battle of Dunkirk, if it mattered. By any name, it was the most crushing defeat Holland had ever suffered at sea—and with the destruction of the fleet, the United Provinces' coasts lay naked before the threat of Spain. The ring of fortresses guarding the southern border could be outflanked any time the Spanish wished. And . . .

With the treachery of England and France—especially France—there would be nothing to stand in Philip IV's path. For decades, whenever the Spanish army had pressed the Dutch too hard, the intervention of the French forces perched on the borders of the Spanish Netherlands had relieved the pressure. Even when the French had not intervened, the simple threat of intervention had been enough to tie down a large portion of the Spaniards' forces.

"Why?" he heard one of his officers croak softly. "Why did they *do* it? Insane."

Tromp did not answer aloud, because he was still chewing on the problem in his own mind.

The motives of the English seemed clear enough, in retrospect. King Charles' desperate need for money to keep control over England with mercenary troops was probably enough in itself to explain it. Money which, Tromp was quite certain, had been quietly emptied out of French and Spanish coffers. But there was more, now that he thought about it. In fact, in many ways the English king's treachery would probably increase his popularity with his own subjects.

Certainly with English seamen and merchants! The Dutch had

often been their greatest commercial rivals. And Tromp was well aware that Englishmen, especially seamen and merchants, were still bitterly angry over the Amboina Massacre of 1623, when the Dutch East India Company had tortured and murdered thirteen English merchants in the Spice Islands.

It was the *French* role in the betrayal which was so puzzling. Religious affinity be damned. For decades, Catholic France had opposed the ambitions of Catholic Spain and Austria—supporting Protestants against them, more often than not—because the Bourbon dynasty which had ruled France since 1589 was far more concerned about the threat posed by the Habsburg dynasty than they were over problems of Christian doctrine. As had been the Valois dynasty before them.

Now . . .

"What was Richelieu's *thinking*?" muttered the same officer. "It's crazy!"

On the surface, the man was quite correct. If the Spanish could reconquer the United Provinces . . .

Then France—already faced with a Habsburg threat from Spain itself, not to mention the threat which the Spanish possessions in Italy posed to French interests there—would be faced as well with a Spanish Netherlands on their northeastern frontier which had grown far mightier. The population and resources of the *entire* Low Countries, reunited under the Spanish crown, would truly be something for the French to fear.

Tromp reviewed in his mind the secondhand reports he'd gotten of the warnings the American delegation in The Hague had tried to pass on to Dutch officialdom. With hindsight, he now realized that the reports he'd been given had undoubtedly been distorted by the prejudices and preconceptions of the officials who had received them directly. And he felt a moment's anguish that Frederik Hendrik had chosen not to listen to those warnings in person. The prince himself, for all his canniness, would have been misled by those same self-satisfied official distortions.

*Damn all fat burghers, anyway! And damn—twice over!—all religious fanatics. Where is your "Predestination" now, O ye sectarians?*

Despite the distortions and the fragmentary nature of what he had been told, Tromp was now almost sure he could see the French cardinal's strategy. Enough of it, at least.

"We were not Richelieu's true target," he said grimly to the officers assembled around the table. "We were just in the way—a sacrifice to obtain the free hand he wanted elsewhere."

His mental chuckle was harsh. *You were right, Cornelisz. The Americans were dangerous. We simply didn't recognize how. And we should have. If anyone should have remembered how twisty Richelieu's scheming mind truly is, it should have been us.*

The same officer who had muttered about Richelieu's sanity stared at him. Tromp tried to remember his name, but couldn't. One of the newer and younger officers of his fleet, recently promoted and in command of a ship for the first time.

But Tromp had seen the condition of the man's ship for himself. He was satisfied that whatever the officer might lack in the way of strategic acumen, he did not lack courage. So, despite the effort not to snarl, he forced himself to provide a calm explanation.

"It's those cursed American history books everyone's been grabbing, Captain . . . ah . . ."

"Cuyp, sir. Emanuel Cuyp."

"Captain Cuyp." Tromp drew a deep breath, which, exhaled, became something like a laugh. Or, maybe, a crow's caw. "History! Now everyone thinks they can determine the future—except, of course, they immediately try to change that history to their own satisfaction. And, in the doing, transform cause into effect and effect into cause. 'Insane,' as you say—but on a much deeper level than mere statecraft."

From the blank look on his face, Cuyp obviously still did not understand. Tromp tried again.

"I'm quite certain that Richelieu is thinking two steps ahead of everyone else, Captain. He will set everyone to war here in Europe, accepting whatever short-term losses he must, in order to free his hands to seize the rest of the world. As much of it, at least, as he can. North America for a certainty."

One of the other captains grimaced. Hans Gerritsz, that was, older and more experienced than Cuyp. "That's quite a gamble, sir. It won't do the French much good to have their hands on a few overseas settlements if they lose half of France itself. Or all of it."

Tromp shook his head. "There's no real chance of that, Hans. Not for many years, at least. Think about it. Does a fresh-fed lion attack the keeper of the menagerie? Or does he go into a corner of his cage to sleep and digest his meal? Especially if it was a *big* meal."

Gerritsz considered those words for a moment. Then, nodded. "I see your point. Richelieu is counting on the Spanish being pre-occupied in the Low Countries." He grunted, scowling. "And not a bad guess! It's not as if we had our fleet when we *began* our rebellion against Spain. Who is to say we can't resume it?"

A little growl went around the table. Despite the darkness of the moment, Tromp felt his spirits lifting at the sound.

"True enough. The English, of course, will be preoccupied with their own affairs for the next few years. And by handing the Habsburgs such a triumph—not to mention removing from the board of play the one fleet which might have come to Gustavus' aid in the Baltic—Richelieu has almost guaranteed the eruption of a new major war between the Habsburgs and Gustavus Adol-phus. A war, mind you, which will be fought on Habsburg or Swedish soil—not French."

*Not unless that foul churchman has misgauged Gustavus Adolphus. Or—which might be even worse for him—the Swede's American allies.* But Tromp left the words unspoken. In his heart, he could hope that the same Americans whose warnings had been unheeded could bloody the cardinal. But, for the moment, that was simply a hope grounded on not much of anything. He, Tromp, had immediate responsibilities—and pressing decisions of his own to make. *Now.*

He drew a deep breath and forced himself to consider the grim implications of his position. There was no point even contemplating a return to Holland, not with Oquendo, Tobias, and Martignac between him and Amsterdam. He might sneak past them, but it was . . . unlikely, to say the very least. All of his ships were dam-aged, three of them severely indeed. If he was sighted and inter-cepted at all, he would lose at least those three, and probably all six.

No. Returning home was out of the question. He could only hope that there had indeed been other escapees and that one of them might manage to reach The Hague or Amsterdam in time to give Frederik Hendrik and the States General at least a little warning before the Spanish tempest burst upon them. For himself . . .

"We'll make for Recife," he said. One of the other captains flinched. The others only looked at him.

"We'll make for Recife," he repeated. "It's the closest base we can hope to reach, and the West India Company will have at least a few ships to reinforce us. And we have to warn them before the Spaniards launch a fresh attack on them, too."

"What about Batavia?" Hjalmar van Holst asked.

He had been the officer who flinched, and Tromp snorted softly in understanding. Holst's family had immigrated to Zeeland from Denmark three generations ago. He looked the part—tall, thick-shouldered and powerful, like some shaggy, blond bear—and he, his father, and all three of his brothers held large blocks of stock in the *East* India Company.

But the fact that the captain of the *Wappen van Rotterdam* had a huge financial stake in what happened to Holland's Far East empire didn't rob his question of its legitimate point.

"Batavia? In the condition *our* ships are in?" All the officers at the table grimaced, van Holst no less than the others. Tromp shook his head firmly. "We need somewhere to make repairs. I see no real hope that our ships, as badly damaged as they all are, could circumnavigate half the globe. We'll have no easy time of it just getting across the Atlantic—especially with the hurricane season upon us."

Having made his point, Tromp decided to relent a bit. "We have to make certain Governor-General Brouwer is warned, as well," Tromp acknowledged. "I think it's almost certain that at least a few of our merchantmen will get through with the news, though. And in the meantime—I *need* your ship, Hjalmar. We're going to be hard pressed enough to hold on in Brazil and the Caribbean as it is."

Holst looked for a moment as if he wanted to object. But then he subsided in his chair, and if the bear's nod was angry and exhausted, it also carried true agreement.

"We'll send someone from Recife, just to be sure," Tromp reassured him. "But to be perfectly honest, Hjalmar, I think they'll be too busy closer to home to worry about Batavia or the Indies anytime soon."

Fresh gloom seemed to descend upon the cabin as his words reminded every man in the cabin once again of Holland's nakedness before the Spanish scourge.

"In the meantime," Tromp told them levelly, meeting their eyes unflinchingly across the table, "it is our duty to rally what we can. It may not be much, but at the very least we must hold the empire. As long as we do, neither Philip nor that bastard Richelieu can afford to simply ignore us."

"Perhaps not," Klaus Oversteegen, captain of the *Utrecht*, agreed with gallows humor. "But I suspect we're going to spend more time losing sleep over them than they are over us!"

"You may be right," Tromp agreed, and smiled thinly. "But if they *do* ignore us, I intend to make them regret it. We'll send out the word for every ship which can to rally to Recife. We ought to have at least the strength to hold the Spanish at bay while we gather our strength."

"The Spanish, perhaps," Holst agreed. "But what of the English and French?"

"Unless I'm much mistaken," Tromp replied, "Charles of England is going to be too busy concentrating on his arrests and executions of men who haven't yet done anything to spend much time concerning himself about us. And as for Richelieu . . ."

He smiled thinly. "All of his spiderweb plans depend on one other assumption: that his Spanish and English allies—Danish too, be sure of it—can fend off Gustavus Adolphus for him. The Swede, and his American mechanical wizards. But what if they *can't?*"

Tromp shrugged. "We will do what we must. For the rest, I suspect everyone in the world is about to discover that predestination is a province restricted to God Himself alone. History may record that we were not the only ones who failed to listen to warnings."

# Chapter 21

When Melissa entered the suite of rooms in St. Thomas' Tower, Rita and Tom Simpson trailing behind her, she saw Gayle Mason and Darryl McCarthy crouched over the lid of the trunk where the radio equipment was kept hidden except when it was in use. Night had fallen and the lighting provided by the tapers was too poor to see exactly what they were doing, but Melissa was quite sure they were in the process of extracting the radio. Gayle and Darryl would have heard the sound of the escort accompanying Melissa and the Simpsons back to the Tower of London—the more so since, this time, the escort had been much larger than usual. They'd have assumed that Melissa would want to send off a radio message reporting on today's meeting with the earl of Strafford.

"Don't bother," she said. "We're going to have to wait as long as we can tonight. We may not be able to send a radio message at all."

Feeling all of her years, Melissa moved over to the window overlooking the moat and the Thames beyond. That was the window they normally used to set up the antenna. Gazing down, she saw that there were English troops patrolling the wharf. Half a dozen, that she could see in the moonlight, with at least one officer on horseback overseeing them.

Not Yeoman Warders, either. Melissa wasn't positive, but she thought this was a detachment from the new mercenary companies whose soldiers she and the Simpsons had seen patrolling London on their way to Whitehall Palace and back.

She'd expected to see them. Normally, at night, the English did not bother patrolling the wharf. Nor did she think that Strafford had any particular suspicions concerning the United States' diplomatic delegation. The earl had given no indication, thus far, that he had any conception of American capabilities with radio. For all she knew, in fact, he still didn't even know what "radio" was in the first place.

"And why didn't Richelieu warn them?" she asked herself, in a murmur. "I'm damn sure *he* knows about radio."

Tom Simpson had come up to stand next to her—although, in his usual courteous manner, keeping just far enough away to not crowd Melissa aside. As big as he was, "sharing" a window with Tom Simpson pressed up close would be like sharing a window with a bear. But he was close enough to overhear her murmured words.

"Yes and no, Melissa. I'm sure Richelieu 'knows' about radio. But knowing about it in the abstract and really understanding the implications . . . that's two different things. He's a cardinal, after all, not a technocrat. And I think Mike's scheme with the big radio towers in Grantville and Magdeburg is probably paying off."

Melissa pursed her lips. The issue of whether or not to build those radio towers had been the subject of an argument at the time between her and Mike Stearns. One of the many little contretemps that she, as a cabinet member, had had with the President who had appointed her. Cabinet meetings, under the Stearns regime, were not infrequently raucous affairs. Mike was one of those rare people who, despite being very strong-minded, had no difficulty listening to people disagree with him. That was one of the many things about the man which, despite their differences, Melissa had come to cherish deeply.

The argument over the radio towers had been typical of the disputes she usually had with Mike. To Melissa, devoting the major resources necessary to build huge stone-construction towers—*taller than most cathedrals, fer chrissake!*—when there were still plenty of people in the United States living in shacks, had been absurd. The more so since the towers were mainly "prestige projects." They were designed to enable the U.S. and the CPE to broadcast throughout central Europe, bringing news of the day to hordes of citizens listening on their crystal set radios—of which there were not more than a handful in existence. A fancy and expensive "Voice of America" which . . . had nobody to listen to it.

Her lips quirked, in a little smile of remembrance. Melissa had been her usual acerbic self in the dispute. *Oh, great! We can be one of those damn banana republics which build palaces while their people are scrabbling for food!*

She could also remember Mike grinning at her, completely unfazed by the heat of her remarks. *We'll have the crystal sets one of these days, Melissa. Sooner'n you think, unless I miss my guess. And in the meantime, whatever else, it'll be what the Russkies call* maskirovka—*a masking; deception. When our enemies see us putting up towers hundreds of feet tall, built like cathedrals—it'll take months to do it, with hundreds of men working on the construction—maybe they won't realize that you don't need anything like that for military radio. It'll confuse them, at least. Nor forever, but maybe for long enough. And isn't that what we're doing everywhere? Buying time?*

"Well, maybe I was wrong," she muttered. Out of the corner of her eye, she could see Tom smiling faintly. Tom, like all officers Melissa knew personally in the little army of the United States, was a "Stearns loyalist." Heinrich Schmidt was almost scary on the subject. Melissa knew full well that if Mike were so inclined, he'd have no trouble getting his army to carry out a coup d'état on his behalf.

But . . . Mike Stearns was not so inclined. Whatever her differences with the man, on that subject at least Melissa slept easily at night. A strong-willed leader, yes; a dictator in the making, no.

"Maybe I was wrong," she repeated, pushing herself away from the window. She turned back into the room and looked toward Gayle and Darryl.

"If at all possible, I'll want to send a message tonight. But it may not be." A thumb over her shoulder indicated the soldiers on the wharf. "They'll be watching us closely, for a bit, and we can't afford to have them spot the radio antenna."

Rita chimed in. "The velvet glove is off, folks. That's why Strafford summoned us to the palace today. The king has announced the imposition of a state of emergency in England. New 'Royal Regiments' have been brought into London—from what we can tell, they've got 'em in most of the other bigger cities in the country too. And, yup, we're at war. It's official. The 'League of Ostend,' they're calling themselves. England and France and Spain and Denmark."

She made a face. "'Forced to unite,' you understand, in order to resist Swedish aggression."

Her husband's expression was equally sarcastic. "Exactly why 'resisting Swedish aggression' requires them to start by attacking the Dutch remains a little mysterious. Strafford got pretty fuzzy when he got to that part of the business."

"'Fuzzy!'" snorted Melissa. "That man could give lessons to the old Greek sophists."

Wearily, she lowered herself onto the nearest couch. "But it doesn't really matter, does it? We're at war, whether we like it or not. And while Strafford was polite as could be about the whole thing, he made it very clear that we—" Her head made a little sweeping motion, indicating everyone in the room; which included the entire delegation, now, since Friedrich and Nelly Bruch had entered from their own little alcove in the suite. "Like Rita says, the gloves are off. There's no more pretense that we're being kept here to protect us from disease. We're prisoners. Hostages, when you get right down to it, although the earl was too couth to use the term outright."

Darryl looked a bit alarmed, and glanced at the trunk where the radio was kept. Gayle had already lowered the lid and was sitting on it, half-protectively.

"Relax, Darryl," chuckled Tom. "I doubt very much if we'll be having any surprise inspections. 'Couth,' like Melissa says. Strafford's doing his best to keep the thing as civilized as possible. He assured us that our stay here would remain as comfortable as ever. They'll be watching us more closely, I imagine, but I'm pretty sure—so are Melissa and Rita; we talked about it on the way back—that Strafford will continue to respect our personal privacy."

Darryl muttered something under his breath. Melissa wasn't positive, but she thought it was *"Oh, sure—Black Tom Tyrant!"*

For a moment, her exasperation with the whole situation flared up. "For God's sake! Darryl—*just once*—can you stop thinking in clichés? Thomas Wentworth, the earl of Strafford, is not a villain out of a comic book. The truth is, I think he's basically a rather decent sort of man. Just one who takes his responsibilities and duties seriously, according to his own lights. He'll do what he thinks he has to do, in the interests of his king and country—as he sees it—but he's not going to start pulling wings off of flies."

Darryl's face settled into mulish stubbornness. It was an

expression Melissa well remembered, from the days he had been one of her students. *I knows what I knows; don't confuse me with the facts.*

The memory lightened her mood, oddly enough. Her next words came with a chuckle. "Oh, never mind. Hopeless! But I wonder, sometimes, how you and Harry Lefferts managed to rebuild so many cars. I'm sure the manual sometimes disagreed with your preconceptions."

A bit guiltily, Melissa remembered that one of those cars had been her own. On a teacher's salary, she hadn't been able to afford a new car, and the repair bill estimate the garage had given her had caused her to blanch. Until the next day, much to her surprise, the two most obstreperous and unruly students in her class had offered to do it for her. Free of charge, as long as she paid for the parts.

And . . . the jalopy had run as smooth as silk, afterward.

"It's not the same thing," Darryl protested. "Engines ain't people. They don't have bad hair days and they're never on the rag." Gayle smacked him. "Uh, sorry 'bout that last. No offense intended."

Gayle was smiling; so was Melissa, for that matter. *No offense intended*—and, the truth was, he meant it. Darryl could no more help being uncouth than a leopard could change its spots. And, now that she thought about it, Melissa was just as glad. The day might come when her own life depended on an uncouth young leopard's ability to deal with suave and aristocratic lions. Looking at him, Melissa suspected that she'd picked the right sort of champion for the fray.

*Yeah, it was a jalopy—but it did run smooth as silk after Darryl and Harry were done.*

"We'll wait," she announced, returning to the subject at hand. "Whatever else, we can't afford to have them spot the antenna. That's the one thing that might make Strafford change his mind about inspecting our quarters."

"Wait, for how long?" asked Gayle.

"As long as we have to. We're in for the long haul, now, so the one thing we can't afford is to arouse anyone's suspicions." Melissa glanced out the window. "Still too much of a moon, unless it gets overcast, which it doesn't look like it's going to do tonight."

Decisively, she planted her hands on knees and levered herself upright. "Tomorrow night, or the next day, whatever. In the meantime, we'd better figure we're going to be wintering over in the Tower this year. That means we can't fool around with the risk of disease." She glanced at a different trunk, which held their medical and preventive supplies. "Good thing we brought that stuff, I guess."

She heard Tom chuckle, and couldn't help smiling ruefully herself. "That stuff" referred to several pounds of the DDT which the fledgling American chemical industry was starting to produce. Mike Stearns had insisted the diplomatic delegations take what was available—over Melissa's objections, needless to say.

Firmly, however, Melissa squelched all feelings of self-doubt. She was going to need her well-honed Schoolmarm Authority to enforce her next command.

"And we'll set Operation Ironsides under way," she pronounced.

Immediately, Darryl scowled. "The guy's a monster, Melissa! Let him rot in hell for eternity!"

"You *will* obey orders, soldier," growled Tom.

Darryl looked mulish and stubborn. "'Orders' got nothin' to do with it. I didn't say I wouldn't *do* it. I just think it's nuts. Really really *nuts.*"

He looked to Melissa, and spread his hands in a gesture of appeal. "Come on, Melissa. I'm begging you! Just consider—just think about it!—that maybe you're making a big mistake here."

Melissa burst into laughter. So did Tom—who, like Melissa herself, had spent the months leading up to the departure of the diplomatic mission studying everything he could find on the history of 17th-century England. And Tom, furthermore—being a soldier himself—with a particular concentration on all of the famous military figures of the day.

"What's so damn funny?" demanded Darryl.

"You are," came Tom's immediate reply. "You don't know it, of course, but you just quoted the monster himself."

"Huh?"

"'I beseech you in the bowels of Christ—think it possible you may be mistaken.'" Melissa grinned. "It's a rather famous little saying. Made by Oliver Cromwell addressing the Church of Scotland."

That same night, in Paris, a young French general named Turenne examined the eight officers assembled in the salon of the house which Richelieu had provided for him. Most of the officers were as young as Turenne himself, and all were known to him personally. He had handpicked them to be the staff of the new army the cardinal had ordered him to create. An army which, in private and to himself, Turenne had given the whimsical title *New Model Army.*

Turenne gestured toward a long sidetable positioned next to a wall. There were eight little manuscripts resting atop the piece of furniture.

"One for each of you. The cardinal had some monks copy the books he obtained. I have been through them all and summarized what seemed to me the key points." There was another and larger manuscript atop a small table in the corner. But Turenne did not mention it. That was for later, and only for one of them.

"I will expect you to have the manuscript studied thoroughly within a week, at which time we will have another staff meeting. For the moment, just read it. In the months to come, I have no doubt we'll all be arguing the fine points." The smile he gave them was both friendly and . . . self-confident. Already, Turenne had begun to establish what he thought was a good rapport with his immediate lieutenants. He did not want slavish obedience. At the same time, he would insist that his leadership be respected. From what he could determine thus far, he seemed to be maintaining that needed balance.

One of the officers, Henri Laporte, cocked his head. "Is there any point in particular which seems to you of special importance?"

Turenne shrugged. "Hard to say, of course, without some experience. But I suspect the most useful—immediately, at least—will be my summary account of the American Civil War. Pay particular attention to the depiction of cavalry tactics used by such officers as"—he fumbled a bit over the pronunciation of the names; Turenne's English was not fluent—"Forrest, Morgan, Sheridan . . . a number of others." Again, he shrugged. "You will understand that I was forced to interpret a great deal. The histories which Richelieu obtained were more often than not rather vague on precise matters of tactics . . . when they addressed them at all. Still, one thing seems clear enough."

Most of the officers assembled in the room were cavalrymen. Turenne gave them a long, sweeping—and very cold—stare. "Whatever romantic medieval notions of cavalry warfare you may still possess, I strongly urge you to abandon them now. Or I will have you dismissed, soon enough. This war we are entering now will be a war like no other. The cardinal—"

He hesitated. Turenne owed his unexpected elevation and

influence entirely to Richelieu's favor. He was hardly inclined to criticize the man openly. Still, he was convinced that success would depend, as much as anything else, on the extent to which his newly formed officer staff could absorb the lessons of the future.

He cleared his throat. "Cardinal Richelieu, as you all know, is an extremely astute and wise leader. But he is not a soldier—"

Again, he broke off. That wasn't *quite* fair, after all. The cardinal had overseen several military campaigns, and from a close distance.

"Even if he were," he added a bit hastily, "he'd be likely to misgauge the situation." Again, he gestured toward the manuscripts. "You'll find a pithy little saying somewhere in those pages, which I was so taken by that I adopted it for my own. 'Generals always plan to fight the *last* war.'" A soft little chuckle went up from several of the officers.

"In any event, it is my belief that the cardinal is underestimating the effect which the new technology of the Americans is going to have on the tactics and methods used by Gustavus Adolphus." Harshly: "For certain, judging from my one brief meeting with him, Bernhard of Saxe-Weimar will make that mistake."

Most of the officers were now either scowling or wincing, or both. Bernhard of Saxe-Weimar led the mercenary army which controlled Alsace, on the payroll of the French crown. His reputation for arrogance and rudeness had become something of a byword among the officers of the French army, especially the ones who were young or not of noble birth.

"Bernhard, full of vainglory, will go straight at the Swede," predicted Turenne. "And—have no doubt of it—the Swede will crush him. And would crush us as well, did we make the same mistake." Again, the little gesture toward the manuscripts. "The weakness in the Swede will be his logistics. And that is where we will strike, gentlemen. So forget any fancies you might have about dramatic cavalry charges. Dragoons, we'll be, more often than not. Raiding, where we can, not fighting; and, when we must fight, doing so on the defensive as much as possible. If any of you finds that beneath your dignity, best you let me know at once. There will be no dramatic wheeling caracoles in *our* tactics, and precious few if any thundering charges."

He paused, waiting. Not to his surprise, none of the officers indicated any discomfort at his words. Turenne had handpicked them carefully.

"Good," he said, nodding. "Robert, would you be so kind as to remain behind?"

It was a clear dismissal. The officers moved over to the sidetable, each taking up one of the manuscripts, and quickly left the room. When they were gone, only Robert du Barry's stack remained.

Turenne gave the stack a glance. "You should read them also, of course. But I have something more important for you immediately." He led the way toward the little table in a corner where rested a larger manuscript.

"This is more technical in nature, Robert. I put it together as best I could from the material I had available." Quickly, Turenne sketched out the assignment he had in mind. When he was finished, du Barry's already florid face was almost brick red with suppressed anger.

"I have given you no reason—neither you nor the crown nor the cardinal—to doubt my loyalty. Furthermore—"

"Oh, do be quiet!" snapped Turenne. "Robert, I have never once inquired as to your religious beliefs. Neither has the cardinal. The fact that you—like me—come from a long line of Huguenots is irrelevant." *A long and notorious line,* he could have added. Robert du Barry's ancestor Jean de la Vacquerie had been the central figure in the so-called "conspiracy of Amboise" in the previous century.

" 'Irrelevant,' I say—except in one respect. Which does not reflect badly upon you in the least." Turenne placed a hand on the manuscripts. "It's all here, Robert," he said softly. "Everything we need—most of it, anyway, I'm convinced—to meet the Swedish king and his American wizards on level ground. Not immediately, no; hopefully, though, soon enough. But the books give us precious few specifics. In almost every case, they tell us only what the weapons could do, not how they actually did it. Perhaps that's because their readers already knew those things, while we do not. But the mere fact that we know what can be done will guide us in determining how to do it, of that I am confident. Yet it will take a large number of the best mechanics and gunsmiths in the world to carry this out—and they won't be able to do it unless they are properly organized and led. By a man who understands them and has the skill to manage them."

Du Barry's face was still flushed, but the color was beginning to fade a bit. "Can't do it without Protestants," he gruffed. "Does the cardinal understand that?"

Turenne smiled, a bit savagely. "I think he does more than simply 'understand' it, Robert. He is *counting* on it." He jerked his head toward the northern wall of the room. "Where will all those fine Dutch artisans go, once the Spanish bootheel is back on their necks? Eh?"

Turenne's thumb rifled idly through the first few pages of manuscript. "To Germany, some, to be sure. Looking for work from the Swede. But our spies tell us the Dutch are already resentful of the growing American reputation for being the world's best craftsmen. So . . ."

A slow smile spread across du Barry's face. "So the cardinal will offer them exile, will he?"

"Exile—*and work*. And at good wages." Turenne smiled himself. "When you think about it, the ports and manufacturing towns of northern France are much closer to Holland than central Germany, after all. And there will be no overweening and cocksure Americans to tell stout Dutch master gunsmiths and metalworkers that they are novices at their own trade. Just the firm leadership of a French officer who understands Protestants and can gently lead them to the light of a newer day."

"Ha!" By now, du Barry's flush was back to normal. He only made one last token protest.

"I should not like anyone to think I am flinching from the field of battle."

"Please, Robert! With *your* reputation?" Du Barry had been one of the only two officers in the room who was well into his thirties. He had quite an impressive record in the various French campaigns since the beginning of the war.

"And, besides," added Turenne smoothly, "I will explain to everyone that I was able to prevail upon you to undertake the assignment solely by dint of much pleading and begging."

He and du Barry shared a little laugh. Given the warmth of the moment, Turenne saw no reason to add what he could have added. *And, if I'd had to, I would have used the secret information the cardinal gave me to blackmail you into it. There's no doubt about your loyalty, true enough. But your brother could be sent to the executioner tomorrow.*

But he left the words unsaid. Turenne would have found saying them distasteful in the extreme, for one thing. For another, like Cardinal Richelieu himself, Turenne did not really care much about a man's private conscience—so long as he was faithful, in his public activities, to his duty to crown and country.

"Ha!" repeated du Barry. Turenne had chosen him for the assignment because Robert, unlike most officers, was familiar with the world of manufacture. As Turenne had suspected—and planned—he was finding the challenge an interesting one.

Du Barry picked up a sheaf of pages and began leafing through them. "Any suggestions for where to start?"

Turenne, as it happened—and much to his own surprise—had become quite fascinated with the challenge himself. "I can tell you where *not* to start," he growled. "You'll be working closely with Yves Thibault—you know him, I believe?"

Robert nodded.

"Well, don't let the old man convince you to devote much effort to"—again, Turenne stumbled over the pronunciation—"these 'breechloaders' he's become a fanatic about. Oh, to be sure, he's a master gunsmith—so let him fiddle around with a few. Who knows? We might even find he can make enough to be of use. But keep his nose to the wheel, Robert. *Simplicity.* Learn from the Americans themselves—you'll find more than a few spy reports in that stack also. 'Gearing down,' they call it. Make what you can *now,* in large enough quantities to affect the world in time."

Du Barry nodded, but Turenne could see that he was already becoming engrossed in what he was reading.

*Good enough. What I need.*

"Percussion caps, Robert. I can't tell, from the materials I had, exactly how they were made. But from the hints, we should be able to find out. And rifled muskets—not much different from today's hunting pieces. But with a clever American adaptation which enables quick loading on the battlefield. Again, I don't know exactly how it works. Richelieu's books weren't detailed enough. So find out—try different things. But it *can* be done, Robert. Huge armies, larger than any in Europe today, fought pitched battles with rifled muskets—muzzleloaders, not breechloaders—with which they could somehow maintain a fantastic rate of fire. Three shots a minute—and accurate to several hundred yards."

Du Barry's eyes widened. Turenne grinned.

"The best of it all, however . . . They called it a 'Minié ball.' Which—*ha!*—they got from a Frenchman in the first place."

Du Barry's eyed widened. Turenne barked another laugh.

"Oh, yes! Welcome to the new world, Robert—and who is to say it can't be a French one?"

# Chapter 22

"The streets are in chaos," Rebecca said, as soon as she came through the front door of the U.S. delegation's house in The Hague. "I never even made it to my interview with the prince."

Heinrich Schmidt came in after her, and closed the door. "It probably doesn't matter, anyway. According to most rumors, Frederik Henrik left The Hague yesterday. On his way north, according to some, trying to find out what happened. Others claim he went south—or east—in order to bolster the Dutch forces guarding the line of fortresses."

Rebecca sighed and rubbed her face. "Rumors, rumors—everywhere. Every corner is filled with knots of people arguing and exchanging rumors. Who knows what's really happening?"

Gretchen scowled. Jeff, sitting next to her on a couch, took a deep breath. "Well . . . if Frederik Henrik's really gone . . . there went our best chance to get a hearing from anybody who'd listen."

Rebecca went over to a nearby chair. "Yes, true enough." As she sat down, her hands slapped the arm rests in a gesture of exasperation. "Damn the Dutch and their obsessive sectarianism! Ever since we got here, the burghers and the regents have had us pigeonholed as 'Arminians.' As if we care in the least about their stupid doctrinal disputes!"

Heinrich leaned back against the door and grinned coldly. "Calvinists, what do you expect? If you support freedom of conscience—as we do—you are no better than a spawn of Satan,

Rebecca. Arminians—the devil's wolves already—dressed in sheep's clothing."

Wearily, Rebecca nodded her head. "Arminianism," in the parlance of the day, was what hardcore Calvinists called the moderate tendencies within Calvinism itself. The term was a vague one, measured by any objective intellectual standards, since it swept under one label such very different men and schools of thought as the Dutchman Grotius—now in exile—or the forces gathered around Bishop Laud in England.

But that very vagueness was an advantage to the hardcore Calvinists in the United Provinces. Under the official theology lurked hard-headed immediate material interests; and the real issues at stake were at least as much political and economic as they were religious. The bastions of hardcore Calvinism in Holland—the Counter-Remonstrants, as they were called—were in such towns as Haarlem and Leiden and Utrecht: manufacturing towns, basically, whose prosperity depended largely on the textile trade. A state of hostility with Spain worked to their advantage, since the Dutch blockade of the Flemish coast and their control over the outlets of the Rhine served to protect them against their Flemish and Brabantine competitors in the Spanish Netherlands. And thus they were hostile to any tendency within the United Provinces which, along theological lines, suggested the possibility of a compromise with Spain.

For its part, Arminianism in Holland had an equally material underpinning. The strongholds of the Arminians were the major port cities—Rotterdam and Amsterdam, along with the smaller towns of Dordrecht and Alkmaar and Delft. These cities depended for their prosperity on the carrying trade and fishing, and for them the continued state of hostilities since the end of the Twelve Years Truce in 1621 had been a major burden. Fine for the manufacturers of textiles—or the Zeeland merchants who depended on the inland trade—to wax hot and eloquent about the Anti-Christ and the devious ways of Popery. It wasn't *their* ships which were seized by the Spanish-backed privateers operating out of Dunkirk; nor was it *their* trade with Iberia and the Levant which had been destroyed; nor was it *their* herring fisheries which were suffering.

Complicating the mix was the long-standing political tug-of-war between the various levels of Dutch government, which was a complex entity: Holland versus the other six provinces; between the town councils and the States of Holland and the States General;

the ongoing conflict between the merchant oligarchs who domi- nated the town councils of Holland and the nobility who were still the dominant class in the more agricultural areas.

Overriding everything else, perhaps, was the role of the House of Orange, the premier noble family of the United Provinces. In the summer of the year 1618, Mauritz of Nassau—the stadtholder of Holland and Zeeland provinces as well as the prince of Orange— had carried through, with the support of the hardcore Calvinists, what amounted to a coup d'état. The existing Arminian regime led by Oldenbarnevelt and Grotius had been overthrown. Olden- barnevelt had been executed, and Grotius cast into prison.

For the next seven years, until his death in 1625, Mauritz had wielded greater personal authority in the United Provinces than any man since his father William the Silent had been assassinated in 1584. He had used that power to entrench the forces of hardcore Calvinism throughout the country. By the time of his death, however, the rigidities of the Counter-Remonstrants had produced a great deal of unrest, and under his successor Frederik Hendrik the balance had begun swinging the other way. Mauritz's half brother, if he lacked some of the martial glamour of other members of the illustrious House of Orange, possessed in full measure the political adroitness and skill of their great father William the Silent. So, steadily but surely, he had worked toward a more even balance of power between the various factions of Dutch society.

And, just as steadily, toward achieving a long-lasting settlement with Spain. Frederik Hendrik had used the prestige of his victo- rious siege of 's-Hertogenbosch in 1629—which had caused a sensation; the first really major defeat for Spanish arms in Europe since the Great Armada of 1588—to launch an effort to reach out and achieve an acceptable compromise with the Spanish Habsburgs.

As she reviewed this history in her mind, Rebecca had to con- trol her own anger. There were times, she thought, when the history of Europe in her era could be summed up with a phrase from her father's beloved Shakespeare: *sound and fury, signifying nothing.*

Nothing beyond death and destruction, that is, tearing a con- tinent apart and leaving millions slaughtered in its wake. And for no reason beyond the narrow and petty interests of the various factions in European society which ruled the lands—just as petty, on the part of Holland's merchants, as any princeling of Germany.

For months now, since December of 1632, Dutch and Spanish representatives had been negotiating a new peace. By the spring of 1633, it had appeared that a settlement was in the making—and a very good one, all things considered, from the long-term interests of both the independent and Spanish portions of the Low Countries. If anything, even more favorable to the United Provinces than to the Habsburg provinces in the south.

But the Counter-Remonstrants dug in their heels, and by the time Rebecca and the U.S. delegation arrived in Holland the talks had already collapsed. The hardcore Calvinists had been certain that, backed by France, the Dutch had no need to make *any* settlement with the Spanish, and so Spain had withdrawn from the talks and turned to its fleet and Don Antonio de Oquendo. And still the hardcore had been confident, for Richelieu's France, as always, had stood ready to support them against its traditional Habsburg enemies.

Now, it seemed, their little world was being turned upside down. The Mantuan War between France and Spain had ended two years earlier, freeing up the still-great strength of the Spanish empire to be brought to bear once again on the Low Countries. And if the rumors sweeping The Hague were true, and the French had set aside their long quarrel with Spain and turned against their Dutch allies . . .

Jeff said it for her: "Sow the wind, reap the whirlwind, huh?"

"Yes," she said, almost biting the word off. "Damnation! Just when I'd finally managed to cut my way through all the obstacles to get my first meeting with the prince of Orange himself!"

Exasperation drove her to her feet. "Enough. What is done is done. Until the situation settles down, there will be no way for us to meet with Frederik Hendrik. Nor do I see the point in any further 'discussions' "—the word was almost sneered—" 'with bigoted officials whose fine theological phrases are no more than a cover for greed. So—what should we do next?"

For a moment, there was silence. Then Heinrich, pushing himself away from the door, said forcefully: "Get out of The Hague, for a beginning. I do not share your confidence that there will be *any* 'settling down' of the situation, Rebecca. If the French have really switched allegiance and the English are in it also—which makes sense, given the message we just got from Melissa last night—then I think the Dutch are facing disaster."

"They've held out for over fifty years," protested Jeff.

But it was something of a feeble protest. Not even his wife agreed with him. "Don't be foolish, Jeff," said Gretchen. "Without France to back them up, the Dutch survival depends on their fleet alone."

"Best fleet in—"

"Not *that* much better," she growled. "And if the fleet is defeated, the Spanish will be able to get behind the line of fortifications at the frontier."

"And don't think for a minute," Heinrich added, "that the Spanish army isn't still the best in Europe. Their infantry, at least. For fifty years, everything has favored the Dutch—the political terrain even more than the physical. Change the French factor in the equation . . ."

For a moment, Rebecca was distracted by the expression. She could remember a time—not so long ago, really—when Heinrich Schmidt would not have used the language of mathematics in his metaphors. That, too, was one of the multitude of little ways that a few thousand Americans had begun a transformation in central Europe.

She took courage from the thought, and remembered her husband's oft-repeated little mantra: *Buying time, Becky, that's what we're doing. Buying time, until all the little changes we're making start merging into a river that can't be stopped.*

"I do not disagree, Heinrich," she said firmly. "So—yes. There is no point remaining here. If the war goes badly for the Dutch, The Hague will be too exposed. Amsterdam is where they will fall back. Best we get there quickly, before the roads become flooded with refugees. But relay Melissa's message to Julie and Alex in Scotland first. Hopefully, it will get through to them. They should be in Edinburgh by now."

Heinrich nodded, glanced at two of his soldiers standing against the far wall, and nodded again. Immediately, understanding the gesture, they headed for the door. Those were the two members of their party who spoke fluent Dutch, and the ones they'd come to rely upon to make whatever practical arrangements were needed. They would see to the task of hiring the necessary carriages for the journey to Amsterdam.

"We should leave someone behind," said Gretchen. "Two of us, with a radio—not Jimmy, we'll need him to set up the big radio again in Amsterdam—so we can keep informed of what's happening."

"Me," said Jeff immediately. "And either Franz or Jakob."

Gretchen froze for a minute, staring at her husband. Her face seemed to pale a bit.

Jeff shrugged. "With only two of us here, one of us has to speak the language well enough. I can't speak it hardly at all. And I've got to stay because, like you said, Jimmy has to go with the rest of you to Amsterdam. That leaves me. The only—" He broke off, for an instant. Then, harshly: "That leaves me."

Rebecca understood the meaning of that hard, clipped statement. Jeff was skirting around an issue which ran deep beneath the surface in the new society emerging in what was called the United States. Would the "old Americans"—the *real* Americans, as some thought of it—share in the risks and dangers of what they were forging? Or would they simply guide others in the doing? *Rear echelon motherfuckers,* in their own crude phrase, whose skills and knowledge were too valuable to risk on the front lines.

It was an old and long-running argument, both of whose sides Rebecca could understand. The fact was that almost any of the people who had been transplanted from the West Virginia of the future—any of them, at least, who were in their late teens—had a level of knowledge and skill which made them almost invaluable. Even with no more than a high school education, someone like Jeff Higgins understood more about science and technology than any European of the day. He could debate Galileo on astronomy—and win; Harvey on medicine—and win. Absurd to place such knowledge at the risk of being destroyed by a stray bullet or the diseases of a war zone.

And yet . . .

Perhaps—in the winning itself—lose everything. Saddle the world coming into being with an aristocracy of the robe which was no better, in the end, than any aristocracy of the sword. Create a world where, insidiously, American blood came to count for as much as the precious *limpieza* of the haughty Spanish hidalgos.

She hesitated, torn. As much as anything, because she had come to feel a deep love for the young American who had once saved her life—just as he had saved the lives of his German wife and her family.

The wife herself settled the issue. "Yes, you must," said Gretchen softly. Her hand slid into Jeff's and gave it a tight squeeze. Her eyes were moist. "You must."

❋          ❋          ❋

The U.S. delegation set off for Amsterdam very early the next morning. Gretchen was the last to board, hugging Jeff fiercely until the last moment. Then, with a final kiss, climbed into the second one.

Jimmy leaned out of the window. "You *sure* you don't want the incendiaries too?"

Jeff shrugged. "What for? They're anti-shipping." His head jerked a little, indicating the surroundings. "The Hague's an inland town, in case you hadn't noticed. Besides . . ."

He bestowed on Jimmy a grin which he hoped had an aura of bravado about it. Instead of reflecting the fear which seemed to be coiling in his belly. "Besides, who's to say *you* won't be the ones catching all the grief? Hell, Jimmy, before too long you might find yourself on the docks of Amsterdam firing those incendiary grenades at the Spanish fleet. You'll be glad you have them, then."

His friend grinned back. Like Jeff's own, the expression was one of pure bravado. Jeff suspected Jimmy was probably as nervous as he was himself. But, dammit, he'd keep up the front.

"So long, buddy," Jeff said softly, as the carriage lurched into motion. "See you soon. I hope."

He watched until the carriage rounded the corner and vanished from sight. Then, with a little shrug, turned to face the other U.S. soldier who had volunteered to stay behind.

"I guess we might as well spend the rest of the day cruising the town, Jakob. Hell, who knows? We might even hear a piece of actual news mixed in with all the rumors."

"Not likely," grunted Jakob. "But we have nothing else to do, so why not? I need to buy us some more food, anyway. We may be on short rations, soon."

Julie burst into the room where Alex's father lay in his bed, recuperating from his injuries. Her face was flushed with anger. "I don't believe this sh—"

She broke off abruptly, remembering that she had just met her father-in-law a few days before. The trip to Scotland had been a long one, and while Alex's family had welcomed her readily enough, she was not exactly on comfortable Appalachian-cussing terms with them.

Not yet, at least. She had hopes for her father-in-law, if not the solemn woman he had married after his youthful escapades. (One of which, of course, had produced Alex himself.) Robert Mackay, even tortured by constant pain as he was, seemed like a rather cheerful soul.

Still—

"Must be the English, eh?" said Robert Mackay slyly, glancing at Alex. He winced as his son helped him rise up a bit from the pillows. "Nothing else, in my experience, produces quite such a sudden rush of fury. If I mistake me not, your lovely wife was about to utter a most indelicate term."

Julie flushed. Her father-in-law chuckled, glancing now at the corner where his bedpan was kept discreetly tucked away in a small cabinet. "*Especially* indelicate for a man in my position, given the miserable contortions I must go through just to take a simple shit."

Julie tried to keep from laughing. And . . . couldn't. Her father-in-law's grin at her raucous glee was good-natured. Amazingly so, really, for a man who was now paralyzed from the waist down and whose chances of survival for more than a few months were dim. Horsefalls could be as devastating as car accidents, Julie had learned over the past two years—but without 21$^{st}$-century medical care to repair the damage on those who survived.

Alex was smiling broadly. Not so much at the little exchange between Julie and her father itself, she knew, but simply because he was glad to see the developing warmth between two of the three people he cared most about in the world. She knew he'd been worried about that, though he'd never spoken of it to her.

*17$^{th}$-century Scot Calvinist nobleman esteemed father—meet my, ah, not-Calvinist, not-noble, ah, not-entirely-respectful, ah, sometimes-downright-impudent, ah, new wife. Did I mention she's from the future and thinks we have the toilet habits of wild animals? And thinks Edinburgh is probably the asshole of the universe?*

She kept laughing. Now that she'd come to know her father-in-law a bit, she suspected that Robert Mackay might well have agreed. With the last, anyway. Edinburgh *did* have the reputation, even among the people of the time, for being the foulest and least sanitary town in Europe. And whatever aristocratic notions Robert possessed—plenty, of course—he did seem able to look reality in the face.

Perhaps awakened by the levity in the nearby room, the third of Alex's most beloved people began making her presence known. Loudly and insistently, as was her habit.

Julie began to turn around. "Oh, leave it be, lass!" exclaimed Robert. "T'won't hurt the girl to learn the world is a cold and callous place. I swear, you coddle Alexi."

Julie danced back and forth, torn between her new mother's reflexes and her desire not to quarrel with her father-in-law.

"What's the news, Julie?" asked Alex.

"Oh." Julie scowled. "I just got a message from Becky. Would you believe—?"

By the time she finished summarizing the developments for her husband and father-in-law, Robert was scowling as fiercely as she was.

"So it begins," he growled. "I *knew* it. I knew those sweet words from the king's new man were a disguise for tyranny."

Alexi's yowls grew louder. Julie, with the tender skin of a first-time mother, could no longer resist. Mumbling apologies, she hurried from the room.

After she was gone, Alex turned to his father. "Explain. Please."

Robert shrugged. The little motion caused him to wince. "Don't ever smash your spine, son," he muttered. "T'isn't worth the thrill of the hunt, I assure you."

He paused, waiting for the worst of the pain to subside. Then, speaking in short, clipped sentences:

"Wentworth. You may remember him. Was Lord President of the North when you left to take Swedish colors. Strafford, now. The king made him an earl. He gave the presbyters all they wanted. No interference with service. No English prayer book. Do as we will. But don't meddle in England."

Alex frowned. "What bothers you about that? I'd think—"

His father, visibly, restrained himself from making a violent gesture that might flood his ruptured body with pain again. "Don't be as stupid as the presbyters. Sorry damn churchmen. Sure and certain, Wentworth will leave us be. For *now*. Why not? Leave Scots to their own—do I need to explain this to *you*, whom I've never been able to legitimize because of it?—and within a year they'll be ripping at each other again. Damn all clans and sects and factions anyway."

He stared bleakly at his son. "We've always been pawns in their hands, Alex. Only the Irish are worse. At least they have the excuse of being sorry superstitious priest-ridden papists." Another pause, fighting down pain. Then: "Five years from now, ten at the latest . . . after Wentworth has his French state, he'll be leading his troops to the north. Promises be damned, then. England's promises are as worthless as Scotland's leaders."

Jeff and Jakob got back to their quarters by early afternoon, not having learned much of anything. The rumors were still flying all over, but they were hopelessly contradictory. Jakob disappeared thereafter, saying he had business to attend to. By the time he returned, shortly after sundown, it had all became a moot point. Jeff had just received a radio message from Rebecca. Traveling by coach, on the good road to Amsterdam, she and her party had been able to make the trip in one day.

The message was short and to the point:

ARRIVED IN AMSTERDAM. RUMORS CONFIRMED. GET OUT NOW. DO NOT WAIT. START TONIGHT IF POSSIBLE. DAWN TOMORROW LATEST. LOOK FOR US AT—

The rest was convoluted directions to find a tavern in Amsterdam where someone would meet them. Jeff didn't even try to memorize it.

"For Pete's sake," he muttered, glancing helplessly at Jakob. "Start *tonight*? As badly as I ride a horse in the daytime? And where are we going to get horses that fast anyway?"

Jakob smiled. "Relax. I thought of everything. While you were lounging about, I bought us some horses with the money Becky left us. Unlike you silly optimistic up-timers, I know the world stinks and news is always bad." He motioned toward the door with his thumb. "Get packed. The horses are in a nearby stable. We can be out of town in an hour. The weather is as good as possible and there's enough of a moon. Ride all night and we'll be in Amsterdam sometime in the afternoon tomorrow, even as badly as you ride. We'll be exhausted, sure, especially you. But exhaustion can be fixed. Dead is forever."

"I'll fall off," Jeff whined. "Horses don't like me."

"I bought 'mounts,' I should have said. I told you I thought of everything. For you, I bought a mule. Looks like a very nice and gentle beast." Jakob's chest swelled. "For me, of course, a proper charger! Well, of sorts."

❀          ❀          ❀

The mule *did* seem like a reasonable creature, Jeff decided, after riding on it for a bit. Fortunately, Jakob was not trying to drive the animals any faster than a walk, visibility was not terrible, and the Dutch road was in fine shape.

Eventually, Jeff concluded he would survive the experience. That left him enough energy to dwell on his *other* grievance.

He glowered up at Jakob. Jeff was a large man, riding a small mule. Jakob, a small man riding a full-size horse. The German-born soldier seemed to loom over him.

"This is ridiculous," Jeff complained. "How did *you* get to play Don Quixote and I'm stuck being Sancho Panza?" After a moment: "Well, maybe it's not such a bad deal. At least *you* get to fight the windmills."

He could barely see Jakob's frown of puzzlement in the moonlight. "Never heard of them. And why would anyone fight a windmill?"

"They're characters in a book."

"Oh." Jakob's serene smile returned. "Another problem with you up-timers. You wrote too many books. All of them with those silly happy endings."

"It's *already* written," grumbled Jeff. "Thirty years ago, now. Something like that. By a Spaniard named Cervantes."

"Ah! Then why bother reading it at all? Written by a Spaniard—in the here and now? The story will end in death and destruction and horror and misery. The Spaniards are no fools, except the one who wasted his time writing it. Who needs a book to figure that out?"

# Chapter 23

Jesse watched carefully as Hans completed his third landing of the flight and let the aircraft roll to a stop, as instructed. Saying nothing, Jesse motioned for Hans to taxi back to takeoff position and made a last notation on his kneeboard. Though within tolerances, the landing had been the roughest of the three and none had been close to Hans' best.

*Well, you can't wait forever,* Jesse mused.

"Okay, stop here and keep her running," he told Hans, when they were again pointed into the wind. He watched Hans' eyes go round as he unbuckled his harness and took off his kneeboard.

"I think I'll go talk to Kathy for a minute," Jesse said. "Why don't you take her up and do a couple of touch-and-gos, followed by a full stop?"

He opened his door and stepped out. "And—Hans!" he yelled, over the prop noise at the gaping student, "Don't screw the pooch, okay?"

Jesse secured the door, blocking the view of his startled student, and walked around the tail. He waved at the usual onlookers lounging by the edge of the field. A few of them, judging from the way their own eyes seemed to widen a bit, were suddenly realizing they were seeing something different today. The man the Germans had begun calling "Der Adler"—*the Eagle*—was walking swiftly away from the still-running aircraft, leaving Hans alone.

The nickname embarrassed Jesse, but he'd stopped trying to

prevent people from using it. It came naturally enough to the Germans, who were still in some awe of the man who actually *flew*.

And now . . . for the first time, a German himself would be *flying*. Alone, with no eagle from the future to watch over him.

Jesse deliberately averted his eyes from the aircraft as he strode on, knowing that Hans would need the time to gather his wits. He heard the engine run up as he approached the control tower and saw that Kathy and Sharon had come out to meet him. Behind them came the other eight youngsters—six young men and two young women—who, along with Hans, constituted the first class of the fledgling air force. Jesse put his arm around Kathy's waist and turned back to watch the birth of a pilot.

"Do you really think he's ready?" Sharon asked nervously.

"Dunno," he replied, eyes glued to the aircraft. "We'll find out."

"Ouch!" he said, as Kathy's sharp elbow struck his ribs. "Don't worry, Sharon, I wouldn't let him go if I didn't think he was ready."

Jesse gave Sharon a smile, which she returned weakly.

"Watch carefully, now. I guarantee he'll want to talk about it later."

She looked into his calm, green eyes and nodded.

Jesse turned back to observe the takeoff with the realization that much more than his precious aircraft was at stake here. In some way, he understood, another brick was being laid in the forging of a nation—a *true* nation, not simply a crazy-quilt patchwork of tribes and customs. Once a boy—young man—born and bred in 17th-century Germany could demonstrate that he, too, could do the impossible . . .

He took a deep breath and tried to settle his own nerves. It was easy enough, really. Truth be told, Jesse wasn't overly concerned about the outcome of the flight. Hans was a good pilot and Jesse had intentionally delayed this moment to make sure he had all the skills he needed. Still, a crash would be disastrous, both for Hans and his country.

The aircraft passed them, lifted smoothly off the grass, and climbed steadily outward. Jesse looked down into his wife's knowing eyes and absently kissed her forehead, then looked up to follow the aircraft. Kathy said nothing, which he appreciated. She knew he was still deeply in his instructor mode and would stay there until Hans returned.

The three of them waited together as Hans flew the traffic pattern in the brilliant blue sky. They'd been getting a lot of good weather lately, and Jesse had taken full advantage of it. The one thing the *Las Vegas Belle* was *not*—not even close—was an all-weather aircraft. On days with bad weather or even poor visibility, Jesse didn't go up at all. He'd trust himself in bad conditions, even with such a primitive airplane—within limits, at least—but he didn't want to risk it with trainee pilots at the controls.

As the aircraft at last turned onto final, Jesse felt Kathy's arm slide around his own waist and give him a reassuring squeeze. Out of the corner of his eye, he saw Kathy look at Sharon and, seeing the young woman about to speak—no doubt wanting some reassurance herself—shook her head slightly. Again, he was grateful for his new wife's understanding. Jesse's concentration was entirely on Hans and the airplane.

*On course, on glideslope.* Jesse mentally repeated an approach controller's standard reassuring advisory, almost as a mantra. His practiced eye detected no deviation, no wild control movements. *On course, on glideslope.*

The aircraft slid over the field boundary and settled onto the grass without a trace of a bounce, so sweetly that Jesse had to stifle the urge to yell an exultant "Yes!" Instead, as Hans added power and took off again, Jesse slowly exhaled and smiled at Sharon.

"What'd I tell ya?" he demanded. "Piece of cake."

Hans' second circuit was almost as uneventful as the first. Though at one point he allowed the aircraft to slide below the proper glide path, he quickly corrected and made a good, if firm, landing. All the while, Jesse's eyes never left the aircraft, mentally projecting instructions to his student, willing him to succeed.

The third and final approach was as precise as the first and, true to the old saying that a good approach makes for a good landing, the touch down was again perfect. As Hans taxied toward them, Jesse could no longer restrain himself.

"Damn, that kid is good! He reminds me of—me!"

"Jesus, pilots and their egos," Kathy said, looking meaningfully at Sharon. "Don't say I didn't warn you."

Jesse snorted, "Hush, woman! Get ready to hail the conquering hero."

"I still say we should have had someone here from town," Kathy complained.

"What, and listen to Stearns or somebody give another speech?" Jesse smiled. "Not likely. Besides, this is Air Force business today." He went to grab a set of chocks.

With the aircraft chocked and shut down, the three of them waited for Hans to emerge. Behind them, the other trainee pilots lined up and came to attention. As the door opened and Hans stepped out, a cheer rose from the group of onlookers at the perimeter fence—a very loud cheer, and one which went on and on. In fact, it seemed to be picking up steam as it went. Two young men, on horseback, began galloping toward the town.

Hans looked slightly dazed, as if just now realizing what he had done. Snapping into focus, he gave Sharon a smile, but, for the moment, his primary attention was on his instructor, the man who had taught him to fly. He walked over and stood at attention in front of Jesse. He did not salute, although Jesse could see the boy's arm practically twitching in his desire to do so. But Jesse had always thought saluting—like wearing hats—was a silly damn thing to do in the vicinity of aircraft. And since *he* was the commanding officer in *this* universe's version of an air force, he'd damn well seen to it that his own relaxed attitudes set the new traditions. Salutes were dramatic, sure, but they distracted people who should be paying attention to the aircraft around them. And hats invariably just wound up getting blown off. A waste of time, at best, chasing after them.

Coming to attention, on the other hand, was a reasonable military custom. Jesse did the same himself, and looked sternly at Hans.

"Cadet Richter." The older man raised an open hand holding a set of silver insignia. He'd quietly had it made the week before— along with a number of others—by Grantville's major jewelry store, Roth, Nasi & Rueckert. "Or perhaps, I should say, 'Lieutenant' Richter, because these will be yours in a minute and the rank goes with them. On the occasion of your having successfully completed undergraduate pilot training, I am pleased to announce in my capacity as Chief of Staff that you have achieved the rating of pilot in the United States Air Force."

Jesse looked at Sharon. "Miss, would you kindly do the honors?"

Hans stood stiffly at attention as Sharon took the insignia from Jesse, carefully pinned them over Hans' left breast pocket, and gave him a quick kiss. As she stepped back, Jesse could see tears beginning to well in her smiling eyes. He looked down at the insignia on Hans' chest—shiny silver wings with the radiator shield in the center—and felt a sudden lump in his own throat.

Jesse stepped forward and solemnly offered his hand.

"Congratulations, son. Very well done. I'm proud of you."

"Thank you, sir," Hans choked out.

Jesse smiled at him, "Oh, Hans, try to remember one thing, will you?"

Hans smiled broadly in return, "Yes, sir. I promise to remember. 'Don't screw the pooch.'"

Whatever Jesse might have wanted, soon became a moot point. Within an hour, Mike Stearns was out at the airfield along with, this time, what looked to be the *entire* cabinet except those members of it who were out of town. All of them tried to cram their way into the lower floor of the combination control tower and Air Force headquarters. Mike and Frank Jackson were the only ones actually able to get in, because the room was already packed with those people Jesse himself considered its proper habitués—himself, Hans, the other youngsters he was training as pilots, and their various womenfolk or boyfriends.

"I am *not* a politician," growled Jesse, as soon as Mike came in. "So spare me the lecture. I told you—"

"Oh, be quiet," chuckled Mike. "I didn't come here to give you a hard time, you old grouch. I just wanted to invite you to the parade."

"*What* parade?"

Mike and Frank were both grinning. "The one I just told Henry Dreeson to organize," replied Mike. "*You* may not be a politician, but I am." He shrugged. "Hey, sure, it's a dirty job—but somebody's got to do it."

"It's gonna be one hell of big one, too," Frank added. Jesse frowned. He was a little surprised by the very evident tone of satisfaction in Frank's voice. As a rule, the head of the U.S. Army shared Jesse's own skepticism about the often rough-and-tumble nature of politics in the new United States.

Frank shook his head. "Don't be stupid. We just got another message over the radio this morning. From Becky. She's in *Amsterdam* now, Jesse. The first rumors about the destruction of the Dutch fleet seem pretty well confirmed. And from what she can tell, the Dutch are starting to fall apart. Apparently—we still don't really know how they pulled it off—the Spanish have taken Haarlem. That means they've cut Holland in half, and they've got their troops behind the Dutch line of fortifications. You know what that means, in this day and age."

Jesse sucked in a breath. In the 17th century, warfare was mainly a matter of siegecraft, not field maneuvers. For decades, the Dutch had held off the Spanish with their walled towns and fortresses along the outlets of the Rhine. If the Spanish had gotten *behind* those lines . . .

"It's probably even worse than that," added Mike. "Becky's not sure yet, but from what reports they've been able to piece together—the news from England matches, too—it looks as if Richelieu's alliance is moving into the Baltic. With the Dutch fleet destroyed, that means the Swedes will be facing the French and the Danes and the English alone."

"What about the Spanish?" asked Hans. "Uh, sir." Despite the gravity of the moment, Jesse had to fight down a smile. The mere fact that young Hans could even ask a question in such august company was a subtle but sure sign of the effect on his self-confidence of that new insignia on his chest.

But Jesse didn't have much trouble suppressing the smile. *He's going to need that self-confidence, soon enough. God damn it all to hell.*

"From what we can tell, the Spanish seem to have dropped aside," Frank replied. "Makes sense, when you think about it. This alliance of Richelieu's—they're calling it 'the League of Ostend,' apparently—is a devil's alliance if you ever saw one. Each of the parties to it has their own agenda and their own axes to grind. It's bound to fall apart, eventually, but in the meantime . . ."

Mike picked up the thought. "In the meantime, like Frank says, it all makes sense. The Danes get the control of the Baltic they've always wanted, the Spanish get the Low Countries, and King Charles gets the French and Spanish money he needs to clamp down in England and keep his throne—and his head. We've gotten word from Melissa that the streets of London are being flooded with newly hired mercenary troops."

"But what do the *French* get out of it?" asked Kathy. "For themselves, I mean. Just looking at it, it seems like they're doing a lot of fighting—not to mention shelling out money—and not getting much in return."

Mike shrugged. "They slam a hammerblow at Gustav Adolf, if nothing else. With the Baltic under their control, Sweden is cut off from the rest of the Confederated Principalities of Europe. And, while I'm not positive, I think . . ." He hesitated, for a moment.

"I don't want to get into *how* we know, but we have gotten some news from the French ports."

Jesse, as commander of the little air force, was privy to the U.S. government's intelligence secrets. *That'll be Uriel and Balthazar Abrabanel's network of Jewish sailors.* A considerable number of the "Portuguese" seamen of the time were actually *marranos*—"secret Jews," keeping their identity hidden from the Spanish Inquisition.

"An expedition left a few weeks ago—pretty big one; six ships and over a thousand soldiers—heading for North America."

Kathy frowned. "But . . . if the French try to conquer the English settlements—"

" '*Conquer*' isn't the right word," said Mike harshly. "According to our information, they are simply going to take 'rightful possession'—of properties which King Charles of England signed over to them as part of the deal. I assume, of course, that the soldiers will be used to overrun the handful of Dutch settlements in the New World."

Frank Jackson's face was twisted into a grimace. "Yeah, a bit of twist. 'Plymouth Rock' is about to become a French colony—whether the Puritans like it or not. So's Jamestown."

Jesse closed his eyes, and brought up the image of a world map into his mind. "Jesus Christ," he muttered, "do you really think Richelieu is looking *that* far ahead?"

"Yes, I do." Mike's voice was even harsher, now. "I think we've been underestimating Richelieu all along. He's not like the rest of them, Jesse. Charles—even Wentworth—Olivares in Spain, King Christian of Denmark—God knows that narrow-minded bigot Emperor Ferdinand of Austria and the greedy pig Maximilian of Bavaria—they're all just looking at what's in front of their noses. Say what else you will about him, Richelieu is a *statesman*. He's considering the long-term interests of France. As smart as he is, with the history books he's gotten his hands on, I think he's seen the overall pattern for the next several centuries: whoever controls North America is going to have the edge. So I think he's carrying through a radical realignment of French foreign policy. I think he's decided that squabbling over little pieces of territory in Europe is short-sighted and stupid. Why drain France for twenty-five years in a war with Spain, just to wind up with a handful of extra towns? When he can let the Spanish and the Danes and the English—and whoever else he can rope in—hammer away at the CPE while he swipes an entire continent? Dirt cheap, at the price."

Suddenly, Hans shot to his feet and stood at attention. "I am at your command, sir!" Immediately, the other trainee pilots followed his lead.

Mike smiled at them. "Good enough. The *first* thing you're going to do—right now—is be the stars in a parade."

Jesse was back to scowling. Mike transferred the smile to him. "A grouch, like I said. Don't be shortsighted yourself, Jesse. Me, I think Richelieu just goofed. And I intend to prove it by swiping a bit from French history."

"What are you talking about?" gruffed Jesse. "What I know about French history . . ."

Frank snorted. "You *have* heard about something called 'the French revolution,' I hope."

"Well. Sure. What's that—"

"What blew it wide open was when the surrounding powers of Europe invaded France. Pissed the average Frenchman off right proper, that did. And so before you knew it the volunteer columns of the revolutionary army were forming up, and . . . the world was never the same afterward. War stopped being something princes and mercenaries fought on top of the bodies of helpless civilians. The civilians became *citizens,* you see. With their own kind of army."

Frank was grinning again. "Hell, Jesse, I even learned the tune. *Allons enfants de la patrie, le jour de gloire—*"

Everybody in the room winced. Jesse shot to his feet. "Enough! Enough! Even a damn parade beats listening to you trying to sing!"

By the time the parade was over, late in the afternoon, Jesse was willing to concede that Mike had been right. Truth to tell, he was beginning to suspect that Mike Stearns had the makings of a great politician—or, at least, a great politician for the times. Even, maybe—though the word made Jesse uncomfortable—a "statesman."

Mike too, he knew, was thinking in the long run. A war, in itself, is just a war. History recorded thousands of them, all but a relative handful forgotten by anyone except scholars. Every now and then, though, a war became something else.

The crucible of a nation. The forge on which a new society was hammered.

Listening to the chants and slogans which thundered throughout the streets of Grantville that day, Jesse realized he was hearing the hammer blows of that forging. The town was packed, with people pouring in by the minute from the surrounding countryside. He'd seen at least four places where the Committees of Correspondence had set up impromptu enlistment booths, recruiting people into volunteer regiments. Every one of the booths had a long line of young men standing patiently before it. Almost all of them, young Germans—and almost all of those, German commoners. The sons of farmers and artisans—paupers, too—now signing up to engage in an enterprise which, for their society, had always been the business of kings and nobles and mercenaries.

Lambs, deciding they were lions. *Choosing* to be lions.

Not simply civilians. Not even simply civilians who were allowed to vote.

*Citizens.*

There had been many slogans chanted that day. But, always, one slogan rose over the rest whenever Jesse and his little crew of fledgling pilots rode by the crowd in the pickups which had been commandeered for the purpose.

*Der Adler! Und seine Falken!* The Eagle, and his Hawks.

"Oh, Jesse," Kathy whispered into his ear at one point, hugging him tightly. "I'm so proud of you. They think they can do anything, now. That's because you showed them they could even *fly.*"

# Chapter 24

Momma hadn't wanted her to come.

Kristina wasn't entirely sure why that was. On the other hand, there were a lot of things she didn't understand about Momma. Not that Kristina didn't love her mother. But there were times when Momma seemed just a little . . . odd. She seemed to change her mind a lot. And it was important to her that people appreciated her—and told her so.

Kristina was only seven years old—well, almost eight—but it seemed to her that some of the people who kept telling Momma how much they appreciated her wanted things from her. Usually things Poppa and Chancellor Oxenstierna wouldn't give them . . . or let Momma give them. Which could make things around the palace very uncomfortable.

Things were especially uncomfortable in the palace just now. Everyone seemed very upset and worried about the Danes and the French. Kristina knew where France was, of course. She loved maps. And she knew all about that awful old Richelieu, who ran France instead of the French king. But only a year or so before, Richelieu had been Poppa's friend. Now, he was an enemy.

It was all very confusing. She understood why King Christian was an enemy. Danes were nasty. They wanted to keep Sweden penned up in the Gulf of Finland while they had the Baltic all to themselves. Which was ugly and greedy of them. Especially since the Baltic belonged to Poppa, exactly as it would someday belong to Kristina. So, of course, King Christian was going to do whatever he could to hurt Poppa. But just why Richelieu would help him was something Kristina was still working on figuring out.

It would have helped if someone would explain it to her. People ought to explain things to her. After all, she was the crown princess of Sweden. Someday, she would be queen, too. But except for Poppa, and sometimes her tutors (who were usually so *boring* about it all), people very seldom explained to her. They didn't care that she was a princess; they just treated her as if she were a baby who couldn't understand anything. Which was really, really unfair of them, because how was she supposed to understand things if no one bothered to explain them to her in the first place?

That was one of the reasons she was so happy that she was going to Magdeburg, whatever Momma thought about it. Poppa had made Magdeburg his new capital, which meant she would finally get to see him sometimes. Poppa was the most wonderful man in the world. Everybody in Stockholm said so, and even if they hadn't, *Kristina* thought he was the most wonderful man in the world. But he was always so busy, always off fighting the bad people. The Poles, the Russians, the Danes, the Spanish, the Germans—some of them, anyway; the *good* Germans were on Poppa's side—and now the Danes (and the French) all over again. He beat them all, of course. But because he had to spend so much time doing that, Kristina had never really gotten to spend very much time with him. So she was looking forward to changing that.

On top of that, it was September. It wouldn't be very long before the snow began, and they got a lot of snow in Stockholm. It wasn't that Kristina didn't *like* snow. It was just that once the snow began, it stayed so long. From what her tutors had told her, Magdeburg wouldn't get snowed on as much as Stockholm did.

But most exciting of all to Kristina, Magdeburg had Americans in it. *Real* Americans. Americans from the future, not just from Germany. Kristina had heard all sorts of wonderful tales about the Americans and their machines. Some of them, she suspected, were the sort of made-up stories people told to little girls because they expected little girls to believe anything. But it even half of them were true . . .

She stood on the deck of the forty-gun *Margaret* as the warship glided further into Wismar Harbor. Sailors hurried about the decks and swarmed up the rigging as they furled the sails. The ship slowed even more, barely moving forward at all, and then the anchor splashed into the water and disappeared. The anchor cable streamed out after it, and then, a moment later, *Margaret* gave a tiny shiver as the cable went taut and snubbed away the last of her movement.

Kristina wanted to dash to the rail and stare curiously at the shore. But she was a princess, and princesses (as Momma had explained to her at great length) didn't go running around gawking at things like some ill-bred peasant. So Kristina made herself stand still on the poop deck beside Lady Ulrike, her governess. Lady Ulrike had a tiresome habit of agreeing with Momma about things like running to see what was happening. Actually, Kristina was pretty sure that that was the reason Momma had wanted Lady Ulrike as her governess, and she wondered if there were some way she could convince Poppa to pick someone else. Momma wouldn't like that, of course, but Poppa was the only person Kristina knew who was perfectly willing to tell Momma to do things his way. Of course, Poppa was *very* brave. Everyone said so.

Kristina smiled to herself at the thought even as she tucked her hands primly and properly into her fur muff. It was cool enough out here on the water to make her genuinely grateful for the muff's warmth, but mostly she did it to keep Lady Ulrike happy and avoid any words like "hoyden."

The sailors were running around doing all sorts of mysterious sailor things. Some of them were coiling ropes neatly, others were scampering about in the rigging, tying the folded-up sails to the yards. But some of them were also bringing Kristina and Lady Ulrike's baggage up on deck, and Kristina saw a big rowboat coming across the harbor toward *Margaret*.

It didn't take the boat long to reach *Margaret*. A man in a leather coat and cavalry boots, with a sword at his side, climbed up the wooden battens fastened to the ship's side. He nodded at *Margaret*'s captain, but he also walked straight across to Kristina.

"Your Highness," he said, bowing gravely to her. "Welcome to Wismar. I am Colonel Ekstrom. Your father, the king, has instructed me to escort you to join him at Magdeburg."

Colonel Ekstrom had a big nose, almost as strong as Poppa's (or Kristina's, for that matter), and a thick, closely trimmed brown beard. And he had nice eyes, Kristina decided. They looked very serious at the moment, but there was a twinkle hiding somewhere down in their gray depths.

"Thank you, Colonel," she told him politely.

"No thanks are necessary, Your Highness," Colonel Ekstrom assured her. "It will be my pleasure. Unfortunately," he looked across at Lady Ulrike, and the twinkle Kristina had thought she'd seen in his eyes disappeared completely, "it will be necessary for us to begin our journey immediately."

Lady Ulrike's face tightened the way it did whenever Kristina did something naughty. She opened her mouth as if she were going to say something, but then she closed it again and simply nodded. Kristina recognized that nod. It was the sort of nod grown-ups used when they didn't want to talk about something in front of children. Usually something interesting.

"If you would see to stowing the princess's baggage in my boat, Captain," Colonel Ekstrom continued, turning back to *Margaret*'s captain, who had followed him across the deck, "we can be on our way now."

Kristina decided that she was in favor of whatever was obviously worrying the adults about her. Well, maybe not actually in *favor* of it, because it was pretty clear that Colonel Ekstrom and Lady Ulrike were *really* worried about whatever it was they were carefully not discussing in front of her. But whatever it was, it couldn't be all bad from Kristina's viewpoint, because no one was making her ride in a carriage. Kristina hated carriages. They were stuffy, and uncomfortable. Even on a good road, they bounced and jounced whenever they weren't actively swaying, and most of the time they made Kristina sick to her stomach. And, of course, there were very few good roads. Certainly, the one they were on today was a terrible one. She was pretty sure she would already have been throwing up if they'd made her ride over it in a carriage, but they hadn't. Instead, they had provided her with a horse. A wonderful horse Poppa had captured from the Austrians just for her!

Kristina loved horses, and they liked her. She was just as happy Momma wasn't here to see this one, though. Momma worried. Momma hadn't wanted Kristina to stop riding ponies, and she would have had a fit if she'd seen Kristina perched atop her new horse. Lady Ulrike didn't look especially happy about it herself, but one thing Kristina had to admit about her governess was that Lady Ulrike was one of the best horsewomen in Sweden. In fact, Kristina had heard one of the other court ladies say once that the only reason Poppa had agreed with Momma to make Lady Ulrike Kristina's governess was that he'd seen Lady Ulrike riding on the hunting field. Whether that was true or not, Lady Ulrike never fussed over Kristina's horses . . . although she was as quick to correct a fault in her charge's seat in the saddle as she was to correct any other error in deportment.

Kristina was so happy to be riding the new chestnut mare that it took her a little while to realize that they were riding almost due south. That didn't seem right. She'd sneaked into Poppa's study in the palace when she heard they were going to send her to Magdeburg and spent two cheerful hours with his big maps. Professor Belzoni, her favorite tutor, had started teaching her geography last year, and Kristina had put his instruction to good use as she pored over the maps of Northern Germany. Which was how she knew that Magdeburg was on the Elbe River. And the Elbe River was west of Wismar. So why were they heading south up a muddy dirt road beside a great big ditch full of water?

Colonel Sigvard Ekstrom rode just behind the princess and her companion. Although Ekstrom had become a member of Gustavus Adolphus' personal staff shortly after the Battle of the Alte Veste, he'd never previously met Princess Kristina. But he was himself the father of no fewer than three sons and two daughters of his own, so he'd been prepared to put the king's descriptions of his daughter's intelligence down to the natural pride and fondness of any father for his only child. Now, as he watched Kristina riding as naturally as if she were a part of the chestnut Andalusian mare, he realized that, if anything, the king had understated the blond-haired princess' intelligence. It was already evident to him that Lady Ulrike found herself hard pressed to stay ahead of the girl. It wasn't so much anything Kristina had said. Truth to tell, she hadn't actually *said* very much at all. A very well-behaved child, Ekstrom thought approvingly, especially compared to some of the highbred brats he had encountered among the ranks of Germany's aristocracy!

Yet the princess' eyes were very like her father's, windows on a sharp, incisive brain that watched everything about her. Unless he was sadly mistaken, she also nourished a healthy sense of mischief and deviltry . . . *also* very like her father, come to that. If he hadn't known how old she was, he would have guessed her age at closer to twelve than to seven, although she certainly wasn't particularly large for her age. When she actually did approach twelve, he thought, she was probably going to be quite a handful.

"Excuse me, Colonel," she said, turning to look at him almost as if she'd heard him thinking about her, "but are we headed the right way?"

"I beg your pardon, Your Highness?" he asked in some surprise.

"We're going south," she explained, pointing ahead along the muddy road—if calling such a track a "road" wasn't a gross insult to that fine and ancient noun.

"Yes, Your Highness, we are," he acknowledged.

"But we're supposed to be going to Magdeburg," she said reasonably. She gazed up at the sun for a moment, as if orienting herself, and then pointed to the west. "Shouldn't we be heading for the Elbe?" she asked.

Ekstrom felt his eyebrows rise, despite his best effort to suppress his astonishment. He'd known cavalry officers, some of them considerably senior to himself, who wouldn't have realized that, at the moment, they were headed away from the Elbe.

"In a way, Your Highness," he explained, urging his horse a little closer to hers, "we are headed for the Elbe. But not directly. This"— he pointed at the muddy ditch beside the road—"used to be a canal, which connected Lake Schwerin to Wismar. Lake Schwerin connects to the Elde River up ahead of us—" he pointed to the south, "—and another canal connects the Elde to the Elbe up at a town called Dömitz. And Dömitz is quite a bit closer to Magdeburg than Lauenburg, where the canal from Luebeck reaches the Elbe."

He was surprised, as he listened to his own voice, to find himself explaining in such detail to a child. But Princess Kristina listened closely, one hand gently stroking the thick, wavy mane of her horse. Then she nodded, but her expression was pensive.

"So, actually," she said, "it's faster to go this way?"

"Exactly, Your Highness."

"But if it's faster to go this way, why did this canal"—she gestured at the water-filled ditch—"get into such a mess? I mean, wouldn't it be smarter to use it instead of horses? Of course," she added quickly, "I really like horses. But boats can carry more."

"Indeed they can, Your Highness," Ekstrom agreed, doing his level best to keep his fresh surprise at her perceptiveness from showing. "In fact, your father the king thinks the same thing. That's why he's having this canal repaired and rebuilt. When it's finished, we'll be able to ship things straight from Wismar to Magdeburg."

"But why did whoever dug it in the first place let it get all clogged up?"

"Well, Your Highness, that's a bit difficult to explain," Ekstrom said. "I suppose the main reason is that it costs a lot of money to keep a canal like this working properly. The people who dug it ran out of money, so they couldn't maintain the canal and it started silting up. I mean, it started filling up with mud."

"But now Poppa is going to dig it out again," Kristina said with obvious pride, and Ekstrom nodded.

"That's precisely what the king intends to do," he said. *Assuming, of course, that Richelieu and Christian between them don't finally manage to bring him down,* he added mentally. But that wasn't anything to be sharing with a child. Not even one as frighteningly precocious as this one.

"It's awfully twisty, though," Kristina observed after a moment. "Wouldn't it be better if it was straighter?"

"Yes, it would, Your Highness." Despite himself, Ekstrom looked over his shoulder at Lady Ulrike. The princess' companion gave him an ironic smile, as if welcoming him into her own sometimes exhausting race to stay ahead of her charge's restlessly questing mind. For just a moment, the colonel found himself in complete sympathy with the governess. Like the rest of Gustavus Adolphus' staff, he frequently found himself feeling exhausted trying to keep up with the king. So he supposed there was no real reason he shouldn't experience the same fatigue trying to keep pace with the king's daughter.

"As a matter of fact, Your Highness," he said after a moment, "your father agrees that a straighter canal would be better. In fact, he has a team of engineers with American advisers planning a straighter route a bit west of here. But digging that canal is going to be a long and difficult task, so in the meantime, he's going to repair and improve this one."

"Why? I mean, why is it going to be harder to dig a straight ditch than one that twists and turns all over the place? Wouldn't a nice straight one be easier, since it would be so much shorter?"

"The problem, Your Highness," he explained, "is that the new route is going to require a lot more digging because of the way the land it goes through is shaped. In fact, when they dug the original canal, they followed the easiest path. As you can see, it goes around hills instead of through them or over them, and it stays down in the lowest spots along the way. It may be longer than a straight canal, but they had to do less actual digging this way than we'll have to do with the new route. And staying in the low spots made it easier for them to get the water through it, as well, although even so, they had to use locks. Like that one."

As it happened, they were just passing one of the old locks. It was in very poor repair, as was most of the canalbed, but if one knew what one was looking for, its intended function was fairly obvious. He doubted that the princess had ever seen one before, and he watched her closely, if unobtrusively, wondering if she would grasp its function.

She frowned in obvious thought, then cocked her head as she looked back at the colonel.

"It's like a little lake between two dams, isn't it?" she said, and he nodded.

"That's exactly what it is, Your Highness," he agreed. "They let water in or out through the gate at one end—when it's working, anyway—until the level in the lock is equal to the level that a boat needs to be at to keep going. That's how you get enough water to float a boat uphill."

"That's really clever!" Kristina approved in delight, and he felt himself smiling at her. She grinned back at him, every inch a little girl, then shot an almost guilty look at Lady Ulrike. "Thank you for explaining that to me, Colonel Ekstrom," she said with conscious dignity, and he inclined his head in a graceful seated bow.

"It was my pleasure, Your Highness," he told her, and allowed his horse to drop back beside Lady Ulrike. He glanced at the governess, and then fought down a most unbecoming urge to chuckle as she smiled wryly at him.

He looked away again, and the desire to chuckle faded as his eyes rested once again on the slender, slight child riding so gracefully on the horse which stood almost twice her height at the shoulder. She was as much a little girl as any child he had ever met, and yet, there was something almost frightening about her intelligence.

Perhaps it was because she was a girl, he thought. He'd been exposed to enough up-time Americans since joining the king's personal staff to come to recognize the sheer, frightening capability of many of the American women. Quite a lot of men he knew were uncomfortable around such women. Some of them, in fact, felt considerably more strongly than that, and Ekstrom had heard a few muttered comments about the unnaturalness of it all. Of course, they were careful not to utter such thoughts anywhere around the Americans themselves. Or, probably with even more cause, around the king, who had made it perfectly clear that he was not prepared to tolerate any insults to his uncanny allies. And, come to that, no one but an idiot—and probably a suicidal one, at that—was even going to think about making any such comment where Julie Mackay might hear him!

But the point was that American women, and not just up-timers—he shuddered internally as he considered Gretchen Richter—considered themselves just as capable as any man and acted accordingly. Which might be all very well for them. In fact, the colonel was prepared to admit that however unsettling he might find the concept himself, the Americans were probably onto something. Certainly it didn't make any sense to tell someone who could shoot like Julie Mackay that her place was solely in the kitchen and the nursery! None too safe to try, for that matter.

But Princess Kristina wasn't an American, any more than Gustavus Adolphus was, "Captain Gars" or no. This little girl was going to grow up to become the queen of Sweden. And if her father succeeded in his plans—as he had a habit of doing, Ekstrom reflected with a certain complacency—she would also become empress of the Confederated Principalities of Europe. No doubt brilliance would be very useful to her in that case, but how prepared would her subjects—and especially her aristocracy—be to accept a brilliant queen and empress who'd been . . . contaminated by American modes of thought?

He didn't have an answer for that question. But one thing he did know, even on this short an acquaintance with the princess: the razor-sharp mind behind that child's eyes was not the sort to accept compromises or subterfuges which required it to pretend to be less than it was.

Which could have all sorts of . . . interesting consequences for the future of Europe.

# Chapter 25

After she finished tightening the gauze mask over her face, Melissa took the spray gun handed to her by Darryl. She gripped the device much the way a devout Christian might grip a heathen fetish: on the one hand, with great and squeamish reluctance; on the other, very tightly—lest the horrid thing escape and inflict unknown havoc upon nearby innocent children.

Everyone in the room burst into laughter. After a moment, Melissa couldn't help smiling herself.

"God, do I feel stupid," she chuckled.

Darryl's laugh faded into a simple grin. "Hey, Melissa—I told ya. I'll be glad to do it myself. The stuff doesn't bother *me* any."

Melissa sniffed. "All the more reason for you not to do it! It *should* bother you. You'll be careless."

Darryl's eyes rolled. "Fer Chrissake," he muttered. "It's just DDT. You're acting like it's nerve gas or mustard gas, or sumthin'."

Melissa eyed the spray gun with distaste. "Besides, I'm by far the oldest person here. So whatever the foul stuff does to me it isn't likely—I suppose—to kill me off until I'm dead of old age anyway. And since I'm past menopause, there's no problem with effects on my offspring."

Now it was Rita's turn to roll her eyes. In the two years since the Ring of Fire, Mike Stearns' sister had devoted her energies to nursing and medical studies. Although she was no doctor—nor even a nurse, by the strict standards of a pre-Ring of Fire RN—

she had far more medical expertise than anyone else in the U.S. delegation to England.

"Melissa," she said, almost sighing, "how many times do we have to go over this? The health hazards involved in using DDT are long-term, and have a lot to do with how frequently you get exposed to it. It's not likely to hurt any of us to spray it once in a while, especially if we take simple precautions like wearing a breathing block—" Here she nodded toward the gauze mask on Melissa's face. "—wash the clothes used afterward, keep the windows closed while spraying so it'll settle quickly. Hell, people have even been known to *eat* the stuff and not die from it." A bit hastily: "Not that it's a good idea, of course. It *is* toxic, no doubt about it. And for a rich country like our old U.S. of A., it made plenty of sense to stop using it. But—"

Melissa waved her hand impatiently—just for a brief moment, before she resumed her firm clutch on the heathen device.

"Spare me the lecture," she grumbled. "I admit I'm probably a little eccentric on the subject—old habits die hard—but I'm not actually crazy. I know perfectly well that the fatality rate from typhus or bubonic plague makes the toxic side effects of DDT look like cotton candy. I *still* don't have to like it."

She waved the spray gun around, almost threateningly. "Now get out of here, all of you. To quote the Bard—whoever the hell he is, and that's something else I'd like to find out while we're here because I still don't quite believe Balthazar about the earl of Oxford anymore than I believed those slick-talking company spokesmen I can remember swearing that benzene was harmless—until the poor slobs on the factory floor who were making it started dropping like flies from cancer of the liver—and dammit, I *liked* the idea that the English language's finest poet and playwright was a nobody from the sticks—"

Everybody's eyes were now almost crossed, trying to follow the convoluted thought processes. Melissa stopped her prattle, cleared her throat noisily, and got to the point:

" 'If t'were done at all, best t'were done quickly.' *Scat!*"

The Schoolmarm's Voice, that last. Everyone scatted—hastily—while Melissa marched toward the far corner of their rooms in St. Thomas' Tower. Darryl was the last one to emerge onto the walkway connecting their suite to the inner walls of the tower. By the time he closed the door, he could hear Melissa's growls interspersed with the *spish-spish* of a manually operated spray pump being furiously worked.

He grinned, and pressed an ear against the door. "That's telling 'em, girl!" His voice took on a little falsetto, mimicking Melissa. "'Die, bug, die! Out, damned louse!' And then there's something in . . . sounds like Latin, maybe. 'Sick sumper rickets perwacky,' I think."

Rita was grinning too. "'Sic semper Rickettsia prowazekii,' I bet. That translates more or less as: *thus to all the damned critters that cause typhus.* Rickettsia prowazekii is the germ involved in that disease. It's sorta like a bacterium."

"Only good bug is a dead bug," said Darryl, nodding approvingly.

Tom Simpson chuckled. "Don't let Melissa hear you say that, Darryl—not unless you want a lecture on how most bugs are our friends and you shouldn't squash spiders."

Darryl winced. Tom started to add something else, but felt a hand on his elbow. Turning his head, he saw that one of the Yeoman Warders standing guard on the walkway—as always, keeping the Americans from entering the inner Tower except under escort—had come up behind him. Politely, the man was leaning his partisan away.

Away, yes—but the great blade of the weapon was still honed sharp, and gleamed in the morning sun.

"Yes, Andrew?" he asked. By now, Tom had made it a point to learn the names of all the Yeoman Warders assigned to stand guard over the American delegation. They all had.

"If you'll pardon my asking, m'lord—ah, sir—what are you *doing* in there?"

The words were not spoken in a hostile tone. This was not the query of a guard investigating suspicious conduct, simply the question of man puzzled—not for the first time—by the sometimes odd conduct of these rather eccentric Americans.

"We're spraying our rooms with a chemical we brought with us. It's called 'DDT' for short." Tom nodded toward Rita. "You'd have to ask my wife what the letters actually stand for. I've forgotten. Some long bunch of chemical terms."

Andrew frowned. "Why?"

"The stuff kills most kinds of germs—small things; you can't see them with the naked eye—that carry disease. Well, some diseases, anyway. It'll work against the germs that carry typhus—what you all call 'Gaol fever,' I think—and bubonic plague, I know that."

Rita chimed in. "Tom doesn't have it quite right. DDT doesn't kill the bacteria directly, what it does is kill the lice which transmit it."

By now, Andrew's two companion guards had come up also. All three of them were frowning fiercely, obviously lost in the "explanation." But one word did register.

"That . . . ah, 'DDT,'" said Andrew. "It kills *lice.*" Reflexively, all three Yeoman Warders started scratching themselves.

"Yup," said Tom. "Deader'n doornails. Of course, you have to keep spraying an area now and then to get the full effect. But we brought quite a bit of the stuff with us, and it really doesn't take that much. I imagine we've got enough to spray all the places in the Tower where people actually live. Rita?"

She nodded firmly. "Not often," she qualified. "Some places— except the sleeping areas—probably not more than once. But DDT decays at a very slow rate. The stuff'll last for years—which is a good part of the reason, of course, that back in the U.S. of A.— the old U.S. of A., I mean—we finally decided—"

She broke off, obviously realizing that this was neither the time nor the place to delve into the long-term drawbacks of using DDT. Her husband charged into the breach.

"And it helps a lot—a *lot*," said Tom firmly, "if you also have your clothing and bedding regularly cleaned. They need to be steam cleaned, though, to kill the lice. Regular washing won't do it."

The three guards stared at each other. Then, back at Tom. "What is, ah, 'steam cleaning'?" asked Andrew.

Tom started to answer, but Rita interrupted. "We can show you— *but*, you'll have to give us some help."

Immediately, the frowns on the faces of the Yeoman Warders changed from those of puzzlement to suspicion. "We canna—" Andrew started to say.

Rita shook her head. "I'm not talking about any kind of private or secret 'help.' You'd have to get the agreement of your own commanding officer, or whoever"—she waved her hand—"is really in charge of this place. Which I never have quite figured out. For all I know, it's the earl of Strafford himself."

The frowns of puzzlement were back. Rita smiled sweetly. "In order to 'steam clean,' we'd have to set up something we call a 'laundry.' Which doesn't mean exactly the same thing you probably think it means. We'd have to build some kind of big central heating area, run water through it to make steam, then—"

Now at a bit of a loss, she glanced appealingly at Friedrich Bruch. As was his usual manner, the always-quiet Friedrich had been standing toward the rear of the little crowd gathered in conversation on the walkway. Seeing Rita's eyes upon him, he shuffled forward.

"I worked for a time in the big public laundry in Grantville," he said softly. Softly, but not hesitantly. "I can design a steam-cleaning system for the Tower, given the necessary resources and labor. It's really pretty simple, when you get down to it."

The guards stared at him. Stared at Tom and Rita. Then, stared at the door to St. Thomas' Tower. The door was opening now, Melissa almost charging through.

*"Faugh!"* she exclaimed, tearing the mask from her face. Then, imperiously, handed the spray gun to Darryl. "Take this thing, would you? I've had enough of it."

Seeing the three guards, almost ogling her, Melissa gave them a somewhat savage smile. "I will say this, however. I won't be scratching myself to sleep every night. Typhus and plague be damned! That alone is worth its weight in gold."

Three Yeoman Warders, as one man, started scratching reflexively.

After the earl of Strafford had explained the situation to the man who was considered probably England's foremost doctor of the day, Sir William Harvey frowned.

"If I understand you correctly, my lord, you are concerned that this might be a subtle ploy on the part of the Americans? An attempt, perhaps, to poison the entire population of the Tower."

Strafford pursed his lips. "Not that, exactly. Perhaps." Suddenly, he heaved a great sigh. "Sir William, to be honest I don't *know* what it is I fear—or might fear, or should perhaps fear. If anything. For all I know, their proposal—their offer, if you will—is quite genuine. I simply . . ."

His voice trailed off into silence. Harvey's lips quirked a bit, into something that was half a smile of understanding and half a grimace of shared exasperation.

"Ah, yes, Lord Strafford—I *do* understand. Believe me! The short time I spent in Grantville was often, ah, frustrating. Never quite knowing what to believe, and what not. The great discomfort—great discomfort—of old sureties being rattled by new and—to me, at least—outlandish theories. Still—"

The doctor swiveled his head and stared out the window of the palace. His eyes seemed slightly unfocused.

"I do not think . . ." He took a long breath. Then, abruptly: "You've read, I suspect, the long report I wrote for His Majesty on my experiences in Grantville?"

Strafford nodded.

"Do you recall my account of a public session I attended of what they call their 'Congress'? It's a bit similar to our own Parliament."

Again Strafford nodded; the gesture, this time, accompanied by a thoughtful running of his fingers through his thick hair. "You are referring, I imagine, to the dispute that took place over the use of—what did they call it? 'Chemical warfare'?"

"Yes. 'Chemical and biological warfare,' to be precise. I sat through the entire debate, my lord. There's a gallery from which guests can observe the proceedings. I was quite fascinated—and more by the political struggle taking place, really, than the scientific aspects of the question."

Strafford grunted. "You don't believe, then, that the whole thing was a staged performance?" He hesitated for a moment, then added: "That seems to be the opinion of His Majesty himself, and most of his courtiers. Laud thinks so as well."

Harvey barked a little laugh. "'Staged'? For my benefit, you mean? So that I might scurry back and warn everyone that the Americans have the capability of slaughtering entire nations?"

Strafford nodded. Harvey barked another laugh. "To be honest, my lord, I doubt if many of their officials were even aware that I was in the gallery. And that hardly explains the speech given by their President, when he insisted on addressing the Congress directly. You did read that portion of the report also?"

Strafford smiled. "Yes, I did. I was rather amused, despite the man's appalling language. He seems a blunt and direct sort of fellow." The earl closed his eyes for a moment, summoning his memory—which was, as always, excellent—and began reciting:

"'If you pass this stinking bill, I will veto it. If you override my veto, I will refuse to implement the provisions in my capacity as the head of the armed forces. I will also give it a development budget too small to pay for a child's toy. If you try to impeach me for so doing, I guarantee you will be in the worst damn brawl of your lives. We outlawed this crap in the world we came from, for Chrissake—and for good reason!—so why is anybody here such a fucking idiot as to think it's a good idea in the new one? Do I make myself clear? Go ahead, try me."

Harvey smiled. "Mind you, my lord, I doubt if the proposal would have been adopted anyway. But after that little speech—he broke custom, apparently, by even appearing to give it in the first place—the thing was dropped immediately."

Strafford studied the doctor. "And what do you think? *Could* the Americans make such weapons?"

Harvey shrugged. "From what I could tell, based on conversations I had with various people . . . the answer is both 'yes' and 'no.' Yes, they could *make* them. But not without great difficulty, and not in such quantities as to enable them to poison entire nations."

"But possibly in enough quantities to poison a much smaller place," stated Strafford immediately. "Such as, for instance, the Tower of London."

Harvey hesitated, then nodded. He began to add something, but Strafford shook his head.

"No, that doesn't solve the problem. Obviously, they wouldn't want to poison themselves at the same time. But who is to say they don't have an antidote of some kind already with them? We've never searched their rooms or their luggage, you know. Nor, given the need to maintain at least the appearances of diplomatic niceties, am I prepared to order such a search. I am violating established custom badly enough as it is, by keeping them sequestered."

The doctor was silent. Strafford kept studying him. "And I would remind you, doctor, that according to the accounts we've received— three of them, now, from independent sources—the Americans did not hesitate to use some sort of fiendish incendiary weapon against the Spanish troops they trapped in the Wartburg."

Again, Harvey began to speak; but, again, Strafford shook his head. "No, doctor, that won't do either. I am aware, also, that the Americans seem to have taken care at the Wartburg to keep the Spanish casualties to a minimum. I am not suggesting these people are a new tribe of Tatars. Still, we cannot make too many assumptions about what they will and won't do. It seems odd to me that they make such a fuss about *some* forms of what they call 'chemical warfare,' but don't seem to have any qualms about roasting a man to death with another. Contradictory, that is, from any philosophical or theological or ethical standpoint I can imagine. So, at least, it seems to me."

Harvey was silent. Finally, Strafford allowed a little smile to come to his face. "Oh—say it, doctor. I am not trying to browbeat you. Simply, if you will, playing the good sophist by arguing the other side of the case."

Harvey returned the smile with one of his own. "Nor, for that matter, should you assume I am their partisan, my lord. There was much about the Americans that, frankly, I found quite distasteful. But the fact remains—"

He squared his shoulders a bit. "The fact remains that one thing I did notice, while I was there—impossible *not* to notice it, save you were a blind man—was the great care they take of children. Much better care, to be honest, that we often do in our own kingdom."

Strafford's lips tightened, but he did not argue the point. He had often been appalled himself, since his youth, at the condition of many of England's children. Especially those of paupers.

"The Tower is full of children, is what you are saying."

"Yes, My Lord. And I remind you that the one woman—" For a moment, Harvey's lips twisted into a grimace. "The one who seems to fancy herself some kind of 'lady.' Well. The point being, that whatever her pretensions now, she was—by all accounts—"

"A teacher of children. And for most of a lifetime."

Harvey nodded. Strafford turned slightly away from the doctor and clasped his hands behind his back. "Do not be misled by your own habits, doctor," he said softly. "I have, as it happens, spent a number of hours in the company of *Lady* Mailey." There was just a slight emphasis on the title. "Which you have not, I believe. That she *is* a 'lady,' in some fundamental sense of the term, is not subject to doubt."

Harvey accepted the mild reproof without demur. Strafford swiveled his head back toward him. "Still, as you say, a former teacher of children. And I believe you are correct in this matter, doctor. Whatever else that woman might be capable of, I find it impossible to imagine her deliberately poisoning dozens of innocent children. True, it is a sinful world. But some crimes, at least, we may have safely left behind us."

He smiled crookedly. "Which, now that I think upon the matter, is exactly what their President said to their own Congress. If not, admittedly, with such a fine turn of phrase as my own."

For a moment, he and William Harvey shared a little laugh. When that was over, Strafford issued his commands.

"We shall do it, then. Give the Americans in the Tower whatever they ask for—within reason—in the way of resources and labor. If nothing else, this might prove to be an interesting and valuable test of their claims. Their moral claims, even more than their mechanical ones—which, I think, will prove in the end to be the most important thing to know about them. I would ask you, however, to oversee the affair from the standpoint of the crown."

"Yes, my lord. Ah—"

"No need, I think, to concern King Charles over such a small matter as building a clothes-cleaning apparatus and killing insects. Nor, of course, do I expect you to take any time away from the medical demands of His Majesty and the queen."

"Ah, yes. my lord. You understand—"

"Yes, yes. I am aware that the queen's health is frail and she requires a great deal of attention. Simply give this affair at the Tower as much attention as you can."

"Yes, my lord."

On the third day of the spraying of the Tower of London, Darryl McCarthy was manning the spray gun. Toward the end of the day, he insisted on spraying the special dungeons where the most dangerous criminals were kept.

"Doesn't do any good," he said forcefully, "if you don't kill *all* the lice—and you know as well as I do, Andrew, that the damn things will be worse in there than anywhere else!"

By this time, the Official Sprayer was a title of great—even if informal—respect. Somewhat helplessly, the Yeoman Warder looked to Doctor Harvey for guidance. After a moment's hesitation, Harvey nodded his approval.

"But the prisoners will not be allowed to leave their cells during the process," he said firmly. "If they suffer some ill-effects, so be it. Most of them will be dead soon enough anyway."

Darryl didn't argue the point. Truth be told, he agreed with the good doctor.

When Darryl entered the fourth cell, the Yeoman Warder accompanying him curtly ordered the prisoner into a corner. Once the man was there, Andrew fastened his manacles and hastily backed out of the chamber, closing the heavy door behind him.

The moment he heard the sound of the bar being dropped across the outer door, Darryl began by spraying the prisoner himself. Most vigorously.

"Take that, you Sasanach bastard. If the Brits don't chop you, I hope this gives you cancer. Black-and-Tan asshole. Butcher of Ireland." *Spish-spish-spish.* "I didn't have orders, I'd shove this thing down your throat and let you have the whole lot."

The prisoner was covering his face with his hands. Still snarling obscenities, Darryl turned away and finished spraying the rest of the chamber. Then, started fumbling beneath the heavy protective garment he was wearing. Rita and Nelly had designed and sewn the thing. It was something like a combination of a poncho and a pair of "heavy duty pajamas." Very bulky—certainly bulky enough to conceal a small object like a walkie-talkie.

"Orders," muttered Darryl. "I *still* say this is a bad idea. Here, fuckwad—take it. Keep it hidden." He smacked the prisoner on the top of his head with the spray gun. "Dammit—pay attention! You see this button?"

Bleary-eyed, the prisoner stared up at him. Then, down at the button on the strange device. Darryl smacked him again. The prisoner nodded.

"That turns it on and off." He glanced up to make sure the cell had an arrow slit through which the prisoner could tell if it was day or night. "Keep it off except just after sundown. Then turn it on until you hear a voice. Then do what the lady says. See this button? Looks kinda like a little black wheel sticking out on the side."

*Smack.* The prisoner nodded.

"That's the volume control. That means the voice will sound louder or softer. Turn it down as low as you can and still hear it. So the guards don't. The gadget's set for VOX, so you just talk into it. But remember that when you're talking, you can't be listening. So shut up when you're done so she can get a word in. And that's it. Even a stinking murderous shithead like you should be able to figure it out."

For good measure, Darryl gave him a few last spurts of DDT—*spish-spish-spish*—and stalked over to the door. By the time Andrew opened it, in response to his hammering fist, Darryl was humming the tune of "The Men Behind the Wire."

Shortly after sundown, the prisoner did as he had been instructed. He heard a woman's voice coming out of the strange little box. Hastily, he followed the orders he had been given and swiveled the little wheel until the voice was barely loud enough to hear.

"—*mwell. Oliver Cromwell. Come in. Are you there?*"

A bit hesitantly, he spoke. "Aye. 'Tis I."

There was a little pause. Then he heard the woman muttering something. It sounded something like "*damn Darryl—didn't he—*" He didn't catch the rest.

A moment later, the woman said: "—*can barely hear you. You need to hold the—ah, the thing—up close to your mouth. Talk into the grille—ah, the crosshatch-looking part—ah, what do you call it—*"

He smiled. "I understand. Is this better?"

"*Yes. Good! Now, listen. This thing is called a 'walkie-talkie.' With it, we can talk to you from where we are, which is in a part of the Tower called St. Thomas' Tower. But you don't have a lot of power to spare—*"

He didn't understand the sentence or two which followed. Something involving "batteries," though he didn't see where massed guns had anything to do with the subject at hand.

"—*only right after sundown, you understand? If you leave it on, you'll drain it.*"

That seemed clear enough. "Aye. Only after sundown, and then turn it off when you instruct me to do so."

"*You got it. Good.*" There was another pause. "*That's really all I've got for tonight. Any questions?*"

The prisoner thought for a moment. Then, in a mild tone of voice: "Yes, actually, I do have a question. Why did the man you sent to deliver this device strike me on the head—several times—spray what I suspect is poison in my face, and bestow a truly monumental string of curses upon me? I don't recall ever meeting the fellow."

He heard another muttered string of phrases. The only part he understood was: "—*kill the stupid kid, I swear I will—*"

She broke off abruptly. "*It's because he's Irish and you—well, the 'you' that would have been—conquered Ireland once and apparently—depends who you hear this from—either killed half the Irish or—ah, hell, never mind. He's holding a grudge for something you did about fifteen years from now. In another universe.*"

"Ah." The prisoner nodded. The little smile on his face widened. "It seems fitting enough. The king is peeved with me for a similar reason. So why should my—ah, allies—not feel the same?"

"*Well.*" Another pause. "*It's all pretty complicated. To be honest, I'm not sure what I think about the whole thing myself. Not just you, I mean—everything. We're from the future, you know. Americans. You may have heard about us.*"

"Oh, to be sure. The earl of Strafford has waxed eloquent on the subject to me, once or twice. I confess I was somewhat skeptical. Apparently I was wrong."

Silence. Then: "*Okay. Well, I guess I'll sign off now. Remember to turn the walkie-talkie off.*"

"A moment, please. What is your name, Lady of the Walkie-Talkie? And do you have any thoughts on the subject of predestination? I have been puzzling over that matter myself, these past many weeks. Nothing much else to do, of course."

"*My name? It's Gayle Mason. As for predestination . . . oh, hell, Oliver Cromwell. I haven't got the faintest idea. I always just figured a person should try to do the right thing and let God figure out the rest of it.*"

"Ah. Splendid. A Puritan after my own heart."

He heard what sounded like a snort. "*Ha! 'Puritan,' is it? That's sure as hell not what my ex-husband called me.*"

"The more fool him, then." The prisoner's smile became something rather sad. "Enough. I'll not keep you, Lady Gayle. I suppose it is just that I have not heard the sound of a woman's voice since . . . since my wife died. It's a sound I miss a great deal."

Again, there was silence. The prisoner began to push the button, then paused. "Is there some proper signal I should give, before shutting down this little machine?"

"*Oh. Yeah. 'Seventy-three.' But—*"

"Aye?"

"*Ah . . . never mind. I'm sorry about your wife and your son. We heard what happened from some of the Yeoman Warders. Ah . . . never mind. I'll call you again tomorrow night, Oliver Cromwell.*"

"And the nights after that?"

"*Oh, yeah. Sure. Every night. And now, ah—*"

"Seventy-three, Lady Gayle. May the Lord watch over you."

# Part IV

*A tattered coat upon a stick*

# Chapter 26

"Goddamit, Mike, we've got to put a stop to this! We're too sloppy, I tell you. We might as well be handing out all our technical secrets on street corners."

Mike leaned back in his chair and studied Quentin Underwood for a moment, before he replied. He was trying to gauge exactly how much he would be forced to let Quentin know, in order to head off another one of the man's typical bull-in-a-china-shop rampages. There was a part of Mike—no small part, either—that wished Underwood would finally sever his connection with the July Fourth Party and go it on his own politically. Granted, the immediate damage would be significant. But, in the long run—

*At least I'd be spared these constant clashes with him,* Mike thought sourly. *Quentin may be one of the best industrial managers the world's ever seen, but what he understands about how a society works could be inscribed on the head of a . . .*

For a moment, Mike indulged himself in a little fantasy where he set all the world's scientists to find a pin small enough to fit Quentin Underwood's "social consciousness" on its head.

*Can't be done,* he decided. *We left all the electron microscopes behind in that other universe.*

He realized he couldn't stall any longer. Underwood's flushed face showed the man was working himself up to another explosion.

"Oh, calm down," he growled. *What the hell, let's try it one last time.* "Quentin, I've told you this before, but you never even listen to me. Whatever short-term damage might be done to us because of our 'open books' policy isn't a pittance compared to the long-term damage that clamping down would do. I don't have a problem with locking up a *few* books, and I've done it. But that only applies to stuff that involves immediate and specific details about weapons-making that really *can* be kept a secret, at least for a while. An example is that old 1910 book on guns by Greener that Paul Santee owned and all the gunmakers slobber over. Or Chapelle's books, with the building drafts for all those 19th-century frigates and ships-of-the-line."

Underwood, from his sullen expression, wasn't moved in the least. Mike decided to match Quentin's temper with his own. He slammed the palm of his hand down on the desk. He was a very strong man, with a large hand. The sound bore a reasonable resemblance to a thunderclap.

"Damnation! Do you even *listen* to the reports Dr. Nichols gives the cabinet?"

That jarred Quentin. A bit, at least. Underwood leaned back in his own chair, his hands braced on the armrests, and said defensively: "Hey, c'mon! I've been up in the Wietze oil field for the last stretch. Just got back a few days ago."

"James has been giving us the same message for a year," growled Mike in return. He wasn't going to let Quentin off the hook that easily. "Longer than that—and you've *never* paid any attention."

He levered himself out of his chair and took two steps to the window. Jabbing a forefinger at the teeming little city of Grantville below, he said:

"Thirty percent, Quentin. That's probably the lowest fatality rate we can expect, if we get hit with a really good dose of the plague. *Or* typhus. *Or* smallpox. *Or*—hell, you name it." Frowning: "And it could be worse than that, especially if it's plague. Some of the Italian cities have suffered a death rate in excess of sixty percent, from what we've heard. Every city in Europe in this era is a mortality sink. People die in them faster than they get born. The only reason urban areas exist at all is because paupers and poor peasants keep drifting into them hoping for a better chance. And most of them are young, too—which gives you some idea of how badly disease hits the cities."

He heard Underwood shifting in his chair. "I thought . . . I mean, dammit, I still don't like the idea of relying on a hippie drug-dealer, but he does seem to know what he's doing. I thought you were

pretty sure we'd have some of this—what do you call?—cloram-
something or other. Ready by now. Supposed to be some kind of
wonder drug, even if"—his voice was a bit skeptical now—"I never
heard of it."

Mike smiled thinly. "Chloramphenicol. Also known as Chlor-
omycitin. And it *is* a wonder drug, Quentin. Very effective against
typhoid fever and syphilis as well as plague and typhus."

He turned away from the window. "James tells me it was real
big back in the 1950s. Which, of course, is before your time or
mine. That's why neither one of us heard of it before, because they
dropped it in favor of other stuff, back in the universe we came
from. The problem, apparently, is that about one in twenty-five
thousand people has a really bad reaction to it. Bad reaction, as
in fatal. Kids—not many, but some—were dying just from being
treated for an ear infection. So, with penicillin and other drugs
available, it pretty much got put back on the shelves. But, for us,
it's the one major antibiotic we can make quickly. And a one-in-
twenty-five-thousand fatality rate in a world facing epidemics of
bubonic plague just isn't worth worrying about."

He moved back to his chair and almost flopped into it. Mike
was feeling bone tired, more from what seemed like never-ending
stress than any actual physical weariness. Becky's absence was
especially hard on him.

"Yeah, we can *make* it, Quentin. Stoner already has, in fact. Just
like he and Sally over at the pharmacy—your son-in-law at the
chem plant too, for that matter—have been able to make some
of the sulfa drugs and DDT. But we can't make *enough*. That's the
problem. We're doing better with DDT, but as far as the medi-
cines go . . . right now, we've got enough stockpiled to treat a few
thousand people. That's it, and the stockpile only grows slowly.
A trickle—with, by now, maybe a million people just in the United
States alone. Ten million, probably—maybe more, who knows?—
in the CPE as a whole."

He gave Underwood a stony gaze under lowered eyebrows.
"Stainless steel, Quentin. That's what we need in order to move
from home-lab bucket-scale production to real industrial production. That's what we need in order to turn antibiotics from a social
and political nightmare into an asset. From a *privilege*—who gets
it? and who decides?—into a *right*." He waved a hand at the
window. "Yeah, sure, we've been able to scrape up some stainless
from what we brought with us in the Ring of Fire. Enough stock

in the machine shops to make valves, that kind of thing. A couple of small dairy tanks, the lucky break of having a tanker truck in town when the Ring of Fire hit. Some other stuff. But we need *lots* of it, Quentin. Thick slabs of it, too, not just thin sheet. Some of these chemical processes require a lot of pressure as well as high temperatures."

As always, given a technical problem, that impressive part of Quentin Underwood's brain which wasn't half-paralyzed by bias and preconception was now working. "How about—"

Mike laughed. "Leave off, Quentin! You've got enough on your plate as it is getting our petroleum industry up and running. Without that—also—everything else is moot anyway. Besides, you're missing my whole point."

He leaned forward and tapped the desk with stiff fingers. "Forget *us* doing it, in the first place. There are tens of millions of people in Europe today, Quentin. They are just as smart as we are—smarter, some of 'em—and plenty of them have as much initiative and get-up-and-go as we do. And they're often—more often than not—in a better position to do something than we are. For stainless steel, just to name one instance, you've got to have access to chromium. Which they already *have* in Sweden. In fact, Gustav's sent out an expedition to examine some place called Kemi, somewhere in or near Finland.

"So let them do it. Hell, let the *French* do it, if that's how it winds up shaking down. Once anybody starts making stainless steel, you won't be able to stop it from spreading. Provided—"

Here he gave Quentin his best glare. "Provided that *we* didn't put a roadblock in the way by locking up every book that might have a so-called 'technical secret' in it."

Quentin tried to match the glare, but gave it up after a few seconds. "Well, I guess," he grumbled. "But I still hate to just see us standing around with our thumb up our ass while these bastards rob us blind."

Mike was tempted to respond. *I didn't say we weren't going to do anything, Quentin.* But, with a little mental sigh, he left the words unspoken. The worst thing about having state secrets, Mike had discovered, was that you couldn't brag about it over a beer after work.

Not long after Underwood left, Mike was handed a radio message. From Gustav Adolf himself, in Luebeck. After he finished reading it, he had a powerful urge to drink something a lot stronger than beer.

"Very good," murmured Francisco Nasi, as his eyes scanned down the pages. He gave Freddie Congden a quick smile of approval.

Freddie, slouched on his couch, responded with a sullen scowl. But he didn't snarl or make any excessively overt indication of his disapproval of the Sephardic Jew who was, for all practical purposes, his lord and master. Since the "new arrangement" had been made, Freddie Congden had at least been civil, if not polite. Clearly enough, he was too terrified of Harry Lefferts to do otherwise.

Francisco did not blame him. Harry Lefferts, except for his casual Americanisms, reminded the Sephardic banker of some of the Ottoman emperor's *spahis*. To be precise, the ones the emperor tended to use as his personal guards. Not men anyone in their right mind took lightly when they issued threats.

"Very good," he repeated. That was, in some ways, a lie. Freddie Congden's handwriting was so bad that Francisco had difficulty understanding some of the scrawled words which Freddie had copied from one of his son's books. But, under the circumstances, the semi-legibility of the writing simply added authenticity to the text.

"Now, I need you to add something." Francisco set the pages down on the edge of the table. Sullenly as ever, Freddie rose from the couch, slouched over, and slumped in a chair.

"You may continue from the point where you left off, in your history of the California Gold Rush. I shall dictate the words to you."

With no enthusiasm at all, Freddie picked up the pen. Francisco cleared his throat. The next words came slightly stilted, as words will issued in dictation.

"Despite the wealth of the California gold fields, they were very difficult to reach and the ore was hard to extract. So, the California Gold Rush was soon overshadowed by new discoveries of gold in that part of Florida—"

"*Florida?*" choked Freddie, his scrawling suspended for a moment. "Hey, I *been* to Florida. There ain't no gold—"

Sternly, Francisco's finger indicated the page. Freddie resumed his scrawling.

"—known as the Everglades."

❈        ❈        ❈

When he was done, Freddie scowled at Nasi. "What you got against Florida, anyway?"

"Absolutely nothing," replied Francisco with a smile. "I am especially taken by the prevalence of malaria. And, of course, by the fact that the French and the Spanish, once they get to fighting over it, will find the place a swamp. In more ways than one."

When Francisco Nasi returned to the converted office building in downtown Grantville which served as the quarters for the executive branch of the U.S. government, the soldier standing guard outside Mike Stearns' office began to open the door as soon as Francisco appeared on the landing. Nasi recognized the man as readily as the soldier had recognized him. Sergeant Gerd Fuhrmann, that was, one of the small group of soldiers whom Captain Harry Lefferts had begun assembling around himself in what amounted to a semi-informal special unit.

Nasi was tempted to call it a Praetorian Guard, but he knew the term would be inaccurate. True, "Harry's guys" had the task of guarding the President of the United States. But Francisco suspected their real function was—or would be, soon enough— much closer to what the English term "commando" captured.

"*Señor* Nasi," Gerd murmured politely. Nasi nodded and returned the greeting, appreciating the subtlety. Among the Sephardim themselves, Francisco Nasi was considered a hidalgo. Sephardic Jews, even those like Nasi who had been raised in the Ottoman Empire, still retained the cultural trappings of their Iberian homeland. But most Americans and Germans were oblivious to such matters, and would have simply called him "Mister" or "Herr."

As he walked through the door, Francisco found himself mulling over that unexpected subtlety. It did not come from Gerd himself, of that Nasi was quite certain. Gerd had been one of Tilly's mercenaries captured after the first battle at Badenburg, who had enlisted afterward in the U.S. Army. A German commoner of some kind, prior to that.

Mike was standing at the window overlooking the town, his hands clasped behind his back. "I think Harry Lefferts has currents beneath the surface," said Francisco cheerfully.

Mike turned his head, showing his profile. A thin smile came to his face. "Oh, I'd say so. Just two days ago I caught him actually reading a book."

Francisco and Mike shared a little laugh. As Mike pulled out the chair to his desk and sat down, the smile broadened. "Not just any book, either, but a genu-ine I-will-be-good-goddamned history book. He's starting to learn French, too, I heard. His Italian's already pretty good."

"Mazarini's influence, I think."

Mike nodded. Harry had been sent along as something of a bodyguard for the Vatican diplomat Mazarini who had returned to Italy after a visit to Grantville the previous year. The young American had spent months in the company of Mazarini—a man who was already, even at a young age, recognized as one of Europe's premier diplomats. And who would someday, under the Francofied name of "Mazarin," have become Cardinal Richelieu's successor in another universe.

"Mostly, yes. But give Harry himself some credit too. I think he's finally realizing it was time he grew up. All the way, if you know what I mean."

Francisco started to report on his latest little session with Freddie Congden, but Mike waved him silent before he'd finished the second sentence.

"Enough, Francisco. I trust you to handle that situation just fine. To be honest, it's pretty small potatoes now anyway. I'm dead sure Freddie wasn't the *only* leak, so the best we can hope for is just to keep the other side confused a bit." He paused briefly. "Actually, I'd just as soon you turned the Freddie business over to somebody else. Unless I miss my guess, we're going to have a lot bigger fish to fry before much longer."

Slowly, Francisco eased himself into a chair across the desk. "That's right. I'd forgotten. Today was to be the opening of the special session Gustav Adolf called for the Chamber of Princes in Magdeburg. How did it go?"

"I don't know yet. Simpson told me he'd pass word over the radio as soon as he heard anything."

Francisco cocked a skeptical eyebrow. Mike shrugged. "Oh, I don't think he'll play any games with it. Not that he won't be tempted. But don't forget that he's got Eddie Cantrell—Nat Davis too, for that matter—more or less watching him."

"Simpson is—ah—very strong on military discipline, I understand."

"So what? Eddie won't try to buck Simpson over any *military* matter. But if Simpson should try to start mucking around in political waters while he's in Magdeburg, Eddie will at least make sure I know about it."

In a half-irritated manner, Mike rubbed his jaw. "Ah, hell. The truth is—much as part of me hates to admit it—I think John Simpson is doing a hell of good job up there. And if he's diddling around in imperial politics on the side, he's at least keeping it under the table. I never expected the guy to act the saint. But as long as he doesn't sup with the devil in broad daylight on the terrace, I'll more or less look the other way."

Francisco's smile was rather crooked. "You are such an oddly tolerant man, for a 'ruler.' I fear for your sanity, at times. And for your life, quite a bit more often."

Mike's returning smile was equally crooked. "Method to my madness, I'm telling you. Not sure what it is yet, but I know it's there." He planted his forearms on the desk and leaned forward. "But I think the real reason we haven't heard anything is way simpler than John Chandler Simpson playing petty games when it comes to relaying important news. I don't think there *is* any news yet, because the session isn't over. And unless I miss my guess, won't be over for some time. Days, for sure, maybe for many weeks."

Francisco drew in a deep breath through wide nostrils. "Ah. You think, in other words, the princes will try to use this crisis to extort concessions from the emperor. Stall as long as they can, quibble, fuss—they're *so* good at that—while Richelieu and his allies put the squeeze on."

He made a face. Extorting anything from a man like Gustavus Adolphus was . . . what the Americans called "a dicey proposition." But German princes were notorious for combining caution—to the point of cowardice—over major things with recklessness over petty ones. Like a man who'd let a fire grow until it burnt his house down, because he was unwilling to risk his favorite boots stamping out the initial small flames.

Mike snorted. "'Princes,'" he mimicked. "What a pretentious title. For a handful of them, the word might mean something. John George of Saxony, George William of Brandenburg—even, to a degree, Wilhelm of Hesse-Kassel. The rest? The so-called 'Hochadel'? A pack of puffed-up peacocks. Hundreds of them—'high nobles' one and all—most of whom rule over territories which aren't much bigger than a good-sized cattle ranch in my old U.S.A."

"Still," cautioned Francisco, "with the legal and political structure as it currently exists, they have a great deal of influence. And, what is probably even more important, a multitude of ways in which they can serve as impediments and stumbling blocks."

"Tell me about it," snarled Mike. "We *still* haven't been able to negotiate something as simple and straightforward as free passage down the Elbe. Don't even think about a common imperial currency, as desperately as it's needed. Much less—ha!—a coherent and systematized tax structure."

For a moment, he left off in order to glower at a painting on a nearby wall. The innocuous landscape seemed quite undeserving of the displeasure.

Mike himself apparently felt as much; for, within seconds, he was chuckling softly. Nasi felt a momentary surge of affection for the man. Mike Stearns was one of those rare leaders who combined intelligence, shrewdness, decisiveness—and good humor, far more often than not. With a bit of a shock, Francisco realized that over the past months he, too, had become something of a "Stearns loyalist." Which was quite an odd sentiment, really, for a man brought up in the knife-in-the-back atmosphere of the Ottoman court. In Istanbul, Machiavelli would have been considered a neophyte. A dabbler and a dilettante.

Nasi chuckled as well. Not the least of Mike Stearns' talents was the ability to spot and use the talents of others.

"So. You wish me to go to Magdeburg. I warn you though, Michael, most of those 'princes' will refuse to meet with a Jew."

Mike's curled lip was not quite a sneer. The sentiment was there, to be sure. But the expression conveyed almost too much in the way of contempt—as if the subject of the curled lip was not even worth the effort of a full sneer.

"Don't care about *them*," he grunted. "Unless I miss my guess, I think *that* lot is going to discover very very soon that trying to twist Gustav Adolf's tail when he's in the middle of a fight is as risky a proposition as twisting a bear's tail when his fangs are bared."

He leaned back from the table, spreading his arms a bit. "What I *do* care about is how the rest of them act. Hesse-Kassel most of all. Our own Wilhelm—Saxe-Weimar, I mean—is at the session also. He's always been friendly to you, and he's on good terms with Hesse-Kassel. Try to move in that crowd, Francisco. I think..."

After a pause: "Guessing, sure. But I'll be surprised if we don't see a quiet little flurry of deals being offered to us. Under the table, as it were."

Nasi nodded. "I will set off first thing tomorrow. When do you want me to report back?"

Mike chuckled again. It was a harsh-sounding chuckle. "I won't be surprised if I'm up in Magdeburg myself, soon. Emperor Gustav is in Luebeck, you know. If all hell breaks loose—which is the way it's looking to me—I'll probably have to make some rush trips to Magdeburg. For all I know I could get there before you do."

When the meaning registered, Nasi's eyes widened. "You can't—!"

"Oh, don't be silly. I'm no *hick*, y'know, even if I am a country boy." Mike squared his shoulders and puffed out his chest in mimicry of a boy's bravado. "I've flown in planes *lots* of times."

# Chapter 27

The light from the single 75-watt bulb cast shadows in the dim corners of the kitchen. Rain pattered on the windows. Papers littered the table, agendas, lists, crude diagrams, and hastily scribbled notes, competing for space with the remains of dinner and a prized Mason jar, lid set aside.

"Another touch, Hal? Jim? Kathy?" Jesse asked as he reached for the jar.

"Not just now, Jesse, thank you," said the aerospace engineer, looking up from his notes. "Perhaps when we finish."

"No thanks, sir." The young officer barely glanced up from his own lists and duty rosters.

Jesse looked up at Kathy who had started clearing the dishes. She gave him a quick shake of the head and a meaningful nod toward his own glass. He hesitated and carefully put the jar back in its place without pouring. There *were* some disadvantages to married life. Kathy had grown up in a family riddled with alcoholism, and wasn't too happy with Jesse's somewhat hard-drinking habits. He chafed, sometimes, at her attitude on the subject. On the other hand . . .

*What the hell. It doesn't hurt me any.* He shoved the jar a little farther away from him and gave his full attention to the young captain.

"Okay then, Jim, you start off."

"Yes, sir. Operational support squadron manning stands at thirty-seven, including Sergeant Tipton and three men up at Magdeburg. I have four Americans and thirty-three Germans—but only fifteen of *them* speak English all that well."

Jesse frowned. The United States, as a political entity, was letting the language question settle itself out however it would. The Stearns administration had ruled out anything even resembling an "official language." That had been one of things which Simpson had demanded in the election campaign; Mike had just as firmly denounced the idea—and, once elected, had been true to his campaign promise.

On a strictly political level, Jesse agreed with Mike. By leaving the issue a purely voluntary and social one, Mike had taken the political tension out of it. Some people used English, some German, some—more and more—were effectively bilingual. And already, in the slang and patois which was beginning to emerge everywhere, Jesse thought the first signs of a new language were perhaps discernable. He knew enough history to know that "English" itself had come into existence that way—a largely Germanic language, in its basic structure and everyday vocabulary, which had over time been transformed by the influence of the French brought by the Normans. A language, as a wag once put it, forged by Norman men-at-arms trying to seduce Saxon barmaids.

But Jesse was running an *Air Force,* not a country. The needs of flying—even in peacetime, much less in time of war—didn't leave any room for linguistic confusion. So, since all the technical terms and most of the concepts involved were only expressed in English, he had quietly insisted that every airman at least had to start learning English. He knew that Simpson was following the same policy in the Navy. Frank Jackson, commanding the less technically oriented army, seemed not to be worrying about the issue at all.

As usual, of course, theory was one thing. Practice another.

"Uh, we lost four today, sir," continued Jim, proving the point. "They just wandered off and didn't report at dinner. The usual story, probably. All single men. They didn't mind working, but drill bored them."

Jesse repressed a sigh. "Go on."

"Yes, sir. Um, the barracks are nearly completed, including the fireplaces at both ends. Family quarters are next, but for the time being the women and kids of the married troops are in the barracks. We should finish before the snow comes, so at least no one will freeze."

"Good, good," Jesse said. "What about operational facilities?"

"Well, we've finished cutting down the trees and moving the field fence farther out. We filled in that ditch in front of the normal landing area. I'm afraid our neighbor, Mr. Sterling, is angry at us. He's claiming we've stolen five acres of his best ground."

"We did, Jim. Governments can do that. Don't worry about it, I'll speak to President Stearns. He'll compensate Sterling somehow. And I'll speak to Sterling myself. Go on. What about fuel storage?"

The captain smiled. "That's the best news. Capacity is two thousand gallons with eight hundred sixty gallons of M85 methanol fuel on hand. We've finished building the berms around those salvaged house fuel-oil tanks and the plumbing is finished to the hand pumps in the refueling area. No more flash fires, I think."

Jesse smiled. "Now that *is* good news. Fine work, son. And remind me tomorrow to send a note of appreciation to Kerry over at the methanol plant."

"Uh, yes sir. Uh, Kerry told me to pass on to you that you owe him five dollars."

Jesse's eyes widened. "What for?"

Behind him, Kathy snorted. "You don't remember? I'm not surprised, as blotto as you were. About two weeks ago, over at the Thuringen Gardens, you bet him five bucks he wouldn't make his methanol production goal. I tried to stop you, but ...'"

Jesse grimaced. "Anything else?"

Captain Horton referred to his notes. "Not at this time, sir. Sorry about the runners."

"Can't be helped, I suppose," Jesse said. "But take a word of advice. These newcomers don't understand us, yet. Ease up on the drill."

He held up his hand. "I know, I know, it instills discipline and a sense of teamwork. But consider—we're not going to ask these men to stand in a battle line. Their job is to serve those aircraft out there and this airfield. Most of them are only here for the food and shelter, at this point. So keep 'em busy and too tired to run. So long as we are flying, we can expect the majority to stick. I'll work on getting them uniforms and we'll hand out a few promotions. You made a good decision by making Danny Tipton the squadron first sergeant. He's a steady sort and he's done a fine job organizing the airfield up at Magdeburg. But while he's gone, you need another NCO. That mean-looking tall German, what's his name—Krueger? Make him a sergeant. If he hasn't been one before, I'm Queen of the May. He'll help keep the Germans in line. And work on your German. Just because we're requiring them to learn English doesn't mean we shouldn't speak German ourselves."

"Yes, sir."

"Okay, then. Now get out your list, because I'm about to give your squadron some more work."

The young officer obediently bent to his paper.

Jesse ticked off the items on his fingers.

"First, airfield lighting. With us 'to-ing and fro-ing' back and forth from Magdeburg, eventually someone's going to get caught up at night. It doesn't have to be fancy. Maybe a line of methanol-filled tin cans on each side of the 'runway.' Have the men practice lighting them off a couple of times.

"Second, I want three aircraft shelters ready before winter. Again, nothing fancy—three-sided covered affairs, facing south. You figure out where it's best to put them. Oh, and find some small tarps. I want one in each aircraft to cover the engine when it's away from home station. Got it?"

"Yes, sir."

"Good. Third, start detailing an enlisted man to assist the Tower Officer. They're to be taught basic radio procedures and traffic control. Now that we have two aircraft, I don't want an accident because someone went outside to take a leak. We'll eventually transfer tower operations over to your men entirely.

"Lastly, I want you to start investigating the possibility of paving the entire runway. That includes taxiways and parking ramp—the whole nine yards."

Jim protested, "Sir, that's impossible!"

Jesse grinned. "Sure, right now, it is. I said 'investigate,' didn't I? Next time you're in Magdeburg, go talk to Mr. Simpson. I understand he's got plans for producing some sort of paving material. Find out what it is, concrete, macadam, whatever, and what it will take to get it down here to the field. We're talking long range here, son. But in case you haven't noticed, that field out there gets pretty sloppy when it rains and takes just about forever to dry. Can do?"

"Okay, Colonel."

"Fine, then." Jesse leaned back in his chair. "Oh, and remember to salute Admiral Simpson when you meet him. He goes in big for that kind of stuff."

"Roger that, sir."

Jesse paused as Kathy placed a cup of tea in front of him. He leaned his head against her hip for a moment.

"Thanks, honey."

"Jess, I think I'll go to bed. Don't be long and don't forget to turn down the stove," said the tall blonde. "G'night Hal, Jim."

"Good night, Katherine."

"G'night, Mrs. Wood."

Jesse admired the view as his wife left and turned back to the men at the table. He saw Hal grinning around his pipestem. The retired aeronautical engineer had kept his pipe habits, even though Grantville's tobacco supply had long since vanished.

"What?"

Hal removed his pipe, unconsciously tapped it in his palm, and smiled even more broadly.

"Nothing, Jesse, nothing. These days, it's just nice to see such a scene of domestic bliss. Makes me miss my Dorothy."

"Heh." Jesse grinned back. "You'll see a different aspect of 'domestic bliss' if we don't get on with it. So go ahead, please. Materials, problems, construction status."

"Right." Hal checked his list momentarily.

"Engines. As you know, we've obtained first right of purchase or salvage of light-block, aircraft-compatible engines from the strategic resources board. I've identified at least a dozen engine types in town that will probably serve, but I would prefer using those that I can find in multiple units. A one-of-a-kind engine presents obvious spare problems. The best news is that most newer engines tend to be smaller and lighter, turbocharged, with higher compression ratios and horsepower than older models. Suitably stripped down, with such things as the air conditioning, power steering and anti-pollution devices removed, we can even use water-cooled engines. The town mechanics really got enthusiastic when I explained what we needed."

Hal paused. "By the way, I hired Harvey Matowski as chief mechanic—for the firm, that is. If you want him in the Air Force, you'll have to talk to him."

"Right. I will," Jesse noted. "So what kind of engines did you find?"

"Well, we've found good engines to power the "X-2.""

Jesse interrupted, "X-2?"

Hal looked up. "Oh, Yes, sorry. I've gotten tired of referring to it as 'it.' I assume at some point you'll want to give it a suitably warlike name."

Jesse smiled. " 'X-2' is for test-pilot types, Hal. When you get it ready, we'll come up with something else. I'd go with *Hellcat* except we already get accused of witchcraft often enough as it is, without fueling the flames."

*"Thunderbolt,"* Jesse mused to himself. *Or "Liberator." Hell, maybe the "Gustav." It kinda looks like an ME-109 from the side and our Swedish ally might think it's named after him.*

He mentally shook himself.

"But you were saying about engines?"

Hal beamed. "Yes, a fine pair of Mazda 13B power plants. Thank God for young men and their sports cars. Imagine, two RX-7s in a town like this. Wonderful engines. They should produce over a hundred sixty horsepower, easily. Very sturdy with a superb crankshaft. Good cooling system, though we're going to remove the electric oil cooling bypass valve. That just wastes space, you see, and . . ."

"Hal. Hal, please," Jesse interrupted. "Not now."

"What? Oh, sorry," Hal said sheepishly. "Where was I? Oh, yes, engines.

"There are four Saturns in town with 2.2-liter engines that will work. Two Honda Preludes. Perhaps ten or so Chevy S-10s, since they're already methanol compatible. We're even looking at a number of V-6, twenty-four-valve engines, with horsepower in the one eighty to one ninety range. Plenty of makes and models to choose from, there; but, of course, it will depend on the reduction drive. When modified, they should all have power-to-weight ratios above .35 and some considerably higher. Here's the list. I should think we'll want to take out options on the whole lot."

"Thanks. What's next?"

"Wood, or, rather, wood storage. Rudi says he can get as much as we need from Weimar, but he can't keep it dry here. That barn needs a new roof."

Having already run afoul of the irascible German carpenter several times, Jesse grimaced. "Well, whatever Rudi wants, Rudi gets, I suppose. Jim, there's another job for your list."

"Yes, sir."

"And speaking of wood," Hal continued, "I'm not having much

luck with that three-bladed prop design. The balance is much more difficult than with two blades. I'm afraid we'll have to settle for a two-bladed prop on the new model, at least initially. That will mean we can't obtain peak performance, of course. Perhaps one twenty knots at cruise and a top speed of no more than one fifty knots."

"That will be fine, Hal," Jesse said. "Remember, we're looking for reliability, first and foremost."

Hal nodded. "Well, if that's the case, we'd also better take the props off the Belles and cap the ends with something. I've noticed some wear and splitting along the leading edges, too. Hmm, thin brass, I think. Drill small holes and put long brass rivets right through. That should work. No dissimilar metal problems."

"You're the engineer, Hal." Jesse smiled.

Hal snorted. "More like a shade-tree mechanic, these days. Look at the trouble I'm having coming up with a reasonable attitude indicator. If I could just find some small, reliable gyros . . ."

"Don't beat yourself up too much," Jesse said. "Besides, if we had good attitude indicators, we'd just be tempted to fly in bad weather. And without any navaids, someone would come to grief, sooner or later. So, where do we stand with modifications and construction?"

"Well, now that the 'Belle II' is fully operational, we're concentrating on production of the X-2. Naturally, we've learned some things about construction techniques from building the 'Belles.' Provided the power-plant design proves out, we should be ready to test by midwinter, weather permitting. As you realize, this is a much more advanced aircraft. Trim tabs, windscreen anti-icing, tandem seating and controls—that means duplicate instruments, such as they are—semi-wooden wings with cloth only from mid-chord rearward, landing lights in the wingroots. It'll even have brakes. Not to mention it's a low-wing, strutless planform with much more power than the 'Belles.' Much heavier too, of course. Fully aerobatic and capable of something like five gees. And I've decided the fuel tank must be placed somewhere under the rear seat to maintain proper weight and balance. You don't know the difficulties we've already overcome—"

Jesse held up a hand. "Wait a second, Hal. Slow down. First things, first. Is there anyone we don't have whose particular skill you need?"

Hal thought a moment. "Well, I could use a glazier."

Jesse stared. "A what?"

"You know, someone who can fit glass."

"I know what a glazier is, Hal. Um, why do you need him?"

"Well, you've insisted that the X-2 have a closed cockpit . . ."

"You're damned right, I did," Jesse groused. "Do you know how *cold* it gets up there?"

"Certainly, I do. That's why I agreed on this design. But as you know, the cockpit will have two hinged segments, a way to get into each seat. That means using at least thirteen cut pieces of auto safety glass, frames, supports, bracing. Remember how many leaks you found on the *Las Vegas Belle*, once it rained? Who did the work on the windscreen? I should think you'd want an expert to do it this time."

"Uh, point taken," Jesse conceded readily, since he had installed the *Belle*'s windscreen. "We'll get someone from the auto glass place."

He changed the subject.

"Let's go back to the 'Belles' for a moment. Now that I've flown the Belle II, I'm anxious to get the improvements retrofitted on the original Belle. For example, that stall warning device you came up with. That could save a pilot, one of these days. Good going."

Hal beamed. "Nothing, really. Just a short piece of angle iron attached to the underside of the left wingroot. At a sufficiently high angle of attack and low enough airspeed, the propwash gives you a little shake. Ten minutes work. I should have thought of it earlier. I can show you the equations, if you like."

"Never mind, I'm just a simple airplane driver. It works and that's good enough for me. I also want that dual throttle control lashup copied on the Belle I. Can do?"

Hal nodded.

Jesse checked off that item on his list. "Okay, how about the rocket wiring and the flashguards?"

Hal sucked on his pipe for a moment. "Should be no problem. Perhaps half a day's work, once we find the tin sheets and insulation. We'll have some loss of airspeed due to increased drag, though. You can tell the government 'weapons board' we'll be ready to test next week. You'll be able to carry eight rockets solo, perhaps four with a second person on board. Each rocket will have an individual switch, all in a row in front of the left seat. But I warn you, if one of those things explodes under the wing, you'll have to walk home."

Jesse grimaced. "Yeah, right. Well, the President says he expects we'll soon be at war and our pilots will have to take a warrior's chance. How about the bomb racks and releases?"

Hal waved dismissively. "Couldn't be simpler. Four racks under the fuselage ahead of the airscoop. Shouldn't disrupt the airflow overmuch. The releases will be mechanical—just pull the handles back. We'll have to drill through the floor, of course. And, with the 'Belles' it should be one thing or the other, rockets or bombs."

Jesse nodded again. "That gives us operational flexibility. Chances are, we won't have any time to practice dive bombing before we see action, but, hell, six months ago, nobody believed we'd ever get anything flying. Next week, we'll have an Air Force."

He reached for the Mason jar with an air of satisfaction. *How's that for military efficiency, Admiral Simpson?*

After pouring, the Air Force Chief of Staff lifted his glass. "Gentlemen, I give you a toast. 'To the First Air Squadron, the best damned flying unit this side of the Ring of Fire!' "

# Chapter 28

The Luebeck sun was bright in a sky of washed-out September blue as Larry Wild hurried toward the shipyard. It was a trip he'd made often enough since arriving at the Swedish Army's encampment outside the city with his small party of Navy personnel, but that didn't prevent heads from turning as he jogged by. Partly, perhaps, it was because of his obvious haste, but there were other people moving through the narrow streets almost as rapidly as he was, and no one turned to gawk at them. Then again, none of them wore the unofficial "uniform" of a transplanted American: blue jeans, denim shirt, and sneakers.

Despite the urgency of the message in his shirt pocket, Larry was tempted to smile at the thought. Admiral Simpson badly wanted to put his entire Navy into proper uniform, but it was going to be quite some time before he managed it.

The problem wasn't manufacture, as such. The textile industry of 17th-century Europe was perfectly up to the task, technically speaking. But since European armies of the time rarely used standard uniforms, and even those uniforms varied wildly from unit to unit, there was no real uniform manufacturer as such in existence. Thus—given the exacting standards that Simpson insisted on—producing a significant lot of genuinely identical clothing was something that any regular manufacturer was going to charge a premium for, since making sure the dyes remained standard was not business-as-usual.

That meant increasing the naval budget, simply to provide "proper" uniforms instead of workable clothing. When Simpson had tried get Mike Stearns to agree to that, the answer had been short and none too sweet. The U.S. government's budget was stretched like a drum to begin with. Larry had heard from his "inside sources" that Simpson had had the bad luck to submit his budget request the day after Mike had, with great reluctance, struck an item from the budget which would have provided money to help Willie Ray Hudson's granges spread the techniques of modern silage to Thuringia's farmers.

"I can't fucking help *feed* people and this asshole wants me to pay for shiny buttons?!" had been, according to reports, Mike's explosive outburst when he read the request. The written response had not contained the profanity. It *had* contained the sentiment.

Simpson, stubborn as always, would eventually figure out a way to wrangle his uniforms. Of that, Larry had no doubt at all. In the meantime, the clothing which had made the trip back from the century of Larry's birth was enough to provide a uniform of a different sort, though scarcely the kind Simpson had had in mind. So Larry enjoyed his blue jeans while he still had the chance.

But the admiral had at least managed to get an official table of ranks and insignia worked out. Worrying about something like that might be typical of his taste for empire building; but Larry was by now willing to agree that whatever his other faults, John Simpson was an excellent organizer. He'd gotten his military table of organization worked out in detail and presented it to the President while Frank Jackson was still busy trying to avoid the entire question.

Simpson's suggestions had been adopted for the Navy. Personally, Larry suspected that the smoothness with which they'd gone through had resulted at least in part from Mike Stearns' decision that he could afford to indulge Simpson in that regard. No doubt he thought of it as more of the typical Simpson Mickey Mouse bullshit. Something he could accede to as a way to stroke the man's ego harmlessly.

Larry had been inclined to see it the same way, until he and Eddie Cantrell had wound up as the United States Navy's very first pair of lieutenants. Simpson had surprised him considerably when he handed over the silver bars he'd ordered from Roth, Nasi & Rueckert, Grantville's major jeweler. He'd had them made at his own expense and presented them with a degree of formality neither

Larry nor Eddie had anticipated when they were officially commissioned lieutenants junior-grade.

Even now, Larry wasn't prepared to admit it to anyone else except Eddie. But the solemn little ceremony Simpson had insisted upon had left a lasting impression. Larry and Eddie had done their best to laugh it off privately afterward, and there probably had been a more than slightly ludicrous aspect to it. There they'd been, two West Virginia hillbilly youngsters—at nineteen, still technically teenagers—standing at the closest they could come to a proper position of attention while the city slicker from Pittsburgh, with his very distinguished-looking head of gray hair, pinned shiny silver bars onto the collars of their very civilian shirts. All this, to formally commission them as officers in a navy which didn't even exist yet!

And yet . . .

There were more jay-gees now, and there would soon be even more as the new ships began to come into service, which was how he and Eddie had become senior-grade lieutenants after less than six months. The way things were going, they could probably count on turning into lieutenant *commanders* before very long, too. All of which put them in the peculiar position of finding themselves senior officers of a rapidly expanding military organization. And all of which also put Larry and Eddie in a position which was not just peculiar, but downright bizarre.

Despite everything, and however much they might fight the process kicking and screaming every inch of the way, Larry Wild and Eddie Cantrell were becoming naval officers. Which meant, in practice . . . John Chandler Simpson's men. There was just no way around it, no matter how much Simpson often rubbed the youngsters the wrong way. Whatever else, Simpson was building one hell of a fine little navy. And Larry, like his friend and fellow senior-grade lieutenant Eddie Cantrell, was increasingly proud to be a part of it.

Larry trotted into the harbor area mulling in his mind a remark Eddie had made the last time he saw him. *Yeah, sure, Simpson's a bastard. But dammit, Larry, he's our bastard.*

Now that he'd reached the harbor, Larry headed for the bustle of activity around the looming skeleton of Gustavus Adolphus' ironclad-to-be.

The ship wasn't very large by the standards of the 21$^{st}$

century . . . but this was the 17th century, and the partially planked hull loomed over the waterfront like a Titan.

The basic building plan had come from a book by Howard I. Chapelle, who'd once headed the maritime history section of the Smithsonian Institute. Eddie had picked it up in a used-book shop somewhere, along with a couple of Chapelle's other books, when he'd been doing the research for one of the "Four Musketeers' " war games. Once Eddie had approached Mike Stearns with the proposal for the ironclads and casually mentioned the rest of his esoteric collection of military reference works, Mike, Frank Jackson, and John Simpson had descended upon his library in force. A lot of what it contained wouldn't be very useful until the infrastructure to build it could be constructed, but Chapelle's books had been pounced upon by the Swedish shipwrights as if Eddie had been Galahad, returning to King Arthur with Holy Grail in hand. The looming skeleton of what would become the Swedish Navy's flagship was only one result.

A fairly substantial result, Larry conceded. The flush-decked U.S. Navy sloop-of-war upon which the design was based had been one hundred and forty-eight feet long between perpendiculars, with a beam of just under thirty-nine feet. That meant her hull was about thirty feet shorter than the ironclads Simpson was building in Magdeburg, but since she was going to have a bowsprit over sixty feet long, Eddie suspected no one would notice. And whereas Simpson's ships were going to be ugly, boxy vessels, with an uncompromising brutality of line and form, Gustavus' ship retained the graceful lines crafted by her original 19th-century architect. The only real change the emperor's builders had made in the enlarged builder's draft Grantville copiers had produced from Chapelle's carefully redrawn plans had been to increase the height of the bulwarks from just under five feet to approximately seven. Once the armor plate being produced in the local rolling mill was bolted to the outside of the hull, that would provide head-high protection for her gun crews. Of course, hanging that much iron plate on the outside of the hull was going to add about two hundred tons to her weight, so even with the reduction in her broadside armament, she was going to draw close to twenty-four feet, which was a bit deep but manageable for the Baltic.

Personally, Larry suspected that the impressiveness of Gustavus' new ship was the real reason the emperor had insisted upon building her here in Luebeck. Certainly, she made a lasting impression on anyone who entered or visited the city's harbor . . . including the town's burghers and authorities.

The harbor itself swarmed with shipping of every description. According to Ms. Mailey, Luebeck had managed to sit out the Thirty Years War in the past of Larry's own world pretty much unscathed, maintaining its neutrality with shrewd diplomacy. This time around, it didn't look like it was going to be quite so lucky, because in *this* 17th century, Gustavus Adolphus hadn't gotten himself killed in battle—so far, at least. He was very much alive, and while he was willing to use the velvet glove instead of the iron fist when he could, he also wasn't about to put up with any evasion of his requirements.

Gustav Adolf needed a solid base for his logistics, and Luebeck was one of only a few North German ports suitable for the part. Wismar, Rostock and Stralsund were already held by the Swedes and incorporated into the CPE, and it was fairly obvious to everyone that Luebeck was going to join them in the end. The only real question was how much independence the old Hanseatic League city was going to retain, and that was what Gustavus' current diplomatic dance with the city's authorities was all about.

Unlike Hamburg, which dominated the estuary of the Elbe, Luebeck was on the Baltic side of the Jutland Peninsula. That was important, because as long as Denmark was in a position to close the Kattegat to shipping and so deny Sweden access to the North Sea, Hamburg was completely unsuitable as a supply port connecting Sweden itself to the continental portions of Gustav's CPE.

Not that Luebeck was a perfect substitute for Hamburg. The Stecknitz Canal, which linked the city to the Elbe River at Lauenburg, upriver from Hamburg, had been designed only to accommodate the barges of the salt trade. Those were large enough to haul cargos that could be broken up into fairly small chunks, but not for the sort of heavy transport the CPE and the United States envisioned. That could be fixed, however, and Gustavus' engineers, assisted by American survey crews, were already busy designing the new and improved Stecknitz which would serve their needs just fine.

More immediately, however, there was the fact that any of the North German ports were close enough to Christian IV's Denmark for the Danish Navy to threaten their lines of communication with Sweden. Luebeck, in fact, was more vulnerable to Danish interference than most of them. But that was what the Swedish Navy was for. The Danes had learned the hard way that the Swedes were not to be trifled with, and the squadron of Admiral Karl Karlsson Gyllenhjelm had been stationed at Luebeck to remind Christian of that.

Luebeck itself was in two minds about Gyllenhjelm's presence. The city's burghers were far from blind to the enormous beneficial impact the sort of canal Gustavus envisioned would have on their economy. The king and his Swedish and American team of engineers were planning for a canal whose locks would admit barges as much as a hundred feet in length and thirty or forty feet across the beam—larger than many seagoing merchant ships. Coupled with the improvements on the Elbe itself which were already underway, the new and enlarged Stecknitz would turn Luebeck into the focal point for the entire Baltic's trade with Northern and Central Germany, just as Hamburg dominated the North Sea trade. Given that Luebeck was already the largest and most important of the German ports on the Baltic, its economic prospects looked bright indeed.

Unfortunately, those same burghers were only too well aware of the downside of the situation, as well. Leaving aside the loss of their cherished independence—Luebeck had been the leading city of the Hanseatic League for centuries—there was a crude and simple matter of self-preservation involved. The more important they became to Gustavus and the CPE, the more attractive their destruction would appear to Gustavus' enemies, which made his plans for the Stecknitz very much a two-edged sword. Especially since Luebeck was none too sure Gustavus was going to survive, even with his American allies and their mechanical marvels.

Despite that, it was clear to everyone that sooner or later the city would have no choice but to accept Gustavus' terms. Even to a political neophyte like Larry Wild, it was obvious that the pressure upon Luebeck's authorities was enormous. Gustavus had done everything he could to sweeten the pot, sure; but he had no qualms about turning the screws, either. Even if he was—at least in Larry's opinion—about the only 17th-century king worth a damn, the terms "17th-century monarch" and "one hell of a sweet guy" were a ridiculous match. What was called an "oxymoron," if Larry was remembering his high-school English properly.

Among other things, Gustav had *insisted*—politely, to be sure, but backed by the threat of Gyllenhjelm's guns—that he be allowed to build his new seagoing ironclad in Luebeck's shipyards. Just as he had *insisted* on the need to station a thousand or so men here—a full regiment—as a guard for the ironclad. True, he'd agreed that his men would encamp outside the city's walls. True also, Gustav had agreed to allow no more than thirty or forty of those men to enter Luebeck at a time. But their encampment was clearly visible from the city's southern bastions. And if the behavior of the troops in that encampment had been mannerly enough—downright excellent, in fact, by the standards of the day—their presence was a constant, discreet reminder that the king of Sweden's patience was not infinite.

The banners which flew over that encampment were another reminder of the facts of life. Gustav Adolf had assigned the task of guarding the ironclad to the well-known Tott's Regiment, a veteran unit which had fought at the great Swedish victory at Breitenfeld. The cavalry regiment, a very high percentage of whose troopers were Finns, had been named after their founding commander.

Åke Tott was most often described as "a fierce man." The banners he'd chosen for his regiment certainly fitted the description. Black banners, with a white skull in the middle resting on a green backdrop. In some of the banners, flames protruded from the skull's eyesockets; in others, various types of evil-looking plants or flowers sprouted from those same sockets; in one—Larry's personal favorite—the head of a serpent.

In the meantime, however, Gustav was prepared to allow Luebeck its official neutrality as an independent city in the Hanseatic League. For the moment, at least.

Despite some doubts, Larry thought the king was being smart. After all, in practical terms, Gustav already controlled their city, however careful he was to avoid any words like "occupation" or "garrison troops." The Luebeckers had no real option but to accede to his polite requests and gentle insistence upon the use of their port facilities . . . and if they happened to be making a fortune off of servicing his army's needs, well, the laborer was worthy of his hire, after all. And so a ceaseless flow of men and supplies poured into Luebeck under the protection of the Swedish ships' guns protecting Mecklenburg Bay. They came aboard the merchant vessels crowding the harbor, and from there flowed onward to Gustav's army further south.

It was a process which was neither spectacular nor draped in martial glory. It came without trumpets or battle flags, but Larry had come to understand that without it, there would be no trumpets, no glorious victories. Without the vital logistical link Luebeck represented—along with Wismar and Rostock—Gustavus' army would wither and starve. Or, what would in some ways be worse, find itself forced to start plundering the very population it was supposed to protect.

All of which, put together, was what made the folded message slip in Larry's pocket so terrifying.

An officer of Tott's Regiment looked up as Larry headed purposefully for the building ways. The officer and a dozen of the regiment's troopers sat their mounts between the half-completed warship's hull and the rest of the harbor.

Larry's gaze was drawn to their weapons. The new rifle shops in Magdeburg, set up by partnerships between Grantville's machine shops and some German gunmakers, had reached a production rate of just over a hundred and fifty weapons a week. They'd already supplied Gustavus with more than five thousand of the new rifles, and Tott's Regiment had been one of the first to profit from them.

Tott himself was no longer in command. But the regiment remained one of Gustav Adolf's favorites under its new commander, Colonel Karberg. So, all of the troopers carried brand new flintlock rifles in saddle scabbards. They continued to carry two or three huge, cumbersome wheel-lock pistols apiece, as well, but Larry suspected that would be changing soon. The Swedes were still feeling their way into the new realities of 17th-century warfare, American-style. Once they'd adapted fully to it, he thought, cavalry pistol charges were definitely going to become a thing of the past.

It wasn't a completely satisfied thought. Not because Larry disapproved of the changes to come, but because they were coming so much more slowly than he would have preferred.

The troopers' rifles were a case in point. They were much shorter and handier than any of the Swedes' previous shoulder arms, and with their new, American-designed hollow-based bullets, steel ramrods, and conical touch holes, they were vastly more lethal. Their effective range, despite their shorter barrels, was several times that of any standard infantry weapon. Or, rather, any other army's standard infantry weapons, because the rifles being produced for Gustavus' infantry were even longer-ranged than the cavalry version.

They were also equipped with the first socket-mounted bayonets in European history, which was going to come as a nasty surprise to someone, one fine day.

But they were still *flintlocks*, and that offended Larry's sensibilities. It might be possible to fire them three or even four times as rapidly as some clumsy matchlock, but they still couldn't be fired as rapidly as a decent breech-loading design. And like any flintlock, they were much more vulnerable to misfires than a percussion cap design.

Larry and Eddie had been strong supporters of the group which had argued in favor of producing a breechloading, cartridge-firing weapon, instead. Failing that, they'd at least wanted a proper caplock design, and they'd been initially supported by Gustavus Adolphus. But they—and the king—had been overruled by no less than the President himself.

Larry had been at the meeting where that decision had been made, serving as a very nervous staff officer accompanying Admiral Simpson. Mike Stearns, General Jackson and several American and German arms manufacturers and technical advisers had come to Magdeburg specifically for the purpose, to confer with Gustav Adolf and his own advisers and military staff.

"Yes, we've been able to create a small cartridge industry," Mike had acknowledged at the meeting, "but it's barely enough to keep our existing up-time weapons supplied. And not all of them, for that matter. We're not even trying to maintain ammunition except for the most common calibers. There is no way at all we could supply more than a trickle to a new line of cartridge-using breechloaders, even if you could make those in large numbers. Which I doubt we could, at least for the next couple of years or so."

Gustav had glanced around the room, seeing the agreement so obviously manifest on the faces of the Americans (and now, a few Germans) who were the experts on the subject.

"Very well. I will accept that. But why are you also opposed to the introduction of *caplock* muskets? Those would be simple muzzleloaders."

Mike turned toward Greg Ferrara. The former high school science teacher—now quickly emerging as one of the new United States' premier inventors/industrialists—cleared his throat.

"We're not *opposed* to them, Captain General Gars. We think a caplock industry can and should be started. But . . . ah . . ." Ferrara coughed. " 'Your Majesty,' I meant to say. Sorry, I forgot where we were."

Gustav grinned. A little laugh went around the room—a bit of an embarrassed one, on the part of the Americans; simply amused, on the part of the Germans and Gustav's Swedish officers.

Larry himself had joined in that laugh, once he understood the meaning of Ferrara's quick little apology. When Gustav Adolf visited the United States, under the terms of agreement by which the U.S. had affiliated to the Confederated Principalities of Europe, he did so in his persona as "Captain General Gars"—thus maintaining the formality that the U.S. itself was a republic, not a constitutional monarchy. In certain respects, there was a parallel between Gustav Adolf's position in the U.S. and the position of the House of Orange in the United Provinces. *Officially,* the United Provinces was a republic. In practice, the "unofficial royalty" of the House of Orange carried a great deal of real authority.

In the CPE proper, however—certainly those areas like Magdeburg, which were under direct imperial rule—these convoluted formalities did not apply. In his own imperial capital, Gustav II Adolf was "Your Majesty" and no fancy-dancing around it. King of Sweden, emperor of the CPE, not to mention a host of other titles.

Fortunately, the King-and-Emperor-Etc was usually good-tempered about the whole business. Today, as well. After the laugh faded away, Gustav inclined his head, politely urging Ferrara to continue.

"It's like this, Your Majesty. Eventually, sure, we'll want to switch everything over to caplock muskets. But we think it would be a bad mistake to try to jump too quickly. The problem is with the caps. There are just too many 'ifs' and unknown quantities involved."

Ferrara ran fingers through his hair. "Despite what seems to be my growing reputation, I am in fact just a high-school science teacher, with a particular background in chemistry. And as good as the libraries and other data sources we have in Grantville are, given the circumstances, they are very far removed from the resources of a university research library."

For an instant, a look of longing crossed his face. "If the Ring of Fire had just stretched a little—brought all of Morgantown along with it, along with West Virginia University . . . not to mention Fairmont and all the industry in *that* town . . ."

Frank Jackson barked a laugh. "Hell, Greg, if we'd had Fairmont and WVU with us—"

He, too, broke off, coughing. Larry had to suppress a grin. He could complete the thought in his own mind:

*We'd sure as hell not be doing this silly dance with kings and emperors and dukes and earls. You betchum. Gimme Fairmont's National Guard Armory and 30,000 professors and students at a modern state university and all those machine shops and factories—not to mention prob'bly half the membership of UMWA District 31—*

*West Virginia über alles, that's what . . .*

Ferrara hurried past the awkward moment: "The point is, Your Majesty, we're groping a lot of the time. I don't know *exactly* how to make percussion caps. I've got a pretty damn good idea, mind you, especially after kicking it around with some of the gun collectors in Grantville. So, with a little experimenting, I'm quite sure we'll be able to start making them. But not *enough* of them—not soon enough—for what you need."

He grimaced. "The one thing that's clearest of all to me is that we do *not* want to be messing around with fulminate of mercury. I repeat: *not.* Well . . . not in any kind of hurried-up rush production program, anyway. The problem—again—is that our needs are outrunning our resources. Of which the most important, ultimately, is skilled human labor." He gave the emperor a look of appeal, with a trace of exhaustion under it. "Your Majesty, I don't have enough *chemists.* Not more than a handful. What I've got are half-trained kids that I'm trying to train at the same time as—"

Gustav Adolf interrupted him. "I understand. You are afraid that—this is dangerous material I take it?—disasters will result if the thing is rushed."

Ferrara nodded wearily. "I'm scared as it is, Your Majesty. There are so *many* ways we've been cutting corners. With chemistry, some kinds of it, you can only do that for so long. Sooner or later . . ." He shuddered a little. "Some of this stuff will kill a man in a heartbeat. And some of it can do the same to a whole town, if something goes wrong badly enough."

He straightened and shook his head, as if to clear it. "Give me some time—time to train people properly, take it slowly—I'll give you percussion caps. Other stuff, too. Guncotton, for instance, which—*if* you make it properly, making sure you rinse—" Again, he shook his head. The emperor didn't need or want a detailed technical lecture. "Besides, I need time anyway, even leaving aside the shortage of skilled labor. Most of this stuff depends on something else being ready also—which it usually isn't. Guncotton, for instance. Making guncotton is no big deal, in itself, but it does presuppose a supply—a plentiful supply—of nitric acid. And, as you know from yesterday's discussion of our overall progress in building a chemical and antibiotic industry, nitric acid is probably *the* biggest—"

"Yes, yes," said Gustav, waving his hand. "You explained. 'Bottleneck,' was the term you used. The problem is an insufficient supply of what you call 'stainless' steel."

Ferrara nodded. "Exactly. So what we'd be faced with is the same thing we're faced with time after time with so many of the chemical products we need: what amounts to a mom-and-pop bucket-and-bathtub production line. To sum it up: yes, we could make caplock muskets and percussion caps; no, we couldn't make enough of them, quickly enough, to provide the armed forces of the King of Sweden and Emperor of the CPE what it really needs right now. Uh. In my opinion, that is. Uh, Your Majesty."

Gustav smiled thinly. Then, after stroking his mustachios, looked at Axel Oxenstierna. "Mine also, I think, now that you have explained. Chancellor?"

"As you well know, I am generally more conservative than you in all things. So I am hardly going to disagree here." Oxenstierna frowned. "This much I know for sure: it has happened to me, on campaign—you also, Gustav—where I have found myself required to use captured enemy gunpowder because our own supply train collapsed or was inadequate. With *flintlocks,* we can do that. With this new caplock design . . ."

The king's face took on a frown of its own. "We might find ourselves in a battle, and out of percussion caps. Surrounded by plenty of gunpowder we can't use—but could have used if we'd stayed with a more primitive design. Which is still, let us not forget, much better than anything our enemies have at the moment."

"Maybe Clarke had it right. 'Superiority,'" Larry muttered under his breath.

Or so he'd thought. A moment later, the king's head swiveled and Larry found himself under Gustav Adolf's blue-eyed gaze.

"Yes, Lieutenant? You have something to add?"

Larry was paralyzed. He'd had absolutely no intention of speaking at all at this conference. In point of fact, the admiral had *ordered* him to keep his mouth shut, unless he was asked a direct question.

111111111111

Which, of course, the king had now done. But only because Larry had interrupted the meeting. He found himself wishing desperately for a hole to crawl into.

Simpson cleared his throat. "What my aide is referring to, Your Majesty, is a story written by a well-known author of our time. 'Up-time,' as people seem to be putting it now. A science fiction author—think of it as a type of fantasist—named Arthur C. Clarke. In this story, 'Superiority,' Clarke imagines a situation where one side loses a war because of its obsession with the most technically advanced weapons. None of which work the way they are supposed to, or can be made in the quantity predicted. So the enemy overruns them, using cruder and simpler weapons—but ones which work, and of which they have a plentiful supply."

"Ah! An excellent cautionary tale, I think." The king nodded approvingly. "Is there a copy of this story available? I think it would be a good idea to have it printed up and distributed to our officers."

Casually, Simpson swiveled his head to look at Larry, who was standing behind him. "I'm afraid my own copy was left behind in Pittsburgh, Your Majesty. Lieutenant?"

Larry managed to jolt himself out of his state of shock. "Uh, yessir. I've got a copy in one of my anthologies. Uh . . . it's back at my house—I mean—the Dreesons—uh . . . it's in Grantville. Uh, sir. Uh, Your Majesty."

"Not a problem, then. See to it, Lieutenant. I agree with His Majesty. It's a good suggestion. Have a local printer run off . . . oh, make it two hundred copies to begin with. We'll pay for it out of the Navy's budget."

He swiveled back, and the meeting continued. But Larry never did remember much of the rest of it. His shock had simply deepened at the realization that not only had the admiral slid him out of a jam but he was himself . . .

*John Chandler Simpson? A freakin' science fiction fan?*

After the meeting, on the way back to the shipyards, Larry had simultaneously tried to thank and apologize to the admiral. Simpson had cut him short.

"Two things I want you to learn from this, Lieutenant." The admiral came to a stop and glared down at him. Simpson was a big man, even if not the semi-giant that his son Tom was. "First.

When I tell you to keep your mouth shut at a meeting, I mean *shut*. Is that understood?"

"Yessir."

"Good. Second thing."

A wintry smile came to Simpson's face. "I imagine by now both you and Lieutenant Cantrell call me 'the bastard' more often than not. In private, that is. If I ever catch you doing it in public, I'll have your ass. But you might as well understand the other half of it. The Navy takes care of its own, son. Always. So if I'm a bastard, at least you can count on me to be your bastard."

Larry jerked his mind out of reminiscence. He'd just noticed that four of those new rifles were being slid free of their saddle scabbards as he jogged toward the Tott's Regiment troopers. Their officer started to say something to them, but before he could, someone else spoke up sharply. The troopers looked over their shoulders at the huge blond shape of Anders Jönsson and put their rifles back with the sort of hasty "I-wasn't-doing-anything" air of small children caught out by an irate tutor. Jönsson glowered at them for a moment; then said something else, gesturing at Larry's 21st-century clothing, and shook his head.

Under other circumstances, Larry would have chuckled at the troopers' hang dog attitudes. Unlike the cavalrymen, Jönsson was not armed with a flintlock rifle. In fact, he didn't carry a rifle at all, and he'd already discarded all of his wheel locks, as well. Instead, he wore a shoulder holster which contained a single HK .40-caliber USP automatic. It was one of the half-dozen or so most expensive handguns to have made the trip back from the 21st-century, but no one in Grantville begrudged it or the four high-capacity magazines which had accompanied it when Mike Stearns presented the black, polymer-framed pistol to Jönsson. Given that assassination was an acknowledged if officially frowned-upon way of dealing with problems in this day and age, anything which made it more difficult for someone to get past Gustavus Adolphus' personal bodyguard struck most Americans as a very good idea indeed.

Larry reached the side of the building slip just in time to hear the tag end of Jönsson's caustic homily. It was in Swedish, which was still a foreign language—in every sense—for Larry, but he didn't need to be able to understand the words to grasp the meaning. He tried hard not to grin at the discomfited troopers.

Actually, when he thought about it, he was in favor of paranoia on their part where the safety of their monarch was concerned. As long as that paranoia wasn't expressed by pointing rifles at his own personal body, at least.

"Can I help you, Lieutenant?" Jönsson inquired, switching to heavily accented but clearly understandable English and nodding courteously as Larry trotted up to him. The bodyguard carried no official rank, but Larry had privately decided that his effective rank had to be somewhere around that of a colonel, so he paused to come to attention and salute in the fashion Simpson insisted upon. It still felt more than a little unnatural, but it no longer felt silly; and Gustavus' bodyguard returned the formal military courtesy with unsmiling dignity.

"I have an urgent message for the king," Larry told him, puffing slightly for breath after his hurried trip.

Jönsson regarded him for a moment, then nodded. He said something to the Tott officer in Swedish, then gestured politely for Larry to accompany him and led the way up a ladder to the deck of the incomplete warship. A couple of workmen glowered at them for getting in the way as they stepped onto the partially planked deck, but Jönsson ignored them as he and Larry crossed to the powerfully built figure of the king of Sweden.

At the moment, that regal monarch was covered in sawdust from head to toe while he stood glaring down at the building draft spread out over a pair of sawhorses and waved his arms energetically. The man facing him across the sawhorses was much smaller and even more heavily coated in sawdust, and he did not appear to be greatly daunted by his king's vigor. He stood with his arms folded, frowning ferociously, then shook his head firmly. He stepped forward, tapping an index finger on the building plans, and spoke emphatically. Gustavus frowned back, even more ferociously, and tapped his own finger on the plans, but the other man was singularly unimpressed and only shook his head again. Gustavus glared at him, then threw both hands in the air, and turned to stomp away from him.

Jönsson made a beeline toward the king, and Larry followed in his wake. Gustavus looked up, still frowning, as Jönsson spoke to him in Swedish. Then the king's expression altered. The frown remained, but the emphasis was completely different.

"You have a message, Lieutenant?" he said. His accent was much heavier than Jönsson's. In fact, it was more than a bit difficult for

Larry to follow at times, but he knew Gustavus read English as readily as he did several other languages.

"I do, sir," he replied, and unbuttoned his shirt pocket to extract the single sheet of paper upon which Adam Jeffreys—now officially Petty Officer 1/c Jeffreys—had copied the transmission from Grantville.

The king took it with a courteous nod, unfolded it, and began to read. The blue eyes moved rapidly across the neatly lettered text, then froze. They moved back to the beginning and then down the lines once again, reading slowly and carefully, and his lips compressed. That was absolutely all the change in expression he allowed himself, but it was enough for Larry to sense Jönsson's entire body tightening in reaction.

Gustavus reached the end of the brief message, then refolded it with slow, meticulous care before he turned back to Larry.

"Thank you for delivering this so promptly," he said. "Now, you will take me to your . . . 'radio room,' it is, yes?"

"Of course, sir," Larry replied.

"Good. I need to ask your President a number of questions."

# Chapter 29

Jesse and Hans were seated in the overstuffed chairs near the tower, reviewing the fourth in a series of instructor training flights. Jesse was determined to ensure that Hans could train other pilots as well as he could fly himself. Otherwise, the growth of the Air Force would be limited to the strength of Jesse's back. *Which*, he reflected, *isn't any too strong, now that cooler weather is settling in.*

On this flight, Jesse had played the part of a particularly dense student, unable to properly combine the use of rudder with ailerons. Hans was patiently explaining the theory and feel of coordinated flight when Woody, the tower duty officer, leaned over the rail and yelled down.

"Colonel Wood! Telephone!"

Jesse reflected that an extension phone on the ground floor would be handy, as he ran up the rickety stairs of the tower. He stepped inside and noted Woody standing at attention.

"At ease. Who is it?"

"The operator at Government House, sir," the young officer replied. "A message from the President, he said."

Jesse picked up the phone. "This is Colonel Wood."

"Colonel Wood, this is Capitol," came the immediate response. "Be advised that President Stearns requires immediate transportation to Magdeburg."

"Understood, Capitol. Transportation to Magdeburg. Anything else?"

"No, that's it. He's on his way now."

Jesse nodded at the duty officer and burst out the door. Hans was standing below looking up at the tower.

"Lieutenant Richter!" he bellowed. "The Belle II should be fully fueled. Go preflight her. The President is going flying."

Fifteen minutes later, Jesse had told Kathy where he was going, grabbed his homemade aeronautical chart, and reached the Belle II. He noted gratefully that Hans had already started the engine, as concerned as his commander that the cold engine might balk with the President looking on. Jesse returned the thumbs-up Hans threw him and saw the President's pickup pull into the yard.

Mike Stearns was obviously in a hurry. He ran up to the aircraft.

"Hello, Jesse," he said, shaking the pilot's hand. "Are we ready to go? Simpson swears he's got the landing strip shipshape and ready for us."

Jesse nodded. He and Hans had both made the Magdeburg trip twice—once together, once each solo. He didn't doubt that Simpson had the landing strip "shipshape." From what Jesse could tell, Simpson had a fetish about always having *everything* shipshape, and at all times.

*The man probably has an exact routine for how he folds toilet paper.* But Jesse let the thought drop, almost as quickly as it formed. Partly because a considerable part of him—certainly the part which was going to have to land a plane in Magdeburg before too long—actually approved of Simpson's precision. Mostly, though, because Jesse didn't like to think about toilet paper. Or, more precisely, its absence.

"Let me get in and then you take the right seat," he told Mike. "Mind the prop, okay?"

A minute later, Jesse began to taxi as the President struggled to strap himself in. The radio was already on Tower frequency.

"Grantville Tower, this is Belle II. Check that, Tower, this is *Air Force One* taxiing for takeoff."

"Roger, uh, Air Force One. Cleared for immediate takeoff. Wind is three-four-oh at twelve knots."

After takeoff, Jesse turned right and began to climb. *Magnetic heading of 025 for now,* he thought to himself.

Leveling off above scattered clouds at six thousand feet, he checked his chart. *Yeah, 028 degrees to Halle, no wind. But not today.* He peered at the scudding clouds and noted his cowling string inclined to the right. *At least seven or eight degrees right drift.*

He settled the aircraft heading on approximately 020 degrees by his whiskey compass and set 75-percent power for high cruise. The airspeed settled on a steady 95 knots. He noted they were abeam Weimar and hacked the clock. Only then did he look over at his passenger. He was puzzled to see Mike Stearns chuckling.

"Damn, this is a real aircraft, isn't it?" Mike said.

"Well, yeah. And I'm a real pilot and everything." Jesse was suddenly irritated. "What did you think it was?"

"No offense, Jesse. It's just that I haven't given much thought to the reality of what you and Hal have done. Sure, I get the reports, but there's nothing like the real thing. And Simpson doesn't think much of the Air Force. I can see he's mistaken."

Jesse couldn't help himself. "With all due respect to the admiral, Mr. President, he's a friggin' squid. His brain can't keep up with anything that travels faster than ten knots."

Stearns was laughing now. "Maybe it's a good thing you've missed what few meetings we've had of the Joint Chiefs of Staff. Admiral Simpson would probably have challenged you to a duel by now."

Slightly chagrined, Jesse tried to calm down. "I guess Simpson knows what he's doing, most of the time. Sorry about the meetings, but I have one, repeat, one instructor pilot—me. That'll change soon, but I saw it as my primary duty that the Air Force has trained pilots. Given that Simpson insists he can't leave Magdeburg and it takes too long to get there from here unless I fly—and I had better things to do with our one and only airplane until last week when the Belle II here got finished . . ." He twitched his shoulders. "I get the written summaries, anyhow."

Changing the subject, he handed Stearns the chart. "Hold this for a minute, would you, sir?"

Digging out his 'whiz wheel,' the circular aeronautical slide rule he'd had since pilot training, Jesse stared hard at the clouds darting past. He marked the wind side of the computer, moved the outer ring, and pursed his lips at the result.

"Good thing we took off when we did," he explained to his passenger. "We've got a front moving in from the north. Looks to me like about a fifteen-knot headwind component into Halle. After that, probably thirty knots into Magdeburg. We won't have much daylight left."

Checking the clock, he made a quick calculation. "Seventy-five nautical miles to Halle. About eighty-five miles to Magdeburg after that. We'll get there around 1615 or so. Uh, that's 4:15 P.M. I hope you know we might not be able to fly back tomorrow, if that front closes in. What's the rush, anyway?"

"I've got to meet with the admiral about helping Gustav Adolf," Mike replied. "There could be some work in it for you, so I'll want you at it as well as Simpson." He took a breath and looked around. "Kinda bumpy today, isn't it?

Jesse shrugged. "Maybe a little."

He settled back to concentrate on his heading, though that was becoming a tad difficult. They were traveling through what he called light chop and the whiskey compass was bouncing around quite a bit.

He'd missed lunch, but Kathy had fixed him up. He pulled a sausage out of his flight jacket pocket and took a bite out of it. Remembering his manners, he looked over at Stearns. And realized he wouldn't have to share his meal.

Mike stepped down from the plane, delighted to feel his stomach settling down, turned, and froze as a stentorian voice bellowed a command. Two dozen men, most of them armed with up-time shotguns, but six of them armed with the new-model muzzle-loading rifles being turned out by the Struve-Reardon Gunworks, snapped to attention and presented arms. Their clothing could scarcely be called a "uniform," but every one of them wore a brassard with the fouled anchor-and-muskets design Simpson had adopted for his "Marine Corps" insignia, and one of those brassards carried the three embroidered chevrons of a sergeant.

Eddie Cantrell stood beside the sergeant, clearly torn between embarrassment and enjoyment. He snapped to attention and saluted far more sharply than anyone who had known him before the Ring of Fire would ever have believed he could.

Mike was still staring at the youngster, wondering where the changeling had come from, when John Simpson stepped forward and saluted even more sharply than Eddie had.

Somewhere, Simpson had managed to have a very credible duplicate of a 21st-century officer's cap produced. The cap cover was a spotless white, and genuine gold leaf glittered on its polished black brim with eye-watering intensity in the bright afternoon sunlight. A single golden star flashed equally brightly on either side of his collar, and he carried a holstered 9mm automatic on a brilliantly polished Sam Browne belt he'd probably had made by whoever had made the cap for him.

He ought, Mike reflected later, to have looked absolutely ridiculous. But that thought came considerably later. What happened at the moment was that Mike Stearns, former president of a union local and now President of the United States, felt his own shoulders square themselves automatically, without any conscious thought at all, in acknowledgment of the formal courtesy.

Simpson held the salute for perhaps two heartbeats. Then the leather-lunged sergeant bellowed another order, and Simpson's hand came down from his cap brim at the exact same instant the honor guard snapped from present arms to stand easy.

"Welcome to Magdeburg, sir," Simpson said formally.

*It has to be for the benefit of the troops,* Mike told himself. *Even if it* does *feel like I've just stepped through the looking glass.*

"Thank you, Admiral," he said after a moment, deliberately pitching his voice to carry. Then he gave himself a mental shake. "We have to talk," he said much more quietly, and Simpson nodded curtly.

"It's a five-minute walk to my office," he said equally quietly.

Simpson's office was another surprise. This was the first time Mike had been to Magdeburg since the meeting with Gustav and his staff to confer on matters of military production. He'd been too pressed at the time to take up Simpson's offer to tour the "naval base." He realized now that he'd been making some automatic—and erroneous—assumptions about exactly what Simpson had been up to. The office boasted a handsome desk and window glass, true. But aside from that, and an obviously locally manufactured filing cabinet in one corner, it was remarkably plebeian and utilitarian. Nothing at all like the "Douglas MacArthur Oriental Splendor" HQ which one of Mike's great-uncles who'd fought in the Pacific Theater had once described to him, and which Mike had assumed Simpson would mimic.

Or, for that matter, the lavish CEO suite which Simpson's son Tom had once described to him that had been Simpson's before the Ring of Fire. Simpson's wife Mary, according to Tom, had been quite a connoisseur of art and a mover and shaker in Pittsburgh's upper-crust social circles. She'd had the executive suites in her husband's petrochemical corporation decorated in good taste, and at great expense. Here, the only things on the walls were a calendar, what looked to be a series of production charts and a Table of Organization, and . . .

Mike tried to suppress a grin, but found it impossible. There *was* some art up on one wall, but it was hardly the kind of work that would have adorned the walls of Simpson's CEO suite in uptime Pittsburgh. Three paintings, all told:

The first—more of a professional sketch than a painting—was a straightforward depiction of one of the ironclads. The sketch was precise, done in pencil, and had almost the look of a diagram or blueprint. Mike wasn't certain, but he thought it had probably been done by Nat Davis, who he knew had a good hand for such things.

Next to it was the illustration which was the cause of Mike's grin: a large, cheaply framed canvas which depicted the ironclads under construction once they'd gone into action. Guns blazing in full glory. From the vaguely 'science-fictiony' flavor of the painting, Mike suspected that Eddie Cantrell himself was the artist. He knew Eddie was something of an illustrator, and had had ambitions in that direction before the Ring of Fire.

Simpson came to stand next to him. When Mike glanced over, he saw that for once the stiff-faced admiral had something of a smile on his face.

"Eddie's, right?"

Simpson nodded. "He's actually got some talent for it, I think. So does my wife."

"I'm surprised you let him put it up."

"I almost didn't. But I agreed, once Lieutenant Cantrell agreed to leave off the gorgeous young woman in skimpy armor and wielding a sword perched on the bow he'd had his heart set on. He claimed that was 'the tradition.' I told him I couldn't imagine anything sillier in a naval battle, since she'd be mincemeat in five seconds."

Still smiling, Mike moved over to the third painting. "Who did this? I'm no connoisseur of the arts, but . . ."

"The man's name is Franz Knopf. Mary found him doing this painting on the wharf and took him under her wing." The stiffness was back in his face. "My wife *is* a connoisseur of the arts and claims he's got the genuine touch."

Mike studied the painting. There was no question that the technical skill involved was far superior to that displayed in Eddie's painting. Yet, in its own way, this third painting also had something of a futuristic quality. It depicted one of the still-unfinished ironclads in its full glory, with a cavalryman staring up at it. But the ironclad, as the 17ᵗʰ-century artist envisioned it, bore little resemblance to what the warship would actually look like. It vaguely reminded Mike of photographs he'd seen of pre-World War I era dreadnoughts.

"Impressive damn thing," he murmured.

Simpson smiled thinly. "Isn't it? And don't I wish I'd *actually* have something like that, when we're done. I'm seriously tempted to have it duplicated and use it for a recruiting poster." He examined the painting, for a moment. Then, softly: "I put it up partly because Mary would have been upset if I hadn't. But, more than that, to remind myself of how we must sometimes seem to the people of this era. Bigger than life. Much bigger, at times."

The perspicacity of the last remark intrigued Mike. But before he could pursue the thought, Eddie Cantrell came into the room and moved to stand against the office wall. Immediately, Simpson was all business. He offered Mike a chair, and then walked around to seat himself behind the desk.

There was absolutely no warmth in the look Simpson gave Mike, after they were both seated. But there was none of the bluster or posturing he'd more than half expected, either, he realized. It left him feeling off-balance, like someone prepared for a fight who isn't getting it. Almost uncertain, in fact, which was rare for Mike. He wondered if that was the reason Simpson was doing it.

Then he shook himself mentally and he drew a deep breath. "We've got a problem," he said bluntly.

Simpson nodded. "So I gathered from your radio message."

Mike drew a folded piece of paper from his pocket. "Here," he said. "It'll probably save a little time if you just read Gustavus' message yourself, while we're waiting for Jesse to finish securing the plane. Especially the last two sentences."

Simpson unfolded the sheet and laid it on his desk. The message wasn't a very long one:

YOUR MESSAGE RE DESTRUCTION DUTCH FLT RECEIVED. BALTIC ONLY LOGICAL TARGET FOR RICHELIEU. EXPECT JOINT DANISH-FRENCH NAVAL ATTACK SOON. PROBABLE TARGETS STOCKHOLM, LUEBECK, WISMAR, ROSTOCK, STRALSUND,

GOTEBORG, OLAND. STOCKHOLM, LUEBECK, WISMAR ALL VITAL TO WAR. AM PREPARED TO ORDER ADMIRAL GYLLENHJELM TO DEFEND STOCKHOLM AND PERSONALLY UNDERTAKE DEFENSE LUEBECK. GARRISON FOR LUEBECK HOWEVER CAN ONLY BE DRAWN FROM WISMAR, ROSTOCK, STRALSUND. I CAN AFFORD LOSE ROSTOCK AND STRALSUND. NOT WISMAR. URGENTLY REQUIRE ALL POSSIBLE SUPPORT. MOST URGENT YOU ADVISE ME IMMEDIATELY ON AVAILABLE SUPPORT WISMAR. ALSO ADVISE IF YOUR IRONCLADS CAN ENTER BALTIC TO NEUTRALIZE DANISH-FRENCH NAVAL FORCES THERE.

He read it through twice, carefully. By the time he was done, Jesse Wood had entered the room and taken another chair. Simpson handed the message silently to Eddie and looked up at Mike.

"Yes," he said simply. "But not immediately."

"Are you serious?" Mike asked. "You think you really can get these monsters—" he gestured through the office window at the flank of a looming armored vessel which looked far larger in the flesh than he'd ever envisioned from the plans "—through to Luebeck?"

"I said I could," Simpson replied a bit more testily, then gave his head an impatient twitch. "Oh, it won't be easy. And there's no way in hell you can get one of these ships—not even one of the timberclads—through the Stecknitz, much less across the Schwerin to Wismar! If you're really serious about our neutralizing the Danes, we're going to have to go through Hamburg, into the North Sea, up the Helgoland Bight, through the Skaggerak, and down through the Kattegat. We'll have to fight our way through the Belt to break into the Baltic, but that shouldn't be a problem. As a matter of fact, I'm more worried about making the trip than I am about what we may have to fight at the other end. When we modified the original design for the ironclads, we made them a little more seaworthy than most river defense vessels, but they were never really intended to operate in the open sea, even in coastal waters. Fortunately, the Baltic is fairly sheltered. We should be able to handle any conditions we're likely to meet there."

His confidence, Mike realized, was not at all assumed. He meant it, and the President felt his gloom ease ever so slightly.

*My God,* he thought. *Who would ever have thought* Simpson *could actually make me feel better about something?*

He glanced at Jesse. The head of the Air Force was scowling slightly, but it was simply a thoughtful expression, not a hostile one.

"What about your schedule?" Jesse asked. "Last I heard, you were still predicting that you couldn't have them completed until next spring."

"We can do somewhat better than that," Simpson told him. "But not without some prioritizing. My existing estimates were based on completing all four of them, but I can get two of them—*Constitution* and *United States*—launched within six to eight weeks. This is September; call it mid-November, and I can have them in the water. I can only do that if I pull the crews off of the other two, though, and I'll need not just Nat Davis but Ollie Reardon and Greg Ferrara up here, as well. It's going to take an all-out effort to get them launched that quickly, and I'll need the best mechanics and machinists we've got to deal with any unforeseen problems."

"What sort of problems?" Mike asked.

"If I could tell you that, they'd hardly be 'unforeseen,' now would they?" Simpson replied, with an acidity Mike found oddly comforting, under the circumstances. Then the admiral relented—slightly, at least.

"We've done our best to test the machinery as we went along, but there's no way to really know what problems we may or may not have until we actually get the ships into the water. And although Mr. Ferrara and I have checked our estimates as rigorously as we can, we can't absolutely predict how they're going to handle or what their actual top speeds are going to be. It may turn out that we have to make some last-minute modifications to the steering arrangements, for example. If we do, I'll need the best technical people we've got to deal with them promptly. And I'll need them *here,* not in Grantville."

"All right, I can see that," Mike acknowledged. "But even if you get them launched that quickly, and even if there are no technical problems at all, you've still got to get them down the river to the North Sea. Are you certain you can do it?"

"I'll get them down the river," Simpson said flatly.

"What about these *wehrluecken*? We still don't have agreements for all of them."

"Fuck agreements." The harsh-voiced obscenity startled Mike, and Simpson laughed without humor at his expression. "I said I'll get them down the river," he said. "I didn't say it would be pretty. But there's a time for diplomacy and negotiation, Mr. President, and there's a time to be direct. I'm willing to go on working for voluntary agreements right up to the last minute. But if we don't get them, then I'll by God blast my way right through any fucking *wehrlueck* in my way!"

Mike blinked, then darted a glance at Eddie. The young man's expression surprised Mike more than a little. He looked just as determined as Simpson. Even more surprisingly—and importantly—his entire manner radiated agreement. And confidence. Whether Simpson really could pull it off or not, *Eddie* thought he could. Out of the corner of his eye, Mike saw Jesse smiling coldly. Apparently, he did too.

Mike felt a moment's amusement, then. He suspected that his top military officers sometimes found his diplomatic and political subtleties a bit frustrating. Whatever differences there might be between John Simpson and Jesse Wood, after all—or Frank Jackson—they had all at one time been officers or soldiers in the world's most powerful military. The prospect of—for once, dammit—just *blasting through the crap* must have a certain appeal to them.

For that matter, once he thought about it, *Mike* found the prospect had an undeniable charm. He knew all about Freiherr von Bleckede and his obstructions over his precious little *wehrlueck*. Bleckede was a fine sample of the German petty aristocracy at its worst. Mike allowed himself a moment's pleasant reverie, imagining the expression on the good baron's face after Simpson's ironclads . . .

He shook it off.

"That still leaves Hamburg," he observed. "They've been hesitant to sign on with us from the beginning because of how close to Denmark they are. They don't have any particular love for Christian IV. In fact, they've been all but at war with him themselves for the past two or three years. But everybody in the region knows that sooner or later Christian and Gustavus are going to have it out to decide who's top dog in the Baltic, and they haven't wanted to get caught in the crossfire. Now that France and England and Spain are obviously signing up with Denmark and the Dutch are completely out of the equation, Hamburg's authorities are going to be even more unwilling to openly support Sweden in any way. Especially with Bernhard of Saxe-Weimar's army perched in Alsace, French troops even closer, and the Spanish—from what Becky can tell—rolling into the eastern Netherlands."

"With all due respect, that's your problem, Mr. President," Simpson said with a tight smile. His eyes locked with Mike's. "It comes with winning elections, I believe," the admiral added.

Mike felt himself smiling back thinly. "I believe you're right," he agreed. "And I promise we'll give it our best shot. All the same, I doubt that anyone is going to be able to talk them into just letting you sail through their harbor."

"Well, if Porter could run his gunboats past Vicksburg, I can run mine through Hamburg if I have to." There was an undeniable edge of arrogance in Simpson's voice, but to his own surprise, Mike found the other's flat confidence immensely reassuring. He looked over at Jesse and saw the cold smile was still there. That, too, was reassuring.

"But by your best estimate, it's going to be six weeks before you can be ready to start," he pointed out.

"No," Simpson corrected. "I said it would take six to eight weeks to get them *launched*. I'll need at least one more week, probably two, to get any problems worked out and the crews sufficiently familiarized with them. Especially if I'm going to be taking them into the North Sea!"

"All right," Mike accepted the correction. "Two and a half months, then. How long will it take you to get them to Luebeck or Wismar once you're ready to go?"

"Um." Simpson leaned back in his chair and looked thoughtful. "It's roughly a hundred and fifty miles from here to Hamburg, as the river flows, and another fifty from there to the sea. Then up around the Skaw . . ." He rubbed his chin, then shrugged. "Call it six hundred and seventy-five miles from Hamburg to Luebeck."

He sat back up and focused on Mike.

"I estimate that it should take us somewhere between three and ten days to get down the river itself. It depends on a lot of factors, including how much rain we get over the next few months, given how shallow parts of the river are between here and Hamburg. Once we get to sea, we should be able to make Luebeck within another three days, maximum. So take a worst-case estimate and say the entire trip will take two weeks."

"That makes a total of three months," Mike said. "Late December, at best, then."

"At best," Simpson agreed. "And while we're thinking about timetables, let's not forget that December gets us well into winter and that the Baltic sees a lot of ice in winter. I'm not sure what sort of icing conditions we can expect, either. From last winter's numbers, though, I don't expect it to be good."

He paused, and Mike nodded. Average temperatures in the 17th century were lower than in the 21st, and the previous winter had been colder than any of the up-timers had expected.

"There's no reason to expect this winter to be any warmer," Simpson continued, "and ice is the reason Baltic shipping is so extremely seasonal in this century. It's entirely possible that by the time we can get them to sea, the ice situation will be too bad for us to operate in the Baltic. By the same token, however, if *we* can't operate there, then sure as hell no sail-powered navy's going to be able to, either. So if winter shuts us down, it'll also shut the other side down. And by the time the spring thaw sets in, I damned well *know* we'll be ready to go after them."

"I see," Mike said, then frowned. "Either way, though, December is a long time to expect Gustavus to hold out in Luebeck. Especially if the Danes and this League of Ostend have complete control of Mecklenburg Bay for the next couple of months. Possibly even the entire Baltic; the western part of it, at least. And it sounds from his message like the only way he can get a garrison into Luebeck soon enough to do any good would be to strip it away from Wismar and the Stralsund Peninsula."

"Of course he will." Simpson sounded almost as if he were surprised Mike felt any need to comment on something so obvious. "He has to find the troops for Luebeck *somewhere*—where else could he look?" The admiral shook his head. "From my last information on his deployments, he ought to be able to scrape up enough additional troops to hold Wismar, at least. Probably have to just write off Stralsund and Rostock, though, at least for now. He can always take them back later, assuming we survive, but hanging onto Luebeck and Wismar will split the Danes' attention. If he thinks he can do it, it's certainly worth trying. But if he reduces Wismar's garrison to cover Luebeck, we're going to have to do something to keep the enemy from just walking in and taking it away before he can shift in fresh troops to cover it. He's pretty much *got* to hold on to Wismar. With Luebeck invested in a siege, and Rostock and Stralsund in enemy hands, Wismar would be his only good outlet on the Baltic."

"Do something? Like what?" Mike asked.

Simpson glanced at Jesse. "Colonel Wood will have to speak for the Air Force. As for the Navy, I've been thinking about that ever since you radioed that you were coming. And I had Lieutenant Cantrell do some resource analysis for me. He tells me that there are several speedboats in Grantville, including a couple of good-sized launches and at least one cockpit cabin cruiser. He also informs me that there are at least two or three people who scuba dive as a hobby. And he reminds me that Mr. Ferrara and his rocket club have been working on a ship-launched surface-to-surface missile for us."

The admiral gave his youthful lieutenant a long, sharp look, then turned back to Mike.

"If we commit those resources to Wismar with orders to hit and run, try and keep the French and the Danes off balance, they ought to be able to disrupt enemy naval operations to at least some degree. Long enough for Gustavus to bring in fresh troops, at least. And I assume that General Jackson ought to be able to provide at least a few surprises for them on the land front, as well."

For the first time, Jesse spoke up.

"We can commit the two Belles to it, too, if we can get some kind of airfield ready in or near Wismar. The X-2s, unfortunately, won't be ready in time, no matter how much we try to rush things.

"That'll mean delaying flight training for the new batch of pilots, but ... Depending on the circumstances, I might take one or two of the first group with Hans and me. There's no point in me staying back in Grantville when our only functioning aircraft is on the Baltic coast. And the truth is my original pilot group—especially the best of them, like Hans and Woody—are actually at the point where the experience would do them good. Assuming, of course, they survive the experience at all."

The Air Force colonel's face was grim.

"This is going to be a bitch, don't think it won't, especially this time of the year. As it happens, I've flown a lot in Germany and some around the Baltic. But not in the simple machines we've got. We'll be able to fly on the days between the passage of succeeding storm fronts—of which there will be an increasing number as winter approaches. Then subtract some of the calm days because of fog, which is frequent on the coast."

He gave Simpson a hard stare; Simpson returned it, after an instant, with a curt nod. Mike realized he was witness to a little inter-service . . . not "rivalry," precisely. More like a mutual demand for respect.

Apparently satisfied with Simpson's response, Jesse continued. "Here's how it is. You can take off in clear weather and not be able to return two hours later. Or it might be clear for days on end. As a best guess, I'd say we'd have at least marginally VFR weather about one-third of the time. On the other days, it would be asking for death to take off in these machines. Not because you couldn't fly, but because we have no radio navigation aids to guide us to landing and because they aren't really equipped for instrument flying. A half-trained pilot—which is what I've got—would likely get into a classic death spiral after entering heavy cloud formations. There are chances an older pilot like me might take, because they have a feel for weather that surpasses that of new pilots. Plus an older pilot won't panic, which is often what kills you in weather."

He drew a deep breath and let it out.

"Mr. President—Admiral Simpson—I'm not going to kid either one of you. Flying in the Baltic doesn't appeal to me, with winter coming on. I'd say you can bet on perhaps fifty to sixty percent of flyable days in September. Maybe forty percent in October and November. Don't count on more than twenty-five to thirty percent from December through February. Foggy days will be very common on the coast."

Simpson grunted. "I remember the year when two F-111s just disappeared during fighter operations in NATO's BALTAP exercises—that stands for 'Baltic Approaches,' Mr. President. I was involved in that, from the naval side. They never were found. One in September and one in March, as I recall."

"Yup," echoed Jesse. "Of course, they probably flew into the sea while on 'hard ride' autopilot, but thinking about it is still not pleasant. Even in the world we came from, there are places where, if someone goes down, you don't bother looking very long. That's just the way it is—and will be for us."

Mike felt his own expression tighten at Simpson and Jesse's matter-of-fact assessment of the risks involved. He'd suspected it was coming, of course. And the fact that Simpson had been the first to actually suggest it didn't mean Mike was blind to the logic. It was just that the up-timers were already so thinly spread. The thought of sending his people into Wismar and all of the horrors of a 17$^{th}$-century siege was not one that he wanted to contemplate.

But that was cowardice speaking, he told himself coldly. That was the fear of a man who was unwilling, when it came down to it, to pay the price his own beliefs demanded. Or even worse, of a man who was willing to let *someone else's* people pay for his beliefs.

He looked down at his hands for a moment, then drew a deep breath and raised his eyes once more.

"If Gustavus takes personal command in Luebeck and we assume responsibility for covering Wismar until he can reinforce it, it sounds like anything we commit will have to be more on the naval side. I think that means one of your people appropriately ought to be in charge, with the Air Force in a supporting role." He saw Jesse nodding out of the corner of his eye, and felt a moment's relief that whatever else he was facing Mike wouldn't have to play referee in some petty interservice brawl. "So who do you recommend, Admiral?"

Simpson's jaw clenched, and he turned to look out the dockyard window, as if this part of the decision was one he, too, would have preferred to pass to someone else. He stared out the window for several seconds, then turned back to Mike.

"Lieutenant Wild is already at Luebeck to set up the commo station with the Swedish encampment there. Once that's done, he's supposed to move on to do the same thing at Wismar. He's got a couple of petty officers with him, but his primary function is to coordinate communications. That's going to be just as important as anything else, and we're going to need a reliable commo link with anyone we send to Wismar. We're going to need it pretty badly, in fact, so I don't want to pull him off that. And, frankly, I'm not sure he'd be the right person for a combat assignment, anyway." His nostrils flared, and he turned his head to look directly at Eddie at last. "I think Lieutenant Cantrell is probably the best available choice."

"Eddie? I mean," Mike corrected himself almost instantly as he saw Eddie flush, "Lieutenant Cantrell?"

"He's here in Magdeburg, closer to Wismar than anyone back

in Grantville, so we can get him there that much quicker. And we're going to have to establish the support infrastructure in Wismar now, before the city gets itself invested."

"What infrastructure do you have in mind?" Mike asked just a bit warily.

"Colonel Wood will have to assign some Air Force personnel for his end of things. The Navy will cooperate with them fully, of course. Speaking for the Navy itself..." He paused for a moment, thinking. "At the very least, we're going to need refueling facilities in the city. We can stow extra ammunition aboard the ironclads and probably even tow some supplies with us on barges, but I'm not about to put half of our total armored combat strength out at the end of a supply line that may or may not be there when it arrives. I want technical support personnel, fuel, and spare parts in place in either Wismar or Luebeck before we get there. Fuel, at least, in both, preferably. Most of that sort of thing is going to have to come from right here at Magdeburg, down the Elbe and through one or the other of the canals. Fortunately, the advance warning we've gotten from your wife's reports gives us a few days to work with. The enemy won't be expecting that. If we use both tugs, we can get anything here in Magdeburg to Lauenburg and through the Stecknitz to Luebeck within forty-eight hours. But it's going to take longer to get anything to Wismar, because the Swedes still haven't finished rebuilding the stretch from Lake Schwerin to the coast. That means we're going to have to move fast to get what we need into position, and Lieutenant Cantrell is very well versed in what we have here and how it all goes together.

"And, finally, he's the one I had figuring out what our available resources are. That means he's completely informed on what we have in Grantville, as well. And that he's probably in the best position to make effective use of them, for that matter."

Mike stared at the admiral for several seconds, and a memory played itself mercilessly in the back of his brain. The memory of an argument with Melissa Mailey and Ed Piazza that first night when he'd beaten back Simpson's argument that the up-timers must turn Grantville into some sort of Fortress America and refuse to grant asylum to starving, terrified refugees from the madness of war lest they all be overwhelmed. He'd disagreed then—and still did—with Simpson's logic, but he hadn't been blind to the necessities of his own. That same night, Melissa had called him a "warmonger" for proposing that high school seniors be called upon for military service in defense of Grantville.

*So now it's my turn,* he thought. *My turn to say "But he's just a kid!" And he is . . . by the standards of the 21ˢᵗ century. But even in our own world, plenty of teenagers died fighting our wars. Sure as hell, Eddie—and Larry, and Hans—aren't "kids" here. Simpson's right, here and now, just as I was back then.*

"All right." He turned from Simpson and looked at Eddie. "You heard what Admiral Simpson said, Eddie. You understand how important this is?"

"Of course I do," Eddie replied. "And don't worry, Mike. Uh, Mr. President. Larry and I will kick their asses! Speedboats and rocket attacks, maybe throw a few limpet mines at them." He grinned with the ferocious enthusiasm of the very young. "We may not be able to lift the siege all by ourselves, but we'll sure as hell keep them from getting very much done!"

"You'll do what you *can,* Lieutenant," Simpson said coldly. Eddie looked at him, obviously surprised by his tone, and Simpson showed his teeth. "I know you think of me as an ancient and decrepit military bureaucrat," he said. "It may surprise you to know that that wasn't always the case. I spent my time in gunboats on another river, Lieutenant. The same one General Jackson spent some time wading in. And I saw a lot of people die—as often as not because they thought technology and 'advanced weapons' made them invulnerable. Well, they didn't. And they won't make *you* invulnerable, either. I expect you to use good judgment. To *think,* damn it!"

Mike heard Jesse grunt approvingly. Eddie's eyes widened for just a moment, and then he nodded sharply. It was obvious from his expression that he was considering coming to attention, as well, but he didn't. Perhaps, Mike thought, he was too stunned to do anything that active. The President wouldn't have been a bit surprised if that were the case, for *he* was a bit stunned himself. Just as Mike had expected Simpson's HQ to resemble the fabled ones of MacArthur, he'd expected Simpson to be prone to the same glorious posturing.

But this was no time for that. He turned to join Simpson in glaring at the young man. "I agree wholeheartedly," Mike said forcefully, "and I expect you to do exactly what Admiral Simpson just told you to. Is that clearly understood?"

"Yes, sir!" Eddie blurted, and this time he *did* snap to attention.

"Good!" Mike growled. He turned away to consider John Chandler Simpson, who was still giving Eddie his best admiral's glare. And, for the very first time since he'd met the man, realized he was feeling something surprisingly close to genuine respect, not simply cold-blooded assessment of his talents.

"Good," he repeated softly.

That night, Mike and Jesse settled into their rooms in the new building very close to the shipyards which was the official U.S. embassy in Magdeburg. As he tossed his little traveling bag onto the bed, Mike found himself smiling whimsically. The very title of the building—*embassy*—was somewhat amusing. Given the tortuous complexity of the political structure of the Confederated Principalities of Europe, which resembled one of the mythical creatures made up from the parts of different animals—a manticore, or a sphinx, or a winged horse—the United States was a part of the CPE as well as an independent realm in its own right.

But Mike found the situation only somewhat amusing. The advantage to the arrangement was that each realm—including his own U.S.—enjoyed a great deal of autonomy to manage its own affairs. The disadvantage, of course, was that when faced with a real external threat the resultant beast was as unlikely to fight effectively as . . .

Mike's smile widened, and grew more crooked.

Jesse entered the room. "What's so funny?"

"Just the man I wanted to see. I have a technical question for you, O great experienced pilot. What do you think would really happen if Pegasus took a flying leap off a cliff?"

Jesse snorted. "Are you kidding? Horsemeat for dinner, that's what. Mind you don't break your teeth on all the splintered bones and little rocks mixed into the mess."

"Yeah, that's about what I figured."

"Ready to eat?" asked Jesse. "The guard tells me there's a very nice new restaurant just opened down the street. Um. Using the term 'street' loosely, anyway."

Mike sighed regretfully. "No, you go ahead, Jesse. I'll scrounge up what I can here. Oh, and, by the way—figure we'll be here at least another day."

Jesse cocked an eyebrow. Mike's whimsical smile came back. "I'll be in the radio room most of the time, I imagine, whenever I'm not meeting some of the people who showed up here for the Chamber of Princes."

"Doing what?"

"Trading horses—before we all wind up a lot of mangled horsemeat."

# Chapter 30

The prince of Orange looked older than a man still short of his fiftieth birthday. As he ushered her to a chair in his private chambers, Rebecca was struck by the haggardness in his face. His drawn expression contrasted sharply with what was obviously the man's normal appearance. Frederik Henrik had an almost archetypical "Dutch" face: rather handsome, if on the fleshy side; pale-complected; brown hair offset by a very gingery goatee and flaring set of mustachios. Only his eyes were a bit exotic. Instead of the normal blue or green or brown, they seemed some off-color combination of slate gray and hazel.

It was a face which, Rebecca suspected, was normally full of ruddy good cheer. But not now.

That was hardly surprising, of course. The double Spanish victories—first the naval triumph at the Battle of Dunkirk, followed by the lightning seizure of Haarlem—had driven his country to its knees in less than two weeks. Panic was sweeping everywhere, with refugees now pouring into Amsterdam. One after another of the frontier fortresses and towns were reportedly surrendering to advancing Spanish troops—and the Counter-Remonstrant towns no less readily than others, once assured that the Spanish would leave their churches alone and refrain from reprisals against the inhabitants.

According to all reports, the United Provinces were coming apart at the seams. The Spanish seizure of Haarlem had cut Holland itself

in half. Then, the cardinal-infante—whether from his own acumen or because he was listening to Oquendo—had not made the
mistake of the Spanish who had seized Haarlem after a long siege
in 1572. On that occasion, the Spanish commander, Don Fadrique
de Toledo—the duke of Alva's son, in spirit as well as flesh—had
frittered away his strength by attacking northern Holland. The
cardinal-infante would leave northern Holland for a later time.
Leaving enough of a garrison to hold Haarlem, he was now driving
south on Leiden, and everyone Rebecca had talked to seemed to
think that city's fall was inevitable.

Most of Zeeland and Utrecht had already fallen, it seemed, as
well as the southern half of Gelderland. And the northern provinces of Friesland, Groningen and Drenthe, still largely Catholic
and long resentful of the heavy thumb of the Counter-
Remonstrants, had erupted in full revolt. The United Provinces,
born sixty years earlier in a rebellion against Spain, now found
three of its provinces rebelling in *favor* of Spanish rule.

That left the prince of Orange the effective ruler of one and a
half provinces—Overijssel and what was left of Gelderland—along
with the city of Amsterdam. But Amsterdam—on this no one
seemed to have *any* doubt—would very soon be completely surrounded and under siege itself.

After taking a seat on a chair a few feet away, Frederik Hendrik
gave Rebecca a wan smile. "So, Madame Stearns. We meet at last."
His French was fluent and impeccable. "I cannot begin to tell you
how many times I have cursed myself for listening to the advisers who urged me to keep a distance from you."

This was no time for smug *I-told-you-so's*, Rebecca told herself
firmly. "It might very well not have made a difference anyway,
Prince. Perhaps, yes. But . . . by the time you could have investigated my warnings—admittedly based on sketchy evidence—
Richelieu's scheme would already have been underway. Could you
have called back Tromp's fleet, in time to save it?"

Frederik Henrik shrugged. "Quite possibly not. But I still would
have been better prepared myself. The disaster was not *simply* a
naval one." For a moment, he glowered ferociously. "What in the
name of God were those idiots in Haarlem *thinking*, anyway? A
flotilla of Dutch ships—badly battered—arrives in the waterway
leading to the Harlemmermeer, and they do nothing more than
gawk at them? Cretins! Why would Dutch vessels damaged in battle
not have docked at Amsterdam?"

Rebecca hesitated. She did not want to increase the prince's gloom, of course. On the other hand, she thought Mike and Gustav would appreciate better information than she'd been able to provide them so far, based on the fragmentary and rumor-laden reports she'd received.

"What exactly *did* happen in Haarlem, Prince?" she asked. "I know that the Spanish seized the city, but not really how they managed to do it."

Frederik Hendrik's lips twisted. "They did it by a combination of reckless impetuosity on the part of that young prince of theirs—the 'cardinal-infante,' they call him—combined with Dutch stupidity. Admiral Oquendo, as you may know, was apparently injured in the sea battle. Though not fatally, alas, because he remained in command of the main body of the Spanish fleet. The Spanish prince, Don Fernando, took command of a flotilla made up of a number of captured Dutch vessels. Then, loaded them with Spanish soldiers and sailed into the Zuider Zee, past Amsterdam—in broad daylight, no less!—and landed them on the eastern side of Haarlem. Meanwhile, Oquendo ordered the bulk of his fleet to disembark most of the Spanish troops on the North Sea coast."

The Prince made a little squeezing motion with his hand. "A pincer attack, if you will. Investing the city from east and west simultaneously, avoiding the very strong fortifications on the south." He erupted in what seemed a combination of a cough and a laugh. "Exactly the kind of flashy and dramatic maneuver beloved of dramatic young princes and storytellers! And which—in the real world—almost never works."

Gloomily: "But it worked this time. From what I can determine, the idiots at Haarlem decided that Don Fernando's flotilla was a relief force. So instead of rushing the troops garrisoning the city itself to meet the disembarking Spanish soldiers—who could have been easily hammered as they were trying to come ashore—they rushed them instead to reinforce the soldiers fighting off the main body of Spanish troops on the western side of the city. That left Haarlem's eastern approaches effectively unprotected. The prince led his men ashore and more or less stormed into the city. That, of course, panicked the Dutch troops on the North Sea fortifications. Soon enough, everything was chaos, Oquendo's troops surged forward, and our soldiers either fled or surrendered."

He threw up his hands. "My whole life, spent mastering the genuine art of war! And—now *this*! A stripling Spanish prince makes a mockery of it all with something that belongs nowhere outside of a troubadour's tale!"

Rebecca swallowed.

"Was there . . . ah, a massacre thereafter?"

Frederik Hendrik took a deep breath, and then abruptly shook his head.

"No massacre. Neither there nor, so far as I have been able to determine, anywhere the Spanish have overrun us. In fact—"

He gave her a smile which, for the first time, was not simply sardonic. "They've taken Rotterdam and The Hague also. As of three days ago."

Rebecca felt herself grow tense. By far the largest Jewish community in the United Provinces was in Amsterdam. But there had also been, for decades, a small Jewish population in The Hague. And while Rebecca did not consider herself "Jewish" in the sense of that term which was the most common one in the Europe of her day—religiously observant—the ethnic sense of the term was already gaining ground. The Spanish Inquisition had begun that process, with their obsession over "secret Jews" and maintaining the "pure blood" of Christian Castile—*limpieza,* as the Spanish called it.

"It seems that as soon as the Spanish took the city," the prince continued, "a few Inquisitors took it upon themselves to round up the Jews. From the reports I've gotten, the cardinal-infante immediately ordered them to release their prisoners. And—" Here the smile widened. "When the Inquisitors objected, he promptly had three of them executed."

Rebecca's eyes widened. The Spanish Inquisition, unlike the Papal Inquisition, was officially under the authority of the crown of Spain. In the century and a half since its foundation, however, the Spanish Inquisition had developed a great deal of autonomy. Now, it seemed, a Spanish prince had decided to remind them—in the crudest way possible—that they *were* subordinate to royalty. Rebecca doubted if the cardinal-infante was any less anti-Semitic than any other Spanish hidalgo. But prejudice was one thing, a challenge to his authority another. And he might even be cunning enough to realize that Protestants, seeing a Spanish prince protect Jews, would be that much more likely to believe his promises of toleration.

Frederik Hendrik's smile faded away, replaced by the drawn and haggard look which had been on his face when Rebecca entered his chambers. "Which speaks well for the prince's humanity, of course. Or his shrewdness, at least. But—I will not lie to you, Rebecca Abrabanel—I almost wish he were another Alva."

He raised a hand abruptly. "*Almost*,' I say. Not . . . quite. But I must now think like a prince myself. And if I am to rally what remains of the Dutch republic, my task would be far easier if I faced another Alva."

Rebecca understood the point, just as she understood the prince's subtlety in using her maiden name. Rebecca might not consider herself "Jewish," but that did not mean that others would agree with her estimate—especially her enemies. Amsterdam would be under siege, soon, along with its three thousand Jewish inhabitants. If the duke of Alva were overseeing that siege . . . every one of those Jews could look forward to death and torture if the Spanish took the city. As great an incentive as possible, in other words, to throw themselves into the fight.

And not just them. *Any* "heretic." When the duke of Alva had been given the task of suppressing the Dutch Revolt by Philip II, he had followed the most savage policy possible. Even the Mongols, after all, had spared people who surrendered soon enough.

Not Don Fernandez Alvarez de Toledo, third duke of Alva. From the moment he arrived in the Low Countries, in 1567, the duke conducted himself like a beast. An old man when he landed, he had spent sixty years of his life accumulating a full store of religious bigotry, Castilian harshness and hidalgo arrogance. The gout and other bodily ailments which plagued his final years made him more vicious than ever.

Almost immediately, his brutality drew objections from the Spanish authorities on the spot. Archduchess Margaret, the Spanish regent in the Low Countries, resigned in outrage after Alva executed two leading magnates who had remained loyal to the Church—and had been assisting Margaret herself in trying to find a peaceful settlement.

But Alva did not *want* a peaceful settlement. Alva intended to simply terrorize the Netherlands into submission to the Spanish crown, and he set about it with a vengeance. The *Conseil des Troubles* was established under his supervision, with a staff of 170 prosecutors, and began the activities for which they soon became notorious. Thousands were investigated and sentenced for treason and heresy, more than one thousand of them executed outright.

In the southern provinces of the Low Countries, Alva's brutality succeeded in squelching the revolt. But in the northerly provinces, where Protestantism had sunk deeper roots, they had exactly the opposite effect. The Dutch rallied in 1568 under the leadership of William the Silent—the father of the man sitting across from Rebecca this moment—and the long war began.

It was a war which, in its early years, was marked by pure savagery. Alva set the pattern and never wavered from it. When the town of Mechelen threw open its gates at the approach of his army, Alva allowed his soldiers to sack the city and massacre its inhabitants. Another massacre followed when he took Zutphen. And, at Naarden, Alva set the seal on his reputation. He ordered the entire population of the city slaughtered—men, women and children alike.

The moral reputation of the Spanish empire would never survive Alva, in the universe which had produced the history books which Rebecca had read in Grantville. She knew that for a certainty. Coming atop the Inquisition and the conquistadores, Alva would ensure that history's memory of the Spanish in their heyday—that much of it written in the English language, at least—was one of simple cruelty, brutality and intolerance.

Which, in truth, was hardly fair. Spain would produce Parma and Spinola, also, just as it produced the line of shrewd and tolerant archduchess regents of the Spanish Netherlands beginning with Margaret and ending now with Isabella, reported to be lying on her deathbed. The same nation which produced Torquemada and Pizarro would also produce Bishop de las Casas and Miguel Cervantes. As a Sephardic Jewess, Rebecca understood the contradictions perfectly. Her own people had been driven out of Iberia by that Castilian darkness—yet still retained the culture of a land which was actually quite sunny. To this day, in private, she and her father Balthazar spoke to each other in Spanish. And why not? It was their tongue also.

But it mattered not. Alva had burned too deeply.

And, in the end, for no purpose. Alva's policy would backfire—and backfire badly. Whether they wanted to or not, the population of the northern provinces really had no choice *but* to fight a ferocious war of resistance. So, a cruel and vicious old man would create a rebellion which not only defeated him, but would endure for as long as he had lived himself. Sixty years, now.

She and the prince stared at each other. Yes, sixty years—*until* now. But what would happen next?

"I am still glad of it," she said softly. "The world does not need another Alva, Prince. However greatly that may burden your task."

Frederik Hendrik squared his shoulders. "And I am glad of it also, in the end. I am only a prince to a certain point. Or, it might be better to say, beyond a certain point I need to consider what the very word 'prince' means in the first place."

He tilted his head to one side, eyeing Rebecca shrewdly. "But let us move now to the immediate circumstances. What do you want from me, Madame Stearns? And what do you offer?"

Rebecca's response came instantly. "I can offer you an immediate alliance with the United States. And I am quite certain—although I cannot speak for him—with the king of Sweden."

The prince said nothing, for a moment. Then, bringing his head level, he pursed his lips. "I find myself—quite astonishing, really, for a prince—possessed by an overwhelming urge to speak the truth. Madame Stearns, I will gladly accept your offer. But I must warn you in advance that, in the end, I will almost certainly betray you."

Rebecca nodded. "Of course. You will seek a settlement, not a victory. Which is, in my opinion, exactly what you should do."

Frederik Hendrik hissed in a breath, his eyes widening. "Good God, am I *that* transparent?" He seemed genuinely aggrieved.

Barely, Rebecca managed to keep herself from emitting a nervous giggle. "Oh . . . not to most people, I think."

"I had heard you were shrewd," the prince murmured. "The reputation does not do you justice."

"Ah . . . I think that is because people underestimate my husband, actually. They see me, and estimate the intelligence of a cosmopolitan Jewess, sired and raised by the philosopher Balthazar Abrabanel. And so they miss the influence—and training—of the man I married."

The prince spread the fingers of his hands, inviting her to continue.

"Insofar as Europe's nobility knows much at all about my husband—insofar as they *deign* to do so, I should say—what they see is simply a man who is reputed to have once been a leader of unruly workmen." Again, Rebecca suppressed a giggle. Truth be told, Mike's coal miners *were* a fairly unruly lot. "But that is only part of it, Prince. The American trade unions of his time were not a mob of apprentices in the streets, hurriedly assembled and waving torches about. It was an *organized* movement—and one which had more than a century of history behind it before he was even born. So he also knows how to negotiate as well as fight; retreat, as well as advance; concede, as well as demand. Most of all, he understands when a settlement is worth making, and when it is not. Or, as he puts it, when a settlement allows for later victory, whatever it costs at the moment."

She fell silent. Frederik Hendrik looked away and studied one of the paintings on the wall of his chamber. It was a Brueghels—the Younger, Rebecca thought, although she was not certain—and depicted a tranquil scene of daily life in a Flemish town.

"Yes," he said softly. "I, too, you know, have gotten my hands on a few of these now-famous history books of yours. Copies of them, rather." His eyes moved back to her. "I am curious. When you read them, did you ever consider what that future history looks like—from the perspective of a *Dutchman*?"

Rebecca was a little startled by the question. "Ah . . . no. No, Prince, as a matter of fact. I never did."

He nodded ponderously. "Of course not. That is because Holland is a *little* country, in the world which produced those books. One which enjoyed—would enjoy—a century in the sun. This century, as it happens, the Seventeenth. 'The Golden Era,' they would call it. Thereafter . . . just a little country. Like our neighbors—relatives, really—just south of here. Two little countries, Holland and what will be called Belgium, surrounded by greater powers. Prosperous little countries, to be sure." His lips tightened. "And, about every quarter of a century, from what I can determine, destined to be overrun and plundered by foreign armies."

Now, he was scowling. "I find myself not very thrilled by that prospect. And I find myself also wondering what the world would look like—from a Dutchman's point of view—if Alva's savagery had not forever separated the two halves of the Spanish Netherlands. If, instead, that *single* country had been able to mature slowly. Still a smallish country, to be sure. But not *so* small—and also a country which, even divided as it is now, has a population and wealth which is already the envy of Europe."

"The Spanish—"

He waved her down. "Oh, don't be silly, Rebecca!" he snapped. Then, realizing at the same time she did that his unthinking use of the familiar name had allowed a certain genuine warmth into their relationship, gave her a friendly smile. "You know as well as

I do that—in almost any world I can imagine—the grandiose and creaking empire built by Charles V is destined to disintegrate sooner or later. It was all Philip II could do to hold onto most of it—and he was quite a capable king, you know. Now . . ." He shook his head. "Spain has grabbed too much; certainly more than it can handle any longer. That was true even before your Americans arrived and stuck a very large spoke in history's wheel."

Rebecca leaned back in her chair, her thoughts leaping ahead, following the prince's. *God in Heaven, the man is right. Mike and I never considered* this *possibility . . .*

"An interesting point, Frederik Henrik." The informality was calculated. *Might as well find out how friendly he's prepared to be.* "A very interesting point. It is in the nature of things that a Spanish viceroy resident in Brussels—especially one who oversees the *entire* population and wealth of the Low Countries—will soon discover that he has different interests from those of Castile."

"Not an accident, you know," murmured the prince, "that almost every archduchess regent wound up clashing with the king of Spain. Those were genteel ladies, however—and often elderly. So I find myself wondering how a brash young prince—especially one who is now covered with glory from the greatest feat of Spanish arms in a century—is going to react to the admonitions of his older brother. The older brother, perched in Madrid, in that pile of stones they call the Palacio Real; surrounded by Castile and its narrow-minded provincial hidalgos. The younger brother, in Brussels—or perhaps even in Amsterdam." His eyes moved back to the painting. "Surrounded by what is today—I'm boasting, I admit it—perhaps the world's greatest collection of artists—"

"Hardly boasting!" chuckled Rebecca. "Rubens, Van Dyck, not to mention Rembrandt—who's only what, now? Not more than thirty years old, I'm sure."

"Twenty-seven, I believe," said Frederik Hendrik with satisfaction. "With—assuming all goes well—a full lifetime ahead of him."

Again, they exchanged warm smiles. "Yes, indeed," Rebecca said. "It *is* an interesting thought. Surrounded by artists, philosophers, scientists, cosmopolitan merchants and financiers—not to mention that the populace as a whole is the best-educated in Europe, which is hardly true of Spain's. Craftsmen, artisans, manufacturers, seamen. For that matter, you have the world's most advanced farmers here, also."

The prince was almost grinning. Almost, but . . . not quite. And then the smile closed down abruptly, replaced by a face which was no longer haggard but still grim enough.

"All of it is true, Rebecca. But it is only a possibility. Nothing more than idle speculation, at the moment. It would need to be *made* true." He drew another deep breath. "And, for that, I will need both time and breathing space. After Dunkirk and Haarlem, the prince of Spain will be too full of himself to listen to anyone. I will need to bloody him a bit. More than a bit, in fact. I— or someone—will need to buckle his knees and smash his head about. *Then* . . . maybe."

He gave her a level stare. "So. There it is. Are you still prepared to make an alliance with me? Knowing—in advance—that I will someday almost certainly tear it up. And bend my knee to your enemy, the prince of Spain." Softly: "I will have no choice, Rebecca. The disaster is too great. All I can do now is try to force the best settlement possible—which will still be a settlement on Spanish terms."

"Yes, we are." The words came instantly and firmly. Rebecca hesitated a moment. Then, decided that it was worth the risk to be on frank speaking terms with the one ruler in Europe she had encountered thus far—even including Gustav Adolf—who seemed genuinely able to think the unthinkable.

"My husband calls it 'buying time,' Frederik Hendrik. Win what you can, cede what you must; compromise where possible, do not where it isn't. Most of all, never lose sight of what you are striving for in the first place." Her voice hardened. "Which is *not* the aggrandizement of princes, whether they be noble or common of birth. It is not even 'victory' at all, except insofar as a midwife might use the term when she successfully brings a new life into the world."

She pointed a finger at the painting, depicting Flemish townsfolk about their daily life. "*There* is victory, Prince of Orange. Nothing else is worthy of the name."

The prince nodded. "My father would have enjoyed meeting your husband, I think. Do you know why they called him 'William the Silent'?"

Rebecca shook her head.

"A bit of a mysterious name, really. My father was as far removed from taciturnity as possible. A most loquacious and voluble man, in fact. So everyone who knew him tells me. I can't remember him myself, of course, since he was assassinated the same year I was born."

Frederik Henrik chuckled. "I think the name was actually coined by his enemies. They called him 'the Silent' because they accused him of never saying what he really thought. But I think, myself, that is simply the surliness of defeat. What my father *was*, was the most adroit statesman in Europe. Who used his victories on the field of battle to disguise the blade in his left hand, which he wielded at the negotiating table."

He rose to his feet. "Done, then, Madame Stearns. You may tell your husband that the prince of Orange sends a workman his warmest regards. And will pray every night that the day comes when a cardinal of France, thinking he stands astride the world, glances down and discovers he has been disemboweled in the process. And never noticed it at the time, so craftsmanlike was the hand that did the deed."

# Chapter 31

That night, after he got Becky's message, Mike walked out of the radio room before answering. The radio operator assured him he'd have at least two hours to send a reply before transmission became too difficult, and Mike needed time to think. The decision he had to make was, in more ways than one, the most difficult he'd ever had to make in his life.

When he left the embassy building, he found his feet taking him down to the Elbe. Mike had always found the sight of moving water both restful and a help to concentration. This was a decision he needed to make standing on a wharf, watching the flow of a river, not staring at the walls in a room. The chill in the autumn air was just enough to be invigorating, given the heavy jacket Mike had brought for the flight up here.

Fortunately, the sky was clear and there was enough of a moon to see. The "street lighting" in the area was not even a joke. There wasn't any at all except an occasional lamp in an open window or signaling the entrance to a tavern. So Mike had no great difficulty picking his way through the mud puddles and finding the occasional patch of half-finished cobblestones, and was confident he could make it back to the radio room within a few minutes once he'd made his decision.

But when he arrived at the wharf, he instantly regretted having done so. By bad luck, Simpson was already there, standing on the wharf himself with his hands clasped behind his back. Apparently he found staring over water as relaxing as Mike did.

He was a lonely looking figure, staring down at the water in the moonlight. Mike's dislike for the man had been so constant, for so long, that he'd never really given any thought to what Simpson's own life must have been like, since the Ring of Fire. He had simply been a political opponent to be defeated.

Now, for the first time, he found himself wondering about it. And didn't take more than a moment to conclude that the lonely-looking figure on the wharf was a lonely man in truth. Neither Simpson, nor certainly his wife, could have found the transition easy—the more so after having, from their own sheer haughtiness and arrogance, alienated their own son so completely.

*Well, that's a small horse or two I can trade easily enough,* Mike thought. *But I'll worry about that later.*

He began to turn around, planning to retrace his steps. Staring at the walls of a room was not an attractive prospect, to be sure, but it beat trying to make small talk with Simpson while he wrestled with *this* decision.

But, then, he hesitated. Turned back around and studied Simpson again. The admiral had still not spotted him, standing in the shadows where the street debouched onto the wharf.

*What the hell. Maybe I owe it to him. Or, let's put it this way: maybe I owe it to myself to remember what Simpson and I were fighting about in the first place.*

Mike was decisive by nature. A moment later, he was striding toward the wharf.

Simpson, hearing him come, turned his head. When he recognized who it was, the expression which flitted across his face almost made Mike laugh aloud. Simpson, clearly enough, was no more pleased than Mike had been himself to see the other man in the area.

"My apologies for disturbing you, Admiral."

"Not at all, Mr. President. What may I do for you?"

"For starters—for tonight, at least—I'd like to dispense with the 'Admiral' and the 'Mr. President' business. If that's all right with you, John."

Simpson hesitated. "Very well." His shoulders shifted a bit, as a man's will when he feels uncomfortable. "I'm not actually as formal as you may think. Believe it or not, I did not require my executives—any of my subordinates—to call me 'Mr. Chief Executive Officer.'"

He unclasped his hands and waved one of them toward the

flowing river. "Back in my days in Pittsburgh. In fact, when I met with the president of the local union which represented the production employees in my petrochemical plant, he called me 'John' and I called him 'Henry.'"

The hands reclasped; then, tightened. Simpson's next words came in a harsh voice. "Since you've chosen informality, at least for the moment, I'd like to get something off my chest."

Mike nodded. "Shoot."

"During the political campaign, the one accusation which you leveled against me which I deeply resented personally—and still do—was the insinuation that I was a racist. I am *not*, sir, and never have been. The union president I mentioned—Henry—was a black man. And while I have no doubt he'd have choice words to say about me on most other subjects, I don't think you'd find him raising *that* as an issue." Simpson's clasped hands were now very tight. It was obvious even in the poor lighting.

"Yes, Henry and I fought over a lot of things. As you can imagine, being a former local union president yourself. But not *that*. My company had an equal opportunity employment program which I took dead seriously—and saw to it was enforced down the line. We almost never had a grievance filed over discrimination issues." His voice was starting to rise a little in anger. "A few, sure—but you know as well as I do—"

"Yeah, yeah, John, I know." Mike waved his own hand at the river. "In any factory or mine, there's always a few goofballs who'll file a grievance on any grounds, especially if they get in trouble." He smiled thinly. "Of course—in my official capacity as a union president—you'd never catch me admitting that to the boss."

Simpson snorted. "Neither did Henry. Ha! And what a laugh that was, sometimes. I remember one guy—took us forever to get rid of the bum—who seemed to have a grievance every week. Invariably after he got disciplined for something. Henry even managed to keep a straight face whenever it got to me in third-step hearings, and he'd argue the case as if he didn't know just as well as I did that we'd all be better off with the jerk looking for a job somewhere else."

"Gotta keep management honest," said Mike. "And that means, now and then, you fight a grievance on behalf of a guy you'd personally just as soon see get run over by a truck. If you start getting too cozy with the boss . . ." He shrugged. "Way it is. What union was that, by the way? Oil, Chemical and Atomic Workers?

Or PACE, now, as they're called since they merged with the paperworkers."

Simpson nodded. "Good outfit," said Mike. "We almost merged with them once."

He clasped his own hands behind his back. It seemed like the proper gesture, under the circumstances. "I never once, John, stated that I thought *you* were a bigot. What I did say—and I won't retract it—was that your program amounted to a return to Jim Crow. Or, at least, that was the logic of it." Simpson started to say something, but Mike overrode him.

"Hear me out, dammit. Just once—*listen.*" Simpson took a deep breath, then nodded abruptly.

"Whether you ever intended it that way, John, is not the issue to me. Wasn't then, sure as hell isn't now. I'll be glad to grant you the best possible motives—simply trying to figure out the best way to deal with a bad situation. But what was clear to me then—and still is—is that we were in the position of a man who had stumbled badly and was about to fall. And the surface he was going to fall on was nothing but broken glass. You wanted us to throw out our hands to break the fall—which would, at best, have ripped our hands to shreds. And I thought we should get out of the stumble by running faster."

Simpson's jaws were tight, but he said nothing. Mike nodded toward the looming bulk of the ironclads under construction, then swept his head in a circle, indicating the entire city rising up out of the rubble of what had been the worst massacre in the Thirty Years War.

"Look at it, John. Can you honestly say I was *wrong?*"

Still, Simpson said nothing. Mike decided not to push the issue any further. Whatever were the good qualities of John Chandler Simpson—many, obviously, as those same ironclads indicated— the ability to admit error was clearly not one of them.

*Besides, this horse is easy to swap.*

"I realize—" Mike broke off, as if he were momentarily a bit embarrassed. (Which . . . he was, perhaps. Just a tiny bit.) "I realize that I'm a bare-knuckle kind of guy, in a political brawl. So if I insulted you personally, please accept my apology."

After a moment, Simpson nodded. Very stiffly, to be sure, but . . . a nod was a nod.

"Beyond that, I'll do what I can to make amends. I imagine, ah . . ."

Simpson smiled coldly. "Oh, indeed. One of the reasons I've grown so fond of my assistant, Dietrich Schwanhausser, is because he's one of the few Germans here who doesn't assume I eat German babies for breakfast. Thanks to you, and your campaign, my reputation has preceded me." Bitterly: "And it's even harder on my wife, who sits at home most days as if she were a leper. If she didn't have that school expansion project of Veronica Dreeson's to work on I think she'd go nuts entirely. As least in Grantville, she had some American friends. Here—"

Now, finally, some of the anger seeped into his voice. "For God's sake, Stearns, half of my ancestors on my mother's side are German. *Her* maiden name was Schreiber. How in the world—"

"*John!*" The half-shouted word cut Simpson off. "If you don't want to accept a man's apology, then don't. But don't accept it one minute and throw it back in his face the next."

Simpson froze. Then, abruptly, nodded again. "Fair enough."

"Besides, you should have told me sooner. I didn't realize—" Mike let out a breath. "Sorry. My fault. I hadn't really thought about it. Or, when I did . . ." For a moment, his lips twisted. "Truth be told, I was assuming you and your wife Mary were hobnobbing with the upper crust here in Magdeburg. Letting them all know—privately, of course—that I was indeed the reckless and disreputable and dangerous fellow they thought I was."

Simpson's stance was as rigid as ever. "We have not been invited to any . . . 'hobnobbings,' as you put it. Neither upper-crust nor any other kind. And even if we had, I can assure you—" His voice was starting to rise hotly again.

"*John.*" Again, Simpson broke off. "Give me a break, will you? I wasn't *accusing* you of anything."

Mike motioned toward the ironclads. "As a naval officer in the service of the U.S. government, I will expect you to refrain from public attacks on your commander-in-chief. Or, if you feel strongly enough about something that you can't, I will expect your resignation. But what you say about me in private, as long as you're reasonably discreet about it . . . I won't go so far as to say that I don't *care* about it, but I will look the other way. Is that fair enough?"

Simpson's hesitation was very brief. "Yes," he said curtly. "That's fair enough."

Mike nodded. "Good. That's settled." His smile was now actually a bit warm. "Do keep in mind, of course, that I certainly won't

object either if—just now and then—you find you have something
positive to say about me also."

Simpson chuckled. And, there too, there was a bit of actual
warmth in the sound. "Actually—and just in private, between you
and me—there are a few things I like about you. Not many, mind.
But . . ." He took a deep breath of his own. "I'll give you this much,
Mike Stearns. At least you're not one of those presidents we had
back up-time who shilly-shallied and danced around every time
the shit hit the fan."

The reminder jolted Mike. "Oh, hell," he muttered. He held up
his watch, trying to read the old-style face in the dim lighting.
That was the disadvantage of the somewhat antique mechanical
watch he owned. The advantage, of course, was that it still
worked—where almost everyone else's fancy digital timepieces were
unusable because the special batteries had gone dead long since,
and Grantville had few spares.

"You need to send a radio message, while the window lasts?"

Mike nodded. "Yeah. I've still got a bit of time, though. But I'd
better—"

He was starting to turn away already. Then, struck by a thought,
stopped and turned back.

"What the hell. As it happens, John, I've got a decision to make.
And—in a different way—it's the same kind of decision you and
I fought about once. When a man stumbles, does he try to break
it by running or taking the fall? So I'll be interested to see what
you think about this one."

Quickly, he sketched out Becky's radio message and the choice
he had to make. When he was done, Simpson shook his head.

"Jesus. That one's a bitch." Simpson thought a moment. "Even
leaving aside the decision itself, it's the kind of thing your political
enemies could try to make hay over."

"I'm not worried about *that*."

Simpson smiled thinly. "No, you wouldn't be. If nothing else,
because—with your roughhouse political skills—you'd leave them
bleeding in the street."

"Yeah, I would. Bloody, bruised, battered, and beat to shit. And
I'd make no apologies for it, either." Harshly: "But that's neither
here nor there, John. I wouldn't let that influence me anyway. You
may not *like* my character, but don't make the mistake of thinking I don't have one."

"Oh, I won't make that mistake. I meant what I said. I can think of former presidents of the U.S.A. up-time I wouldn't want in your shoes now, making this decision. I wouldn't trust them—especially that worthless bastard—"

He shook his head. "Never mind. Of all the silly things I can think of, hauling in old partisan squabbles from another universe ranks right at the top."

He gave Mike a sharp glance. "You're inclined to go for it, aren't you? Use a knife in a knife fight—even if it's your own wife who's the blade."

Mike nodded. "Yeah, I am. So's Becky herself, by the way. Her own opinion was, ah, firm."

Simpson nodded. "Cowardly, the lady is not." He thought a moment further. Then:

"Do it, Mike." He glanced at the ironclads. "And for what it's worth, the Navy will back you up to the best of our ability."

"That's worth quite a bit, John. In fact, the time may come when it's worth a *lot*. And now, I'd better go. I'll have more than one message to send tonight."

After taking a few steps, Mike turned back around.

"Before I forget, one other thing."

"Yes?"

"As Admiral of the U.S. Navy, I expect you'll be getting a fair number of social invitations. You and your wife, both. Quite soon, in fact." He raised his fist and coughed into it. "Not to put too fine a point on it, I'll see to it. And I think it would reflect badly on the United States if you didn't accept them. It might give the aristocracy the notion that we don't have any manners, you know. Won't leave our houses because we're afraid we won't know which fork to use in polite company."

For a moment, Simpson's face almost turned puce. "*Mary?* She could—"

His shoulder heaved a little, suppressing a laugh. Then, smiling: "Thank you, Mike. I'd appreciate that."

Mike nodded and began to turn away.

"Mr. President."

"Yes . . . Admiral."

Simpson squared his shoulders. "As a rule, I'd prefer formality. It's not a matter of personality. Well . . . not much. But I'm building a military force here, a *navy*. And while—"

He paused, briefly. "I will not interfere with General Jackson and Colonel Wood. They can create whatever traditions and customs in the Army and Air Force they choose. But I will insist they extend me the same courtesy. And you also."

"Fair enough. Admiral."

Simpson nodded stiffly. Then, for the first time since Mike had appeared on the wharf, the admiral seemed to relax completely.

"Did you have any horse traders in your family tree, Mr. President? I'm just curious."

Mike grinned. "Two, that I know of. And at least one horse thief. Family tradition has it that they never caught and hung 'im, neither." Solemnly: "Even though, of course, everyone agreed that was a great shame and he was a disgrace to the family name."

# Chapter 32

Rebecca returned to the prince's quarters early the next morning. "My husband agrees to the alliance," she said, as she began lowering herself into the seat offered.

Frederik Hendrik smiled. "So. Overnight, no less. How nice to see that my advisers were wrong about something *else*. Your mysterious 'radio,' it seems, does not require gigantic constructions after all."

Rebecca was so startled that she plopped onto the chair instead of sliding gracefully into it. She realized—too late—that she had not even considered what she would be revealing.

Sensing her unease, the prince waved his hand. "Have no fear. Your secret will remain safe with me." As he took his own chair, his expression was odd. Something like a combination of a scowl and a grin of pure glee. For a moment, with his gingery facial hair and ruddy plump cheeks, he looked a bit like a prosperous pirate contemplating another rich prize.

"And let's hope Richelieu doesn't find out until it's too late. Which he probably won't, the cocksure bastard. That's the one advantage to having a cardinal for an archenemy. He thinks God is whispering tactics into his ear."

Once seated, Frederik Hendrik planted his hands on his knees. "What I need, immediately—although I can't see what it would be—is whatever help you can give me in holding Amsterdam. We will be under siege here within a week, and it will be a bitter one.

In fact—as I'm sure you know—the siege has begun already. Spanish warships fired on the city yesterday evening."

Rebecca nodded. She'd heard the sound of the cannonade from the house the American delegation had taken for its quarters. The owners of the house had rented it to them shortly before leaving Amsterdam themselves, seeking refuge in a town further east. They hadn't seemed too concerned about how they'd collect the rent, either. Two months in advance, coin in their hands, and they were off.

"Within a week—two at the outside—the land approaches to the city will be completely invested," the prince predicted. "And since the Spanish also now control the Zuider Zee, there will be no relief from that quarter either. I will do what I can to smuggle supplies into the city, but . . . it will not be much." A bit hurriedly: "More than you might think, though. No Spanish fleet is going to be able to stop Dutch boatmen from getting at least a trickle of supplies into Amsterdam. Certainly not after winter sets in."

Rebecca nodded. She knew, from her studies, that navies of the future would maintain year-round blockades. But that was not something within the capability of 17th-century fleets.

"Still," the prince said grimly, "it will be a very difficult siege. Very difficult. Hunger and disease are certain, epidemic is very likely. Even if we succeed in holding off the Spanish, a large part of the city's populace is sure to die before it is over."

"*Can* you hold the city?" she asked.

"Oh, yes."

She was a bit surprised by the quick and relaxed answer, and it must have shown. Frederik Henrik smiled.

"Trust me on *this* subject, Rebecca. If there is one thing the House of Orange knows, it is siegecraft. Amsterdam is a large city, and well fortified. So long as the populace and the garrison retain their will, the city can be held. For at least a year, probably longer." He frowned. "What we lost thus far was due to treachery on the part of the French, boldness on the part of the Spanish, bad luck, and—most of all—our own complacency. But the cardinal-infante has now used up that treasury, every coin in it. So now *he* will learn the cold facts of life.

"The first thing he's going to learn—has already, unless I miss my guess—is that his victories have outrun his supply train. That means he has one of two choices: plunder the countryside, which would immediately undo everything he has accomplished by his light-handed policies. Or, stop everything except investing Amsterdam, and thereby give me the time I need to organize the resistance in what is left of the United Provinces. While he twiddles his thumbs outside Amsterdam waiting for supplies, money, reinforcements—everything. By the time he can resume his advance . . ."

The prince's chest seemed to swell. "By then, I can and will have a sizeable force back in the field. Or, I should say, behind fortifications in northern Gelderland and Overijssel. The Spanish will be back to a grinding war of attrition—and this, after having paid a heavy price in blood and treasure for what they have gained already. Cardinal Richelieu used them as well as us, you know. By all accounts, it was the Spanish—not the French or the English—who paid the butcher's bill at Dunkirk."

"But you do not think the cardinal-infante will want to negotiate a settlement?"

"Not right away, no. Why should he? He's come this far on audacity and boldness, why should he stop? If he were Spinola, canny from decades of warfare, yes. But he is a young prince, Rebecca—and still undefeated. He will inevitably go for the final and most dramatic stroke, hoping thereby to end the thing entirely on Spanish terms."

"Take Amsterdam."

"Precisely. And I will use that audacity for my own ends. Draw him into a siege of Amsterdam, which will tie him up and give me the time I need to fortify what is left to me in the eastern provinces."

"How long can you maintain that situation?" she asked, frowning. "I am not a soldier, to be sure. But . . . with only Overijssel left and part of Gelderland . . . Spanish to the south, Danes to the north—the French everywhere, it seems—"

"Not *everywhere*, Rebecca." Frederik Hendrik cleared his throat. "As I recall, central Germany is still in the hands of the king of Sweden. Whom the French—and Danes—have now taken it upon themselves to attack also. With the Spanish—and English—having been so foolish as to sign their names to the enterprise."

"But—" She broke off.

The prince was smiling gently. "Yes, yes. I realize that, at the moment, things look rather bleak for Gustav Adolf also. But—unlike me—he has *not* already lost most of his realm. And—also unlike me—he has been fortunate enough, or wise enough, not to have his populace paralyzed by endless disputes over religious doctrine. Indeed, from what I can see, he seems to be increasingly drawn toward your American-style . . . what shall I call it? 'Arminianism Excelsior'?"

Rebecca laughed. "Hardly that, Frederik Hendrik! Arminianism is a religious doctrine itself. What the Americans preach—and practice—is something far simpler. 'The separation of church and state,' they call it. Worship whatever you will, however you will, and do so in peace. The state has no business in it—nor, on the other side, do the churches have any business meddling in state affairs."

The prince grunted. "A month ago—a week ago, even—I would have said you were mad. And I am considered—accused, as often as not—of being an Arminian myself. Now . . ."

For a moment, he studied the same painting he had studied the day before. "Odd, isn't it? The way your husband seems to force people to adopt his own practices in order to fight them. I've been getting continual reports, you know. The Dutch navy may be destroyed, but Dutch merchant vessels continue to ply their trade. It seems that Richelieu is setting up what he calls 'religious havens' in the northern towns and ports of France. Hoping, no doubt, to draw Protestant workmen there in order to build his own armaments industry. And now I hear that Earl Strafford has put a complete stop to any attempts to enforce strict religious adherence in England. Scotland too—even Ireland, if the reports are correct."

He turned back to her, smiling. "Of course, what else can he do? He—like every statesman in Europe now, probably even the Tsar of Russia—*knows* what history is supposed to bring. So, trying to stop it . . . ha!"

He slapped his hands on his knees. "That is my plan. In the long run, obviously, I am counting on Gustav Adolf to humble my enemies. In the short run, I can simply try to hold on to what I can—Amsterdam above all else. To be honest, Rebecca, I do not see what you and the United States can do for me in the short run. Throw your support behind the king of Sweden, of course, which I am sure you will be doing. I think you would be wise, therefore, to leave Amsterdam now. For the next few days, I am fairly confident I can get you safely back to Germany. But once the siege closes in, you will be trapped here for months."

Rebecca took a deep breath. "Well, actually, that is what I came here to tell you. I discussed this with my husband last night—no, you are right, we do not *need* great edifices for all forms of radio—and we are agreed." She took another deep breath. "I, and the entire delegation, will remain here in Amsterdam. If for no other reason, both Michael and I feel that will be a dramatic public gesture making clear that the United States stands firmly with the United Provinces and has confidence in your survival."

"As dramatic as possible," grunted the prince. "The wife of the President herself. But—" He winced. "Rebecca, the risk . . . if I did not make it clear yesterday, the siege is going to be terrible. Disease alone—"

"*That,*" said Rebecca firmly, "is in fact the main reason I am staying. We cannot do much, obviously, to help you fight your Spanish enemies. Not directly, at any rate. But we can do something about the rest of it."

After she finished explaining the American proposal, Frederik Hendrik arose and went over to the painting. He studied it for a moment, his hands clasped behind his back, and then moved over to the next painting on the walls.

"It's what they never show, you know. You can find everything else in these paintings. Portraits, scenes of daily life—even the carnage of war. Occasionally, perhaps—not often—someone is bold enough to allow the painter to portray the smallpox scars. But never the rest of it. Never the endless supply of infants slid into graves before their first birthday. Never the quiet grief of parents who have seen as many children die as live. Never—not once, that I can recall—a portrait of a mother sitting by the bed of a three-year-old child. Just watching—nothing else to do—while Death spreads its pitiless wings."

His voice became a bit shaky. "It has been the silent terror of the world since time began." When he turned back to face her, his cheeks were hollow—but his eyes seemed bright. "Dear God in Heaven," he whispered, "you can *do* this?"

For once in her life, Rebecca would meet the arrogance of nobility on its own terms. She lifted her head and spoke in as haughty a manner as she could manage. "Yes, Prince of Orange. A world forged by commoners can do what kings and princes and dukes and earls and cardinals and archbishops never could. Can give life to children, where you could only watch them die." Coldly: "Your own faces—often enough—scarred and pitted beneath the costumes and the cloaks and the crowns."

He did not flinch from the rebuke in her tone. He did not even lower his eyes.

"Give me *that*, Rebecca, and even I might be convinced." He grinned suddenly. "Who knows? I might even abdicate my title."

Rebecca laughed. Prince he might be, but she *liked* this man. "I hardly think that would be the best tactic. Certainly not at the moment! If you wish to hold Amsterdam, you will need the full support of its commoners. You know that as well as I do—better, I imagine."

"As if I'd have much choice! Most of the real oligarchs have packed up their bags and already left. There aren't more than a handful of regents still in the city. The burghers who remain— lots of them, of course—are the small ones. Their wealth depends on their little shops and enterprises, with them running it with their own brains and hands. No going into comfortable exile for *them*—much less the city's artisans and apprentices and common seamen."

Rebecca nodded. "A commoner city—*but* with the authority and legitimacy of the prince of Orange to give them confidence. Quite a tough combination to crack in a siege, I would think."

The prince was back in full measure, now. Frederik Henrik's next words came with ringing confidence. "That same combination broke the butcher Alva at the siege of Middelburg—and then again, at Leiden." Proudly: "My father, that was."

"Indeed. And you are already well liked by the residents of Amsterdam. Far more so, if you will pardon my frankness, than was your intolerant half-brother Mauritz. Which brings me to the next point. As I am sure you know—better than I do—the existing structure of authority in the city is, ah—"

"As ragged as a pauper's cloak. Half the town council has already fled. Half the remainder will have done so within three days. For all practical purposes, the city is falling under the control of the civic militia. Which—" His head rose a bit. "—is most favorably inclined to the House of Orange. So I can't say I'm all that sorry to see the rats scampering away. Frankly, it will make things easier for me."

Rebecca cleared her throat. "Easier still, I think, if the growing militant sentiment of the city is channeled, organized, given—at least for many—a clarion call and symbol of resistance." She cleared her throat again. "This is, ah, somewhat delicate . . ."

✻         ✻         ✻

When Rebecca finished, the prince broke into laughter.

"*Richter?* You brought that lunatic here with you?"

"She is *not* a lunatic. Quite a dear friend of mine, as a matter of fact." Rebecca shifted a bit in her chair. "I grant you, she has a reputation. Grant you, also, the reputation is not entirely undeserved."

"Ha! Which is the reason, of course, that you never mentioned her name when you arrived. 'One of my servants,' I believe you said, if I recall my spies' reports correctly."

There didn't seem to be any point to denying that, so Rebecca didn't bother to try. Besides, the prince didn't really seem angry. Amused, more than anything else.

"Frederik Hendrik, she is a superb organizer. Public orator too, I might add. And you will *need* that organization, Prince. The chemical substances we will bring to the city—smuggle them in somehow; my husband says he can do it—are not a magic wand. They need to be dispensed in a rational and organized manner, and combined with measures—strict measures—of public sanitation. No civic militia is set up to oversee something like that. Whereas the Committees of Correspondence can and will."

She ran her hands down her thighs, smoothing the rich fabric. "I do not propose that you acknowledge her publicly, of course, or give the Committees themselves any official sanction. That would be most indelicate, given your need to maintain the loyalty of the noblemen in Overijssel. But here in Amsterdam . . ."

The prince leaned back in his chair, his eyes growing slightly unfocused. "Yessss . . . The men guarding the walls will be simple workmen, more often than not. Many of them, apprentices. Essential to keep their spirits up, I agree. Will agree further, for that matter, that I wouldn't mind at all seeing the civic militia organized along less purely military lines." He frowned. "That always starts causing its own trouble, the longer a siege goes on. The soldiers start taking advantage . . . Still . . ."

He chuckled. "Talk about a Devil's bargain! You offer to free me from plague, with one hand, while handing me a different sort of epidemic on the other."

Many times, Rebecca had found Gretchen's unrelenting attitudes somewhat annoying. But now, she discovered—not for the first time—that annoyance only went so far. Much as she liked this particular nobleman, she had no doubt at all where she stood in the great chasm which ran through European politics.

"Call it that if you will," she said, as harshly as she'd ever spoken in her life. "But that 'epidemic' is, in the end, the one which can cure the other. Choose, then, Prince of Orange."

He didn't hesitate for more than a few seconds. "Oh, I'll take my chances with Richter. One enemy at a time."

Rebecca smiled. "Exactly what my husband says."

After she returned to the U.S. delegation's quarters, Rebecca plopped herself onto a couch next to Gretchen. "You're on," she said.

Gretchen sniffed. Rebecca smiled. "I knew you'd wait for permission." Her eyes were drawn to the door leading to the kitchen. There seemed to be an unusual amount of noise coming from within.

"We have guests?"

"Three apprentices," Gretchen replied. "Two journeymen also. All employed in the copper-working shops here in Amsterdam. Heinrich and I met them yesterday. And the daughter of the master craftsman one of the journeymen works for. They're affianced."

That was a common enough situation. What was *not* common, of course, was to have such a group gathered in the kitchen of what was, technically, a prestigious and snooty foreign delegation's quarters. Rebecca didn't know whether to sigh or giggle.

She giggled. Impossible not to, given the bet she'd made with Frederik Henrik.

"By the way," she added casually, fluffing her hair, "the prince of Orange says he'd like to meet you. He's quite curious. It would have to be a very discreet meeting, of course, so you'd need to use the servants' entrance."

"The prince of Orange can kiss my sweet German ass. Discreet is fine. He can wear a disguise. The servants' entrance is out."

"Exactly what I told the prince you'd say," said Rebecca cheerfully. "Now what shall I spend the money I won on?"

"With a siege coming? Get salted herring."

# PART V

*The gold mosaic of a wall*

# Chapter 33

"Oh, for the love of God, husband!" exclaimed Amalie Elizabeth. The wife of the landgrave of Hesse-Kassel rose from her chair and stalked over to a nearby desk. Angrily pulling open a drawer, she withdrew a thick sheaf of letters and waved it in his direction.

"How much longer will you nurse these foolish dreams of yours? Do you really think *these*—" Here she shook the letters fiercely. "These posturers! These cretins! These petty—"

She broke off, slapping the letters down on the table and taking several deep breaths. Her pretty face was flushed with anger.

Wilhelm V of Hesse-Kassel grimaced. Seated next to him on the luxurious couch in the salon, Wilhelm of Saxe-Weimar tried to keep himself from smiling.

"Those are, ah . . ."

Amalie gave him a sour glance. "You know perfectly well what they are, Wilhelm, even if you've never seen them. My husband here—" She jiggled the letters in the direction of the landgrave. "—has been trying for a year now to get the nobility of the Confederated Principalities of Europe to form a common bloc. The smaller princes and nobles, that is. Squeezed the way we are between the king of Sweden, the princes of Saxony and Brandenburg—now, most of all, by the Americans—"

She broke off, sighing. "I told him from the beginning it was pointless. May as well try to herd cats. Particularly vain and lazy and stupid cats, to boot."

The landgrave avoided her stony gaze. "And to what end?" she demanded. "Would you like to know, Wilhelm? Here, I'll read some of them to you! You're an old and close friend of the family, so why not?"

Hesse-Kassel scowled, but did quite dare to object. The landgravine picked up the top letter from the pile and began reading.

"This one is from—well, never mind—but it's a report of a conversation at a dinner table, shortly after my husband's first circular letter went out. Sophia von Markenfeld is reported to have said to her husband: 'Albrecht, I wouldn't trust this for a moment. The count of Sommersburg is certain to be allied to Hesse-Kassel. And do you remember how Sommersburg cheated me out of great-aunt Leopoldine's garnet-and-pearl necklace that she always said that I should have, but he put it into the probate and his daughter Louisa ended up with it?'

"Then, needless to say, Georg von Gluecksburg jumped in—oh, yes, Wilhelm, of course he was there—do you think he wouldn't have been—"

It was Saxe-Weimar's turn to grimace. Von Gluecksburg bore a remarkable physical resemblance to a piglet. The resemblance was by no means superficial.

Amalie continued:

"—said to his brother, 'Ernst, I wouldn't go along with this if I were you. The Sommersburgs were also very unhelpful in the matter of the border between Craichsbach and Altfelden. With a new administration, we can refile the litigation and request a rehearing.'"

Hesse-Kassel sighed. Wilhelm heard him mutter something about incest. It was true enough—certainly on a political level. The nobility of Thuringia, Saxony, northern Franconia, and eastern Hessia consisted of families which had intermarried so many times that the resultant feuds were as rancorous and never-ending as they were picayune.

Amalie had picked up another letter. "This one is too long to quote, but the gist of it is that there was a meeting at Herzfeld to discuss my husband's circular, but only about half of those invited came. The many Heinrichs of the Reuss lines, as you know, mostly hold land east of Jena and so they were more concerned with what was happening in Albertine Saxony. The two lines of Schwarzburgs apparently decided to maintain a position of neutrality for the time being, while the Ernestine Wettins—they were led by you, of course, Wilhelm—sent a message announcing they were thinking of throwing in their lot with King Gustavus Adolphus and the new United States. So none of them bothered to show up at all. Good for you."

She scanned down more of the letter. "Of the ones that came, the wife of the count von Morsburg and her sister-in-law, who are also cousins, revisited—for what is it, now? the fortieth time?—the long-discussed issue of which one had brought the more valuable dowry to her marriage." She barked a sarcastic laugh. "And—it failed only this!—Johann von Rechberg and Margrave Christoph von Thuen continued the tension that has marked their relationship since the unfortunate incident in 1614 of the expensive prostitute in Leiden when both were on their grand tour."

She let the letter slide from her fingers. "In the end, the only decision of the self-proclaimed 'Herzfeld Conference' was to have another meeting the next year."

Again, she took several deep breaths. "I have read, myself, several of the pamphlets written by that Spartacus fellow. Even—God save my soul—a pamphlet written by Gretchen Richter. I would be lying to both of you if I did not confess that I agree with half of what they say." A bit hastily: "If not, certainly, the other half."

She drew out the chair from the desk and sat in it. Then, folding her hands atop the stack of letters, gave the landgrave of Hesse-Kassel and the former duke of Saxe-Weimar a level stare.

"But this much is true, O ye noblemen. With, of course, some exceptions, the aristocracy of Germany has become a plague upon the land. Parasites, nothing else. And while I do not include our own family in this—nor yours, Wilhelm, save that swine Bernhard—nor a number of others—if we insist on sticking together we will all go down together. Do not doubt it for an instant."

The words were, on the surface, addressed to both men on the couch. But, in reality, they were aimed entirely at her husband. The mere fact that the Saxe-Weimar who had appeared that evening at the Hesse-Kassel quarters in Magdeburg did so as a commoner, no longer as a duke, made clear to everyone where Wilhelm stood in the matter. Even if, thus far in his visit, he had said very little about it directly.

Saxe-Weimar decided to rise, a bit, to Hesse-Kassel's defense. "In fairness, Amalie, it is quite a bit more difficult a decision for your husband than it was for me." With a rueful chuckle: "Since, for all practical purposes, my 'duchy' had been slid out from under me anyway."

But Amalie was not so easily mollified. "Nonsense! No one is suggesting that the landgrave should *abdicate*. No such bold measure as you took is needed from him. All my husband has to do is give up this hopeless scurrying after petty noblemen most of whom aren't fit to serve as his valet." She paused, her eyes almost crossing. "Now that I think about it, I would not wish any of them on my husband's valet himself. I'm rather fond of Dieter."

Hesse-Kassel spread his hands and then slapped them on his thighs. It was a forceful gesture. . . .

Not very forcefully done. "What would you have me do, wife?" he grumbled. Casting a somewhat unfriendly glance at the man seated next to him: "Fine for Wilhelm to be so cozy with the Americans. If I did the same—"

Now, Wilhelm decided, it was time to be direct. "There is no need to be 'cozy,' as you put it, with the Americans. But what you *must* do—and no 'cozy' about it—is weld yourself to the emperor. *Weld* yourself, Landgrave! Gustavus Adolphus now faces what is probably the greatest crisis of his life. You *know* the man. Do you think they call him the Lion of the North—even, in Italy, the Golden King—for no reason?"

Saxe-Weimar felt too strongly about the matter to remain seated. He rose and began pacing about, using short and abrupt gestures. "He will *not* cave in, Landgrave. Never think it. He will do whatever he must to defeat his enemies. And if that means—as it surely will, given continued aristocratic foot-dragging—that he has no choice but to weld *himself* to the Americans, he will do so. Yes, he will hesitate. But not for very long. Not when he has the enemy at the gates. And *then*—"

Saxe-Weimar ceased his pacing, almost spinning around to face Hesse-Kassel. "Have you considered what will happen *then*?"

He pointed a stiff finger at the eastern wall of the salon. Somewhere beyond that wall lay the still-unfinished imperial palace where the Chamber of Princes would resume their meeting the next day. The salon wall was covered with a tapestry, to disguise the rough wall of the new and still-unfinished building which Hesse-Kassel had rented for his own quarters during his stay in Magdeburg. Crude, rough, unfinished—like everything in Magdeburg. But only a fool—or an aristocrat lost in reverie—could fail to sense the new strength coiling beneath the surface.

"Those peacocks! They are assuming, all of them—John George of Saxony most of all—that Richelieu and his Ostenders will hammer the Swede into a pulp. Leaving just enough of a 'Confederated Principalities' for Saxony and Brandenburg and their pack of carrion-eaters to pick over the remains and recreate things to their liking."

He paused, a bit dramatically. "But what if they *don't*, Landgrave? What if—not for the first time in his life!—the Swede leaves his enemies bleeding and broken on the battlefield. What *then*? When his victory came entirely from his own strength and the stalwart allegiance of the Americans—and the Committees of Correspondence which you can now find springing up all over Germany? You *have* noticed, I trust, that the recruiting stations for these so-called 'volunteer brigades' have begun operating here in Magdeburg, not just in the United States."

"There's at least one in Leipzig too," commented Amalie. "I heard about it yesterday. Also in Nürnberg and Frankfurt, it's said."

"Meanwhile," Saxe-Weimar continued remorselessly, "Gustav Adolf finds that the back of his legs and his heels are bruised black-and-blue from the blows landed on them from behind by the 'princes' who also swore allegiance to him, but betrayed him—in fact if not in name—in his darkest hour. What *then*, Landgrave?"

The landgrave looked away, studying yet another tapestry. That one, as it happened, depicted a lion devouring a deer. Hesse-Kassel grimaced.

"Oh, indeed!" half-laughed his wife. "Oh, indeed!"

"What do you propose, Wilhelm?" asked the landgrave softly. "Concretely, mind you." He smiled thinly. "Your rhetoric is excellent. But rhetoric is not policy."

Saxe-Weimar had prepared for this moment. The words came flowing quickly and easily.

"You must announce that you are forming a new political league. Other than Saxony and Brandenburg, Hesse-Kassel is the largest and most powerful of the principalities within Gustav's Confederation. Many—not all, not even most—but many of the small princes will follow you." He nodded toward Amalie. "Sommersburg for a certainty, and I can guarantee all of the Ernestine Wettins. A number of the free cities, the Reichsstaedte, will certainly do the same. I can guarantee that Nürnburg and Frankfurt will. I've been in touch with their notables."

"Regensburg too, of course," chimed in Amalie quickly. "All

reports are agreed that when Gustav's General Banér drove Maximilian's troops out of the city—just last month—the populace went wild with jubilation. Right on the border with Bavaria and Austria, as they are, the Regensburgers will certainly want to cement themselves to the Swedes." She fluffed her hair. "And they're saying also that Gustav Adolf will appoint Wilhelm's brother Ernst as the administrator for the entire Oberpfalz. Consider what *that* might mean."

Hesse-Kassel glanced at Wilhelm for confirmation. Saxe-Weimar nodded. "That's what Ernst tells me, anyway. I got a letter from him recently. He was with Banér, you know, when they entered Regensburg. With Frederick V now dead, and his widow Elizabeth and their children almost certainly in Spanish captivity, the whole question of the Upper Palatinate is back up in the air."

"Just what it needed," muttered Hesse-Kassel, sighing. The Thirty Years War had been triggered off in the first place when Elector Frederick V of the Palatine had chosen to accept the offer of the Bohemians to be their new king. Since that would have upset the balance of power in the Holy Roman Empire, Ferdinand II of Austria and Maximilian of Bavaria had invaded Bohemia. At the Battle of the White Mountain in 1618, Tilly's Catholic army had smashed the Protestant forces. Then, for good measure, the imperials and the Bavarians had invaded the Palatinate and seized *that* from Frederick as well.

"The Winter King," he'd been called thereafter, for the only season he'd enjoyed his crown, as he and his wife Elizabeth—sister of King Charles of England—had been forced to flee from one court of exile to another in the years which followed. Frederick had finally died of disease in 1632, but the status of the Palatinate was still one of the most hotly contested issues of European politics.

Today, of course, most of the area was back in Protestant hands. To be precise, in *Swedish* hands. But . . .

The official heir, Karl Ludwig V, was only fifteen years old—and now, at least according to rumor, held by the Spanish after they overran the Netherlands where Elizabeth had been in current exile. So how would Gustav Adolf choose to resolve the situation?

The landgrave glanced again at the man sitting next to him. Wilhelm of Saxe-Weimar. A duke deprived of his duchy who had decided to abdicate in order to strive for power as a commoner in a new republic. But still a man who was very close to the emperor, and now one whose younger brother seemed likely to become the administrator of one of the most important regions in the CPE. The Oberpfalz portion of it, at least—which, perhaps not by coincidence, happened to be one of the great centers of German mining and manufacture.

A commoner now, yes. Out of power? With no influence? Hardly.

"Until the rightful heir returns, no doubt," grumbled Hesse-Kassel. "But by the time that happens—*if* it happens—what might have been transformed in the meanwhile? And transformed permanently."

Saxe-Weimar shrugged. "So it is, Wilhelm. Whether we like it or not, it is a new world."

The landgrave grunted. "And the policies of this new league?"

"Everything the emperor has asked for. Every last thing. And not simply the emergency measures he proposed yesterday, but everything else he and Oxenstierna have advanced since the Confederation was formed last autumn. Free navigation of all waters, drastic reduction in tolls, elimination of all medieval vestiges of forced labor—every shred of serfdom gone—a commission empowered to begin implementing a rationalization of all these idiotic little local practices which interfere with commerce . . ." He hesitated.

"And the currency reform, too, I suppose?" Hesse-Kassel asked glumly. "Wilhelm, you *know* what that will end up with, not too many years from now. An 'imperial' currency which is for all practical purposes an American currency. Damn them and their Jewish bankers, anyway."

Saxe-Weimar shrugged. "It's not really the Jews, Wilhelm, and you know it perfectly well. Yes, the Abrabanels and their allies have provided the immediate liquid currency. But the real reason the American dollar is the hardest currency in the land—even though it's really only paper and everybody knows it—is because it is backed by the wealth being produced in the principality which issues it."

Again, he shrugged. "There is no reason that production cannot be extended quickly in Hesse-Kassel also." He heard Amalie mutter a word or two of agreement. "And . . . I am fairly certain I can manage an arrangement myself, with the Abrabanels. There is also no reason, when you think about it, that a branch of their bank—issuing a new imperial currency—cannot be opened in your principality also."

The landgrave cocked a skeptical eyebrow. Saxe-Weimar shook his head. "They are financiers, after all. Not ideologues, no matter how many of them may have close political and personal ties to the Americans. Don't forget, too, that the Abrabanels are not so much a family as an extended clan. There will be any number of them who care little enough for the Americans and their more extreme political views." A bit sternly: "You *would*, of course, have to guarantee their safety from pogroms and the right to practice their faith, at least in private."

Hesse-Kassel shrugged. "Not a problem, that. For all I care, they could open a synagogue. Most of my subjects are as tired of the zealots as I am. As for the ones who aren't . . ."

He straightened up in the couch. "That's why I have soldiers, after all."

"Well said!" exclaimed his wife. "Besides, look on the bright side. Remember what happened when the count of Schaumburg allowed universal free worship in his village of Altona?"

Her husband did seem to be cheered up, a bit. The episode—scandalous at the time—was well known. Very quickly, Altona found itself well-nigh flooded with every unpopular religious group: Mennonites, Anabaptists, Jews. The count was thought to be crazy—until his coffers began filling up. Whatever else they were, these outcast religious groups tended to be thrifty and industrious.

"And finally—" said Wilhelm.

Hesse-Kassel threw hands. "Yes! Yes! The precious tax reform. The symbol of it all. End, once and for all, the nobility's exemption from taxation."

His wife spoke softly, but firmly. "It is the most important thing, husband. Whatever else they disagree about, there is not a commoner in Germany—Lutheran, Calvinist, Catholic, it matters not—who does not hate and resent that noble privilege. That exemption is a burr under the saddle of Gustav's growing empire—and don't think the Americans will hesitate to ride it, if we do not help the emperor to remove it. Better to lose some income, than to lose it all. When peace comes, don't forget, the taxes from those noble lands will be part of the revenues of those territorial rulers who have ridden the coming storm instead of being drowned by it."

There was silence in the salon, for a moment. Then the landgrave nodded his head. "Done. Do you have a proposal as well for the name of this new political league?"

Saxe-Weimar smiled. "Something simple and to the point, I think. 'Crown Loyalists' should do nicely."

Later that evening, over dinner, Amalie turned to Saxe-Weimar. "And what of you, yourself? Do you intend to form a 'Crown Loyalist' league in the United States?"

Wilhelm laughed. "Not exactly."

He held up a thumb. "First, because it would be redundant. We are at war now, and I can assure you that whatever political quarrels the Americans have with Gustav Adolf, they will back him militarily to the hilt. And they, unlike me, can give that backing real steel and fire. So it would be a bit like a small boy marching around with men claiming to be the captain."

Amalie laughed. The landgrave smiled. Wilhelm held up his forefinger alongside the thumb.

"Two. It would hardly gain me any friends in the United States itself. The Americans—and, increasingly, more and more of their new German citizens—are uneasy at the very notion of monarchy. Diehard republicans, you know, all of them, whatever internal disputes they may have."

Another finger came up. "But, mostly, the answer is no because what is needed in the United States is not a league of noblemen— that will do, for the moment at least, in the Confederation—but a genuine political party as the Americans themselves understand the term. Something with deep roots in the broad populace."

The landgrave and his wife stared at him. Wilhelm, formerly the duke of Saxe-Weimar, smiled serenely. "Oh, yes. My program itself will be based on the best thinking of our German cameralists, with a heavy leaven from the Americans' own political traditions. So far as tactics go, however, I intend to steal many pages from the book of Michael Stearns. I have been studying the man very closely, this past year."

"What do you *really* think of him?" asked Amalie. The tone of the question was simply curious.

"On a personal level, I admire him a great deal. I would go further. Whatever my political differences, as great as they undoubtedly are, I do not in the end really consider him as an 'enemy.' An opponent, certainly. But not an 'enemy.' The distinction is quite critical, I think—and so do the Americans. They have a name for it, as a matter of fact. They call it a 'loyal opposition.' "

The stares of the landgrave and the landgravine were now

skeptical. "Seems to me he has all the makings of a tyrant," gruffed Hesse-Kassel.

"Like the old Greek tyrants?" Saxe-Weimar shrugged. "The *makings* of one, yes. Even quite a terrifying one. And I also think that, if he felt he had no choice, he would take that road. But not willingly, Wilhelm."

He paused, thinking. "He was a professional pugilist once, you know, as a younger man."

The landgrave and the landgravine grimaced. Pugilism for pay was not unknown in their era, but it was a savage and bloody business. On a par with cockfighting and bearbaiting. Its practitioners were considered to be sheer brutes.

Wilhelm smiled. "You misunderstand, I think. In his world, it was a *sport*. Brutal enough, to be sure. Oh, yes! Never make the mistake of thinking that Michael Stearns will refrain from bloodshed. But it was highly organized, you see. They called it 'boxing,' and it was surrounded by rules and regulations. Many things were ruled out, such as what they called 'low blows.' Indeed, a man could lose a match by violating those rules."

He lowered his hand and opened it, palm up, on the table. "I believe that, to pursue the thought, Michael Stearns wants to teach the world how to box, in the political arena. So, in the end, I think it is my responsibility—perhaps the greatest of my responsibilities— to see to it that he never faces the necessity, as he might see it, to become a tyrant. Because he trusts his opponent to box rather than to fight like an animal. So if he loses a match, it is simply a match, not his life. And he might win the next, after all. Because I and—" His eyes flitted back and forth between the two other people at the table. "—others provided him with an acceptable alternative to the stark choice between tyranny and destruction."

Silence fell over the table. After a time, Amalie rose. "Well, I think that's enough for one night. It's late and I'm tired." She smiled down at the two men. Not quite serenely, but surprisingly close. "Though I have no doubt we will be having many such nights, in the years to come."

"It's not as bad as war," observed Saxe-Weimar. "Especially a civil war."

"Certainly isn't," agreed the landgrave, draining his wine glass. "I've seen a real war. Been watching a civil war, in fact, for fifteen years now. It's filthy."

❀          ❀          ❀

Wilhelm spent the night in a guest room in Hesse-Kassel's quarters. Late the next morning, they left to attend the session of the Chamber of Princes scheduled to begin in the early afternoon. On their way out, the doorman handed Wilhelm a letter, saying it had been left for him by a courier who arrived shortly after dawn. Saxe-Weimar broke the seal, opened the letter, and scrutinized it. Then, folded it up and tucked it away.

Since it was a very pleasant day and they had plenty of time— no session of Germany's princelings began punctually—they chose to walk. The imperial palace was no great distance in any event.

As they neared the palace, a strange noise was heard in the sky. Like everyone else on the street, they stopped and looked up. Above, sailing directly over the palace, came the most bizarre-looking contraption anyone had ever seen.

Anyone except Wilhelm, at any rate. The former duke had seen it before, any number of times.

"Is that—?" asked Hesse-Kassel.

"Yes, Landgrave. That is what they call an 'airplane.' President Stearns informed me, in the letter I was handed as we left, that he would be flying back to Grantville this morning."

Hesse-Kassel's head craned, as he gawked at the *Las Vegas Belle* passing overhead. So did everyone on the street except Saxe-Weimar, who took the time to draw out the letter and read it again.

Only after the aircraft had passed out of sight did Hesse-Kassel lower his head. He frowned, and pointed to the south. "But I don't understand. Thuringia is *that* way. So why is he going—?"

Saxe-Weimar sighed. He still had a long way to go, before Germany's princelings—to use an American expression—*got the picture.*

"Why is he flying north? Well, if you ask him—or the head of his little flying military force who is probably the one at the controls of the machine—he will claim it was due to the necessities of wind direction, or whatever. A technical explanation which you will not be able to follow very well."

The same peculiar droning sound began to fill the sky again, coming now from the north. Like a giant wasp, perhaps.

"The real reason, of course—" Wilhelm fell silent, waiting for the noise to subside. Coming back, Mike Stearns' aircraft was flying *very* low. As it passed directly over the imperial palace and then above the thoroughfare where Saxe-Weimar and Hesse-Kassel were standing, Wilhelm realized that this was the first time he had ever stood directly *under* the flying machine.

"I believe they call this 'buzzing'!" he half-shouted.

The aircraft, and the noise, faded away.

"As I was saying, the *real* reason he did it was to remind everyone who is attending the session today—none too subtly—" Saxe-Weimar poked a finger toward the imperial palace. "—that we can either reach an accommodation with Gustavus Adolphus or—" He jerked his thumb over his shoulder, pointing to the now-vanished aircraft. "—we will someday have to try reaching an accommodation with *him*."

Hesse-Kassel grunted. "Indeed. The Swede looks better all the time."

"Does he not?"

They took a few more steps and then Wilhelm handed Hesse-Kassel the letter.

"Most of this is really for you, I think, even though it's addressed to me. It's all very polite. But the gist of it is that the President of the United States feels that—with war now here—it would be a good gesture—show our enemies that we stand united—if the American admiral residing here in Magdeburg—and his wife—were to be invited to some of the social functions which surround this gathering of so many of Germany's princes. And since you're the most important of them, Wilhelm—we'll leave aside Saxony and Brandenburg, no chance of *them* doing it—I think you should take the lead. Besides, Amalie always has the best soirees anyway."

Hesse-Kassel's face looked as sour as a pickle. But, as his eyes came toward the end of the message, the expression began to lighten.

"Huh," he grunted. "I thought this Simpson fellow was some sort of semi-barbarian. You told me—"

Saxe-Weimar looked slightly embarrassed. He'd had no good words to say himself, about the campaign which Simpson had run against Mike Stearns the year earlier. Simpson himself could claim, as he had once to Wilhelm in private, when Wilhelm had raised objections to him, that he had no personal prejudice against Germans. Saxe-Weimar was even inclined to believe him. But Simpson's *followers* had certainly not been so meticulous in their distinctions. Saxe-Weimar could still remember the sign which had adorned at least one tavern in Grantville: *No dogs or Germans allowed.*

"An injustice to the man," he said firmly. "I'm quite convinced of it now. Yes, he certainly made some mistakes. Bad ones too, in my opinion. But—" He gave Hesse-Kassel a glance. "Which of us can say he has *not,* eh?"

They'd reached the steps to the palace. Hesse-Kassel lowered the letter for a moment, to negotiate the steps. Glancing up at the still-unfinished but massive edifice, he grunted again. "Not Germany's princes, that's sure and certain."

He tapped the letter with his thumb. "And I will say this last part certainly seems promising. Impressive, even, though of course I don't recognize any of the names."

Wilhelm didn't need to look at the letter again to know what Hesse-Kassel was talking about. Mike Stearns had ended the letter with a list of the various organizations Mary Simpson had once belonged to—in some cases, been the leader of.

"Yes, it is. Especially for Amalie, I think, given her patronage of the arts and sciences."

Hesse-Kassel grunted agreement again, walking up the steps and still reading the letter.

"What do you think this means? '*Board of Directors*'? Sounds impressive, whatever it is."

Up in the sky, now many miles south of Magdeburg, Jesse gave Mike a somewhat sarcastic smile.

"Well? Do you feel better now, Mr. President? After wasting all that valuable fuel, I mean."

Mike's responding smile was serene. "I'd rather waste gas and ink than waste blood, Jesse."

"Um. Okay. I'll buy that."

# Chapter 34

The cabinet meeting that began that evening, soon after Mike returned to Grantville, was the stormiest one in months. In some ways, the stormiest ever.

It began with a squall and escalated from there. Throughout, not to Mike's surprise, Quentin Underwood was at the center of it. Like the eye of a hurricane, except this eye was not calm at all.

"Look, I know it's going to be a pain in the ass! Unfortunately, that doesn't mean we don't have to do it. So quit telling me all about how we can't, and figure out how we *can!*"

Mike Stearns glared at the available members of his cabinet. At this particular moment, he missed Rebecca badly, and not just because she was his wife. And he missed Melissa Mailey almost as badly. This was definitely not the sort of crisis Melissa was best equipped to cope with, but her uniquely astringent version of calm would have been far more welcome than the exasperated expressions looking back at him.

"It's all fine and good to sit there waving your hands in the air telling us we have to do something," Quentin Underwood growled. "Have you really considered exactly how we're supposed to accomplish this miracle for you?"

"Eddie was already pulling together the first barge loads before Jesse flew me home again," Mike said flatly. "They've recalled *Meteor* and *Metacomet* to tow the barge strings downriver, and Eddie and

Simpson promised me they'd have *Meteor* underway with the first consignment before dark. If they can manage that, then I am *not* going to accept any bullshit about how we can't do our part!"

Mike was genuinely annoyed. *Meteor* and *Metacomet* were the first pair of several planned sternwheel river tugs powered by Grantville-built steam engines. They weren't fast, but they were much faster than tow horses, and their two-foot drafts were shallow enough to navigate virtually any water deep enough to float a barge—all of which Quentin knew perfectly well, since he was counting on them to provide much of the transportation for the petroleum he was starting to produce at Wietze.

"But they're already on a damned river!" Underwood snarled. "In case you haven't noticed, we're not!"

"Gosh, really?" Mike glared at the other man, and for just a moment, they were once again union and management locked in mortal combat. But then both of them drew deep breaths, almost simultaneously, and shoved themselves back in their chairs.

"Look, Quentin," Mike said in his most reasonable tone, "I know we're looking at a major operation here. Hell, why do you think I've been pushing the rail link to Halle so hard?"

"Which," Underwood pointed out, "we'd have been in a far better position to have finished by now if we hadn't diverted all of those railroad rails to Simpson's damned fleet."

Mike glared at him, and this time several of his fellow cabinet members—including Frank Jackson and Ed Piazza—joined him.

"Quentin, don't be a fuckhead," Jackson said bluntly. The ex-mine manager turned an interesting shade of red, but Jackson went on before he could explode. "You know I was just as pissed off as you were when Simpson—well, Eddie and Simpson, if we're going to be picky—skimmed off all those rails. Not for the same reasons, maybe. But I purely hated to see all that high-grade steel disappearing. But just you ask yourself where we'd be right now if Simpson hadn't been sitting over there in Magdeburg building his little empire . . . and the boats that're going to kick the Danes' asses!"

"All right," Underwood allowed after a moment. "I'll grant that much—assuming he does get them finished and floated all the way out to sea! But," he rejoined in a voice which was calmer but no less stubborn, "that still doesn't change the fact that we don't have a railroad link from here to Halle. And *won't*, not for some time." His lips curled a bit. "Not even these dinky wooden rails with an iron cap we're calling a 'rail line,' with pathetic cargoes being pulled as often as not by 'locomotives' made up of a pickup truck—or even just a team of horses."

Mike grit his teeth. One of the many things he didn't like about Underwood was the man's refusal to let anything drop. For better or worse—and in Mike's opinion they'd had no choice—the decision to go with "light" railroads had been made months earlier. Quentin had been opposed, for the same reason the man always was whenever stretched resources required compromises. He wanted what he wanted, damnation, there's an end to it—and he'd make sure to let you know how he felt about it forever afterward. "Spilt milk" and "what's done is done" were not in Underwood's list of stock phrases. "Beat a dead horse," on the other hand, seemed to be right at the top. If he'd been present at the Creation, Mike thought sourly, he'd still be nattering at God for having made the waters out of sequence.

"But we do have a road link," Mike pointed out, through tight jaws. "And we still have some of the coal trucks and the three semi tractors. We've been holding them for use in case of an emergency. Well, Quentin, just what do you call this?"

"Jesus, Mike," Underwood said. "Do you realize what kind of hole that's going to make in our reserve fuel stocks?"

" 'Hole,' my ass," Mike said steadily. "It's going to use up most of it. But the alternative is worse. You and your oil fields are just going to have to take up the slack, along with the methanol plant. And we're getting a fair amount of oil now from the gas wells right here in Grantville, too, since we upgraded them. Don't forget that either." He held up a hand, forestalling another outburst. "Sure, sure, Quentin—call it a 'trickle' if you want to. For what we're doing, a 'trickle' is enough. We are *not*, fer Chrissake, trying to restage the invasion of Normandy."

"Even if we use the trucks," James Nichols pointed out, "we're not going to set any speed records. We've at least graded the roadbed most of the way to Halle, but it's still going to be a long, slow drive."

"I know," Mike agreed. "But two of the boats Eddie's asking for have their own trailers. If we winch George Watson's boat up onto one of the converted semitrailers and use one of the coal trucks, we can move Eddie's entire 'flotilla' in a single trip."

"George?" Jackson looked up quickly and laughed when Mike nodded. "Well I'll be dipped in shit," the general said with a nasty grin. "You mean to tell me that idiot's fancy toy is going to be useful for something after all?"

"Looks like it," Mike agreed. "Assuming we can get it to Wismar."

"You only want two of the coal trucks?" asked Ed Piazza.

"Of course only two of them," Underwood growled. "If we're going to do this at all, it only makes sense to send the rest of Simpson's damned shopping list overland to Magdeburg. The speedboats can't haul all that crap downriver; we'll have to send it to Simpson and let him barge it down. And at least we ought to be able to get all of it into one of the coal trucks. Probably." He shrugged. "If we can't, we can always hang an extra trailer off the back. We've got several of them. Sending it cross country will get it to Simpson faster than stacking it on barges from Halle down the Saale to Magdeburg. He can probably get it all cross loaded onto his own barges before even the power boats could get that far following the river. It'll sure as hell get it there sooner than barging it from Halle would!"

"Exactly," Mike said.

Underwood was still gloomy. "The worst of it's going to be the wear and tire on the truck tires. Fortunately, boats are a lot lighter load than what those tires were designed for. Still and all . . . we've got plenty of car tires, what with all the cars sitting around unused. But there's hardly any spares for the trucks. Once those tires are gone . . ."

"Then they're gone, and that's that," said Mike forcefully, hoping to cut Quentin off before they got tied up in another pointless wrangle. Underwood had turned a cabinet meeting some months earlier into a brawl, by insisting that developing a rubber industry should be a top priority. Exactly *how* that was to be done, when the world's existing rubber supply didn't exist in the first place, and the natural resources were halfway around the world under the political control of other nations—leaving aside the fact that even the CPE, much less the U.S., was effectively almost landlocked—was not Underwood's concern. He wanted what he wanted. Period.

"That's a problem for another day, Quentin. This is a problem for now."

"But we're not ready to be shipping weapons off," Ferrara said, more than a little anxiously. "We're still at least a month or so from putting the heavy rockets Simpson wants into production." He grimaced. "My fault, I suppose. The last time Eddie and I talked,

I thought the schedule was going to look a lot better than this. And then I got pulled off onto the chemical plant design—what I'd give for just *one* heavy stainless-steel pressure tank—"

He shook his head. There was no point in dwelling endlessly on the fact that, while Grantville had quite a bit of stainless steel lying around in one form or another, almost all of it was in the form of thin sheet. And they were still a long ways off from being able to make stainless steel from scratch.

"That doesn't really matter right now," he continued. "What matters is that I can't give you what I don't have, and what I don't have is a standoff rocket."

"What's the matter with the ones we've got?" Underwood asked. "They worked just fine before."

"Sure they did," Frank agreed, his tone a bit sarcastic. "Of course, we were using 'em from nice, steady land-based launchers at fairly short range. And against targets the size and speed of Spanish tercios. Oh, and on thinking about it, we fired lots of them at once, so that when half of 'em missed, we'd still get enough hits to do the job." He shook his head. "I know the rocket Simpson and Eddie are talking about. It's a hell of a lot heavier than anything we've used in the field, Quentin. And it's got two or three times the range."

"And better accuracy, and a heavier warhead," Ferrara added.

"But if it's that much heavier, they'd have trouble mounting it on a speedboat anyway, wouldn't they?" Nichols asked.

"Mounting rockets on a speedboat is going to be a pain in the ass however you look at it," Ferrara told him grimly. "We're going to have to rig up some sort of blast shield to deflect the exhaust when they launch. And aiming them is going to be pretty much hopeless. We'll have to go with a scattergun effect if we want to produce hits . . . and they're going to have to run in close."

"How close?" Mike asked.

"I can't really say," Ferrara admitted unhappily. "I don't know enough about the conditions to have the foggiest idea. It's going to have to be something they work out as they go, but, frankly, I'll be surprised if they could hit the *Titanic* at much over a hundred fifty yards."

"That close?" Mike couldn't hide his dismay . . . and he didn't try very hard. *Cry, havoc! And set loose the dogs of war.* Youngsters—whom *he* sent into harm's way—were going to be dying soon.

"And this limpet mine idea of Eddie's?" Underwood asked skeptically.

"Actually, I think the kid's got something with that one," Jackson replied. "I know Sam and Al, and Al was always pretty handy when it came to blowing stumps or boulders. Never did understand what the two of them saw in swimming around in old quarry pits and flooded mines—is there a sillier sport in Appalachia than scuba diving?—but, hey—man's got to have a hobby, right?" He grinned. "Point is, they're both used to swimming around in the dark, and Al, at least, is a good man to have gluing dynamite to the bottom of somebody else's boat. And just happens that we've still got half a dozen cases of dynamite over in the armory. Been saving it for something just about like this, as a matter of fact."

"Really?" Ferrara perked up. "You've got that much dynamite left?"

"Well, yeah," Jackson said again, this time a bit defensively. "I didn't want to make a big thing out of mentioning it, seeing as how if everybody knew we had it, we'd have people over there every day explaining why they just *had* to have a stick or two for some vital project or other. Just seemed simpler not to admit we had it."

"And what else are you hoarding away over there?" Underwood inquired.

"We can worry about detailed inventories later," Mike interrupted, to Jackson's obvious relief. "The point Frank's making is that we've got the capability to plant underwater explosives on the other side's ships."

"Maybe we can even do a little better than that," Ferrara said. "A half or quarter stick of dynamite could make our rocket warheads a lot more destructive."

"But given how many we're going to have to launch to score a hit, we'd burn through our entire dynamite supply pretty damned quick," Jackson pointed out.

"I wasn't thinking so much about the rockets we've got now," Ferrara told him. "I was thinking more about the long-range job we're working on down at the shop. It's going to be a lot more accurate, Frank. That's one reason I'd like the best warhead I can put on it. I hate to waste a hit on anything less than that."

"Well, we can talk about that later," Jackson said. "For now, the important thing is that I can send a couple of cases along with Eddie."

"What about the rest of his 'wish list'?" Piazza asked.

"We send everything on it," Mike said decisively. "We're lucky Gustavus picked this particular week to go inspect his ironclad. If anybody can organize the defense of Luebeck effectively, he can. But by the same token, the fact that he's going to be commanding the city's defense ups the stakes all around. As soon as Richelieu and the Danes realize he's in the city, they're going to be more determined than ever to take it . . . and take him off the board with it."

"The same thought had occurred to me," Nichols said quietly. "Are you sure we want to risk him this way?"

"*Want* to risk him?" Mike barked a laugh. "James, the man leads cavalry charges for a living! And he couldn't even wear armor while he was doing it until you cut that musket ball out of his neck! What in the world makes you think he's going to turn a hair over something as tame as holding off the entire Danish army with a garrison of less than four thousand men? The idiot will probably think it'll be fun!"

"That might be putting it just a tad strongly," Jackson said. "I've spent a little more time in the field with him then you have, Mike. I'll admit, he's got a hasty streak in him. Just as well, come to that. Think where Jeff Higgins would be if 'Captain Gar' hadn't dived into that fight at the school. All the same, I think he's taken all of Melissa's and your lectures to heart. He's not going to risk getting himself killed off the way he did in our past. Not if he has any choice, anyway."

"The problem is that he's a lot more likely to decide he doesn't have a choice than I wish he'd be," Mike grumbled.

"It's what makes him so damned effective," Jackson said with another shrug. "Don't much like it myself, but I can't argue with his results. So far, at least."

"Maybe." Mike frowned, then sighed. "But what matters is that there's no way in hell I can *order* him out of Luebeck. And, truth to tell, the fact that the garrison—and the city population, for that matter—know that he's there in person will be worth another thousand or two men all by itself."

"Not to mention the fact that the Swedish army will move heaven and earth to dig him out of the trap," Jackson predicted confidently.

At that very moment, the subject of their discussion was convening a conference of his own in Luebeck. It was somewhat smaller than the one in Grantville . . . and some of its members were also restive.

"Your Majesty, you can't be serious!" Axel Oxenstierna objected. Gustav Adolf's chief minister had just returned from Sweden. In fact, he'd arrived early that same afternoon aboard one of the many ships crowding Luebeck's harbor, and he was more than a bit aghast at his king's plans.

"Of course I can, Axel," Gustavus said calmly.

"Then you certainly shouldn't be!" Oxenstierna said sharply. "This city may be important, but it isn't as important as your own person is!"

"It's no use," Lennart Torstensson told the minister gloomily. "I've spent all morning arguing with him." He glowered at his monarch. "No moving him at all. It's Captain Gars all over again!"

"Nonsense!" Gustavus said cheerfully. "That reckless officer has no business dealing with something as serious as this matter. No, no! It would never do to put *him* in command."

"It's all very well to make jokes, Gustavus," Oxenstierna's tone was far more serious. "But you're the one who told me about the consequences which followed your death in the world the Americans came from. If anything, you're even more important to the future now than you were then. We literally cannot afford to lose you, and you know it."

"Axel, my friend," Gustavus said softly, "caution is all very well, but I can't let it rule my life. I won't. I serve a monarch of my own, and if it happens that I must risk my life in His service, then risk it I will. And if He chooses that I should die, then I will die, trusting in Him to look after my people for me."

"I beg you to remember that He did not do so in that other history," Oxenstierna said very quietly, and Gustavus scowled. The chancellor didn't shrink from the genuine anger in his king's blue eyes. He simply stood there, gazing back into them, and, after a moment, Gustavus drew a deep breath and shook his head.

"Perhaps that is the reason—or one of them—He sent the Americans and the Ring of Fire in *this* history," he said. "There are implications of that entire extraordinary event which I have no idea how to interpret. But this I know, Axel: I cannot permit what happened in that other world I will never know to dictate my decisions in this one. Be warned by those events, yes. But I will not allow the fear that they will somehow repeat to divert me from my clear duty. And at this moment, my duty is to see to it

that this city does not fall to Christian IV and his French pay-
master!"

"I don't disagree," Oxenstierna replied, with the stubbornness
that was the hard-earned right of his unrivaled record of loyalty
to Gustavus. "I only argue that you have generals expressly to
execute your commands. Lennart here," he waved at Torstensson,
"could just as readily command the defense here while you rally
our relief force."

"No," Gustavus said, and this time his tone was flat. "I do not
undervalue Lennart. But it will be months before any relief force
can be mustered for Luebeck, Axel, and you know it. And, even
then, if at all possible I would prefer to use them in a counter-
attack." He clenched his heavy fist, almost hissing the next words.
"I intend to *defeat* Richelieu and his allies, not simply beat them
off."

Torstensson, the most pugnacious as well as the youngest of
Gustav's generals, grinned cheerfully. Even Oxenstierna allowed
himself a smile.

The king continued. "Any troops we can find immediately must
go first to Wismar, to make good the forces I will withdraw from
there to reinforce Luebeck, and it will take time to free up more
than a few thousand even for that task. Horn is nailed to the
Palatinate, keeping watch on Bernhard and the French on the
Rhine. Banér and his corps must remain in the south, of course.
Neither Maximilian of Bavaria nor Emperor Ferdinand is going
to quit simply because we've now taken Regensburg." He took a
deep breath, his jaws tightening. "And—curse the lot of them!—
Otto Sack and his troops must remain in Magdeburg and the surrounding country to stiffen the spines of my so-called 'affiliated
princes' in Saxony and Brandenburg. Not to mention—"

He gave Oxenstierna a very sharp glance indeed. "—the need
to keep an eye on Wallenstein in Bohemia."

The chancellor nodded in unwilling—and silent—agreement with
his last sentence.

"You know our commitments, Axel," Gustavus went on. "And
so you know it will take many weeks, probably months, to free
up sufficient strength to hope to break the siege which will soon
begin here. It is for that task, to organize the defense of Wismar
and the ultimate relief of Luebeck, that I will use Lennart. And
while he sees to that, *I* will see to the defense here."

Oxenstierna started to continue the argument, then closed his mouth with a click. He knew his monarch too well, and recognized the futility of attempting to sway him from the decision he had so obviously made.

"Better," Gustavus told him with a smile. Then he turned to the other officer seated at the table. Karl Gyllenhjelm was an experienced naval commander, and he was obviously unhappy about what he'd been hearing.

"And so we come to you, Karl," the king said.

"With all due respect, Majesty," Gyllenhjelm said stiffly, "neither Wismar nor Luebeck are yet under siege. Nor will they be until my squadron has been defeated!"

"Against the Danes by themselves, I would back you without qualm," Gustavus told him. "But the Danes won't come alone. They will be accompanied by the French, at the very least; and by the English, as well, unless I miss my guess. You have parity against Christian's ships. Against the Danes and the forces Richelieu committed to the defeat of the Dutch, you would be outnumbered by more than two to one." He shook his head. "I will not commit you at such odds. And even if I were willing to," he admitted honestly, "it would achieve little beyond your heroic death."

"But I could at least anchor my ships in the Wismar harbor approaches," Gyllenhjelm protested. "Even as no more than floating batteries, they would take much of the pressure off of the defenses there. Here, so far up the river—" He shook his head. "We would be helpless as rats in a trap at Luebeck, but from Wismar the possibility of a sortie would still exist, and the enemy could never be certain when we might attempt to sever *their* supply lines!"

"So you might," Gustavus agreed. "But this is not the only point they will attack, Karl. Think about it. For the first time, the Danes have the full-fledged support of not simply one outside kingdom, but at least two of them—three, if Richelieu has entangled Ferdinand in his webs. And Christian has that support while our main strength is committed to Germany. And scattered from the Rhine to Dresden, at that! Do you truly believe that with that advantage he will restrict himself to attacking only Luebeck and Wismar?"

Gyllenhjelm's expression stiffened. Clearly, he saw exactly where Gustavus' logic was headed and had no desire to go there.

"They will attack us at home, as well," Gustavus said. "Unless they're fools—and we dare not assume they are—then their objectives must be our German supply ports, to starve our army, and

Stockholm, to crush our fleet and destroy its base. We do not have the strength to defend both of them on the water, Karl, and we can better afford to lose Luebeck and Wismar both than to lose Stockholm, if we're honest about it. So I won't argue this point with you further. You will take your ships to sea no later than the morning tide, and you will sail for Stockholm. And you, Axel," he turned on Oxenstierna once more, "will sail with him."

Oxenstierna's head came up as he stiffened in instinctive protest, but Gustavus continued, rolling over any objection he might have voiced.

"You will return to my capital, Chancellor of Sweden," he commanded, "and you will hold that capital for me. I charge you with that duty upon your oath of fealty to me."

Oxenstierna closed his mouth a second time, and bent his head in submission. He might argue with his king with all the stubbornness of Swedish iron, but in the end, he recognized the man he served. The only monarch in Europe truly worthy of the title "King." When that man commanded, Axel Oxenstierna would obey.

"Thank you," Gustavus said, clapping him on the shoulder. "And don't look so glum, Axel! I have no intention of leaving my bones in Luebeck! And, for that matter, I rather doubt the Americans have any intention of allowing me to."

# Chapter 35

Old-fashioned torches and modern spotlights threw a glare of illumination over the small convoy, and Frank Jackson stretched and yawned wearily. It had been a long day, and the commander in chief of the Army had no business doing grunt work. Unfortunately, Frank still found it easier to recognize the concept of delegation than to practice it. Or, if he wanted to be more accurate about it, he could delegate just fine . . . as long as he didn't have any choice about it.

He grinned at the thought and scratched the neatly trimmed beard he'd decided to grow since arriving in a Germany which had never heard of replaceable razor blades, much less disposable razors. Then he shook himself and headed out on one last walk-through inspection.

The flatbed tractor-trailer rig was ugly as sin—a single-axle tractor pulling a standard semitrailer whose walls and roof had been torched off and hauled away for salvage. The ability of the resulting visual abortion to handle outsized cargos had proved extraordinarily useful quite a few times, but it had never carried a load like the one chocked and strapped down on it tonight.

Three boat trailers, one behind each of the two coal trucks and another hitched firmly to the rear of the flatbed, each carried a power boat. Quite large power boats. Jack Clements' thirty-two-foot Century 3200 measured ten and a half feet across the beam, and Louie Tillman's twenty-eight-foot Chris Craft launch was very nearly as big. Neither of them really had any business in a place like Grantville, far from any coasts or large lakes or inland waterways except the Monongahela. But, in any town of several thousand people, a few of them are bound to buy something that everyone else considers ludicrous. At least Jack Clements could argue in self-defense that he'd bought his boat to take to Florida with him when he retired. And Louie Tillman *had* spent a lot of hot summer days on the Monongahela River in his Chris Craft before the Ring of Fire.

But the third boat, sitting in massive, lordly majesty atop the flatbed . . .

Frank shook his head. George Watson's Outlaw 33 was thirty-three feet long, with an eight-and-a-half-foot beam, and the damned thing weighed over three and a half tons. The weight, of course, was picayune for a tractor-trailer combination designed to haul well over twenty tons. But it was so big that it overhung the trailer front and back and a bit on the sides, braced in position by lumber and held down by nylon straps. It looked like some kind of high-tech, fiberglass torpedo sitting up there, gleaming with polished stainless-steel fittings and embellished with bright red lightning bolts down either side of the hull. Frank had no idea how much the thing had cost, and Watson had always refused to tell anyone—probably because he'd figured they'd all *know* he was insane, instead of just suspecting it, if he ever admitted how much he'd paid for it.

"I still say you've got no right to steal my fucking boat," a voice grated, and Frank turned his head. George stood behind him, glaring up at his expropriated property, and Frank barked a laugh.

"Jesus, George! You've had the damned thing in the water—what? twice? three times?—in the entire time you've owned it! I can't begin to imagine what you thought you were doing when you bought it. Except maybe watching reruns of *Miami Vice* again!"

"If I want to buy a boat, it's my own frigging business," Watson shot back belligerently. "And you got no right to steal it from me. You *or* Mike Stearns!"

Frank didn't like George Watson, and he never had, even making allowances for the fact that George was a fellow member of the UMWA. Watson was the kind of sour, surly man who, almost fifty years old now, liked to brag that he was a lifelong bachelor—a brag which drew the invariable response that no woman in her right mind would have him.

So he saw no reason to be polite to him. With Watson, being polite was a waste of time anyway. "We didn't 'steal' it," he said forcefully, "we nationalized it. And we're gonna use it to save your ass right along with the rest of us, so quit bitching about it."

"I'll sue," Watson threatened. "You see if I don't!"

"You do whatever you want, George," Frank said, shrugging. "You'll get compensated for it by the government. Now, beat it. It's done. And I've got other things to worry about."

Watson stalked off. Frank turned to another, older man whose hair gleamed like fresh snow under the lights.

"You sure about this, Jack?" he asked more quietly.

"Yeah, sure I am," Clements replied cheerfully. "Hell, you think I'm going to let anyone else drive *my* boat?"

"Actually, I'm thinking we'll probably need you worse for Watson's Folly, here," Frank told the man who had once served in the U.S. Coast Guard before coming home to the West Virginia mountains, and jerked a thumb at the massive boat on the flatbed. "You've got the most boat-handling experience of anyone we've got, and that thing's gonna be a real handful for whoever gets behind the wheel."

"Maybe," Clements said in an unconvinced voice, and Frank chuckled.

"Hell, you're in the Naaaaavy now, Mr. Volunteer Lieutenant Clements, sir!" He waved in something which could, with a sufficient stretch of the imagination, have been called a salute. "*Admiral* Simpson's gonna have his own ideas about how to use you best. And much's I hate to say it, the prick seems to know what he's doing, so you listen to him, hear?"

"You say so, Frank," Clements agreed dubiously, and Frank chuckled again. Then he turned back to his inspection.

Clements', Watson's, and Tillman's were the three boats Eddie had specifically requested. After that, the Grantville boating selection ran down through smaller ski boats to bass boats and simple dories, but Frank had picked out one more as a backup for Eddie's requests: a sixteen-foot Boston Whaler which had belonged to Harry Rousseau before Harry and his family went to visit his mother in Duluth the day before the Ring of Fire struck. It was on the small size for what they had in mind, but it was the next biggest boat in Grantville, and he wished fervently that he had an entire fleet to send with the four of them.

*Hell, while I'm wishing, I might's well wish for a frigging destroyer—or even an aircraft carrier!* he told himself sourly.

He started tugging on the tie-down straps and checking the hull chocks, but left off when he spotted Jerry Yost glaring at him. The truck driver, clearly enough, did not appreciate the interference of an amateur, "General of the Army" or not. Frank gave Yost a half-apologetic smile and moved down the line of trucks. The coal trucks, he decided, would provide him with a safer avenue for venting his overseer reflexes. They were, after all, officially the property of the U.S. Army.

He glanced into the back of the first coal truck. At the moment, it was loaded with additional fuel drums and cans, two deflated rubber Zodiac boats that belonged to Sam and Al Morton, and the odd case of dynamite. The second coal truck, also towing Rousseau's Boston Whaler on its trailer, would be leaving Grantville for Halle early next morning with its own load of supplies too bulky to be transported by the speedboats themselves—including several hundred rockets and the modified launch frames the machine shops were working frantically to complete even as Frank stood in the dark and worried.

He still had his doubts about the entire operation, whether he was prepared to admit them to anyone else—besides Mike, of course—or not. But if the defense of Wismar failed, it wasn't going to be because Frank Jackson hadn't done everything he could to prevent it.

He reached the end of his inspection trip and grunted in satisfaction, then looked at his own addition to the relief force.

James Nichols and Frank's niece Julie had personally overseen the training of the Thuringian Rifles, the first company of true long-range snipers in history. Most of them, American and German alike, had been experienced hunters before the Ring of Fire. The Germans were mostly youngsters who hadn't picked up any bad habits when it came to firing a gun from serving in arquebus-wielding mercenary units, and had been eager to learn. The up-time Americans among them, on the other hand—about a fourth of the unit—had already thought they understood the finer points of marksmanship. Julie and Dr. Nichols had shown them otherwise, and on any one-for-one basis, the forty-two men and three women of the understrength "company" were undoubtedly the most dangerous marksmen in the world. Aside from their official commanding officer, Julie Mackay, that was. In fact, they were too dangerous for Frank to justify committing all of them to Wismar, but he'd decided that he could reinforce that city with their first squad, at least. Second Squad would be leaving for Luebeck with the second coal truck.

He didn't think he'd need to send more than that, anyway. Mustered up not far away from the Thuringian Rifles, their horses already saddled, was a larger body of men. Thirty-four of them, all with the long beards they favored, and all wearing their special blue uniforms and distinctive "montero" headgear. The montero was an odd-looking hat, which the Germans sometimes called an "English foghat." In cold weather, the beak of the hat could be pulled down, serving much the same function as a balaclava.

They were all Swedish woodsmen and gameshooters, under the command of Nils Krak. Gustav Adolf had ordered the unit's formation early in 1632. Unlike most other soldiers of the time, these men used small-bore rifled hunting muskets and the unit had been designed for sniping and skirmishing, not volley fire in the line. Once the alliance with the Americans had been made, Gustav had sent Krak's Shooters down to Thuringia. Krak and his men had all been issued brand-new flintlocks with longer barrels and a tighter rifling twist, and they had now trained for months alongside the Thuringian Rifles. The two units got along well, and were accustomed to joint operations. True, the Swedish sharpshooters did not have the range of their U.S. counterparts, but their weapons had been fitted with aperture sights which made them very nearly as accurate over the range they had. Compared to any other body of 17th-century soldiers, they were a unit of elite riflemen. Some of the best shots among them had actually been issued telescopic sights from the carefully hoarded store of them which had come back from the 21st century, and to compensate for the technical inferiority of their equipment, almost all of them had a lot more in the way of actual combat experience than most of the U.S. soldiers did.

They were also trained as dragoons, so they would make the trip on horseback. On the crude roads ahead of them, especially with the unwieldy trucks setting the pace, they would have no trouble at all keeping up. The ten members of First Squad, along with their carefully packed 21st-century weapons and ammunition, were now loading into a pair of pickup trucks at the end of the procession. These trucks, unlike most of the ones in service, still ran on gasoline rather than natural gas. The one big drawback to natural gas engines for military operations, even leaving aside the danger inherent in the more flammable fuel, was that gasoline engines had more range for the same weight and bulk of fuel.

Frank nodded to Stan Wilson, their sergeant.

"Ready to go, Stan?" he asked, through the rumble of waiting engines.

"Ready as we're going to be, anyway, I reckon," Stan drawled back.

"Well, then," Frank said, reaching in through the truck window to pat him on the shoulder. "You watch your ass—all of you! I'd take it as a personal favor if you'd remember we don't want any dead heroes around here."

"Oh, I think you can count on us to remember that," Stan assured him with a slow smile.

"Bet your ass," Frank agreed, and slapped him on the shoulder again. Then he stepped back and twirled one hand over his head in a "wind-them-up" gesture. Stan's pickup truck honked its horn in response, and the lead tractor-trailer moved forward in a grumbling snort of diesel exhaust. The snort had a vaguely derisive sound to it, as if Frank Yost was still miffed that Frank—friggin' coal miner, what does *he* know?—had had the presumption and gall to double-check his expert tie-down.

Frank Jackson stood there, watching them head off down the dirt roads of southern Thuringia until their tail lights vanished into the blackness.

When he returned to the executive branch building in downtown Grantville, Frank found Mike sitting at the desk in his office. He'd expected to find him there, since he'd known Mike would wait to hear his report.

What he hadn't expected to see was the cheerful smile on his face.

"What are you so happy about?"

"This," said Mike, pointing at a piece of paper lying on his desk. "Quentin Underwood just handed it to me an hour ago. It's his resignation from the cabinet."

Slowly, Frank lowered himself into his seat. "Resigned, huh?" He thought about it, then shrugged. "Well, that'll hurt us politically, of course. But at least it might keep James Nichols from killing him at the next cabinet meeting. For a moment there, I thought he was going to do it today."

Mike made a face. The cabinet meeting that day had ended in the worst brawl his Cabinet had ever had—and, with its strong-willed personalities, it had never been a cabinet characterized by mild manners. It had begun badly, with Quentin—as usual—insisting on bringing up again his disagreements over the issues thrashed out and settled the day before.

Mike had squelched that quickly—*it's settled; that's it; forget it*—because he needed to leave as much time as possible for the cabinet to consider his next proposal. That was, of course, the decision to leave Becky and the U.S. delegation in Amsterdam with a Spanish siege about to close in.

Underwood had kept his mouth shut while Mike explained the political and diplomatic aspects of the question. In fact, Mike suspected he really wasn't paying much attention at all, since he was brooding over his defeat over yesterday's issues. But when Mike had finally gotten to the "kicker," Underwood had exploded.

"Are you out of your *mind*?" he'd roared, rising from his chair and planting his hands on the table. "You want us to send off our whole supply of antibiotics—every drop of chlora-chlora—whazzit and most of the sulfa drugs we've slowly accumulated? Sending some of it to Gustav in Luebeck is one thing—but to the fucking *Dutch*?"

Slammed his fist on the table. "No, dammit! Let the Dutch handle their own mess! The whole problem with you, Stearns, is that you've forgotten that you were elected to be the President of the *United States*—not the 'President of Europe.' That stuff should be kept here for—"

And that was as far as he'd gotten. For the first time since anyone in Grantville had met the doctor, arriving in town the day before the Ring of Fire to accompany his daughter Sharon to Rita's wedding, James Nichols lost his temper.

He shot to his feet, spilling his chair. The sound of *his* fist slamming the table was like a gunshot.

"*You insufferable jackass! You stupid, ignorant, self-satisfied moron!*"

Nichols came stalking around the table toward Quentin. For all that James Nichols was a smaller man than Underwood—he stood only five feet eight inches tall and was not especially heavily built—the advance radiated sheer menace. For a few seconds, the well-educated and urbane doctor in his late fifties vanished, and everyone caught a glimpse of the ghetto hooligan who, as a teenager, had been given the choice by a judge between the Marines and a stay in prison. Mike started to rise, thinking he would have to physically restrain James from beating Quentin into a pulp. And that he *could* pummel the larger and younger man into a pulp, Mike had no doubt at all.

Neither, from the shocked pallor on his face, did Underwood himself—and Quentin was by no means a timid or cowardly man.

But, by the time Nichols reached Underwood, he'd brought himself under control.

More or less.

"*Sit . . . down,*" he commanded, pointing a rigid finger at Quentin's chair. "Now!"

As Quentin fumbled to comply, James spoke through teeth which were not quite clenched, but closely enough that the words came as a hiss.

"Let me explain something to you, Underwood. Maybe this time you'll finally get it. There is no such thing as a 'Dutch disease.' There is no such thing as a 'United States immune system.' The bacteria and viruses which carry epidemics don't give a flying fuck about your precious borders and your fine political distinctions. They could care less, fathead. Do you think a germ stops when it gets to your nose and says: 'Oh, no! Mustn't infect *this* man. He's a fine and respectable Murikun, 'e is. I'll just have to find me a scruffy no-good Dutchman or Kraut or Frog or Dago. Huh? Do you?"

Underwood stared up at him, wide-eyed.

"*Do you?*" James demanded. His hand reached out, as if he were tempted to grab Underwood by his jacket and shake him. But he drew it back. Mike was relieved to see that Nichols had his temper back under control, even if he was still steaming mad.

"Let me explain to you, Underwood," James grated, "what's going to happen to you—or your wife, or your sons—if you get infected with *Yersinia pestis.* That's the germ that carries bubonic plague. I'll start with the less fatal form. Then I'll move on to describe what often happens in cold weather—*shut the fuck up, Underwood! I am sick to death of you!*"

Quentin's attempt to interrupt James was cut off by that angry shout. James drove on relentlessly. "You *will* listen. This once, you *will* finally listen to me."

In the time which followed, carefully and slowly, Nichols explained—in the truly graphic and gruesome detail which a doctor can—*exactly* what would happen to a human body infected with bubonic plague. Even Mike, who knew far more about the subject than Quentin had ever bothered to learn, found himself getting a little sick to his stomach. Most of the people sitting frozen around the table seemed to share his reactions.

By the time James finished, the tone in his voice was more that of an old, tired anger than a fresh and hot fury.

"—come cold weather—and the sieges in Luebeck and Amsterdam will for sure and certain last through the winter—the form of the plague often changes. The infection migrates from the lymph nodes to the lungs. At that point it becomes what we call 'pneumonic plague,' which is the most virulent form of the disease. Along with the septicemic variety, where it gets into your blood."

He wiped his face. "I've had nightmares about pneumonic plague since the Ring of Fire," he said, almost whispering. "It's airborne, so it can spread like wildfire. Except for some of the exotic Ebola strains of hemorrhagic fever—which, thank God, we don't have to worry about—there is no disease I know of which has a worse fatality rate. No mass disease, anyway. Regular bubonic plague is bad enough. That'll kill half of the people who contract it. But *pneumonic* plague . . . With that form of the disease, the fatality rate is at least ninety percent."

He glared down at Underwood, his dark eyes like agates. "The Black Death of the fourteenth century was bubonic plague, by the way—and it started in China. But, hey," he sneered, "who cares about China, right? If we aren't going to worry about some Dutchmen, why lose any sleep over a bunch of coolies? Right? Well, here's how it *really* works, Mr. Borders-and-Frontiers. After killing an estimated twenty-five million Chinese, the epidemic reached Europe, probably through India and the Middle East. Maybe Istanbul. Who knows? The bacterium's invisible to the human eye, Underwood—you do know *that* much, I hope? Ain't no border guard checking papers gonna spot it, trust me."

He moved away from Underwood and started walking back toward his side of the conference table, talking as he went. "It started in the Italian port cities. By the summer of the year 1348 it had reached Paris; by the end of the year, London. By 1350—two years, that's all—it had spread throughout Europe. Everywhere, from Scandinavia to Spain to Russia. By the time it ran its course, the Black Death killed a third of the continent's population, all told. The estimate of historians is another twenty-five million people. Add that to the death toll in China, and you're looking at the same numbers as World War II and the Holocaust—in a world which had a far smaller population than the twentieth century."

He reached down, picked up the chair he'd knocked over, and resumed his seat. Then, clasping his hands in front of him, he swept the room with a long and stony gaze.

"I have been telling all of you for over two years now that we're living on borrowed time. There is *no way*—I don't care how you try, barbed wire around the borders, it doesn't matter—that you can insulate our little United States here from the rest of the world. For Christ's sake, people, even with the resources the *old* U.S.A. had, millions of so-called 'illegal aliens' came across our borders every year. From everywhere—China to South America—where there were poor people looking for something better, or fleeing from persecution and oppression. And in case you haven't noticed yet, 17th-century Europe in the middle of the Thirty Years War has more poverty and persecution and oppression and desperation than we did back up-time—and, God knows, we had plenty of it."

He paused, letting that sink in. "What we are faced with here is basically the same choice we've been faced with since Day One. This is the same argument Mike had with Simpson at that first public meeting. The same argument he had again with him during the campaign. The analogy Mike likes to use is whether a man who stumbles should try to take the fall—on broken glass—or run faster. I think of it like a man in the surf who sees a tidal wave coming. He's got a choice between trying to get to dry land—with not enough time to do it—or swimming out to meet the wave and trying to ride it in. Either way, the odds are crappy. But what looks like the safest course in the short run is sure to be the most dangerous one in the end."

Quentin was frowning. Clearly enough, the parallel James was drawing between the current issue and the old battle between Mike and Simpson had gone right over his head. James sighed.

"I'll put it a different way. The *only* way we've really got to protect ourselves from epidemics—sure as hell in the long run—is to spread our knowledge and our sanitary and medical techniques, throughout Europe. The whole world, eventually. I've always known that. The *problem*, however—compared to which deciding what to do with the piddly supply of antibiotics we've got on hand is meaningless—fucking *meaningless*, people—is that most of Europe doesn't believe us. Half the time, even our friends and allies don't really believe us. For every Balthazar Abrabanel who does, there's at least ten people who think our notions are either witless babble or heretical theology or—or—God knows what they think. Not the least of the reasons I supported Mike during the wrangle over chemical warfare was because I knew that if we set *that* monster loose we'd never get anyone to trust us when it came to medicine. Nobody in their right mind goes to a poisoner for remedies."

He lifted his clasped hands and thumped them on the table. Not angrily, so much as forcefully. "Who *cares*, goddammit, if we give up enough existing antibiotic to treat a few thousand people? If an epidemic hits the U.S., we'll run through that much antibiotic inside of a week. And then what?" He shook his head. "It's penny-wise and pound-foolish. We'll keep making the stuff, of course, and rebuild the stockpile. But it's way better for us, right now, to send what we've already got on hand to Luebeck and Amsterdam. Why? Because—are you listening, Underwood?—think what's going to happen there this winter. In a siege, rampant disease is a given. It's a fact of life. Everybody in this day and age knows it perfectly well. Right?"

Several people nodded. James smiled coldly. "Okay, then. Think what happens—what people all over Europe think—when they see Spanish besiegers dying in droves . . . and Dutchmen in Amsterdam surviving. When they see Danish and French soldiers being shoveled into mass graves outside of Luebeck—and Swedish and German troops surviving inside the city. Because of what *we* sent them."

He opened his clasped hands and spread them wide on the table. "Sure, Europe's princes don't give a damn—well, most of them—what happens to their commoners. But they *do* give a damn about their wars. Show them—in as graphic a way as possible—how a war can be impacted by modern sanitary practices, prophylaxis and medical treatment . . ."

Mike was watching Underwood. *Still*, the man didn't understand. He never would, Mike realized. It was odd, really, how a man so very intelligent could be so blind. Could see 'victory' only in terms of scoring points in a game. As if politics were a game to be won in the first place, instead of—what it should be, at least—the methods by which a civilization governs all "games" in the first place.

He decided he'd try one last time. "Quentin," he said softly, "I don't *care* who ends the danger of epidemic. I don't *care* if it's done by us—or by some French cardinal trying to beat us, or an ally emulating us, or just some Italian city council trying to keep their tax base intact. *As long as it gets done.*" He breathed in; out. "Just like I don't *care* how freedom of religion gets established all across Europe. If Wentworth and Richelieu start implementing it to *fight* us, then as far as I'm concerned the whole basis of the 'game' has been shifted in the direction I want it. We aren't scoring points here, for the love of God. You score points with a ball. Not with peoples' lives."

Silence fell on the room. After a few seconds, Mike said: "The decision's mine, of course, in the end. But I'd like a formal vote of the cabinet. All in favor of my proposal to send our existing stock of chloramphenicol and most of our sulfa drugs to Luebeck and Amsterdam, along with as much DDT as we can manage, raise your hands."

Nichols' hand was up before he'd finished speaking. Ed Piazza's and Willy Ray Hudson's hands came up almost as fast. Within five seconds, the hand of every member of the cabinet was raised.

Except Quentin Underwood's. He looked around the room, shook his head, and said quietly: "Sorry, folks. I can't see it. That stuff belongs to us. We made it. We should keep it here for our own people. I just don't understand how anyone can see it any other way."

Then he rose and left the room.

"So when'd he resign?" asked Frank.

"Not long after. The cabinet broke up within a half hour. He came in maybe half an hour after that and—" Mike nodded toward the letter.

Frank thought about it for a bit. "Well . . . Personally speaking, I'm tempted to jump for joy. He's been a pain in the ass to deal with for months, now, and it seems like it's been getting worse all the time. Kinda strange, really. I'd have thought he'd have put old quarrels behind him."

Mike shook his head. "This isn't an 'old quarrel,' Frank. It's got nothing to do with the fact that he used to be the manager of our mine and we used to be the officers in charge of the union. Quentin's narrow-minded, yeah, but he's not *that* narrow-minded." Shrugging: "It's just the way the world works. When it comes to politics, anyway. Given XYZ set of circumstances, some people are going to argue one side, somebody else the other. Change the circumstances a bit—WXY—and the alignment changes. Some, anyway."

He chuckled, a bit ruefully. "Would you believe that under *these* circumstances, I'm starting to warm up to John Chandler Simpson?"

Frank made a face. Mike laughed. "C'mon, Frank! The man's not a devil. Neither one of us thought that even when he was at his worst. What he *was*, in those days, was an arrogant and take-charge kind of guy who, faced with a crisis, tried to drive through what he thought was the *safe* alternative. Too sure of himself—too obsessed with his own position, also—to consider the long-term risks."

"So? How's anything changed? According to James, anyway—and it sounds like you agree with him—we're facing the same choice now. Always have been."

"Don't oversimplify. Broadly speaking, yes. In detail, it's a lot different." Mike levered himself up from his relaxed slouch. "Right *now*, John Chandler Simpson has two big advantages Quentin Underwood doesn't. And I think—not sure yet—I just handed him a third."

Frank cocked an eye. Smiling, Mike continued. "The first advantage he's got is that he's already taken a big set of lumps from me. False modesty aside, I give pretty big lumps in the political arena. Quentin hasn't. Yet."

Frank's shoulder heaved a little with amusement. "You figuring you will?"

"Pretty soon. Not right away. First thing Quentin will do is go talk to Wilhelm Saxe-Weimar about forging a united opposition. Let's call it a 'conservative' opposition. Wilhelm will agree, of course—he's a very sharp cookie—without letting Quentin understand exactly what the problems are. Which won't be hard, since it'll never occur to Quentin to consider that the term 'conservative' covers a lot of ground. Cats and dogs are both conservative too, y'know—I've raised 'em, so have you, and if you don't believe me try changing their routine—but that doesn't mean they necessarily get along or have the same attitudes and personalities."

Seeing Frank's little frown of incomprehension, Mike waggled his fingers. "I'll get to that in a minute. The *second* advantage Simpson has over Quentin, now that he's gotten the stuffing knocked out of him—enough of it, at least—is that he has an intrinsically wider view of the world to begin with."

"'Intrinsically,'" Frank muttered. "Dammit, ever since you married Becky you've been starting to talk like a city boy."

Mike grinned. "You shoulda heard the way I talked those years I lived in Los Angeles. I mean, like, man, when in Rome kick back like the Romans do."

Frank chuckled. "All right, all right. And your point is?"

"What's so complicated about it? Quentin was born and raised in West Virginia, spent his whole life here. There, I should say. Started in the mines right out of high school, picked up an education at college while he was working, wound up the manager. He's not exactly what you'd call a 'hick,' but sure as hell a country cousin."

"Hey!" protested Frank. "The same's true for me. You too, for that matter, leaving aside those three years you spent in La-la-land."

"Not the same thing, Frank," replied Mike, shrugging. "The problem with Quentin is that his *mind* never left the place. Yeah, sure— you and me were coal miners. But did you take the job home with you?"

"Fuck no," snorted Frank. "Washed it off with the coal dust, fast as I could."

"Exactly. Whereas Quentin . . ." Mike shook his head. "He spent an entire adult lifetime thinking about not much else beyond his job and getting ahead. I used to wonder, sometimes, how he ever found time to get Roslyn to marry him, much less raise his kids."

Mike spread his hands. "And that's . . . still pretty much his world, Frank. Put a problem—especially a technical or managerial one— right in front of his nose, Quentin will do fine. Do very well indeed, more often than not. That's why he was so good—and he was, let's not deny it—in the first stretch after the Ring of Fire. But try to get him to consider the world beyond the little hills and hollers of his view of it, once things start getting complicated and confusing . . ." Mike shook his head.

"Can't be done. God knows, I've tried, these last two years. Simpson, on the other hand—to get back to the subject—is a different breed altogether. Give the man some credit, Frank. Yeah, in a lot of ways he's narrow-minded. It might be better to say, a narrow kind of man. But he's no *hick*, that's for sure. He's been all over the world—and not just as a tourist—he's run a major petrochemical corporation, been a naval officer, rubbed shoulders with generals and admirals and politicians in Washington D.C.— *and*—"

Mike's grin was very wide. "Is married to a woman from old Eastern money who is a genuine connoisseur of the arts, a former wheeler-dealer in very high social circles, *and* happens to speak fluent French. Pretty decent Italian, too, Tom tells me."

"I don't—"

"Figure it out, Frank. Wilhelm of Saxe-Weimar will launch *his* kind of political party. One that not only suits him but can appeal to a broad range of people in the United States—a lot of whom find me pretty scary. A *lot,* Frank. Don't ever make the mistake of thinking it's just a handful of sour-grapes noblemen and those bigoted goofs who hang out at the Club 250. All the way from old widows worrying that I'll remove their rent income because it derives from some kind of old medieval land tenure, to religious fanatics or just people who really believe in witchcraft, you name it. But most of them are *German,* and so they'll be thinking in their own terms. Wilhelm knows that. So he'll put together a party based on a platform which can 'bridge' the gap. Draw mass support from Germans but be acceptable—enough, at least—to a lot of Americans."

Mike shrugged. "It'll be 'conservative,' sure, but *his* definition of the term. Not Quentin's. I'm not sure yet, but I think Wilhelm will base most of his program on the theories of the cameralists, who've been the rising new reform movement here in Germany for quite some time. Interesting stuff, actually. Becky's uncle Uriel is quite a fan of the cameralists, in a lot of ways, and I've been talking to him about them over the past few months. Then Wilhelm will graft onto it, probably, a hefty dose of stuff from the Anglo-American political tradition back in the late eighteenth and early nineteenth centuries. Edmund Burke, for sure—and you might be surprised how conservative a lot of the Founding Fathers were. They didn't all see eye to eye with Tom Paine and Sam Adams."

Frank was frowning again. "Becky is *ruining* you. I lost count, exactly, but I know there was more than one three-syllable word in those sentences you just rattled off. Keep it up, buddy, and I'm taking away your Caterpillar hat. Don't even think of applying to the Ancient Order of Hillbillies for a Harley-Davidson decal."

They shared a laugh. When it was over, Mike shook his head and said cheerfully: "The reason I'm not too worried about the political hit I'm going to take from Quentin's resignation is because I know what's going to happen. Bet you dollars for donuts. Wilhelm's going to agree to form an alliance with Quentin because Wilhelm is plenty smart enough to know that for an opposition party here in the U.S., having some well-known and respected

American adherents and leaders is critical to success. A purely German-based party won't have enough credibility that it can keep the tech base up and running—and *nobody* who lives here, not any longer, has any doubt that's necessary. Having Quentin Underwood signed up, on the other hand, is about as gold-plated as it gets."

"Makes sense. But I still don't understand what you're grinning about."

"I'm grinning about what's going to happen *afterwards*. After Wilhelm's milked Quentin for all he's worth and then has to explain to him that the cameralist definition of 'conservative' is *not* 'what's good for General Motors is good for America.'" Mike leaned back in his chair, lacing his fingers across his midriff. "The cameralists—in some ways, like the founding fathers of conservatism in our own political tradition—were basically a bunch of forward-looking and socially-conscious noblemen and gentry figures who felt that government should, among other things, look out for the needs of the common people. They weren't actually all that fond of unbridled capitalism, which Quentin thinks will solve all problems. Rather the opposite, in fact."

He pursed his lips. "Uriel once told me he thought the best translation of what 'cameralism' meant into modern political concepts—as near as he could figure it out—would be something like 'aristocratic municipal socialism.' Or 'social democracy,' at least, to use the more appropriate European term. Think of it as a mix and match between *noblesse oblige,* Teddy Roosevelt's progressives, and Milwaukee-style 'sewer socialism.' For guys like Wilhelm, the notion of 'deregulation' ranks right up there with fornication and adultery and worshipping graven idols."

Frank's eyes were almost bulging. "Socialism?!" he choked. "Quentin *Underwood*?"

James Nichols entered the room, then, talking as he came through the door. "Okay, Mike, it's set. Stoner's starting to get the stuff packed up and Anne Jefferson's volunteered to lead the medical side of the mission to Amsterdam. Sharon'll go to Wismar and—"

He stared at Frank. "What the hell's so funny?"

Frank, his shoulders heaving, pointed an accusing finger at Mike. "James, this bastard is a sneaky, conniving, scheming—"

"It's taken you this long to figure that out?" Nichols shook his head sadly. "Dumb-ass hillbilly. I figured it out within a week after the Ring of Fire."

He plumped himself onto another chair. "'Course, I did have the advantage of a Chicago street education. He's a *politician*, Frank. For my money, the best one in Europe. I sure as hell hope so, or we're dog meat."

# Chapter 36

*"Monsieur L'Admiral et Madame Simpson!"* cried out the major-domo, in a tone of voice which somehow managed to be stentorian without actually bellowing hoarsely. As he passed by the man into the huge and crowded ballroom beyond, maintaining a stiff and stately progress with his wife's hand tucked under his arm, John Simpson found himself possessed by a sudden and well-nigh irresistible urge to have the man impressed on the spot and shanghaied into the United States Navy. One of the many discoveries Simpson had made concerning naval service in the 17th century was that—in a navy without powered phones—a petty officer with leather lungs and a carrying voice was worth his weight in gold.

The notion, he realized dimly, was a reflection of his own nervousness. Simpson hated being nervous, and handled it with such a rigid external pose that the mind beneath was sometimes prone to mad flights of fancy. He could remember entering a stockholders meeting once, followed by the top officers of his corporation, to give a very pessimistic report. Entering the room and seeing the angry and gloomy faces of the stockholders, he'd had to choke down a sudden impulse to turn around, draw his gold-plated pen, and order the vice-president in charge of marketing to commit seppuku with it on the spot.

But . . . he hadn't. He'd given the report, and weathered the storm which followed, with his usual wooden expression. The same expression had been on his face the next day, when he'd fired the incompetent jerk.

A little tug on his arm distracted him from the memory. "Why are they announcing us in French?" Mary whispered. "I didn't think that had become the language of the courts until Louis XIV came along."

Simpson shrugged. "No idea." He listened to the babble of conversation filling the room. "Most people seem to be talking in German. Of some sort or another. I think. Hard to tell, as many dialects—"

*"Monsieur L'Admiral! Et Madame Simpson! Enchanté!"*

A very pretty woman in her late twenties or early thirties was advancing toward them, hands outstretched. The beaming smile on her face was echoed in fabric and embroidery by every single item of apparel she was wearing. From the top of her well-coiffed hair to the soles of her expensive-looking slippers, she positively radiated splendor and wealth.

The smile was supple as well as wide, somehow conveying *great unexpected pleasure* with *I realize you have no idea who I am* combined with *don't worry about it, I'll get us through the awkward part.*

Simpson remained stiff and wooden-faced. His wife Mary, on the other hand—one old pro instantly recognizing another—had a smile plastered on her face that was just as wide and just as supple. *God knows who this is* welded to *but I'm sure we'll get along* soldered firmly to *no sweat, dearie, give me a lob and I'll get the volley started.*

A moment later, the unknown woman and Mrs. Simpson were chattering away like magpies. In French, a language Simpson neither spoke nor had ever had any desire to learn. To his wife, French was the language of class and culture. Good taste personified. To Simpson, it was the tongue of a nation whose character—as any proper Pentagon-corridor-man could attest—was the very definition of "obnoxious" and "obstreperous." *He'd* learned to speak reasonably passable simple German and Dutch in his NATO years. Useful languages, spoken by useful folk.

He felt a hand on his other arm, and swiveled his head. Wilhelm of Saxe-Weimar was smiling up at him.

"Delighted you could come, Admiral," said Wilhelm in his fluent English. "If I could tear you away from your wife for a moment . . . some gentlemen I'd like you to meet." He gestured in the direction of an archway in the far corner of the huge room. "Like me, they find the din in here tiresome, so we've sequestered a smaller room for more civilized conversation."

Before Simpson could even think of a response, Mary was saying: "By all means, John. You'll be more comfortable there anyway." The smile plastered on her face was as wide as ever. It would remain so, he knew, for the rest of the evening. Supple as always, of course, the variations would change as quickly as clouds passing through the sky. Right now the smile was radiating *thank God I'm in civilized hands* standing at attention next to *and she's got* such *a splendid volley* with *you'll get underfoot, buster* saluting smartly and *get lost but don't go far* holding up the colors.

A moment later, Wilhelm was steering him toward the archway. Again, Simpson had to fight down an almost irrepressible urge. This time, to laugh uproariously. This was not the first time in his life, of course, that he'd seen this same maneuver carried out on the field of social battle. But he couldn't ever recall seeing it handled so surely and effortlessly.

Just before passing through the archway, he turned his head and caught a last glimpse of Mary. By now, there were perhaps half a dozen women in the little group surrounding her. All of them had the same general aura of wealth and position, though their ages and appearance varied widely. Two of them seemed to be as old as Mary, late middle age. It was, as always, difficult to tell. Even for noblewomen, the 17th century was a heavy burden. Simpson wouldn't be surprised if they were ten years younger than his wife.

But he wasn't paying much attention to them, in truth. He was just immensely relieved to see that, for the first time since the Ring of Fire had shattered their well-ordered universe, Mary Simpson actually seemed to be enjoying herself.

An hour later, Simpson was not feeling so cheerful. The small group of men gathered in a small salon in the palace, so much was quickly obvious, were the inner circle of what Simpson could easily recognize from past experience constituted a faction of some kind. And, since his German had become rather good over the past two years, if not fluent, he was able to follow the conversation easily enough. The more so once the men apparently decided he was "safe and acceptable"—several of them had obviously been surprised to learn that he spoke any German at all—and began unbending a little and speaking more frankly in his presence.

There was even something mildly amusing about their increasing relaxation. Some of it, he suspected, was because they assumed the particular dialect most of them favored would be rather opaque to the stranger in their midst. As it happened, however, Simpson's NATO years had left him with an odd combination of half-remembered Dutch as well as German. And the dialect these German noblemen were speaking was riddled with expressions and phrasings which seemed very "Dutch-like" to him.

That was enough to bring the picture into focus. To some degree, at least. Simpson made a stern resolve to pay more attention to what his assistant Dietrich Schwanhausser had been telling him about the internal politics of Germany. He hadn't really done so in the past, partly because of his own preoccupation with the ironclad project, but mostly because he found the subject infuriatingly complex and intricate. Accustomed as he was to the comparative logic and rationality of late 20th- and early 21st-century government administration, Simpson found the traditions left over from feudalism utterly bizarre. "Quaint" was the polite way to put it. As far as he was concerned, "idiotic" was more accurate.

The Holy Roman Empire had been a political mare's nest to begin with. Since Gustav Adolf had sundered away a good portion of it from Ferdinand II of Austria to form his Confederated Principalities of Europe, the situation had—if anything—gotten even worse. As if a bowl of spaghetti had had a heavy layer of Swedish cheese melted over it.

This much Simpson did know:

The Holy Roman Empire's nobility, the "Adel" as it was called, was basically separated into two major classes. At the top were the Hochadel. The Hochadel were also known as the "territorial princes," because they were the ones who had a seat in the Holy Roman Empire's Reichstag and, in theory, dealt directly with the emperor himself. They also had jurisdictional rights over their subjects, since they ran the law courts. It was in this class of noblemen that one found the electors, prince-bishops, prince-abbots, counts, margraves, landgraves, and the like. Despite their legal equality, however, their actual power varied enormously—from the ones as large as John George of Saxony with a million subjects down to a reichsritter with one village.

When Gustav Adolf formed the CPE, he had simply transferred their status to the new Chamber of Princes. He had also transferred with it their *debts* to the Holy Roman Empire—which were considerable, because it had been this class of noblemen whom Ferdinand II had squeezed ruthlessly to pay for his wars.

The rest of the German nobility were called Niederadel, and had at least one layer of the territorial nobility standing between them and the emperor. But all of them, no matter how petty their actual power and wealth might be, were officially classified as being one of the Adel, or nobility. Taken as a whole, Dietrich had told Simpson, the Adel constituted perhaps one out of a hundred of Germany's population—a much higher percentage than the small English aristocracy constituted of that island's population.

Perhaps most critical, at least from the standpoint of taxation and government revenue, was the fact that *any* nobleman was exempt from taxation. And while the Adel constituted only one percent of the population, they controlled perhaps a third of Germany's land. Which removed from the tax rolls a disproportionate share of potential government income—and threw an extra burden on both the commoners at the bottom and the territorial princes themselves, who, come what might, were the ones whom the emperor was going to squeeze when he needed money.

It was even more tortuous than that, because the tax exemption applied to the property itself, not the individual landholder. Over the centuries, as tax-exempt properties passed from one set of hands to another, Germany had become a crazy quilt of tax exemptions. From what Simpson could determine, the situation was roughly analogous to what might have happened in the United States if all taxes owed to the federal government had been the responsibility of the state governors to collect—but one third of all counties were exempt from taxation. And if the governors were forced to do so, moreover, while finding their way through an accumulation of "loopholes" that made the old U.S.A.'s much-derided 1040 tax form look like child's play. *And* had to deal with a judicial system at the imperial level that was firmly dedicated to the maintenance of every traditional variance, quirk, and local peculiarity—such as a nobleman who had the right to maintain a tavern in his castle.

Hesse-Kassel was the largest and most important of the semi-autonomous princedoms, leaving aside the two major ones of Saxony and Brandenburg. And Hesse-Kassel's principal allies among the secondary and tertiary territorial princes were the so-called counts of the Wetterau. The Wetterau counts traditionally had close ties both with Hesse-Kassel and with the aristocracy of the United

Provinces. Those ties were still alive and strong. The wife of Frederik Hendrik, the prince of Orange, had come from the Solms-Braunfels family.

So it was not surprising that the conversation roiling around Simpson was spoken in a dialect of German that bore certain resemblances to Dutch. Nor—and this was the reason for his ebbing good cheer—was it surprising that the conversations were tense.

The Holy Roman Empire had been a crazy quilt of political allegiances tangled up with centuries worth of accumulated social and economic rights, obligations and privileges. Gustav Adolf had inherited all that from the Habsburgs. But, unlike the Habsburgs, he was bound and determined to bring some order, logic and rationality to the situation. If for no other reason, because until and unless he could do so the vast potential wealth of German manufacture and commerce would remain crippled.

"Order, logic and rationality," of course, was the *Swedish king's* definition of the process. From the point of view of that portion of Germany's Adel who now found themselves within the CPE, on the other hand, the Swedish king bore a remarkable resemblance to a bovine oaf who proposed to tread heavily on their toes—and they had hundreds of toes, each and every one of them very long and tender.

Still, Simpson knew enough about the situation to be puzzled. For the first time since he'd been welcomed into the room, he cleared his throat and spoke.

"I do not understand. I have—would have"—he stumbled for a moment over the grammar, cursing himself; John Chandler Simpson *hated* to stumble—"would have thought you would welcome a tax reform."

The eight men in the room stared at him. Saxe-Weimar shrewdly, the other seven with befuddled expressions. As if they'd just had a grizzly bear ask them a question, and were trying to decide whether to answer or look for an escape route.

Hesse-Kassel was the first to recover, and did so quickly. "Ha!" he barked. Sweeping his hand to indicate the room: "Admiral Simpson, I can assure you that *we* welcome it. So does every Hochadel in Germany—John George of Saxony no less than any other. It would increase our revenues considerably, not to mention making our lives easier. But . . . the matter is tied to everything else. Gustavus Adolphus has made clear that he wants the tax reform adopted as part of a systematic reform. Ah, you may think of it—"

"Americans already have a term for the thing, Landgrave," interjected Wilhelm smoothly. "They call it a 'package deal.'"

Hesse-Kassel cocked his eyebrow. "Indeed?"

"Oh, yes. In fact, the American vocabulary for matters of fine political distinction is quite massive." He smiled sweetly. Simpson suspected Saxe-Weimar was taking the opportunity to drive home a point. "Remind me someday to explain such terms as 'logrolling' and 'pork-barrel' and 'line-item veto.' The concept of the 'filibuster' is particularly enchanting."

Simpson cleared his throat. "In other words, the king of Sweden—ah, 'emperor of the CPE' I should say—"

He paused, a bit nonplussed. Once again, the noblemen in the room were staring at him as if he were a speaking bear.

"Did I mention Americans are fond of acronyms?" mused Wilhelm. "An odd habit, I thought at first. But then, when I saw the enthusiasm with which the Americans proliferate administrative and regulatory bureaus, I realized the logic of it. They're quite an efficient folk, much given to order and routine. They even have a name for that, too: 'red tape.'"

Now, the noblemen were staring at *him* as if he were a speaking bear. Or, perhaps, a man they thought they knew suddenly transformed into one. Saxe-Weimar's smile was still on his face, but it could no longer be described as "sweet." Indeed, it was rather grim.

"They ruled a *continent,* lords. They had provinces larger than any realm in Europe. Do you think they did that by the methods of anarchy?"

Simpson sat stiff, wooden-faced. There had been times in his life—not many, but some—when he'd cursed that also. That inability of his to "unbend," however useful it was in many situations, had cost him in others. In his most honest moments, he knew it had played a large role in losing the affections of his own son. But tonight, in the here and now, it was invaluable. He could tell, just by the look on the faces of the German landgrave and his supporting counts.

*To hell with you snots. I've forgotten more about efficient administration than the pack of you amateurs will ever learn.* But the stiff and wooden face removed the insult, while passing along the fact itself.

"Ah," said one of the counts. "By 'CPE' you refer to—"

Hesse-Kassel chuckled. "It is more efficient, I admit."

The point having been made well enough, Simpson continued. "In short, Gustav Adolf is demanding that you adopt *all* of his measures. He will not permit you to pick and choose."

One of the counts nodded. Glumly: "And some of those other measures are . . . highly distasteful. Speaking for myself, for instance, losing the tolls will cost me—"

"Oh, enough!" exclaimed one of the other noblemen. "Enough, I say! We've already agreed to support the emperor and we've formed a league to do it. So why waste the rest of the evening fretting over it?"

He bestowed a smile on Simpson which, for the first time coming from any of them except Saxe-Weimar, was the kind of expression a man gives to another man, not the formal grimace one presents to a potentially savage animal.

"I am Ludwig Guenther, Admiral. The count of Schwarzburg-Rudolstadt. And, speaking for myself, I think we will—certainly in the long run—gain far more than we will lose from the emperor's policies." His nostrils flared. "If nothing else, abolishing the rule of derogation will mean that my lazy cousins will no longer have any excuse to drain my larder."

"Surely you won't turn away the prince of Orange?!" exclaimed Hesse-Kassel, half-laughing and half-grimacing.

Ludwig Guenther smiled thinly. "If my first cousin Frederik Hendrik shows up at my door looking for asylum, I will gladly give it to him. But my second cousin Ernst—to give just one example—can hardly claim Orange's necessities. Much less his talents! If Ernst can do anything beyond ride a horse and drink himself into a stupor, I have yet to see any evidence of it."

The count of Schwarzburg-Rudolstadt's face grew stern. "Half the noblemen of Germany are pure and simple parasites. I know it and you know it—all of you. Well, no longer! Not after the reforms are instituted. Henceforth, they will have no excuses. They will be able to take up any occupation—trade, commerce, whatever—without losing their precious status as members of the Adel. I can assure you that as soon as I return home, those cousins of mine are out the door. Louts, all of them! I'll give them enough to get started. That's it."

Two of the other noblemen chuckled. "You think your cousins are bad?" demanded one. "My brother-in-law . . ."

Hesse-Kassel interrupted. "What do *you* think, Admiral?"

For a moment, Simpson froze. (And, fortunately, because of his wooden face, was able to hide the moment.) He had a flash of memory; being asked a question, once, at a stockholders' meeting, for which his staff had not prepared him. He'd gotten through the question, fumbling his way—he *hated* to fumble—and had then stripped the hide from his staff the next day. Rubbed salt into the bleeding flesh, in fact.

But . . .

*I can hardly blame Dietrich for this, after all. Not as if he hasn't tried. John Chandler, you've been goofing off on your homework. An 'Admiral,' you stupid jerk—how much time did you spend in the Pentagon?—has to be a political animal also.*

He cleared his throat. "I'm sorry, but I've been so preoccupied with my own naval affairs that I haven't paid as much attention to this matter as perhaps I should have." The pro forma apology issued, Simpson glided forward smoothly. He *had*, after all, gotten through more than one bad moment at a stockholders' meeting.

"But it seems to me that you need to step back and consider the long-term—ah—" His lips tight, he fumbled for the word. Wilhelm, sitting next to him, leaned over and murmured: " 'Consequences,' I believe, is the word you're looking for."

He flashed Saxe-Weimar a grateful glance. "Yes, consequences." He swiveled his head and looked at the nobleman who had complained about losing his tolls. "Let me give you an example, using a subject I *am* very familiar with. The matter of the tolls. Yes, immediate revenue will be lost. Although I should point out that the emperor has no objection to tolls levied for works which are actually being maintained—such as locks, for instance. It's simply the endless bleeding of money from the merchants for a thousand fees that he wants removed, most of which—let us be honest—are simply a monopoly surcharge for no service rendered. Add it all together—which I have done—and you will find that, as a rule, those tolls wind up adding a third to the price of something shipped simply across half of Germany."

The nobleman scowled, but did not try to object. *And you'd better not, buster. On* this *subject, I've got the facts and figures damn well memorized.*

"What this will produce in the long run, however—and much sooner than you might think—is a rapid increase in Germany's internal trade. Foreign trade as well, for that matter. That, in turn, will produce an accumulation of money in the hands of Germany's commoners. Some of them, at least. What will they *do* with it? Reinvest, that's what. And where will they do so? Many of them, of course, in the same place where they exist already. But many of them will look for opportunities elsewhere. Especially—"

He swiveled his head, giving all the noblemen in the room his very fine and well-polished *confident CEO regard*, lingering for an extra moment on the count of Schwarzburg-Rudolstadt. "Especially in the lands of those territorial princes who have the good sense to encourage them to come. And there are a multitude of ways to do so. For instance—"

Simpson spoke steadily for half an hour, interrupted only on occasion by the need to determine the right word, or to clarify a few terms for the noblemen. The concept of 'tax-free enterprise zones' was especially challenging for some of them. Although Simpson was ignorant of most of the specific circumstances, the subject in general was one on which he was a genuine expert.

When he was done, the room was silent for a moment. Then Hesse-Kassel started chuckling.

"So. We are not doomed after all, it seems."

Wilhelm, the former duke of Saxe-Weimar, started to say something. Then, pursed his lips and remained silent. Simpson glanced at him, and for an instant a look of complete understanding passed between them.

*God, he's a smart one. Saxe-Weimar knows the truth. No, Hesse-Kassel. As a* class, *you are in fact doomed. Sooner or later. But as individuals, as families . . . If you're smart—and that's a big "if"— you could wind up better off than ever. So what do you care?*

A dim thought seeped into Simpson's mind. Dim . . . and unpleasant. So he pushed it aside almost instantly. But, for just a moment, he found himself contemplating the possibility that maybe—just maybe—that coal miner roughneck knew what he was doing. Better, even—maybe—than the CEO had.

*Bah. He was just lucky.*

# Chapter 37

Mary Simpson chattered gaily all the way home, not even complaining once about the wretched conditions of the half-cobblestoned streets and the way their vehicle was lurching about. They were riding in what amounted to a palanquin suspended fore-and-aft between two horses, with a rider on the lead horse. That was a far more practical conveyance for a city with such rough streets as Magdeburg's still were than an actual carriage would have been. Still, the ride was very far from a smooth one.

Simpson was glad to hear the undertone of happiness in his wife's voice, but paid little attention to her actual words. Her monologue was mostly meaningless to him, anyway, involving Mary's detailed—even exhaustive—assessment of the various personalities she'd encountered at Hesse-Kassel's soiree. As opaque as his own shop talk would have been to her.

It was a practiced and polite sort of ignoring, on his part. He'd had plenty of experience, in the long years before the Ring of Fire, accompanying Mary to a multitude of social occasions. He'd always tried to get out of as many as he could, except during his stint at the Pentagon, but Mary ran a tight ship and didn't let him slip too often. She'd even forced him to attend more operas than he could remember, a form of entertainment he found positively excruciating.

But . . . he'd never complained, either. Simpson was honest enough to admit, even to himself, that his impressive career in the

Navy had been helped along considerably by Mary's talents and discipline. She'd been the perfect "Navy wife," just as, in later years, she'd given him more influence in the social circles that mattered than he'd ever have been able to get simply from his status as the head of a sizeable industrial firm. Without Mary, John Chandler Simpson would have been a powerful and respected man, of course. But no newspaper or magazine would ever have bestowed upon him—as one of them once had—the title of "Mr. Pittsburgh." The title had been given out in a gingerly manner, to be sure. There would always be too much of the ruthless corporate shark about John Simpson to make people completely comfortable around him, even those as wealthy and powerful as he had been.

There'd been no such reservations, on the other hand, about the title which many magazines and newspapers had bestowed upon Mary. "The Dame of the Three Rivers" was a phrase you could have found, on any given day of the week, in the society columns of western Pennsylvania's periodicals. She'd been on the board of directors or otherwise highly connected with practically all of the Carnegie establishments in Pittsburgh, ranging from museums to Carnegie-Mellon University; and the same for at least half of the city's major artistic and musical foundations. Whenever someone wanted to tap into philanthropical circles in Pittsburgh, they eventually wound up knocking on the door of Mrs. John Chandler Simpson—and those of them already in the know started there in the first place. With a quick phone call, followed by lunch at any one of Mary's favorite restaurants.

Her enthusiasms had cost him money, to be sure, and now and then he'd grumbled about it. But not too loud, and not too often. Partly, because money hadn't been everything to John Simpson, despite what people assumed. Mostly, though, because he was more than sophisticated enough to understand that what goes around, comes around. He was certain that at least one big contract he'd landed—balanced on a knife edge between him and a competitor— had come his way because the prospective customer, on a visit, turned out to share Mary's enthusiasm for Benjamin Britten's opera *Peter Grimes*. The customer's wife—no accounting for taste—had even shared Mary's fondness for Renaissance music.

By an odd coincidence, no sooner had they entered the house which he'd rented next to the shipyard and lit the lamps than his drifting thoughts intersected Mary's full-bore monologue.

"—still *alive*. God, John, think of it! *Monteverdi himself.* Of

course, he's getting on in years—must be somewhere in his six-
ties by now—but if I remember right he lived to a ripe old age.
Even down there in Italy, where they always have such terrible
epidemics. And the landgravine of Hesse-Kassel—that's Amalie—
was telling me that she heard from her cousin Luise that although
Monteverdi took holy orders after that horrible sack of Mantua
and he moved to Venice—"

The name "Monteverdi" finally rang a bell. An alarm bell. Mary
caught the slight wince on his face and laughed.

"Oh, please! I am *not* going to apologize for forcing you to sit
through—once only, for pity's sake—a performance of the entire
*Vespers of the Virgin Mary.*" Firmly: "No person who claims to be
civilized should go through life without hearing it. I will admit,
I'm personally more partial to his operas."

She broke off her monologue as she went to the side table and
rang a little bell. Almost instantly, a young German girl appeared
in the doorway. Their house servant, having heard them enter, had
obviously been waiting for a summons.

"We'll have some tea, please, Hilde." She spoke in English, not
her still very-poor German. Hilde had been hired in part because
she was fluent in English.

The girl nodded and left for the kitchen. "That's one good thing
about this century," said Mary, lowering herself onto a divan. "The
service is not only cheap, it's good. And I'll say this, too—"

She patted the divan she was sitting on. "Furniture like this
would have cost us a fortune back then. Even if we do have to
spray it with DDT before taking it into the house."

When Mary looked at him, her smile was a bit sly. "But, to get
back to what I was saying, Monteverdi himself, of course, is probably immovable. But the Landgravine tells me that her cousin Luise
tells her that Monteverdi's student Cavalli is very frustrated with
the situation in Venice. Frightened too, of course. The epidemic
there two years ago took off a third of the city's populace, you
know."

Knowing the decision Mike Stearns had made to send all of the
chloramphenicol to Luebeck and Amsterdam, Simpson winced
again—and no slight wince, this time.

Mary shook her head. "Horrible, isn't it? But let's look on the
bright side. Cavalli's not the genius that Monteverdi is, to be sure—
I saw his opera *Giasone* once, and while it wasn't bad at all it
certainly didn't match up to *Orfeo* or *L'incoronazione de Poppea*—

but he's the other great composer of the day in Italy. Will be pretty soon, anyway. He's still a young man. And Cavalli's apparently just as upset about the state of musical affairs in Venice as he is about the danger of plague. He wants to build a theater especially for opera—opera houses don't exist yet, as amazing as that seems—and with the city's desperate situation he's having a hard time getting the financial backing—*what's so funny?*"

"You are," said Simpson, shaking his head. "Mary, I hate to break the news to you, but you are no longer 'the Dame of the Three Rivers.' And—" He shrugged. "While I'm reasonably well-off by today's standards, with my salary as admiral, I am no longer 'Mr. Moneybags.'"

He lowered himself on the divan next to her. "I'm sorry, Mary, but we have to face it. We lost everything."

Her face was pale, and even stiffer than his own. "No, John. That's not quite right. We didn't *lose* everything. What we lost was our money. What we *threw away* was our life—starting with our son."

Simpson felt the wooden mask clamp down.

"Oh, God help us," she whispered. "Here it comes again. John Chandler Simpson, the man who can never be wrong about anything." She turned her face away from him, her eyes starting to water. "I *hate* that man. Now, more than I ever have."

"Mary—"

"Shut up. Just shut up." She rose to her feet, hands pressed to her thighs, and stared at the far wall. There was nothing on the wall. No painting, no tapestry, nothing. Simpson's salary had been enough to cover the house and the furniture and the servant. There had been nothing left over for Mary's beloved art works.

She seemed to be reading his mind. Not surprising, perhaps, for as long as they'd been married. "I don't blame you for that. I don't blame you for not having the money you used to have. The Ring of Fire was not your fault. I don't even blame you for Tom. That was probably my fault more than it was yours, to be honest. I think I was even nastier to his fiancée than you were."

Simpson's jaws were clenched. He was filled with the anger of a man who, always sure of himself, wanted desperately to drive home the lesson again. *Probably? Are you kidding? I was just stiff and cold to the girl. Okay, even rude, I suppose. But you were the one, the first time Tom brought her up to Pittsburgh to meet us, who reduced her to tears at the dinner table by ridiculing her tastes in music. You were the one who wouldn't let her slide out easily when you pressed her on her knowledge of the world's 'great lit'rat'chure.' You were the one, you snotty—*

Barely, thankfully, he managed to hold it in check. Even through the anger, Simpson retained enough clarity of thought to realize that his marriage was at the breaking point. And realized also, in something of a crashing wave of recognition, how desperately he did not want that to happen. On a personal level, his wife was all he had left in the world. They'd gotten married the day after he graduated from Annapolis. He couldn't imagine his life without her.

"Mary, please—"

"John, be quiet. For once—just once—listen instead of talking." She turned around to face him. The anger was still there on her face. But he was relieved to see, lurking somewhere behind the tears, the affection of a lifetime shared.

"You are not good—to put it mildly—at ever admitting you were wrong about anything." She swallowed. "I suppose I'm not much good at it either, for that matter. I know I can be even pettier than you are, lots of times. But I'm not in your league when it comes to unyielding self-righteousness. Not even close. I don't think I know anybody who is."

Hilde came into the room then, carrying a tray with a teapot and two cups. There was neither milk nor sugar on the tray. Milk was too much of a headache for casual use, needing to be boiled first; and sugar was far too expensive. Willy-nilly, Mary Simpson had learned to take her tea plain. She'd even stopped complaining about it, months before.

The servant froze, after taking two steps in the room, as servants will when they suddenly realize they've walked into the middle of a quarrel between the master and lady of the house.

When she wanted to be, Mary Simpson could be graciousness personified. For a moment, the anger and hurt and sorrow on her face vanished, replaced by the serene dame. "Thank you so much, Hilde. That will be all for the night."

The servant nodded nervously, set the tray down on a sidetable, and hurried from the room.

The break in the tension came as a relief for Simpson. All the more so, when he saw that Mary's "dame persona" had settled her down. The expression on her face was now stern, but no longer had any trace of hysteria.

"Tonight, John Chandler Simpson, I am going to tell you the truth. Two years ago, when the Ring of Fire turned our universe inside out, Mike Stearns was right and you—we—were wrong. Just as *he* was right—not us—during the political campaign."

She waved her hand impatiently. "Oh, stop looking like a boy being forced to swallow a pill. I didn't say he was right about *everything*, for God's sake. He's still a crude and uncouth man, as vicious in a brawl as anyone you'll ever meet, and I think he's reckless and short-sighted about a lot of things. *But—*"

The word was spoken almost like a gunshot. "He understood something, right from the beginning, that we didn't. Although, looking back on it now, it's clear as day to me. Those few thousand Americans who came through the Ring of Fire were almost petrified with terror. You saw that also, and—I know you, John, you're not a bad man, never have been—reacted to it by trying to *organize* the fear in order to save them. And what he saw, and understood, was that fear—*organized*—would just turn into savagery. No matter how well it was administered. So, he used you—and me—like a punching bag. Hammered on us to dispel the fear by offering them . . ."

She paused, wiped her face. "Oh, hell, call it inspiration, if you will."

"Mary, that's the most one-sided—"

"Shut *up*. Can't you *ever* listen?" The fury was returning to her voice. "*I was at those campaign rallies at the Club 250, John.* Tonight—now, after it's all over—look me straight in the eye and tell me we weren't staring down the throat of a Ku Klux Klan in the making."

Her shoulders shivered. "I always felt like taking a shower afterward. Would have, too, if the hot water hadn't been rationed. God, those *animals.* 'No dogs and Germans allowed.' 'Pale niggers.' 'I got nuthin' 'gainst no Kraut—ev'ry Murikan should own one.' That's what they were saying in the *crowd,* John, it doesn't matter what fine words you were spouting from the speaker's platform."

Simpson swallowed. He'd hated those rallies, himself. But, given Stearns' savage and relentless campaign, he'd had no choice—

He groped for . . . *something.* "Damn it, his program and policies were incredibly *reckless.* Without our traditions, our customs, letting tens of thousands of Germans—I don't care about their so-called 'race,' it's got nothing to do with that and you know it—

let them have the franchise—swamping us under with their medieval attitudes and superstitions—God knows what they'd do with it . . ."

The words petered off. Mary laughed drily.

"Yes? And then what? *What have they done with it?*" She glanced at the bare wall, and managed a smile. "Having no pictures up isn't really the end of the world, you know. It's been two years now, John. And if the man was wrong about a lot of things—and I think he was, and still do—he wasn't wrong about *that*. He may have screwed up around the fringes, but he didn't screw up at the core. Did he? Whatever else this new United States is and may become, at least it's nothing we or anybody else needs to be ashamed of. And—be honest, John—are you so sure you'd be able to say the same thing today, if *you'd* been running the show?"

He tried to say it, but . . . couldn't. Quite.

"Terror is a horrible thing, John," she said softly. "A monster, if it's set loose. Much less if it's whipped up. And I think, no matter how hard you tried, you wouldn't have been able to control it. Not after you'd done everything you could to ride terror into power. Which—to be blunt—is exactly what you tried to do."

Again, she wiped her face. "Yes, yes, me too. I'm not trying to put the *blame* on you, John. Just . . . oh, *fuck it.*"

The profanity jolted him. Mary was usually fastidious in her use of words. More than anything, in fact, it had been Rita Stearns' unthinking use of profanity—and the way it seemed to have infected Tom—which had so instantly turned Mary's prejudice against their son's fiancée into unyielding opposition to the marriage.

Suddenly, they were both laughing. Almost hysterically, in fact—Simpson himself as much as Mary. Some of that was his own relief at the realization that his marriage was going to survive. But as much—even Simpson could understand it—because the laughter would let him release all errors. Wash them away into the past, without ever actually having to come right out and . . .

*Admit* it.

"All right, Mary," he said after the laughter died down. "Tell me what you want."

She sat down next to him and took his hands in hers. "I want *us* back, John. I want my *life* back. I want our son back, if we can manage it. You've had your work with the Navy to keep you going. I've had *nothing*."

He nodded, acknowledging the truth of that. "I'll do—"

"Oh, shut up!" This time, though, the snapped words were friendly, not hostile. "John, *you* don't have to do anything. Well . . . not quite. I'm going to need you to call in the favor Mike Stearns put in your bank account."

She laughed at the stiffness in his face. "Come *on*. Whatever else he is, the man's as slick a politician as you'll ever meet. That much ought to be obvious to anyone with half a brain—especially *you*, Mr. Black and Blue All Over and Still Wondering What Truck Ran Over Him."

Again, laughter. And again, a wave of relief. Mary and he hadn't shared this much in the way of warmth since before the Ring of Fire. He'd missed that intimacy, and desperately—all the more so because he'd had no way of telling her. He wasn't good at that. Marriages don't lend themselves well to efficient administration.

"That's what that personal apology was, John, that he gave you on the wharf. It wasn't just an olive branch. It was also an offer. So take him up on it, you dimwit. Or would you rather stay all cooped up, festering in resentment?"

She rose to her feet, moved over to the one window in the room, and drew aside the curtain. There was really nothing much to see, of course, in the middle of the night.

"Let's steal a page from Mike Stearns' book, John. Down there in Grantville, he's groping his way when it comes to imperial politics. But up *here*, in Magdeburg . . . I can *feel* it, John. *Feel* it, I tell you. It was all through the air at that soiree tonight. Those people are perched on a knife's edge between exhilaration and terror. Some of them—The Landgravine of Hesse-Kassel, for instance—are even smart enough to know it. And if you think *Amalie's* a smart cookie, you ought to meet the abbess of Quedlin-burg. I spent more time talking to her than anyone."

"I don't understand what you mean. Steal a page from Mike Stearns' book? How?"

"Give them *confidence*, John. Give them *hope*. Gustav Adolf's not seeing that either, I don't think. 'I want this, I want that. Give up this, give up that.' They all recognize that he's *right*—the ones who were at that soiree, anyhow. And there's even a part of them—the best part—that's a bit thrilled that they're going to be bold enough to do what everyone has known for—oh, for centuries now!—needs to be done, if Germany is ever going to be more than a basket case. But they're *scared*." She stared out into the dark-ness. "If there's one thing I've come to know, these past two years,

it's the way fear can eat a human being alive. Terror is a dangerous thing, John. Let's not—this time—be on the wrong side of
that equation."

He shook his head. "Mary, I'm not trying to argue with you.
I just don't understand—"

She spun around, her hands spread wide and a great smile on
her face. For just an instant, his heart swelled, remembering the
young woman he'd met and married so many years before.

"Give them an *empire,* John. Not just money and power. Hell,
you're trying to take *that* away from them. So—so—" She groped
for words. Then, softly: "Give them an olive branch, extended on
a wharf. Give them a place of their own. Give them an *imperial*
city for a capital, not just a great, ugly, monster of an industry
town. Give them universities that they can send their children to.
Give them opera houses and libraries and museums. Give them
a city they'll want to live in—and it won't hurt any to have them
here under Gustav's guns instead of festering out in their country mansions, now will it?—while they spend their energies in a
social whirl. There's no harm in it, and a lot of good. I know you
think my hobbies are a bit silly, but I will tell you this, John Chandler Simpson. *Culture* is not just a pretentious word for rich bitches
with nothing better to do."

She smiled, seeing his jaw sag at her language. "Oh, phooey. Since
I'm broke now, anyway, why not? If you've got the name, why not
have the game?"

She shook her head firmly. "It's *not,* John. However foolish the
trappings often are. Culture is what transforms raw power into
civilization. So if we're going to do this, then, damnation, let's do
it right. If Gustav wants his empire, fine. I just insist that the thing
has to *shine.*" She spurted a little half-laugh, half-giggle. "At the
very least, I insist that it *glitter.*"

"But—but—" He took a deep breath of his own. "Mary, who
is going to *pay* for all this? We're already strapped—"

"Men!" She rolled her eyes. "And you're no better than Mike
Stearns or Gustav Adolf!"

She lowered her eyes and gave him a twisted half-grin. "'Mr.
Pittsburgh.' What a laugh. *Tax breaks,* you dumbbell. Gustav Adolf
is about to strip away the tax exemption from Germany's nobles.
Well . . . those of them, at least, who are willing to vote for it. And
a lot of them are going to, I'll give them full credit for it. But then
what? How easy is it going to be to *collect* the taxes?"

He winced.

Mary's half-grin twisted still further. "You know as well as I do—you ought to, John, as many accountants as you had on your payroll—how energetically they're going to try to dodge the bullets. And they'll have all the advantages you didn't have. A poorly educated civil service, for starters—not like those sharpies in the IRS, you can be sure of that—a population which doesn't even consider it 'corruption' unless the stealing takes place in broad daylight—"

Now, he was scowling. He understood her point, and perfectly. After all, he *had* spent untold hours closeted with his accountants and tax lawyers, in years gone by, figuring out every angle to shave money from his tax bill. But . . .

Even in his day and age, up-time, with all the complex dodges a highly industrialized and well-educated society provided, the key to efficient tax collection had been the basically cooperative attitude of the tax-*payer*. Sure, everybody would look for the legitimate loopholes. But, in truth, not all that many people really tried to break the law outright. Especially when—

"Jesus, you're right," he whispered. "Give them a *legal* loophole . . ."

"At last. The dawning light." Her smile was positively serene. "You let me trot around and show all those noblewomen how their husbands can swindle the emperor all the way to their opera houses—as founding contributors, of course, they'll be entitled to their own box seats—and they'll cough up the money he needs for his soldiers and his ironclads. Gladly enough, believe me. They won't want any surly foreigners sailing up the river to interrupt their parties. And Gustav Adolf doesn't really lose anything in the process, because—you know this as well as I do—he'd never get his hands on that money anyway. They'd hide *that* much from him, be sure of it. So why not have them hide it in broad daylight? And, while you're at it, provide this place with universities and art institutes and musical centers—which anybody can use, after all—and also make them feel like they're *important*. A part of it, not just the sheep that got shorn."

He stared up at her. Then, rose abruptly to his feet.

"Let's try it. What the hell." He took her coat off the rack by the door and held it up. "Come on."

"Where are we going?"

"Radio station at the naval base. I'm going to call the President. If the idea comes from him, Gustav Adolf will listen."

434 *David Weber & Eric Flint*

"It's the middle of the night!"

"So what? It's not far to walk."

Still, she hesitated. Simpson gave her that same twisted half-grin.

"Come on, Mary. In for a penny, in for a pound. We're living in the middle of the so-called 'radical district,' in case you didn't know. Sure, those CoC youngsters are just barely this side of ruffians. They rub me the wrong way just looking at them. But I'll give them one thing: this is the *only* part of the city that's pretty much crime free."

Harshly: "They call it 'knee-capping.' Except they do it with a hammer instead of a gun. That's the established penalty for robbing or stealing. First offense. You don't want to know where it goes from there. Let's just say it ends up in the Elbe and leave it at that."

Mary's eyes were wide. "You're kidding." She turned to face the door, her expression apprehensive, as if worried that wild-eyed anarchists would break in any moment.

"No, I'm not kidding. But"—this with a bit of a chuckle—"I assure you that *we* don't have to worry about them. Say whatever else, those CoC roughnecks approve of the United States. The Navy in particular, I think, the way I see them coming down to the wharf all the time to admire the ironclads."

He helped her on with her coat. "I don't approve of their conduct, of course. But I also never hesitate to walk home from the naval base after dark. I guess it's not a perfect world, is it?"

She was still wide-eyed when he opened the door for her, after taking up a lamp. "'Knee-capping,'" she muttered. "That never happened in Pittsburgh. Well. Not in *our* neighborhood."

"No, it didn't. On the other hand, I can also remember you complaining that the courts coddled criminals. No danger of that happening *here*."

By the time they neared the naval base, picking their way slowly in the light shed by the lamp in Simpson's hand, Mary's apprehension seemed to be fading away. Simpson realized now that she'd never made this walk before. Not at night, at least. So she, unlike him, was not accustomed to its . . . peculiarities.

Young people—most of them young men—standing on street corners with their hands in their pockets, was not the sort of thing which people of John and Mary Simpson's class were accustomed to look upon with favor. Especially in a city which had no streetlights. But, after the first two such little groups did nothing more than nod politely, Mary began to relax. By the time they reached the third and largest group, standing not far from the entrance to the navy yard, Simpson decided it was time he put his own lingering doubts to rest.

So, as they drew alongside the cluster of half a dozen people, five young men and a girl—teenagers, half of them—Simpson came to a halt. The murmured conversation among the youngsters died away and one of the group, a man in his twenties, stepped forward a pace or two.

"Excuse me. My name is John Simpson and I'm—"

"We know who you are, Admiral," the young man said softly. He nodded his head politely to Mary. "Frau Simpson. My name is Gunther. Gunther Achterhof. I am in charge of this district. What may I do for you?"

*In charge? 'District'?* Simpson was taken off-balance for a moment. Then cleared his throat and said:

"My wife may, in the future, wish to come down to the shipyards. I would appreciate it if you would . . . ah . . ."

Achterhof smiled, his crooked teeth gleaming in the lamplight despite the dark spots left by caries. "We can provide her with an escort, if you wish. But there's really nothing to fear. Your house is under guard at all times. Even when you are not there, since Frau Simpson arrived in Magdeburg."

Simpson stared at him. Mary was practically goggling at him. Her German was good enough to follow the conversation.

"The enemies of the revolution. Richelieu has agents everywhere—Ferdinand and Maximilian too. Desperate and vicious men. They will stop at nothing."

Achterhof added a word in German which Simpson did not recognize. From the venom roiling under the syllables, he suspected that it was the CoC's version of slang terms which had been found throughout history when the anger of the long-downtrodden began to congeal and harden. *Sasenach. Bouzhoi. Honkie.* Sometimes national, sometimes racial, sometimes simply a matter of class. The simple definitions of people who had had *enough!*—and were none too concerned about the fine points.

"The United States, of course, is their most feared and hated enemy. So—" Gunther shrugged. Or, it might be better to say, shifted his shoulders into a fighter's stance. "We guard."

There seemed nothing further to say. Simpson realized, suddenly, that he would never really understand how to talk to someone like this. So . . .

*Let Stearns deal with them. He can, I can't. I'll deal with the Navy. That I know how to do.*

He nodded, murmured a few words of thanks, and went on his way.

"He seems a nice enough young man," said his wife hesitantly.

"Mary, he is absolutely nothing of the sort. On the other hand, he's on *our* side."

After a few more steps, she said, "Best figure out how to keep him there, then. I'm telling you, John. *Culture.*"

The radio operator was on duty of course, but he was obviously surprised to be called upon. As a rule, since reception was always best in the hours after sundown, the radio was only used then. But, with the higher power and full-sized antennas available to the radio stations in Magdeburg and Grantville, radio communication was quite possible at any time.

"Uh, sir," said the radioman as Simpson gave him the opening words of the message, "the President'll still be asleep. I send this 'urgent top priority' they'll—"

"I know how to tell time, sailor," rasped the admiral. "And I don't recall asking for your opinion. Just send it. If the President loses some sleep—"

He bit off the next words. *Serve the bastard right, all the sleepless hours he's caused me.* He realized, even if still only dimly, that he was going to have to stop calling Mike Stearns *the bastard.* Even under his breath.

"Do as you're told."

"Yessir." The sailor hastened to comply.

Two hours later, the sailor's eyes were no longer bleary with sleep. Indeed, by now he was downright astonished. Not so much by the content of the messages flying back and forth—most of which he barely understood to begin with—but simply by the fact that it was happening at all.

*Nobody's gonna fucking believe this. Not even about the Old Man, much less Mrs. Pruneface. And she's doing most of the talking.*

By dawn, it was over. The radio operator, now too tired to be astonished any longer, handed over the final transmission from the President.

WILL SEND PROPOSAL TO EMPEROR. EXPECT HIM AGREE ALSO. U.S. INFLUENCE HIGH RIGHT NOW. SUSPECT VERY HIGH.

COMING UP MYSELF, AS YOU SUGGEST. AGREE THAT WITH CRISIS LOOMING, APPEARANCE OF UNITY AS ESSENTIAL AS FACT ITSELF. WILL BRING VERONICA DREESON, IF SHE AGREES. PROBABLY WILL. TOUGH OLD BIDDY. APPROVES HIGHLY OF MRS. SIMPSON ALSO.

"That seems to be it, sir."

Simpson passed the message over to his wife, smiling about the last two sentences. He'd suspected it was true, as hard as it was to believe. Granted, Veronica had married Henry Dreeson, the mayor of Grantville. However, she was also the grandmother of Gretchen Richter—and Richter's dislike of the Simpsons was well-known.

But Veronica Dreeson had wound up traveling with his wife, when Mary had finally moved up from Grantville. Having established a school in Grantville, Veronica had been bound and determined to set up a branch of it in the new imperial city. Odd as it may have been, in the days of their shared journey up the rivers, the two women had discovered they had several things in common. First, firm convictions on the subject of child discipline. Second, a passion for setting up schools. Third—probably most important—the mutual esteem of tough old biddies.

Mary, new to the city herself and—it was obvious to Simpson now, looking back on it—mired in a quiet, deep depression, had still done what she could to help Veronica's project. Apparently the experience had left Veronica with as high an opinion of Mary as Mary had of her. Which, given the new situation, probably boded well for Veronica's ambitions.

Mary smiled also, reading the message. But, by the time her husband rose, the smile was gone.

"That's it then, Mary. We've done all we can. It's late—early, I should say. We need some sleep."

"No, John." She shook her head firmly. "There's still one last message to send. And this is not a message that can be sent to 'Mr. President.' It's a message that has to be sent to Mike Stearns. Our son's brother-in-law."

She took a deep breath, her nostrils flaring. "If you can't do it, I will."

Simpson sighed. Then, turned to the radio operator.

"Last message. Address this one, 'Dear Mike.'" Simpson almost laughed, seeing the man's efforts to keep a solemn face. *They'll never believe this in the barracks. What, sailor, you think I don't know that you'll gossip about the Old Bastard?*

"Dear Mike," he dictated. One glance at Mary told him not to try compressing the language for the sake of transmission brevity. "Mary and I would much appreciate it if you would do what you can . . ." He groped for the words. Then just said, quietly: "We'd like our son to speak to us again. We miss him. Thanks, John."

The reply came back immediately.

WILL DO MY BEST. MY WORD ON IT.

"As much as I can ask," said Simpson quietly, handing it over to Mary.

"He'll keep his word," she said. Even confidently.

"Oh, yes. He's quite good at that, actually."

On the way back to their house, walking much faster in the light of daybreak, Simpson spoke only twice.

"I *still* don't like the man."

"Of course not," replied Mary, matter-of-factly. "What is there to like? Yes, he'll keep his word. But, beyond that . . ."

Her breath steamed in the cold morning air. "He's crude and uncouth—he is, too; his language is vulgar beyond belief—I hate the way he panhandles everybody, shifts his language to suit the crowd—fancy here, as good-ole-boy as you could ask for over there—ruthless as a snake; just as brutal, too, when it comes to infighting. Devious, manipulative, a backroom horse trader and wheeler-dealer with the scruples of a carnival huckster fleecing the crowd—I could go on and on."

She took a long, slow breath, steaming into Germany's autumn. "But I won't, John. Not any more. And the reason I won't is because *I* majored in history in college. And there is this little nagging voice in my head that is reminding me how much proper society detested another president the United States once had. And for exactly the same reasons. He was a crude bumpkin from the sticks, with a low sense of humor—and undoubtedly the most capable politician the country ever produced. I think it was the last part they hated the most. Couldn't forgive, anyway."

Simpson's knowledge of history was, in general, not the equal of his wife's. But there were some exceptions, especially when it came to American history. Given Simpson's own brown-water experience in Vietnam, he'd read a great deal on the Civil War. He'd been mainly interested in naval history, of course, especially the use of gunboats on the interior rivers. But, obviously, studying the Civil War involved constantly running across a certain famous politician.

"You *can't* be serious," he protested. "How can you possibly compare Mike Stearns to—to—"

She just gave him a sideways stare. He never did finish the sentence.

# Part VI

*Those dying generations*

# Chapter 38

The last few miles were the worst.

Eddie Cantrell was quite certain he'd never been so exhausted in his entire life. He stood watching as the long, worn-out column reached more or less level ground south of Wismar at last and rubbed his eyes wearily.

Thank God Gustavus' canal-building crews had begun their efforts by hacking out a roadway (of sorts) to parallel the channel's course from Lake Schwerin to Wismar Bay! Without that, the entire trip would have been impossible . . . or, at least, so difficult trying to make it wouldn't have been worth the effort. He'd been this way once before already since Becky's warning had reached Grantville, but this time was different. *Very* different.

Louie Tillman's Chris Craft groaned past him on its improvised cart, fiberglass hull lurching as the clumsy wooden wheels found every uneven spot in the muddy, crudely graded roadbed. A long line of horses stretched out in front of it—thirty or forty of them, he couldn't really remember which in his exhausted state—and harness creaked as they leaned into it. Nor were they the only source of motive power. Scores of men, virtually all of them civilians from Wismar, conscripted for the task by the small garrison of Swedish troops Gustavus had left in the city, heaved and grunted right alongside the draft animals.

That launch had a dry weight of just over three tons. Intellectually, Eddie had known all along that 17th-century Europeans were accustomed to moving such weights by brute muscle strength. After all, some of their heavier artillery pieces weighed at least half again as much. But that knowledge had been dry and theoretical, harvested from histories of events long past. Even now, after two years here, he hadn't been prepared to see something the sheer size of Tillman's launch moving, however slowly and clumsily, under nothing but the power of straining muscle and sinew.

"How much longer, do you think?" a weary voice asked beside him, and he turned to look at the speaker.

"I'd guess another six to ten hours," he replied, and Jack Clements shook his head.

"Have to say I thought you were out of your mind to try it," he admitted. "Of course, I'd already decided you and Mike were *both* out of your minds to even contemplate something this crazy. I never thought we'd make it as far as the lake, much less cross-country from this end of it." His thick thatch of white hair gleamed in the gradually strengthening light of a very early dawn, and his face was etched with deep lines of fatigue as he shook his head again.

"Never thought *you'd* make it as far as the lake?" Eddie snorted. "Hey, you had the easy part! At least you got to use internal combustion engines! Best I could do was steam. And not very good steam, either!"

"If you think getting those monsters down the Saale was 'easy,' internal combustion or not, you're out of your frigging mind, whippersnapper," Clements riposted with a tired chuckle.

Eddie grinned back at him. He hadn't known Clements very well before the Ring of Fire, but all of Grantville's younger people had been fond of him. Despite his own age, rapidly approaching that of mandatory retirement, Clements had spoken up for their interests before several meetings of the Grantville town council. He'd also been a member of the local school board, where he'd done his best to ensure that the board considered how the *students* might feel about the various issues which came before it.

"Damn," Clements continued, kneading the sore muscles of his back, "but that river is one shallow son-of-a-bitch. Couldn't even begin to tell you how many times we grounded. Even as slow as we were taking it, there was a time or two when I thought we'd never get Watson's Folly to float off again. Good thing Frank sent the zodiacs along. At least I could send them out ahead with Al's fishing fathometer to look for the really shallow spots." He shook his head. "Even then . . ."

His voice trailed off as Watson's Outlaw came creaking and groaning along in the Chris Craft's wake. The huge, angular slab of fiberglass loomed above the men and horses straining to move it, and Clements grunted.

"George Watson," he declared roundly, "is even stupider than I ever thought. Putting that monster," he pointed at the rakish hull, "on any river—except maybe the Mississippi or the Amazon!—is like trying to use a transfer truck for a golf cart. The damned thing is a speed machine, pure and simple. Sure as hell whoever designed it never expected some landlocked hillbilly to plunk down umpty-ump thousand dollars for it!" He snorted derisively. "Course, only a lunatic would've done it, lottery win or not."

"Maybe," Eddie agreed, then he grinned again. "All the same, I've got to admit I always really wished I could take it out and play with it myself. Seemed unfair someone like George had it sitting behind his house all that time."

"That's because your poor teenaged brain is too awash in testosterone for rational thought," Clements told him. "Besides, you'd probably have killed yourself with it in nothing flat." He hawked and spat on the ground while he absently massaged his chest with one hand. "I know you kids. You'd have taken that over-powered bastard out on a river somewhere and shoved the throttles to the stops, wouldn't you?"

"Well . . ."

"Sure as hell that's what you would've done. And when you did, you really would have killed yourself. Trust me, Eddie—comparing that son-of-a-bitch to any bass boat or ski boat you've ever handled is like comparing an F-16 to some Piper Cub." He shook his head. "I spent eight years in the Coast Guard when I was about your age, son. Put in a lot of time handling small craft, and I've owned half a dozen good-sized boats of my own since. But this sucker is like a rocket on slick grass."

"Then I guess it's a good thing Frank and Mike sent you along, isn't it?" Eddie chuckled. "Without you to drive it, we'd have to trust Larry with it."

"*Larry Wild?*" Clements shuddered. "Eddie, I've *seen* him steering a ski boat. Trust me, it would be like . . . like giving Hans Richter a Corvette!"

"Nothing could be like giving Hans a Corvette," Eddie replied firmly. "Personally, I always figured the best thing about Jesse's teaching him to fly was that at least in the air there's nothing he can run into!"

" 'Cept the ground," Clements agreed.

"Well, yeah," Eddie conceded. "On the other hand, Jack," it still felt . . . odd to him to be calling Clements anything besides "Mr. Clements," but officially, he actually outranked the older man, "it'd probably be a good idea for you to check Larry and me both out on the Outlaw." Clements raised both eyebrows, and Eddie shrugged. "Well, Larry, at least. Seems pretty obvious that it's going to be our 'flagship,' " he pointed out. "It's the biggest, fastest thing we've got. And Mr. Ferrara managed to put together an eight-cell launcher for her, and we can carry at least three or four complete reloads in the cabin. The Chris Craft and your boat are both slower, and they're both completely open-cockpit designs, too." He shook his head. "That's going to make stowing extra ammunition dicier. Too much chance of the exhaust from one launch touching off the backup rounds. So seems to me it only makes sense to have a backup driver just in case, well . . ."

He shrugged again, but this time the gesture carried a completely different meaning.

Trying resolutely to ignore the ache in his chest, Jack Clements looked at the young man standing beside him with his denim jacket buttoned against the October chill. The youngster could have used a shave, he thought. And for all the gold bars pinned to the collar of his plaid shirt, he looked like exactly what he was—a kid who'd stopped being a teenager less than two months ago. But there was nothing particularly kidlike about the eyes watching the Outlaw dragging its way past them. Or about the thoughts behind those eyes at this particular moment.

"Of course," Clements said after a moment, his voice deliberately light, "the proper Navy term is 'coxswain,' not driver, you ignorant lout."

"Coxswain, driver—whatever," Eddie allowed with a dismissive wave of his hand.

"Jesus, and you a full lieutenant!" Clements shook his head. "I see I'd better take you in hand and teach you what's what Navy-style before Admiral Simpson has to do it."

Colonel Holtzmüller tried not to hover anxiously as Lieutenant Cantrell and Lieutenant Clements oversaw a rowdy gang of dockside workers. In Clements' case, it was apparent that he actually understood what he was doing. Lieutenant Cantrell's expertise was less obvious, but his German was far better than Clements'. No doubt that had made him particularly valuable to the American Admiral Simpson in Magdeburg, and it certainly stood him in good stead now, as well.

"*Achtung!*" he shouted as Clements made a frantic hand-sawing gesture. "Ease up on the left line!" he added, and Clements heaved an unmistakable sigh of relief as the thirty-three-foot boat slid stern-first into the waters of Wismar Harbor.

Holtzmüller heaved a deep breath of relief of his own. Personally, he had his doubts about this entire project. His king's orders had stripped his garrison to the bone—at the moment, he had fewer than three hundred troopers from his own regiment, whereas manning the extended fortifications the Swedes had erected around Wismar's original walls required a minimum of almost four thousand. Even at that, there would be precious little in the way of any central reserve.

He could make up some of the shortfall by impressing civilians from the city itself, plus the crews of any Swedish merchant ships which found themselves trapped in the port when the inevitable Danish blockaders arrived. Even at best, however, that wasn't going to give him the number of live bodies he needed. Worse, Wismar's civilians lacked much of the motivation Protestant cities in other parts of Germany might have had. After all, the Danes were also Protestants—fellow Lutherans, in fact. It hadn't been so very long ago that Christian IV had been the anointed champion of Protestantism. True, he hadn't been very good at it, but he was unlikely—to put it mildly—to indulge his troops in any massacres or introduce a religiously repressive regime if he should take the city. Which meant that any of the local civilians were more likely to be thinking about the consequences to their families' health and their own property rather than fighting defiantly to the death if the siege proved long and arduous.

"All right," Lieutenant Cantrell announced. "Let's get the Century into the water, and we can all take a break."

His labor gang headed for the third of the large speedboats obediently. One or two of its members seemed less than fully enthusiastic, although they were scarcely likely to object with a half-dozen of Holtzmüller's rifle-armed dragoons standing around. The fact that four of Krak's Shooters were also keeping an eye on things didn't hurt, either. But most of the dock workers seemed as fascinated as Holtzmüller himself by the huge, sleek up-time craft floating majestically in the harbor.

Like so many of the Americans' mechanical marvels, the speedboats radiated a refined grace, a fusion of line and form. There was something indefinably "right" about them. Holtzmüller didn't pretend to understand the mechanical principles upon which they operated. Like most of the rest of Gustavus Adolphus' subjects, he was prepared simply to take the Americans' word that they would perform as promised. Yet, just as he could recognize the grace and power of a well-conformed horse, he could recognize those same qualities in these sharply carved, alien watercraft.

The one the Americans called the "Outlaw" was half as large as most of the seagoing merchant vessels anchored in the harbor, and it seemed still larger. Perhaps that was because he'd seen its size and arrogantly shaped hull before its gleaming propellers disappeared into the water.

"That's right!" Lieutenant Cantrell encouraged as Lieutenant Clements said something into his ear and his straining laborers swung the bow of the "Century" around so that they could ease it into the water stern-first. "Keep that stern rope tight, Gunther!" Cantrell admonished a moment later, then scurried over to lend his own weight to the line.

The big boat moved with ponderous grace, simultaneously urged into motion and restrained by the ropes and hands of its attendants. It slid slowly and carefully into the water, and Holtzmüller watched Lieutenant Clements drop down into the open cockpit while mooring lines made it fast to the wharf.

Another work gang, this one headed by no less than three of the up-time Americans, had already swung into action. The wooden wheels of a wagon creaked and clattered across the stone-ballasted quay, and Holtzmüller watched one of the up-timers climb down into the Outlaw.

"Let's get the base mount down here first," the American said. "After that, I guess we need the blast shield." His two fellows nodded agreement and began passing down the first components of the "rocket launcher."

Holtzmüller turned away with a mental shake of his head. In the end, he knew, it was going to be a race between whatever forces General Torstensson found to replace his own stolen garrison and the Danes. And it was going to be up to these Americans and their outlandish devices to buy time for Torstensson to win the race. On the face of it, the notion that so few men—less than sixty, even counting the native Germans assigned to the American reinforcements—could delay a force the size the Danes were bound to throw against Wismar even temporarily was ludicrous.

But Holtzmüller recognized confidence when he saw it; perhaps even more importantly, he'd seen enough bravado to know when "confidence" was only another word for desperation. These bizarre Americans truly believed they could slow the Danes down enough to make the difference. And as he looked back at the harbor one last time, at those white "fiberglass" hulls and the ungainly framework of the "rocket launcher" already taking form on the Outlaw's foredeck, he actually found himself believing that perhaps—just perhaps—they might be right.

Perhaps.

"I assure you, Compte, that we will move as soon as possible," Captain-Admiral Aage Overgaard told the insufferable Frenchman.

"I accept your assurance, of course, Admiral," the compte de Martignac replied with exquisite politeness. "My only concern is that the season grows late. It is already the second day of October. We do not have many weeks left before my own ships and those of Admiral Tobias must return to their home ports."

"I am well aware of how hard our Northern winters can be," Overgaard assured him. "And, in all honesty, I am fully as impatient as you are yourself. Unfortunately, as I am certain you are aware, it was impossible for anyone to predict precisely when the Spanish and Dutch would meet in combat." He did not add "and you and your fine English colleague could betray the Hollanders," although he felt quite sure Martignac heard the unvoiced thought, anyway. "Because of that uncertainty, we dared not press our own preparations too openly. Gustavus, and especially that devil of a chancellor, Oxenstierna, have spies everywhere. Had we made it apparent that we were preparing an expedition, they would quickly have divined our intentions, which could been disastrous. Their navy is very nearly a match for our own, and the first thing Fleming and Gyllenhjelm would have done would have been to seek a decisive engagement with us before you could sail to reinforce us. Even had they failed in that purpose, Gustavus would have been given sufficient warning to redeploy his troops to meet us."

"That much is understood. Yet my fear is that if our blow is delayed much longer, that delay will have the same effect as fore-warning them might have. By now, word of Dunkirk must have reached Magdeburg, and Gustavus will already be redeploying his forces."

"Of course he is," Overgaard acknowledged. "And that is a less than good thing in many ways. Yet even Gustavus must have been prey to at least a brief uncertainty as to our intentions. No doubt he is repositioning his forces, but it will take him some time to move significant numbers of them. Moreover, our own spies' reports indicate that he has personally undertaken command of the garrison at Luebeck."

"He has?" Martignac's gaze sharpened suddenly, and Overgaard nodded.

"He has. And if he truly intends to hold that city, then he will be forced to reinforce its garrison. Which means he must strip forces from other positions . . . like Wismar, Rostock, and Stralsund."

"I see," Martignac said slowly.

"I'm sure you do," Overgaard agreed. "If Gustavus chooses to pen himself up in Luebeck, so much the better. It is he, and he alone, who binds this Confederated Principalities of Europe together. And it is he alone who stands protector to the Ameri-cans. If he can be swept from the board, then all he's managed to build must come tumbling down. In which event, of course, my king will become master of the Baltic once and for all, and yours will have what he seeks elsewhere."

"An alluring prospect, indeed," Martignac observed. "And if he is given time to draw the garrisons from those other northern ports into Luebeck, then he denudes them of their own defenders."

"Exactly. We have no intention of delaying a moment longer than we must, but neither are we blind to the possible advantages accruing from our unanticipated delay. It would have required true magic for him to have learned about the Battle of Dunkirk quickly enough to issue his movement orders in time to cover the rest of the North German coast. At the moment, the troops he had cov-ering Wismar are undoubtedly most of the way to Luebeck, which is unfortunate in some ways. It effectively removes any possibil-ity of our convincing the city to surrender without resistance, and it also means that his garrison there will be sufficiently strong to foreclose any chance of seizing it by a sudden assault. No, Compte. Luebeck will require a siege now, and the army required to prosecute that siege is completing its embarkation even now. As is the second army which will reinforce Gotland to provide us with a base for the investment of Stockholm when the time comes.

"But the same moves which have strengthened Luebeck have weakened him everywhere else along the coast. We will be able to move in almost unopposed and secure control of all the ports well before he is able to assemble the forces to do anything about it. And with those ports in our hands, his Confederated Principalities will starve and wither like a tree cut off from its roots."

# Chapter 39

"Melissa says we should stay put here," Alex said softly, leaning over his wife's shoulder. "I just got her message on the radio. Nothing we can do anyway."

Julie was silent, sitting on a chair next to the bed in their sleeping chamber. Alex was not sure she'd even heard him. The young American woman's face, normally full-cheeked and rosy, was pale and drawn. Her eyes, showing the tension of someone trying not to cry, were fixed on the little figure of their daughter, bundled up and lying on the bed. Alexi was not wailing any longer. The disease had already carried the infant past that point.

He laid a hand on Julie's shoulder, giving it a little reassuring squeeze. At least, he hoped it would be taken as reassurance. Alex had no great expectations himself, although he'd never said so to his wife. He was one of nine children his father had sired, legitimately or otherwise. Only three of his siblings were still alive. Four of them had not made it past the age of five, and three of those had died in their first year. Their little bodies were interred not far away, in the Mackay family's portion of a nearby graveyard.

"I'll never forgive myself if she dies," Julie whispered. "Never." The words sounded hollow. As hollow as the little coffin Alex's father had already ordered his cabinetmaker to construct.

Julie didn't know about that coffin. Neither Alex nor his father had seen any point in mentioning it to her. In this, as in so many things, Julie's history worked against her. She would see the coffin as a prediction, a lack of faith. Where, in fact, it was quite the opposite. It was simply acceptance; practicality in this world, and deep faith in a better afterlife.

*Americans,* thought Alex. *They still think, deep in their souls, that their new world is not quite real.*

It was not a sarcastic thought. That same semi-fantastical view of things was much of what he admired about them—even treasured. None more so than the young American woman he'd married. Still, it often disarmed them.

A strange folk, Americans. Bold in so many ways, timid in others. Daring to go where no sane man would, yet flinching from perils which any sane man accepted as given. Like sculpture, Alex sometimes thought, remembering statues he'd seen years earlier on his tour of northern Italy. Beautiful beyond flesh, serene, confident as only marble can be. Even hard as stone, in some respects. But, like marble, also brittle and easily chipped.

"I'll never forgive myself," she repeated, the tears beginning to leak. "I should have listened to you, and stayed behind. Or at least left her behind."

He'd often had that thought himself. Hotly, even, when he realized that Alexi had been stricken by one of the diseases—which one? God only knows, take your pick—which periodically swept through Edinburgh. As that same sickle swept through every part of the world.

But he'd restrained his temper then, and felt none of it any longer. Such was the nature of things. There was all of human wisdom, if not science. It was not his province, to heap a husband's wrath atop a mother's grief.

He stooped, folded his arms around her and held her close.

"Don't be a fool, love," he whispered into her ear. "She could have been struck down in Grantville also. 'Tis the way of things, that's all. If she dies, we'll have another child. Never forgetting her, of course, and the joy she brought us. But not letting that memory blacken itself either."

Julie started to cry. Slow, quiet sobs. Alex kissed the tears.

"Please, Julie. You have given me so much, this past year, from your future world. Now let me give you some of Scotland. 'Tis God's will, that's all, whatever it be. The child's soul is in no peril, only her mortal sheath. The loss will be ours, not hers. If God chooses to bring her early, 'tis only because He could not bear to wait Himself for the joy of her company."

She turned her head into his shoulder. The tears flowed still, but the sobs ebbed away.

"You think so?" she asked softly.

"Of course," he replied. There was no need to fake assurance now. However much he might have changed in many ways, in this matter Alex Mackay was still a son of Scotland.

"Let me give you some of *my* world now, beloved wife. For the world we are creating will need that also."

"Yes," she whispered. "Yes, it will. Me, most of all."

When Darryl McCarthy entered the prisoner's cell, bearing the spray gun, the prisoner did not flinch. He did not even give him a stony gaze. Simply watched, seeming more curious than anything else.

Darryl waited until he heard the door being barred behind him, then moved quickly over. He reached into a pocket of his poncho and pulled out some batteries.

"Gimme the walkie-talkie," he muttered. "Quick. We haven't got all that much time. I talked the Warders into thinking these cells need regular spraying, but . . ."

He fell silent, while he switched the batteries. They'd recharge the old ones in their suite in St. Thomas' Tower, using the same pedal-operated generator that powered the radio. The batteries in the walkie-talkie were probably still good, but Darryl had no way of knowing how often the English would allow him back into the cell.

"Tell me, if you would," the prisoner said softly, "the nature of your grievance."

Darryl scowled. He made no reply, at first. But then, as he sprayed the cell, began a recitation of the reasons for his anger. By the time he finished, even Darryl was wondering how coherent the explanation was.

"So," mused the prisoner. "Killed half the Irish, did I? Odd, that. Are you familiar with the island? In this day and age, I mean."

Darryl said nothing. His scowl deepened.

The prisoner nodded. "I thought not. I've never been there myself, you understand. But 'tis a well-known place. Full of hills and rocks and little valleys—and precious little in the way of roads. So I am wondering, a bit, how I managed such a fearsome slaughter. How many years did I spend at the task, hunting down all those Irish that I might slay the half of them? And what, exactly, was my purpose in doing so? I've not much use for the Irish, mind you. I'll not claim I love that priest-ridden folk. But I've no fierce animosity against them, either. And it does seem like a great deal of effort for no conceivable good end."

Finished with the cell, Darryl moved over to the prisoner and squatted next to him. "I dunno. I'll find out. Now lift your arms and stretch out your legs. This stuff ought to be sprayed under your clothes, too. Especially wool like you're wearing. Keep your mouth and eyes closed and hold your breath."

He started to continue with an assurance that the DDT wouldn't actually poison the man, but the prisoner followed his orders with no hesitation. Darryl found the man's calmness unsettling. It rattled him some.

After he returned to their suite in St. Thomas' Tower, and put away the spraying equipment, Darryl handed the used batteries to Gayle. Then, he studied Melissa for a moment. As usual, Melissa was sitting on one of the couches reading a book. If nothing else, their imprisonment had given her the opportunity to study texts which would have turned any historian of her time green with envy. The earl of Strafford had been gracious on the matter of giving her access to his own considerable library. Not directly, of course. But he always brought some books on his periodic brief visits.

Darryl did not appreciate the man's courtesy. Not in the least littlest bit. "Black Tom Tyrant," damnation, was not *supposed* to be gracious.

He dismissed, with almost no thought at all, the notion of asking Melissa. She'd inevitably accompany the facts with a lecture. Darryl was in a bad enough mood already.

His eyes ranged down the room, falling on Tom Simpson. The big army captain was standing by one of the windows overlooking the Thames. He was alone. Rita was probably taking a nap, as she often did in the early afternoon.

Darryl made his decision and walked over to stand next to him.

"Weather's clearing," Tom grunted.

Darryl wasn't interested in the weather. Not the world's, anyway. He was preoccupied with the storm front moving through his own heart.

"How long was the son-of-a-bitch in Ireland?" he demanded. "I know you've been reading about him."

Tom swiveled his head and looked down at Darryl. A little smile came to his face.

"What's the matter, Darryl? The real world not matching your blueprint?"

Darryl glared at the river. The sun was out, now, so the Thames had no difficulty at all in glaring back.

"He was in Ireland for nine months," said Tom. "Landed near Dublin in August of 1649. Less than a month later, he took the town of Drogheda and ordered most of the garrison massacred after they refused to surrender once the walls had been breached. That's the incident that's most notorious during his campaign. But—cut the crap, Darryl, you've been living in the seventeenth century for two years now; you know how it works—by the standards of the time that was no war crime."

Darryl kept glaring, but said nothing. By now—long since, in fact—Darryl understood the realities of 17th-century combat. The tradition went back well into medieval times. Once the walls of a fortified town were breached, the garrison was expected to surrender. Further fighting was pointless, after all, since a besieging army which could manage a breach could certainly take the town. The garrison had now proven its courage, well enough, and any further bloodshed would be on their hands.

If the garrison did surrender, quarter was given. If they didn't . . .

Tom had read to him, once, the passage in Shakespeare's *Henry V* where the consequences of refusing to surrender after the breach were spelled out. In very graphic detail, by King Henry V to the defenders of Harfleur. Darryl could still remember the phrase *naked infants spitted upon pikes*.

Harfleur had surrendered.

"The truth is, Darryl," said Tom softly, "by the standards of the time, Cromwell was actually considered to be a merciful soldier. The garrison was put to the sword, yeah, but the civilians were spared. You know damn well that, more often than not, a full-bore massacre follows. In fact—how's this for a little irony?—the only actual *Irish* in Drogheda lived in a ghetto, which Cromwell's men didn't touch. The garrison he massacred was made up of English Catholics. Settlers, most of them, who'd been grabbing land from the Irish themselves."

Darryl's lips tightened. Another precious little certainty gone. Damnation.

Tom's great shoulders moved in a little shrug. "Drogheda's still an atrocity by our standards, of course. But you really can't judge one period of history by the standards of another. And, however savage it was, Drogheda didn't hold a candle to Magdeburg. Which, you might remember, was a massacre carried out by Catholic soldiers.

"And for *that* matter," he continued remorselessly, "you might also want to remember that when the Irish rebellion started in 1641, the rebels slaughtered thousands of Protestants."

"They shouldn't have been there in the first place!" snapped Darryl.

Tom eyed him for a moment. "Yeah, maybe not. But you might want to consider the fact, Darryl—if, just once in your life, you can tear yourself away from self-righteousness—that any American Indian can say exactly the same thing about the whites they massacred from time to time in America. But if that ever stopped *your* ancestors from grabbing the Indians' land, it's news to me. It sure as hell didn't stop mine."

Darryl was back to his silent glaring at the river. The Thames didn't seem to care much. He was starting to regret having asked Tom the question.

The regret deepened, as Tom pressed on.

"Oh, yeah. God, there's nothing in the world like a self-righteous hypocrite. Let me ask you something, Darryl. You know *this* much history. What do people call George Washington? Huh?"

" 'Father of Our Country,' " mumbled Darryl. He dredged up another loose fact. " 'First in peace, first in war, first in the hearts of his countrymen.' "

"Well, not quite. Yeah, that's what *we* call him. But do you know what the Iroquois call him?"

Darryl's eyes widened. The thought of what the Iroquois might call George Washington had never once crossed his mind, in his entire life.

Tom chuckled. "About what I figured. Well, Darryl-me-lad, the Iroquois call him 'the Town Burner.' That's because, during the American Revolution, the Iroquois were allied to the British. Can't blame 'em, really. They knew if the colonists won, they'd be pouring onto Indian land even worse than ever. So good old George Washington threw another coin across the river. He ordered an army under the command of General Sullivan to march into Iroquois territory and crush them. Washington's orders were just that explicit, Darryl. 'The immediate objects are the total destruction and devastation of their settlements.' I remember the exact words, 'cause I was struck by them when I read the history as a teenager. I admired George Washington. And I still do, by the way. But I've also got no use for people who try to sugarcoat stuff like this, when it's done by the 'good guys.' The difference between the good guys and the bad guys isn't always that easy to separate, especially when you look at things in isolation. And it depends a lot which angle you look at it from."

He paused, considering the tight-faced young man standing next to him. "It's a pretty close parallel, actually, as these things go in history. Washington was leading a revolution against the English crown, and he needed to secure his rear. So he did, the way the man did things. Decisively, effectively, and ruthlessly. It worked, too. Sullivan pretty well destroyed the Iroquois as a nation, and drove most of them out of New York. And that's basically what Cromwell did in Ireland. The Irish were King Charles' 'reservoir,' if you will. That's the role they played in those days—these days— for the English monarchy. If the English commons get uppity, just bring over an Irish army to squelch 'em. That was the threat posed to the English revolution—and Cromwell ended it."

"It's not the same thing!" protested Darryl. "Those were Injuns! Wild savages!"

The moment the words went out of his mouth, Darryl regretted them. Not least of all, seeing the way Tom's huge shoulders bunched. But he was relieved to see the man's hands remained clasped behind his back. He'd seen those same hands bend horseshoes, on a bet.

"Don't piss me off, Darryl," growled Tom. The huge captain was now glaring at the river himself. "This much I'll say for my old man—my mother, too. They never tolerated racist shit. That much of their upbringing I don't regret at all."

"I didn't mean it that way," mumbled Darryl. "Hell, Tom, you know I'm not—"

"Oh, shut up, will you?" Tom's glare faded, and he sighed. "Darryl, I know you're not a racist. Although, I swear, sometimes you can do a damn good imitation. But, since we've descended into this little pit, I'm not going to let you off lightly."

He jerked his head toward the east. "What in the hell do you think your precious *Irish* are, in this day and age? Huh? You think Ireland in 1633 is the land of poetry? James Connolly giving socialist speeches before he leads the Easter Uprising?"

Darryl said nothing. Tom's chuckle was dry as a bone. "Fat chance. We're a long ways off from William Butler Yeats and James Joyce, Darryl. Much less James Connolly and his Irish Socialist Republicans. Today—right now—the Irish are every bit as much 'wild savages'—your words, not mine—as any American Indian."

Mercilessly: "It's an island full of superstitious illiterates—sorry, Darryl, but they *are* 'priest-ridden'—whose main export is probably mercenary soldiers. Who have a particularly bad reputation, by the way, for savagery. Ruled over—wherever the English haven't grabbed the land—by the sorriest pack of mangy clan chiefs you'll ever find. Frankly, comparing them to the Iroquois is an insult to the Iroquois. The Iroquois managed to pull together a real confederacy. More than your precious Irish have done! Every one of those so-called 'kings'—and you've got hundreds of them—isn't anything more than a sheep-stealing bandit with delusions of grandeur. The reason the English rolled right over them for centuries is because they could always find one Irish so-called 'king' eager and willing to sell out any other at the drop of a hat."

He stopped, challenging Darryl to contradict him.

But Darryl didn't even try. His romanticism about Ireland was deep, but . . .

That, too, after all, was part of the nationalist tradition he'd been brought up in. "*Such a parcel of rogues in a nation,*" he half-muttered, half-sang.

Tom smiled. "That's actually from a Scot tune, but it's appropriate enough. The Scots in this day and age aren't much better than the Irish. Which, of course, is why the English have usually been able to run them ragged too."

Darryl sighed, and wiped his face.

"For Pete's sake," said Tom, "you don't have to look as if I'm asking for your family heirlooms. I'm not asking you to give it *all* up, Darryl. There's no need to. It's not as if I'm any fan of England's policies in Ireland over the centuries. And if we were in the days of the Men of '98, we'd be playing in a whole different ball game. But we're not. Wolfe Tone won't even be born for another century. At least. So . . . are you willing to listen, for a change? To me, at least, if not Melissa?"

"Yeah. Shoot."

Tom paused, marshaling his thoughts. "What Cromwell did in Ireland, for those nine months, was crush a rebellion allied to King Charles that threatened the revolution he was leading. He carried out the campaign the way the man did everything. I told you once before, he was one of the greatest generals of his day. And he didn't have any time to waste, because he needed to get back to England as soon as possible. So, he went through Ireland like a thunderbolt. Mostly, it was a string of sieges. None of the Irish rebels—who were mostly English Catholic settlers, by the way, not Irishmen the way you mean the term—wanted to face him in the field. Don't blame 'em. Nobody did, after Marston Moor and Naseby, except maybe Prince Rupert.

"Speaking of whom . . ." Tom's eyes moved back to the Thames and grew a bit unfocused. "Hm. I wonder what'll wind up happening to him, now? Hell of a guy, Prince Rupert. He's King Charles' nephew, by the way. Thirteen or fourteen years old, right at the moment, if I remember right."

"'Bout Cromwell," gruffed Darryl.

"Yeah. Well, anyway, it was all over within nine months. There was another bad massacre at Wexford in October. About two thousand people died. Some of them were civilians, including women and children fleeing the town, who drowned when the boats they were in capsized. But it doesn't seem that Cromwell himself ordered that massacre, the way he did at Drogheda. From what the historians can figure out, his troops ran into resistance inside the town after the garrison was supposed to have given up, and ran wild. On the other hand, there's also no evidence that Cromwell tried to stop it, or gave much of a damn afterward. He was a hard man, no doubt about it, even if he wasn't deliberately cruel. And he had good reason to be, frankly, because if the royalists had won they would have been a lot more savage than he was. Don't ever believe any of this crap about the sweet English aristocracy, Darryl. Take a look at what the English did to the Scot Highlanders after Culloden, you don't believe me."

Darryl snorted. As if *he'd* be likely to have fond thoughts about English kings and noblemen!

Tom grinned. "Coal to Newcastle, I guess, saying that to you. And the 'harrowing of the glens' after Culloden happened in the eighteenth century, during the so-called Enlightenment. So you can just imagine what *this* century's royalist revenge would have been like. As it was—ha!—after the Restoration, the silly buggers dug up Cromwell's body and beheaded his corpse."

Darryl made a face. "You're kidding."

"Nope. That's a big part of Cromwell's reputation, of course.

The English establishment had their own big grudge against the guy, over the next few centuries, so they were hardly likely to object about what the Irish nationalists did to blacken his name."

Tom thought for a moment. "Other than that, from what I can determine, all the legends about Cromwell's 'butchery' are just that. Legends. The truth is, Darryl, that Cromwell was known to be merciful, as they count such things in this day and age. He generally offered good terms to towns which surrendered—and kept his word. His soldiers, in Ireland as they had been in England itself, were the best-disciplined troops in these islands. Probably anywhere in Europe, in fact, except for maybe Gustav's Swedes. Like Gustav, Cromwell would hang a man for plunder or rape or murder."

The thick shoulders made that somewhat awesome movement that did Tom for a shrug. "I'm not trying to pretty him up, Darryl. He was a hard man, like I said. And 'merciful' by the standards of the seventeenth century isn't all *that* merciful. You know that as well as I do. He'd execute the officers of a garrison that fought too long, for instance. Did that more than once. But I can't see anywhere in the books I read where he did it out of any ingrained viciousness. He had a revolution to fight and win, and he was damn well going to do it. If that meant shooting or hanging some royalist officers to encourage those in the next town to surrender faster, he'd do it. And . . . just as with Sullivan's campaign up the Hudson, it worked. Nine months and it was all over. He took ship for England and never came back to Ireland for the rest of his life.

"He traumatized the Irish, sure enough. But it was mainly just because his campaign was so decisive and effective. And I think as the years went by—the centuries, actually—the Irish read back into the memory of that frightening military campaign everything that happened later. But . . . come on, Darryl. Fair's fair. Blaming Cromwell for the Irish potato famine and the cold-blooded shooting of James Connolly and Bloody Sunday and the men behind the wire and all the rest of it makes as much sense as blaming George Washington for the massacre at Wounded Knee."

Darryl wasn't going to let go that easily. "Well, yeah, sure. But don't tell me there isn't any connection."

"Of course there's a connection. If Cromwell hadn't crushed the Irish rebellion in 1650, maybe the potato famine wouldn't have happened. Then again, maybe it would have. Hard to say for sure. But cause and effect isn't that simple, Darryl. I can't remember the terms any longer—been some time since the course on philosophy I took in college—but there's a difference between a direct cause and something that sets up the conditions for it.

"And why am I telling you this?" Tom snorted. "Darryl, cut the bullshit. You may not have studied philosophy in college, but I know you've rebuilt plenty of engines. So don't pretend you don't understand the difference."

Darryl didn't argue the point. He *did* understand the difference. Any good car mechanic understood it. *The reason your piece-a-junk car's not running is such-and-such. The reason your car's a piece-a-junk in the first place is because you're a sorry goofball who never bothered to change the oil.*

"Aw, hell," he sighed. "I just don't know what to think any more."

Tom smiled. "Well, you're hardly alone in *that.* Neither do I, most of the time. But . . ." He paused, breathing in and out for a few seconds. Then, continued in slow and soft words.

"Here's what I think about all this, Darryl. I think we ought to avoid making the mistake all these goofy kings and cardinals are making. I don't think we can 'read history' any better than anybody else."

He gave Darryl a glance. "You with me so far?"

"Yeah, sure. I agree." And he did, too. That much he could say firmly.

"Then why don't we start by forgetting all about some guy named 'Oliver Cromwell'? Who lived in another universe, and did this-and-that when he was a man in his forties and fifties, under the conditions of another world. Why don't we concentrate instead on the man *we* know, a little bit, at least—in this world that we've been busy as bees trying to change. The man who's squatting in a cell not far from here. How's that grab you?"

Darryl thought about it, for a moment. "Okay. I'll buy that."

"Then let's consider *that* man. A man in his early thirties, who's done nothing so far in his life except irritate his king in a parliament a while back, raise a family—raise 'em well, too, not even his enemies ever tried to claim Cromwell wasn't a good family man—and led some dirt-poor fenmen in their fight against a bunch of land-grabbing rich gentry in his part of England. Who now finds himself in a dungeon because a genuinely foul and treacherous and stinking-rotten king of England is scared of what he might do years from now. Filled with grief because his wife and son were murdered before his very eyes. You got a problem with *that* man, hillbilly?"

The clarity came with relief. "Hell, no. My kinda guy."

"Yeah, that's what I figured. Mine too. To hell with 'predesti-nation,' Darryl. A man is what a man does—what *he* does. And there's an end to it."

"I'm with you on that. All the way."

Darryl stuck out his hand. Tom's big one closed over it. For a moment, a son of Appalachian coal miners made the power salute with a scion of one of Appalachia's wealthiest families. But Darryl missed the irony of it completely. Tom Simpson, too, had long since become his kinda guy. And Darryl, whatever his other faults, was one of those country boys who didn't look back.

"So. We gonna spring him, then? For real?"

"That's the plan." Tom shrugged. "Whenever we decide to spring ourselves, anyway. Won't be for quite a while, though, if ever. Mike told us to stay put till we hear otherwise. If nothing else, we're a source of valuable information. Besides, winter's coming. I don't know about you, but speaking for myself—"

Tom grinned wryly, and gestured with his head toward the fireplace which dominated the room. It was a big fireplace. A king-sized one, actually. In real and actual fact, not the fancies of Madison Avenue. Three hundred and fifty years earlier, King Edward I had warmed his bones before its flames.

Darryl made a little thumbs-up. "I'm with you there, too. Screw winter. Spring's when a young man's fancy turns to wine, women and taking it on the lam."

Tom smiled and clapped Darryl on the shoulder. Fortunately, he didn't put much into it. "So. Any other questions?"

Darryl's brow wrinkled. "Well, yeah, now that you mention it. I mean—I'm not objecting, you understand—but, uh, given what you just said, why *are* we planning to spring the guy? It's a bit risky, and if he's nobody in *this* universe—" Darryl's lips tight-ened. "Not that I'm worried about the risk. Piss on these sorry English bastards. But . . ."

Tom's smile was now serene. "I said I didn't believe in *predes-tination*, Darryl. I do, on the other hand, believe in personal *character*. So does Melissa." He gestured with his thumb toward the Chapel Tower, where Cromwell was immured. "And that man has character coming out of his ears, don't think he doesn't."

The smile faded. "Here's what I do know about the man called Oliver Cromwell, Darryl. His deeds are one thing, the man who could do them, another. And in that other world, he wasn't just a great general. He was also a devoted husband and father. A man who, by the standards of his time, was tolerant on matters of religion. It's not an accident, you know, that Cromwell was the first ruler of England in centuries who considered removing the ban on Jews. Who, once he became dictator of England—more because of circumstance than because of any lust for power—ruled as much as possible with the consent of others." A brief flash of teeth. "Well . . . *some* others. He gave royalists short shrift. Still, he was no autocrat, Darryl. Ruthless he might be, when he felt it necessary. But he was never given to tyranny for its own sake."

Tom paused, studying Darryl. Not for the first time, Darryl was struck by the big man's eyes. An odd shade of gray, they were, pale rather than slate. He'd inherited them from his mother, Darryl knew. Darryl had never cared—not in the least—for the super-cilious look he'd always thought he detected in the mother's eyes. Icy, her eyes were. But in the son, the color was simply very clear. Darryl trusted those eyes.

"He rattled you, didn't he?" Tom asked. "Shook you some."

Darryl swallowed. "Yeah, he did. He just . . . I dunno. Hard to explain. He just always seemed so calm, like. No matter what I said or did to him."

Tom nodded. "Part of that's his faith. Most of it's just him." He turned his head and studied the slowly moving Thames, now gleaming. The sunshine was back. Autumn sunshine, to be sure, but sunshine nonetheless.

"Any world I can think of, Darryl, I think that man will rattle it. Shake the bars of its cage the same way he did those of another world. So, push comes to shove, I think I'd much rather have him on my side than anywhere else."

He gave Darryl a sidelong glance. "Hell, who knows? He might wind up in Ireland yet. Would you rather he went there with or without you?"

Darryl pondered the same river. "No contest," he pronounced firmly. "Just gotta make him a good hillbilly first."

When Darryl told Gayle he'd decided to give up his feud with Cromwell, she smiled.

"Oh, good. That'll save us some hassles. I think I'm starting to get sweet on him."

"*Gayle!*"

❀    ❀    ❀

At the same window, another decision was made. As soon as Rita came up to him, risen from her nap, Tom gave her a smile. It was the same serene smile he'd given Darryl earlier, and he silently thanked the young Irish-American for that serenity. Thrashing through another man's confusion had enabled him to resolve his own.

"You're right. We'll do it the way you wanted."

Rita blew out her breath. "Thank God. For a while there, I was afraid you were gonna turn all fucking upper-crust on me."

Tom chuckled. "You do realize, don't you, that you *will* have to watch your language around her? The 'gonnas' won't cut it, much less the four-letter words."

Rita's grin was as broad and sun-filled as the river, and Tom fell in love all over again. He did that about four times a day, and hoped he would for the rest of his life.

"Sure. So fucking what? My language could use a lot of improvement. I don't mind at all—wouldn't have then, either—if she'll just be *nice* about it."

# Chapter 40

*"Jesus!"* Eddie Cantrell snatched desperately at his seat to keep himself in it as the Outlaw heeled in a sharply angled, sliding turn to port. "You're gonna kill us all, Larry!"

Larry paid him no attention. In fact, it was extremely unlikely that he'd even heard Eddie in the first place. The big cruiser was smashing across the lively outer waters of Wismar Bay at a speed of over forty miles per hour. That had never seemed particularly fast to Eddie driving a pickup truck down a well-paved road. On a chill, gray October afternoon in the Baltic, with white water flying back from a knifelike prow like huge, angry wings and icy spray lashing his cheeks while the shock of the big boat's collision with each succeeding wave slammed through him like a train wreck, it seemed *extremely* fast.

He sat in one of the bench seats at the rear of the cockpit, watching Larry hunch over the big chrome wheel while the huge, twin inboard engines howled against Eddie's spine. At that particular moment all he wanted to do was to strangle his friend. But that would have required him to climb out of his own seat, which was something he had no intention whatever of doing just now.

Larry straightened the wheel, and the boat snarled around onto a new heading. At least there was plenty of open water, so it wasn't like they were likely to run into anything, Eddie consoled himself. And Jack Clements was perched in the left-hand seat, watching

Larry like a hawk. Now if only the hawk would take the wheel back from the lunatic sitting behind it!

"Slow it down, Larry!" Eddie shouted into the wind of their passage. Uselessly, of course. Neither of the two maniacs driving this death machine showed the least interest in anything their putative superior might have had to say. All Eddie could do was grit his teeth, hang on for dear life, and remind himself that it had been his own stupid idea to have Larry "checked out" at the Outlaw's controls. He also tried to find some peace of mind with the thought that Jack *must* know what he was doing, and the old man didn't actually seem too worried himself.

Jack leaned close to bellow something into Larry's ear. Larry nodded, then reached for the throttle quadrant at his right hand. He inched both levers open a little further, cautiously, and the Outlaw lunged ahead, faster than ever. Eddie found himself staring at the ungainly framework of Ferrara's rocket launcher as it bounced up and down, obviously trying to shake itself to pieces. It was ugly as hell, and he hated to think how George Watson was going to react to the gaunt abortion which had been permanently epoxied just forward of the hatches on his pride and joy's once-sleek foredeck. At least the work had been done solidly enough to survive the beating Jack and Larry were giving it, Eddie told himself moodily.

Jack sat back and watched Larry for perhaps another ten minutes, although it seemed much longer to Eddie. Then he slapped the younger man on the shoulder and made a "shut it down" gesture with his other hand. Larry looked up, nodded obediently, and throttled back the howling engines.

The boat lost speed quickly. The repetitive shocks as it leapt across the waves eased, but its motion became even more lively as it lost way and started pitching up and down. Jack waited until they were moving at no more than a few miles per hour, then waved for Larry to get up and took his place at the controls. He cracked the throttles a little wider, to put a bit more speed back onto the boat and ease its motion, then swiveled the comfortable chair around to face Larry and Eddie.

It was hard to believe they were still in the same boat. The ear-smashing bellow of wind, wave, and engine noise had eased into a gentle burble of exhaust, and the furious sense of movement had abated into something that was almost lulling. It was actually possible to hear someone speaking in normal tones, as Jack proceeded to demonstrate.

"All right, boys," he said, paying no attention to their official ranks with no other ears present to hear. "Larry got her up to about forty, forty-five knots. That's about the speed of one of the old World War II PT boats. It's also not a whole hell a lot more than half of what she's capable of."

"*Half?*" Eddie knew the word had come out half-strangled, but he couldn't help himself, and Jack laughed.

"A bit more," he conceded. "In smooth water, this baby will turn out about sixty-five, sixty-eight knots. Call it seventy miles an hour." Eddie's eyes bulged, and he shrugged. "Give us some wave action like today's or maybe a little stronger, and at full throttle you'll get her up to maybe seventy-five miles an hour."

"She's faster in waves than smooth water?" Larry asked.

"Sure. This is basically a racing hull, Larry. Get a little air under it and you reduce drag even further." He shook his head. "George always was an idiot. Oh, I'll agree that getting behind the wheel on something like this can be a hell of a lot of fun, sometimes. I'll go further, and admit I've enjoyed playing with it even under these circumstances. But I'll also say it again—fun or not, this thing is nothing but a speed machine, and I've seen him handling a dinky little fifteen-footer. He'd've killed his sorry ass in nothing flat the first time he cranked her wide open."

"I wouldn't've been surprised, either," Larry said. "I thought I'd seen fast fooling around with Uncle Evan's ski boat, but this thing—!"

"That's the point you need to keep in mind, if it comes down to it," Jack told him soberly. "Truth to tell, I'd sooner never see you behind the wheel for real. Nothing personal, Larry, but this is a lot bigger handful than you're used to. In some ways, she actually handles better at higher speed—that's what she's designed for, after all. And as long as you've got plenty of open water to play with and you're careful, you ought to be all right. But when we actually have to go in against the Danes, we're not going to have a lot of open water. So, while I agree with Eddie that it makes sense to train someone to back me up, I trust you won't be offended by the fact that I hope to hell you never have to do it."

"You and me both," Larry said with a fervor which surprised Eddie. Larry had always been up for the craziest, most risky stunts he or any of the other Four Musketeers had been able to come up with for dirt bikes or skateboards. And if Eddie wanted to be honest, the four of them had also occasionally stepped ever so slightly across the line from driving habits their parents would have been likely to approve. But there was no mistaking the sincere respect in his eyes when he gazed back at the Outlaw's controls.

"Yeah, well," Jack said, "the one other thing you've got to remember here is that people on the other side are gonna be shooting back at us. I know, I know!" He raised a hand as Eddie opened his mouth. "We're gonna be a hard target to hit, especially with those damned smoothbores of theirs. But hard ain't the same thing as impossible, and speed—even the speed this thing can crank out—ain't the same thing as a cloak of invulnerability, either. You two just keep that in mind. And at the same time, you remember you can kill yourselves just as dead with this thing as the bad guys ever could."

"Where are they?" Colonel Karberg muttered.

He'd thought his voice was too low to be overheard as he stood in Luebeck's Teuffelsorth Bastion and gazed down the Trave River toward the Baltic, but the King of Sweden had surprisingly acute hearing.

"I presume you mean the Danes," he observed, and Karberg flushed.

"Forgive me, Majesty," he said quickly. "It was only an idle question, not—"

"Come, my good Colonel!" Gustavus chided. "It was not at all an idle question. It was, if I may be permitted, something of a *burning* question, in fact."

Karberg's flush darkened, and the king chuckled. Karberg looked up quickly to meet his blue eyes, and relaxed as he realized Gustavus had chosen to be amused rather than angered.

"Well, yes, Majesty," the colonel acknowledged. "If I'm honest, I suppose I really must admit it preys upon my mind."

"And mine, Colonel," Gustavus assured him in a tone which was far less amused than it had been. "On the other hand, I'm not inclined to question God's goodness in granting us this delay. This city is as close to prepared to withstand a siege as it could hope to be. In that regard, it's most fortunate that we had made it one of our major supply magazines, because it is as well provisioned as any city awaiting a siege has ever been. And thanks to the advance warning the Americans' radio was able to give us and

Christian's tardiness, our troops are ready here and General Aderkas is no more than a week's march from Wismar."

He smiled, and that smile was thin and cold.

"They've missed their best chance, Colonel. They may still strike in time to secure Wismar, unless the Americans truly are able to work a miracle to stop them. And we cannot, I fear, prevent an attack on Stockholm before winter closes the Baltic. But they will not take Luebeck, and so long as Axel Oxenstierna can draw breath, they will not take Stockholm, either. And when the Americans are ready, and their ironclads enter the Baltic *behind* Christian's ships . . ."

The smile which had been thin and cold became a razor of ice.

As Jesse sized up the situation, there was a very good chance he would die today.

*No, things are much worse that that,* he berated himself. *Odds are you're going to kill yourself, three others, and the whole concept of an Air Force, all at one time.*

He looked over at his copilot, Lieutenant Eugene Woodsill. Woody appeared to be having the time of his life. Right at the moment, he was making faces at Hans and Sharon, who were in the Belle II, just ten yards off Jesse's right wing. He'd been doing it all flight, at first surreptitiously and then, as Jesse hadn't seemed to care, more and more openly.

*Ignorance is friggin' bliss,* Jesse thought, though he didn't bother to make the young man stop. *Time enough for him to be frightened later.*

He understood the young man's high spirits, of course. When the prospect of their first combat assignment had presented itself, Jesse had naturally chosen the two best pilots—himself and Hans— to do the honors. The other pilot officers had been almost inconsolable, especially since the mission required taking both of the Belles, leaving nothing for them to do but study and bother Hal Smith.

Things had changed soon after he and Hans had arrived at the field outside of the coastal town of Wismar, on their first flight up there. The field was a good one. Located on a slight rise above the beach, it was easily equal to the Grantville airfield; large, smooth and covered with short grass, thanks to the local sheep.

There was a somewhat boisterous reunion scene once Jesse and

Hans were down. Eddie Cantrell and Larry Wild were good friends with Hans, whom they'd lived with in the same trailer complex after their best friend Jeff had married Hans' sister Gretchen. But, soon enough, the two lieutenants settled down and gave Jesse a tour of the facilities they'd manage to prepare for the Air Force.

He was genuinely impressed. However rambunctious they might be, the two youngsters had done well, in the short time they'd had available. They'd even erected a makeshift windsock, something which he hadn't expected young naval lieutenants to even think of. They'd also managed to shift a sizable quantity of fuel and rockets up to the field, storing it all in an old shed of some kind. Before the tour was over, Jesse decided to commend them to Admiral Simpson at the first opportunity and told them so. Their boyish grins in response went a long way toward making him forget the misgivings he had about this shoestring operation.

A long way, but not all the way. "Don't get too cocky," he'd warned Hans. "Enthusiasm and hard work will get you far. But the weather doesn't give a damn, just for starters. And you can backslap a handful of rockets and some fuel cans all you want, and tell them how great they are. They're still just a handful of rockets and some fuel cans."

He gave Hans a crooked grin. "Trust me on this one. The engine in your aircraft isn't going to be impressed if you run out of gas, just because you assure it you're still in high spirits."

After unloading the two aircraft, he and Hans had immediately refueled the Belle II and had gone on an area familiarization flight. Jesse would have made that his first business anyway, but he also wanted to impress on Hans that their *main* function up here was to provide the Navy and Gustav Adolf with reconnaissance—not dramatic heroics.

They'd started with a circuit of Wismar Bay, then ventured along the coast to the west, marking their charts all the while, turning north and continuing across to the Isle of Ruegen before returning. They hadn't seen anything larger than a fishing smack the entire flight.

When his early morning flight the following day had given the same results, Jesse had made his decision. They would fly to Magdeburg that afternoon, returning with First Sergeant Tipton and some tools. After all, there was no telling how long they'd have to operate from their remote location. Besides, Lieutenant Cantrell had gotten word over the radio that Mike Stearns and Veronica

Dreeson had arrived in Magdeburg. Jesse wanted a chance to confer briefly with the President and Admiral Simpson one more time, just to make sure nobody had any signals crossed.

And . . .

He'd stared at Hans, standing on the field and gazing out to sea. Such a fine and splendid young man he looked—and was, too. The confidence with which Hans stood there was almost palpable.

Jesse sighed. And that was something else that, all too often, the world didn't give a damn about. At his age, Jesse had no illusions. So he also wanted to give Hans a chance to see his grandmother, for what might be the last time. The tough old biddy, as people tended to think of her, who had shared with his older sister Gretchen the task of mothering him after his own mother vanished into the cauldron of the Thirty Years War.

The wind remained strong out of the south—dead foul for any invasion fleet. Since immediate combat seemed unlikely, Jesse had also decided to bring another pilot to Wismar and left word for Woody to get ready—they'd two hop it to Grantville the next day and get him. And capping all of those fateful decisions, when the son of the Wismar burgermeister suffered a severe head injury while playing near the American speedboats, Jesse had confidently agreed to bring modern medical assistance. He'd like to have that available anyway, in case of casualties.

In retrospect, with Hans involved, he should have counted on that medical aid being Sharon. Still, Jesse hadn't worried overmuch, particularly when he saw the young pilot's joyous face. And after all, what could happen on the flight to Wismar?

*This could happen*, Jesse thought grimly. The barometer had started falling while they were at Grantville, wispy mare's tail clouds had begun to gather in the east while they were at Magdeburg, and the wind had started to shift westerly. A storm was approaching. Fast.

*I should have seen it, damn it*, Jesse told himself. *Winds move counterclockwise around a low pressure area. And this must be one hell of a low.*

They were still okay for the moment, of course. Flying in formation at ten thousand feet, they were in bright sunshine and smooth air. As the three young people enjoyed themselves, Jesse alone had noticed the low clouds closing in behind, then beneath, and now ahead of them. The undercast looked innocent enough, a white, smoothly undulating blanket at about six thousand feet. He wondered how thick it was, realizing it would inevitably get thicker. As he had done every minute for the past half hour, Jesse looked to the western sky and knew he saw death in the distance. Dark, bulky thunderstorm cells, their high tops obscured by flying scud, marched shoulder to shoulder across the western horizon. Any of those cells would be fatal to enter in these aircraft—probably in any aircraft. They had to get on the ground ahead of them. Magdeburg was out of the question. They were well past the equal time point, the point of no return, even with the wind shift.

"Ah-huh." Jesse cleared his throat. "Lieutenant, if you're finished amusing Lieutenant Richter, will you take the stick for a minute?"

"Certainly, sir," Woody said, as he turned a bright pink. "Copilot's aircraft."

Jesse reached for the radio mike, considering how to tell the others. *Hans will need confidence.*

"Two, this is Lead."

Hans answered promptly enough, "Lead, Two."

"Ah, Two, I'm going to push up the power. Pull it in a bit and stay with me."

"Roger, Lead."

Jesse shook the stick. "Pilot's aircraft."

"Pilot's aircraft," came the standard acknowledgement. Jesse felt Woody staring at him. The young man was finally starting to realize that something was wrong.

*Thank God, Hans is flying the Deuce,* thought Jesse, as he pushed the throttle up. *More than enough power to keep up. He's gonna need it.*

With the throttle near redline, Jesse watched the airspeed climb and settle at about 110 knots. *Where the hell are we? At least, Hans is hanging in there.*

"Woody?" Jesse looked over at his copilot.

"Yes, sir!"

"Take the stick for a minute, will you? Stay on this heading and keep your eyes peeled for Lake Schwerin, okay?"

Jesse picked up his whiz wheel and forced himself to concentrate, to not look out to the west. *Assume the wind has blown us, what? Twenty miles east. At a 110 indicated, we must be going . . . Christ, Jesse, this is just guesswork.*

Slowly, deliberately, Jesse reached up and carefully wound the clock on the instrument panel. He tapped the wheel against his teeth and stared at the white clouds below. Referring to the computer again, he made some calculations, checked them, and nodded to himself.

"Woody, turn ten degrees left to a heading of three-four-five degrees."

"Roger, three-four-five."

There was no talking now and Jesse realized that Woody was staring at the wall of clouds off to the left. *Probably Hans and Sharon, too.* A glance in the mirror told Jesse the storm had curled behind them.

No going back now. Time passed slowly, as they raced for the coast. The white undercast stretched endlessly before them. Curiously, Jesse felt calm, as if the bet had been made and he was just waiting for the results of the game. He spent the time thinking about how to get down.

*How deep is it?* he considered. *Maybe all the way down to the ground, but if that's true, who gives a shit? Okay, so there's a ceiling down there, somewhere. Can Hans fly formation in the soup? No formation lights. He's good. But how good? How good are you?*

Jesse rubbed his chin, looked up and stared at the storm, a moving juggernaut looming closer.

*Come and get us, you bastard. If you can.*

He noted the time and checked his kneeboard. Time to go down. He picked up the mike.

"Two, Lead. Hans, bring her up the reference line into fingertip. Just keep your reference marks in place and stay with me. We're going down. One thousand feet per minute. Copy?"

Hans answered promptly, all business. "Copy, Lead. Two's in." He had brought his plane within six feet of the other, slightly behind Jesse's right wing.

Jesse took the stick. "Pilot's aircraft."

The undercast looked peaceful, harmless as they slid down to it. As they neared, it became less smooth, less uniform. Jesse unconsciously braced himself and concentrated on his turn and slip. He deliberately loosened his grip on the stick, using only his fingertips, as they touched the mist.

Darkness. Jesse felt the aircraft heave, buck, as it passed through succeeding layers of cloud. He used a light touch, didn't fight it, small corrections, sought to swim down through it.

*One thousand feet per minute. Ball centered. No bank. Keep it straight. Needle, ball, airspeed, altitude.* His crosscheck became a blur, eyes darting, his mind working, not thinking. *Ball. Airspeed. Bank.* He couldn't tell how long it had gone on. He wasn't steering, he was the aircraft, sliding down ever deeper. Smooth, wingtips bouncing, no rudders, touch of down, now up, down elevator. Gently sinking, sinking. *Airspeed. Needle. Ball.*

Jesse was surprised when he burst out. Over water at 600 feet. *Made it, by God!*

His next thought: "Hans!"

Woody was shouting beside him, "Still there, still there! God, I swear he disappeared a couple of times!"

Jesse didn't have time to be relieved, they weren't down yet. *Heading.* He was shocked to see they were still on heading 345, steady as a rock. He saw land ahead, which could only be possible if . . .

*Mary, Mother of God.* It was the north shore of Wismar Bay. There. The shore battery guarding the entrance to the bay. He'd hit it on the button.

He cleared left and made a gentle turn, rolling out south toward the field. Ten minutes later they were both down.

Jesse switched off and looked out. The first big drops of rain splashed on the Belle's windscreen. He looked over at Woody.

"Lieutenant Woodsill, would you mind getting out the chocks? I think I'll watch the rain for a bit."

"Colonel Wood and Captain Richter are on the ground in Wismar."

Mike looked up quickly at the announcement. John Simpson stood in the doorway of the office Mike had appropriated here in Magdeburg with a folded piece of paper in his hand.

"The radio room just got word from Lieutenant Wild," Simpson continued. "Apparently the weather was closing in and they just got down in time, but they made it safely. I thought you'd like to know."

"You certainly thought correctly," Mike told him, and heaved a deep sigh of heartfelt relief. The pounding rain which had swept over Magdeburg just before sunset had made him more than a little anxious about Jesse and Hans. Wismar was over a hundred miles from Gustavus' capital, so there was a lot of room for local differences in weather. But, judging from the difficulty they'd been having with radio transmission to Holland, the rain seemed to be part of a storm front crossing over a large stretch of northern Europe.

"Sounds like things are looking up in Wismar," he said after a moment.

"Yes," Simpson agreed, but his own expression was much less relieved than Mike's. "At the same time, however, the situation there is scarcely what I'd call secure. Lieutenant Cantrell and Lieutenant Clements seem to have managed rather better than I'd allowed myself to hope they might where jury-rigging the speedboats is concerned. But General Aderkas is still several days from the city. And until he arrives, the prospect for Wismar's managing to stand off a serious Danish attack is hardly a favorable one."

Mike started a quick, caustic retort about how the suggestion which had sent Eddie and Larry to Wismar had come from Simpson in the first place. But the quick comeback died unspoken before the worry in the other man's eyes. Yes, it had been Simpson's idea. But Mike had signed off on it, and he'd done that because it had also been the *right* idea. And if John Simpson was worried about the safety of the men his suggestion had sent into harm's way, then Mike Stearns had no intention of mocking him for it. Particularly not when it was a worry—and a responsibility—he shared in full.

"Yeah," he agreed instead. "We're still hanging in the wind at Wismar. But the situation's getting better, even there. And Luebeck, on the other hand, looks pretty damned secure. Which," he acknowledged, "is largely due to the effort you made to get reinforcements and supplies into the city."

"Only common sense," Simpson replied a bit gruffly. "Like I said, I'm not going to put half of our ironclads out at the end of a supply line which might not be there when they arrive."

"Of course," Mike said.

"And whatever the situation in Luebeck," Simpson resumed in a stronger voice, "the fact remains that we still don't know what the Danes think they're—"

"Excuse me, Admiral. Mr. President." A lieutenant (junior grade) had trotted up behind Simpson. The stocky young German came to attention as Simpson and Mike turned toward him. "This dispatch just came in from Luebeck, sir," the jay-gee said, extending another folded slip of paper to Simpson.

The admiral took it with a crisp nod of thanks and unfolded it quickly. His eyes flipped over the neatly printed lines, then stopped. He raised them to meet Mike's gaze, and his voice was flat.

"A fishing boat just put into Luebeck, Mr. President," he said formally. "According to her crew, the Danes aren't more than an hour behind her."

# Chapter 41

Jack Clements wished, not for the first time, that he was better at languages. Unfortunately, he wasn't. What he really needed right now was Eddie or Larry, or one of the other up-timers who'd acquired sufficient German to explain what he wanted done. He'd had Larry up until a few minutes before, but then the runner had arrived from the radio shack with the news that Larry was urgently needed to supervise an incoming message from Luebeck. Which was how Jack came to be struggling with the Outlaw's rocket launcher and ammunition stowage in the poor illumination provided by dockside torches. His two German assistants were eager enough to help; he just wasn't able to tell them what sort of help he needed, and gestures could only go so far.

He straightened his aching back and beckoned for one of the Germans to climb back up onto the wharf. More hand gestures, and the younger German nodded enthusiastically and began dragging another rocket from the cart parked beside the mooring bollard. In fact, he was rather more enthusiastic about it than Jack might have liked, given the size and weight—and explosiveness—of the projectile. He shook his head, trying to slow the youngster down, but the message clearly wasn't getting through, and he had to jump quickly to catch the heavy rocket before his overeager assistant dropped it straight into the Outlaw's cockpit.

He staggered as the solid weight hit his arms, but he managed to keep his footing and lower the black-powder missile in more or less controlled fashion.

The German on the dock obviously realized, after the fact, what Jack had been trying to get across. His expression was hard to make out in the poor lighting, but what Jack could see of it was—as his wife would have put it—"covered with chagrin." The up-timer chuckled and waved one hand in a reassuring gesture, but he also beckoned for his enthusiastic assistant to give him a moment to catch his breath.

*Not as young as you used to be, Jack,* he told himself, sinking down into one of the Outlaw's luxuriously upholstered seats. *Not even as young as you were when you started out for Halle!* He closed his eyes for a moment, one hand rubbing his chest in an effort to relieve the tightness in his lungs. *Weather isn't helping any, either, he thought irritably. Cold and wet. Gets into a man's muscles and joints. Makes the bastards ache like hell, too.* He rubbed his chest harder. *Still, I can't just sit here all night. We've got too much—*

The pain hit like a sledgehammer. It seemed to explode through his chest like a bomb, and his grunt of anguish was that of a man who'd just been kicked in the belly by a mule. His eyes popped open, and he saw both of his German assistants turning toward him in sudden alarm even as the sledgehammer smashed him again and he felt himself sliding helplessly out of his seat.

"God*damn* it!" Frank Jackson's left fist slammed down on his kitchen table and the knuckles of his right hand went white where it gripped the telephone. He snarled another curse before he could make himself stop, then he paused and drew in a deep breath.

"How bad does it sound, James?" he asked in a more nearly normal voice. He listened again, lips firmly compressed. Then he closed his eyes, and his square shoulders sagged. "Okay," he said. "Okay. I understand. Just . . . let me know if you hear anything else, all right?" He listened a moment longer, then nodded as if the other man could see him. "Thanks. I'll talk to you later."

He hung up the phone very, very carefully, and turned to his wife.

"What is it?" Diane Jackson asked. She'd been heating water to brew tea when the telephone rang. Now she studied her husband's expression with the same eyes which had seen the fall of one homeland, the loss of a second, and the painful birth of yet a third.

"Jack," Frank told her flatly, and his nostrils flared as he inhaled deeply. "Stubborn old bastard. Why the hell didn't he *tell* me he had a heart condition when I asked him to go to Wismar?"

"Don't be foolish," she scolded, and snorted when he looked at her in surprise. "Men! All of you just alike!" She shook her head. "Would you have told you if you'd asked you to go to Wismar?" she demanded.

Despite himself, Frank found himself smiling as she glowered at him. Diane's English sometimes got just a bit . . . convoluted, even after all these years. Not that his was always any great prize, he reminded himself, and shook his head at her.

"Point taken," he conceded. "I'm just as stubborn and pigheaded as he is, I suppose. But, Jesus, Diane! He could've at least warned me there might be a problem instead of leaving it all up to Doc Adams!"

"And if he had, you wouldn't have sent him," Diane pointed out inexorably. "But you needed him. So he didn't tell you." She shrugged.

"Guess you're right," he sighed.

"So," she said. "How bad?"

"James couldn't really say," Frank said sadly. "Sharon was right there on the spot, thank God. But good as she is, she's not as good as her dad. And she doesn't begin to have what she really needs in the way of supplies and equipment." He sighed again and shook his head. "Sounds to me like James was trying to tell me he doesn't expect Jack to make it."

"I must go to Alice's," Diane said.

"I'll come along," Frank said. "After all, my fault he went."

"You will not come along," Diane informed him. "First, Alice does not need for you to come and beat yourself in front of her. Second, you must tell Mike and Admiral Simpson. They should know."

"Yeah." Frank nodded. "Yeah, you're right. Not that much we can do about it, of course, but I guess somebody should tell them that the only real pilot we had for Watson's Folly isn't available anymore."

"Can you think of anything at all we can do about it?" Mike asked.

"No." Simpson's face was drawn, and he shook his head. "There's not anything. We're here; they're there. And even if that weren't true, I doubt there's anyone else here in Magdeburg or in Grantville who's really qualified to handle that boat properly. We'll just have to hope Lieutenant Wild did pick up enough from Mr. Clements while he was available."

"I don't like it," Mike muttered, and Simpson snorted.

"I don't like it either," he admitted. "Unfortunately, what we like has very little to do with the situation. It never does. Especially when it's time for the shooting to start."

Mike leaned back in his chair and cocked his head at the older man. He gazed at him for several seconds.

"You don't have to answer this if you don't want to . . . John," he said, deliberately putting his question on a non-official basis with the use of the other's first name. "But I can't help wondering. It's obvious to me from some of the things you've said—and the way you talked to Eddie, before we sent him off—that you'd seen combat before we ever wound up here. A lot, I'd guess. Probably at least as much as Frank Jackson. But you never mentioned it until we needed you to build our navy. And to be honest, I've got the distinct impression you'd never mentioned it to Tom at all."

Simpson looked at him steadily, and Mike gave a tiny shrug. "John, I really don't think the fact that your son hasn't answered the radio message I sent to him just before I left means anything. That storm front has scrambled all our communications with Becky—and God knows what it's done to the relay between Amsterdam and London."

Simpson nodded once, jerkily, but his face was still tight.

Mike sighed. "Oh, hell . . . I guess if I'm asking for confidences, I should spill one of my own. Even though Rita swore me to silence."

Mention of Simpson's daughter-in-law caused his eyes to widen a bit.

"When the Ring of Fire hit," Mike asked, "what did you and your wife do? Right away, I mean. You didn't have anything left except a rental car—and we nationalized all the gas within a week—and a couple of suitcases. Every credit card in the world, I'm sure, and a wallet full of cash and the world's best wristwatch. Lot of good that was."

Simpson stared at him. "Well . . . a family took us in. Very nice people. The—"

"I *know* who took you in, John. The reason I know is because Rita set it up. The Wendells' son Jerry is an old friend of Rita's.

Boyfriend, to be precise, back in high school. But they stayed on good terms after they broke up."

"Your sister . . ."

Mike snorted, half-angrily and half-wearily. "John, just because we West Virginia hillbillies like to brag about the fact that we won the Hatfield-McCoy feud doesn't mean we really think old Devil Anse Hatfield was a role model. So relax about your son, will you? My kid sister's got her faults, but spitefulness is not one of them."

Simpson looked away. For a moment, the stiff wooden face seemed slightly embarrassed. And relieved.

"So, to go back to my question—why?" Mike asked again.

Simpson said nothing at all for several seconds. Then he drew a deep breath.

"I never really wanted to go into the 'family business,'" he said. "I don't imagine that that's something you expected to hear, but it's true. There were always two traditions in my family—business, and the Navy. There's been a Simpson in the Navy in every generation since the War of 1812. Until Tom's, of course."

He looked away, and his tone was distant, as if he were speaking of someone else entirely.

"I loved the Navy. And I didn't start off on an engineering track, either. Not me. I was headed for a major surface command of my own one day. Sea duty—that was what I wanted, and I volunteered for river duty in Vietnam right out of the Academy. And I got it, too. I got there about the time our riverine forces were reaching their maximum size, and I fitted right in. Within six months I was the squadron XO. Another six, and I was the 'Old Man.' At the grand and glorious age of twenty-four."

He shook his head, his eyes sad.

"You may not believe this, but in some ways, those were the best months of my life. I didn't like combat. Some people actually do, you know. I wasn't one of them. But whether I liked it or not, I was *good* at it. I was . . . effective. And my people and I were . . . Well, 'family,' I guess."

He swiveled his eyes back to Mike, almost defiantly, as if he expected the other man to laugh at him. But Mike only sat there, waiting, and Simpson looked away once more, gazing back into the distance across the vista of vanished years.

"And then, one day, I found out it doesn't always matter whether or not you're good. I never did find out whether it was a communications screw-up, or an intelligence failure, or just plain stupidity, but we were ordered to move in to cover what was supposed to be the extraction of a battalion of ARVN paratroopers . . . and found out it was a battalion of North Viet regulars, instead.

"They blew the crap out of us. I lost three boats, almost a third of my people, and my right foot."

Despite himself, Mike stiffened in surprise, and Simpson chuckled mirthlessly.

"Oh, yes. I do so well with my prosthesis that no one ever guesses, but it's nylon from right about here." He leaned over and rapped his right calf just above the ankle. The sound was surprisingly loud and hollow.

"That was the end of my Vietnam tour," he went on after a moment. "Almost the end of my career, for that matter. They wanted to give me a medical retirement. Seemed surprised when I turned it down, actually. But the loss of the foot, coupled with the McNamara build-down and the general reductions in manpower after Vietnam, changed my plans. I went into engineering, instead, which is what led me to the Pentagon. And you know what? I was good at that, too. Very good. Had a promising future.

"And then, just about the time I was put on the captain's list, my older brother was killed in a plane accident. Thomas was the one who'd been going to take over from my father. That was why I'd been free to be the one to pursue a Navy career. But now Thomas was gone, and I didn't have any other brothers, which made me the only choice to manage the family business interests. So I resigned my commission, went home to Pittsburgh, and took over when my father retired."

He was silent for two or three endless minutes, then shrugged.

"Sometimes," he said softly, "I think that's where Tom and I first got into trouble. I was so pissed off with him because he didn't want the Navy *or* the business. He wanted to play football, from the time he was just a kid, and I never understood. Mary did. Or, at least, I think she came closer to understanding than I did. And probably it was my fault. I was never very good at putting things into words to begin with, and I never really talked to Tom. I talked *at* him. I told him what I expected him to do, but I never got around to explaining why I wanted him to do it. Just like I never told him about my own Navy career, or even exactly how I came to lose my foot. I wanted . . . I wanted him to be like me. To realize that sometimes you have to give up a dream because you have responsibilities. To recognize how 'silly' it was to be so focused on playing a stupid game instead of preparing himself for his 'real' career. And I was so busy wanting him to do those things that I never quite got around to recognizing the sheer determination and discipline he was showing in pursuit of what *he* wanted to do with his life."

He was silent again, still gazing frowningly into the past. Then he inhaled sharply and gave himself a vigorous shake.

"Anyway," he said briskly, "that's the deep, dark secret of my naval past."

He smiled tightly, a man uncomfortable with confidences settling back into his familiar armor, and Mike nodded in acceptance. He wondered how much of Simpson's willingness to reveal his past stemmed from Mike's own effort to help him find reconciliation with his son. A lot of it, he suspected. But not all. Perhaps not even the majority of it. No, the real source, Mike thought, was the two youthful lieutenants at Wismar. Lieutenants even younger than he had been on a muddy, bloodsoaked river three and a half decades before.

Lieutenants who, in many ways, had become almost replacements for the son from whom he had estranged himself so thoroughly.

# Chapter 42

"Well, it seemed like a good idea at the time," muttered Jeff, peering forward from the bow of the fishing boat, desperately trying to see anything in the darkness through moisture-beaded glasses. "The damn rain doesn't help things any."

"It *is* a good idea," hissed Jimmy, crouched next to him. "You watch and see." Judging from the tone of his voice, Jeff's friend wasn't any too certain about the proposition himself.

Still, Jimmy—like any proper mountain boy having steeled himself for folly—pressed on, bound and determined to make a silk purse out of a sow's ear. "Besides, the rain's working for us. If we can't see the Spaniards, they can't see us either. And you can bet your sweet ass any Spanish sentry standing on a deck is going to be spending most of his time trying to keep from getting soaking wet."

Insistently: "It *is* a good idea."

"That's what you said that time we snuck into Mr. Ferrara's lab and swiped—"

"That was your idea too," protested Jimmy.

"I know it was," grumbled Jeff, feeling another cold trickle of rain water starting down his back. "Just like this harebrained scheme was my idea. But what's the point of having friends if they don't restrain you? You're as bad as Eddie and Larry, when it comes to that."

Jimmy eyed him for a moment. Then, smirking. "Well, yeah. But look at the bright side. The most harebrained idea you ever came up with in your life was proposing to Gretchen on the same day you met her. Ha! Had to use a dictionary to do it. And we didn't restrain you then, either. In fact, we were the only ones backing you up, right at first."

That was true enough, of course. But, at the moment, Jeff didn't appreciate being reminded of Gretchen. Gretchen, and her warm and luscious body. Gretchen's smile in the morning—even better, late at night. Gretchen, when—

He yanked the thoughts away. Gretchen was back *there*, standing on the wharf and staring into darkness. He was *here*, in the bow of a thirty-foot fishing boat. And if he couldn't see any Spanish ship in that darkness, he *could* see the pitch-covered cask full of gunpowder sticking a few feet beyond the bow of the boat.

*Spar torpedo,* he thought sourly. *Seems nifty as hell, reading about it in a book. Seemed nifty as hell, too, when we convinced a buncha crazy CoC volunteers to go in with us on the scheme. Now . . .*

"Reminds me of that wisecrack I read once. Remember, Jimmy? You and me both thought it was funny. At the time."

A frown came over Jimmy's face. At least, Jeff *thought* it was a frown. It was hard to tell, between the darkness, the falling rain— not to mention the rain on his glasses—and the shapeless hat Jimmy was wearing. But he knew Jimmy well enough to guess that he was seeing a frown of puzzlement. Jimmy was a smart enough kid, but . . . not fast-thinking. Nothing at all like Eddie Cantrell, that way. Jimmy could and would slowly chew his way through to a problem's right answer, but he always took some time getting there.

"What are you talking about?"

Jeff's lips quirked. "That quote I showed you once. 'Adventure is somebody else having a miserable time someplace far away.'"

"Oh. That one. Yeah." He chuckled. "There was some British actor once—maybe Paul Newman—said kinda the same thing. His idea of adventure was carrying a mug of beer from one smoke-filled room to another."

Jeff rolled his eyes. "Paul Newman's not English. He's American. *Why* do you always think every classy old actor is English?"

"'Cause most of 'em are," came the confident reply. "Take a look at Cary Grant. Or Katherine Hepburn. Get past Humphrey Bogart and Jimmy Cagney, that's about it. Well . . . I'm not sure about that Olivier guy. His accent's a little much. I think he might have been faking it. Probably came from someplace in Kansas."

Jeff closed his eyes tightly. Partly to shelter them from the rain, which had suddenly turned into a driving, almost-horizontal sheet. Mostly to dispel the pain.

"There are so many errors in what you just said it makes my head hurt. Besides, I think it was Peter O'Toole who made the wisecrack about the smoke-filled rooms. And if I remember right, it was 'a pint of bitters,' not a mug of beer."

"Um. Yeah, that makes sense. I figure that's why he stuck with Elizabeth Taylor so long. Sure, she's too hefty, but she's English like he is. Or maybe they're Welsh."

Jeff stifled a groan. He started to snarl something, when he felt a hand on his shoulder. He turned his head and saw one of the fishermen who'd agreed to accompany them on this harebrained scheme.

"Push it now, ha?" the man asked, nervously. He gestured toward the torpedo.

Jeff didn't blame him for being nervous. A hundred pounds of black powder perched just a few feet away would make anybody nervous. The fact that the bomb was designed to be set off by a weird American triggering device was guaranteed to make any Dutchman twice as nervous.

*That's just 'cause he doesn't understand how it works. I do—which is why I'm twice as nervous as he is.*

He felt a powerful urge himself to order the spar holding the torpedo to be run out to its maximum extension. But he restrained it. That extra few feet of distance wouldn't really help that much, in the event of an accidental explosion. Not Jeff and Jimmy, anyway, right in the bow of the boat. And lowering it into the water now, when they had no idea where their target was, would just be foolish.

He shook his head firmly. "Must wait until—" He groped for the words for *diversionary attack* for a moment. Not long, though. The sophisticated terminology was hopelessly beyond the rudimentary Dutch-German pidgin he was speaking.

"Other sailors," he managed, pointing off somewhere into the darkness to port. "Must wait them."

The Dutch sailor grimaced, but didn't press the point. Instead, he scurried back to the men laboring at the oars. Jeff suspected he'd been sent forward as their emissary. The crew manning the boat was a volunteer force, patched together from a few fishermen, seething at the destruction of their livelihood, and the boldest of the city's apprentices who'd joined the Committee of

Correspondence Gretchen had set up in Amsterdam over the past two weeks.

"And that's another thing," Jeff muttered, dragging off his glasses and drying them—well, smearing the water into fresh patterns, anyway—before he jammed them back onto his nose. "In the history books, at least the screwballs pulling off this stunt all spoke the same language."

Jimmy combined a shrug with a shiver. The rain was *cold*. Naturally.

"What we got. They volunteered. More than you can say for those civic militia assholes."

Jeff didn't say anything. In truth, Jimmy's sour characterization of the civic militia wasn't really fair. Not, at least, as applied to the soldiers themselves. The problem was that the militia's officers were drawn mostly from the city's burghers and master craftsmen. And, like most such, were not inclined toward approving harebrained schemes.

*Which is probably why they managed to get rich in the first place. No fools, they.*

The only official authority Jeff had managed to convince to come in on the project was two captains of the Dutch navy. What was left of the navy, that is. In their case, both were not even regular officers. Their ships were armed merchantmen, some of the few which had managed to escape the destruction at Dunkirk. Truth to tell, Jeff didn't much like either one of them. Angry men—even nasty, he suspected. But, under the circumstances, their choleric temperaments had been turned toward the Spaniards. Which was good enough for the purpose.

Suddenly, to port, he saw flashes of light that splintered in the droplets on his glasses. They were followed, moments later, by the rolling sound of cannon fire. The sound was muted, partly by the rain and partly by the fact that the cannons involved weren't any larger than nine-pounders. But it was all Jeff needed.

The Spanish fleet in the Zuider Zee was anchored just far enough from Amsterdam to be out of range of the city's heavy artillery, but close enough to blockade the port. Under those circumstances, they were bound to be on guard against a cutting-out expedition. Judging from what he'd seen since the fleet arrived, the Spaniards would have four launches out on patrol, serving as a picket line.

That was the job of the two little Dutch warships. Just get in range and fire off a few broadsides, then scamper—hopefully—

out of harm's way. But drawing off the picket boats—or at least directing their attention elsewhere—while the real strike went in.

*The "real strike." Yeah, right. The harebrained scheme, cooked up by two American kids out of some books they read on the Civil War.*

But he didn't have time to dwell on the sarcastic thought. Jimmy was urgently squeezing his arm and giving it a little shake.

"Look! D'you see it?"

Jeff squinted along the line of Jimmy's pointing finger. His friend had better eyesight than he did, even with his glasses on. Leaving aside the fact that Jeff's glasses were covered with rain water.

He saw nothing. Then . . . It was just a thicker darkness, at first. But, much faster than he would have expected, the darkness congealed into a shape.

"That's it, all right. A Spanish galleon, sure as shit. Good-sized one, too. Okay, Jimmy, we're on. Get the guys up here."

Jimmy motioned urgently. Four of the men left off rowing on the oars and hurried forward. Moving quickly but carefully, they slipped the heavy spar holding the torpedo forward until it had reached maximum extension. Behind them, the men remaining at the oars threw their backs into it. Again, moving a bit slowly— even with muffled oars, no one wanted any noise—but digging into the pulls with as much power as they could muster. The fishing boat began to surge forward.

Jimmy watched Jeff, waiting for the signal. Jeff was studying the distance to the enemy ship, trying to gauge the right point at which to lower the torpedo into the water. Too soon, and the boat's speed would be slowed right when speed was most important. Too late, and the splash might alert whatever sentries were on deck. *Really* too late, and the whole exercise would be wasted. For the torpedo to work properly, the explosion had to happen underwater.

Part of him, too, was studying himself. All through the night, and the days leading up to this event, Jeff had been . . . wondering. Hoping desperately, really. Hoping that a thing which had happened to him only three times in his life would happen again.

The first time, at the age of sixteen. When, driving his father's car on a two-lane highway through the hills, he'd suddenly seen an oncoming car in his own lane. The stupid idiot had tried to pass a truck on a curve. Jeff had saved his life and his mother's that day, calmly and steadily—not a trace of panic; his nerves like ice—steering his own vehicle onto the shoulder and narrowly missing the head-on collision.

The second time, when he'd come around another curve on his motorcycle and seen Becky Stearns sprawled on the road with Croat cavalrymen about to kill her. Again, without any thought on his part, the ice shield had come down. He'd laid down his bike— almost casually—and slain all of them, never feeling anything at the time beyond calculation.

Later that same day, it had happened again, when other Croat cavalrymen had come smashing into the gym where some of the Americans were fortified. Jeff had killed several of them as coldly as a snake. He'd not even felt anything when he saw Mr. Trout cut down in front of him. Not even, that he could remember, when he himself had been sent to the floor from another saber cut. He *could* remember being puzzled a little, when he saw the Croat about to kill him have his head split open by a saber in the hands of Gustav Adolf.

That he *could* handle himself in combat, Jeff knew already. What he didn't know, crouched in the bow of a boat on a dark and rain-swept night, was whether he could do the same thing when the danger did not come upon him by surprise. When, to the contrary, he'd had days to plan for it in advance. Days in which his fear and apprehension could slowly and steadily saturate every nerve in his body.

He was still considering the problem, with a part of his mind, when the other part said—calmly, icily—"Okay, that's it. Now, Jimmy."

The torpedo slid into the water. Jeff watched it disappear into the Zuider Zee until he was sure the warhead was positioned the necessary five or six feet below the surface. Then, again speaking calmly and steadily, said: "Get back, Jimmy. I'll take it from here."

Jimmy started to protest, but Jeff shook his head. "Don't be stupid. It only takes one of us to pull the trigger. You got no idea what that spar's going to do. It could sail back right through you like a spear."

The exact same risk was posed for him, of course. But his voice was so steady, so sure, that Jimmy didn't argue the point. He just nodded, whispered a quick "good luck," and scurried back to the oarsmen amidship.

Jeff hunkered himself down in the bow, getting as far away as he could from the spar holding the torpedo while still being able to see what he needed to see. The Spanish warship was very close now, almost looming above him. It was close enough that Jeff could see, even in the darkness, that the torpedo would strike below the turn of the bilge.

*Perfect.*

Very close, now. Still, no shouted cry of warning. He decided that Jimmy had been right. On this miserable night, Spanish sentries would be trying to get whatever shelter they could from the rain. Those few of them, that is, who weren't at the rail on the other side of the ship watching the fireworks in the distance.

Now, he closed his eyes and ducked his head. There was no doubt at all in his mind that the torpedo would strike. What remained was simply to trigger the bomb at the right instant. For that, eyesight was useless anyway (fortunately, perhaps, given the state of his glasses), so he might as well protect himself as best he could. Besides, the closed eyes would help him concentrate. It was his sense of touch that mattered now—that, and his hearing. His entire mind was focused on that. That little vibration/jolt/noise which would tell him the bomb had finally touched the hull of its target.

He held the firing device firmly in his hand. It was a simple thing, just a lanyard tied around a stick. One good quick pull—and it would have to *be* quick—and the jury-rigged firing pin they'd made with the help of an Amsterdam watchmaker would set off the shotgun shell fixed firmly into the bomb at the end of the spar.

His mind saw what amounted to a diagram. Pull too soon, and most of the force of the blast might be wasted. Too late, after the torpedo struck the hull and recoiled, and the same might happen. Or, worse, the spar itself might break, sending the torpedo to the bottom. Jeff didn't really think that was likely—it was a pretty hefty piece of wood—still . . .

He just had time to realize that the ice shield was firmly in place—time, even, to realize that he would never again have to doubt himself, not, at least, when it came to *this*—when he felt the tremor.

His arm flashed back, all the steadiness of his nerves translated into the speed of his hand.

Afterward, he could never remember hearing anything that even vaguely seemed like an explosion. Just the sudden sensation that Leviathan had risen, roaring its monster fury, determined to consume entire the pitiful boat that had blundered across its great ridged spine. He glanced up—almost straight up, the boat had been driven at such an angle by the dome of water—a bit curious to see how long Leviathan's fangs were. He'd never really believed the illustration he'd once seen in a book.

Later, Jimmy told him the spar had gone sailing overhead. No danger at all, Jimmy claimed.

Of course, he also claimed the spar had landed somewhere in Brunswick. And made the claim, furthermore, while insisting that Katherine Hepburn *had* to be English. Since, in that movie *African Queen,* she'd managed to look dignified all the way through, even when she was sopping wet.

Which was more than two scruffy young Americans and a bunch of scruffier Dutch fishermen and apprentices could say—for damn sure—as they desperately bailed water out of their boat while trying to avoid angry Spanish warships in the dark.

That was actually the most dangerous part of the whole escapade, Jeff realized later. But, at the time, he hadn't been afraid at all. Not because of any mysterious quirk in his nervous system, but simply because he'd been too exasperated.

"And that's *another* thing they don't tell you in the books," he grumbled, pitching another pail of seawater overboard. "It's all a fucking spongy mess."

Jimmy was more philosophical about it. "Beats what happened to the *Hunley.*"

Gretchen was still on the wharf when they returned, along with a small number of other women whose husbands and sons had participated in the mad affair. For obvious security reasons, Jeff had kept the enterprise as much of a secret as possible. He hadn't even seen fit to notify Amsterdam's authorities, and was now finding himself a bit apprehensive about how they were going to react.

Not too apprehensive, and certainly not for long. Gretchen's body and lips pressed against his, her breath coming heavy, was enough to dispel almost anything except love and lust.

"I was so frightened," she whispered into his ear. "I was certain you would be killed."

"I was scared too," he admitted, "until the very end. But don't tell anybody about that part. It'd ruin my image as a geek."

"Stupid," she murmured, her lips back and eager. "You have never been a geek to me. Or the children. Who else matters?"

He found himself agreeing to that sentiment. Though not, of

course, verbally. Gretchen's kisses, when she was in the mood, made conversation impossible.

The next day, when the news spread through the city, Amsterdam erupted. The city's populace had been mired in something of a gloomy depression since the siege closed in. Not despairing, to be sure. Dutchmen had been through many sieges since the Revolt began, decades earlier. Some of them lost, to be sure, but more of them won.

Still, they had no illusions as to the price they would pay, even in the event of victory. "Winning a siege," to those experienced at the business, is a bit like hearing that your life will be saved and you'll "only lose a leg."

The announcement of the alliance with the United States had lifted their spirits a bit. But only a bit. It had aroused more in the way of curiosity than hope, really. The fables about the Americans had already spread through Europe—and now, for long enough that most people had concluded they were probably fables indeed. What was *known* was that the United States was, first, a small nation; and, second, nowhere close enough to render much in the way of immediate aid.

Overnight, that had changed. A Spanish warship lay on the bottom of the Zuider Zee. The force of the explosion, most of it channeled by the unforgiving near-incompressibility of water against the fragile wood, had ruptured the ship's hull. Most of the crew had survived, but the Spaniards had not made more than a token attempt to prevent the ship from sinking. Not after experienced seamen came up onto the deck and described the size of the hole the mysterious explosion had created.

But the city's glee and elation was not really a matter of military calculation. The Spanish had plenty of other warships, after all. True, the blockading fleet had withdrawn a bit farther from the city. Far enough, in fact, to make a few smuggling runs feasible. But only a few. The Spaniards had also doubled the number of launches they set out at night for a picket line.

No matter. The old enemy, now grown so huge and seemingly unstoppable, had finally been dealt a blow. And the fact that the blow itself had been delivered under the leadership of the very small delegation from the United States gave that new alliance a luster it had not possessed the day before.

Jeff Higgins did for that. By nightfall, he was the best-known public figure in Amsterdam except for the prince of Orange himself. And, in all likelihood, even more popular. By noon of the following day, the fledgling Committee of Correspondence in Amsterdam would have dozens of new members.

In mid-afternoon of that day in early October, Gretchen would give her first public speech in one of the city's squares. Most of the hundreds of people who would show up to hear the speech did so because they were curious to see the wife of Higgins, the now-famous American ship-killer. But, by the end, they would be listening to Gretchen Richter.

By the morning after that, the Committee of Correspondence would have another dozen new members. And by the end of that day, Gretchen would have started looking for a suitable building in which to establish Amsterdam's Freedom Arches.

On the day after the torpedo attack, however, it was a time for whoopee. Amsterdam's population poured into the streets to celebrate, the weather having cleared also. Many of them went to the walls of the city, to taunt the Spanish army in its entrenchments.

At Gretchen's firm command, Jeff and Jimmy—indeed, all the members of the U.S. delegation, including Rebecca—were paraded around the city by members of the Committee of Correspondence. The crowds which met these little parades cheered wildly. Even the Dutch gunners manning the great cannon on the walls were grinning.

Jeff noticed that one of their officers seemed a bit gloomy, true. Possibly because his own guns hadn't gained any such public acclaim. Or, possibly, because he came from a noble family—what the Dutch called the *ridderschap*—and was beginning to suspect that a Spanish ship wasn't the only thing which might be sinking.

If there was glee, there was also tragedy. The crowd had been foolish, often risking too much in their taunts at the Spanish besiegers. Spaniards, of course, were also experienced in siegecraft. So they responded to taunts with taunts of their own. Sixty-four-pound taunts, in their case, iron balls sent sailing into the city. Most of those Spanish cannonballs simply damaged homes and warehouses, but several of them struck the crowd itself.

And, in the case of one, destroyed a family. A Jewish family, as it happened; who, in most wars, would have sheltered in the ghetto. But these were Amsterdam Jews, more accustomed than most to feeling—at least to some extent—a part of the world around them. And the father of the family, like the *ridderschap* artillery officer, had a sense that the world might be changing.

So, he'd come, a merchant bringing his wife and infant to see the parades. By sheer bad luck, a Spanish ball ranged onto the street just as Rebecca and her little entourage passed by. At the last instant, sensing the oncoming destruction, the man had grabbed his wife and tried to shelter her behind his own body. But a human body is a pitiful shield against sixty-four pounds of iron. The shot cut them both in half, spilling the infant to the ground.

Rebecca—crouching against a stone wall, where the experienced Heinrich had yanked her as soon as he heard the oncoming shot— saw the whole thing happen, almost before her very eyes. For a few seconds, her face turned pale with shock. She tried desperately to control her heaving stomach. Blood and intestines had been scattered everywhere, some of it spattering the wall against which she was sheltered.

The sight of the infant steadied her. The boy was unhurt. His father's body had not protected his mother, true; but that same body—a portion of it, at least—had been enough to cushion the shock of the child's fall. He was lying on the bloody cobblestones, coated with blood himself, wailing his protest at the universe.

Without thinking about it, Rebecca lunged from her shelter, snatched up the boy, and hurried back.

"Idiot," growled Heinrich, pulling her down. "You should have left him there."

She stared at him, clutching the bloody little body. Heinrich's callousness left her as aghast as the carnage.

The veteran mercenary soldier scowled. "Not *forever*, damn the world. You should have waited—picked him up when the barrage passed." His shoulders, pressed against the stone, moved in a little shrug. "Little chance of another ball striking such a tiny target. What does it matter if the child shrieks with fear? It won't be the last time he does it, be sure of that, not if he survives. Not in this damned world."

When he was sure the firing had stopped, Heinrich immediately rose to add his share of jubilation to the crowd. Rebecca remained behind, still crouched against the wall. If there was no shelter needed against guns, any longer, she still felt a desperate need for the comfort of stone against the world.

"Don't worry," she whispered, "I'll take care of you. I promise."

The boy seemed to be settling down, a bit. Rebecca began wiping the gore from him, using her own dress for a rag. The garment would need to be cleaned anyway, and very thoroughly.

Jeff and Jimmy found her there, some time later. The sight of her, ashen-faced and clutching an orphan to her chest, stripped away every trace of warrior self-satisfaction.

"Aw, shit," said Jimmy. He looked away, his eyes bleak beyond his years.

Jeff's eyes were not bleak so much as simply grim. Nor did he look away. "Next time," he said softly, almost hissing the words, "let's make sure we've got some real torpedoes."

# Chapter 43

"I'm sure glad you're here, Jesse—I mean, Colonel."

Eddie corrected himself quickly, but not quite quickly enough to keep him from blushing.

"That's all right, Lieutenant," Jesse assured him gravely. "But I remind you that, as I understand it, the Navy's been designated the senior service here in Wismar. That makes sense to me, too. The Air Force—such as it is, and what there is of it—is very much a clear-weather-only force just now. Your surface units are going to have a lot better round-the-clock capability than we are, so it's only sensible to put a Navy officer in overall command."

"It may seem sensible to you," Eddie said, grimacing, "but I sure as hell don't *feel* like an officer in overall command of anything!"

"It'll grow on you," Jesse assured him. "Besides, it comes with the territory, I'm afraid."

"Always seemed a lot easier than this in war games," Eddie muttered, but his voice was just low enough that Jesse decided he could pretend not to have heard it.

"Now that I am here, and more or less for good this time," he said instead, "what can I do for you?"

"Larry just copied a message from Magdeburg," Eddie told him. "The Danes are landing troops in Luebeck Bay."

"I see." Jesse was surprised that his own voice sounded so calm. Or perhaps he wasn't. On one level, at least, the news was almost a relief. It certainly wasn't unexpected, and at least the Danes' arrival brought an end to the drawn-out anticipation.

Unfortunately, it also meant enemy troops were coming ashore no more than thirty miles from Wismar, as well.

"Well," he went on after a moment, "what does Colonel Holtzmüller have to say about it?"

"Not a lot," Eddie admitted with a crooked smile. "According to our latest reports, General Aderkas is still at least four days out from Wismar. Larry handed Colonel Holtzmüller the same dispatch first, and he headed out to check his pickets immediately."

"And Captain Stecher?"

"I've already passed the warning on to him," Eddie said, and Jesse nodded. Jochaim Stecher was a German Lutheran fishing boat skipper. Actually, he owned no fewer than six small fishing vessels operating out of Wismar and Rostock. Eddie had entrusted one of his precious citizens-band radios to him, along with a German-born U.S. Navy sailor trained in its use. At the moment, Stecher was somewhere out on Wismar Bay, looking as innocent as possible while he kept a sharp lookout for the first sign of the Danish fleet. The chance of his seeing anything in the middle of a rainy fall night wasn't particularly great, but in this pre-radar era, invasion fleets were going to want at least minimal daylight before they tried to put any troops ashore. And as long as his boat showed no signs of trying to run past the Danes toward shore, they were likely to leave it alone . . . since there was no way for them to know it had a radio aboard.

"I guess what I really need to know," Eddie went on after a moment, "is how likely it is that you and Hans can get into the air tomorrow, Colonel."

"That's the sixty-four-dollar question," Jesse said with a humorless smile. "Right this minute, I'd say the chances were at least a little better than even. Judging from the way the rain's slacked off, it looks like the front's pretty much passed through, and while I was walking over here from the field, it looked to me like the cloud cover was breaking up. Of course, this time of the year in the Baltic, the only thing anyone can say for sure is that no one can be sure what the weather is going to do. Damn, what I wouldn't give for a decent weather service!"

"I can certainly agree with you there," Eddie said feelingly. "But to be honest, better than even is a lot better chance than I'd figured on."

He leaned forward, gazing down at the large-scale chart of Wismar and its approaches pinned down on the table between him and Jesse, studying it so intently that no one would ever have guessed he didn't actually see it at all.

"What are your intentions?" Jesse asked quietly.

"Um?" Eddie looked back up quickly and shook himself. "Well, Captain Stecher's supposed to be staying in line-of-sight from our antenna overnight, so we should be able to catch any transmission from him if he spots anything out there tonight. If he does, Larry and I may try a night attack with the low-light gear." He paused, and Jesse nodded in understanding. Given all of the deer hunters in and around Grantville, it had been inevitable that several someones would have acquired low-light vision equipment. As it happened, no less than thirteen Russian Army surplus night-vision glasses had turned up, along with four low-light telescopic rifle sights. Batteries would become a problem eventually, but not for quite some time. And in the meantime, they provided a limited, potentially invaluable night combat capability.

"And if Stecher doesn't spot anything?" Jesse asked.

"In that case, we're going to have to go looking for them ourselves," Eddie replied. "Either that, or just sit here and wait for them, and that's not what the admiral had in mind when he sent us up here. Which is why I hope you can get into the air tomorrow."

"Understood." It was Jesse's turn to step closer to the map table and frown down at the chart. "At the very least, we can probably get up under the cloud deck and circle above the city. That would extend Stecher's range; you could send him further out and still give him a good line-of-sight to the radio in the plane. And we could get back onto the ground in a hurry if the weather went bad on us again.

"Of course," he continued, "his detection range is going to be limited. I doubt the Danes could slip an entire fleet past him, but it certainly wouldn't be impossible. Depending on how far he can actually see, we might need to send one or both of the planes out to do the scouting for you." His hand traced an arc across Wismar Bay toward the open waters of the Baltic beyond. "I'd be a lot happier about trying that if the weather really cleared instead of just improving, of course. But if we can get up at all, we should be able to see a lot further than you could from sea level. And we've got the camcorders rigged in both planes. So if we do see anything, we should be able to bring back pretty decent reconnaissance footage."

"What about the rockets?" Eddie asked in a suddenly toneless voice, and Jesse's frown deepened. He understood the need to throw every possible weapon at the Danes. And there wasn't any technical reason why they couldn't strap a couple of rockets under either wing. The problem was that Jesse didn't see much chance that weapons that short-ranged and inaccurate were likely to do much damage, whereas their weight would certainly decrease the aircraft's safety margins. Not to mention their potential to explode in a bad landing . . . or takeoff.

On the other hand, he reminded himself, the amount of actual damage they did might be pretty much immaterial compared to their morale effect.

"All right," he said reluctantly. Then he sighed. "I suppose there never really was much question," he admitted. "Not after Greg Ferrara went ahead and wired the damned hard points for them!"

Mike looked over the pile of equipment Harry Lefferts had brought to Magdeburg with him, now stacked in a well-shielded and guarded part of the naval yard. He shook his head, partly in bemusement at the weird assemblage, but mostly at the thought of Harry himself. And the barely veiled glee with which he and his handful of cohorts had so obviously put it all together.

"*Two* outboard motors?"

Harry grinned. "Don't be a cheapskate, Mike. We're on a mission of mercy, remember."

Mike's eyes moved over to the truly impressive stock of firearms and other weapons Harry had also brought up from Grantville. Some of those weapons . . .

"What the hell is *that*?" he demanded, pointing a finger.

Harry's grin seemed fixed on his face. He nodded toward the German soldier standing at his side. "Something Gerd came up with. He can't shoot a gun to save his life, except close range— where he's purely hell on—well . . ."

Harry managed to keep the grin, but let the sentence trail off. Mike didn't push the matter. He knew, from private sources, of the personal revenge which Gerd had taken on several of Tilly's mercenaries shortly after he'd arrived in Grantville. The police had chosen to look the other way, at the time. The killings had taken place outside their jurisdiction, for one thing. For another . . .

Some people just plain *needed* killing. Harry and Gerd saw eye to eye on that, and Mike couldn't really say he disagreed. Certainly not on this evening, waiting in Magdeburg while his wife was under Spanish siege in Amsterdam and several young men he thought the world of were about to face war's destruction in Wismar.

Harry glided on through the momentary, awkward pause. "But he's a whiz with a crossbow, and we decided we could fix us up some kind of—well, what would you call it? Think of it as a poor man's mortar, howzat. And we've got several different kinds of ammo for it too, that's the best part."

Harry spent the next minute or so cheerfully explaining the variations he'd be able to play in the future on the general air of havoc. A projected fugue of mayhem; composed by a 17th-century young German veteran of Tilly's savage armies, and orchestrated by a young hard-ass from the hills of West Virginia.

Mike made a token protest. "You're just trying to get into Amsterdam," he pointed out.

Harry shook his head firmly. "Stick to politics, Mike. You're not thinking ahead, the way us secret agent types gotta do. What happens *after* we deliver Anne and the stuff to Amsterdam? Huh?"

As it happened, Mike *had* given some thought to that, but he'd kept his speculations entirely to himself. They were too wild and woolly at the moment to advance openly.

He looked back and forth from Harry to Gerd. *Captain Wild and sidekick, Sergeant Woolly.*

"It's England next, for sure," pronounced Harry. Gerd nodded firmly. "Gotta be."

The grin was still there, but it was a lean and savage thing now. "Keep *our* people locked up, will they? Including my good buddy Darryl? Fat chance."

"We'll start in Scotland first," added Gerd. "We're not rash, you know. Just bold. So it'd be nice to have Julie and her rifle along. For that matter, Alex Mackay is a nasty character in a pinch." He swelled out his chest. "Can't shoot a gun either, of course. Men of our times! Brave, fearless. Muzzle-in-the-belly types, stare the Devil in the eye."

Mike didn't know whether to laugh or roll his eyes. He wound up doing both.

David Weber & Eric Flint

"Just make sure you wait for orders," he growled. He gave Harry the sternest look he was capable of. "You're a soldier now, you know. Full-grown, too. So I want none of your wild and woolly kid-stuff stunts."

Both Harry and Gerd looked aggrieved. "Well—hell, yes!" protested Harry. "Who ever heard of James Bond types not following orders?"

Remembering several movies he'd seen, Mike was not entirely reassured. But . . .

They were the best he had. Nor was he sorry of it. Mike was quite certain that if anyone could bring life into Amsterdam and death into London, it would be Harry Lefferts and his hand-picked wrecking crew. Especially with Darryl and Tom Simpson and the Mackays waiting at the other end in Britain.

"Oh, well," he muttered. "I guess the tourist trade was pretty well shot anyway."

Later that evening, after sundown, Harry and Gerd invited Mike to join them for a drink at the tavern near the naval yard which had become the unofficial watering hole of the U.S. Navy and the CoC militants who were their fierce partisans. Mike hesitated, for a moment. Then, deciding that there was really nothing further he could do until news came the following day of the impending battle at Wismar, he gave his assent.

On the way to the tavern, however, he was suddenly struck by a thought. Brought on, as it happened, by the sight of the building they were passing by.

"Hold on a minute. Let me see if the admiral's still in. He might care to join us."

Gerd, full of the simple and straightforward attitude of the Army toward the Navy in general, and its pissant admiral in particular, glowered fiercely. Harry, on the other hand, curled his lip at the sergeant and nodded.

"Crude bastard," he commented. "Can't be helped, Mike, he's a Kraut. Uneducated. Me, on the other hand—" He patted his chest proudly. "I've read some books. So I know my history!"

Mike's expression must have been skeptical. Harry pouted.

"Hey, s'true! Well . . . okay, not much. But I know all the good quotes."

"Like what?"

"Franklin Roosevelt's famous speech after Pearl Harbor, how's that? 'We must all hang together, or assuredly we shall all hang separately.'"

Mike winced. "Harry, I'm pretty sure that was said by Ben Franklin during the American Revolution."

"Really? Hm." Harry shrugged. "What the hell. Close enough. I got the continent right."

Simpson hesitated also. But, like Mike, only for a moment.

"Sure, why not? I'm not really doing anything here anyway, not any longer, except spinning my wheels and waiting to hear the news tomorrow. A drink might do me good."

When they arrived at the tavern and commandeered a table, Harry ordered beer for himself and Gerd. So did Mike. But the barmaid didn't have time to even turn away before the admiral countermanded the order.

"Not tonight, Gisela," he said firmly, pointing to Harry and Gerd. "Not for these two gentlemen. Please bring some of my special stock, if you'd be so kind. For me as well."

She scurried off instantly. Clearly, Simpson came here often enough to have established his authority. Of course, given John Chandler Simpson, "often enough" might only have required two visits.

Harry and Gerd were trying—not very hard—to hide their glares at Simpson. The admiral glanced at them and snorted.

"Please! You are about to embark on a desperate and daring mission into enemy territory. A beer just won't do."

The barmaid was back quickly, bearing a large mug of beer for Mike, three smaller mugs, and an unlabeled bottle of some truly suspicious-looking beverage.

And, indeed, Harry and Gerd both looked at the thing with dark suspicion.

"Don't ask," commanded the admiral. "You probably don't want to know. I'm afraid it was the best I could have them do, given the circumstances. But I think you'll find it tasteful. It's a bit strong, of course."

Whether by design or not, the last comment was enough to make sure that Harry and Gerd would accept the challenge. As soon as Simpson filled the mugs, they reached out for them. The admiral's scowl stopped them short.

"Please, gentlemen! These things must be done properly."

Simpson took their mugs and handed them over, giving them a little jiggle as he did so.

"Shaken, not stirred. I insist."

# Chapter 44

"All right, I've got them."

Sergeant Elizabeth Buchholz, A Company, Thuringian Rifles, leaned on her elbows and peered at the estuary of the Trave River through the night-vision glasses. She and her small party were safely invisible in the misty darkness, but she could easily make out the riding lights of the Danish vessels anchored in the river. They were far enough downstream to be safe from any of Luebeck's guns, and Gustav Adolf had been careful not to station any of his own troops in the area. After all, he'd wanted the Danes to feel completely comfortable.

From here, it looked as if they did . . . and as if they'd done about what Gustavus had predicted they would. They'd placed a handful of warships upstream of their main body, to protect the merchantmen and transports from anything Lubeck's defenders might try to sneak downstream, but the bulk of their men-of-war were anchored further out. Obviously, they weren't as confident as they would have liked about the location of the Swedish Navy, and most of their warships were positioned to defend the transports tucked safely away in the sheltering estuary against any sudden pounce from the open Baltic.

"Here, Al," she said, and passed the glasses to Al Morton. "Take a good look," she said.

Al took her at her word and raised the glasses to his eyes. Unlike the sergeant or any of her troopers, he wore a diver's wet suit rather than a camouflaged poncho, and he sucked quietly on a piece of local candy something like toffee while he hummed to himself. After several minutes, he nodded in satisfaction and lowered the glasses once more.

"Sort of what we expected," he murmured.

"So you think you and Sam can pull it off?" Buchholz asked.

"Oh, no problem!" Al replied confidently. "And we'd damn well better, too. If Jeff Higgins and Jimmy Andersen can sink a genuwine Spanish galleon with a fishing boat and a jury-rigged blackpowder torpedo, we're going to look like pure fools if we can't do the same with all the fancy modern gear we've got. In fact, I intend to do better."

"That water's damned cold, Al," Buchholz pointed out. "When they briefed us on this, they said that someone who goes into the water has maybe ten minutes. After that, he's gone. What do you call it?" She fumbled for the word. Elizabeth's English was fluent, even colloquial, but her technical vocabulary was still somewhat limited. " 'Hypothermia,' I think."

"E-yup," Al agreed. "But that's why me and Sam have these real nice wet suits, Lizabeth. Don't worry. We'll be fine, won't we, Sam?" He looked over his shoulder at his younger brother, who grinned back in a flash of spotless white teeth.

"You betcha," he agreed cheerfully. Then he frowned. "Only thing really bothers me, Al, is not being able to use our lights."

"Hey, nothing's perfect," Al told him philosophically. He sucked on his toffee for a few more seconds, then shrugged and turned back to Buchholz. "Looks to me like our best bet is to go in right about . . . there," he said, pointing to a flat patch near the riverbank. "Doesn't look like there's a lot of current in close along the shore through there, and that'll help when we head back. I'll plant the beacon before we go in."

"Right." Buchholz nodded. "We'll watch the back door for you. I just wish we could talk to you while you're under."

"Hey," Al repeated with another shrug. "You do what you can. And at least Sam and I can talk to each other."

"There's that," Buchholz agreed, watching the two brothers as they began to don the rest of their equipment. They moved with the calm, smooth, unhurried precision of a dive team which had done precisely the same thing scores of times before. Buchholz found their obvious competence more than a little reassuring and concentrated on her own responsibilities while they got on with it. By the time they were ready, with facemasks, regulators, and radios checked, she had her four troopers deployed to secure their recovery point.

"Well," Al said laconically, "guess we'll be going now. See ya."

The two of them waded out into the river, submerged, and vanished.

Aage Overgaard stepped out from under the break of the poop aboard his flagship and inhaled a deep breath of the wet, cold night. It was getting colder, he noted. Nippy and raw for so early in October, even here on the coast of the Baltic. But there were still at least a couple of months, he reassured himself. Ample time to carry out his responsibilities before winter closed in in earnest.

He crossed to the bulwark and leaned on it, gazing out over the anchored transports. His eyes particularly sought out the warships scattered among them, especially at the upstream end of the anchorage, just in case the Swedes had any ideas about sending cutting-out expeditions down from Luebeck. He wouldn't put such a ploy past Gustavus Adolphus for a moment—especially not now that he'd put the bulk of his troops ashore. A few large row boats full of soldiers could easily overwhelm the crew of any transport—or even a smaller warship—if they took it by surprise. Which was why he had four guard boats rowing steadily back and forth across the river channel to watch for just that sort of enterprise.

Things were going well, he thought, then instantly scolded himself for succumbing to such a moment of complacency. It was always just when a man thought things were going best that something resoundingly unpleasant happened. Nothing but superstition, of course. Still—

*KAAAAAAAA-BOOOOOOOM!*

The explosion wasn't really as ear shattering as it seemed at the time, he realized later. It was the total unexpectedness of the sound which made it seem that way. That, and the towering column of white water and mud that erupted from the Trave as the thirty-four-gun *Falken* seemed to leap halfway out of the river. Then the 300-ton ship sagged back, masts folding in on one another as her back broke. Even as Overgaard watched, the shattered ship settled to the bottom with only the very top of her stern galleries still above water. Two of the guard boats pulled frantically toward the wreck to rescue anyone they could. Overgaard doubted that they would find many to save, between the icy temperature of the water and the fact that so few sailors ever learned to swim.

For a moment, the captain-admiral was certain *Falken*'s magazine must somehow have exploded. But, no. There'd been no visible flash. That explosion hadn't come from inside the ship—it had come from *underneath* her. But how—?

The Americans! It had to be those uncanny allies of Gustavus! But how could even they have contrived something like *this*? No diver could survive long enough in water this cold to place a charge beneath a ship. And even if someone could have, fusing such charges was always a delicate and dangerous business. Certainly not something to be attempted in the middle of a dark, foggy night!

For the first time, Overgaard found himself truly believing the wilder tales about the American marvels. And as he did, it suddenly occurred to him that if the Americans could do it once, there was no reason they couldn't do it more than—

*KAAAAAAAA-BOOOOOOOM!*

It was one of the transports this time, he noted almost numbly. The ship went down even more rapidly than *Falken* had, and this time Overgaard could hear the terrified screams of at least some of her crew.

The captain-admiral shook himself out of his momentary stupor with a venomous curse. Was he going to just stand here while the American devils blew up one of his ships after another? He started to bellow orders, then made himself stop as he heard the thunderous patter of hundreds of feet. Other voices were shouting orders, axes were thudding on anchor cables, and windlasses creaked and groaned as the entire Danish fleet began frantically preparing to get underway.

*KAAAAAAAA-BOOOOOOOM!*

Yet another transport collapsed in on herself in a folding curtain of white foam and river-bottom mud. Overgaard cursed more venomously even than before as he recognized the precise timing between explosions. They were marching through his fleet as steadily as some demonic metronome. They had to get clear of whatever the Americans had left in this stretch of the river! And, he told himself grimly, it was already obvious that they wouldn't be able to come back. Not, at least, until they knew exactly what the Americans had done to them and how to make sure it couldn't be done again!

More and more of his ships were getting underway, cutting their cables in desperation and allowing themselves to be carried by the current more than the weak and fitful breeze. His own flagship was moving slowly, but steadily, and—

*KAAAAAAAA-BOOOOOOOM!*

He gritted his teeth as a *fourth* explosion ripped through the river water. But this time it wasn't one of Overgaard's ships, and he laughed with a sort of hysterical glee as he realized it was Martignac's flagship. He watched the arrogant French nobleman's ship settling rapidly while an entire flotilla of small craft hurried toward her to take off any survivors.

Overgaard turned his back upon her, wondering how many other ships—and how many of those his—would be killed before they could get free. Perhaps there wouldn't be many more. Perhaps it was only that one stretch of the river, and once they escaped from it everything would be—

*KAAAAAAAA-BOOOOOOOM!*

"Think we used enough dynamite there, Butch?" Al Morton asked his brother with a huge grin as the carefully placed charge's timer detonated it and sent a fifth Danish ship to the bottom.

"Looks like it to me," Sam agreed gleefully. "I admit, I figured we'd need bigger charges, but looks like you pegged it just about right."

"Sure," Al said expansively. "Water's not all that compressible, 'specially not with the river bottom so close and all. Doesn't take a really big explosion to break a wooden ship's back under those conditions, now does it?"

"How many did you get charges under?" Sergeant Buchholz asked in half-horrified awe.

"Actually, only half a dozen," Al admitted. "It's *dark* down there, Lizabeth. And cold, even with the suits. Six was the best we could do and still get out within the safety margin on the timers. On the other hand, I don't 'spect most of those ships are gonna take a chance on hanging around where we might do it to them again."

"I think you can say that again," Buchholz agreed, still shaking her head.

"Well," Al said cheerfully, "when Admiral Simpson explained what he wanted, he did say that was the name of the game. Reckon he'll be kinda pleased by how well it came out?"

*KAAAAAAAA-BOOOOOOOM!*

# Chapter 45

Jesse felt the mist on his face and pulled up the zipper on his leather flying jacket as he walked past the aircraft toward the sea. Though the fog looked as thick as it had the last two days, he sensed a difference in the air, a slight freshening from the sea.

*This stuff is gonna lift soon*, he decided. *About time.*

For the past two days, he had chafed at the weather, knowing the enemy was out there somewhere, headed this way. While the fog wasn't as dramatic as the storm that had almost killed him three days ago, it could be just as deadly to a pilot caught above it while trying to land. So they had all waited helplessly for the fog to lift.

*That's the problem with a seaside airfield*, Jesse reflected.

Not that they had wasted the time. Jesse had carefully coordinated his reconnaissance schedule with the U.S. Navy contingent, making it clear to Lieutenants Cantrell and Wild that though he was the senior officer present, *they* were in charge of the defense of Wismar. The Air Force contingent was present in a supporting role, a fact he'd made abundantly clear to Hans and Woody, just as Admiral Simpson had made it clear to him. He might have his doubts about the naval plan, but he knew his duty. And right now, his duty was to get airborne and provide some useful intelligence.

*Where is the invasion fleet?* He wondered. He knew the Navy had a fishing vessel out there somewhere, but it couldn't be very far from the coast. *I'll bet anything they're approaching from the north right now while my butt is here on the ground.*

Jesse looked up and saw the disk of the sun trying to burn its way through the fog. Rubbing his unshaven jaw, he made his decision and turned back toward the aircraft.

Lined up into the slight wind, Jesse thought he could already see a lessening in the fog. Visibility varied between a sixteenth and an eighth of a mile as the fog eddied. The sky was still completely obscured. He had chosen the Belle II because of the slight power advantage it had over the original Belle and, for the same reason, had removed the four rockets that had been loaded on it. He wasn't taking much of a risk, probably, but after the near disaster of three days ago, he wasn't in the mood for any sort of risk. As Jesse reckoned, even if the fog closed back in, he could contact the captain of the fishing boat acting as their picket to seaward, perhaps orbit for a couple of hours and then divert to Magdeburg. If the fog lifted, Hans and Woody could go on a familiarization ride in the Belle I, just as they had planned for the past two days, while he would land to refuel and rearm. The Belle I was already armed with four rockets. All he had to do now was get airborne.

Advancing the throttle, he started rolling through the fog toward the end of the field and the sea beyond. The fog whipped past as he accelerated, lifted the tail, and let the aircraft fly off. He was immediately on the turn and slip, glancing at the altimeter to make sure he kept a positive rate of climb. He knew better than to look out at the fog—he could think of no faster way to get vertigo and crash. No more than twenty seconds later, he emerged from the fog into a dull sky dimmed by successive, thin cloud layers. As he climbed, he saw that almost the entire bay was enshrouded in fog. As he passed four thousand feet, he could no longer see much to the west, due to another cloud layer. If he remembered correctly that was where the friendly fishing boat waited. Jesse momentarily thought about going to find it. But in the distance straight ahead, he saw open water, and so he continued his climb and headed north. *Piece of cake.*

An hour later, he was reluctantly coming to the conclusion that he'd guessed wrong. The enemy wasn't coming from the north, as he had suspected. He'd swept the entire quadrant, going as far north as he dared, and hadn't seen a damned thing, except empty sea.

*Perhaps they're not coming at all,* Jesse thought as he flew back toward Wismar. *Maybe they've gone on to Rostock, or something.*

He was perhaps forty miles away from the town when he heard a partial radio call from what he surmised was the fishing boat.

"They come! The Danes come!" an excited voice said.

Despite his own jumpiness, Jesse tried to calm the disembodied voice.

"Station calling, this is the Belle II. Please identify yourself and give your location, over."

The reply was immediate, if only a little more helpful. "This is the *Elizabet,* on the port tack, west of Wismar. The Danish fleet is two leagues to the west of us with the wind on its port quarter. We're coming about. Uh, over."

Jesse puzzled over the *Elizabet*'s message, but only for a moment. *So much for airborne reconnaissance.*

"Roger, *Elizabet.* Belle II understands and will relay your message. Break, break, Outlaw, this is Belle II. Did you copy the *Elizabet*?

"Negative, Colonel." Jesse recognized Cantrell's voice. "We only copied your transmission. Say again, *Elizabet*'s message."

Jesse passed the message while looking at the conditions in Wismar Bay. The fog had burned off, just as he had predicted. He ended with a request.

"Outlaw, request you send someone to the airfield. Inform Lieutenant Richter that Colonel Wood directs him to take off and assist the defense of Wismar. I will land, load rockets, and return as soon as I can."

Hans must have been listening in the Belle I.

"No need, Colonel. I am rolling now."

"Roger, Belle I. Good hunting."

"I wish Jack were here," Larry muttered as the Outlaw went purring out of the harbor.

"You and me both," Eddie agreed. He stood in the well between the cockpit's two consoles, peering ahead through a pair of binoculars. Then he lowered the glasses and looked at his friend. "Sorry, Larry! Didn't mean to sound like I don't trust you, or anything. It's just—"

"Just that we both want him to be okay . . . and that he's a hell of a lot better at this than I am," Larry finished for him with a grin which combined nervousness with true humor. "That's the same reason *I* wish he were here, dummy."

"That's 'Dummy, *sir*,' from you, Lieutenant!" Eddie corrected him. They both laughed, and if the strength of their laughter owed itself to the tension coiling deep inside them, that was their business.

Eddie raised the binoculars again, sweeping them back and forth. They ought to be seeing something soon, he told himself, and wondered again if he'd made the best available dispositions.

The sheer speed and power of the Outlaw, even with Larry at the wheel instead of Jack, made it the logical choice for the first strike at the enemy. The Chris Craft and the Century were tagging along behind, but they were there strictly for backup this morning. The Chris Craft carried an eight-cell launcher like the one on the Outlaw's foredeck, but the Century had only a six-cell launcher . . . and neither of them carried any reloads. They were both slower than the Outlaw, as well. So the plan was to use the Outlaw to attack the enemy and the other two speedboats as threats. After all, the Danes could hardly be expected to recognize the differences in the capabilities of up-time power boats, so the Chris Craft and the Century ought to seem just as dangerous and threatening to them as the Outlaw.

Of course, if everything went perfectly and the Danish formation came unglued, the other two boats could certainly close in, as well. But for right now, Eddie would settle for just convincing the Danes to hesitate long enough for General Aderkas' reinforcing column to reach Wismar.

"I see them." Eddie lowered the glasses again as Hans' voice came from the Outlaw's radio. He looked up at the airplane buzzing steadily along above them. Jesse was still on the ground at Wismar, refueling while the understrength ground crew mounted rockets on the improvised hard points, but Hans sounded confident.

Eddie reached for the radio microphone and hit the transmit key.

"You're supposed to tell me *where* you see them, Hans," he said dryly. "Over."

"Oh!" Hans chuckled just a bit nervously. "Sorry, Eddie," he said. "I see them about eight to ten miles ahead of you, bearing roughly northwest and headed straight for Wismar."

Eddie frowned, picturing the chart in his mind, then nodded. If Hans was right about the distance and bearing, it sounded like the Danes must be coming directly from Luebeck, swinging around the curving headland between Luebeck Bay and Wismar Bay. Actually, Wismar Bay was virtually an inlet on Luebeck Bay's southeastern flank, and the oncoming enemy was about to enter it.

"It looks like there are half a dozen warships, and twice that many merchant ships," Hans continued. "They're not moving very fast, and there must be thirty or forty smaller ships and boats with them. I think they're using the little ones to carry the infantry. Over."

"Understood," Eddie replied. "Let me think about this for a minute. Over."

He gazed in the indicated direction, but although the morning sky had largely cleared, conditions remained too misty here at sea level for him to see anything of the enemy yet. So he lowered the glasses once more, and frowned in thought.

"What do you think, Larry?" he asked. "Think we should head further out to hit them, or let them come to us?"

"I'd just as soon get it over with, actually," Larry admitted with a quick, nervous chuckle of his own. "And remember what Jack said. The further out we hit them, the more sea room I'm going to have to handle this brute in."

"There is that," Eddie agreed. He frowned for a few more moments, rubbing the tip of his nose in thought, then shrugged.

"Makes sense to me," he said, and keyed the mike again. "Hans, we're going to attack," he said. "Head straight for them. We'll use you to make sure we're lined up properly. Over."

"Understood," Hans replied. "I'm changing course now. Over."

Eddie and Larry both craned their necks, staring up as the airplane adjusted its flight path. Then Larry eased the wheel to port, slowly and carefully, without waiting for orders from Eddie.

He opened the throttles slightly, and the purring engines snarled a deeper, harsher song. The *Outlaw* dug in its stern and headed for the enemy with the other two speedboats forging along in its wake.

"Look! What's *that?*"

Captain Tesdorf Vadgaard, commodore of the small squadron escorting the eight thousand men assigned to sweep up undefended Wismar, looked up irritably at the semi-coherent shout from his flagship's lookout. The man at *Christiania*'s mainmast head was unaware that he had aroused his captain's ire, and Vadgaard started to open his mouth to administer a scathing rebuke. But that rebuke died stillborn as someone else shouted the same question and the lookout pointed wildly to port.

*Christiania* and the rest of Vadgaard's command were headed southeast, standing steadily into the mouth of Wismar Bay. The wind was on his ship's port quarter, blowing almost directly out of the north, with gradually increasing strength. The waves were making up as the chill wind strengthened, and the mist which had clung to the surface of the water since dawn was breaking up and rolling away on the breeze. The day wasn't going to be warm, but it was still a vast improvement over the last two days' rain and fog. The growing patches of sky between the broken banks of charcoal-gray cloud were a bright autumn blue.

The lookout was pointing at one of those patches of blue, and Vadgaard felt his own eyes widening in astonishment.

The shape headed directly toward his ship was formed like a cross, or perhaps like some seabird, wings outstretched as it glided effortlessly across the heavens. But small though that shape might appear, he knew that was an illusion. Whatever it was, it was bigger than the greatest bird the world had ever known. It must be, for him to see it at all at its vast height.

"Glass!" he snapped to the deck officer beside the helmsman. The officer handed over his telescope promptly enough, but Vadgaard could tell he didn't really want to. What he *wanted* to do was raise the glass to his own eye while he peered through it at the apparition. Vadgaard could understand that, but his sympathy for the other man was strictly limited by his own curiosity and instinctive dread.

He leveled the glass at the shape. Finding it was harder than he'd expected, partly because the shape was so small, but also because he was unaccustomed to looking up through a telescope at such an acute angle. The motion of the deck under his feet didn't help, but Vadgaard had first gone to sea over twenty years before. He'd looked through a lot of telescopes in the course of that career, and eventually he managed to find what he was trying to examine through this one.

His jaw clenched as he examined the bizarre sight. It was a machine of some sort, he realized. It was too unlike anything he'd ever seen before for him to fit all the details together into a coherent mind picture, but as he stared at it he remembered the spy reports. He'd dismissed them as the sort of wild, fantastic exaggerations Gustavus Adolphus' "American" allies seemed to generate so effortlessly. Winged machines? Machines that could *fly*? Ridiculous! Exactly the sort of fables someone trying to impress credulous fools might spin.

But it seemed he owed the spies an apology, and he wracked his brain in an effort to dredge up the details he had dismissed so cavalierly. There was supposed to be something on the front of the machine, the . . . "airplane," they'd called it. Something like the sails of a windmill, but smaller, and with only two arms. He didn't see anything like that through the telescope, but perhaps it was still too far away.

He lowered the telescope and blinked his eye against the muscle strain of his intense scrutiny. He could sense the shock coursing through his officers and men, not least because the same shock still echoed inside him, as well. If the Americans could truly fly like the birds of the heavens themselves, then perhaps they actually were the witches or wizards wild-eyed rumor had initially insisted they were. And if they could fly, who knew what *else* they might accomplish?

*No*, he told himself firmly. *Whatever they may be, they aren't witches. For all of his faults, no honest man would ever accuse Gustavus of Sweden of consorting with servants of Satan. It's just one more of their wondrous machines, and surely it can do us no harm from so high above! Not even if whoever is controlling it has one of the long-ranged American muskets we've heard so much about. But if it can't harm us, then why is it headed so unerringly in our direction?*

Then he heard the lookout's fresh cry of astonishment. The man was pointing to port once again, but not at the sky this time, and Vadgaard felt his mouth tighten as he raised the telescope once more.

*So*, he thought, studying the strange white shapes coming out of the vanishing fog in a rolling pile of even whiter bow waves. *Perhaps it can't harm us, but it would seem it can lead toward us those who can.*

# Chapter 46

Eddie raised his binoculars and studied the oncoming Danish fleet nervously. Hans' estimate of their numbers had been accurate, he decided, though it was difficult to get any sort of a definitive count. Too many of the vessels overlapped and merged into one another when he tried to make one out.

Most of the twenty or thirty ships he could see seemed to have gun ports, but that didn't mean a lot, he reminded himself. Most 17th-century seagoing merchant ships carried at least a few guns to ward off pirates, if nothing else. The majority of the ships in that straggling formation had to be transports, not regular warships. Of course, the fact that they weren't officially warships didn't mean that any anti-pirate guns they carried couldn't be sufficiently dangerous.

He swung the binoculars gently back and forth while he tried to analyze the Danish formation . . . such as it was, and what there was of it. The larger ships appeared to be in what was supposed to be a single column, heading toward Wismar at perhaps three or four miles an hour. If it was supposed to be a column, it wasn't a very neat one, but he and Larry were scarcely in a position to criticize anyone else's seamanship.

His mouth twitched in an almost-smile at the thought, and he turned his attention to the smaller vessels Hans had reported. There were more of them than of the larger ones, clustered around the untidy column like goslings around geese. Most of them looked like no more than large row boats, although the majority had at least some sort of sail, but four or five of them were larger, lower, and sleeker. And—his binoculars stopped moving, and his jaw muscles tightened—those larger "row boats" each had what looked like a good-sized cannon mounted in its bows.

*They can't be as big as I think they are,* he told himself sternly. *The damned boats would capsize if they tried to fire thirty-two-pounders at us! But even a teeny-tiny one-pounder can take someone's head off without any trouble at all. And those ain't one-pounders, Eddie! Probably more like three-pounders, maybe even sixes . . . or nine-pounders.*

He let his eyes linger on the gunboats for a few moments longer, then made himself look away. The odds of a single 17th-century cannon's actually managing to hit a 21st-century speedboat were minute. *That* was going to take an entire broadside—or blind luck. He couldn't do much about the latter, but he intended to see to it that no broadsides got a clear shot at him.

"All right." He lowered the glasses and turned to look at Larry and their single additional crewman. "I don't want to get any more tangled up in them than we can help, Larry. But if we can manage it, I'd like a shot where at least a couple of them overlap. That way, anything that misses the closest ship still has a chance of hitting something else."

Larry cocked his head, lips pursed while he contemplated the Danish formation, then he nodded slowly.

"Looks to me," Eddie continued, "like our best bet is going to be to get inshore of them. We ought to have enough water, and we'll keep an eye on the fathometer." He tapped the digital depth display, and Larry nodded again. "The main thing though, is that if we come at them from the coastline, we'll have the choice of breaking left or right after we fire without having to worry about running *into* the coast, right?"

"Sounds reasonable to me," Larry agreed. His effort to project an air of nonchalance was not an outstanding success, but Eddie decided not to hold that against him under the circumstances.

"What I'd really like to do," he explained, "is to take out some of their warships. That's where their commanding officer's most likely to be, and I'll bet that most of those merchant ships would just as soon be somewhere else, anyway. If we can pick off a couple of their escorts, they may turn and run for it. And it looks to me like most of their regular navy units are concentrated toward the back of their formation." He pointed across the water. "That's probably so that they'll have the wind behind them if they have to run down to intercept us if we try to get at the transports."

Larry nodded again, and Eddie turned to the other member of their three-man crew. Bjorn Svedberg was a bit on the scrawny side for a proper Viking, but he certainly had the blond hair and beard for the role. More to the point, however, he'd been chosen for the Outlaw's crew because his English, although heavily accented, was excellent.

"I want to make at least two attack runs, Bjorn. You and I will let Lieutenant Wild manage the helm while we reload between shots. Right?"

"Right," Svedberg agreed, and nodded so enthusiastically that Eddie chuckled. Bjorn *really* wanted to see the rocket launcher in action. Well, so did Eddie, come to that. Although now that the moment was approaching, he seemed to be experiencing a small degree of difficulty where bladder control was concerned.

He drew a deep breath, held it for a moment, then let it out.

"All right, then, Larry," he said. "Cut around to get between them and the shore."

"Right. I mean, yessir."

The big speedboat swung to port as Larry eased the wheel over.

Hans concentrated conscientiously on his flying as he floated between the chasms of cloud, but it wasn't easy. The surface of the Baltic was a dark blue carpet below him, wrinkled by moving lines of white as waves marched across it. From up here, it was easy to imagine that all he saw below him were toys, but he knew better.

This wasn't like the day he had gone into battle the first time as a terrified young recruit whose only fragile chance of protecting his extended family had depended on "proving himself" in the eyes of the very men who'd murdered his father and gang raped his sister. Then he'd faced battle not because he'd wanted to, but because he'd had no choice. Because he'd had to fight as one of those he hated with all his heart and soul, for the sake of those he loved.

Today was different. Today he sat in the cockpit of this wondrous airplane because he'd chosen to. Because he'd found something he would never have believed might have existed just two years ago: a nation and a cause that was actually worth dying for.

A world which would protect those he loved even if he was no longer in it, and which would extend that protection to *everyone*.

Hans Richter wasn't made of the same unflinching steel as his sister. He knew that, and he accepted it. After all, *no one* was as strong as Gretchen . . . or as ruthless where her loved ones were concerned. But he was her brother. Some of that same steel infused him, even if in lesser measure, and he felt it now at his core.

He had nothing personal against any of the Danes on those ships below him. More than that, he knew they were being used just as surely as he'd been used during his brief career as one of Tilly's mercenaries, and that the subtle mind which had truly chosen them as tools resided in Paris, not Copenhagen. But that didn't matter. However they came to be here, they were a mortal threat to everything in the universe that mattered to Hans, and he would remove that threat. He and his brothers from the future, he thought, gazing down at the white arrowhead of foam curving around to attack the enemy.

He watched the Outlaw circling around, and even as he kept his wary hand light upon the stick, a part of his mind was down on that arrowhead with Eddie and Larry, accompanying two more of those he loved into battle.

Tesdorf Vadgaard watched the same white arrowhead—and the two behind it—slice through the water and felt an even greater sense of awe than he had when he first saw the flying shape. A corner of his mind insisted that he shouldn't have. That the miracle of flight far surpassed anything that might happen upon the mundane surface of the sea. But that was the point. The very concept of humans in flight was so alien to him that even now the flying machine seemed more like a mythical creature from some fabulous tale than reality. More than that, he was a professional seaman. He'd spent two-thirds of his life mastering his craft, and he knew beyond any shadow of a doubt that no vessel in the world could do what *these* were doing.

It wasn't simply the way they moved without oars or sails, however profoundly unnatural that might seem. It was the *speed* at which they moved. For the first time in his life, Vadgaard found himself completely unable to estimate the speed of another ship. He'd never seen one move that quickly, never imagined one could. Whatever his guess, he knew that it was low, that they were moving even faster than that, and he felt his jaw muscles tighten as he considered what that impossible speed would mean for his gunners.

On the other hand, he told himself, studying the oncoming threat through his telescope once more, he saw no sign of artillery aboard any of them. For that matter, the more he gazed at those sharp-sided hulls, the more he realized that they *couldn't* mount guns. There was simply no place to put them.

But they had put something on their foredecks, and Vadgaard muttered an oath under his breath as he cudgeled his brain, trying to remember everything from the spies' reports he had paid so little attention to.

One thing was obvious, he decided, watching how smoothly the Americans maneuvered their vessels—they had some means of communication. They couldn't possibly have responded so quickly, moved so adroitly and with such assured coordination, if they hadn't. It must be another example of that mysterious "radio" from the rumors, and he felt a deep, burning sense of envy as he contemplated it. No seaman who had ever attempted to maneuver more than two or three ships could *not* have envied it. Not when he watched the other ships under his command slipping and sliding into action any way they could, all too often completely blind to opportunities he saw because there was no way for him to tell them about it.

That wouldn't happen to the Americans, he told himself. Which made them even more dangerous than the impossible speed of their vessels and whatever mysterious weapons they mounted might otherwise imply.

And speaking of weapons . . .

He steadied his glass on the lead American. It was the biggest of the three, and Vadgaard nodded to himself as he realized the other two were falling back slightly. Obviously the American commodore was aboard the lead ship of his squadron. He intended to open the attack himself, holding his other two units in reserve— a luxury his ability to communicate with them made possible. He could afford to commit them separately because of his ability to control their movements with as much confidence and sureness as he did his own flagship.

That much was obvious, but what interested Vadgaard most intensely at the moment was that angular framework on the flagship's foredeck. It was obviously a weapon, but not like any weapon he'd ever seen before. He stared at it until his eye ached, watching the enemy flagship moving steadily northeast along the Mecklenburg coast. It wasn't a gun, so what *was* it? It looked like . . .

His blood seemed to freeze suddenly in his veins as he remembered the stories about what the Americans had done to the Spaniards at the Wartburg, and to German armies at Badenburg and the Alte Veste. They'd used several new and demonic weapons no one had ever heard of, one of which had spread hellfire across the Spaniards trapped in the ancient castle. True, the tales Vadgaard had heard sounded as if the Americans had used an old-style catapult of some kind to launch the bombs used at the Wartburg. There was certainly no room for such on the boat hurtling its way toward him, any more than there was for cannon.

But . . . there had also been tales of other weapons. Like the ones they called "rockets." Intellectually, Vadgaard suspected that the chilling tales of the range, accuracy, and devastating effect of the American weapons must be exaggerated. After all, the tales came from Spaniards and Germans, not Danes! And all questions of national courage aside, anyone so resoundingly defeated by such novel weapons would be certain to overestimate their effectiveness. And not necessarily just to cover the humiliation of their defeat, either.

But whatever Vadgaard's intellect might suspect, his emotions were something else. They didn't care about his intellect, and he swallowed hard as the American flagship altered course once again. The American commodore had obviously reached the position of advantage he'd wanted. Now he was turning to launch his attack, maneuvering his units with cold-blooded, professional skill.

The silhouette of the enemy flagship altered as it settled onto its new course, and Vadgaard lowered his spy glass.

He no longer needed it to see the American ship. Not when it was so close and aimed straight at his own.

"Here we go!"

It was scarcely a proper military announcement, but Eddie felt no temptation to reprimand Larry for it. Not under the circumstances.

The Outlaw made its final turn, the engines' snarl rose in power and pitch as Larry advanced the throttles, and Eddie reached forward and slammed the hinged steel plate of the rocket launcher's blast deflector into the upright position. He threw the old-fashioned dead bolt which locked it there, and glanced sideways at Larry.

His friend was leaning forward in the comfortable chair, a bit closer to the wheel than he had been, in order to peer through the heavy glass plate in the deflector. It wasn't very big, and from the way Larry was craning his neck, Eddie suspected that the launcher blocked even more of his forward view than they'd expected it to. He kicked himself mentally as soon as the thought occurred to him. They ought to have gone ahead and loaded the launcher and let Larry practice handling the boat with all eight cells filled and the deflector up. At least then his friend would have had a little experience managing the Outlaw when the launcher was no longer simply an open framework of welded steel rods.

But there was nothing they could do about that at this point, and Eddie leaned forward to peer through his own glass-protected slot in the blast shield. His was different from Larry's. In fact, his was positioned dead center behind the launcher, giving him an unobstructed view through what would have been its ninth cell. It was the crudest sighting mechanism conceivable, but it ought to work. Assuming, of course, that the axes of the other eight cells were accurately aligned with it. And that the rockets would fly straight.

And that the damned boat wouldn't bounce at exactly the wrong moment, he told himself grimly.

"Right! We have to come right!" he shouted to Larry, never taking his eyes from the simple wire crosshairs in the center of the launcher's missing cell.

"Gotcha!" Larry shouted back, and nudged the wheel. Eddie's sight picture changed, and he shook his head.

"Too much—too much!"

This time, Larry didn't reply; but the Outlaw altered its course again, ever so slightly, and Eddie nodded hard.

"On! You're on!" he shouted. "Now kick this bitch in the ass!"

"*All right!*" Larry screamed, and rammed the throttles forward.

Eddie clung desperately for balance, managing—somehow—to keep his eyes glued to the crosshairs, as the Outlaw stopped bouncing. It was climbing up onto its own bow wave, now—hydroplaning as it sliced across the three-foot Baltic waves like a bullet.

❋          ❋          ❋

"Stand ready! But if any man fires before I give the order, I'll have him hanged!" Vadgaard shouted to his gunners, then glanced up at *Christiania*'s hovering sailing master.

Unlike the captains of most non-Dutch warships, Vadgaard was a seaman, not one of those "captains" who were chosen (in theory, at least) for their experience in battle, without regard as to whether that battle had taken place afloat or ashore. There was no doubt in the mind of *Christiania*'s sailing master that *he* ought to be handling the ship's maneuvers, but Vadgaard had no intention of delegating that to anyone. Not when *Christiania* was the only ship in his squadron which he could hope to control directly.

"Bring her a point to larboard," he told the helmsman quietly.

"Aye-aye, sir," the helmsman acknowledged. *Christiania*'s bowsprit swept around to point further east while feet thudded on her deck as seamen hurried to trim her sails.

He'd been wrong, Vadgaard realized as he watched the oncoming American. The attack wasn't aimed directly at *Christiania*. But it wasn't his fault he'd been fooled; he simply hadn't realized how much speed that fiendish craft had still had in reserve. What had looked like a turn to align itself on *Christiania* had actually been a turn to align on the *Anthonette*, two full ship lengths ahead of Vadgaard's flagship.

The American vessel had leapt to starkly impossible speed in what seemed less than a heartbeat. It was no longer slashing through the water like some unnatural plowshare, piling the white furrow of its bow wave to either side. Now it was tearing *across* the waves, half its sleek, knife-sharp length completely out of the water as it charged straight into the heart of his command.

Hans watched the Outlaw accelerate. Eddie and Larry had told him what Jack Clements had said about the big speedboat's maximum speed, but Hans hadn't really believed it. In fact, he'd been privately convinced that they were "putting him on," as the uptimers were fond of calling it. It just hadn't seemed possible that a *boat* could be almost as fast in the water as a Belle was in the air!

Now he knew they hadn't been "putting him on" at all. Then again, the Outlaw wasn't being that fast *in* the water. Even from Hans' altitude, he could see the way the bows rose up out of the waves, like some shark coming to the surface for its prey.

*           *           *

The universe was wings of white foam, flying across icy blue water. It was a fiberglass hull, half-airborne and half-afloat. It was engine snarl, the ear-battering impacts of that hull as it smashed across the crests of the Baltic waves, and the roar of wind around the angular barrier of the blast shield.

Eddie Cantrell hung onto the edge of the cabin hatch with his left hand, still managing to watch their target growing through his crude sight, while his right reached for the simple doorbell pushbutton incongruously fastened just below the sight. He hadn't been prepared for how quickly the range would drop, but at least the Outlaw's sheer speed had taken the bouncing effect out of the equation. The boat was no longer bouncing—despite the shocks, it was steady as a rock as it hydroplaned toward the Danes.

There was another sound, now. One that cut through even the howling chaos of the Outlaw's passage like thunder and sent clouds of dirty-white smoke spurting and rolling like fresh banks of fog. Waterspouts rose in white stalagmites as the Danish ships began to fire. But the men behind those guns, however experienced and skilled they might have been otherwise, had no experience at all in estimating the speed of a target like the Outlaw. None of the shots landed anywhere close to the charging speedboat. In fact, Eddie scarcely even noticed them. He was too focused on his sight picture and the plunging range.

It was all happening too quickly. There was no time to stand back and estimate ranges carefully. Besides, at this speed they were going to have to change course quickly . . . unless they wanted to bury the Outlaw in the target of their attack right along with its rockets!

He waited one more fleeting second, then stabbed the bell push with his thumb. A circuit closed. Current flashed suddenly through simple insulated wire to the igniters an ex-high school chemistry teacher had installed in eight eight-inch black-powder rocket motors.

For just an instant, Vadgaard thought the American had blown up.

The entire vessel seemed to disappear in a huge flashing, gushing roar of flame and an enormous burst of smoke. But the illusion of the American's destruction vanished as swiftly as it had come.

The ship itself came charging through the cloud of flame, trailing smoke behind it . . . and eight fiery projectiles screamed ahead of it like dragon's breath.

Straight at *Anthonette*.

# Chapter 47

The blast deflector worked. Eddie felt as if every hair had been singed off his head, but the shield had protected them from the rockets' incredible back blast. What no one had expected or allowed for was its disorienting effect. The sudden, blinding fury as eight powerful black-powder rockets ignited as one directly in front of them was indescribable. It didn't actually *hurt* them in any way, and if they'd realized it was coming, it probably wouldn't have had anywhere near the effect it did.

But they hadn't realized. Larry Wild had never before experienced the explosion of flame and smoke across a thick glass plate barely two feet in front of his eyes, and he would have been more than human not to flinch.

Tesdorf Vadgaard recoiled from the missiles. It wasn't as if he'd never seen smoke and flame before. In fact, in many ways, the new weapon was less terrifying than staring directly into an enemy ship's broadside and seeing dozens of gun muzzles vomiting their flaming hatred. But no one of Vadgaard's time and place had any experience of something like this. Of ruler-straight lines of smoke. Of roaring black monsters with tails of flame. Or of the brutal explosions as five of them smashed into *Anthonette*'s side like the hammer of Thor itself.

Three of them missed her completely. One of those hit nothing at all. A second hit one of the fishing boats Vadgaard had impressed to help transport the troops under his protection. It exploded squarely in the middle of the hapless infantrymen, slaughtering them like so many tightly packed animals and blowing the thinly planked hull apart. What was left of the fishing boat rolled over and sank within minutes.

The third of the "misses" exploded against the mainmast of a transport brig. The mast snapped like a sapling in a tornado, and the ship staggered aside as the flaming remnants of its mainsail set fire to her standing rigging. An inferno roared and bellowed as it consumed the heavily tarred cordage.

Vadgaard had no idea how much powder each of those missiles carried. Nor did it matter. One of the ones which hit *Anthonette* skipped off of her stout planking. Another exploded in the instant of contact, blowing a smoking, splintered crater in the surface of her side. Two more of them buried themselves in her thick timbers before they exploded. Those two ripped huge, ragged holes and shattered planking like sledgehammers. They also threw geysers of flaming debris into her rigging and cordage. No doubt, Vadgaard thought, the fires that debris started would have doomed her anyway, just as surely as the blazing brig beyond her, but it scarcely mattered. Because the fifth missile plunged directly into an open gun port and exploded *inside* the ship.

The force of the blast ripped up through *Anthonette*'s deck in a hurricane of smoke, fire, and splinters. Pieces of men came with it, and some of the men from whom those pieces came shrieked in agony. The mainmast fell—slowly, at first, but with rapidly gathering speed—as the shattering explosion cut it off like an ax just below the level of the deck. More blazing debris started still other fires all along her topsides, but that was nothing compared to the wavefront of flame cascading through her mid-deck spaces.

The wavefront that found her magazine.

Eddie felt the explosion like a body blow, and elation flashed through him on a wave of triumph. It had worked!

But even as he realized that, he had to grab suddenly for whatever handhold he could find. The Outlaw slewed wildly to port as Larry flinched instinctively away from the rockets' back blast. At a lower speed, it would have been a scarcely noticed bobble, a small kink in the Outlaw's wake. At their actual speed, it sent the thundering boat sprawling to port in a sliding, fishtailing, spray-shrouded momentary loss of control.

It was a small thing, really. It only seemed larger because of their speed.

And because that unplanned change of course carried them directly through the arc of *Christiania*'s broadside.

Time seemed to have stopped. Bits and pieces of what had been *Anthonette* rose into the air like the petals of some obscene, fire-hearted flower, and Vadgaard cringed away from its fury. Fire was the most deadly foe of any wooden ship, and he sensed the panic which possessed *Christiania*'s sailing master as the flaming shower of wreckage began to descend once again. It was a panic Vadgaard understood perfectly, but he had no time to feel it himself.

The Americans had destroyed three of his ships and killed hundreds of his men with their horror weapons, but for all of their marvels, they weren't gods. They were mortal, and as they put their helm hard over to break away from their attack, their course brought them where he could get at them. They were moving so quickly there was no possibility of adjusting his gunners' aim. Indeed, there was no point trying to aim at all, but Tesdorf Vadgaard would see himself damned and in Hell if he didn't at least try.

His sword was in his hand—not that he remembered drawing it—and he thrust it wildly at the careening American vessel.

"*Fire!*" he screamed.

It was the end of the world.

Actually, only a single shot from *Christiania*'s entire broadside found a target. The eighteen-pound roundshot was what pilots three hundred years in the future would call a "golden BB"—a fluke hit, that should never have happened.

But it did.

Eddie Cantrell had a fleeting moment to see the starboard edge of the *Outlaw*'s cockpit shatter as a spherical iron ax five inches in diameter smashed into the fiberglass. Splinters flew like smaller, flatter axes, and Bjorn Svedberg screamed as one of them ripped through his chest.

Larry didn't scream. He had no opportunity to as the same roundshot literally cut him in half ... an instant before it struck Eddie's left leg.

❋        ❋        ❋

Hans saw it happen.

One instant he was pounding his knee with a jubilant fist as he watched enemy ships exploding. The next, he saw the Outlaw go staggering aside and the gout of muzzle flashes and smoke from *Christiania*'s side. The big speedboat reeled, then turned crazily, almost capsizing. It porpoised and rolled, spinning through yet another sharp turn that almost sent it completely over, and an icy fist seemed to squeeze his heart as he realized no one had it under control.

Eddie couldn't believe he was still alive.

There was no pain, not really. That was shock, a distant corner of his brain observed, since he no longer had a left foot. *That has to hurt like hell,* that isolated corner thought almost calmly, but he couldn't feel a thing. He raised his head, looking for the rest of his crew, then looked away instantly. There was nothing he could do for Larry or Bjorn, and that same dispassionate observer in his brain told him that if he didn't act quickly, there wouldn't be anything anyone could do for him, either.

His hands moved as if they belonged to someone else, unbuckling his belt, wrapping it around his calf, yanking it as tight as it would go. It wasn't much of a tourniquet, but it was the best he could do . . . and at least it slowed the bleeding some.

The Outlaw's engines were still bellowing their fury, and he felt the boat lurch through yet another unguided turn. That part of his brain which continued stubbornly to function wondered why it hadn't capsized or collided with something yet, but he didn't have time to worry about that, either. The shore was out there somewhere, and if he ran into it at this speed . . .

He dragged himself across the blood-smeared cockpit on his belly, trying not to think about Larry or Bjorn while he did so. It seemed to take an eternity, but finally he reached Larry's broken seat. He felt a tiny stab of gratitude that the roundshot which had killed his friend had also thrown Larry's mangled body out of the way. He didn't know if he could have made himself move it to get at the wheel.

He clawed himself upright, forcing himself somehow up onto his remaining foot, and bent to peer through the blast shield view slit.

He'd taken just a little bit too long to reach the wheel, he realized almost calmly in the seconds he had left.

﹡          ﹡          ﹡

Hans banked sharply, fighting to keep the Outlaw in sight as it looped and wove through yet another impossible, writhing turn. He was lower now, trying desperately to see, and he thought he saw someone moving in the cockpit. But he couldn't be sure, and his teeth ground together as the speedboat turned yet again.

The white fiberglass arrowhead trailed spray and foam as it settled briefly onto its new course, and Hans heard his own voice crying out in useless protest as he realized what was going to happen.

More Danish guns were firing now—firing more in desperation than in vengeance. They shrouded the morning in smoke and muzzle flashes, pocked the surface of Wismar Bay with white waterspouts all around the Outlaw, but now the speedboat seemed to lead a charmed life. It charged through the waterspouts, ignoring the Danes' frantic efforts to destroy it.

But then again, it didn't need the Danes. It had its own howling engines, and those engines were its executioners. A three-and-a-half-ton sledgehammer loaded with over a hundred gallons of gasoline and twenty-four eight-inch rockets smashed into an eight-hundred-ton, fifty-eight-gun warship at something in excess of seventy miles an hour.

Vadgaard felt his elation turn to horror as the American ship collided with the *Johannes Ingvardt*. He'd realized at once that his desperate broadside had managed somehow to score a hit, despite his target's incredible speed. He'd also realized that only blind luck had made that possible, and he'd watched in disbelief as the American's wake twisted and knotted like a berserk serpent writhing in its death agony, obviously with a dead man at the helm.

But then it turned one last time and hurled itself into the very center of his squadron like some arrowhead of vengeance upon its killers. *Johannes Ingvardt*'s frantic effort to repeat *Christiania*'s lucky hit failed, and then both ships vanished in yet another explosion that sent fresh wreckage arcing into the smoke-sick heavens.

The explosion seemed to rip Hans' heart from his body. He stared down at the rising smoke cloud where two of the up-time brothers who had saved his life—and his family's—had ended their own lives, and something snarled inside him.

There. That was the ship. The one whose fire had first crippled the *Outlaw* and sent it into the weaving dance to its own death.

He banked around, then dropped the nose and lined it up on his brothers' killer.

Vadgaard never knew what prompted him to tear his eyes from *Johannes Ingvardt*'s death. Perhaps it was no more than instinct. Or perhaps it was something else. It didn't really matter.

He looked up to see the flying machine headed directly toward *Christiania*. There was something about it, about the straight, unwavering line of its course, that suddenly told him he'd been wrong about how harmless it might be.

There was no way he could possibly elevate *Christiania*'s guns high enough to engage a flying target, but his ship, too, was loaded with infantry destined for Wismar, and he bellowed frantic orders.

Hans' target grew rapidly as he peered through his improvised sight. There was movement on the ship's deck, but he paid it no attention. His entire being was focused on stick and rudder pedals, on keeping that ship pinned at the heart of his fury, and he reached out for the firing switches. Given their crude accuracy, Hans was determined not to release the missiles until the last possible moment, at point-blank range. With the plane armed with only four rockets, at stations 3, 4, 5 and 6, he could fire all of them with one flip of his fingers.

Fresh flame spouted from the flying machine, and Vadgaard heard someone screaming. It might have been curses, or it might have been prayers. Either would have worked as well . . . or as poorly.

Three more missiles came scorching down out of the heavens, and this time there was no question about where they were aimed. One of them missed. A second slammed into and through the main deck, but miraculously failed to explode. And the third hit squarely in the center of the foredeck and exploded on contact. Blast and splinters plucked men away like angry hands, the foremast swayed drunkenly and collapsed, and smoke poured up out of the wreckage. Orders warred with panic as officers and petty officers fought to impose order and extinguish the flames before *Christiania* followed *Anthonette* and *Johannes Ingvardt* into destruction.

Vadgaard screamed for the musketeers he had assembled

amidships to fire as the flying machine continued directly toward them. Their volley crashed out, discipline overcoming fear.

The flying machine flashed by very low, crossing *Christiania* in a stuttering buzz of sound. Vadgaard couldn't tell if they had hit it, though he prayed fervently that they had.

The hammer hit Hans in the abdomen, and for a moment, he was back on a bloody field outside Badenburg.

It was the second time a bullet had hit him there, but this time he didn't lose consciousness. Not that it mattered.

He looked down, then covered the hole in his jacket with his left palm. It scarcely slowed the pulsing flood of scalding blood, and then the pain hit, and he knew.

Another memory flashed through his mind. The first time he'd ever seen Sharon, when he'd thought she was the angel of death come to claim him—only to discover that she was an angel of life, who had saved him, instead. But this time, close as she was, she was too far away. He felt his strength flooding away with his blood, carried on the crest of anguish, and there was no way he could last long enough to return to Wismar and land. Not with that wound.

He wasn't the only target the musketeers had hit, either. The controls felt heavy, stiff—heavier and stiffer than his own injuries alone could explain. He didn't have as much control of the aircraft as he would have liked, but it would have to do.

"Hans! Hans, damn it—talk to me!" Jesse half-shouted into the microphone as he pushed his own aircraft as hard as he could toward the clouds of smoke rising from the sea.

There was no answer, and Jesse's jaw clenched tight.

He didn't have a complete picture of what was happening, but the radioed reports from Louie Tillman had told him enough. Eddie and Larry's initial strike had been far more successful than Jesse had ever allowed himself to hope ... only to disintegrate into disaster. The Outlaw was gone—that much Tillman knew for certain—and with it both of the boys. But that wasn't what frightened Jesse, because there was nothing he could do about it. It was too late for that. But Louie had also reported Hans' insane, low-level attack on the Danish ship which had destroyed the Outlaw. Hans hadn't reported. In fact, he had yet to transmit a single word.

"Hans, I know you can fucking well hear me!" Jesse snapped. *"Now answer me!"*

Silence. But he was close enough now to see the smoke and wreckage to which the invasion force had been reduced. Some of the Danes had already put about, clawing back toward Luebeck and away from the demons which had ravaged them. Others looked as if they were trying to continue toward Wismar, and a few of them were engaged in frantic rescue operations, trying to snatch men from the icy waters before hypothermia killed them. But most of them seemed to be milling around in confusion, still shocked and confused by what had happened. He could see the remaining speedboats hovering between the invaders and Wismar, and even as he watched one of the brigs which had been holding its course turned away rather than face them.

But Hans. Where was *Hans*?

Jesse searched desperately for the other Belle. It had to be here somewhere, but where—?

Then he saw it. Saw it crabbing back around in a wide, awkward circle. One rocket still hung on its hard point under the port wing. Obviously, the firing mechanism had malfunctioned—not surprisingly, given the crude nature of the jury-rigged installation— but that wasn't what brought Jesse's heart into his throat. That was left to the thin streamer of vapor trailing behind it, and he bit his lip. That silvery skein of blood could only be gasoline . . . which meant Hans had been hit at least once.

Jesse held his heading, racing to meet the other plane, then swung in to match Hans' course.

"Hans?" he tried the radio again. Again, no response. Carefully positioned off the other's left wing and looking at the half-dozen holes punched through the formica skin of Hans' aircraft, he felt chillingly certain why.

He edged in as close as he dared, and he bit his lip harder as he saw Hans. The boy's head hung forward wearily, and he seemed unaware Jesse was even there for at least a minute and a half. But then, slowly, his head turned. He was too far away for Jesse to see his expression, but everything about the way he sat, how slowly he turned his head, told Jesse he was badly hurt.

Jesse frantically gestured the hand signal to land, pointing vigorously back toward Wismar in an order to return. Hans stared at him across the emptiness between their aircraft, and then, slowly, he shook his head.

Jesse pointed again, even harder, and Hans altered course. But not toward Wismar. Instead, he slowly rolled to the right, turning back out to sea, and Jesse knew what he intended to do.

"No, Hans," he whispered. "Please. It's just a fucking battle, and we've already won it anyway." But even as he uttered the plea, he knew it was useless. Even if Hans' radio wasn't damaged at all, he wouldn't have listened. Not now.

There was nothing Jesse could do to stop him. Nothing *any-one* could do. For Hans Richter, it wasn't just a battle. It wasn't even just a war.

*They* fought wars, for whatever remote purposes seemed good to them, sitting in their palaces. Fought them atop the broken bones of German families; trampling their way through the entrails of German mothers; slaughtering fathers in their little shops. Hans Richter was fighting a crusade.

Just an orphaned brother, in the end, flesh of his sister's flesh. She had been his steel angel, often enough. Now, he would be hers.

Jesse watched the other plane as its nose dropped. Watched Hans adjust his course with all the assurance and skill he had learned so well. Watched the aircraft accelerate.


"It's coming back!"

Vadgaard turned away from the fire fighters at the shout. The flames were almost under control, but if the flying machine hit them with still more missiles...

Only it wasn't *a* flying machine this time. There were two of them now, and Vadgaard's heart plummeted. How many of those devil machines did the Americans *have*? And what was he supposed to do with them and two more of their accursed naval vessels between him and his objective?

Then he realized that one of the flying machines was diving.

It wasn't quite like its first attack. This dive was steeper, faster. And it wasn't headed for *Christiana* this time. This time it was headed for *Lossen*, one of his two remaining warships.

He held his breath, waiting for the deadly rain of missiles to begin once more.

But it didn't. And it only took Vadgaard a moment to understand the reason.


Hans wished his radio had been working.

It wouldn't have mattered, in one sense. He already knew what

Jesse had been ordering him to do, and there would have been no point in obeying the command. Not as badly as he was bleeding. His thoughts were growing wobbly with shock and blood loss, but he knew that much. Still, he would have liked to say good-bye. To Jesse . . . most of all, to Sharon.

He watched the thirty-gun ship growing before him, but he didn't really see it. Not any more. All he saw was a dark-skinned face, smiling at him, and he smiled back.

# Part VII

*In God's holy fire*

# Chapter 48

*Admiral Simpson:*
    *1. The purpose of this report is to provide details regarding the activities of U.S. forces engaged in combat in defense of the city of Wismar on 7 October, 1633. On that date, joint elements of the U.S. Navy and U.S. Air Force under the command of Lieutenant Edward Cantrell, USN, successfully repulsed a Danish invasion fleet commanded, it was later determined, by Admiral Tesdorf Vedgaard of the Kingdom of Denmark (details of opposing forces at Tab A). During the action, several U.S. military personnel were killed, including the commander of the defense, Lt. Cantrell . . .*

Jesse poured himself another three fingers of the local hooch and stared at the beginning of the after action report before him. He didn't know which would run out first—the hooch or his nerve.

*You coward,* he berated himself. *Your knowledge of military operations was a thousand times greater than that kid's. You should have helped him more, come up with a more coordinated plan. What was that "we're only here to provide assistance" crap?*

He bent back to his duty. Eventually, he neared the end.

> *As the still dangerous enemy fleet attempted to rally, Capt. Richter pressed his final attack against a large, as yet undamaged, Danish warship, the* Lossen. *Despite his wounds, Capt. Richter maneuvered his damaged aircraft above and, by the expedient of ramming, set the warship ablaze amidships. The warship was subsequently totally destroyed by an explosion, probably as the fires reached the ship magazine. After the destruction of the* Lossen, *the remainder of the Danish fleet withdrew to the west, under continued harassment by the remaining U.S. forces until all anti-shipping munitions had been expended. Estimated enemy losses are at Tab D. The supplementary report of the surviving U.S. naval assets is at Tab E. After the withdrawal of the Danish fleet, all surviving U.S. forces returned to Wismar.*
>
> *7. A full report of weapons effectiveness will follow under separate cover. However, in the opinion of the Chief of Staff, U.S. Air Force, rockets, such as can currently be constructed, are not the optimum choice for aerial attack. The effectiveness of the rocket attack against the Danish flagship* Christiania *was due more to the intrepidity of Captain Richter in the attack, than to the inherent suitability of the weapon. It should be noted that the same weapons, when fired from longer distances by surviving elements of the U.S. Air Force, resulted in only minor additional damage to the Danish fleet. In the opinion of the Chief of Staff, U.S. Air Force, a maximum effort should be made to develop an efficient dive bomb technique for use in future hostilities.*

Jesse poured himself another drink.

*So why didn't you press in, like you wanted to, hero? Oh yeah, that magic word, "duty." Only one aircraft left in the entire world, after all. Are you sure it wasn't cowardice?*

> *8. In conclusion, the defeat of the Danish invasion fleet was due more to the effect of surprise and the determination of U.S. forces under the leadership of Lieutenant Cantrell, than to any superiority of weaponry or tactics. U.S. military forces*

*should immediately review pre-Ring of Fire concepts of joint operations, in order to ensure greater effectiveness in the application of combat power.*

Joseph J. Wood
Colonel, Chief of Staff, USAF
Richter Field, Wismar

*Attachment:*
Admiral Simpson, it looks as if it is our mutual responsibility to recreate a system of awards and decorations. I thought it likely you would prefer to write any award recommendation you thought appropriate for Lts Cantrell and Wild, though I would, of course, be pleased to endorse anything you submit. I attach my own recommendation for Capt. Richter at Tab F. I would have preferred the Medal of Honor for Hans, but, as I see it, the DFC is within my personal discretion. I find myself unable to wait for the politicians to do the right thing.

Jesse Wood, Col, USAF

Finally finished, Jesse rose to take the messages to the radio operator. For a moment, he stared at what was left of the hooch on the table. A bit to his surprise, there was still half a bottle left. He started to reach for it; but then, almost angrily, turned away and strode out of the room.

*The least you can do now is face Sharon half-sober.*

After a bit of searching, he found Sharon where he'd first seen her when he landed his plane. At the edge of the airfield, staring out to sea. All that had changed in the hours since, while Jesse had radioed an immediate short account and then forced himself to write what needed to be written, was that Sharon was now sitting on the ground instead of standing up.

It was after sundown, but there was still enough light in the western sky to allow him to see her face clearly. The tears had dried. He thought she had none left to weep.

Awkwardly, he sat down next to her. "Sharon, I'm sorry—"

"Don't apologize, Jesse," she said softly, not moving her eyes from the same spot on the now-invisible horizon where, hours earlier, columns of smoke had marked the funeral pyres of her fiancé and two of his closest friends. "You owe Hans that much, at least. The *world* owes him that much."

Her dark eyes were shadowed, but Jesse was relieved to see the composure in them. Grief-stricken Sharon Nichols might be, but she was not struck down by it. In that moment, Jesse could see the lines of her father's face in the daughter. Not the roughness and near ugliness of his features, simply the strength in them.

"Hans was not a complicated man, Jesse. Bright, yes. But not complicated. I think that was the reason I fell in love with him, even though part of me thought the whole idea was nuts. I just . . . couldn't resist that simple, uncomplicated adoration." The last word ended with something of a gasp. She covered her mouth, holding in the sorrow.

Jesse took a long, deep breath, fighting off his own tears. "No, he wasn't complicated. Paladins never are. I guess, anyway. Not sure. Hans is the only paladin I think I ever met."

A half-sob, half-laugh came from behind Sharon's fingers. "Paladin!" She lowered her hand, exposing a sad little smile. "Not a bad word, actually. If we ignore the 'chaste' part of the business. *That* he wasn't, I can tell you. He threw himself into lovemaking with the same enthusiasm he did everything else."

After a bit, the smile faded away. "Oh God, Jesse, I'm going to miss him. So much."

"Yeah. Me, too."

She shook her head. "But—promise me. No apologies. That would detract from his sacrifice. From his whole life. He was no boy, led astray. Never think it, just because he wasn't complicated. Never think it."

Jesse started to weep. Sharon put her arm around his shoulders and hugged him close. Her own eyes were moist, but no tears came.

She lifted her head a bit. The stars were coming out, with all the clarity of a sky not polluted by a later century's flood of lights.

"The only reason they seem to twinkle," she murmured, "is because the air gets in the way. The stars themselves are pure and bright and simple. Don't confuse what you see with what there is, Jesse. Hans Richter was our bright shining star. And that's all there is to say. Now, and forever more."

That night, Mike found Veronica Dreeson at the Simpsons' house. Hans' grandmother had been staying there since she arrived in Magdeburg.

Admiral Simpson was still at his office in the shipyard. Mary Simpson, who had left the naval base an hour earlier, let him in the door.

"I haven't had the heart to tell her yet, Mr. President," she whispered as he came through. "I should have, I suppose, but . . ."

"Not your job, Mrs. Simpson. Mine." He saw that Veronica was preoccupied with reading something, and was seated far enough away not to hear them. "God damn it all to hell," he muttered wearily. "How do you tell someone that the nation which saved half her family just shattered it again?"

But he didn't have to tell her. Once he stepped forward into the room and Veronica looked at him, something in his face did the job.

"Which one?" she asked.

Mike looked away.

"How many?" she asked.

Still, he couldn't meet those hard old eyes. "Gretchen and Jeff are fine, Veron—"

"How *many*?"

"All three. All of them."

Silence. Then, quietly, Veronica spoke. "They drove them off, then. Yes?"

A bit surprised by the words, Mike was finally able to look at her. He was even more surprised to see that the hard face showed no signs of grief beyond something faintly discernable in the set of her eyes.

"I could tell by your face. You understand very little, Michael Stearns. Someday you may come to understand the difference between sorrow and despair. But I hope not. I would like to think my young boys did not live and die in vain."

That same night, after getting the news from Frank Jackson, James Nichols stared at the walls of an empty house. Realizing for the first time how much he had been looking forward to a grandchild.

An empty house. Melissa gone. Sharon gone. Hans gone forever.

There was a knock on the door. When he opened it, Tom Stone bustled through with his three teenage sons. One of them was carrying a cardboard box.

"Bummer, man," Stoner pronounced. "Really is."

"How'd you know?" James asked.

"The whole town probably knows by now," said Tom's oldest son Frank. "There's a line of people standing outside Mayor Dreeson's house, waiting to give their condolences."

"We just came from there ourselves," added one of the other boys. Ron, that was. "Annalise is taking it pretty hard, but she's trying to bear up. It'd be a lot easier for her if Gramma were still here."

"The whole town's bummed out," said Stoner. "Really bummed out. Those kids were . . . you know. Special."

He gave Nichols a scrutiny. "I figured you'd be in bad shape too. That's why we came over. Keep you some company and—"

He gestured toward the cardboard box in the hands of his son Gerry. The box was covered, so Nichols couldn't see what was in it.

Given Stoner, on the other hand, he thought he could guess.

"I am *not* in the mood to get high," he growled.

Stoner's eyes widened. "Hey, doc, take it easy. It's not grass. It's flowers. I grow them *too,* y'know."

"Oh." James felt a bit sheepish. "Thanks."

He started to reach for the box but Stoner took his outstretched arm and started leading him toward the door. "They're not for *you,* man. They're for the shrine. But we thought—you being Sharon's dad, and all—that the honor of placing the first flowers should go to you."

"What shrine?"

When they showed him, James felt his spirits lift. Not much, but some. Stoner and his boys had already set up the receptacles for the flowers—two very large terra-cotta pots, placed on either side of a little walkway. The walkway led to the trailer complex where, in the days after the Ring of Fire, Jeff Higgins and Jimmy Andersen and Eddie Cantrell and Larry Wild had taken into their home and hearts a man named Hans Richter and his family.

It was fitting, he decided. That somewhat ramshackle trailer complex was perhaps the truest symbol of what those courageous youngsters had died for. And, somehow, an old hippie had figured out the perfect memoriam to paint on the flowerpots.

One read: *Gone but not forgotten.*

The other: *We remain.*

The next morning, sitting at his desk, Admiral John Simpson finished reading Colonel Wood's after action report—for perhaps the tenth time since it had arrived the night before. His jaws tight, he set it aside and picked up the attachment. That, he had read perhaps twenty times. Whatever comfort there was to be found, would be found there.

CITATION TO ACCOMPANY THE AWARD OF
THE DISTINGUISHED FLYING CROSS
TO
*CAPTAIN HANS RICHTER, U.S. AIR FORCE*

> *Captain Hans Richter, assigned to the 1st Air Squadron, U.S. Air Force, distinguished himself in aerial combat against enemies of the United States, during the defense of Wismar, 7 October, 1633. On that date, Capt. Richter was ordered to support U.S. naval forces defending the strategically vital city of Wismar against a Danish invasion fleet. In response to orders, Capt. Richter provided vital tactical information to U.S. naval forces preparing to attack the enemy. He continued to conduct essential reconnaissance until, in the course of combat operations, the chain of command of U.S. forces was disrupted. Capt. Richter, recognizing that continued offensive operations could rout the enemy, immediately pressed an independent attack against the enemy flagship. In this attack, he severely damaged the enemy ship, at the cost of severe personal injury and damage to his aircraft. Despite his wounds, Capt. Richter continued his attack against the enemy armada. He subsequently attacked another Danish warship, which he destroyed, though suffering fatal injuries. This last attack broke the fighting spirit of the Danish fleet and ensured the safety of Wismar. Through his courage and determination against superior enemy forces, Capt. Richter brought great credit upon himself and the United States Air Force and is hereby awarded the Distinguished Flying Cross.*

*By Order of*
Jesse J. Wood, Colonel, USAF
*Chief of Staff*

Not much comfort, but some. John Chandler Simpson had spent the time since the news came, much as he was sure Colonel Wood had done. Berating himself.

*Chain of command. Senior service. Strategy. Tactics. The whole panoply. And in the end, what did it all come down to? The courage of young lions. Nothing else.*

For the first time in his life, he felt like an old man.

When Mike walked into Simpson's office, the admiral was sitting behind his desk. Stiff, upright; the chair slanted so he could stare out the window. He glanced at Mike, then returned his eyes to the glass.

Mike studied him, as he closed the door and stepped forward. Simpson's face was not "wooden" now. It looked as if it were carved from stone. Pale stone. That was grief, Mike understood, being controlled the only way the man knew how to do it.

"I'll want the Navy Cross for Lieutenants Cantrell and Wild," Simpson said abruptly. "And the Silver Star for Gunner's Mate Bjorn Svedberg. They'll all get the Purple Heart, of course."

He glanced back, still stone-faced. "Excuse me. Bad manners. Please have a seat, Mr. President."

As Mike lowered himself into the chair across from Simpson's desk, the admiral added: "I can do that on my own authority. I established the Navy's system of decorations some time ago, you know." The words were not quite a challenge. Not quite.

"You'll get no argument from me," Mike said mildly.

Simpson jerked his gaze from the window and stared at Mike. Then, even more abruptly:

"And what do you propose for Captain Richter?" He gestured toward the citation, which Mike had seen the night before. "Colonel Wood's already awarded him the Distinguished Flying Cross. Most he can do. But I agree with him—it's not enough. Mortally wounded, Captain Hans Richter deliberately flew his plane into an enemy vessel. That calls for the Congressional Medal of Honor, Mr. President. Posthumous, as most of them are."

Anger was starting to seep into his voice now, coloring the ice. Mike was glad to see it come. The anger of a man like Simpson, he could reach. He could do nothing with a man of stone.

"In our *old* universe, I should say," Simpson half-snarled. "In this new one, who knows? I don't believe you even *have* a Congressional Medal of Honor. Forgot about it, naturally."

"Yes, I did," said Mike calmly. "My apologies. I'll see to correcting that immediately." He said nothing else; just waited.

Simpson's icy glare held for a few more seconds. Then, he closed his eyes. Took a deep breath, and slowly let it out through half-open lips. By the time the exhalation was finished, the lips looked human again.

"Sorry, Mr. President. That was quite uncalled for on my part."

"No, it wasn't. It was a screw-up. Mine. I guess I never really thought—wanted—ah, hell." He took a deep breath of his own. "I'll see to it, John. Today, if possible. There won't be any problem, believe me."

Simpson's shoulders slumped. With the slump, went all trace of stone from the face. It was still a wooden face, true, but . . .

Such was the nature of John Chandler Simpson. Mike had his full measure now. He could live with wood.

Wearily, Simpson rubbed his face. "Ah, it's all crap anyway, Mike. Just the last parting shot of a man who hates to admit he was wrong about anything." When he removed the hand, to stare back out of the window, he was almost smiling. "You were right, weren't you? When all is said and done. I thought you were insane to think we could build another United States your way. Throw it open overnight to people who had none of our background, customs, traditions."

Mike's mouth twisted. "Well . . . it *was* a risky enterprise. And still is, John. Risky as hell. I could use your help, that's for sure."

"You'll get it." The words came as sure and certain as John Chandler Simpson could say any words. Which was sure and certain indeed. "I'd be betraying those dead boys if I didn't. The proof is in the pudding. The first Congressional Medal of Honor will go to a German boy—and rightly so. And the other two young heroes were among those who first took him in, and welcomed him with open arms. Which I sure as hell didn't."

He made a fist and rapped the desk with it. The gesture was not an angry one; simply . . . firm. The way, Mike imagined, Simpson had often in times past pronounced that something involving his business was settled and done.

"That's what it all came down to in the end, Mike," he said sadly. "Just the raw courage of four young men. Two Americans, a German and a Swede."

"Two lashes is enough, John." Mike's chuckle was dry; even harsh;

but not caustic. "We country boys have lower standards, y'know, than you High Church types. There's no apology needed, and sure as hell no penance. You trained them, remember? You built this Navy, not me, not anyone else. Just like Jesse built the Air Force. Their sacrifice will give you—all of us—the tradition we need. The start of it, anyway. But it couldn't have happened without you either."

Simpson turned his face back to meet Mike. There was pain in those eyes. Not that there hadn't been before; but now, it was plainly visible.

"I like to think so, Mike," he said softly, almost whispering. "I'm not sure I could get through this otherwise."

"Yeah, I know. It's keeping me going too. But it won't happen without—"

An interruption came, in the form of a very worried-looking Dietrich Schwanhausser almost barging through the door.

"Excuse me, Admiral, but General Torstensson—"

Torstensson himself came through the door, shouldering the aide aside. He took two steps into the room, and planted his boots. Then gave Mike and Simpson a look that was part-glare, part-challenge, and . . . oddest of all, more than a trace of simple curiosity.

"So!" he exclaimed, in his thickly accented but quite good English. "Now we will see. The city is erupting beneath our feet, President and Admiral. What do you propose to do about it?"

# Chapter 49

By the time Mike and Simpson neared the entrance to the naval yard, Mike was pretty sure he understood what was happening. The hurried words spoken by Nat Davis as he came up to meet them confirmed it.

"I don't know what's happening, Admiral," said Nat, his face creased with worry and confusion. "Almost nobody showed up to work today. Sergeant Kohler tells me a lot of the sailors didn't either."

Mike cocked his head, listening. He could hear what sounded like a low murmur in the distance. Words were impossible to make out, but he knew that was the sound of a huge crowd in the making. He recognized the odd feeling it gave to the air itself, like an echo in a cavern. He'd felt it before, from time to time, when he'd participated in mass demonstrations in Washington, D.C. called by the labor movement.

Except the crowd at those demonstrations had not been angry so much as simply resolved to exercise—as the First Amendment to the Bill of Rights put it—"the right of the people peaceably to assemble, and to petition the Government for a redress of grievances."

But that right was *not* established in the CPE as a whole, even if it had been in the new United States. And, in any event, the population of Magdeburg was not one accustomed to the fine etiquette of a long-established democratic society. That they were gathering in the city to demand a redress of grievances was clear. It was also clear to Mike, just listening to the undertone of fury in that distant murmur, that the crowd was going to be paying little attention to any notions of "petition" and "peaceable assembly."

"It's blowing wide open," he pronounced. "The news from Wismar must have been the last straw."

General Torstensson was gazing at him with a kind of detached curiosity. As if he was an observer of a heretofore unfamiliar phenomenon, interested to hear what a self-professed expert might have to say on the subject.

Simpson was frowning. He, clearly enough, was simply confused.

"But . . . *why*? We won at Wismar! Whatever else—whatever it cost us—that much is crystal clear. Why are they angry? Why aren't they celebrating?"

For a moment, Mike felt a flash of anger. For all that he'd come to understand and respect Simpson—even, to a degree, develop a certain liking for the man—he was forcefully reminded of the enormous gap that still existed between them. In the end, Simpson would always look at the world from the top down. Mike, no matter how high he rose, from the bottom up.

*Try watching men you love choking their lives out with black lung, you rich bastard, fighting the companies tooth and nail*—and *their so-called "experts" and 90% of the government*—*for every dime they can get. Try*—

He broke off the thought. Snapped it off, rather. This was no time for it.

"Why are they *angry*? Well, John, let's start with the fact that for fifteen years they've watched Germany's princes—and every other prince in the world except maybe Gustav Adolf—grind their lives under. Even Gustav is only on probation, as far as they're concerned. Add to that the fact that their lives before the war weren't exactly a commoner's paradise."

He shook his head. "Wismar didn't make them *angry*. Anger, they already had—anger and rage and grief and bitterness, drunk to the dregs. And I can guarantee you that the spectacle they've been watching right here in Magdeburg for the past few weeks"—Mike pointed a rigid and accusing finger in the direction of the palace where the Chamber of Princes had been holding their sessions—"did nothing but rub salt in the wounds. Once again, Germany's princes will bicker and dawdle and protect their privileges, while Germany's millions stare at their blood and intestines spilling on the ground."

Torstensson grunted. The sound was that of a detached observer, acknowledging that the expert had made a valid point.

"What Wismar did," Mike continued, "was finally crack their *doubt*. Not doubt in the princes—they've long ago given up any faith in princes—but doubt in their own ability to do anything about it."

He took a long, almost shuddering breath, fiercely controlling his own grief. "Hans Richter didn't simply destroy a Danish warship, John," he said softly. "He also broke the last chain the princes had on Germany. When all is said and done, he belongs to *them*. Not us. Or, at least, we only had a part of him. We can give whatever medals we want to that part. But Germany's people will lift his memory to the skies, and use it for their own standard. And that standard—don't doubt this for a moment—is a battle standard. The standard of people who, for the first time, think they can *win*. Understand for the first time, really, that 'winning' can even be a part of their world."

"True," pronounced Torstensson. "The first elements of the crowd moving toward the palace were chanting his name when I left the palace grounds. And, as you say, it was a battle cry." He smiled thinly. "I know the sound of such."

"But—" Simpson shook his head. "Who are they going to fight? Here, I mean?"

"Me, most likely," growled Torstensson. "Or the Saxon troops. John George has already summoned them into the city. To protect himself and the princes from mob violence. That is his excuse, at least, and—" Torstensson cast a quick glance toward the swelling murmur. "I cannot honestly say it's simply an excuse. Some of the crowd is already calling for his head. As well as the head of the elector of Brandenburg."

Now, Torstensson looked every inch the 17th-century general. Still interested, perhaps; but also sure of his duty. His eyes were hard and narrow.

"Who, may I remind you—yes, George William is a swine; and so what?—has a son to whom Princess Kristina is unofficially betrothed. And since I am the commanding officer of Gustav's army in this city—where the Princess also lives now—I must put a stop to this. However brutal that may become."

Simpson's eyes widened. "My God, this could be a disaster!"

"Screw that," Mike snapped. "Yes, it could be a disaster. It can also be a triumph and a victory. And a *big* one, too. But that's up to us, gentlemen." He gave both Simpson and Torstensson a hard look of his own.

"Will you follow me?" he demanded. The question was addressed at both men.

Torstensson's answer came immediately. "Yes—to a point." He smiled somewhat grimly. "And do not ask me what that point may be. I do not know yet. But . . . this much I can promise you, Michael Stearns. So long as I retain confidence that you can control the situation, I will do as you say."

"Good enough. John?"

Simpson drew himself up stiffly. "Mr. President, the Navy is always under your—"

"*John!* Cut it out, goddamit. Now is not the time for this. I know you will obey orders. That's not what I asked. Will you—this time—*follow* me?"

Simpson hesitated and looked away. Then, his lips quirking a little, nodded his head. "Yes, Mike. This time I will. I just hope—"

He shook his head. "Never mind. If *you* don't know what you're doing in a situation like this, I'm damn sure nobody else is even going to come close. So. What do you want?"

Mike's thoughts had been racing ahead. "First. Did you ever get those fancy uniforms?"

Simpson snorted. "They're sitting at the tailor's, still. All made up and—no money to pay for them. You wouldn't approve the expense, you may recall."

Mike grinned. Now that he was sure he would be going into combat fully armed—his kind of combat, the kind he understood and knew he was genuinely superb at—he was full of cheer and confidence.

"We'll fix that, right now." He drew a small notebook from his shirt pocket, scribbled a few letters on it, signed it, tore the page off and gave it to Simpson. "Here. Have one of your men take that to Abrabanel Bank." The small building was nearby, since—no fools, they—the Abrabanels made sure they located in the radical district, and close to the U.S. military base. "They'll issue the funds immediately, with that code. As fast as possible, I want you and all your men in the fanciest dress uniforms you have."

Simpson passed the sheet over to one of the petty officers who

had started gathering around. He didn't even have to give instructions. The noncom had been listening to the conversation and was
already trotting toward the gate. Simpson nodded toward another
man, this time one of the German-born commissioned officers.

"You heard, Lieutenant Kelleher. Go to the tailor and make sure
the uniforms are ready when the money arrives." He turned back
to Mike. "What next?"

Mike waved his arm, encompassing in the gesture the entire navy
yard. "Now, I want you and Nat to turn this whole place into
Disneyland. Today the U.S. Navy is going to throw an open house,
with all the trimmings. Guided tours, let the kids play on the boats,
the whole shot. For the first time, we're going to let Germany's
people come and see *their* Navy. The one whose heroes fought
alongside the great Hans Richter."

"Fuck *yes!*" exclaimed Nat Davis. "That's a great idea, Mike. For
damn sure, all the missing sailors and workers will pour in. And
they'll bring their families with them too, sure as shooting."

Mike was watching Simpson, expecting an outburst on the
subject of security. But, instead, Simpson nodded. Mike had forgotten that Simpson had also run a major factory.

"Yes, I agree. Nothing pleases working men so much as showing off their place of work to their wives and kids. Every time we
held an open house in the plant, the place was packed."

Mike was not surprised. *Because it's the one place where, even
in our old world, much less this one, a common man can really feel
like a man. Here is where I spend much of my life, wife and children, doing what only real men can do. Here, I am a master of my
trade. Screw the suits. They don't count.*

But this was no time for idle thoughts. "Next thing. I need you
to pull out the loudspeaker system you set up in the plant. Have
some electricians bring everything to the palace. While you're
organizing Disneyland, I've got to organize as fine a filibuster as
any politician ever pulled off. I've got to *talk* to that crowd—and
my own voice just isn't loud enough or strong enough. Not for
a whole day. Won't surprise me if it turns into a two-day stint.
Maybe three. That crowd is *pissed.*"

"Done." Simpson started to issue orders to yet another petty
officer, but, again, the man was already racing off. By now, the little
knot of confused noncoms and junior officers gathered around
Mike and Simpson and Torstensson was neither little nor confused.
The air of sure command and authority had returned, and if it

was centered on their President rather than their admiral, all the better. The confidence of those men was pouring back in like a flood.

Quickly, Mike pictured in his mind the layout of the city in the vicinity of the imperial palace. Fortunately, the palace opened directly onto a large square, into which three broad avenues emptied. Mike was certain that Gustav Adolf had ordered that layout with cannons firing grapeshot in mind. But a square large enough to commit mass slaughter was also large enough to bring order to the masses before slaughter became necessary. There was room there for a large enough part of the crowd to assemble, and for him to transform an inchoate burst of fury into a political rally.

True, the crowd would be baring its teeth. A "petition for redress of grievances" with real fangs. All the better. Let Germany's princes cower for a change. So long as Mike could keep the blood from flowing, he could turn a potential disaster into another nail—a very, very *big* nail; a spike, in fact—driven into the coffin of Europe's aristocracy.

He glanced at Torstensson. *Easier said than done, of course. Since I'll need a Swedish nobleman general to hold the spike while a Swedish king swings the hammer. Oh, Mike. Mama done told you not to walk on tightropes. And look at you now!*

It was a cheerful thought, though. Mike Stearns, for the first time in months, felt as if all his blood was flowing. He would need that confidence, he knew, just as any master craftsman needs it when he faces one of the top challenges in his trade. But, also like a master craftsmen facing such a challenge, he could not deny the sheer exuberance involved. That, too, was necessary.

"The next thing we'll need, John, is for you to provide General Torstensson with secure radio communications with Gustav Adolf in Luebeck. That means secure from *us*, too. Unless I miss my guess, the emperor and I are going to be trading a lot of horses over the next day or three. But he can't do that unless he's sure he can talk privately to his own man on the spot, without me eavesdropping." His eyes flicked back and forth between the American admiral and the Swedish general. "Do we have a Swedish soldier who can use the radio well enough?"

"Yes." The word came simultaneously from both men. Torstensson nodded to Simpson, allowing him to answer.

"We've got two, in fact." Simpson's eyes ranged the small crowd, coming almost immediately to rest on a short and thickset man.

"That's one of them. They've been training for weeks with us. By now, they should know how to handle all of it."

Torstensson cocked his head, looking at the man Simpson was pointing to. The gesture was inquisitive. The Swedish radio operator was fluent in English, of course, given his assignment, so he'd been able to follow the conversation.

The man nodded firmly. "Good," said Torstensson. "That will help. A great deal."

He gave Mike a smile that was still grim, but also a bit amused. "I must warn you, however, that while it is most disrespectful to suggest that His Majesty would stoop to something as low and common as horse-trading, he is actually very good at it."

"You're telling me," chuckled Mike. "I've swapped horses with him before, you know. It's still a painful memory."

*But not all* that *painful. Sure as hell not compared to a civil war, if it can be avoided. Some can't, but this one can.*

"Anything else?" asked Simpson.

"Send an immediate radio message to Wismar. I want Jesse back here ASAP, with the plane. And tell that stubborn apolitical character that if he doesn't overfly the palace at least three times before he lands, I'll have his liver for dinner. Gas is cheap; blood isn't. But, most of all, I want Sharon here. Desperately. She'll be worth her weight in gold."

"Done. Anything else?"

Mike thought a moment.

"Yes. Please send a runner to your wife. I'll want—very much want—Mary and Veronica to be standing on the palace steps next to me."

Again, Simpson was caught off-balance. "Mary? Why? Sharon and Veronica I can understand, sure—Hans Richter's betrothed and grandmother. But Mary—"

The admiral groped for words. "Mike, please. She'd be like a fish out of a water at something like that. Not to mention scared out of her wits. Ask Mary to give a speech to a crowd of—well, you know. Rich people sitting at fancy tables in a fancy banquet room while she tries to squeeze money from them for her latest project. But—"

"John, be quiet." Mike's voice was low, but almost steely. "What you—or Mary—understand about this stuff could be written on the head of a pin. You're not *in* that universe, any longer. You're in this one. And in this one . . ."

He groped for words himself. As he did so, his eyes ranged across the area, coming to rest on the small crowd of Germans gathered just beyond the gate to the naval yard. Except it was no longer a small crowd, he saw. Several hundred people, he estimated. Not hostile. Simply . . .

Watching. Waiting. Wondering.

Most of all, sitting in judgment.

He recognized one of the men standing at the front of the crowd. Gunther Achterhof, that was, one of the CoC's militants. Shortly after Mike had arrived in Magdeburg, he had noticed Gunther and several other men following him everywhere. A self-appointed bodyguard, he suspected. Which Gunther had immediately confirmed when Mike went up to him and asked. He'd then spent some time in conversation with the man. Idle conversation, in one sense; a probe, in another.

The sight of Achterhof brought everything into full and final focus. In that one man, Mike knew, could be found the soul of the mob now rising throughout reborn Magdeburg. And soon enough, he knew, pouring into the city from the nearby area.

All of it. Beginning with the rage which could kill and mutilate a soldier, but not . . . necessarily ending there. Perhaps no longer even needing to start there, or even go to that dark place at all. Because there was also hope, and yearning. Most of all, the dawning half-recognition that perhaps *victory* was within his grasp, not simply vengeance. The beginning of it, at least.

"I'll bet on Gunther," Mike murmured, more to himself than anyone else. "I'll always bet on the world's Gunthers."

He turned back to Simpson. "Do you know what they call Mary? The people who live around here, I mean. The most ferocious of the CoC's militants. The same ones, by the way, who watch your house—her house—day and night, to make sure no enemy strikes."

He didn't wait for Simpson's answer.

"They simply call her 'the American Lady.' That's 'Lady' with a capital L, John. You can hear it in the way they say the word. And do you know *why* they call her that? It's not because of her table manners, I can assure you of that. They wouldn't know whether she was using the right fork or not themselves. No, the reason's simple. It's because your servant Hilde is one of them, and they know how she treats her servant. She says 'please' and 'thank you,' and—most important of all—she looks at Hilde when she says it."

Torstensson grunted. This grunt had more than a trace of surprise in it. But, again, also contained the sense of an observer acknowledging an expert's point.

Simpson didn't really understand. It was obvious in the blank look on his face.

"You just don't get it, John. You *still* think—you and Mary both—that these noblemen are just this world's version of your old familiar upper crust. Well, they're not. They've got all the vices, oh, yeah, in spades—but damn few of the virtues."

His smile was very thin, now. "Virtues, mind you, which you only have because *we* beat them into you, over the centuries. Often enough with blood and iron. Usually our blood and your iron, but blood always wins out. If nothing else, it'll rust iron."

Still, incomprehension. Mike almost sighed. *Give it up, will you? The man is what he is, and you can live with that. Just explain it to him.*

He thought of demanding that Torstensson explain. But Mike wasn't actually sure of Swedish custom. He suspected the Swedish nobility, given their own history, lacked some of the sheer unthinking arrogance of Germany's princes.

"When a German nobleman or noblewoman addresses a servant, John, they do not say 'please' or 'thank you.' In fact, they don't even address them at all. They summon the servant and never look at them. Simply gaze at the wall, as if the servant does not exist, and give their orders in the third person. 'He will bring us tea.' 'She will clean the bedroom.'"

Simpson's eyes almost crossed. "You're kidding!"

"No, he is not," said Torstensson. "Such is indeed the custom."

The general swiveled his head. The crowd's murmur was swelling ever more powerfully. "Best we be off, now. These servants will not be satisfied until, at the very least, we look at them. Straight in the face, as you say." He gave Mike a glance. "And maybe not then. Let us hope you can teach them—"

He broke off abruptly. Mike was grinning at the general, and the grin was purely feral. A wolf, daring a nobleman lost in the forest to finish the sentence. Before the wolf tears his entrails out.

"I do not propose to teach *them* manners, General Torstensson. I propose to teach manners to Germany's aristocracy. Who are badly in need of the lesson."

The nobleman flinched from the wolf. The general remained. Mike gave him his instructions for the day, as surely and firmly as might Gustav Adolf himself. "You, Torstensson—come with me. Your job is to keep those fucking Saxons away. Far away. And most of your own troops, for that matter. Just enough for a bodyguard for Princess Kristina. That's it."

"Yes, Mr. President."

Mike turned back to Simpson. "Send Mary," he commanded. "If she can't bring herself to speak, so be it. But I want her standing there with Sharon and Gramma Richter right next to me, facing *our* folks. And beginning the nobility's instruction. They'll either learn to use a fork, Mary's way—and be damn quick about it— or they'll learn what a pitchfork feels like. *My* way, if it comes down to that."

He began to turn toward the gate. But paused long enough to address some final words, both to the admiral from another world and the general from this one. "And it *will* come down to that, gentlemen, if I can't be satisfied at the negotiating table. Never doubt it, not for a minute. I'll compromise, if I can, but don't ever think I don't know whose side I'm on."

He pointed a finger at Gunther Achterhof. "*His.* So you can deal with me, or deal with him. Your choice."

# Chapter 50

By the time Mike and Torstensson got to the big square before the palace, the area was already packed with the crowd. Fortunately, Achterhof and his militants were able to clear a path for them. The task became easier as they passed through the mob, and word of Mike's arrival began to spread. Toward the end, nearing the steps of the palace itself, the biggest problem was clearing aside people who were pressing in to cheer them.

Well . . . cheer Mike, at least. There were precious few cheers coming Torstensson's way, which Mike was quite sure the general had noticed.

*Good. Get the picture, Lennart? Make sure you pass it along to Gustav.*

Still, Mike was relieved not to hear any calls for Swedish blood, either. Fury and rage were obviously roiling through the thousands of people gathered there. But, so far at least, it seemed aimed at Germany's princes and not the Swedish prince who—in theory— ruled them all.

By now, partly under Becky and Melissa's tutelage and partly from his own disciplined reading program, Mike knew enough history to recognize the phenomenon. It was a common pattern, repeated many times. The crowd was still—just barely—willing to give the emperor a pass. *If he did the right thing and got rid of his evil and wicked advisers.*

The emperor seemed a goodly enough fellow, after all. He'd beaten down the Habsburgs, hadn't he—something no German prince could claim. And he slept with his own troops in the field, didn't he—lying on the cold ground right next to them. And, perhaps most important of all, he had greeted the United States with . . .

Well. "Open arms" was a bit much. Still, he *had* greeted them. Which no one could say for German princes.

Except one, who had chosen to give up his princedom.

When Mike saw Wilhelm of Saxe-Weimar already standing on the steps of the palace, not far from Spartacus and—like the young German leader of the CoC—trying desperately to calm down the mob, he gave him a silent nod of respect. And, simultaneously, felt a deep sense of relief and satisfaction.

*If I can head off this civil war—contain it, rather—maybe we won't have to fight the next one at all.*

When Wilhelm and Spartacus caught sight of Mike striding up the steps, the look of relief which crossed their own faces was almost comical.

"Thank God you're here!" hissed Spartacus. "What do we do? I've been trying to reason with them, but . . ."

Mike clapped him cheerfully on the shoulder. Then, as Wilhelm scurried up, did the same for him. Both gestures were purely histrionic. Mike Stearns was on stage now, and the common folk of his new times did not appreciate method acting. They wanted *dramatic* gestures. On this day, they would *demand* them.

Now with one arm around the shoulders of each man, half-dragging them forward with him, Mike stepped up to meet the crowd. To greet the crowd.

No, to greet the *people*.

His people, always. For better or worse. In sickness and in health.

*"Welcome, people of Germany! Rejoice in this day of triumph! Victory is ours! Today—and tomorrow!"*

By the time Simpson's men arrived with the equipment to set up the loudspeakers, Mike was almost hoarse with shouting. But he'd settled things down enough to avert any immediate clash. Torstensson had indeed withdrawn all Swedish troops from the area, except a bodyguard remaining inside the palace for Princess

Kristina. Who was herself leaning out of a window, smiling and waving cheerfully at the crowd. Many people in the crowd were now waving back.

*God bless smart little girls. And I think that one's a genius.*

The Saxon troops John George had summoned to the city were also nowhere in evidence. Torstensson had taken most of his Swedish troops out to meet them beyond the city's limits, and explain the facts of life. Given Torstensson, Mike could just imagine the terse manner in which he'd do it.

*Fact one. We whipped Emperor Ferdinand at Breitenfeld.*

*Fact two. You ran like dogs.*

*Fact three. You've got ten minutes to get out of here. Five, if I don't see your tails between your legs. Now.*

When the loudspeakers went into operation, Mike shoved Wilhelm toward the microphone.

"I need a break. You're on, buddy."

Wilhelm stared at the microphone much like a rabbit staring at a serpent. "What do I say? I don't know—I've never—"

"Piece of cake, Wilhelm. Just give a campaign speech. But, ah, one word of advice."

"Yes." Wilhelm stared at him. Mike grinned.

"Don't run against *me*. Not today. You can save that for the election. Today, you're campaigning against the princes."

Still staring. "What election?"

"The one I'm going to swap a horse with the emperor for. I'll have it by the end of the day tomorrow, I think. Maybe sooner. Gustav's a decisive man, and I do believe the cardinal and the princes, between them, have really and seriously and genuinely pissed him off. The stupid bastards."

Still staring. But Mike's grin never faded. It wouldn't have, even if he weren't on Europe's greatest stage.

"I think it's time the CPE had an actual *government*. Don't you, Wilhelm?" He jerked a thumb at the palace behind them. "Instead of this silly playpen for princes."

Wilhelm's eyes closed. A little smile came to his lips. "Ah. Yes, actually." His eyes reopened, and this time did not seem confused and uncertain at all. "Yes, indeed."

It took the former duke a bit of time to learn how to speak into a microphone. But not much, really, given his unfamiliarity with the device. And once he began talking, the words themselves flowed easily enough. By the time he was done, in fact, he was bordering on Mike's own brand of full-bore rhetoric.

Only bordering on it, to be sure. But it was a border, now, not a frontier.

Mary Simpson never spoke at all, that day. Mike, seeing the sheer terror that held her almost paralyzed, did not press the issue. It was enough, really, that she was standing there on the steps in full view of the crowd. _The American Lady. Wife of the Admiral, who commands the ironclads. Our ironclads._

And, of course, managing that superb professional smile. Mike suspected that Mary Simpson, if condemned to Hell itself, could greet Satan with it.

Besides, Gramma Richter could hold the fort. Which she did, in her own splendid tough-old-biddy manner. By the time Veronica was finished speaking, the crowd had settled down completely. They wouldn't have dared do otherwise.

She was done shortly after noon. Mike took another stint at the microphone. By now, he estimated the size of the crowd at somewhere in the vicinity of forty thousand people. Between thirty and fifty thousand, at any rate. The entire population of Magdeburg, for all practical purposes—along with, by that time of the day, a number of people pouring in from the nearby countryside.

But it was really impossible to get a very accurate count, even though Mike knew the rule-of-thumb methods for doing so. He'd organized rallies himself, in times past, not simply been a participant in them. The problem was twofold.

First, the crowd was simply too large to fit into the square. It spilled down all three of the major avenues, as well, as far as Mike could see.

Second—this he saw with pure relief—the crowd was beginning to circulate. People were leaving as well as coming in. And almost all of them going in one direction—toward the naval yard.

He recognized that phenomenon, also. He'd seen it often enough, in another universe. Working men with families—and Magdeburg was by now the most plebeian city in all of Germany, even including Grantville—do not come to large political rallies very often. Quite unlike students and footloose young people, in that respect. And, when they do, they often bring their families.

To see the capital of their country, as much as to petition for a redress of grievances. Because that was how they saw it, however much or little that image might correspond to reality. *Their* capital, of *their* country; which *they* had built—and *they* had died for.

So, often enough at mass rallies in Washington, D.C., Mike had seen men and women and children go wandering off after a time from the speeches and the waving banners. Just to go, as a family, and admire the Washington monument or the Lincoln Memorial or the Smithsonian.

Magdeburg had no such things, except the palace of a still-alien emperor and . . . the U.S. Navy yard.

Not *yet*.

Mike was standing next to Mary, while Spartacus took a turn at the microphone. He leaned over and spoke softly into her ear.

"You know any good architects?"

"No. But . . . just two days ago, the landgravine—Amalie, I mean, Hesse-Kassel's wife—was telling me—"

"Never mind the details. Find a good one, Mary. We need a great big monument right smack in the middle of this square. Something like . . . I dunno, maybe—"

"Nelson's column? In Trafalgar Square?"

"Sounds good to me. I saw a picture of it once, on a postcard. And then get a good sculptor to do a bronze statue of Hans Richter for the top of it. A *big* statue."

Mary's smile had some actual life in it now. Mike himself was grinning widely, as he had been all day. Professional expressions, the both of them. But still heartfelt.

"Yup," said Mike. "Can't have a Hans Richter Square without a Hans Richter monument."

Mary's eyes widened. "I think they already named it Vasa Square. I know for sure the biggest avenue is named Gustavstrasse."

"Not by tomorrow. Day after at the latest. Gustav can keep the street. I'm not greedy. Gustavstrasse it is. But the square doesn't belong to him. Not anymore."

Mary's eyes widened still further. "Do you really think you can *take* it from him?"

"Me? Hell, no. But Hans Richter can. You watch."

Then, in mid-afternoon, Mike heard the sound that announced victory. Victory for this battle, at least. Victory sure and certain.

Within a few seconds, no one in the crowd was looking at the palace or the speakers standing on the steps before it. All heads were turned up, craning to see the sky. By the time the Belle II passed over the square, the giant crowd had erupted in sheer, frenzied enthusiasm. All traces of fury vanished in that ear-smashing wave of sound. Bitterness washed away by the tide of victory; vengeance dissolved by triumph in full flood.

Not gone. Simply . . . dissolved. Diluted enough, now, not to be toxic. And leaving behind a salted ocean of human will and energy, surging with glorious strength.

Come nightfall, Mike would begin using that strength to reap the fruits of this new victory. But at that moment, in the mid-afternoon sun, he bent his head for the first time that day. The grin disappeared for a time, and he closed his eyes. Even allowed a few tears to come, remembering young men he had once known and would always treasure.

The blood of heroes which had made it all possible. A boy who had learned to fly—and, once again this day, had been the steel angel protecting his people.

The seal was placed on the victory less than an hour later, when Sharon and Jesse finally arrived in the square. There was no need for the small squad of Marines who accompanied them, in flashy dress uniform, to clear a path. The crowd parted before them, as if directed by a single will.

Mike was amused, at first. Moses couldn't have done it better. But then, hearing the new chants going up from the crowd as Jesse and Sharon moved through it, he understood the truth. This was no prophet, using God's power to part the sea. This was the will of the crowd itself, greeting its own new nobility. An informal aristocracy they had *chosen*.

*Der Adler!*

That title Mike was familiar with. The other, he was not.

*Die Fürstin!*

He understood what the term meant. But—

"Why are they calling Sharon Nichols a princess?" Mary Simpson asked, puzzled.

Mike knew the answer before she'd even finished the question. And knew, as well, that another victory had been won. The beginning of it, at least.

"She's black, Mary. None of them have ever seen a black person before. Not more than a handful, anyway. And we're still a lot closer to the Renaissance, when it comes to the way people see race, than we are to later times. The slave trade's only in its infancy. There hasn't been time yet for that raw racism to take root. So . . ."

Whatever else might confuse Mary Simpson about her new world, she *did* know the world's great literature. Backwards and forwards, in fact.

"Othello, you're saying. The Moor. Exotic, mysterious, powerful. Even majestic. Dangerous too, perhaps, but not inferior. Except the sexes are switched, and it ended in a different kind of tragedy. God knows, a much cleaner one."

"Yeah, exactly. And what people *do* know is that her father is some kind of medical wizard from a foreign and fabled land. Almost a sorcerer, maybe. And—" He took a deep breath, as much to savor the man's memory as to control his grief that it was a memory. "And she was betrothed to Hans Richter. Who else would have been suitable as a bride for Germany's great new folk hero, *except* a princess? All the better if she's foreign and mysterious and exotic."

For the first time that day, Mike heard a little laugh coming from Mary Simpson. Thinking about it, he realized it was the first time he'd ever heard her laugh. It was a brittle kind of laugh, perhaps. But that, too, he could live with.

"Did anybody ever tell Hans?" she choked out.

Mike's grin was back, and in full measure. "Which Hans? The one we knew—or the one his own people will choose to remember? Not that it makes any difference, really."

He watched, for a moment, as the young woman walking alongside Jesse slowly approached the steps which formed an impromptu speaking platform. Slowly was the word, too. Sharon was not smiling at the crowd, nor responding to their waves with a waving hand of her own. She was in mourning, after all, and no pretense involved in it at all. Still, she was moving in a stately, regal sort of way, nodding her head to acknowledge the crowd. There was a great dignity to the procession, in fact. No queen of Europe could have done it better.

Thinking of queens of Europe reminded Mike that there was one final stone he could place that day. Possibly even a capstone.

He turned his head and looked up at the window of the palace from which, all day, Kristina had watched a near-rebellion turn into a rally and a celebration. As he had hoped, and half-expected, the girl was watching him. Mike suspected she'd been keeping an

566 David Weber & Eric Flint

eye on him all day. Seven years old she might be, but she was also—in fact and not simply in fancy—a princess born and raised. Very likely, someday, to be the empress of Europe's most powerful realm.

*And sharp as a tack, to boot. Oh, yes. Interesting years, we've got ahead of us. Let's start finding out just* how *interesting.*

The look he gave her was that of an eagle. And, with a subtle but forceful gesture of his finger pointing at the ground by his feet, gave Princess Kristina a mute but unmistakable command.

*Get down here. Right now!*

Sharp as a tack, indeed. The princess' face was split by a grin, her mass of curly hair bobbing eagerly.

*Coming! Just got to bowl over my bodyguards.*

Kristina's face vanished from the window. Even over the noise of the crowd, Mike thought he could hear the shrill tones of a seven-year-old princess issuing commands.

He turned back, chuckling. Mike had no doubt at all the guards would be protesting vigorously. He also had no doubt at all that the daughter of Gustavus Adolphus would go through them like tenpins.

Sure enough. Just as Sharon started up the steps, Kristina came charging through the great front doors of the palace. She even managed to restrain her headlong seven-year-old charge by the time she reached the steps to greet Sharon with a hug—instead of bowling her right back down.

"And the crowd goes wild," said Mike to himself, grinning wider than ever. Quite loudly, in fact. He couldn't have heard himself otherwise.

The crowd had, indeed, gone wild.

"If I didn't know better," Mary said—speaking very loudly herself, or she couldn't have been heard either—"I'd swear you staged this."

Jesse came up just in time to hear the remark. "He did," the Air Force colonel snorted. "Impromptu theater, of course. Mike's specialty."

He gave Mike a look that was half-amused and half . . .

Wondering, perhaps.

"Torstensson's at the base, by the way. I think he's been on the radio to Gustav Adolf for at least two hours. They've already had to switch operators, to give the first one's fingers some rest. So. What next, O great stage magician?"

Mike was watching the princess. Both of them, it might be better to say. They were still hugging.

"The education of royalty, I think. That's got to be put into the right hands."

Mary gasped. "Michael Stearns! You can't take a little girl *hostage*."

"Why the hell not?" he replied, almost snarling. "When Europe's royalty has taken millions of poor girls hostage? Watch me, dammit."

Seeing the look on her face, he sighed. "Forget the Three Rivers, Mary Simpson. Welcome to the Thirty Years War. Gustav Adolf won't blink at the idea, trust me. First, because he knows she'll be treated right. Second, because he'll get his own back for it. Don't think he won't. Royal blood be damned. That man could swap horses with anyone in the hills. Matter of fact, I think he'd have made a champion horse thief."

# Chapter 51

That evening, in Edinburgh, Robert Mackay gazed down on the sleeping form of his daughter-in-law. She had brought his grand-child to him, once the fever finally broke and it was certain Alexi would survive. This disease, at least. Then, exhausted by her own travails over the past days, Julie had fallen asleep herself, lying on the bed next to Robert and cradling Alexi in her arms.

It was a large enough bed, so Robert had made no attempt to rouse her. Nor, truth be told, had he had desire to.

"She must have struck you like a thunderbolt, the first time you saw her."

Sitting on a chair next to the bed, his hand caressing Julie's hip, Alex smiled. "Oh, father, aye and she did. I could not keep my eyes from her. 'Twas a bit awkward, given the circumstances. What with her people standing about with those frightening guns of theirs."

"Life is an awkwardness, son. Why should its most precious moments be otherwise?"

The infant was beginning to stir. Ignoring the pain, Robert leaned over and plucked her out of her mother's arms. Then, cradled her in his own.

"You've still got your first winter ahead of you, babe," he murmured. "But we've a fire, and you've a spirit. So I think God will wait, for the pleasure of your company. For a time, at least."

❄    ❄    ❄

That same evening, in London, the fate of other children hung in the balance.

"Your Majesty," said the earl patiently, "you cannot—"

"Cannot! Cannot! You—*Wentworth*—cannot use that word! Not to me!"

Charles was in full and peevish fury, stomping back and forth in his private chambers—insofar as his somewhat mincing steps could be described as "stomping" at all.

"There was nothing in the books about this! *Nothing!* And I read them all!"

"Please, Your Majesty. We must deal with the matter using our reason. You cann—" He broke off, for a second or two, almost grinding his teeth. "The history in those books presupposed the *events* in those books. Change one—and others change also. As I was saying, it is not possible to bring thousands of mercenary soldiers from the Continent without the risk of disease coming with them."

The queen interjected her own comments. As usual, casting confusion onto muddle. "There was no mention of a plague in the books! None! Not this year! I read them also!"

"Of course not, Your Majesty. There was no sudden flood of mercenaries into the island in those books either. Coming from a continent awash in epidemics."

Henrietta Maria glared at him. Nothing odd in that, of course. The queen of England disliked the earl of Strafford at the best of times. For the past week, since he'd refused to give another of her favorite courtiers a military post—as if the soldiers didn't have enough grief on their hands as it was, trying to contain the unrest swirling throughout the island—the dislike had become open hostility.

"Nothing in the books!" she repeated. "I read them all!"

Strafford realized it was pointless. Best to move on to practical things.

But the king forestalled him there also. "The queen and I will leave London immediately. On the morrow. The city will be a pesthouse within days. We'll winter over in Oxford."

"Your Majesty, I beg you to reconsider. England is still in something of a turmoil. Unrest everywhere. In London, I can guarantee your safety. The new troops have been concentrated here—"

"Exactly why there's a plague!" shrilled the queen. "What were you *thinking*?"

It was all Strafford could do not to lose his temper completely. *What was I thinking, you mindless idiot? I was thinking that every rebellion in England stands or falls on London, in the end. Didn't you read that also, in those books? Lose London, and soon enough— surely as sunrise—you will lose it all.*

Again, there was no point. He tried to plow on. "The Trained Bands have been dispersed. They no longer even dare to come into the streets. In Oxford . . . I cannot be certain what might happen. Besides, there are many who have welcomed the new turn of things, even here in London. If Your Majesties remain, that will signal confidence. With proper procedures—"

A sudden thought came to him. He tried to pursue it, but the king's petulance drove everything under.

"Not possible! My subjects should have confidence in me because I am king, not because of where I choose to reside or what I choose to do. To claim otherwise borders on treason. The dynasty is what matters, *Wentworth.* Our very lives are at stake. We leave tomorrow—and that is *final.*"

The earl bowed his head. "Sire."

"Not *you,* of course," snapped the king. There was more than a trace of spiteful glee in the words. "*You* will remain in London. Your family also. Since you seem so concerned with providing the people with *confidence.*" He waved his hand. "Now be off, about your business. The queen and I have much to do, thanks to your negligence."

By the time Strafford reached his home, his rage had passed, if not his bitterness. He was able to think clearly again.

*So be it. I can hardly complain, after all, since it was what I was going to propose to the king himself.*

His wife Elizabeth greeted him in the hallway. Nan's hand was held in hers.

Strafford allowed himself a moment simply for affection, such as his stiff manner could manage. Then, stiffly, gave instructions to his wife.

"Pack up whatever you can. I am moving all of you into the Tower. I'll remain here, but I want you safe. As safe as London can be, at least."

"The *Tower*?" Elizabeth's face was creased with confusion.

"Trust me, wife. If there's any place in London that will weather this new storm, it will be the Tower."

❆          ❆          ❆

"Will he be all right?" Andrew asked anxiously. His eyes were fixed on the two-year-old child Rita Simpson had just finished examining. Not far away, leaning against a wall in the cramped quarters of a Yeoman Warder, Andrew's wife was standing, her arms crossed tightly over her chest. Her face was pale, perhaps, but composed. If little George died, he would join one of his siblings in the Tower's graveyard. She still had two others, who seemed healthy. One of them was already seven, and the other five. The odds for them were good now.

"I think so, Andrew," Rita replied. Then, sternly: "*If* you follow my instructions. But for the sake of God—and little George—*don't* let them bleed him."

She studied the infant for a moment, her lips pursed. "I don't know exactly what he's got, but I'm sure it's neither plague nor typhus. Could be . . . oh, lots of things. But the deal is, Andrew, even if I can't cure the disease itself, I *can* probably treat the symptoms. And with most diseases, it's usually the symptoms that kill off the kids so quickly."

"Oh, yes, Lady Stearns. We'll follow you in this. Don't much trust the doctors meself."

"I'm *not* 'Lady Stearns,' " she snapped. "Dammit, I'm tired of hearing that silly phrase. The name's Rita Simpson. Mrs. Simpson, if you want to go all formal about it. My mother-in-law's the lady in the family. Ask her yourself, if you don't believe me."

Andrew did not argue the point. But, seeing the set expression on his face, Rita realized that she'd not moved him in the least. Indeed, had just finished confirming him in his opinion.

"Dehydration's the big killer. What the kid needs is plenty of fluids. Water, basically, with electrolytes. Salt'll do, but I'll see if we can scrounge up some sugar also. I'll set up a regimen for you, and I'll check in every day. Okay?"

"Yes, La—ah, Mrs. Simpson."

Rita didn't know whether to laugh or cry. Somehow, Andrew managed to make the term "Missus" sound like "Duchess."

"Guess they've decided to just look the other way," Darryl announced, as soon as he heard the bar drop across the door. "Gave me no argument at all."

He walked over and squatted next to the prisoner. "Melissa says it's because the Warders have heard enough to know you're apparently some sort of demon. I think they've already come to that conclusion about us too. But since we seem like friendly enough demons—or at least calm, cool and collected like you—they've just quietly decided it's best not to rile us any. Demons remember shit. And, who knows? If they ever get loose . . ."

Quickly, he swapped the batteries. Then, drew a photograph out of his pocket.

"It took me a while to finagle it out of her, but this is what she looks like. Why the hell she bothered to hang on to a driver's license in the first place . . ."

He shook his head at the folly of women, and handed over the little card. Then, as the prisoner began studying the small picture filling one portion of it, Darryl shifted uncomfortably.

"Look, it's a shitty picture of her. Those damn things always are. I think they must have some kinda exotic high-tech camera designed especially to make everybody look as bad as possible. Mine looked like Jesse James with a hangover."

He wasn't sure the prisoner even heard him. "I'm telling you—trust me—she's really not bad looking."

He was cramping the truth here, at least as far as Darryl was concerned. Stocky women in their thirties with plain faces and mouse-brown hair—okay, yeah, pretty damn good figure; especially the jugs—just weren't to his taste. In general, Darryl's tastes ran toward young women with blond hair, slim figures, and long legs. In particular, especially lately, toward a certain young woman in the Tower with—what else?—blond hair, a slim figure, and legs he couldn't see but was starting to have lots of fantasies about.

Alas, she was the youngest sister of the Yeoman Warder Andrew. Who was a rough-looking customer in his own right, even leaving aside his two brothers and his uncle. The uncle especially . . . Darryl managed not to wince. Then, thinking of Melissa, he did wince.

*Give peace a chance, my ass. Melissa catches me making a move . . .*

*Eeek.*

The prisoner didn't seem to have noticed any of Darryl's hesitation, though. So he plowed on confidently.

"We'll start looking for your kids, too. Make plans for them, when the time comes."

That brought the prisoner's eyes from the photo. "And how will you do that?" he asked.

"Well . . . I'm not sure yet. But, reading between the lines of the latest radio messages, I think—"

He paused, trying to figure out where security began and ended. Then, with a little shrug:

"I think an old buddy of mine is on his way. Not soon, of course. But when he gets here . . ." Darryl grinned evilly. "Hell on wheels, that country boy. Take it from me."

"'Hell on wheels,'" echoed the prisoner, smiling faintly. "There are times, Darryl McCarthy, when I find myself fearing for your soul. Of course, 'tis true—as an Irishman you're most likely damned anyway."

Darryl jeered. "You wish!" Again, he shifted uncomfortably. "And that's something else. I want a promise from you."

"Aye?"

"You don't ever go to Ireland without me coming along. In an *of-fi-cial* capacity, that is. I checked with Tom—he knows this stuff—and he tells me the Russkies even got a name for it. It's called 'political commissar.'"

The prisoner's smile was no longer faint. "An Irish watchdog, is it, set to keep the demon on a leash?"

"Yeah, pretty much. *Promise me*, Ironsides."

"Done, Darryl McCarthy. My word of honor."

"Good enough for me." Darryl gave him a little clap on the shoulder and rose to his feet.

Then, seeing the prisoner's eyes drop again, he uttered a protest. "Hey, I'm telling you, it really *is* a terrible picture."

The prisoner didn't even seem to hear him. Watching the way he studied the photograph, Darryl winced again. Like most men his age, he didn't like to think he'd someday be afflicted by that dread disease.

"'Tis a strong face," the prisoner murmured. "I like the lines of it."

Darryl fled, as if from the plague itself.

That same evening, in Amsterdam, still another child's fate was decided. Or, at least, subjected to debate.

All the members of the U.S. embassy were gathered in the main room, as they had been since the news had come from Wismar. After sundown, at least. During the daytime, Gretchen had channeled her own grief into sheer willpower, driving forward the organization of Amsterdam's new Committee of Correspondence with a literal vengeance.

Already, a situation of dual power was emerging within the city. In theory, while the prince of Orange was away marshaling his forces in Overijssel, Amsterdam was under the authority of its city council—what the Dutch called the *vroedschap*. In practice, however, real power was beginning to slip more and more into the hands of Gretchen and her rapidly growing band of Dutch comrades. The civic militia's soldiers, if not many of the officers, were beginning—tacitly, if not openly—to consult with the leaders elected by the new CoC. Many of the soldiers were joining the CoC themselves.

The process was neither uniform nor smooth, of course. There had been any number of angry shouting matches, in the streets and in the civic militia's assemblies. But, so far, only one of those confrontations had escalated into outright violence.

And, even then, not much violence. A flurry of fists on a city corner, followed by a pause. Into the pause Gretchen had come stalking down the cobblestoned street. The news of Wismar had by then spread throughout Amsterdam as well, and with it the name of Hans Richter. That she was the older sister of the hero of Wismar was just as well known. As was her reputation for being the more ferocious of the siblings.

She had neither threatened with words, nor drawn her pistol. Simply stared at those who had taken it upon themselves to assault a handful of CoC streetcorner orators.

"Begone," she commanded, and they were.

The infant Rebecca had snatched from carnage was the center of attention in the room. That had also been true, since the news of Wismar came. Grief at the loss of brothers and friends, salved by the sight of a smiling babe.

A cheerful sort of boy, he seemed. Very curious, too, the way his fresh eyes seemed to study everything.

There came a knock on the door. Heinrich answered it.

"For you, Rebecca. A rabbi says he wants to speak to you. In private, he says."

Rebecca rose from the couch, handed the child to Gretchen, and went to the door.

Standing outside, looking very uncomfortable, was a man she recognized. She couldn't remember the old man's name, any longer. But she was certain it was the same rabbi who, two and a half years earlier, had led Amsterdam's Jewish community to expel her father Balthazar for heresy. Excommunicated and banned—what the Jews called in *herem*.

She'd detested the man then; and, judging from the sour look on his face, detested him still.

"Yes?" she asked coolly. "You have discovered the child's identity?"

"We knew that almost immediately," he replied. "The difficulty has been in deciding what to do."

"What is there to *decide*, for the sake of God? If he has family, we will return him to them. If not, we will care for him ourselves."

The rabbi glared at her. "Do not speak of 'God,' heretic. You do not have the right. Nor—" The old man's hard eyes went past her shoulder, looking into the interior of the house. "—does that boy. So we have decided. Even his kinfolk have agreed. He is in *herem*. Best you take him yourself."

"*What?*" Rebecca groped for the logic. The insane logic. "He's not even a year old! He can't be!"

"He was born less than a year ago. What does it matter? He is destined for heresy anyway. Best for all of us if we deal with it now."

Rebecca's temper was on the verge of cracking. She had to grit her teeth for a moment. Then, almost hissing the words:

"Let me explain something, you arrogant old man. Not even such as you can claim to read the future. And it gives me great pleasure to inform you that, centuries from now, you will be quite forgotten by everyone except for—if you are lucky—a handful of scholars. There is only *one* Jew from the Amsterdam of this era who will be remembered by the world, and that is—"

She slammed to a halt, almost choking.

"My God. But—"

Wildly, she turned her head, staring back at the infant perched on Gretchen's lap. "But he was born in . . ." This time she did choke.

"Oh, God," she finally managed to whisper. "What is his *name*?"

He told her. Then added: "November of 1632, yes. We have copies of those books also, heretic. Those which we found of interest. So take him now. We cast him out."

Vaguely, Rebecca felt him leave. Vaguely, she closed the door. Her eyes were fixed entirely on the child.

No one had ever heard Rebecca whoop with glee. It was quite a piercing sound, actually. Something of a cross between sheer unadulterated joy and a warrior counting coup—or collecting a scalp.

By the time they finished wincing, Rebecca had crossed the room and snatched up the baby. Then, holding him high:

"Do you know who this *is*? One of the world's dozen greatest philosophers! *Baruch de Espinoza!*"

She clutched the baby to her chest—the rather bewildered baby, judging from his expression—and babbled on:

"Better knowm as Benedict Spinoza, after they expelled him and he went to live with the Mennonites who took him in—an expert lens-grinder too, he was—although that's what probably killed him, ruining his lungs with the dust—and that won't happen *now*—be sure of that, my husband's a union man—oh, I must tell Michael! We'll adopt him ourselves!"

She thrust the child back into Gretchen's arms, and raced for the stairs leading up to the radio room. "Who is on duty? Jakob?"

"Yeah, he's up there, Becky. He's—"

No point in continuing, so Jimmy fell silent. Rebecca had already reached the first landing, her footsteps—normally so light—sounding like a herd of stampeding buffalo. They could hear her shouting to the radio operator in the room above. "Quickly! Quickly! While the window lasts!"

Everyone still in the room stared at the baby. The infant returned their scrutiny with one of his own. He seemed a bit puzzled by it all.

Which would not be surprising, of course, since the adults were more than simply puzzled. As the minutes went by, in fact, and the enormity of the event came into clear focus, they were downright aghast.

"We *can't* let this happen, buddy," muttered Jimmy. "I mean . . . it's like a crime against nature, or something."

"You got that right," said Jeff firmly. He reached over and lifted the baby out of his wife's arms. Then, holding him up, gave the little boy a look of stern resolve.

"Don't worry, kid. We'll protect you. Think of us as your uncles, or something."

"First thing we do is get him a little Caterpillar hat," opined Jimmy. "Then—fast as possible—teach him D&D."

Jeff nodded. "And I'll tell you what, Jimmy. I actually tried to read the *Ethics* once. Got through the first chapter. This kid is gonna make a *great* dungeon master."

"You idiots," growled Gretchen. "Think *big* for once, can't you? If the boy can write great metaphysics, sure as hell he can write great political tracts."

"Teach him to ride a horse, maybe," chipped in Heinrich, ever the practical man.

"Naw, screw that," countered Jeff. "I've still got my dirt bike, y'know. Get this kid up on it—fast as possible, before he's totally ruined. Betcha I can take up a collection and have a little leather jacket made up for him. Then—"

"Oh, yeah!" exclaimed Jimmy. "That's perfect! I even got a spare one at home!"

"—put a Harley-Davidson decal on it. Plastered right across his little chest. For the arms, maybe—"

That was as far as he got. Rebecca, moving in her usual light-footed and graceful manner now, had come back into the room. Just in time to hear the last exchange.

"*Hillbillies!*" she shrieked. Snatching Baruch from Jeff's hands, she retreated into a corner; clutching the baby to her chest and bestowing upon everyone in the room the glare of a mother determined to save her child from the Devil's horned and cloven-hoofed minions. "*You have no respect!*"

The next day, the destiny of yet another child was determined; and those of all the world's children poured into a new mold.

When he came to Luebeck's Teuffelsorth Bastion, shortly before noon, Colonel Ekstrom found his king already there; leaning on the wall and gazing out over the Trave River toward the Baltic. The colonel was not surprised. In the middle of a campaign, Gustav Adolf frequently took only a few hours sleep. The king, at such times, seemed to have an almost boundless store of energy.

Ekstrom had not gotten much sleep himself, the night before, and was still feeling the effects of it. As Gustav Adolf's only staff adviser in Luebeck, Ekstrom had been a part of the seemingly endless negotiations which had kept both him and his monarch in Luebeck's radio station until well after daybreak.

The negotiations were over. This initial round, at least. The terms of the bargain were established. Clearly enough, at any rate, to get them through the current war. And perhaps beyond it—perhaps, even, well beyond it.

It remained for Gustav Adolf to make his decision. Yes or no.

David Weber & Eric Flint

At the close of the negotiations, the king had announced that he would make the decision only after having gotten some sleep.

The man at the other end had not objected. That also had not surprised Ekstrom. He had never personally met Michael Stearns, but hours of nonstop negotiations give one a sense for such things. Stearns had not only the skill of an expert negotiator, he also had its vital secret: *confidence.*

Not bluster, not threat. Confidence. Confidence in himself, first. Then, as well, the calm certainty of a man that his demands were just—the core of them, at least—and that he *would* get what he wanted. Sooner or later, so why not make it sooner and save everyone time and grief and trouble?

The king of Sweden, of course, possessed that same confidence in himself. Until the past twelve hours, Ekstrom would have sworn he had the same calm certainty in the justness of his cause.

Today, however, he was not sure. He studied his monarch for a moment, as the huge king himself was studying the horizon. Trying to find perspective, perhaps, in that great vista.

Gustav Adolf must have heard his footsteps. Without taking his eyes from the horizon, the king spoke.

"Yes, I was right. Best to make this decision after some sleep. Most of all, make it in the sunlight. Richelieu is wrong, you know."

Ekstrom wasn't certain what the king meant by that remark. But he asked no questions. He was quite sure Gustav Adolf would explain.

"Yes, the Ring of Fire was a warning from God. But it was not a warning concerning ends. It was a warning—to the world's princes—of what means He would tolerate. I am quite sure of it, now. It is as clear to me as that horizon."

The horizon was actually a bit murky, as was common for the Baltic this time of year. But Ekstrom understood that the king was not referring to clarity of vision, so much as depth of perception.

He nodded. "So, you will accept."

"Yes," announced the king. "I will accept."

Ekstrom's eyes moved further east along that horizon, in the direction of his own homeland. "Well. We will still have Sweden, of course."

Gustav slapped the top of the wall. "More than that, Nils! Soon enough!" He pointed toward Denmark. "I will have the Union of Kalmar, damn me if I won't. On Swedish terms, this time, not Danish. And just to make sure that drunken bastard Christian understands what is coming—and soon!—I have decided to create a new Swedish peer. There were only twelve, before I made Julie Mackay a baroness. Time to add another."

He turned his head and gave the colonel a very cheerful grin. "I think it has a nice ring to it, myself. Sharon, baroness of Bornholm."

Ekstrom matched the grin. The large island of Bornholm was perhaps the single most strategic position in the southern Baltic. It was also Danish territory.

"Send the message, Colonel. One word will suffice. 'Yes.' "

Still, Ekstrom hesitated. "Are you—" He steeled himself. He *was* the only royal adviser in Luebeck, after all. True, the king could speak to Torstensson over the radio. True again, Torstensson had advised the king to accept the terms. But Oxenstierna was absent and unreachable, and Ekstrom felt a certain responsibility to try his best to fill the great chancellor's place.

"Kristina—perhaps—"

"*Enough*, Colonel. I say the answer is 'yes,' and I will not quibble. Besides . . ."

The king returned his gaze to the horizon. "Let the world think of her as a 'hostage,' if they will. I do not. And neither, I am quite certain, does Michael Stearns. I have studied the man, Colonel. Very carefully, these past two years. I do not believe—any longer, if I ever did—in predestination. That, too, is the message of the Ring of Fire. I do, on the other hand, believe in character."

Slowly, and with what appeared to be great satisfaction, Gustav Adolf's eyes scanned the entire vista. "This is a man who killed as few Spaniards as he could, at the Wartburg. Prevented his own people from unleashing poison into the world. Managed to reconcile his most bitter enemy, once the time came and that was possible. Such a man will not murder a child, simply for the sake of small political gains. He might be ruthless enough, but he is not that stupid. Because he understands that certain ends preclude certain means. Or victory becomes a meaningless word."

Ekstrom thought upon it; and found himself agreeing.

"There is more," the king continued. "A 'hostage' is also a pledge. And has not Michael Stearns made that same pledge, to the world? Pledged his wife to one nation, and his sister to yet another? There is no triumph without risk, Colonel Ekstrom. Never trust a man who thinks there is. Down that road you arrive at John George."

The king's lips peeled back in a smile which was barely

distinguishable from a snarl. "The elector of Saxony, who is about to discover that he is no longer the greatest of Germany's princes. And will soon enough discover—the stinking treacherous swine—that he is no prince at all. I remember all my wounds. Especially those in my back."

He pushed himself away from the wall and gave Ekstrom a hearty slap on the shoulder. "Go now! Besides, think how thrilled Kristina will be at the news. *She* won't mind at all, I can assure you of that."

Ekstrom didn't have to think upon *that.* "She'll be jumping for joy," he predicted, smiling himself. "As long as they let her keep a good horse."

# Chapter 52

Mary Simpson was relieved to see that Mike Stearns showed up for the soiree in the imperial palace properly dressed. True, he'd *promised* her he would, but . . .

There was at least a part of Mary Simpson left which was uncertain about the peculiar creature known as Mike Stearns. Who knew when the man might suddenly choose to present himself before Germany's princes dressed as an uncouth barbarian?

But, he hadn't. *Properly dressed, indeed.*

She examined him for a moment, as he stood in the archway after having been announced by the stentorian-voiced majordomo. It was not hard to do so, since Mary did not have a milling crowd swirling around to obscure her view of him. The whole room had grown still and silent the moment his entrance was announced.

There were perhaps three hundred people in the great hall. Most of the crowd consisted of the princes who had thrown themselves in with Hesse-Kassel's Crown Loyalists, along with their wives and closest relatives. Perhaps two dozen people from Magdeburg's new class of prominent manufacturers and merchants, looking somewhat uncomfortable and out of place in that glittering noble assemblage. A handful of top officers in Gustav's army, led by General Torstensson, along with the three top officers of the U.S. Armed Forces—her husband the admiral, General Jackson and Colonel Wood. Sharon Nichols and her father James, who had just arrived this morning in Magdeburg. Veronica Dreeson, looking *very* uncomfortable and out of place.

Fortunately, the abbess of Quedlinburg had taken the old lady under her wing as soon as she arrived, along with keeping an eye on the rambunctious Princess Kristina. The sight of the abbess and her two companions—a young princess and an old commoner— caused Mary to shake her head slightly with bemusement. Of all the strange things in 17th-century Germany, perhaps the strangest for her had been discovering a Lutheran abbess, governing an institute of noble bluestockings who took no religious vows; also governing an independent territory of her own which had given her a seat in the Reichstag and then in the Chamber of Princes; a cousin of the Saxe-Weimar brothers; and fearsomely intelligent and well-educated to boot. Spending some time in the abbess' company, as Mary had done for the past period, had dispelled whatever lingering suspicions she might have had that the people of her new world were inferior to those of her old one. She'd have given her eyeteeth to have had the abbess working with her in Pittsburgh.

There were a few other notables present. The three most important of which were: Ed Piazza, who had arrived in the city with James Nichols; Wilhelm Saxe-Weimar—or Wilhelm Wettin, as he was now calling himself; and Otto Gericke. Gericke was a scientist, engineer and government administrator in his early thirties. One of the few survivors of the slaughter in Magdeburg in 1631, he had been appointed to oversee the city's reconstruction. Mary Simpson had grown very fond of him in the past few days. Gericke had an artistic streak in him as well, and was always receptive to her ideas and proposals.

*He looks good,* Mary thought, as she inspected Mike. Then, forcing herself to be completely honest: *No, he looks superb.*

He did, too. The tailor she'd sent him to had managed to combine Stearns' insistence on a certain "plebeian simplicity" with as splendid a fabric and cut as that worn by any of the princes in the room. Mary was quite certain that, soon enough, the style would be copied throughout much of Germany. It was almost bound to be. Style and fashion were always determined, in the end, by the world's most powerful and prestigious people.

Which, today, Mike Stearns was—and looked the part. If the garments he wore had none of the sheer splendor of those being worn by the princes, the lack was more than made up for by the imposing nature of the man who wore them. Stearns was tall, very well built, and had the kind of face which, if not precisely handsome, exuded the manly vigor and self-confidence that made the term "handsome" a moot point.

Princes who *look* the part are almost always handsome by definition. Taken feature by feature, after all, Gustav II Adolf himself was not a particularly attractive man. One could claim that he had a beak of a nose, was usually overweight, on and on—none of which made any difference at all. Put the king of Sweden in a room, dressed for the occasion, and he would instantly dominate it.

Such were the rules in Mary Simpson's world, at least. And she thought the same rules, perhaps diluted and adjusted, would apply in all worlds. But she gave the matter no more thought. Tonight, she was *in* her world again. And knew that, at least for some time, she would be able to remain there. The relaxation which that knowledge produced gave her, effortlessly, the ability to project her own proper persona for the occasion.

And so she did, sweeping forward through the crowd. The official hostess for the event, and one who was already starting to be called, here and there, the "Dame of Magdeburg." Her hands outstretched, the supple professional smile firmly in place, and her eyes—without seeming to—quickly doing a last inspection of her troops.

*The landgravine's in place. Excellent. Didn't expect any less, of course. Amalie's such a smart woman, thank God. The abbess is keeping Veronica and Kristina sheltered. Good, good. Hesse-Kassel has a huge crowd pinned to the Nichols, père et fille. Splendid.*

"Prime Minister Stearns! So delighted you could come!"

She gave not a moment's thought to the title. The majordomo, of course, had presented Mike with his full set of titles: *President of the United States, prime minister of the United States of Europe.* But that was all much too complicated for the purpose of this evening's soiree. Soon enough, in any event, Mike would be resigning as president and Ed Piazza—having gone in quick succession from secretary of state to vice-president, after Frank Jackson's resignation from that post—would succeed him until new elections could be held.

Everything was in flux anyway, Mary knew. It would take months, no doubt—more likely a year or even more—for all the fine points to be settled. Even the names of the territories would have to be changed. The United States of old—that of which Grantville was the capital—would need to be distinguished from the new federation which had almost the same name. A federation of which it would become a mere province. True enough, the largest and most powerful province in the new nation, and its center of gravity—but still only a province. No longer enjoying semi-sovereignty, although more in the way of provincial power than the American states had retained in another universe. But still, formally at least, distinguished from all the others—except probably, the soon-to-be-created province of Magdeburg—only in the fact that when he entered it, the hereditary king of the United States would do so as the captain general.

Mike had insisted on that small formality. But Mary understood perfectly well that he had done so only to smooth the way for his own government to ratify the agreement he had made with Gustavus Adolphus. "My folks'll get stubborn if they can't keep claiming we're still a by-God republic," he'd told her, smiling crookedly.

She'd had her doubts, true. Personally, she thought the whole thing was a bit silly. The cranky quirks of hill people; almost superstition. But she'd said nothing, simply nodded. That much Mary had learned. She would not again make the mistake of second-guessing the judgment of a man whom she had concluded was Europe's shrewdest politician. Not least of all because, whatever her reservations about this or that detail of the settlement, she approved of the thing as a whole.

Once again, Mike Stearns had turned a stumble into a self-confident stride. Not for him, falling on broken glass. *Forward, not down. Always forward.*

For all practical purposes, Mike and Gustav had carved out a new and very real nation out of a goodly portion of the Confederated Principalities of Europe. A compromise, on both parts. It would remain a monarchy, whose king ruled as well as reigned— but only within constitutional limits. Being fairly well-versed in history, Mary thought of it as roughly equivalent to the situation in her own world's England in the late 18th century. The Vasa dynasty would rule; but only within the limits set—and continually reshaped—by a new world's versions of Pitt and Burke.

A compromise, yes—but one with room to grow. Already, Wilhelm V had resolved to cast his own fate into that new mold. He would remain landgrave of Hesse-Kassel. But he had already summoned a constituent assembly—membership to be determined over the next few months—whose job it would be to provide the new province of Hesse-Kassel with a constitution. That new province of the United States of Europe would have a different structure than Grantville's province, of course. As would all of them, variations on a tune. But it would be subject to the same national laws, which set sharp limits to the power of princes—and gave major incentives to those princes shrewd enough to turn a sow's ear into a silk purse.

Which Wilhelm V certainly was. So long, at least, as he kept listening to his wife Amalie and his close friend Wilhelm Wettin. He would certainly be shrewd enough to make sure that the coming constituent assembly would be dominated by Hesse-Kassel's productive classes.

George, the duke of Calenburg, was practically licking his chops. *His* province contained the Wietze oil field—and the Abrabanel interests had already agreed to open a provincial branch of their bank in his capital city of Hannover.

The counts of the Wetterau were both licking their chops and negotiating amongst themselves in something of a frenzy. Their territories would need to be consolidated, to be sure, which would leave some of them holding more than others. But—O happy day—since much of the Wetterau territories lay *outside* of the CPE, they would be the ones whose provincial power would grow the quickest. Assuming, of course, that Gustav's coming counterblow against the League of Ostend was as devastating as they expected it to be.

There were some losers in the deal, of course. Big ones. The former princes of Pomerania and Mecklenburg, first and foremost. But since they were now sheltering under the wing of Saxony and had followed John George's lead in effectively seceding from the CPE—in fact, if not in name—nobody in that great ballroom in Magdeburg gave a damn. Their territories had been under direct Swedish rule for three years anyway, so the official transformation of them into provinces would mean very little "on the ground." Certainly not to Pomerania and Mecklenburg's commoners! Even by German standards, the princes of those regions had been an exceptionally foul lot.

Today, they huddled in Dresden and Berlin. Tomorrow . . . Or, at least, the year after that . . .

No one in that ballroom had any doubt at all that once Gustav Adolf settled his accounts with the League of Ostend, the Swedish eagle's beak would fix itself on Saxony and Brandenburg and their horde of princely toadies.

The man had a short way with traitors, formalities be damned. For all intents and purposes, the CPE no longer existed. The loyal regions would incorporate into the new United States. The disloyal ones would soon enough seek an alliance with the Austrians and Poles. A "cold" civil war would become hot, before too long.

"So, Mary, what do you think?" Mike asked softly, as she took him by the arm and began parading him through the room.

"It's shaping up perfectly. Wilhelm and Hesse-Kassel have agreed to meet with you privately in one of the smaller rooms, later tonight. Give it about an hour, I'd say. First, I need to introduce you around."

"You're the expert. I take it you don't want me charging into the crowd and glad-handing everybody."

She kept the smile firmly in place. "Are you crazy?" she murmured. "You're not at a campaign rally *here*, Michael Stearns. The trick at these things is to be approachable, yes—but let *them* approach you. It's all very civilized, but don't kid yourself. What you're really doing here is establishing dominance, simple as that. *Prime Minister.* You're just doing it in a way which lets them all save face."

She could see the first little tremors in the crowd, which, so far, had kept a respectful distance. "The youngsters will be the first. Make sure you shower them with approval. Nothing gauche, you understand. Dignity, dignity. That's what princelings need, who've thrown themselves into the fire in a burst of enthusiasm and announced their voluntary abdications."

Mike made a little grunting sound. "That happened early in the French Revolution too, if I remember right. Good. I've got high hopes we can manage to avoid the guillotine and whiff of grapeshot side of the business. Most of it, anyway. I'll talk to Frank and Lennart about the possibility of offering them commissions in the new army. It'd have to be staff positions, of course, at least at first. The volunteer regiments are going to be pretty woolly in these early days."

She started to respond but saw the first wave coming. Very quickly, too. She never really had time to finish the introductions before Mike began showering seven ex-noblemen, five of them still teenagers, with a display of reserved-but-sincere approval which she thought would have met even George Washington's standards.

*Dignitas. That's the trick.*

He managed it effortlessly throughout that first critical hour. Adjusting his *dignitas* properly, from one person to the next. Shading it with gravity for the solemn, ardor for the ardent; exuding confidence for the nervous, relaxation and wit for those willing to chance it. Best of all, he managed to keep a serene expression when dealing with the babbling witless idiots who constituted perhaps half the crowd.

*About the same as Pittsburgh,* Mary estimated. *Subtract ten percent for the abbess. God, I love it.*

"So, Michael. How soon do you foresee the first nationwide election?"

"Hard to say, Wilhelm. I'm guessing about one year, but . . . It'll depend on a number of variables. The press of the war, obviously. Things will be quiet there through most of the winter. Just siege warfare, really. Come spring . . ."

Mike shifted in his seat a little. "Then, on the other end, there's the simple mechanical problems involved. Establishing election boards which are trusted to be reasonably honest and efficient. Procedures for counting the votes. On and on. Just *printing* the ballots will be something of a challenge." He smiled cheerfully. "I foresee a rapid expansion of the printing industry in Magdeburg."

Wettin chuckled. "Do you *ever* miss a chance to scheme on two levels? Just what Magdeburg needs! More printers! The most radical artisans in Europe."

Mike shrugged easily. "Don't complain, Wilhelm. Yes, Magdeburg province will be a bastion for me. In some ways, even more so than—ah—"

Hesse-Kassel's smile was very wide. "What *are* you going to call it, have you decided? The 'United States' province of the 'United States of Europe' just won't do. Too confusing."

"Personally," said Mike, scratching the back of his neck thoughtfully, "I'm rather partial to Gustav's suggestion. 'East Virginia' has a nice little sound to it—and it would certainly be a none-too-subtle poke in Richelieu's eye. Seeing as how the good cardinal has chosen to rename Virginia and call it Louisiana. I can't wait to see what he decides to call Louisiana itself, when they get around to grabbing it."

"Cardinalia," snorted Ludwig Guenther, the count of Schwarzburg-Rudolstadt. "You watch."

"It won't be that," demurred Mike. "Richelieu's much too smooth, and he's always careful not to make the fact that he really runs France become so obvious that it would embarrass Louis XIII. But, to get back to Wilhelm's question, I don't know if the people living there will much care for 'East Virginia.' The name will probably rub a lot of up-timers the wrong way, and it just won't mean that much to the rest of them. However—"

He shrugged. "I'm going to stay out of it. As of tomorrow, when my resignation takes effect, Ed Piazza is the new President of the United States. I'm not about to stick my thumb in his pot of soup. He'll handle it, just like he'll handle anything else he has to. I have great confidence in the man. Truth is, he'll be a lot better administrator than I ever was."

An odd sort of silence fell over the small room. Mike was pretty sure it was what authors liked to call a "pregnant silence."

Delayed pregnancy, apparently. Mike chuckled again. "Come on, Wilhelm, spit it out. You're trying to figure out how soon you should launch your new party and start running in opposition to me. My advice? As fast as you can."

Wilhelm cocked his head. "You are that confident in winning, once the emergency period is over and your post becomes elective?"

"Don't be silly. You'll win in a landslide. Not in—ah—East Virginia, of course, or Magdeburg. But when all the votes are counted, all over the new United States, I figure I'll be doing well to get a third of the votes. That's what I'll be shooting for, anyway."

Again, silence.

"The prospect does not seem to bother you," commented Ludwig.

"Why should it? People need to settle down some, now. Start relaxing a bit. Get accustomed to their new set of political clothes. Start growing into them at a pace they feel comfortable with. I make too many people nervous, Ludwig. You know it, I know it—everybody here knows it. Up to a point, that's fine. But I think we've probably reached that point."

He leaned forward in his chair and gave the eight former princes a display of *dignitas* that would have had George Washington hollering with approval. For their part, the eight men listened with as much rapt attention as pupils listening to a world-famous sage. Eight princes-that-were, now leaders-not-sure-what-they-are. Later on, Mike knew, he would be laughing about it all.

Later, not now.

"Lesson number one, gentlemen. Not the least of the reasons a democracy is more stable than any other kind of regime is because it has a self-correcting mechanism. Right or wrong doesn't even enter into it, really, at this level. You can only stretch a people so far, before they snap. Or *you* snap. And don't think you can't, I don't care how powerful you are. So . . . we'll find out, when the election happens, but I think the people of Germany within our borders would prefer Wilhelm. For a while, at least. They need a bit of a rest."

He gave out a rueful little laugh. "For that matter, I could use one myself. Once Becky gets out of Amsterdam, I'd *really* like to spend some time with my family. Especially now that I seem to have acquired a boy also. A famous miniature philosopher, no less. That's three hours a day right there, just making sure the kid doesn't grow up squirrelly. First thing I'm doing—Becky can squawk all she wants—is teach him how to fish."

"What will you do, if you lose?" asked one of the Wetterau counts. Mike wasn't sure of his name.

Which didn't matter, really, since his reply was addressed to all of them. Coming with a grin that would have earned a tiger's approval.

"I'll be keeping an eye on you, that's what. Have no fear, gentlemen. You'll probably have your moment of relaxation. But you won't be able to relax *that* much."

He leaned back in his chair, planted his hands firmly on the armrests, and allowed the grin to fade away. The rest would be *dignitas*.

"In general, the principle is called 'balance of power.' It's usually applied to political structure, but it applies across the board. Do not forget—not for a minute—that although I probably won't get reelected prime minister, Ed Piazza will carry East Virginia in a landslide. And so will whoever we decide to run in Magdeburg. Do not forget—not for a second—that while the armed forces will now be directly under Gustav Adolf's authority, with Torstensson in command, that: first, neither the Navy nor the Air Force can do anything without the willing cooperation of *my* people; and that, second, Torstensson's new army will be made up primarily of volunteer regiments. Most of whom, as I'm sure you know, will be organized and recruited by the Committees of Correspondence."

He allowed a little silence, so they could absorb the point. The eight former princes did not actually swallow. But they did look very thoughtful.

"Then," he continued, "there's the economic and financial side of the balance of power. Do not—"

He broke off, hearing a little sound behind him. When he turned in his chair, he saw Admiral Simpson standing in the doorway. His face was very pale, and he was clutching a sheet of paper in his hands. Mike recognized it as the form used by the radio operators.

"Excuse me, gentlemen, I need to attend to something." He rose, in as unhurried a manner as he could manage, and strode to the door. Then, taking Simpson by the arm, drew him into the hallway.

"What's wrong, John?"

Simpson shook his head. The gesture had a strange, brittle quality, as if the man were afraid he might break.

"Nothing," he whispered. "We just got a message from Luebeck. A courier brought it over here immediately. Gustav Adolf got a message himself, earlier today. From King Christian of Denmark. The Danes—it seems—oh, Jesus—"

Tears were starting to leak from Simpson's eyes. Mike was astonished. He hadn't thought the man *could* cry.

"He's alive, Mike," Simpson whispered. "He—" Now he broke down, in the complete manner that a man will, who has no idea how to do it. Mike had his arms around him, holding him up.

From the other end of the hallway, leading into the main ballroom, Mike could hear a rising swell of sound. Suddenly, he realized that was the sound of a crowd breaking into celebration. A wild hope came to him.

"Eddie," Simpson choked out. "Lieutenant Cantrell, I mean." Then, taking shaky control of himself, lifted his head and gazed at the opposite wall. "God knows how, but he must have gotten off the boat before it hit. The Danes were all over the area, picking up their own, and they fished him out too. He was badly hurt—lost a leg, they say, or part of it—but he came through it. He's conscious again."

He swallowed, visibly trying to regain his composure. "Hypothermia would have been a blessing to him, actually. Kept the blood loss to a minimum. How in hell he survived the impact on the water, though—at that speed . . ."

Despite his own swelling heart, Mike forced himself to think. Coldly and clearly.

"John . . . Look, I hate to raise this. But is there any chance—"

"A Danish subterfuge? A trick?" Suddenly, Simpson started laughing. The laughter, like the earlier weeping, had a semi-hysterical quality to it. Again, as if the man who laughed had no real experience at it. Or, at least, none for many years.

"Not a chance!" he cried, holding up the message slip. "No, it's Eddie all right. Can't possibly be a Danish ploy. He's *already* pissed off the king of Denmark. Apparently he lectured Christian on something called the Geneva Convention and refused to tell him anything except his name, rank, and serial number."

Mike started laughing himself. Truth be told, perhaps even semi-hysterically.

"It gets better!" whooped Simpson. "Christian is most disgruntled. He tells us—no fool, that man, he's already figured out he'd better not burn any more bridges behind him—he's willing to go along with whatever this Geneva Convention business means but—"

Now, the admiral was almost dancing a little jig.

"—but not unless we quit *cheating*."

Weakly, still shaking with laughter, Simpson handed the sheet to Mike. "See for yourself."

Mike's eyes ranged down the page until he came to the end.

—CANTRELL CLAIMS FORGOT SERIAL NUMBER. WE ARE MOST SUSPICIOUS. WILL KEEP HIM AS PRISONER, FOLLOWING WHAT HE CLAIMS ARE YOUR RULES. BUT MUST INSIST HIS SERIAL NUMBER BE GIVEN TO US. ABSOLUTELY INSIST.
                    CHRISTIAN IV, KING OF DENMARK

"Of course," chuckled Simpson, "he's just covering the Old Bastard's ass. Navy takes care of its own. He didn't *forget* his serial number. I never thought to provide people with any."

Mike stared at him. Simpson shrugged. "What can I say? I screwed up. Guess we'll have to figure out a serial number system. Can't use social security numbers, of course, the way the old Navy wound up doing."

"To hell with a 'system,'" proclaimed Mike. "Later for that. Right now, we'll just have to wing it. Eddie needs a number right away."

The cheering crowd in the ballroom was starting to spill into the hallway. Mike knew he'd be surrounded by well-wishers in seconds, burying him.

*Think quick.*

He did. But—

*Is Eddie bright enough? Stupid question.*

*Will he get reckless? That's the real problem. Ah, what the hell. He's lost a leg, what can he do?*

*Um. Eddie? Stupid question.*

*Piss on it, Mike. Go with the ones who got you here.*

*Just do it.*

Pulling his ever-present notepad and pen from the inside pocket of his fancy clothing—another reason he'd insisted on his own modifications—Mike hastily scrawled a message. He just had time to hand it to Simpson before the mob swept him back into the ballroom. *Dignitas* be damned. Let's have a party!

Simpson didn't read the message for perhaps half a minute, until he was sure he had himself back under control. When he did read the message, however, he promptly burst into laughter again.

LT CANTRELL DECORATED NAVY CROSS. CONGRATULATIONS.

LT CANTRELL REPRIMANDED FORGETTING SERIAL NUMBER.

INSIST REPRIMAND BE GIVEN HIM. WITH SERIAL NUMBER.

THUS NO EXCUSE REPETITION OF INCIDENT.

LT CANTRELL SERIAL NUMBER 007

# 𝔄fterword
## by Eric Flint

It is one of the pieces of accepted wisdom in fiction writing that stories written in collaboration are almost invariably weaker than stories written by authors working alone. Since I enjoy sticking my thumb in the eye of accepted wisdom, I like to think I've done it again with this book—as well as a number of others I've written in collaboration with several different authors.

I've never really understood the logic of this piece of "wisdom," beyond the obvious technical reality: until the advent of computer word-processing and online communication, collaboration between authors was simply very *difficult.* I can remember the days when I used to write on a typewriter, and had to spend as much time painfully retyping entire manuscripts just to incorporate a few small changes in the text, as I did writing the story in the first place. (And I'll leave aside the joys of using carbon paper and white-out.) Working under those circumstances is trying enough for an author working alone. Adding a collaborator increases the problems by an order of magnitude.

That's the reason, I think, that authors for many decades, even centuries, generally worked alone. And where exceptions did occur, they usually did so because of special circumstances. Two, in particular:

The first is where one author basically does all the writing. The input of the other author might have taken the form of developing the plot outline, or, not infrequently, simply lending his or her name to the project for marketing purposes.

The second generally involved married couples, or people who were otherwise in position to work in very close proximity. To use a well-known instance from the history of science fiction, just about everything written by Henry Kuttner and C. L. Moore after their marriage was, in fact if not in name, a collaborative work.

Modern technology, however, eliminates all the practical problems involved with collaborative writing. Thus, to use this book as an example, once Dave and I had settled on a detailed plot outline, we were each able to write our respective chapters, swap them back and forth in emails, cross-edit and add new material, rewrite—whatever was needed—just about as easily as a single author would manage his own rewriting and editing.

Of course, that still leaves the creative and personal aspects of the business. Those can be either a challenge—sometimes an insuperable one—or an opportunity. Part of what annoys me a bit about the unthinking assumption of a lot of people that collaboration automatically reduces the quality of the writing to the lowest common denominator, is that they overlook the obvious. Collaborative writing is a *skill,* like any other. Some authors are hopelessly inept at it—or simply don't want to do it all. Others manage it poorly; still others in a workmanlike but humdrum manner; and some—I happen to be one of them—do it very well.

I think there are three key ingredients to the skill. The first, and most important, is that the author himself has to *want* to do it. Any author for whom collaboration is a chore or a nuisance, done only for practical and commercial reasons, is not going to do it well. They will meet the challenges, perhaps; but they will miss the opportunities and potential benefits.

The second is that you have to choose your partner (or partners) carefully. This has both a personal and a professional side to it. On the personal side, your partner has to be someone you're on friendly terms with. On the professional side, they should be someone whose particular strengths and weaknesses as a writer match up well against your own. There's no point in Tweedledum co-authoring a novel with Tweedledee. You want a co-author who is going to *add* something—and whose weaknesses (and all authors have them) can be cancelled out by your own strengths. And vice-versa, of course.

Finally, you have to pick the right story. Not all stories lend themselves well to collaboration. To give an example from my own work: except for my friend Richard Roach, who has been working with me on the project since we were both men in our early twenties—over thirty years now—I would find it very difficult to collaborate with anyone on my Joe's World series. (The first two volumes of which, *The Philosophical Strangler* and *Forward the Mage*, are now in print.) That story is just too bound up with my own view of things and my sometimes quirky sense of humor. I doubt if many other authors would be able to find their way through its surrealistic logic.

On the other hand, some stories lend themselves superbly well to collaboration—and the 1632 universe is one of them. This is a big, sprawling canvas of a story. Or, since I tend to think in musical terms, it's a story that lends itself to something of a cross between chamber music and a jam session. That's not simply because the story allows for it. In many ways, I think, it almost *demands* collaboration.

The reason has to do with the nature of alternate history stories. Those can, of course, be written by a solo author—and written extremely well. But there is an inherent "occupational hazard" involved. A single author will almost inevitably start shaping his story to fit whatever historical schema he develops. And, over time, in the course of a multi-volume work, the story begins to suffer because of it. It's a subtle thing. But what tends to happen is that the complexities and quirkiness and—if you will—unpredictable chaos of real history tends to get washed away.

I wanted to avoid that, once I decided to turn *1632*—which I wrote as a stand-alone novel—into a series. And so I looked for collaborators. I found them in two places.

The first, obviously, was Dave Weber. By then, Dave and I had become friends and I'd had the experience of working with him in the course of writing a short novel for one of the anthologies in his Honor Harrington series. ("From the Highlands," which appears in the third of the Harrington anthologies, *Changer of Worlds*.) Once Dave told me that he'd enjoy working in the 1632 universe, we decided to write the sequel to *1632* together. The result, you have now read. I hope it has pleased you. It certainly pleased Dave and me—so much so, in fact, that we now have a contract to write four more novels together continuing the story. (The first of which, *1634: The Baltic War*, will be the direct sequel to *1633*.)

The other place I looked was in the now very large group of

fans who participate daily in an online discussion of the 1632 universe. That discussion takes place in Baen's Bar, the discussion area which is part of Baen Books' website—see note below—in a conference specifically set aside for it: "1632 Tech Manual." The discussion has now gone on for over two years, with tens of thousands of posts having gone up during that period.

Last year, after discussing the idea with my publisher, Jim Baen, I decided to put together an anthology of stories set in the 1632 universe. I wanted to do it in a way which would incorporate, as much as possible, the bubbling cauldron of ideas which the Tech Manual has become. So I adopted a rather unusual format. As is standard procedure for such anthologies, I asked a number of established authors to contribute stories for the anthology. I invited those I was sure would write stories which fit into the setting and would add something to it. The authors involved are David Weber, Mercedes Lackey, Dave Freer, Kathy Wentworth, and S. L. Viehl—and all of them did exactly as I had hoped. And I'll be writing a novella of my own for it, of course.

But I set aside half the space for new writers, and threw the anthology open for submissions from the participants in the discussion in the "Tech Manual." A number of the participants are aspiring writers as well as fans, and I was confident that they'd be able to produce a number of excellent stories. Which, they did. About sixty stories were submitted, and I selected nine of them for the anthology.

What was most important to me, though, is that the anthology stories—those from the newcomers as well as the established writers—expanded my own view of this world. The basic framework of the 1632 setting remains the one I had created in *1632*, but that theme now has well over a dozen variations on the tune. Aspects of the story to which I had given little thought were now developed into stories in their own right. Characters were introduced who began to shape the ongoing story I was writing myself, and the way I thought about it.

I could give a multitude of examples. The character of Tom Stone, for instance, was first developed by Misty Lackey in her story "To Dye For"—and was then incorporated by Dave and me into *1633* and will become a major character in a sequel which I will be writing with Andrew Dennis. That sequel will develop Andrew's story for the anthology, "Between the Armies." It involves characters who were either minor in *1632*—such as Father Larry Mazzare—or were first developed by Andrew, and will relate the impact which the Ring of Fire has on Italy and the Catholic Church.

To conclude, although I created this setting and will continue to write solo novels in it, I see myself as part of an ensemble. Sometimes as soloist, sometimes as a participant in chamber music—especially in my duets with Dave Weber—and sometimes conducting the orchestra.

One of the members of the orchestra needs to be singled out for special mention in this afterword, and that's Mike Spehar. Mike was in the course of writing a story for the anthology when the events on September 11 required him to break off from it due to his professional responsibilities. Mike is such a good writer that I hated to see his work simply go to waste. So, with Dave's agreement, we incorporated what he had written into some of the earlier chapters of *1633*. The character of Jesse Wood was developed originally by Mike, along with the technical basis for the aircraft. (With some input from Evan Mayerle, I should add.)

Then, as we continued to write the novel, things developed further. Periodically, Dave and I would ask Mike if he could write a new scene for this or that chapter, since Mike—who is a retired U.S. Air Force pilot—could give the flying scenes a vividness and detail that neither Dave nor I possibly could. Mike did so, and the first drafts of many of the scenes in a number of the chapters were written by him. Except for the final battle at Wismar, in fact, all of the flying episodes were originally written by Mike— and he was our technical editor for that final scene.

Mike will continue to play that role for us in *1634: The Baltic War,* and I'll be very surprised if he doesn't wind up writing his own stories—or becoming a full collaborator on a novel—as this series progresses. I expect the same will happen with some other people who have participated for over two years now in shaping the 1632 universe. I will certainly be encouraging them to, and doing my best to help the process.

I *like* to collaborate, accepted wisdom be damned. It's probably not an accident that I tend to think of writing in musical terms. I'm quite sure that if I were a violinist or a pianist, instead of an author, I'd play at least as much chamber music as I would solo compositions or concertos.

Now, I need to publicly thank a number of people who gave Dave and me a lot of help in the way of technical advice and historical expertise. I can't possibly name them all, but I'll start by thanking the hundreds of people who have participated in the 1632 Tech Manual discussions for the past two years. Then, in particular:

Virginia DeMarce, who is a professional historian and a specialist on 17th-century Germany. (Virginia, by the way, is also one of the authors who will be appearing in the upcoming anthology—and with whom I hope to be collaborating on a novel before too long, following up on the story line she developed for it centering on the character of Veronica. Like Mike Stearns, I'm partial to tough old biddies.)

Andrew Dennis, for his advice on naval and historical matters.

Detlef Zander, who has been incredibly helpful in tracking down information for us in his native Germany. His assistance in providing us with diagrams, maps and photos of the north German ports, canals, rivers and the Wietze oil field was invaluable.

Bob Gottlieb, Rick Boatright, Drew Clark and Marcus Mulkins, who provided us with a great deal of assistance on matters relating to chemistry, steel production, medicine and antibiotics. Rick was also our radio expert, and guided us through the complexities of that part of the story.

Ralph Tacoma and Conrad Chu, for general advice on matters of engineering.

And, finally, I'd like to thank Judith Lasker. Not for any particular thing involving *1633*, but just for the help and encouragement she's given me for a long time now.

NOTE: Those of you who enjoyed this book and would be interested in participating in the online discussion regarding the 1632 series are welcome to join it. You can do so as follows:

1) On the Internet, using your web browser, go to: http://www.baen.com

2) Select "Baen's Bar" from the menu across the top.

3) Fill out a quick and simple registration. Thereafter, you can simply log in.

4) Once you get into the Bar, select the conference titled "1632 Tech Manual."

5) Then, lurk or post, as you choose. Most of all, enjoy yourself.